THE CALDWELL CARAVAN

THE
CALDWELL
CARAVAN

Novels and Stories by

ERSKINE CALDWELL

With an Introduction by the Author

THE WORLD PUBLISHING COMPANY

CLEVELAND AND NEW YORK

Published by THE WORLD PUBLISHING COMPANY

2231 WEST 110TH STREET · CLEVELAND 2 · OHIO

By arrangement with Duell, Sloan and Pearce, Inc.

FIRST PRINTING MARCH 1946
SECOND PRINTING AUGUST 1946
THIRD PRINTING FEBRUARY 1947
FOURTH PRINTING APRIL 1947

CONTENTS

Introduction

WHAT can an author say about his own novels and short stories that a reader cannot state in fewer and more expressive words? Nothing, I would say, of any importance. A reader, because he reads with an impartial eye, is much better qualified to appraise a novel or story than the author himself, and certainly a reader's judgment and understanding of a book is far superior to that of a reviewer. In sum, then, these novels and stories were written for the reader's edification and delight, and not for the author's diversion or for a book reviewer's mania.

The present writer has no delusions concerning his work. I can only say that the pieces on the following pages are readable, honest, and the result of hard work. I do not consider them to be examples of artistry, or of earth-shaking importance; they are not indicative of a trend in fiction; and they were not written to make propaganda. The one and only thing they do is tell stories; if they do anything else, something is wrong somewhere.

ERSKINE CALDWELL

Catalina Foothills,
Tucson, Arizona

TOBACCO ROAD

For my Father and Mother

Advertisement

IT IS good to look backward and to be able to see clearly how a novel had its beginning.

My recollection of how *Tobacco Road* had its beginning is stark and vivid.

It was in the heat of midsummer in Georgia, below the Piedmont, and I was walking along a dusty, weed-bordered, wagon-rutted road.

Here I was in my own country, among eroded clay ridges and barren sand hills, a land I had known all my life.

All around me were clusters of stunted, scrawny, scraggly cotton plants trying vainly to exist in the depleted soil.

The land was desolate.

Not far away across the fields were several tenant houses, shabby and dilapidated, two-room shacks with sagging joists and roofs. Around the buildings were groups of human beings. The children were playing in the sand. The young men and women were leaning against the sides of the houses. The old people were merely sitting. Every one of them was waiting for the cotton to mature. They believed in cotton. They believed in it as some men believe in God. They had faith in the earth and in the plants that grew in the earth. Even though they had been fooled the year before, and for many years before that, they were certain the fields would soon be showered with tumbling, bursting bolls of glistening white cotton.

But I had walked along that same road and had stopped and gazed upon those same fields the previous autumn, and I did not know how many autumns before that, and I had never seen any man gather enough cotton from those stunted plants to provide himself with food and clothing.

It was not difficult to survive in summer when it was warm and balmy, and when there was the vision of cotton to look forward to in the autumn. One could always find blackberries and wild onions and, sometimes, rabbits.

But when it was fall and winter and early spring it was a different matter.

I had walked along the road in midwinter and had seen hungry people wrapped in rags, going nowhere and coming from nowhere, searching for food and warmth, wanting to know if anywhere in the world such things still existed.

They asked for only enough food to keep them alive until spring so they could plant next year's cotton.

11

They had so much faith in nature, in the earth, and in the plants that grew in the earth, that they could not understand how the earth could fail them.

But it had failed them, and there they were waiting in another summer for an autumn harvest that would never come.

It all had happened once before.

Not to these same people, but to their forefathers.

Their forefathers had seen tobacco come and flourish on these same plots of earth.

But after its season it would no longer grow in the depleted soil.

The fields lay fallow for many years.

Then came cotton.

Cotton thrived in abundance for several generations, and then it, too, depleted the soil of its energy until it would no longer grow.

First, tobacco, and then cotton; they both had come and gone.

But the people, and their faith, remained.

ERSKINE CALDWELL

Darien, Connecticut

Chapter I

Lov BENSEY trudged homeward through the deep white sand of the gully-washed tobacco road with a sack of winter turnips on his back. He had put himself to a lot of trouble to get the turnips; it was a long and tiresome walk all the way to Fuller and back again.

The day before, Lov had heard that a man over there was selling winter turnips for fifty cents a bushel, so he had started out with half a dollar early that morning to buy some. He had already walked seven and a half miles, and it was a mile and a half yet back to his house at the coal chute.

Four or five of the Lesters were standing in the yard looking at Lov when he put his sack down and stopped in front of the house. They had been watching Lov ever since he was first seen an hour before on the sand hill nearly two miles away, and now that he was actually within reach, they were prepared to stop him from carrying the turnips any farther.

Lov had his wife to feed and provide for, in addition to himself, and he was careful not to allow any of the Lesters to come too close to the sack of turnips. Usually when he came by the Lester place with turnips or sweet potatoes, or for that matter with any kind of food, he left the road half a mile from the house and made a wide circle through the fields, returning to the road a safe distance beyond. To-day, though, he had to speak to Jeeter about something of great importance, and he had ventured closer to the house than he had ever done before when carrying home turnips or sweet potatoes.

Lov's wife was Jeeter Lester's youngest daughter, Pearl. She was only twelve years old the summer before when he had married her.

The Lesters watched Lov closely while he stood in the middle of the road. He had dropped the sack from his shoulder, but he held the neck of it in the rigid grasp of both hands. No one in the yard had changed his position during the past ten minutes. The next move was left entirely up to Lov.

When Lov came to the house and stopped, he had a good reason for doing so; otherwise he would never have come within hailing distance. He wanted to speak to Jeeter about Pearl.

Pearl would not talk. She would not say a word, no matter how persuasive Lov tried to be, nor how angry he was; she even hid from Lov when he came home from the coal chute, and when he found her, she slipped away from his grasp and ran off into the broom-sedge out of sight. Sometimes she would even stay in the broom-sedge all night, remaining out there until Lov went to work the next morning.

Pearl had never talked, for that matter. Not because she could not, but simply because she did not want to. When she was at home, before Lov had married her, she had stayed apart from the other Lesters and rarely opened her mouth from the beginning of one day to the next. Only her mother, Ada, had been able to converse with her, and even then Pearl had never used more than the barest of negatives and affirmatives in reply. But Ada was herself like that. She had begun to talk voluntarily only during the past ten years. Before then, Jeeter had had the same trouble with her that Lov was now having with Pearl.

Lov asked Pearl questions, he kicked her, he poured water over her, he threw rocks and sticks at her, and he did everything else he could think of that he thought might make her talk to him. She cried a lot, especially when she was seriously hurt, but Lov did not consider that as conversation. He wanted her to ask him if his back were sore, and when was he going to get his hair cut, and when was it going to rain again. But Pearl would not say anything.

He had spoken to Jeeter several times before about his troubles with Pearl, but Jeeter did not know what was the matter with her. Ever since she was a baby she had been like that, he said; and Ada had remained untalkative until the last few years. What Jeeter had not been able to break down in Ada for forty years, hunger had. Hunger loosened her tongue, and she had been complaining ever since. Jeeter did not attempt to recommend the starving of Pearl, because he knew she would go somewhere to beg food, and would get it.

"Sometimes I think it's just the old devil in her," Lov had said several times. "To my way of thinking, she ain't got a scratch of religion in her. She's going to hell-fire when she dies, sure as day comes."

"Now, maybe she ain't pleased with her married life," Jeeter had suggested. "Maybe she ain't satisfied with what you provide her with."

"I done everything I can think of to make her satisfied and contented. Every week I go to Fuller on pay-day and buy her a pretty. I get her snuff, but she won't take none; I get her a little piece of calico, but she won't sew it. Looks like she wants something I ain't got and can't get her. I wish I knowed what it was. She's such a pretty little girl—all them long yellow curls hanging down her back sort of gets me all crazy sometimes. I don't know what's going to happen to me. I've got the need of Pearl for a wife as bad as any man ever had."

"I expect she's too young yet to appreciate things," Jeeter had said. "She ain't grown up yet like Ellie May and Lizzie Belle and Clara and the other gals. Pearl ain't nothing but a little gal yet. She don't even look like a woman, so far."

"If I had knowed she was going to be like she is, maybe I wouldn't have wanted to marry her so bad. I could have married me a woman what wants to be married to me. But I don't want Pearl to go now, though. I sort of got used to her around, and I'd sure miss seeing them long yellow curls hanging down her back. They make a man feel kind of lonesome some way. She sure is a pretty little girl, no matter if she does act like she does all the time."

Lov had gone back home that time and told Pearl what Jeeter said about her, but she sat in the chair and made no sign of answering him. Lov did not know what to do about her after that. But he had realized from that time on that she was still a little girl. During the eight months they had been married she had grown three or four inches in height, and she weighed about fifteen pounds more now than she had at the beginning. She still did not weigh much more than a hundred pounds, though she was gaining in weight and height every day.

What Lov wanted to speak to Jeeter about now in particular was the way Pearl had of refusing to sleep with him. They had been married almost a year, and still she slept by herself, as she had done since the first. She slept by herself on a pallet on the floor, refusing even to let Lov kiss her or touch her in any way. Lov had told her that cows were not any good until they had been freshened, and that the reason he married her was because he wanted to kiss her and feel her long yellow curls and sleep with her; but Pearl had not even indicated that she heard him or knew what he was talking about. Next to wanting to kiss her and talk to her, Lov wanted to see her eyes. Yet even this pleasure she denied him; her pale blue eyes were always looking off into another direction when he came and stood in front of her.

Lov still stood in the middle of the road looking at Jeeter and the other Lesters in the yard. They were waiting for him to make the first move; friendly or hostile, it mattered little to them so long as there were turnips in the sack.

Jeeter was wondering where Lov had got the turnips. It did not occur to him that Lov had bought them with money; Jeeter had long before come to the conclusion that the only possible way a quantity of food could be obtained was by theft. But he had not been able to locate a turnip patch that year anywhere within five or six miles. There had been planted a two-acre field the year before over at the Peabody place, but the Peabody men had kept people out of the field with shotguns then, and this year they had not even planted turnips.

"Why don't you come in the yard off the tobacco road, Lov?" Jeeter said. "Ain't no sense standing out there. Come in and rest yourself."

Lov made no reply, nor did he move. He was debating within himself the danger of entering the yard, against the safety of staying where he was in the road.

For the past few weeks Lov had been thinking about taking some plow-lines and tying Pearl in the bed at night. He had tried everything that he could think of so far, except force, and he was still determined to make her act as he thought a wife should. He had reached the point now where he wanted Jeeter's advice before going ahead with the plan. He believed Jeeter would know whether it was advisable from the practical side, since Jeeter had had to contend with Ada for almost a lifetime. He knew Ada had once acted as Pearl was now doing, but Jeeter had not been treated as he was treated, because Ada had borne him seventeen children, while Pearl had not even begun to have the first one.

If Jeeter said it would be satisfactory to tie Pearl in bed, then he would go ahead and do it. Jeeter knew more about such things than he did. Jeeter had been married to Ada forty years.

Lov hoped that Jeeter would offer to go down to the house at the coal chute and help him tie Pearl in the bed. Pearl fought back so fiercely whenever he attempted to catch her that he was afraid he would not be able to accomplish anything without Jeeter's help.

The Lesters stood around in the yard and on the front porch waiting to see what Lov was going to do next. There had been very little in the house again that day to eat; some salty soup Ada had made by boiling several fat-back rinds in a pan of water, and corn bread, was all there was when they had sat down to eat. There had not been enough to go around even then, and the old grandmother had been shoved out of the kitchen when she tried to come inside.

Ellie May stood behind a chinaberry tree, looking around the trunk at Lov. She moved her head from one side of the tree to the other, trying to attract Lov's attention.

Ellie May and Dude were the only Lester children left at home. All the others had gone away and married, some of them just leaving in a casual way as though they were only walking down to the coal chute to see the freight trains. When they failed to return within two or three days, it was known that they had left home.

Dude was throwing a lopsided baseball at the side of the house, and catching it on the rebound. The ball hit the house like a clap of thunder, rattling the loose weather-boarding until the vibration swayed the house from side to side. He threw the ball continually, the ball bounding with unfailing regularity back across the sandy yard to where he stood.

The three-room house sat precariously on stacks of thin lime-rock chips that had been placed under the four corners. The stones had been laid one on top of the other, the beams spiked, and the house nailed together. The ease and simplicity with which it had been built was now evident. The centre of the building sagged between the sills;

the front porch had sagged loose from the house, and was now a foot or more lower than it originally was; and the roof sagged in the centre where the supporting rafters had been carelessly put together. Most of the shingles had rotted, and after every wind-storm pieces of them were scattered in all directions about the yard. When the roof leaked, the Lesters moved from one corner of the room to another, their movements finally outlasting the duration of the rain. The house had never been painted.

Jeeter was trying to patch a rotten inner-tube. He had said that if he could ever get all the tires on the old automobile standing up at the same time again, he would haul a load of wood to Augusta and sell it. Woodcutters were being paid two dollars a load for seasoned pine delivered in the city; but the blackjack that Jeeter tried to make people buy for fuel never brought him more than fifty or seventy-five cents. Usually, when he did succeed in getting a load of it to Augusta, he was not able to give it away; nobody, it seemed, was foolish enough to buy wood that was tougher than iron water-pipes. People argued with Jeeter about his mule-like determination to sell blackjack for fuel, and they tried to convince him that as firewood it was practically worthless; but Jeeter said he wanted to clear the land of the scrub oak because he was getting ready to farm it again.

Lov had by that time moved a few steps nearer the yard and had sat down in the tobacco road with his feet in the drain ditch. He kept one hand gripped tightly around the mouth of the sack where it had been tied together with a piece of twine.

Ellie May continued to peer from behind the chinaberry tree, trying to attract Lov's attention. Each time he glanced in that direction, she jerked her head back so he could not see her.

"What you got in that there croker sack, Lov?" Jeeter shouted across the yard. "I been seeing you come a far piece off with that there croker sack on your back. I sure would like to know what you got on the inside of it. I heard it said that some people has got turnips this year."

Lov tightened his grip on the mouth of the sack, looking from Jeeter to the next Lester in turn. He saw Ellie May peering at him from behind the chinaberry tree.

"Did you have a hard time getting what you got there in the sack, Lov?" Jeeter said. "You look like you is all out of breath."

"I want to say something to you, Jeeter," he said. "It's about Pearl."

"What's that gal done now, Lov? Is she treating you mean some more?"

"It's just like she's always done, only I'm getting pretty durn tired of it by this time. I don't like the way she acts. I never did take to the way she does, but it's getting worse and worse all the time. All the niggers make fun of me because of the way she treats me."

"Pearl is just like her Ma," Jeeter said. "Her Ma used to do the queerest things in her time."

"Every time I want to have her around me, she runs off and won't come back when I call her. Now, what I say is, what in hell is the sense in me marrying a wife if I don't get none of the benefits. God didn't intend for it to be that way. He don't want a man to be treated like that. It's all right for a woman to sort of tease a man into doing what she wants done, but Pearl don't seem to be aiming after that. She ain't teasing me, to her way of thinking, but it sure does act that way on me. Right now I feel like I want a woman what ain't so——"

"What you got in that there croker sack, Lov?" Jeeter said. "I been seeing you for the past hour or longer, ever since you came over the top of that far hill yonder."

"Turnips, by God," Lov said, looking at the Lester women. "Where'd you get turnips, Lov?"

"Wouldn't you like to know!"

"I was thinking maybe we might fix up some sort of a trade, Lov— me and you. Now, I could go down to your house and sort of tell Pearl she's got to sleep in the bed with you. That's what you was aiming to speak to me about, wasn't it? You want her to sleep in the bed, don't you?"

"She ain't never slept in the bed. It's that durn pallet on the floor that she sleeps on every night. Reckon you could make her stop doing that, Jeeter?"

"I'd be pleased something powerful to make her do what she ain't doing. That is, if me and you could make a trade with them turnips, Lov."

"That's what I came by here for—to speak to you about Pearl. But I ain't going to let you have none of these turnips, though. I had to pay fifty cents for this many in a sack, and I had to walk all the way to the other side of Fuller and back to fetch them. You're Pearl's daddy, and you ought to make her behave for nothing. She don't pay no attention to nothing I tell her to do."

"By God and by Jesus, Lov, all the damn-blasted turnips I raised this year is wormy. And I ain't had a good turnip since a year ago this spring. All my turnips has got them damn-blasted green-gutted worms in them, Lov. What God made turnip-worms for, I can't make out. It appears to me like He just naturally has got it in good and heavy for a poor man. I worked all the fall last year digging up a patch of ground to grow turnips in, and then when they're getting about big enough to pull up and eat, along comes these damn-blasted green-gutted turnip-worms and bore clear to the middle of them. God is got it in good and heavy for the poor. But I ain't complaining, Lov. I say, 'The good Lord knows best about turnips.' Some of these days

He'll bust loose with a heap of bounty and all us poor folks will have all we want to eat and plenty to clothe us with. It can't always keep getting worse and worse every year like it has got since the big war. God, He'll put a stop to it some of these days and make the rich give back all they've took from us poor folks. God is going to treat us right. He ain't going to let it keep on like it is now. But we got to stop cussing Him when we ain't got nothing to eat. He'll send a man to hell and the devil for persisting in doing that."

Lov dragged the sack of turnips across the drain ditch and sat down again. Jeeter laid aside the rotten inner-tube and waited.

Chapter II

Lov opened the sack, selected a large turnip, wiping it clean with his hands, and took three big bites one after the other. The Lester women stood in the yard and on the porch looking at Lov eat. Ellie May came from behind the chinaberry tree and sat down not far from Lov on a pine stump. Ada and the old grandmother were on the porch watching the turnip in Lov's hand become smaller and smaller with each bite.

"Now, if Pearl was anything like Ellie May, she wouldn't act like she does," Lov said. "I'd have taken Ellie May at the start if it wasn't for that face of hers. But I knowed I couldn't sleep with no peace of mind at night with her in the bed with me, and knowing how it looked in the daylight. Pearl looks pretty, and she's a right smart piece to want to sleep with, but I just can't make her stay off of that durn pallet on the floor when night comes. You got to come down there and make her do like she ought to act, Jeeter. I been married to her near on to a whole year, and all that time I could just as well been shovelling coal at the chute night and day without ever going to my house. That ain't the way it was intended for it to be. A man has the right to want his wife to get in the bed when dark comes. I ain't never heard of a woman wanting to sleep on a durn pallet on the floor every night in the whole year. Pearl is queer that way."

"By God and by Jesus, Dude," Jeeter said, "ain't you never going to stop bouncing that there ball against that there old house? You've clear about got all the weatherboards knocked off already. The durned old house is going to pitch over and fall on the ground some of these days if you don't stop doing that."

Jeeter picked up the inner-tube again, and tried to make the patch stick to the rubber. The old automobile against which he was sitting was the last of his possessions. The year before, the cow had died, leaving him with the car. Up until that time he had had a way of boasting about his goods, but when the cow went, he did not even mention the car any more. He had begun to think that he was indeed a poor man. No longer was there anything he could mortgage when the time came each spring to buy seed-cotton and guano; the automobile had been turned down at the junk yard in Augusta. But he still had wood to sell; it was the wiry blackjack that grew behind the house. He was trying now to patch the inner-tube so he could haul a load of it to Augusta some time that week. Ada said all the meal was gone, and the meat, too. They had been living off of fat-back rinds several days already, and after they were gone, there would be nothing for them to eat. A load of blackjack would bring fifty or seventy-five cents in Augusta, if he could find a man who would buy it. When the old cow had died, Jeeter hauled the carcass to the fertilizer plant in Augusta and received two dollars and a quarter for it. After that, there was nothing left to sell but blackjack.

"Quit chunking that durn ball at them there weatherboards, Dude," he said. "You don't never stop doing what I tell you. That ain't no way to treat your old Pa, Dude. You ought to sort of help me out, instead of always doing something contrary."

"Aw, go to hell, you old dried-up clod," Dude said, throwing the ball at the side of the house with all his might and scooping up a fast grounder on the rebound. "Nobody asked you nothing."

The old grandmother, Jeeter's mother, crawled under the front porch for the old burlap sack, and went across the tobacco road towards the grove for some dead twigs. No one paid any attention to her.

Wood for the kitchen stove and fireplace was never cut and hauled to the house; Jeeter would not do it, and he could not make Dude do that kind of work. Old Mother Lester knew there was no food for them to cook, and that it would be a waste of time for her to go after the dead twigs and make a fire in the cook-stove; but she was hungry, and she was always hoping that God would provide for them if she made a fire in the kitchen at meal-time. Knowing that there were turnips in Lov's sack made her frantic with hunger. She could sometimes stand the pain of it in her stomach when she knew there was nothing to eat, but when Lov stood in full view taking turnips out of the sack, she could not bear the sight of seeing food no one would let her have.

She hobbled across the road and over the old cotton field that had not been planted and cultivated in six or seven years. The field had grown up in broom-sedge at the start, and now the gnarled and sharp stubs of a new blackjack growth were beginning to cover the ground. She tripped and fell several times on her way to the grove of trees, and her clothes had been torn so many times before that the new tears in the skirt and jacket could not be distinguished from the older ones. The coat and shirt she wore had been torn into strips and shreds by the briars and blackjack pricks in the thicket where she gathered up the dead twigs for fire-wood, and there never had been new clothes for her. Hobbling through the brown broom-sedge, she looked like an old scarecrow, in her black rags.

The February wind whistled through the strips of black cloth, whirling them about in the air until it looked as if she were shaking violently with palsy. Her stockings had been made by wrapping some of the longer of the black rags around her legs and tying the ends with knots. Her shoes were pieces of horse-collars cut into squares and tied around her feet with strings. She went after the dead twigs morning, noon, and night; when she returned to the house each time, she made a fire in the cook-stove and sat down to wait.

Ada shifted the snuff stick to the other side of her mouth and looked longingly at Lov and his sack of turnips. She held the loose calico dress over her chest to keep out the cool February wind blowing under the roof of the porch. Every one else was sitting or standing in the sunshine.

Ellie May got down from the pine stump and sat on the ground. She moved closer and closer to Lov, sliding herself over the hard white sand.

"Is you in mind to make a trade with them turnips?" Jeeter asked Lov. "I'm wanting turnips, God Himself only knows how bad."

"I ain't trading turnips to nobody," he said.

"Now, Lov, that ain't no way to talk. I ain't had a good turnip since a year ago this spring. All the turnips I've et has got them damn-blasted green-gutted worms in them. I sure would like to have some good turnips right now. Wormy ones like mine was ain't fit for a human."

"Go over to Fuller and buy yourself some, then," he said, eating the last of his fourth turnip. "I went over there to get mine."

"Now, Lov, ain't I always been good to you? That ain't no way for you to talk. You know I ain't got a penny to my name and no knowing where to get money. You got a good job and it pays you a heap of money. You ought to make a trade with me so I'll have something to eat and won't have to starve to death. You don't want to sit there and see me starve, do you, Lov?"

"I don't make but a dollar a day at the chute. House-rent takes up near about all of that, and eating, the rest of it."

"Makes no difference, Lov. I ain't got a penny to my name, and you is."

"I can't help that. The Lord looks at us with equal favor, they say. He gives me mine, and if you don't get yours, you better go talk to Him about it. It ain't none of my troubles. I've got plenty of my own to worry about. Pearl won't never——"

"Ain't you never going to stop chunking that durn ball against the house, Dude?" Jeeter shouted. "That noise near about splits my poor head wide open."

Dude slammed the baseball against the loose weatherboards with all his might. Pieces of splintered pine fell over the yard, and rotten chunks dropped to the ground beside the house. Dude threw the ball harder each time, it seemed, and several times the ball almost went through the thin walls of the house.

"Why don't you go somewheres and steal a sack of turnips?" Dude said. "You ain't fit for nothing else no more. You sit around here and cuss all the time about not having nothing to eat, and no turnips—why don't you go somewheres and steal yourself something? God ain't going to bring you nothing. He ain't going to drop no turnips down out of the sky. He ain't got no time to be wasted on fooling with you. If you wasn't so durn lazy you'd do something instead of cuss about it all the time."

"My children all blame me because God sees fit to make me poverty-ridden, Lov," Jeeter said. "They and Ma is all the time cussing me because we ain't got nothing to eat. I ain't had nothing to do with it. It ain't my fault that Captain John shut down on giving us rations and snuff. It's his fault, Lov. I worked all my life for Captain John. I worked harder than any four of his niggers in the fields; then the first thing I knowed, he came down here one morning and says he can't be letting me be getting no more rations and snuff at the store. After that he sells all the mules and goes up to Augusta to live. I can't make no money, because there ain't nobody wanting work done. Nobody is taking on share-croppers, neither. Ain't no kind of work I can find to do for hire. I can't even raise me a crop of my own, because I ain't got no mule in the first place, and besides that, won't nobody let me have seed-cotton and guano on credit. Now I can't get no snuff and rations, excepting once in a while when I haul a load of wood up to Augusta. Captain John told the merchants in Fuller not to let me have no more snuff and rations on his credit, and I don't know where to get nothing. I'd raise a crop of my own on this land if I could get somebody to sign my guano-notes, but won't nobody do that for me, neither. That's what I'm wanting to do powerful strong right now. When the winter goes, and when it gets to be time to burn off broom-sedge in the fields and underbrush in the thickets, I sort of want to cry, I reckon it is. The smell of that sedge-smoke this time of year near about drives me crazy. Then pretty soon all the other farmers start plowing. That's what gets under my skin the worse. When the smell of that new earth turning over behind the plows strikes me, I get all weak and shaky. It's in my blood—burning broom-sedge and plowing in the ground this time of year. I did it for near about fifty years, and my Pa and his Pa before him was the same kind of men. Us Lesters sure like to stir the earth and make plants grow in it. I can't move off to the cotton mills like the rest of them do. The land has got a powerful hold on me.

"This raft of women and children is all the time bellowing for snuff and rations, too. It don't make no difference that I ain't got nothing to buy it with—they want it just the same. I reckon, Lov, I'll just have to wait for the good Lord to provide. They tell me He takes care of His people, and I'm waiting for Him to take some notice of me. I don't reckon there's another man between here and Augusta who's as bad off as I is. And down the other way, neither, between here and McCoy. It looks like everybody has got goods and credit excepting me. I don't know why that is, because I always give the good Lord His due. Him and me has always been fair and square with each other. It's time for Him to take some notice of the fix I'm in. I don't know nothing else to do, except wait for Him to take notice. It don't do me no good to try to beg snuff and rations, because ain't nobody going to give it to me. I've tried all over this part of the country, but don't nobody pay no attention to my requests. They say they ain't got nothing neither, but I can't see how that is. It don't look like everybody ought to be poverty-ridden just because they live on the land instead of going to the mills. If I've been a sinful man, I don't know what it is I've done. I don't seem to remember anything I done powerful sinful. It didn't used to be like it is now, either. I can recall a short time back when all the merchants in Fuller was tickled to give me credit, and I always had plenty of money to spend then, too. Cotton was selling upwards of thirty cents a pound, and nobody came around to collect debts. Then all of a sudden the merchants in Fuller wouldn't let me have no more goods on time, and pretty soon the sheriff comes and takes away near about every durn piece of goods I possessed. He took every durn thing I had, excepting that old automobile and the cow. He said the cow wasn't no good, because she wouldn't take no freshening, and the automobile tires was all wore out.

"And now I can't get no credit, I can't hire out for pay, and nobody wants to take on share-croppers. If the good Lord don't start bringing me help pretty soon, it will be too late to help me with my troubles."

Jeeter paused to see if Lov were listening. Lov had his head turned in another direction. He was looking at Ellie May now. She had at last got him to give her some attention.

Ellie May was edging closer and closer to Lov. She was moving across the yard by raising her weight on her hands and feet and sliding herself over the hard white sand. She was smiling at Lov, and trying to make him take more notice of her. She could not wait any longer for him to come to her, so she was going to him. Her harelip was spread open across her upper teeth, making her mouth appear as though she had no upper lip at all. Men usually would have nothing to do with Ellie May; but she was eighteen now, and she was beginning to discover that it should be possible for her to get a man in spite of her appearance.

"Ellie May's acting like your old hound used to do when he got the itch," Dude said to Jeeter. "Look at her scrape her bottom on the sand. That old hound used to make the same kind of sound Ellie May's making, too. It sounds just like a little pig squealing, don't it?"

"By God and by Jesus, Lov, I want some good eating turnips," Jeeter said. "I ain't et nothing all winter but meal and fat-back, and I'm wanting turnips something powerful. All the ones I raised has got them damn-blasted green-gutted worms in them. Where's you get them turnips at anyhow, Lov? Maybe we could make a trade of some kind or another. I always treated you fair and square. You ought to give them to me, seeing as I ain't got none. I'll go down to your house the first thing in the morning and tell Pearl she's got to stop acting like she does. It's a durn shame for a gal to do the way she's treating you— I'll tell her she's got to let you have your rights with her. I never heard of a durn gal sleeping on a pallet on the floor when her husband has got a bed for her, nohow. Pearl won't keep that up after I tell her about it. That ain't no way to treat a man when he's gone to the bother of marrying. It's time she was knowing it, too. I'll go down there the first thing in the morning and tell her to get in the bed."

Lov was paying no attention to Jeeter now. He was watching Ellie May slide across the yard towards him. When she came a little closer, he reached in the sack and took out another turnip, and began taking big bites out of it. He did not bother to wipe the sand from it this time.

Ada shifted the snuff stick to the other side of her mouth again, and watched Ellie May and Lov with gaping jaw.

Dude stood watching Ellie May, too.

"Ellie May's going to get herself full of sand if she don't stop doing that," Dude said. "Your old hound used never to keep it up that long at a time. He didn't squeal all the time neither, like she's doing."

"By God and by Jesus, Lov," Jeeter said, "I'm wanting turnips. I could come near about chewing up a whole croker sack full between now and bed-time to-night."

Chapter III

JEETER'S reiterated and insistent plea for turnips was having less and less effect upon Lov. He was not aware that any one was talking to him. He was interested only in Ellie May now.

"Ellie May's straining for Lov, ain't she?" Dude said, nudging Jeeter with his foot. "She's liable to bust a gut if she don't look out."

The inner-tube Jeeter was attempting to patch again was on the verge of falling into pieces. The tires themselves were in a condition even more rotten. And the Ford car, fourteen years old that year, appeared as if it would never stand together long enough for Jeeter to put the tire back on the wheel, much less last until it could be loaded with blackjack for a trip to Augusta. The touring-car's top had been missing for seven or eight years, and the one remaining fender was linked to the body with a piece of rusty baling wire. All the springs and horsehair had disappeared from the upholstery; the children had taken the seats apart to find out what was on the inside, and nobody had made an attempt to put them together again.

The appearance of the automobile had not been improved by the dropping off of the radiator in the road somewhere several years before, and a rusty lard-can with a hole punched in the bottom was wired to the water pipe on top of the engine in its place. The lard-can failed to fill the need for a radiator, but it was much better than nothing. When Jeeter got ready to go somewhere, he filled the lard pail to overflowing, jumped in, and drove until the water splashed out and the engine locked up with heat. He would get out then and look for a creek so he could fill the pail again. The whole car was like that. Chickens had roosted on it, when there were chickens at the Lesters' to roost, and it was speckled like a guinea-hen. Now that there were no chickens on the place, no one had ever taken the trouble to wash it off. Jeeter had never thought of doing such a thing, and neither had any of the others.

Ellie May had dragged herself from one end of the yard to the opposite side. She was now within reach of Lov where he sat by his sack of turnips. She was bolder, too, than she had ever been before, and she had Lov looking at her and undisturbed by the sight of her harelip. Ellie May's upper lip had an opening a quarter of an inch wide that divided one side of her mouth into unequal parts; the slit came to an abrupt end almost under her left nostril. The upper gum was low, and because her gums were always fiery red, the opening in her lip made her look as if her mouth were bleeding profusely. Jeeter had been saying for fifteen years that he was going to have Ellie May's lip sewed together, but he had not yet got around to doing it.

Dude picked up a piece of rotted weatherboard that had been knocked from the house and threw it at his father. He did not take his gaze from Ellie May and Lov, however. Their actions, and Ellie May's behavior, held him spellbound.

"What you want now, Dude?" Jeeter said. "What's the matter with you—chunking weather-boarding at me like that?"

"Ellie May's horsing," Dude said.

Jeeter glanced across the yard where Lov and Ellie May were sitting close together. The trunk of a chinaberry tree partly obscured his view of all that was taking place, but he could see that she was sitting on Lov's outstretched legs, astride his knees, and that he was offering her a turnip from the sack beside him.

"Ellie May's horsing, ain't she, Pa?" Dude said.

"I reckon I done the wrong thing by marrying Pearl to Lov," Jeeter said. "Pearl just ain't made up to be Lov's woman. She don't take no interest in Lov's wants, and she don't give a cuss what nobody thinks about it. She ain't the kind of gal to be a wife to Lov. She's queer. I reckon somehow she wants to be going to Augusta, like the other gals done. None of them ever was satisfied staying here. They ain't like me, because I think more of the land than I do about staying in a durn cotton mill. You can't smell no sedge fire up there, and when it comes time to break the land for planting, you feel sick inside but you don't know what's ailing you. People has told me about that spring sickness in the mills, I don't know how many times. But when a man stays on the land, he don't get to feeling like that this time of year, because he's right here to smell the smoke of burning broom-sedge and to feel the wind fresh off the plowed fields going down inside of his body. So instead of feeling sick and not knowing what's wrong down in his body, as it happens in the durn mills, out here on the land a man feels better than he ever did. The spring-time ain't going to let you fool it by hiding away inside a durn cotton mill. It knows you got to stay on the land to feel good. That's because humans made the mills. God made the land, but you don't see Him building durn cotton mills. That's how I know better than to go up there like the rest of them. I stay where God made a place for me."

"Ellie May's acting like she was Lov's woman," Dude said.

Ada shifted the weight of her body from one foot to the other. She was standing in the same place on the porch that she had been when

Lov first came into the yard. She had been watching Lov and Ellie May for a long time without looking anywhere else.

"Maybe God intended for it to be such," Jeeter said. "Maybe He knows more about it than us mortals do. God is a wise old somebody. You can't fool Him! He takes care of little details us humans never stop to think about. That's why I ain't leaving the land and going to Augusta to live in a durn cotton mill. He put me here, and He ain't never told me to get off and go up there. That's why I'm staying on the land. If I was to haul off and go to the mills, it might be hell to pay, coming and going. God might get mad because I done it and strike me dead. Or on the other hand, He might let me stay there until my natural death, but hound me all the time with little devilish things. That's the way He makes His punishment sometimes. He just lets us stay on, slow-like, and hounding us every step, until we wish we was a long time dead and in the ground. That's why I ain't going to the mills with a big rush like all them other folks around Fuller did. They got up there and all of them has a mighty pain inside for the land, but they can't come back. They got to stay now. That's what God's done to them for leaving the land. He's going to hound them every step they take until they die."

"Look at that horsing Ellie May's doing!" Dude said. "That's horsing from way back yonder!"

"By God and by Jesus, Lov," Jeeter shouted across the yard, "what about them there turnips? Has they got them damn-blasted green-gutted worms in them like mine had? I been wanting some good eating turnips since way back last spring. If Captain John hadn't sold off all his mules and shut off letting me get guano on his credit, I could have raised me a whopping big mess of turnips this year. But when he sold the mules and moved to Augusta, he said he wasn't going to ruin himself by letting us tenants break him buying guano on his credit in Fuller. He said there wasn't no sense in trying to run a farm no more—fifty plows or one plow. He said he could make more money out of farming by not running plows. And that's why we ain't got no snuff and rations no more. Ada says she's just bound to have a little snuff now and then, because it sort of staves off hunger, and it does, at that. Every time I sell a load of wood I get about a dozen jars of snuff, even if I ain't got the money to buy meal and meat, because snuff is something a man is just bound to have. When I has a sharp pain in the belly, I can take a little snuff and not feel hungry all the rest of the day. Snuff is a powerful help to keep a man living.

"But I couldn't raise no turnips this year. I didn't have no mule, and I didn't have no guano. Oh, I had a few measly little rows out there in the field, but a man can't run no farm unless he's got a mule to plow it with. A hoe ain't no good except to chop cotton with, and corn. Ain't no sense in trying to grow turnips with a hoe. I reckon that's why them damn-blasted green-gutted worms got in them turnips. I didn't have no mule to cultivate them with. That's why they was all wormy.

"Have you been paying attention to what I was saying, Lov? You ain't never answered me about them turnips yet. I got a powerful gnawing in my belly for turnips. I reckon I like winter turnips just about as bad as a nigger likes watermelons. I can't see no difference between the two ways. Turnips is about the best eating I know about."

Lov did not look up. He was saying something to Ellie May, and listening to what she was saying.

Lov had always told Jeeter that he would never have anything to do with Ellie May because she had a harelip. At the time he had made a bargain with Jeeter about Pearl, he said he might consider taking Ellie May if Jeeter would take her to Augusta and get a doctor to sew up her mouth. Jeeter had thought the matter over thoroughly, and decided that it would be best to let Lov take Pearl, because the cost of sewing up the harelip would probably amount to more than he was getting out of the arrangement. Letting Lov take Pearl was then all clear profit to Jeeter. Lov had given him some quilts and nearly a gallon of cylinder oil, besides giving him all of a week's pay, which was seven dollars. The money was what Jeeter wanted more than anything else, but the other things were badly needed, too.

Jeeter had been intending to take Ellie May to a doctor ever since she was three or four years old, so that when a man came to marry her there would be no drawbacks. But with first one thing and then another turning up every now and then, Jeeter had never been able to get around to it. Some day he would take her, though; he told himself that, every time he had occasion to think about it.

At the time Lov had married Pearl, he said he liked Ellie May more than he did her, but that he did not want to have a wife with a harelip. He knew the Negroes would laugh at him. That was the summer before; several weeks before he had begun to like Pearl so much that he was doing everything he could think of to make her stop sleeping on a pallet on the floor. Pearl's long yellow curls hanging down her back, and her pale blue eyes, turned Lov's head. He thought there was not a more beautiful girl anywhere in the world. And for that matter, no man who had ever had the opportunity of seeing Pearl had ever gone away without thinking the same thing. It would have been impossible for her to dress herself, or even to disfigure herself, in a way that would make her plain or ordinary-looking. She became more beautiful day by day.

But Lov's wishes were unheeded. Pearl, if it was possible, was more determined than ever by that time to keep away from him. And now that Ellie May had dragged herself all the way across the yard, and was now sitting on his legs, Lov was thinking only of Ellie May. Aside from her harelip, Ellie May was just as desirable as the next girl a man would find in the sand-hill country surrounding the town of Fuller. Lov was fully aware of that. He had tried them all, white girls and black.

"Lov ain't thinking about no turnips," Dude said, in reply to his father. "Lov's wanting to hang up with Ellie May. He don't care nothing about the way her face looks now—he ain't aiming to kiss her. Ain't nobody going to kiss her, but that ain't saying nobody wouldn't fool with her. I heard niggers talking about it not long ago down the road at the old sawmill. They said she could get all the men she wanted, if she would keep her face hid."

"Quit chunking that there ball against that old house," Jeeter said angrily. "You'll have the wall worn clear in two, if you don't stop doing that all the time. The old house ain't going to stand up much longer, noway. The way you chunk that ball, it's going to pitch over and fall on the ground some of these days. I declare, I wish you had more sense than you got."

The old grandmother came hobbling out of the field with the sack of dead twigs on her back. She shuffled her feet through the deep sand of the tobacco road, and scuffed them over the hard sand of the yard, looking neither to the right nor to the left. At the bottom of the front steps she dropped the load from her shoulder and sat down to rest a while before going to the kitchen. Her groans were louder than usual, as she began rubbing her sides. Sitting on the bottom step with her feet in the sand and her chest almost touching her sharp knees, she looked more than ever like a loosely tied bag of soiled black rags. She was unmindful of the people around her, and no one was more than passingly aware that she had been anywhere or had returned. If she had gone to the thicket and had not returned, no one would have known for several days that she was dead.

Jeeter watched Lov from the corners of his eyes while he tried to make another patch stick to the cracked rubber inner-tube. He had noticed that Lov was several yards from the sack of turnips, and he waited patiently while the distance grew more and more each minute. Lov had forgotten how important the safety of the turnips was. So long as Ellie May continued to tousle his hair with her hands he would forget that he had turnips. She had made him forget everything.

"What you reckon they're going to do next?" Dude said. "Maybe Lov's going to take her down to the coal chute and keep her there all day."

Ada, who had been standing on the porch all that time as motionless as one of the uprights, suddenly pulled her dress tighter over her chest. The cool February wind was barely to be felt out in the sun, but on the porch and in the shade it went straight to the bones. Ada had been ill with pellagra for several years, and she had said she was always cold except in midsummer.

"Lov's going to big her," Dude said. "He's getting ready to do it right now, too. Look at him crawl around—he acts like an old stud-horse. He ain't never let her get that close before. He said he wouldn't never get close enough to Ellie May to touch her with a stick, because he don't like the looks of her mouth. But he ain't paying no mind to it now, is he? I bet he don't even know she's got a slit-lip on her. If he does know it, he don't give a good goddam now."

Several Negroes were coming up the road, walking towards Fuller. They were several hundred feet away when they first noticed the Lesters and Lov in the yard, but it was not until they were almost in front of the house that they noticed what Lov and Ellie May were doing in the farther side near a chinaberry tree. They stopped laughing and talking, and slowed down until they were almost standing still.

Dude hollered at them, calling their names; but none of them spoke. They stopped and watched.

"Howdy, Captain Lov," one of them said.

Lov did not hear. The Lesters paid no more attention to the Negroes. Negroes passing the house were in the habit of looking at the Lesters, but very few of them ever had anything to say. Among themselves they talked about the Lesters, and laughed about them; they spoke to other white people, stopping at their houses to talk. Lov was one of the white persons with whom they liked to talk.

Jeeter screwed the pump hose into the innertube valve and tried to work some air inside. The pump was rusty, the stem was bent, and the hose was cracked at the base so badly that air escaped before it ever had a chance to reach the valve. It would take Jeeter a week to pump thirty pounds of air into the tire at that rate. He could have put more air into the tires if he had attempted to blow them up with his mouth.

"It looks like I ain't going to get started to Augusta with a load of wood before next week," he said. "I wish I had a mule. I could haul a load there near about every day if I had one. The last time I drove this automobile to Augusta every one of the durn tires went flat before I could get there and back. I reckon about the best thing to do is to fill them all full of hulls and ride that way. That's what a man told me to do, and I reckon he was just about right. These old inner-tubes and tires ain't much good no longer."

The three Negroes went a few steps farther down the road and stopped again. They stayed within sight of the yard, waiting to see what

Lov was doing. After he had not answered them the first time they spoke, they knew he did not want them to bother him again.

Dude had thrown the baseball aside and had walked closer to Ellie May and Lov. He sat down on the ground close to them, and waited to see what they were going to do next. Lov had stopped eating turnips, and Ellie May had eaten only a part of one.

"Them niggers don't believe Lov's going to," Dude said. "They said down at the old sawmill that wouldn't nobody fool with Ellie May, unless it was in the night-time. I reckon Lov would say so himself, afterwards."

Chapter IV

JEETER carefully laid the pump aside and crept stealthily to the corner of the house. He propped his feet and leaned against the rotten weatherboards to wait. From where he stood, he could see everything. When Jeeter looked straight ahead, Ellie May and Lov were in full view; and if he had wanted to see Ada he could have turned his head slightly and seen her standing on the porch. There was nothing for him to do now but wait. Lov was moving farther and farther away from the sack.

Ada once more rolled the snuff stick to the other corner of her mouth. She had been watching Lov and Ellie May ever since they began getting together, and the closer they crawled to each other, the more calm she became. She was waiting, too, to ask Lov to make Pearl come to see her soon. Pearl had not been there since the day she was married.

Pearl was so much like Ada, in both appearance and behavior, that no one could have mistaken them for other than mother and daughter. When Pearl married Lov, Ada had told her she ought to run away from him before she began bearing children, and go to Augusta and live at the mills. Pearl, however, did not have the courage to run away alone. She was afraid. She did not know what would happen to her in the cotton mills, and she was too young to understand the things she heard about life there. Even though she was between twelve and thirteen years old, she was still afraid of the dark, and she often cried through most of the night as she lay trembling on her pallet on the floor. Lov was in the room, and the doors were closed, but the creep of darkness seemed to bring an unbearable feeling of strangulation. She had never told any one how much she feared the dark nights, and no one had known why she cried so much. Lov thought it was something to do with her mind. Dude did not have very much sense, and neither did one or two of the other children, and it was natural for him to think that Pearl was afflicted in the same way. The truth was, Pearl had far more sense than any of the Lesters; and that, like her hair and eyes, had been inherited from her father. The man who was her father had passed through the country one day, and had never been seen since. He had told Ada that he came from Carolina and was on his way to Texas, and that was all she knew about him.

Lately, however, Pearl was beginning to lose some of her fear. After eight months in the house with Lov she had gradually grown braver, and she had even ventured to think that some day she could run away to Augusta. She did not want to live on the sand ridge. The sight of the muddy Savannah swamps on one side and the dusty black structure of the coal chute on the other was not as beautiful as the things she had once seen in Augusta. She had been to Augusta once with Jeeter and Ada, and had seen with her own eyes girls who were laughing and carefree. She did not know whether they worked in the cotton mills, but it made little difference to her. Down there on the tobacco road no one ever laughed. Down there girls had to chop cotton in the summer, pick it in the fall, and cut fire-wood in winter.

Jeeter pushed himself erect from the corner of the house, and began moving slowly across the yard. He lifted one foot, held it in the air several seconds, and put it on the ground in front of him. He had crept up on rabbits like that many times in the woods and thickets. They would be sitting in a hollow log, or in a hole in a gully, and Jeeter would creep upon them so noiselessly that they never knew how he caught them. Now he was creeping up on Lov.

Half way across the yard Jeeter suddenly broke into a terrific plunge that landed him upon the sack of turnips almost as quickly as the bat of an eye. He could have waited a few minutes longer, and reached it with the same ease with which he caught rabbits; but there was no time to lose now, and he was far more anxious to get the turnips than he had ever been to catch a rabbit.

He hugged the sack desperately in both arms, squeezing it so tight that watery turnip juice squirted through the loosely woven burlap in all directions. The juice squirted into his eyes, almost blinding him; but it was as pleasant to Jeeter as summer rain-water, and far more welcome.

Ada took one step forward, balancing herself against one of the porch uprights; Dude jumped to his feet, holding to the chinaberry tree behind him.

Lov turned around just in time to see Jeeter grab the sack and hug it in his arms. Ellie May tried to hold Lov where he was, but he succeeded in twisting out of her arms and dived for Jeeter and the turnips. Ellie May turned over just in time to clutch wildly at his foot, and he fell sprawling from mid-air to the hard ground.

Each of the Lesters, without a word having been spoken, was prepared for concerted action without delay. Dude dashed across the yard towards his father; Ada ran down the porch steps, and the old grandmother was only a few feet behind her. All of them gathered around Jeeter and the sack, waiting. Ellie May still clung to Lov's foot, pulling him back each time he succeeded in wiggling his body a few inches closer to Jeeter. The tips of Lov's fingers never got closer than three feet to the sack.

"I didn't tell you no lie about Ellie May, did I?" Dude said. "Didn't I tell you right, Pa?"

"Hush up, you Dude," Ada scowled. "Can't you see your Pa ain't got no time to talk about nothing?"

Jeeter thrust his chin over the top of the sack and looked straight at Lov. Lov's eyes were bulging and blood-shot. He thought of the seven and a half miles he had walked that morning, all the way to the other side of Fuller and back again, and what he saw now made him sick.

Ellie May was doing her best to pull Lov back where he had been. He was trying to get away so he could protect his turnips and keep the Lesters out of the sack. The very thing he had at first been so careful to guard against when he stopped at the house had happened so quickly he did not know what to think about it. That, however, had been before Ellie May began sliding her bare bottom over the sandy yard towards him. He realized now what a fool he had been—to lose his head, and his turnips, too.

The three Negroes were straining their necks to see everything. They had watched Ellie May and Lov with growing enthusiasm until Jeeter suddenly descended upon the sack, and now they were trying to guess what would happen next in the yard.

Ada and the old grandmother found two large and heavy sticks, and tried to pry Lov over on his back so Ellie May could reach him again. Lov was doing everything in his power to protect his sack, because he knew full well that if Jeeter once got twenty steps ahead of him, he would never be able to catch him before all the turnips were eaten. Jeeter was old, but he could run like a rabbit when he had to.

"Don't be scared of Ellie May, Lov," Ada said. "Ellie May ain't going to hurt you. She's all excited, but she ain't the rough kind at all. She won't hurt you."

Ada prodded him with the stick and made him stop wiggling away from Ellie May. She jabbed him in the ribs as hard as she could, biting her lower lip between her teeth.

"Them niggers look like they is going to come in the yard and help Lov out," Dude said. "If they come in here, I'll bust them with a rock. They ain't got no business helping Lov."

"They ain't thinking of coming in here," Ada said. "Niggers has got more sense than trying to interfere with white-folks' business. They don't dare come."

The colored men did not come any closer. They would have liked to help Lov, because they were friends of his, but they were more interested in waiting to see what Ellie May was going to do than they were in saving the turnips.

Ellie May was sweating like a plow-hand. Lov had got sand all over him, and she was trying to wipe it off with a corner of her gingham mother-hubbard, and to get to him again. Lov made a final and desperate plunge for the sack, and although he succeeded in getting nearly a foot closer to it, Ada hit him on the head with the blackjack stick so hard he slumped helpless on the ground with a weak groan. Ellie May was upon him in a single plunge; her excited, feline agility frightening him almost out of his mind. His breath had first been knocked from him by the force of Ellie May's weight falling on his unprotected stomach, and her knees digging into him with the pain of a mule's kick kept him from being able to breathe without sharp pains in his lungs. He was defenseless in her hold. While Ellie May held him, his arms pinned to the ground, Ada stood over him with her heavy blackjack pole, prepared to strike him on the head if he again tried to get up or to turn over on his stomach. The old grandmother waited on the other side with her stick held high and menacing above her head. She muttered under her breath all the time, but no one paid any attention to what she was trying to say.

"Has these turnips got them damn-blasted green-gutted worms in them, Lov?" Jeeter said. "By God and by Jesus, if they're wormy, I don't know what I'm going to do about it. I been so sick of eating wormy turnips, I declare I almost lost my religion. It's a shame for God to let them damn-blasted green-gutted worms bore into turnips. Us poor people always gets the worse end of all deals, it looks like to me. Maybe He don't intend for humans to eat turnips at all; maybe He wants them raised for the hogs, but He don't put nothing else down here on the land in their stead. Won't nothing but turnips grow in winter-time."

Ellie May and Lov had rolled over and over a dozen or more times, like tumble-bugs; when they finally stopped, Lov was on top. Ada had followed them across the yard, and the grandmother too, and they stood ready to club Lov with the blackjack poles if he showed the first sign of trying to get up before Ellie May was ready to release him.

While the others were in the far corner of the yard, Jeeter suddenly jumped to his feet, hugging the sack of turnips tight to his stomach, and ran out across the tobacco road towards the woods beyond the old cotton field. He did not pause to look back over his shoulder until he was nearly half a mile away. In another moment he had disappeared into the woods.

The Negroes were laughing so hard they could not stand up straight. They were not laughing at Lov, it was the actions of the Lesters that appeared so funny to them. Ada's serious face and Ellie May's frantic determination furnished a scene none of them could look at without laughing. They waited until every one had quieted down, and then they went slowly down the road towards Fuller talking about what they had seen in the Lester yard.

Ada and the grandmother presently went back to the porch and sat down on the steps to watch Ellie May and Lov. There was no longer any danger of him getting away. He did not even try to get up now.

"How many scoops-full does that No. 17 freight engine empty at the chute every morning, Lov?" Dude said. "Looks like to me them freight engines take on nearly twice as much coal as the passenger ones do. Them firemen on the freights is always chunking big hunks of coal at the nigger cabins along the track. I reckon that's why they have to take on more coal than the passengers do. The passenger trains go faster, and the nigger firemen don't have a chance to chunk out coal at the nigger cabins. I've seen near about a whole scoop-full of coal chunked out of the freights at one time. The railroad don't know nothing about it, do they? If they did, they'd make the fireman stop that. They throw out more coal along the tracks than the engines burn, near about, I bet. That's why niggers don't have to cut wood all the time. They all burn railroad coal in their cabins."

Lov was too breathless to say anything.

"Why don't you burn coal in your house, instead of wood, Lov? Nobody would know about it. I ain't going to tell on you, if you want to do that. It's a lot easier than cutting wood every day."

Mother Lester, the old grandmother, sitting beside her bag of dead twigs, began groaning again and rubbing her sides with her fists. Presently she got up, lifted the bag over her shoulder, and went into the house towards the kitchen. She made a fire in the cook-stove and sat down beside it to wait until the twigs burned out. She was certain Jeeter would not bring any of the turnips back for her to eat. He would stay in the thicket and eat every one of them himself. While she waited for the fire to die down, she looked into the snuff jar on the shelf, but it was still empty. There had been no snuff in it for nearly a week, and Ada would not tell her where the full jar was hidden. The only time she ever had any snuff was when she accidentally found the jar hidden away somewhere, and took some before anybody could stop her. Jeeter had knocked her down several times about doing that, and he had said he would kill her if he ever caught her stealing snuff again. There were times when she would have been willing to die, if she could only have for once all the snuff she wanted.

"Why don't the firemen blow the whistles more than they do, Lov?" Dude said. "They hardly blow the whistles at all. If I was a fireman I'd pull the whistle cord near about all the time. They make a noise about as pretty as an automobile horn does."

Dude sat on the pine stump until Lov got up and staggered across the yard towards the tobacco road. Lov looked all around in every direction, hoping he might see Jeeter hiding somewhere close. He was sure that Jeeter had gone to the pine woods beyond the old cotton field though, and he knew it would be a waste of time trying to find him and catch him. It was too late to stop him now.

Ellie May lay where she was; stretched out flat on the ground, on her back. Perspiration had matted her hair against her forehead and neck, and her pink gingham dress was twisted under her shoulders and head in such a way that it made a pillow for her to lie on. Her mouth looked as if it had been torn; her flaming red upper gum looked like a bleeding, painful wound under her left nostril. Her divided lip quivered, and her body trembled.

"You ought to give me them overalls when you're done with them," Dude said. "I ain't had a new pair of overalls since I can remember. Pa says he's going to buy me and him both some one of these days when he sells a lot of wood, but I ain't putting none too much trust in what he says. He ain't going to sell no wood, not more than a load at a time, noway. He tells more lies than any man I ever heard of. I reckon he'd rather lie about it than haul wood to Augusta. He's that lazy he won't get up off the ground sometimes when he stumbles. I've seen him stay there near about an hour before he got up. He's the laziest son of a bitch I ever seen."

Lov went to the middle of the road and stood there uncertainly, his legs wide apart to keep his balance, and his body swaying backward and forward like a drunken man's. He began brushing the sand off of his clothes, and shaking it out of his hair. Sand was in his pockets and shoes, and even his ears were full of it.

"When is you going to buy yourself an automobile, Lov?" Dude asked. "You make a heap of a lot of money at the chute—you ought to buy yourself a great big car, like the ones the rich people in Augusta has got. I'll show you how to run it. I know all about automobiles. Pa's

old Ford ain't much to look at now, but when it was in good running
order I used to run the wheels off of it sometimes, near about. You
ought to get one that has got a great big horn on it. Whistles and horns
make a pretty sound, don't they, Lov? When is you going to get you
an automobile?"

Lov stood in the middle of the road for the next ten or fifteen minutes, looking out over the top of the sagging brown broom-sedge
towards the thicket where Jeeter was. After he had waited until he did
not know what else to do, he staggered up the road in the direction
of his house and the coal chute. Pearl would be at the house when he
reached it, but as soon as he walked inside she would run out the
back door and stay until he left. Even if she did not leave the room
when he entered the house, she would not look at him nor have anything to say. He could look at her long yellow hair hanging down her
back, but that was all. She would not allow him to come close enough
to look into her eyes; if he tried to do that, she would certainly run
off into the broom-sedge.

Ada and Dude watched him until he was out of sight beyond the
rise in the ridge, and then they turned their backs and looked at Ellie
May in the yard.

Dude went to the pine stump and sat down to watch the red wood-
ants crawl over the stomach and breasts of his sister. The muscles of
her legs and back twitched nervously for a while, and then slowly the
jerking stopped altogether, and she lay still. Her mouth was partly open,
and her upper lip looked as if it had been torn wider apart than it
naturally was. The perspiration had dried on her forehead and cheeks,
and smudges of dirt were streaked over her pale white skin.

For nearly an hour she slept deeply in the warm February sun, and
when she awoke, her right arm was lying across her mouth where
Dude had placed it when he left the yard to get some of the turnips
before his father had eaten them all.

Chapter V

Down in the thicket, hidden from the house and road by the four-
foot wall of brown broom-sedge, Jeeter's conscience began to bother
him. His hunger had been abated temporarily, and his overalls pockets
were filled with turnips, but the slowly formed realization that he had
stolen his son-in-law's food sickened his body and soul. He had stolen
food before, food and everything else he had had opportunity to take,

but each time, as now, he regretted what he had done until he could convince himself that he had not done anything so terribly wrong. Sometimes he could do this in a few minutes, at other times it was days, and even weeks, before he was satisfied that God had forgiven him and would not punish him too much.

The sound of Dude's voice behind him in the woods was like the voice of God calling him to punishment. Dude had been crashing through the thicket and beating the underbrush with a blackjack stick for the past half hour trying to find Jeeter before all the turnips had been eaten.

There was a hollow silence in the woods around Jeeter between Dude's yells, and Jeeter felt humble and penitent. He carefully wiped the blade of the knife with which he had pared the turnips, and thrust it into his pocket. Then he jumped up and ran out of the thicket and into the broom-sedge. He could see the roof of the house and the tops of the chinaberry trees, but he had no way of knowing whether Lov had gone home.

Dude saw him the moment he came out of the underbrush and started through the sedge.

"Hey! Where you running off to now?" Dude shouted at him, running across the field to cut Jeeter off from the house.

Jeeter stopped and waited for Dude to reach him. He took out half a dozen of the smallest turnips and laid them in Dude's outstretched hands.

"What made you run off and try to eat them all up for, and not give me none?" Dude demanded. "You ain't the only one what likes turnips. I ain't had no more to eat this week than you has. You're as mean as an old snake at times. Why didn't you want me to have none?"

"The good Lord is against theft," Jeeter said. "He don't make no provision for the future for them that steals. They has got to look out for theirselves in the after-life. Now I got to get right with God and confess my sins. I done an evil deed this day. God don't like for His people to do that. He won't take no notice of sinners. And theft is the worse deed a human can do, near about."

"Hell," Dude said, "you talk like that near about every time you steal something, but you don't never stick to it afterwards. You're just trying to keep from giving me some more turnips. You can't fool me."

"That's a sinful thing to say about a man who's tried all his life to stand right with God. God's on my side, and He don't like to hear people talking about me in that manner. You ought not to talk like that, Dude. Ain't you got no sense at all?"

"Give me some more," Dude said. "Ain't no use for you to try to keep them all by talking like that. That ain't going to get you nowhere.

That don't mean nothing to me. I know better than to get fooled this time."

"You've already had five, ain't you?" Jeeter said, counting the ones he had left in his pockets. "You don't need no more."

Dude thrust his hand into the nearest pocket and jerked out as many as he could hold in his hand. Jeeter hit at him with his elbows, but Dude did not mind that. Jeeter was too weak to hurt him.

"That's all you're going to have," Jeeter said. "I'm taking what's left and give to Ada and Ellie May. I expect they be almost as hungry as I was. They'll be waiting now to get some. Has Lov gone yet?"

"He went back to the chute long ago," Dude said.

They started walking through the broom-sedge towards the house. Long before they reached the road they could see Ada and Ellie May waiting in the yard for them. The grandmother was crouching in the doorway, afraid to come out any farther.

"I reckon the women folks is pretty hungry, too," Dude said. "Ellie May's belly was growling all last night. It woke me up this morning, starting all over again."

Ellie May and Ada sat down on the steps when Dude and Jeeter came into view. They waited patiently while Dude and Jeeter broke through the broom-sedge, and as they came nearer, Ada went up on another step. The grandmother crouched in the doorway, clinging to the frame with both hands. None of them was more hungry than she was.

There was another woman on the porch, too. She sat swaying backward and forward in the rocking-chair, and singing a hymn at the top of her voice. Each time she reached the highest note she could go, she held it until her breath gave out and then she started all over again.

Jeeter jumped over the drain ditch and came across the yard with Dude at his heels. As soon as he saw the woman in the rocking-chair his face brightened, and he almost stumbled in his haste to reach her.

"The good Lord be praised!" he shouted, seeing Bessie Rice sitting on the porch. "I knowed God would send His angel to take away my sins. Sister Bessie, the Lord knows what I needed, all right. He wants me to give up my sinful ways, don't He?"

Ada and Ellie May jerked at Jeeter's overalls pockets, extracting the remaining turnips in desperate hurry. Jeeter tossed three of the smallest ones on the porch in the direction of the door. The grandmother fell on her knees and clutched them hungrily against her stomach, while she munched the vegetable with her toothless gums.

"The Lord told me to come to the Lester house," the woman preacher said. "I was at home sweeping out the kitchen when He came to me and said, 'Sister Bessie, Jeeter Lester is doing something evil.

You go to his place and pray for him right now before it's too late, and try to make him give up his evil goings-on.' I looked right back at the Lord, and said, 'Lord, Jeeter Lester is a powerful sinful man, but I'll pray for him until the devil goes clear back to hell.' That's what I told Him, and here I is. I came to pray for you and yours, Jeeter Lester. Maybe it ain't too late yet to get on the good side of the Lord. It's people like you who ought to be good, instead of letting the devil make you do all sorts of sinful things."

"I knowed the good Lord wouldn't let me slip and fall in the devil's hands!" Jeeter shouted, dancing around Bessie's chair. "I knowed it! I knowed it! I always been on God's side, even when things was the blackest, and I knowed He'd jerk me out of hell before it was too late. I ain't no sinner by nature, Sister Bessie. It's just the old devil who's always hounding me to do a little something bad. But I ain't going to do it. I want to go to heaven when I die."

"Ain't you going to give me a turnip, Jeeter?" she said. "I ain't had so much to eat lately. Times is hard for the good and bad alike, though I sometimes think that's not just exactly right. The good ought never be hard put to it, like the sinful ought to be all the time."

"Sure, Bessie," Jeeter said, giving her several turnips. He selected the largest ones he could find. "I know how you like to eat, about as bad as the rest of us. I wish I had something to give you to take home. When I had plenty, I used to give Brother Rice a whole armful of chickens and sweet potatoes at a time. Now I ain't got nothing but a handful of measly little turnips, but I ain't ashamed of them. The Lord growed them. His doings is good enough for me. Ain't they for you?"

Sister Bessie smiled happily at Jeeter and his family. She was always happy when she could pray for a sinner and save him from the devil, because she had been a sinner herself before Brother Rice chased the devil out of her and married her. Her husband was dead now though, and she was carrying on his work in the sand hills. He had left her eight hundred dollars in insurance money when he died the summer before, and she was saving it to carry on his work when the time came that it was needed most. She had the money in a bank in Augusta.

Some of the people in the sand hills said the kind of religion Sister Bessie talked about was far from being God's idea of what consecrated people should say and do. Every time she heard it, Bessie always said that the other people did not know any more about God's religion than the male preachers who talked about it knew. Most of them belonged to no sect at all, while the rest were Hard-shell Baptists. Bessie hated Hard-shell Baptists with the same intensity with which she hated the devil.

There was no church building to house Bessie's congregation, nor was there an organized band of communicants to support her. She went from house to house in the sand hills, mostly along the crest of the ridge where the old tobacco road was, and prayed for people who needed prayer and wanted it. She was past thirty-five, almost forty, and she was much better-looking than most women in the sand hills, except for her nose.

Bessie's nose had failed to develop properly. There was no bone in it, and there was no top to it. The nostrils were exposed, and Dude had once said that when he looked at her nose it was like looking down the end of a double-barrel shotgun. Bessie was sensitive about the appearance of it, and she tried to keep people from staring at her and commenting on what they saw.

Ada had already told Bessie about the turnips Jeeter took from Lov. Bessie had come prepared to pray for Jeeter for his sins in general, but she was glad she had a specific sin to pray for him to God about. Prayer always did a man more good, she said, if there was something he was ashamed of.

First of all though, she finished eating all the turnips Jeeter would let her have.

"I wish Lov was here so I could ask his forgiveness," Jeeter said. "I reckon I'll have to go down to his house the first thing in the morning and tell him how powerful sorry I am. I hope he ain't so mad about it that he'll try to beat me with a stick. He's got a whopping big temper when he gets good and mad about something."

"Let's have a little prayer," Bessie said, swallowing the last of the turnip.

"The good Lord be praised," Jeeter said. "I'm sure glad you came when you did, Sister Bessie, because I'm needing prayer about as bad as I ever did. I was a sinful man to-day. The Lord don't take up with humans who commits theft. I don't know what made me so bad. I reckon the old devil just came along and got the upper hand on me."

Every one got down on his knees, except Ellie May and Dude. They sat on the steps eating and watching.

"You know," Bessie said, "some people make an objection to kneeling down and having prayer out of doors. They don't like to have me pray for them on the front porch or in the yard. They say, 'Sister Bessie, can't we go in the house out of sight and pray there just as good?' And do you know what I tell them? I say, 'Brothers and Sisters, I ain't ashamed to pray out here in the open. I want folks passing along the road to know I'm on God's side. I ain't ashamed to let folks see me pray. It's the old devil that's always whispering about going in the house out of sight.' That's the way I stick up for the Lord. I kneel right down and pray in the big road just as loud as I do in a school-house or at a camp-meeting. I ain't ashamed to pray in the front yard or on the porch. It's the old devil who's always telling folks to go in the house out of sight."

"The good Lord be praised," Jeeter said.

"Let's get ready to pray," she said.

Ada and Jeeter bowed their heads and closed their eyes. Mother Lester knelt in the doorway, but she did not close her eyes. She stared straight ahead of her, out over the field of brown broom-sedge.

"Dear God, here I is again to offer a little prayer for sinful people. Jeeter Lester and his family want me to pray for them again. The last time helped them a whole lot, and if it wasn't for Jeeter getting in the clutch of the devil to-day, there wouldn't be no need for prayer this soon again. But Jeeter let the devil get hold of him, and he went and done a powerful sinful thing. He stole all of Lov's turnips and wouldn't give them back. They're all et up now, so it's too late to take them to Lov. That's why we want to pray for Jeeter. You ought to make him stop stealing like he does. I never seen a more stealing man in all my days. It looks like he takes to stealing just as naturally as one of us takes a drink of water. But Jeeter wants to quit, though it seems like he goes and does it again almost as soon as we get through praying for him. You ought to make him quit it this time for good and all. Ain't no sense in You letting a man just keep on doing a sinful thing all the time. You ought to put a stop to it and not let him do it no more. You ain't going to let the old devil tell You what to do, is You? That ain't no way for the Lord to do. The Lord ought to tell the devil to get away and stop trying to tempt good folks.

"And Sister Ada has got the pleurisy again pretty bad. You ought to do something for her this time, sure enough. The last time didn't help her none too much. She can't do all her household work when she's got the pleurisy so bad. If You'll make her well of it, she'll quit the devil for all time. Won't you, Sister Ada?"

"Yes, Lord!"

"And old Mother Lester has got a misery in her sides. She's in pain all the time with it. She's kneeling down right now, but she is in such pain she can't do it many more times.

"You ought to bless Ellie May, too. Ellie May has got that slit in her lip that makes her an awful sight to look at. If You was to make——"

"Don't forget to pray for Pearl, Sister Bessie," Jeeter said. "Pearl needs praying for something awful."

"What has Pearl done sinful, Brother Jeeter?"

"Well, that was what Lov wanted to speak to me about to-day. He says Pearl won't talk to him, and she won't let him touch her. When night comes, she gets down and sleeps on a durn pallet on the floor. Lov has got to sleep in the bed by himself, and can't get her to take no interest in him. That's a pretty bad thing for a wife to do, and God ought to make her quit it. Lov is due some rights. A woman ain't got no business sleeping on a durn pallet on the floor, noway."

"Maybe she knows best, Brother Jeeter," Bessie said. "Maybe Pearl is going to have a little baby, and that's her way of telling Brother Lov about it."

"No, it ain't that, Sister Bessie. Lov says he ain't never slept with her yet. He says he ain't never touched her yet, neither. That's what's worrying him so durn much. He wants her to sleep in the bed with him and stop getting down on that durn pallet on the floor every night like she does. Pearl needs praying for to make her quit that sleeping down there on the floor."

"Brother Jeeter, little girls like Pearl don't know how to live married lives like we grown-up women do. So maybe if I was to talk to her myself instead of getting God to do it, she would change her ways. I expect I know more about what to tell her than He does, because I been a married woman up to the past summer when my former husband died. I expect I know all about it. God wouldn't know what to tell her."

"That might help some, but if I was the praying kind myself, I reckon I'd sort of tell God about it and maybe He would do some good. Maybe He's run across gals like that before, though I don't believe there's another durn gal in the whole country who's as contrary-minded about sleeping in the bed as Pearl is."

Dude picked up the baseball and began tossing it on the roof of the porch, and catching it when it rolled down into the yard. The ball knocked loose the rotten shingles, and pieces of them showered the yard. Ellie May sat waiting to hear some more prayer when Bessie and Jeeter got through talking about Pearl.

"Maybe it wouldn't hurt none if I was to mention it," Bessie said.

"That's right," Jeeter said. "You speak to the Lord about it, too. Both of you together ought to get something done about it."

"Now, Lord, I've got something special to pray about. I don't ask favors unless they is things I want pretty bad, so this time I'm asking for a favor for Pearl. I want You to make her stop sleeping on a pallet on the floor while Brother Lov has to sleep by himself in the bed. Make Pearl get in the bed, Lord, and make her stay there where she belongs. She ain't got no right to sleep on a pallet on the floor when Lov's got a bed for her. Now, You make her stop acting like she's been, and put her in the bed when night comes. I was a good wife to my former husband. I never slept on no pallet on the floor. Sister Ada here don't do nothing like that. And when I marry another man, I ain't going to do that, neither. I'm going to get in the bed just as big as my new husband does. So You tell Pearl to quit that. We women knows what we ought to do, and Pearl just ain't old enough to know better. You got to tell her to quit doing that. If it was——"

"What was that you was saying about getting married, Sister Bessie?" Jeeter asked. "Didn't I hear you say you was going to marry yourself a new husband? Who is you going to get married to?"

"Well, I ain't made up my mind yet. I been looking around some, though. Right now it looks like I can't make up my mind. It's my wish to find a man who's got some goods and possessions, but it looks like ain't nobody got nothing around here no more. All the men folks is poor."

"Now, if it wasn't for Ada, there," Jeeter said.

"Brother Jeeter, you hush your mouth!" she giggled. "You make me feel so funny when you talk like that! How'd you know I'd take to you? You're pretty old, ain't you?"

"I reckon you'd better finish up the prayer," he said. "Ada, there, gets sort of peeved when I talk about marrying another woman."

"—Save us from the devil and make a place for us in heaven. Amen."

Chapter VI

You clear forgot to say a little prayer for Dude," Jeeter said suddenly. "You left Dude out all around, Bessie. Dude, he's as big a sinner as the rest of us Lesters."

Bessie jumped up and ran out into the yard. She clutched Dude by the arm and dragged him to the porch by her chair. She kneeled down in front of it, and tried to pull Dude down beside her.

"I don't want to do that," Dude said angrily. "I don't want no praying for me. I ain't done nothing. Pa did all the stealing of Lov's turnips. He took them and ran off to the thicket."

Bessie took his hands in hers and stroked his arms for several minutes without speaking. Then she stood up beside him and locked her arms around his waist. She squeezed him so hard it made the blood rush to his head.

"I got to pray for you, Dude. The Lord told me all you Lesters was sinful. He didn't leave you out no more than He did Ellie May."

Dude looked into her face. She pleaded convincingly enough to make him want to be prayed for, but he could not stop looking down into her nostrils.

"What you laughing at, Dude?" she said.

"Nothing," he snickered, twisting his head until he could see almost behind himself.

"There ain't nothing about prayer to laugh at, Dude," she said. "All of us has got to have it some time or another."

He felt ill at ease standing so close to her. The way she stroked his arms and shoulders with her hands made him nervous, and he could not stand still.

"Quit that jumping up and down, Dude," Jeeter said. "What ails you?"

Bessie drew her arms tighter around his waist, and smiled at him.

"You kneel down beside me and let me pray for you. You'll do that, won't you, Dude?"

He put his arms around her neck, and began rubbing her as she was rubbing him.

"Hell," he said, snickering again, "I don't give a damn if I do."

"I knowed you would want me to pray for you, Dude," she said. "It will help you get shed of your sins, like Jeeter did."

They knelt down on the porch floor beside the chair. Dude continued to rub her shoulders, and Bessie kept her arms around him. Jeeter was sitting on the floor behind them, leaning against the wall of the house and waiting to hear the prayer for Dude.

"Dear God, I'm asking You to save Brother Dude from the devil and make a place for him in heaven. That's all. Amen."

Bessie stopped praying, but neither she nor Dude made an effort to stand up.

"Praise the Lord," Jeeter said, "but that was a durn short prayer for a sinner like Dude."

"Dude don't need no more praying for. He's just a boy, and he's not sinful like us grown-ups is. He ain't sinful like you is, Jeeter."

"Well, maybe you is right," Jeeter said, "but Dude, he cusses all the time at me and his Ma. He ain't got no respect for none of us. Maybe that's as it should be, but I sort of recollect the Bible saying a son shouldn't cuss his Ma and Pa like he does other people. Nobody never told me no different, but somehow it don't seem right for him to do that. I've seen him pestering Ellie May with a stick, too, and I know that ain't right. That's sinful, and it ought to be prayed about."

"Dude won't do that again," Bessie said, stroking Dude's hair. "He's a fine boy, Dude is. He would make a handsome preacher, too. He's mighty like my former husband in his younger days. I sort of feel like there ain't much difference between them now."

Ada twisted around to see why Dude was staying on the porch. He and Bessie were still kneeling down beside the chair, with their arms around each other.

"Dude's sixteen years old now," Jeeter said. "That makes him two years younger than Ellie May. Well, pretty soon he'll be getting a wife, I reckon. All my other male children married early in life, just like the gals done. When Dude gets married, I won't have none of my children left with me, except Ellie May. And I don't reckon she'll ever find a man to marry her. It's all on account of that mouth she's got. I been thinking I'd take her up to Augusta and get a doctor to sew up her lip. She'd marry quick enough then, because she's got a powerful way with her, woman-like. Ain't nothing wrong with her, excepting that slit in her lip. If it wasn't for that, she'd been married as quick as Pearl was. Men here around Fuller all want to marry gals about eleven or twelve years old, like Pearl was. Ada, there, was just turning twelve when I married her."

"The Lord intended all of us should be mated," Bessie said. "He made us that way. That's what my former husband used to say. I'd tell him that a man needs a woman, and he'd say a woman needs a man. My former husband was just like the Lord in that respect. They both believed in the same thing when it came to mating."

"I reckon the Lord did intend for all of us to get mated," Jeeter said, "but He didn't take into account a woman with a slit in her mouth like Ellie May's got. I don't believe He done the right thing by her when He opened up her lip like that. That's the only contrary thing I ever said about the Lord, but it's the truth. What use is a slit like that for? You can't spit through it, and you can't whistle through it, now can you? It was just meanness on His part when He done that. That's what it was—durn meanness."

"You shouldn't talk about the Lord like that. He knows what He done it for. He knows everything. He wouldn't have done it if He didn't have a good purpose in mind. He knows what He makes men and women for. He made Ellie May's face like that with a good reason in mind. He had the best reason in the world for doing it."

"What reason?"

"Maybe I ought not to say it, Jeeter."

"It ain't no secret between you and the Lord, is it, Sister Bessie?"

"No, ain't no secrets between us. But I know."

"You know what?"

"Why He made her lip slit open."

"Ain't you going to tell me?"

"Brother Jeeter, He done that to her lip to save her pure body from the wicked men."

"What men? I'm the only man around here."

"It's you, Brother Jeeter."

"I ain't wicked. I'm sinful at rare times, but I never been wicked."

"It's all the same to God. It don't make no difference to Him which it is."

"What did I do? I don't see how stealing a few measly turnips and sweet potatoes once in a while has anything to do with Ellie May's face."

"Brother Jeeter, the Lord done that to her lip to save her pure body from being ruined by you. He knowed she would be safe in this house when He made her like that. He knowed that you was once a powerful sinner, and that you might be again if——"

"That's the truth," Jeeter said. "I used to be a powerful sinful man in my time. I reckon I was at one time the most powerful sinful man in the whole country. Now, you take them Peabody children over across the field. I reckon clear near about all of them is half mine, one way or another. And then I used to——"

"You wait till I finish accusing you, Jeeter, before you start lying out of it."

"I ain't lying out of it, Bessie. I just now told you how powerful sinful I once was. There was a man and his wife moved here from——"

"As I was saying, you didn't keep none of it hid from the Lord——"

"But Henry Peabody didn't know nothing about it though——"

"—He knowed that you might take it into your head to ruin Ellie May. The Lord knows everything, and He's got his reasons. He knowed you was such a powerful sinful man long years ago that you wouldn't have obeyed Him if He told you to take your eyes out, if your eyes offended Him."

"Looking at her slit with my eyes won't offend nobody. He don't care about my eyes. What would He want to take them out for?"

"Just like I was saying. If the Lord had told you to cut your eyes out because they offended Him, you wouldn't have done it. That showed you was a powerful sinner. Or if He had told you to cut off your hand, or your ears, for the same reason, you wouldn't have obeyed Him. And He knowed if He told you to stop fooling with Ellie May, you wouldn't have cut off the root of the evil like He said do. That's the reason He sent Ellie May into the world with a slit in her lip. He figured she would be safe from a sinner like you, because you wouldn't like the looks of her."

"The Lord be praised," Jeeter said. "You sure have opened my eyes to the way of God. I never knowed before about that, I declare. If I had knowed it, I sure would have cut myself off when I was fooling around over there at Peabody's. Then if I had done that, Ellie May wouldn't look like she does now, would she, Bessie?"

"It's just like I said. The Lord knows more about us humans' ways than we do."

"I've been a powerful sinful man in my time, I reckon. I never knowed I ought to cut myself off before. Maybe it's not too late now. I sure don't want to let the devil get hold of me."

Bessie turned to Dude again, smiling at him and holding her arms tighter around his neck. Dude did not know what to do next. He liked to touch her, and feel her, and he wanted her to hug him some more, as she had done. He liked to feel her arms tight around him, and have her rub him. Yet he could not believe that Bessie was hugging him for any real reason. She had stopped praying fifteen minutes before, but she still made no motion to release him and make him get up.

"Say, Sister Bessie," Jeeter said, leaning forward and squinting his eyes under his heavy black brows, "what in hell is you and Dude doing there? You and him has been squatting there, hugging and rubbing of the other, for near about half an hour."

Dude hoped she would not make him get up, because he liked to feel her pull him tight to her breast and squeeze him in her arms.

Bessie tried to stand up, but Dude would not let her. She sat down again beside him on the floor, running her fingers through his hair.

"Durn if I ever saw a woman preacher take on like that before," Jeeter said, shaking his head. "Looks to me like you ain't going to do no more praying to-day. You and Dude is hugging and rubbing of the other, ain't you? By God and by Jesus, if it ain't so!"

Bessie got up and sat down in the chair. She tried to make Dude go away, but he stood in front of her, waiting for her to touch him.

"The Lord was speaking to me," she said. "He was telling me I ought to marry a new husband. I can't get around much by myself, and if I was to get married to a man, maybe I could do more preaching and praying. The Lord would turn him into a preacher too, and both of us could travel around spreading the gospel."

"He didn't tell you to marry Dude, did He? Dude ain't no preacher. He ain't got sense enough to be one. He wouldn't know what to preach about when the time came to get up and say something."

"Dude would make a fine preacher," she interrupted. "Dude would be just about as good at preaching and praying as my former husband was, maybe better. The Lord and me could show him how to do. It ain't hard at all after you catch on to it."

"I wish I was in my younger days. If I was, I could maybe do it myself with you. I could do it yet, only Ada, there, has got so she don't want me fooling with the women-folks no more. I know I could do as fine preaching and praying as the next one. It ain't that what's holding me back—it's Ada, there. She's got a queer notion that I might take to fooling with the women-folks. Well, I ain't saying I wouldn't if I had half a chance, neither."

"It would require a younger man for me to be satisfied," Bessie said. "Dude there is just suitable for preaching and living with me. Ain't you, Dude?"

"You want me to go home with you now?" he said.

"I got to pray over it first, Dude," she said. "When I come back by here the next time, I'll let you know. You'll have to wait until I can ask the Lord if you'll do. He's sometimes particular about his male preachers, especially if they is going to marry women preachers."

Bessie ran down the steps and over the hard white sand of the yard. When she reached the tobacco road, she turned around and looked at the Lesters on the front porch several minutes.

Presently, without waiting to walk, she began running through the deep white sand towards her house two miles away on the bluff above the Savannah.

Bessie's home, a tenant house of three rooms, and a corn-crib, sat on the edge of the bluff. That was where the country dropped down into the swampy Savannah River Valley. The house, covered with unpainted weatherboards, sat precariously on three piles of thin stones. The fourth pile had fallen down ten or twelve years before, making one end of the house sag to the ground.

"Well," Jeeter said, "Sister Bessie is up to something, all right. It looks to me like she's got her head set on marrying Dude, there. I never seen such hugging and rubbing of the other as them two was doing. Something is going to come of it. Something is bound to happen."

Dude snickered and stood behind a chinaberry tree so nobody could see him. Ellie May watched him from behind the pine stump, smiling because she had heard what Bessie had said.

Jeeter sat looking out over the old field of brown broom-sedge, and wondering if he could borrow a mule somewhere and raise a crop that year. The time for spring plowing had already arrived, and it made him restless. He did not like to sit idly on the porch and let the spring pass, without burning and plowing. He had decided that he could at least burn over the fields, even if he did not yet know how he could get a mule and seed-cotton and guano. He would have gone out then and set the broom-sedge on fire; but he felt comfortable where he was, and the burning of the fields could wait until the next day. There was plenty of time left yet. It would not take him long to put in a crop when once he got started.

Now that he was alone he began to worry all over again about the way he had treated Lov. He wanted to do something to make amends. If he went down to the chute the next morning and told Lov how sorry he was and that he promised never to steal anything from him again, he hoped that Lov would forgive him and not try to hit him with chunks of coal. And while he was about it, he could stop by Lov's house and speak to Pearl. He would tell her that she had to stop sleeping on a pallet on the floor, and be more considerate of

Lov's wants. It was bad enough, he knew, to have to put up with a woman all day long, and then when night came to be left alone, was even worse.

"Ain't you going to haul no more wood to Augusta?" Ada demanded. "I ain't had no new snuff since I don't know when. And all the meal is gone, and the meat, too. Ain't nothing in the house to eat."

"I'm aiming to take a load over there to-morrow or the next day," Jeeter said. "Don't hurry me, woman. It takes a heap of time to get ready to make a trip over there. I got my own interests to consider. You keep out of it."

"You're just lazy, that's what's wrong with you. If you wasn't lazy you could haul a load every day, and I'd have me some snuff when I wanted it most."

"I got to be thinking about farming the land," Jeeter said. "I ain't no durn woodchopper. I'm a farmer. Them woodchoppers hauling wood to Augusta ain't got no farming to take up their time, like I has. Why, I expect I'm going to grow near about fifty bales of cotton this year, if I can borrow the mules and get some seed-cotton and guano on credit in Fuller. By God and by Jesus, I'm a farmer. I ain't no durn woodchopper."

"That's the way you talk every year about this time, but you don't never get started. It's been seven or eight years since you turned a furrow. I been listening to you talk about taking up farming again so long I don't believe nothing you say now. It's a big old whopping lie. All you men is like that. There's a hundred more just like you all around here, too. None of you is going to do nothing, except talk. The rest of them go around begging, but you're so lazy you won't even do that."

"Now, Ada," Jeeter said, "I'm going to start in the morning. Soon as I get all the fields burned off, I'll go borrow me some mules. Me and Dude can grow a bale to the acre, if I can get me some seed-cotton and guano."

"Humph!" Ada said, leaving the porch.

Chapter VII

JEETER did not go down to the coal chute to see Lov. Neither did he go to the house to speak to Pearl.

There were always well-developed plans in Jeeter's mind for the things he intended doing; but somehow he never got around to doing them. One day led to the next, and it was much more easy to say he would wait until to-morrow. When that day arrived, he invariably postponed action until a more convenient time. Things had been going along in that easy way for almost a lifetime now; nevertheless, he was again getting ready to burn off the fields and plow the land. He wanted to raise a crop of cotton.

Having an operation performed on Ellie May's lip was one of those things that Jeeter had been waiting for fifteen years to do. Several times each year he had said he was going to take her to a doctor in Augusta; when he did make an effort to take her there, he usually never got any farther than the store at the crossroad, where something was certain to come up that caused him to change his plans.

In the course of all those years he had actually reached Augusta two or three times with the sole intention of having the operation performed; but it had always resulted in something coming to his mind at the last minute that he thought he needed more than Ellie May needed an operation. Once it was plow-lines that he could not do without another day, even though he had no mule to use them on; another time it was snuff he had to have, and so he had stopped at the store and spent what little money he had, and they returned home with nothing accomplished.

Ellie May did not protest. She could not have been made to believe that her harelip could be sewn together in such a way that only the faintest suggestion of a scar would remain. She had become so accustomed to the gaping narrow opening in her mouth that she could not believe that it was possible for her ever to look any different from the way she always had.

On those very few occasions when Jeeter had made preparations to go to the hospital, and when he had talked to Ellie May about going there, she would stand behind the corner of the house, or behind one of the many chinaberry trees scattered around the house, and grin. The Lesters had spoken so frequently about her harelip that she had come to believe that Jeeter's proposal to have it operated upon was merely another way of making fun of her appearance. She remained hidden behind the house or a chinaberry tree until the subject of conversation was changed, and only came out where she could be seen when she was certain nothing more would be said about her.

"It ain't no sin to look like that, Ellie May," Jeeter had told her. "You came into the world that way from God, and that's the way He intended for you to look. Sometimes I think maybe it would be a sin to change it, because that would be doing over something He made."

"Well, all I got to say," Ada had stated, "is that it's a shame He didn't make Dude with the slit instead of Ellie May. A gal ain't got no business looking like that. Women ain't good for nothing but to marry and work for men, and when one of them has that kind of thing on her, there ain't no man I ever heard of who's going to use her. If it was Dude who had the slit, it wouldn't make no difference at all. Men ain't noticed so much in the face as women is, noway."

Once when Ellie May went to the schoolhouse several years before, to enter the first grade, she returned home before noon and never went back again. The teacher told her she was too old to attend school with little children, but the real reason for sending her home was because the other boys and girls laughed at her harelip so much they could not study their lessons. So Ellie May came back home and never went again. Dude had never attended school, either; Jeeter said he was needed at home to help him do the work.

But if Jeeter was indifferent towards Ellie May's need for an operation, there was one thing in his life he tried to do with all the strength in his mind and body. That one thing was the farming of the land. There had been scarcely a moment in his life during the past six or seven years when he was not thinking about it, and trying to discover some way by which he could raise cotton. When Captain John had moved to Augusta seven years before, it seemed to be the end of all farming as far as Jeeter was concerned, but he would not give up the struggle to break the land each spring and plant cotton.

Jeeter could never think of the loss of his land and goods as anything but a man-made calamity. He sometimes said it was partly his own fault, but he believed steadfastly that his position had been brought about by other people. He did not blame Captain John to the same extent that he blamed others, however. Captain John had always treated him fairly, and had done more for him than any other man. When Jeeter had over-bought at the stores in Fuller, Captain John let him continue, and he never put a limit to the credit allowed. But the end soon came. There was no longer any profit in raising cotton under the Captain's antiquated system, and he abandoned the farm and moved to Augusta. Rather than attempt to show his tenants how to conform to the newer and more economical methods of modern agriculture, which he thought would have been an impossible task from the start, he sold the stock and implements and moved away. An intelligent employment of his land, stocks, and implements would have enabled Jeeter, and scores of others who had become dependent upon Captain John, to raise crops for food, and crops to be sold at a profit. Co-operative and corporate farming would have saved them all.

Jeeter was now reduced to painful poverty. His means of livelihood had been taken away, and he was slowly starving.

The entire section of land around him had originally been owned by Jeeter's grandfather. Seventy-five years before, it had been the most desirable soil in the entire west-central part of Georgia. His grandfather had cleared the greater part of the plantation for the production of tobacco. The soil at that time was better suited to the cultivation of tobacco than to that of any other crop. It was a sandy loam, and the ridge was high and dry. Hundreds of tumbled-down tobacco barns, chinked with clay, could still be found on what was left of the plantation; some of them were still standing, but most of them were rotted and fallen down.

The road on which Jeeter lived was the original tobacco road his grandfather had made. It was about fifteen miles long, and extended in a southeasterly direction from the foothills of the Piedmont, where the sand hills started, and ended on the bluffs at the river. The road had been used for the rolling of tobacco casks, large hogsheads in which the leaf had been packed after being cured and seasoned in the clay-chinked barns; thousands of hogsheads had been rolled along the crest of the ridge which connected the chain of sand hills, and they had made a smooth firm road the entire distance of fifteen miles. Sometimes the casks had been pushed by gangs of Negroes to the river steamboats, other times they were pulled by teams of mules; but always the crest of the ridge was followed, because when off it the hogsheads would have rolled downhill into the creeks which ran parallel with the road to the river, and once wet, the leaf would have been ruined and worthless.

After seventy-five years the tobacco road still remained, and while in many places it was beginning to show signs of washing away, its depressions and hollows had made a permanent contour that would remain as long as the sand hills. There were scores of tobacco roads on the western side of the Savannah Valley, some only a mile or so long, others extending as far back as twenty-five or thirty miles into the foothills of the Piedmont. Any one walking cross-country would more than likely find as many as six or eight in a day's hike. The region, topographically, was like a palm leaf; the Savannah was the stem, large at the bottom and gradually spreading out into veins at the top. On the side of the valley the creeks ran down like the depressions in the palm leaf, while between them lay the ridges of sand hills, like seams, and on the crests of the ridges were the tobacco roads.

Jeeter's father had inherited about one-half of the original Lester plantation, and approximately half of that had quickly slipped through his fingers. He could not pay the taxes, to begin with, and much of it had been sold to satisfy the county's claims from year to year. The remainder he farmed the best he could. He raised cotton exclusively, but because of the sandy loam he found it necessary to use more and more fertilizer each year. The loose sandy soil would not hold the guano during the hard summer rains, and it was washed away before the roots of the plants could utilize it.

By the time Jeeter was old enough to work in the fields, the land had become such a great item of expense that most of it was allowed to grow up into pines. The soil had become depleted by the constant raising of cotton year after year, and it was impossible to secure a yield of more than a quarter of a bale to the acre. More and more guano was poured into the fields, and faster and faster was it washed away through the loose sandy soil before the cotton plants were able to reach it.

When his father died, what was left of the Lester lands and debts was willed to Jeeter. The first thing that happened was the foreclosure of the mortgage. In order to satisfy the creditors, all the timber was cut, and another large portion of the land was sold. Two years later Jeeter found himself so heavily in debt that he did not own a single acre of land, or even a tenant house, after the claims had been settled. The man who purchased the farm at the sheriff's sale was Captain John Harmon. Captain John allowed Jeeter and his family to live in one of the houses, and to work for him on shares. That was ten years before the World War.

From that time forward, Jeeter had sunk each year into a poverty more bitter than that of the year before. The culmination had apparently been reached when Captain John sold the mules and other stock and moved to Augusta. There was then to be no more two-thirds' share of a year's labor coming to Jeeter, and there was never again to be credit for food and snuff and other necessities at the stores in Fuller. With him, Captain John took his credit. Jeeter did not know what to do. Without snuff and food, life seemed not worth living any longer.

By that time, most of the children had left home and gone to Augusta and elsewhere. Jeeter did not know where all of them were now.

There had been seventeen children born to Ada and him. Five had died, and the twelve living were scattered in all directions. Only Ellie May and Dude were still at home; Pearl was only two miles away, but she never came to the house to see Jeeter and Ada, and they had never been to see her. The children who had died were buried in different parts of the farm. The land had been plowed over since their deaths, and as the graves were unmarked, no one would have known where to look for them if he had wanted to find them.

With the exception of Dude and Ellie May, all the children were married. Jeeter thought he knew where Tom was, but he was not certain. He had heard in the stores in Fuller that Tom, who was the oldest boy, was running a cross-tie camp in the next county at a place about twenty miles away.

Nobody had the slightest idea where most of the others were, nor if all of them were still living. Lizzie Belle had been the last one to leave home. She had gone away several years before, saying she was going to work in a cotton mill across the river from Augusta. There were ten or more cotton mills in Horsecreek Valley, but she had not said which one she was going to work in. Jeeter had been told that she was still there, and that she was married and had seven children already. He did not know if it was true or not, because neither he nor Ada ever received a letter.

There were times when Jeeter became lonesome without all his children around him, and he wished some of them would come back to see him, or write letters. He wondered then, too, if it were possible that they had sent him letters he had not received. There was no rural delivery route on the tobacco road, and he did not have a mail box; but he had said several times that he was some day going to the post-office in Fuller to ask if there was a letter for him from Lizzie Belle or Clara or Tom, or any of the others. He knew he would have to get somebody to read the letters to him if he did hear from them, because neither he nor Ada had ever learned to read. He had been in Fuller hundreds of times since he first thought of asking at the post-office for a letter, but he had not yet got around to making inquiry there.

Some day he hoped to be able to get over to Burke County and see Tom. He had been planning a trip over there for several years, but first it was the old automobile that had prevented him from getting started, then it was bad weather and muddy roads that held him back.

The trip to see Tom had been planned for two purposes; he wanted to see his son, of course, and to talk to him, but his main object in going was because he believed Tom would give him some money regularly when he found out how poor he was and how badly he and Ada needed snuff and food. From the things Jeeter had heard in the stores in Fuller, he knew Tom could afford to give him a few dollars every week. The people said that Tom owned fifty or sixty mules, and twice that many oxen, and that he received a lot of money for the cross-ties he sold the railroad. Jeeter had heard that several times in Fuller, and he knew it must be true. He could not believe that Tom would refuse to help him and Ada when he told his son how poor they were. Now that winter was passing, Jeeter hoped to be able to make the trip some time that summer. The roads would not be muddy then, and the days would be much longer.

The passing of winter and the slow growth of early spring had its usual effect on Jeeter. The warm late February days had kindled in him once more the desire to farm the land. Each year at that season he made a new effort to break the ground and to find means of buying seed-cotton and guano on credit from the merchants in Fuller. His attempts had always ended in the refusal of anybody to give him a dime's worth of credit. However, he burned a field here and a field there on the farm each spring getting the growth of broom-sedge off the land so it would be ready to plow in case some one did lend him a mule and give him a little seed-cotton and guano. Each year for the past six or seven it had been the same.

There was an inherited love of the land in Jeeter that all his disastrous experiences with farming had failed to take away. He had lived his whole life there on a small remnant of the Lester plantation, and while he realized it was not his legally, he felt that he would die if he had to move away from it. He would not even consider going elsewhere to live, even though he were offered a chance to work another man's farm on shares. Even to move to Augusta and work in the cotton mills would be impossible for him. The restless movement of the other tenant farmers to the mills had never had any effect on Jeeter. Working in cotton mills might be all right for some people, he said, but as for him, he would rather die of starvation than leave the land. In seven years his views on the subject had not been altered; and if anything, he was more determined than ever to remain where he was at all cost.

When Lizzie Belle left, Ada had said she wanted to move to Augusta, too; but Jeeter would not listen to her argument. There had never been a time when he wanted to leave the land and live in a mill village.

"City ways ain't God-given," Jeeter had said, shaking his head. "It wasn't intended for a man with the smell of the land in him to live in a mill in Augusta. Maybe it's all right for some people to do that, but God never meant for me to do it. He put me on the land to start with, and I ain't leaving it. I'd feel just like a chicken with my head cut off living shut up in a mill all the time."

"You talk like an old fool," Ada had said angrily. "It's a whole lot better to live in the mills than it is to stay out here on the tobacco road and starve to death. Up there I could get me all the snuff I needed. Down here I ain't never got enough to calm me."

"God is aiming to provide for us," he had answered her. "I'm getting ready right now to receive His bounty. I expect it to come most any time now. He won't let us stay here and starve. He'll send us some snuff and rations pretty soon. I been a God-fearing man all my life, and He ain't going to let me suffer no more."

"You just sit there and see! This time ten years from now you'll be just like you is now, if you live that long. Even the children has got more sense than you has—didn't they go off and work in the mills as soon as they was big enough? They had better sense than to sit here and wait for you to put food in their empty mouths and bellies. They knowed you'd never do nothing about it, except talk. If I wasn't so old, I'd go up to the mills right now and make me some money."

"The Lord sends me every misery He can think of just to try my soul. He must be aiming to do something powerful big for me, because He sure tests me hard. I reckon He figures if I can put up with my own people I can stand to fight back at the devil."

"Humph!" Ada had said. "If He don't hurry up and do something about it, it will be too late. My poor stomach gives me a powerful pain all day long when I ain't got the snuff to calm it."

Chapter VIII

THERE was nothing Jeeter could find to do in the sand hills that would pay him even a few cents a day for his labor. There were no farmers within twenty miles who hired help, because practically all of them were in Jeeter's condition, some of them in an even worse one; nor were there any lumber mills or turpentine stills anywhere near the tobacco road that would employ him. The only job in the surrounding country was the one at the coal chute, and Lov had held it since the Augusta and Georgia Southern Railroad was first built. Even if Jeeter could have taken the job away from Lov, the work would have been too hard for him to do. Filling the big iron scoops all day long and rolling them to the edge of the structure where they were dumped into the engine tenders, required a strong back and stronger arms. Lov could do the work, because he had become accustomed to doing it. For Jeeter to attempt such hard labor in the weakened condition he was in would have been foolish even if the railroad would have hired him.

The hope that he would find Tom was Jeeter's sustaining strength. Behind his hopeful belief that Tom would give him some money lay his fear of dying without a suit of clothes to be buried in. He had developed a growing horror of dying in overalls.

Ada, too, talked a lot about getting clothes to die in. She wanted a silk dress, and it mattered little to her whether the color was red or black, so long as it was stylish in length. Ada had a dress she had been keeping several years to die in, but she was constantly worried for fear that the dress might not be of the correct length. One year it was stylish to have dresses one length, and the next year they were mysteriously lengthened or shortened several inches. It had been impossible for her to keep up with the changes; consequently, even though she had a dress put away, she still tried to make Jeeter promise to buy her a new one that would be in style and in keeping with the times when she should die.

Ada believed she would die almost any day. She was usually surprised to wake up in the morning and discover that she was still alive. The pellagra that was slowly squeezing the life from her emaciated body was a lingering death. The old grandmother had pellagra, too, but somehow she would not die. Her frail body struggled day after day with the disease; but except for the slow withering of her skin and flesh no one was able to say when she would die. She weighed only seventy-two pounds now; once she had been a large woman, and she had weighed two hundred pounds twenty years before. Jeeter was angry with her because she persisted in living, and he would not let her have any food when he could keep her from eating it. However, she had learned now to find her own means of sustenance, such as it was. How she did it, no one knew. Sometimes she would boil leaves and roots, at other times she would eat wild grass and flowers in the fields.

Jeeter had already given implicit instructions regarding his own burial. He had impressed upon both Ada and Lov the importance and necessity of carrying out his plans. He expected to outlive Ada; but in case he should be killed in his automobile, he had made her promise to buy him a suit of clothes. If that was impossible, she was to go to Fuller and ask some of the merchants to give her an old suit for him. Lov, too, had had to swear that he would see that Jeeter was buried in a suit of clothes instead of in overalls.

But there was another thing connected with his death that was of equal importance.

Jeeter had a horror of rats. That was strange, because he had lived with them around him all his life, and he knew their ways almost as well as he did those of men. His reason for hating rats was because of an incident that had happened when his father died while Jeeter was a young man.

The older Lester had died in the same house Jeeter now occupied.

and he was buried on the following day. That night, while Jeeter and the other men were sitting up with the body, some one had suggested that they all go to Fuller and get some Coca-Colas and tobacco. They were to sit up all night, and they had felt the need of something to drink and something to smoke. As all of the men, including Jeeter, had wanted to go to Fuller, they had put the body in the corn-crib and locked the door. The crib was the only place on the farm where anything could be locked up and found intact later. Negroes and white men had a habit of coming by the Lester house during the night and carrying away anything that had been left unprotected. None of the doors of the house had locks on them, but the crib door did have a lock. The men had placed the body inside, locked the door and put the key away, and had driven to Fuller for the Coca-Colas and tobacco.

They returned to the house about three or four hours later. As soon as the mules were unhitched from the buggies and tied to the wagon wheels for the rest of the night, the men unlocked the crib door, lifted out the wooden box, and carried it back into the house. The remainder of the night was spent in watching the casket, drinking Coca-Colas, and smoking and chewing tobacco.

The following afternoon at the funeral, just as the casket was about to be lowered into the grave, the top was lifted off in order that the family and friends might take a last look at the deceased. The lid was turned back, and just as it was fully open, a large corn-crib rat jumped out and disappeared in the woods. Nobody knew how the rat had got inside until some one found a hole in the bottom of the wooden box where the rat had gnawed through while it was locked in the crib.

One by one the people filed past the casket, and each time it became the next person's turn to look at the body, a strange look came over his face. Some of the women giggled, and the men grinned at each other. Jeeter ran to the side of the box and saw what had happened. The rat had eaten away nearly all of the left side of his father's face and neck. Jeeter closed the lid and had the box lowered into the grave immediately. He had never forgotten that day.

Now that the time was coming when he would soon die, Jeeter had become more insistent than ever that his body was not to be put into a corncrib or left where the rats could reach it. Lov had promised faithfully to see that the rats did not get to him before he was buried.

"You've got to swear to me you won't let me be left in the box where the rats can get me," Jeeter had said dozens of times. "I declare before the good Lord, Lov, that ain't a fit way to treat the dead. I've regretted my own father's circumstance every day since that happened, and I declare before the Lord, I sure don't want that thing to happen to me when I'm dead and can't do nothing about it."

"You don't need to worry none," Lov had said. "I'll dig a hole and put you in it right after you're gone. I won't wait for the next day, even. I'll put you in the ground the same hour you die, almost. I'll take care of your body. Don't you worry none."

"Just don't put the coffin in that durn corncrib, Lov, no matter what else you do. There ain't no rats staying in there now since I ain't had corn in it for nearly five years, but they take trips back here every once in a while from the place they're staying at now just to make sure there ain't been no corn put in it. Before they left they et up mule collars and everything else they could get hold of, they was that mad at me for not putting corn in there for them. I used to bust them on the head with sticks, but that didn't stop them from coming back every once in a while. I was in there not so long ago getting me some corn cobs and one of them bit my leg before I could get out. They have sure got it in good and heavy for me, because I don't put no corn in there for them to eat up."

Ada, too, had promised Jeeter to see that his body would not be left exposed to the rats that he hated so much. But Jeeter did not worry her as much as he did Lov, because he believed he would out-live her by several years.

Ada herself looked as if she might die before Jeeter did. Her teeth had all dropped out; she had dipped snuff since she was eight years old. Her teeth had not lasted very long after she was married. Her one concern, besides the constant desire for more snuff, was with her own death. The thought that she might not have a stylish dress when she died was bothering her night and day. She did not trust Jeeter any too much to furnish it when the time came; that was the reason she kept the old dress put away to be used in case a more up-to-date one was not bought for her.

"If I could find out where my daughters was living, maybe they would help me get a stylish dress to die in," she had said. "Lizzie Belle used to love her old Ma a lot. I know she'd help me get one if I could find out where she is at. And Clara might help some, too. She used to tell me how pretty I looked when I combed my hair of mornings and put on a clean apron and sunbonnet. I don't know if the others would want to help none or not. It's been such a long time since I saw the rest of them I've just about forgot what they was like. Seems like I can't recall all their names even, sometimes."

"Lizzie Belle might be making a lot of money over in the mills," Jeeter had said. "Maybe if we was to find her and ask her about it, she might come some time and bring us a little money. I know Bailey would bring us some snuff and rations if I knowed where to find him. Bailey was just about the best of all the boys. He was good to me even when he was just a little boy. He was never stealing all the molasses we had saving for supper, like the rest of them. I expect maybe he's got to be a pretty big merchant somewheres by now. He always said he was going to make a lot of money so he wouldn't have to go barefooted in the winter-time like Tom and Clara did when they went away."

Ada talked to Jeeter whenever the subject was that of their children away from home. It seemed as if she were not interested enough in other things to talk about them any more. She answered Jeeter's questions most of the time, and she scolded him when there was nothing in the house to eat. The rest of the time she had very little to say. But whenever Bailey's name, or Lizzie Belle's, or Clara's, or Walker's, or any of the children's was mentioned, she lost the hollow look in her eyes and wanted to talk about them for the rest of the day. None of the children who had left home had ever been back to visit, nor had they ever sent a message. Because Ada and Jeeter had never received one, they believed that all of the children were alive. There was no way of knowing whether they were dead or not.

"I'm going over to Burke County and see Tom," Jeeter had told Ada. "I've made up my mind that I'll go over there and see him before I die. Everybody in Fuller tells me he's hauling cross-ties out of the camp by the wagon load day and night. They say he's got a whopping big cross-tie camp over there. From what people say about him, I reckon he's a powerful rich man now. He sure ought to give me some money. Though it sometimes looks like a rich man will never help the poor; whereas the poor people will give away everything they has to help somebody who ain't got nothing. That's how it looks to me. Don't seem like it ought to be that way, but I reckon the rich ain't got no time to fool with us poor folks."

"When you see Tom, tell him that his old Ma would like powerful much to see him. You tell him that I said he was near about the best of the whole seventeen. Clara and Lizzie Belle was about the best, I reckon; but Tom and Bailey led the boys when it came to being good children. You tell Tom I said he was the best of them, and maybe he'll send me some money for a stylish dress."

"Pearl is the prettiest," Jeeter said. "Ain't none of the other gals got pretty yellow hair like she has. Nor them pale blue eyes, neither. She's the first Lester I ever saw who had yellow hair. It's funny about her having it, ain't it, Ada?"

"Pearl is my favorite, I reckon," Ada said. "I wish she would come to see me sometimes. I ain't seen her since she left last summer to get married to Lov."

"I'm going to tell Tom he ought to give me some money," Jeeter said. "The folks in Fuller say he's a powerful rich man now."

"You better not forget to mention to him that his old Ma sure would like for him to get her a stylish dress to die in. I know he won't stand back with a little of his money for a little thing like that."

"I'm going to mention it to him when I see him, but I don't know how he'll take it. I expect he's got a wife and a raft of children to provide for. Maybe he'll give it to me, though."

"Reckon Tom has got some children?"

"Maybe some."

"I sure would like to see them. I know I must have a whole lot of grandchildren somewhere. I'm bound to have, with all them boys and girls off from home. If I could see Tom maybe I wouldn't mind it so bad that I can't see the rest of them. I just know I ought to have grandchildren somewhere in the country."

"Lizzie Belle and Clara has got a raft of children, I reckon. They was always talking about having them. And they say over in Fuller that Lizzie Belle has got a lot of them. I don't know how other folks know more about such things than I do. Looks like I ought to be the one who knows the most about my children."

"Maybe you could get Tom to bring his children over here for me to see. You tell him I want to see my grandchildren, and maybe he'll consent to bring them."

Ada had talked several times about Tom bringing his children to see her. Every time Jeeter said anything about going over to Burke County where Tom's cross-tie camp was, she reminded him not to forget to tell Tom what she had said. But from year to year, as Jeeter failed to start, she had become less inclined to talk about the possibility of seeing any of the grandchildren. Jeeter could not get started. He would say he was going the next day, but he always put off the trip at the last minute.

Jeeter made a false start somewhere nearly every day. He was going to Fuller, or he was going to McCoy, or he was going to Augusta; but he never went when he said he would. If he told Ada at night that he was going to McCoy early the next morning, he would decide at the last minute to go to Fuller or Augusta instead. Usually he would have to stop and walk out over the old cotton fields and look at the tall brown broom-sedge, and that made him think about something else. When he did walk out into the sedge, the chances were that he would lie down and take a nap. It was a wonder how he ever got the wood cut that he hauled to Augusta. Sometimes it took him a whole week to cut enough blackjack for a load.

Just then it was the beginning of the new season that was causing him to change his mind so frequently. The smell of the burning broom-sedge and pine undergrowth was in the air every day now. Some of the land was even being broken away off in the distance, and he could detect the aroma of freshly turned earth miles away. The smell of newly turned earth, that others were never conscious of, reached Jeeter's nostrils with a more pungent odor than any one else could ever detect in the air. That made him want to go out right away and burn over the old cotton fields and plant a crop. Other men were doing that all around him, but even if he succeeded in borrowing a mule, Jeeter did not know where to begin begging for credit to buy seed-cotton and guano. The merchants in Fuller had heard his plea so many times that they knew what he was going to ask for as soon as he walked in the door, and before he could say the first word they were shaking their heads and going back where he could not follow them. He did not know what to do about it.

Jeeter postponed nearly everything a man could think of, but when it came to plowing the land and planting cotton, he was as persistent as any man could be about such things. He started out each day with his enthusiasm at fever pitch, and by night he was still as determined as ever to find a mule he could borrow and a merchant who would give him credit for seed-cotton and guano.

Chapter IX

THE sun had been up only half an hour when Bessie reached the Lester house on the morning after her sudden departure. She had said then that she was going home to ask God to let her marry Dude. Jeeter had not expected her to come back for several days.

No one was in sight as she crossed the yard and ran through the front door calling Dude.

"Dude—you Dude! Where is you, Dude?" she called.

Jeeter was just getting out of bed when he first heard her; she ran into the bedroom while he sat on a chair pulling on his shoes.

"What you want with Dude, Bessie?" he asked sleepily. "What you want Dude for?"

Bessie ran around the room looking into the beds. There were three beds in which all the Lesters slept. Ada and Jeeter used one of them, Ellie May and the grandmother another, and Dude slept alone.

Ellie May sat up in bed, awakened by the disturbance, and rubbed her eyes. Bessie jerked back the quilts on Dude's bed, and ran into the next room where the roof had fallen in. It was the other bedroom, the room where most of the children had formerly slept, and it had been deserted because one section of the roof had rotted away. It was filled with plunder.

Bessie came back and looked under Ada's bed.

"What you want with Dude this time of day, Bessie?" Jeeter asked.

She still did not stop to answer Jeeter's questions. She ran through the kitchen calling Dude at the top of her voice.

As soon as he could lace his shoes and put on his jumper, Jeeter followed her out into the backyard. His drooping black felt hat was on his head, because his hat was the first thing he put on in the morning and the last he took off at night.

Dude was drawing a bucket of water at the well, and Bessie reached him before he could tip the bucket and get a drink. She threw her arms around his neck and kissed his face excitedly. Dude fought back at first, but as soon as he saw it was Bessie he smiled at her and put his arms around her waist.

Jeeter went closer and watched them. Presently Bessie took a side-comb from her head and began combing Dude's stiff black hair and smoothing it down with the palms of her hands. Dude's hair was coarse and bristly, and it stood straight on its ends no matter how much it was combed and brushed. Sometimes he could manage to make it lie down for a few minutes by sousing his head in a pan of water and then combing it hurriedly; but as soon as the water began to dry, the hair would stand straight up again as if it were attached to springs. Dude's hair was as wiry as hog-bristles.

"I never seen a woman preacher carry-on over a young sapling like that before," Jeeter said. "What you want to do that to Dude for, Bessie? You and him is hugging and rubbing of the other just like you was yesterday on the front porch."

Bessie smiled at Dude and Jeeter. She leaned against the well-stand and tucked up her hair. She had not waited that morning to pin it up.

"Me and Dude is going to get married," she said. "The Lord told me to do it. I asked Him about it, and he said, 'Sister Bessie, Dude Lester is the man I want you to mate. Get up early in the morning and go up to the Lester place and marry Dude the first thing.' That's what He said to me last night, the very words I heard with my own ears while I was praying about it in bed. So when the sun came up, I got out of bed and ran up here as fast as I could, because the Lord don't like to be kept waiting for His plans to be carried out. He wants me to marry Dude right now."

Dude looked around nervously as if he was thinking of trying to run off to the woods and hide. He had forgotten how anxious he had been to go home with Bessie the evening before when she first mentioned marriage.

"You hear that, Dude?" Jeeter said. "What you think about doing it with Sister Bessie?"

"Shucks," he said. "I couldn't do that."

"Why can't you do that?" Jeeter demanded. "What's ailing you? Ain't you man enough yet?"

"Maybe I is, and maybe I ain't. I'd be scared to do that with her."

"Why, Dude," his father said, "that ain't nothing to be afraid about. Bessie ain't going to hurt you. She knows how to treat you. Sister Bessie, there, has been married before. She's a widow-woman now. She knows all about how to treat men."

"I wouldn't hurt you none, Dude," she said, putting her arm around his neck and drawing his arms tighter around her waist. "There ain't nothing to be scared of. I'm just like your sister, Ellie May, and your Ma. Women don't scare their men-folks none. You'll like being married to me, because I know how to treat men fine."

Ada elbowed her way past Jeeter and Dude. She had not waited to plait her hair when she heard what Bessie wanted. She stood beside Dude and Bessie, with her hair divided over the front of her shoulders, plaiting one side and tying a string around the end, and then beginning on the other braid. She was as excited as Bessie was.

"Bessie," she said, "you'll have to make Dude wash his feet every once in a while, because if you don't he'll dirty-up your quilts. Sometimes he don't wash himself all winter long, and the quilts get that dirty you don't know how to go about the cleaning of them. Dude is just careless like his Pa. I had the hardest time learning him to wear his socks in the bed, because it was the only way I could keep the quilts clean. He would never wash himself. I reckon Dude is just going on the same way his Pa done, so maybe you had better make Dude wear his socks, too."

Ellie May had come out of the house and was standing behind a chinaberry tree in order to hear and see what was taking place beside the well-stand. The grandmother was in the yard too; she was peering from behind the corner of the house lest any one should see her and make her go away.

"Maybe you and Dude will help get me a stylish dress," Ada suggested shyly. "You and him know how bad I want a dress of the right length to die in. I've long ago give up waiting for Jeeter to get me one. He ain't going to do it in time."

All of them stood by the well looking at each other. When Jeeter caught Dude's eye, Dude hung his head and looked at the ground. He did not know what to think about it. He wanted to get married, but he was afraid of Bessie. She was nearly twenty-five years older than he was.

"Do you know what I'm going to do, Jeeter?" Bessie asked.

"What?" Jeeter said.

"I'm going to buy me a new automobile!"

"A new automobile?"

"A brand-new one. I'm going to Fuller right now and get it."

"A brand-new one?" Jeeter said unbelievingly. "A sure-enough brand-new automobile?"

Dude's mouth dropped open, and his eyes glistened.

"What you going to buy it with, Bessie?" Jeeter asked. "Is you got money?"

"I've got eight hundred dollars to pay for it with. My former husband left me that money when he died. He had it in insurance, and when he died I got it and put it in the bank in Augusta. I aimed to use it in carrying on the prayer and preaching my former husband used to like so much. I always did want a brand-new automobile."

"When you going to buy a new automobile?" Jeeter asked.

"Right now—to-day. I'm going over to Fuller and get it right now. Me and Dude's going to use it to travel all over the country preaching and praying."

"Can I drive it?" Dude asked.

"That's what I'm buying it for, Dude. I'm getting it for you to drive us around in when we take a notion to go somewheres."

"When is you and Dude going to do all this riding around and praying and preaching?" Jeeter said. "Is you going to get married before or after?"

"Right away," she said. "We'll walk over to Fuller right now and buy the new automobile, and then ride up to the courthouse and get married."

"Is you going to get leave of the county to get married?" he asked doubtfully. "Or is you just going to live along without it?"

"I'm going to get the license for marrying," she said.

"That costs about two dollars," Jeeter reminded. "Is you got two dollars? Dude ain't. Dude, he ain't got nothing."

"I ain't asking Dude for one penny of money. I'll attend to that part myself. I've got eight hundred dollars in the bank, and some more besides. I saved my money for something just like this to happen. I've been looking for it to happen all along."

Dude had been dropping pebbles into the well for the past few minutes. Suddenly he stopped and looked at Bessie. He looked straight into her face, and the sight of the two cavernous round nostrils brought a smile to his lips. He had looked at her nose before, but this time the holes seemed to be larger and rounder than ever. It was more like looking down into a double-barrel shotgun than ever before. He could not keep from laughing.

"What you laughing at, Dude?" she asked, frowning.

"At them two holes in your nose," he said. "I ain't never seen nobody with all the top of her nose gone away like that before."

Bessie's face turned white. She hung her head in an effort to hide her exposed nostrils as much as possible. She was sensitive about her appearance, but she knew of no way to remedy her nose. She had been born without a bone in it, and after nearly forty years it had still not developed. She put her hand over her face.

"I'm ashamed of you, Dude," she said, wiping the tears from the corners of her eyes. "You know I can't help the way I look. I been like that ever since I can remember. Won't no nose grow on me, I reckon."

Dude dug the toes of his shoes in the sand and tried to laugh. But almost as suddenly as he had first looked at Bessie's face and broken into a smile, he stopped and scowled meanly at himself. It was the remembrance of the new automobile that made him stop laughing at Bessie. If she was going to buy a brand-new car, he did not care how she looked. It would have been all right with him if she had had a harelip like Ellie May's, now that he could ride all he wanted to. He had never driven a new motor car, and that was something he wanted to do more than anything else he could think of.

"I didn't mean no harm," he said uneasily. "Honest to God, I didn't. I don't give a damn how your nose looks."

Bessie smiled again, and put her arms around his waist. She looked up at him again, her face so close to his that he could feel her breath. He had to stop trying to see down into her nose, because it hurt his eyes, and made them ache, to focus them on an object only a few inches away. Her nostrils were only a dark blur on her face when they were standing so close together.

"Can I drive the new automobile, sure enough?" he asked again, hoping he had not made her change her mind. "Is you going to let me drive it?"

"That's why I'm getting it, Dude. I'm getting it for you to drive all over the country in. Me and you is going to get married, and we can ride all the time if we want to. I won't stop you from going somewhere when you want to go. You can ride all the time."

"Will it have a horn on it?"

"I reckon it will. Don't all new automobiles come with horns all ready on them?"

"Maybe so," he said. "You be sure and find out if it's got one when you buy it, anyway. It won't be no good at all unless it's got a horn."

"Dude is pretty durn lucky," Jeeter said. "I didn't get a durn thing when I married Ada, there. She didn't have nothing but some old dresses of her own, and her people was that durn poor they had to eat meal and fat-back just like we do now. I didn't get nothing when I married her, except a mess of trouble."

Ada walked over to Bessie and laid her hand on Bessie's arm.

"Maybe if you got all that money, Bessie, you and Dude could buy me a jar of snuff in Fuller. Reckon you could do that for Dude's old Ma? Being that Dude is my boy, you ought to get me just a little jar of snuff anyway. I'd sure be powerful pleased if you was to get three or four jars while you was about it, though. Snuff drives away the pains in my poor stomach when I can't get nothing to eat."

"I been needing a new pair of overalls for the longest time, Bessie," Jeeter said. "I declare, I'm almost scared to go a far piece from the house any more, because I don't know but what my clothes will drop right off of me some time when I ain't noticing. If you could get me a new pair in Fuller, I'd be powerful pleased."

Bessie led Dude away from the well. They walked around the house, and when nobody was looking, she stood behind him and hugged him so hard he could not breathe until she released him.

"What you doing that to me for?" he said. "I ain't never had that done to me before."

"Me and you is going to get married, Dude. Don't you know that?"

He walked around behind her, looked at the back of her head, and came back in front again.

"When is you going to get a new automobile?" he asked.

"Right away, Dude. We're going to Fuller right now and get it."

Dude was more excited over the prospect of driving a new automobile than he had ever been about anything in his whole life. The automobiles he had seen had all been old ones like Jeeter's, except the ones the rich people in Augusta drove. He could not make himself believe that he was actually going to drive one like those he had seen in the city. He wanted to start for Fuller without another minute's delay.

"Come on," he said. "We ain't got no time to lose."

"Ain't you glad we is going to get married, though?" she said. "It's going to be real nice, ain't it, Dude?"

The rest of the Lesters had followed them to the front yard, and they stood by the corner of the house waiting to see Dude and Bessie leave for Fuller. Ellie May followed them down the road for about half a mile before she turned around and came back to the house.

Dude walked in front, and Bessie followed him several yards behind. When they reached the top of the first sand hill, they stopped and looked back at the Lester house to see if Ada and Jeeter were watching them. Bessie waved her hand until Dude told her to hurry up so they could get to Fuller.

The long walk to Fuller took them nearly two hours, because Bessie had to stop several times and rest beside the road. The sun was hot by that time, as it was nearly ten o'clock when they left the Lester place; and it was difficult walking through the deep sand, especially for Bessie. In some places the sand was a foot deep, and her feet sank down so far that the sand ran down her shoe tops. Dude would never sit down and wait for Bessie to get ready to start walking again. He waited several hundred feet away, urging her to hurry.

Dude had started out walking slowly enough for Bessie to keep up with him; but as they got closer to Fuller, Dude could not hold himself back. He ran ahead several hundred yards, and then had to walk back to meet Bessie. He would have gone on to town without her, but he did not know what to do when he got there. He was afraid, too, that if he got out of Bessie's sight she might turn around and go back without buying the new automobile.

Neither of them talked the whole time. Bessie hummed a hymn to herself, occasionally raising a note to the shrill pitch she liked so much, but she did not try to talk to Dude. They were too engrossed in their own thoughts to talk.

Chapter X

DUDE waited outside the garage and looked at the new automobile on display in the show window. Bessie had gone inside. Dude had said he would stay on the street and look through the window a while.

Bessie waited in the middle of the floor several minutes before any one came out of the back room to ask what she wanted. Presently a salesman walked over to her and asked her if she wanted anything. He noticed that there was something unusual about her nose the moment he first saw her.

"I came to buy a new Ford," she said.

The salesman was so busy looking down into her nostrils that he had to ask her to repeat what she said.

"I came to buy a new Ford."

"Have you got any money?"

He glanced around to see if any of the other men were in the room. He wanted them to take a good look at Bessie's nose.

"I've got enough to buy a new automobile if it don't cost more than eight hundred dollars."

He looked up into her eyes for the first time. It was hard to believe from her appearance that she had as much as a penny.

"How'd you get it?" he said.

"The Lord provides for me. He always provides for His children."

"He ain't never sent me nothing, and I been here thirty years now. You must be on the inside some way."

The salesman laughed at what he had said, and looked down into Bessie's nostrils again.

"That's because you don't put your trust in the Lord."

"You ain't got that much money sure enough, have you?"

Bessie took the check-book from her skirt pocket and showed it to him. While he was looking at the name of the bank and the balance to her account tabulated on the stub, she walked to the door and motioned to Dude to come inside.

"Who's that?" the man said. "Is he your kid?"

"That's Dude Lester. Everybody's heard of the Lesters on the tobacco road. Me and Dude is going to get married to-day. As soon as we can get the new automobile we're going to ride around to the courthouse and get leave to marry."

The salesman shoved the check-book into her hands, and ran to the door of the office.

"Come here quick, Harry!" he said. "I got a real sight to show you."

An older man came out of the office and walked over to where Bessie and the salesman stood.

"What's up?" he said, glancing from one to the other.

"This woman here is going to marry that kid, Harry—what do you know about that! Have you ever seen anything like it before?"

The older man asked Dude how old he was.

Dude was about to tell him that he was sixteen when Bessie pushed him behind her.

"That's none of your business, how old he is. I want to buy a new automobile. That's what I came here for. I walked five miles this morning to get here, too."

The two men were whispering to each other when she had finished talking. The older one looked at her face, and when he saw the two large round holes in her nose, he stepped forward and tried to see down into her nostrils. Bessie covered her nose with her hand.

"Good God!" he said.

"Ain't it a sight, though?" the salesman said.

"Has she got any money?" Harry asked him. "Don't waste no time fooling with her if she ain't. There's a lot of them just like her who come in here from the country and never buy nothing."

"She's got a check-book on the Farmers' Bank in Augusta, and she said she's got eight hundred dollars in her account. The stub shows it, too."

"Better call them up and find out about it first," Harry said. "She might be telling the truth, and she might be lying. Some of them people out in the country do some tricky things sometimes. She might have found the check-book and filled it out herself."

They went back into the office talking about Bessie's nose, and closed the door. After the salesman had called the bank, they came out again where Bessie and Dude were waiting.

"How much do you want to pay for a car?" the salesman said.

"Eight hundred dollars," Bessie told him.

Harry nudged the salesman with his elbow.

"Now, this is a nice little job here," he said, leaning against the fender of a new touring model. "It's eight hundred dollars. You can drive it away to-day, if you want to. You won't have to wait for the tags. I'll get them for you some time next week. You can drive a new car anywhere in the State for seven days while you are waiting for the tags to come from Atlanta."

They winked at each other; every time they wanted to put over a quick sale they told that lie about the registration laws.

Dude went to the car and blew the horn several times. The tone of it pleased him, and he grinned at Bessie.

"Do you like it, Dude?"

"Ain't nothing wrong with it," he said, blowing the horn again.

"We'll take that one," Bessie said, pointing at the car.

"Let's see your check-book," the other man said, jerking it out of Bessie's hand before she could give it to him.

He took the check-book, tore out a blank, and hastily filled it out for eight hundred dollars.

While the man was writing the check for Bessie to sign before she could change her mind or leave the garage, the salesman was again trying to look down into her nose. He had never seen anything like it before in all his life.

"Sign your name here," she was told.

"I always have to make my mark," she said.

"What's your name?"

"Sister Bessie Rice."

"You must be a woman preacher," the man said. "Ain't you one?"

"I preach and pray, both."

She touched the end of the pen while an "x" was crossed after her name on the check.

"The automobile's yours," she was told. "Is the boy going to drive it home for you?"

"Wait a minute," Bessie said. "I clear forgot about praying—let's all kneel down on the floor and have a little prayer before the trade is made."

"It's all over with now," one of them said.

"No it ain't, neither," Bessie insisted. "It ain't over till the Lord sends his blessings on it."

The two men laughed at her insistence, but Bessie had already knelt down on the floor and Dude was getting down on his knees beside the automobile. The two men stood behind her so they would not have to kneel on the floor.

"Dear God, we poor sinners kneel down in this garage to pray for a blessing on this new automobile trade, so You will like what me and Dude is doing. This new automobile is for me and Dude to ride around in and do the work You want done for You in this sinful country. You ought to make us not have wrecks with it, so we won't get hurt none. You don't want us to get killed, right when we're starting out to preach the gospel for You, do You? And these two men here who sold the new car to us need your blessing, too, so they can sell automobiles for the best good. They is sinful men just like all the rest of us, but I know they don't aim to be, and You ought to bless their work and show them how to sell people new automobiles for the best good, just like You would do if You was down here selling automobiles Yourself, in Fuller. That's all. Save us from the devil and make a place for us in heaven. Amen."

Dude was the first to get on his feet. He jumped up and blew the horn six or seven long blasts. The two men came around in front of Bessie, wiping the perspiration from their faces, and laughing at Dude and Bessie. They looked at her nose again until she put her hand over it.

Dude and Bessie got into the automobile and sat down. Dude blew the horn again several times.

"Wait a minute," the salesman said. "We'll have to roll it outside first and fill up the tank with gas. You can't drive it like it is now."

Bessie got out, but Dude refused to leave the horn and steering wheel. He sat where he was and guided the car through the door while the men pushed.

After the gasoline had been pumped into the tank, Dude started the engine and got ready to leave. Bessie got in again, sitting in the centre of the back seat.

"Where you going now?" the salesman asked Bessie. "To get married?"

"We're going around to the courthouse to get leave of the county," she said. "Then we'll get married."

The two men whispered to each other.

"Did you ever see a nose like that before, Harry?"

"Not when I was sober."

"Look at them two big round holes running down into her face—how does she keep it from raining down in there, you reckon?"

"I'll be damned if I know. Maybe she puts cork stoppers in them to keep the water out. She would have to do something like that in a hard shower."

Bessie leaned over and prodded Dude.

"Drive off, Dude," she said. "Ain't no sense in staying here no more."

Dude put the car into gear and turned the gasoline on. Being unaccustomed to the new model, he did not know how to gauge the amount of gasoline, and the car jerked off so quickly that it almost lifted itself off the ground. The two men jumped out of the way just in time to keep from being hit by the fender.

Bessie showed Dude which way to turn to find the courthouse. When they reached it, Dude got out reluctantly and followed Bessie inside. He wanted to stay in the car and blow the horn, but Bessie said he had to go with her to get the license.

The Clerk's office was found at the end of the hall on the first floor, and they opened the door and went inside. There was a cardboard sign on the door that Bessie remembered seeing when she came there with her first husband.

"I want leave to get married to Dude," she stated.

The Clerk looked at her and spread out a blank on the table. He gave her a pen and motioned to her to fill it in with answers to the questions.

"You'll have to write it for me. I can't write the words down."

"Can't you write?" he asked. "Can't you sign your name?"

"I never learned how," she said.

He was about to say something, when he looked up and saw her nose. His eyes opened wider and wider.

"All right, I'll put it down for you. But it ain't my business to do that for you. You ought to do it yourself. I don't get paid for writing people's names for them."

"I'll be powerful much obliged if you will do it for me," she said.

"What's your name?"

"Sister Bessie Rice."

"You must be preacher Rice's widow, ain't you?"

"He was my former husband."

"Who are you going to marry, Sister Rice?"

"That's him back there by the door."

"Who?"

"Dude. His name is Dude Lester."

"You ain't going to marry him, are you?"

"That's what I came here to get leave of the county for. Me and him is going to get married."

"Who—that kid? Is he the one who's going to marry you?"

"Dude said he would——"

"That boy ain't old enough to marry yet, Sister Rice."

"Dude, he's sixteen."

"I can't give you a license—you'll have to wait a while and come back next year or so."

"Dear God," Bessie said, dropping to her knees on the floor, "this man says he won't give me leave to marry Dude. God, You've got to make him do it. You told me last night to marry Dude and make a preacher out of him, and You have got to see me through now. I'm all excited about getting married. If You don't make the county give me leave to marry, I don't know what evil I might——"

"Wait a minute!" the Clerk shouted. "Stop that praying! I'd rather give you the license than listen to that. Maybe we can do something about it."

Bessie got up smiling.

"I knowed the Lord would help me out," she said.

"Has that boy got the consent of his parents? He can't get married unless he's got the consent of both parents, according to the law for his age. What does he want to marry you for anyway? He's too young to marry an old woman like you. Come here, son——"

"Don't you try to talk him out of it," Bessie said. "If you start that, I'll pray some more. God won't let you keep us from marrying."

"What do you mean by coming here to marry this old woman, son? You ought to wait and marry a girl when you grow up."

"I don't know," Dude said. "Bessie, there, brought me along with her."

"Well, I can't give you a license to marry," the Clerk said. "It's against the law for a boy under eighteen years old to marry without his parents' consent. And no amount of praying can change the law, neither. It's down on the books and it won't come off."

"Dear God," Bessie began again, "You ain't going to let this man put us off, is You? You know how much I been counting on marrying Dude. You ought not to let nothing stop——"

"Wait a minute! Don't start that again!" the Clerk said. "Who are this boy's folks?"

"His Ma and Pa don't care," Bessie said. "They're glad of it. I talked to them both early this morning on the way down here to Fuller."

"What's his daddy's name?"

"Jeeter Lester is Dude's Pa, and I don't reckon you would know his Ma if I was to call her name. Her name is Ada."

"Sure, I know Jeeter Lester, and I don't reckon he does care. Nor his wife, either. I had to give Lov Bensey a license to marry one of the young girls, because Jeeter said he wanted it done. She wasn't but twelve years old then either, and it was a shame to marry her so young. But it's in the law, and I had to do it. She was a pretty little girl. I never seen a girl before in all my life with such pretty yellow hair and blue eyes. Her eyes was exactly the same color as robins' eggs. I swear, she was one pretty sight to see."

"Dude is older than that," Bessie said. "Dude, he is sixteen."

"How old are you, Sister Rice? You didn't tell me your age."

"I don't have to tell you that, do I?" she said.

"That's the law. I can't give you the license if you don't state your age."

"Well—I was thirty-eight not so long back."

"How old are you now?"

"Thirty-nine, but I don't show it yet."

"Who's going to support you two?" he asked. "That boy can't make a man's wages yet."

"Is that in the law, too?"

"Well, no. The law doesn't require that question, but I thought I'd just like to know about it myself."

"The Lord will provide," Bessie said. "He always makes provision for His children."

"He don't take none too good care of me and mine," the Clerk said, "and I been a supporting member of the Fuller Baptist church since I was twenty years old, too. He don't do none too much for me."

"That's because you ain't got the right kind of religion," Bessie said. "The Baptists is sinners like all the rest, but my religion provides for me."

"What's the name of it?"

"It ain't got no regular name. I just call it 'Holy,' most of the time. I'm the only member of it now, but Dude is going to be one when we get married. He's going to be a preacher, too."

"You'll have to pay me two dollars for the license," he said, writing on the sheet of paper. "Have you got it?"

"I've got it right here. I don't see, though, why folks has to pay to get married. It's God's doings."

"There's something else I'm going to ask you. It's not required by law, and some clerks don't ask about it, but being a good Baptist I always feel like I ought to."

"What's it about?"

"Has either of you got any disease?"

"Not that I know about," she said. "Has you, Dude?"

"What's that?"

"Disease," the Clerk said again, pronouncing the word slowly. "Like pellagra and chicken-pox, or anything like that. Is there anything wrong with you, son?"

"I ain't got nothing wrong with me that I know about," Dude said. "I don't know what that thing is, noway."

"You sure you haven't?" he asked Bessie. "Did your husband leave you with disease of any kind? What did he die of?"

"He died of age mostly, I reckon. He was well on to fifty when he was married."

"Has either one of you got venereal disease?"

"What's that?" Bessie asked.

"You know—" he said, "venereal disease. Maybe you call it sex trouble."

"I used to take a powerful number of bottles of Tanlac, but I ain't lately because I ain't had the money to buy them with."

"No, not that. What I'm talking about comes from women sleeping with men, sometimes."

"My former husband had mites on him pretty bad sometimes. I had to wash both him and me off with kerosene to get rid of them."

"No, not mites. Lots of people get those on them. It's something else—but I reckon you ain't got it, if you don't know what I'm talking about."

"What other things do you want to know?" Bessie said.

"That's all, I reckon. Now, you give me the two dollars."

Bessie handed him the two soiled and ragged one-dollar bills she had been gripping in her hand. She had several more in her skirt pocket, all of them rolled in a handkerchief and the ends tied together. It was all the money she had left, now that the eight hundred dollars had been paid for the new automobile.

"Well, I reckon you two will get along all right," the Clerk said. "Maybe you will, and maybe you won't."

"Is you a married man?" Bessie asked.

"I been married fifteen years or more. Why?"

"Well, I reckon you know how pleased me and Dude is to get married, then," she said. "All married folks know how it is to get married."

"It's all right at the beginning, but it don't keep up like that long. After you been married a year or two a man wants to go out and do it again all over, but it can't be done. The law puts a stop to it after the first time, unless your wife dies, or runs off, but that don't happen often enough to make it of any good."

"Me and Dude is going to stay together all the time, ain't we, Dude?"

Dude grinned, but he did not speak.

Bessie had the license in her hand, and she did not wait to hear the Clerk talk any more. She pulled Dude out of the room, and they left the courthouse and ran to the new automobile.

They got in to ride home. Dude blew the horn several times before he started the motor, and again before he put the car into gear. Then he turned it around in the street and drove it out of Fuller towards the tobacco road.

Bessie sat erect on the back seat, holding the marriage license tight in both hands so the wind would not blow it away.

Chapter XI

THE Lesters heard Dude blowing the horn far down the tobacco road long before the new automobile came within sight, and they all ran to the farthest corner of the yard, and even out into the broom-sedge, to see Dude and Bessie arrive. Even the old grandmother was excited, and she waited behind a chinaberry tree to be among the first to see the new car.

"Here they come!" Jeeter shouted. "Just look at them! It's a brand-new automobile, all right—just look at that shiny black paint! Great-day-in-the-morning! Just look at them coming yonder!"

Dude was driving about twenty-miles an hour, and he was so busy blowing the horn he forgot to slow down when he turned into the yard. The car jolted across the ditch, throwing Bessie against the top three or four times in quick succession, and breaking several leaves of the rear spring. Dude slowed down then, and the automobile rolled across the yard and came to a stop by the side of the house.

Jeeter was the first to reach the new motor car. He had run behind it while Dude was putting on the brakes, and he had held to the rear mudguard while trying to keep up with it. Ellie May and Ada were not far behind. The grandmother came as quickly as she could.

"I never seen a finer-looking automobile in all my days," Jeeter said. "It sure does make me happy again to see such a handsome machine. Don't you reckon you could take me for a little trip, Bessie? I sure would like to go off in it for a piece."

Bessie opened the door and got out. The first thing she did was to take the bottom of her skirt and rub the dust off of the front fenders.

"I reckon we can take you riding in it some time," she said. "When me and Dude gets back, you can go riding."

"Where is you and Dude going to, Bessie?"

"We're going to ride around like married folks," she said proudly.

"When folks get married, they always like to take a little ride together somewhere."

Ada and Ellie May inspected the car with stifled admiration. Both of them then gathered up the bottoms of their skirts and shined the doors and fenders. The new automobile shone in the bright sun like a looking-glass when they had finished.

Dude climbed over the door and ordered his mother and sister away from the car.

"You and Ellie May will be ruining it," he said. "Don't put your hands on it and don't stand too close to it."

"Did you and Dude get married in Fuller?" Jeeter asked Bessie.

"Not all the way," she said. "I got leave of the county, however. It cost two dollars to do that little bit."

"Ain't you going to get a preacher to finish doing it?"

"I is not! Ain't I a preacher of the gospel? I'm going to do it myself. I wouldn't allow no Hardshell Baptist to fool with us."

"I knowed you would do it the right way," Jeeter said. "You sure is a fine woman preacher, Sister Bessie."

Bessie moved towards the front porch, twisting the marriage license in her hands. Every one else was still looking at the new automobile. Ellie May and Ada stood at a safe distance so Dude would not run them away with a stick. The old grandmother had gone behind a chinaberry tree again, awed by the sight.

Dude walked around in a circle so he could see all sides of the car. He wanted to be certain that nobody put his hands on the car and dulled its lustre.

Jeeter sat down on his heels and admired it.

Bessie had gone half way up the front steps, and she was trying to attract Dude's attention. She coughed several times, scraped her feet on the boards, and rapped on the porch with her knuckles. Jeeter heard her, and he looked around to find out what she was doing.

"By God and by Jesus!" he said, jumping to his feet. "Now wasn't that just like a fool man?"

The others turned around and looked at Bessie. Ellie May giggled from behind a chinaberry tree.

"Ada," Jeeter said, "Sister Bessie is wanting to go in the house. You go show her in."

Ada went inside and threw open the blinds. She could be heard dragging chairs around the room and pushing the beds back into the corners.

"Didn't you and Dude stop off in the woods coming back from Fuller?" he asked Bessie.

"We was in a hurry to get back here," she said. "I mentioned it, sort of, to Dude, but he was blowing the horn so much he couldn't hear me."

"Dude," Jeeter said, "don't you see how bad Sister Bessie is wanting to go in the house? You go in there with her—I'll keep my eye on the automobile."

While Dude was being urged to go into the house, Bessie went slowly across the porch to the door, waiting to see if Dude were following.

Ellie May drew herself up on her toes and tried to look into the bedroom through the open window. Ada was still busily engaged in straightening up the room, and every few minutes she would push a chair across the floor and jerk an end of one of the beds into a new position.

"What is they going to do in there, Ma?" Ellie May asked.

Ada came to the window and leaned out. She pushed Ellie May's hands from the sill and motioned to her to go away.

"Sister Bessie and Dude is married," she said. "Now you go away and stop trying to see inside. You ain't got no business seeing of them."

After her mother had left the window, Ellie May again raised herself on the sill and looked inside.

Dude had gone as far as the front door, but he lingered there to take one more look at the automobile. He stood there until Ada came out and pushed him inside and made him go into the room with Bessie.

There was barely any furniture in the room. Besides the three double beds, there was a wobbly dresser in the corner, which was used as a washstand and a table. Over it, hanging on the wall, was a cracked mirror. In the opposite end of the room was the fireplace. A broom-sedge sweeper stood behind the door, and another one, completely worn out, was under Ada's bed. There were also two straight-back chairs in the room. As there were no closets in the house, clothes were hanging on the walls by nails that had been driven into the two-by-four uprights.

The moment Dude walked into the room, Bessie slammed the door, and pulled him with her. She took the marriage license from her skirt pocket and held it in front of her.

"You hold one end, Dude, and I'll hold the other."

"What you going to do?"

"Marry us, Dude," she said.

"Didn't you get that all done at the courthouse in Fuller?"

"That wasn't all. I'm doing the balance now."

"When is we going to take a ride?" he asked.

"It won't be so very long now. We want to stay here a little while first. We got plenty of time to ride around, Dude."

"You going to let me drive it all the time?"

"Sure, you can drive it all the time. I don't know how to drive it, noway."

"You ain't going to let nobody else drive it, is you?"

"You is the only one who can drive it, Dude," she said. "But we got to hurry and finish marrying. You hold your end of the license while I pray."

Dude stood beside her, waiting for the prayer to be finished. She prayed silently for several minutes while he stood in front of her.

"I marry us man and wife. So be it. That's all, God. Amen."

There was a long silence while they looked at each other.

"When is we going for a ride?" Dude said.

"We is married now, Dude. We is finished being married. Ain't you glad of it?"

"When is we going for a ride?"

"I got to pray now," she said. "You kneel down on the floor while I make a little prayer."

They knelt down to pray. Dude got down on all fours, looking straight into Bessie's nose while her eyes were closed.

"Dear God, Dude and me is married now. We is wife and husband. Dude, he is an innocent young boy, unused to the sinful ways of the country, and I am a woman preacher of the gospel. You ought to make Dude a preacher, too, and let us use our new automobile in taking trips all over the country to pray for sinners. You ought to learn him how to be a fine preacher so we can make all the goats into sheep. That's all this time. We're in a hurry now. Save us from the devil and make a place for us in heaven. Amen."

There was a rustle of skirts as Sister Bessie jumped to her feet and began running excitedly around the room. She came back and pulled at Dude, making him put his arms around her waist.

Outside in the yard, Jeeter and Ellie May had been standing on their toes looking in through the window to see what Dude and Bessie were doing. There were no curtains over the windows, and the board blinds had had to be opened so there would be light in the room.

Dude stood for several minutes watching Bessie as she tried to pull him across the room. She finally sat down on one of the beds and attempted to make him sit beside her.

"You ain't going to sleep now, is you?" he asked her. "It ain't time to go to bed yet. It ain't no more than noon-time now."

"Just for now," she said. "We can go out again after a while and take a ride in the automobile."

Dude ran to the window to look at the car. For the moment, he had completely forgotten about it. When he reached the window, he saw Jeeter and Ellie May holding to the sill with the ends of their fingers and trying to see inside.

"What you doing that for?" he asked Jeeter. "What you want to look at?"

Jeeter turned away and looked out over the brown broom-sedge. Ellie May ran around to the back of the house and tip-toed into the hall through the kitchen.

Bessie came to the window and pulled Dude around until he faced her. Then she made him go back and sit down on the bed.

Suddenly, without knowing how it happened, Dude found himself on the bed with a quilt over him. Bessie had locked her arms around him so tightly that he could not move in any direction.

Outside, he heard a ladder scrape against the weatherboards. Jeeter had found the ladder under the crib and had brought it to the window.

Chapter XII

WHEN Dude looked up, he saw that the door had been opened and that Ellie May, Ada, and the grandmother were crowding through it. He did not know what to do, but he tried to motion to them to go away.

He could not see Jeeter, because Jeeter was behind him, standing half-way up in the window with his feet supported on one of the rungs of the ladder. Bessie saw Jeeter, but she could not see the others.

Dude heard his grandmother groan and walk away. He could hear her feet sliding over the pine boards of the hall floor, the horse-collar shoes making an irritating sound as she went towards the front yard. He paid no more attention to the others.

After a while Jeeter cleared his throat and called Bessie. She did not answer him the first time he called, nor the next. Neither she nor Dude wanted to be disturbed.

When she persisted in not answering him, Jeeter climbed through the window and walked across the room to the bed. He shook Dude by the collar until he turned around.

Jeeter, however, did not have anything to say to Dude. It was Bessie he wanted to speak to.

"I been thinking just now about it, Sister Bessie, and the more I think it over in my mind, the more I convince myself that you was right about what we was discussing yesterday on the porch."

"What you want with me, Jeeter?" she asked.

"Now, about that place in the Bible where it says if a man's eye offends God he ought to go and take it out."

"That's what the Bible says," she answered.

"I know it does. And that's what's worrying my soul so bad right now."

"But you is a religious man, Jeeter," she said. "Nothing ought to bother your conscience now. I prayed for you about them turnips you took from Lov. The Lord has forgot all about it now. He ain't going to hound you none on that account."

"It ain't about the turnips. It's about cutting myself off. Now, I reckon what you said was right. I ought to go and do it."

Dude turned around and tried to push Jeeter to the floor. Jeeter clung to the bedstead, and would not move away.

"Why you want to do that?" Bessie said.

"I been thinking about all you said so much that right now I know I ought to go ahead and cut myself off, so the Lord won't let me be tempted no more. I offended Him, and I know I ought to cut myself off so I won't do it no more. Ain't that right, Sister Bessie?"

"That's right," she said. "That's what the Bible says a man ought to do when he's powerful sinful."

Jeeter looked at Bessie. He pulled back the quilt so he could see her better.

"Maybe I can put it off a little while, though," he said, after thinking several minutes. "Now, maybe it ain't so bad as I thought it was. This time of year puts a queer feeling into a man, and he says a lot of things he don't stop to take into account. Along about when the time to plow the land and put seed in the rows comes around, a man feels like he ain't got no control over his tongue—and don't want none. It's the same way with his actions. I feel that way every late February and early March. No matter how many children a man's got, he always wants to get more."

There was a silence in the house for a long time. Ellie May and Ada made no sound in the doorway. Jeeter sat on the bed deep in thought until Dude pushed him to his feet. Dude climbed out behind him.

When all of them were out in the yard again, Dude sat in the automobile and blew the horn. The women were busy wiping off the dust that had settled on the hood and fenders. The grandmother, though, did not come close to the car. She took her place behind a chinaberry tree and watched every movement of the others.

Jeeter sat on his heels beside the chimney, and thought over what

Sister Bessie had said in the house. He was more convinced than ever that God expected him to fix himself so he would not have any more sinful thoughts about Bessie.

He decided, however, not to carry out his intentions just then. There was plenty of time left yet, he told himself, when he could go ahead and cut himself off, and so long as he did it before he offended God any more, it would be satisfactory. In the meanwhile, he would have time in which to try to convince himself more thoroughly that he should do it.

There was a little fat-back on rinds left in the kitchen, and Ada had baked some cornbread. The bread had been made with meal, salt, water, and grease.

All of them sat down at the table in the kitchen and ate the fat-back and cornbread with full appetite. It was the first time that day that any of them had had food, and it would probably be the last. After the meat plate had been wiped clean of grease, and after the last of the cornbread was eaten, they went out into the yard again to look at the new automobile. The grandmother had hidden a piece of the bread in her apron pocket, and she put it under the mattress of her bed so she would have something to eat the next day in case Jeeter failed to buy some more meal and meat.

Jeeter wanted to take a ride right away. He told Bessie he wanted to go, and that he was ready.

Bessie had other plans, however. She said she and Dude were going to take a little ride that afternoon all alone, so they could talk over their marriage together without any disturbance. She promised Jeeter she would let him ride when they came back.

She and Dude got in, and Dude drove the car out of the yard and into the tobacco road towards the State highway. Jeeter thought they might be going to Augusta, but before he could ask them if they were, they had gone too far to hear him call.

"That Dude is the luckiest man alive," he told Ellie May. "Now ain't he?"

Ellie May started down the road through the cloud of dust to see them leave. She heard Jeeter talking to her, but she was too much interested in seeing the new car go down the road and in hearing Dude blow the horn to listen to what Jeeter said.

"Dude, he has got a brand-new car to ride around in, and he's got married all at the same time," Jeeter continued. "There's not many men who get all that in the same day, I tell you. The new car is a fine piece of goods to own. There ain't nobody else that I know of between here and the river who has got a brand-new automobile. And there ain't many men who has a wife as fine-looking as Sister Bessie is at her age, neither. Bessie makes a fine woman for a man—any man,

I don't care where you find him. She might be just a little bit more than Dude can take care of though, I fear. It looked to me like she requires a heap of satisfaction, one way and another, for a little woman no bigger than a gal. I don't know if Dude is that kind or not, but it won't take long for Bessie to find out. Now, if it was me, there wouldn't be no question of it. I'd please Sister Bessie coming and going, right from the start, and keep it up clear to the end."

Now Ellie May heard what Jeeter was saying, and it interested her. She waited to hear more.

"Now, you, Ellie May, it's time you was finding yourself a man. All my other children has got married. It's your time next. It was your time a long while ago, 'way before Pearl and Dude got married, but I make allowances for you on account of your face. I know it's harder for you to mate up than it is for anybody else, but in this country everybody has got to get mated up. You ought to go out and find yourself a man to marry right away, and not wait no longer. It might be too late pretty soon, and you don't want that to happen. It ain't going to get you nowhere fooling around with Lov like you was doing, because you can't get him that way. He's already married. It's the unmarried men you has got to get. There's a fine lot of boys running that sawmill over at Big Creek. You can walk over that way some day and make them take notice of you. It ain't hard to do. Women know how to make men take notice of them, and you're old enough to know all about it at your age. Them boys at the sawmill down there at Big Creek ought to take a liking to you in spite of the way you look in the face. When a man looks at you from behind, he ought to want to mate up with you right there and then. That's what I heard Lov say one time, and he ought to know, because he's mated up now. Just don't show your face too much, and that won't stop the boys from getting after you."

When Jeeter looked at Ellie May again, she was crying. It was about the first time he had ever seen her cry since she was a baby. He did not know what to do about it, nor to say about it, because he had never before had the occasion to try to calm a crying woman. Ada never cried. She never did anything.

Before he could ask her what the matter was, she had run off into the old cotton field; she ran towards the woods behind the house, jumping through the brown broom-sedge like a frightened rabbit.

"Now, I never seen the likes of that before," Jeeter said, "I wonder what it was that I could have said that made her carry-on like that?"

Chapter XIII

Jeeter remained seated on his heels by the chimney in the yard for half an hour after Ellie May had run away crying. He stared at the tracks left in the yard by the new automobile, amazed at the sharpness of the imprint of the tire-tread. The tires of his own car, which was still standing in the yard between the house and the corn-crib, were worn smooth. When they rolled on the sand, they left no track, except two parallel bands of smoothed sand. He was wondering now what he could do about his tires. If he could pump them all up at the same time, he could haul a load of wood to Augusta and sell it. He might even get as much as a dollar for the load.

It was fifteen miles to the city, and after he had bought enough gasoline and oil for the trip there and back, there would not be much left of the dollar. A quarter, possibly, with which he could buy two or three jars of snuff and a peck of cotton-seed meal. Even a quarter would not buy enough corn meal for them to eat. He had already begun buying cotton-seed meal, because corn meal cost too much. Fifteen cents would buy enough cotton-seed meal to last them a whole week.

But Jeeter was not certain whether it was worth the trouble of hauling a load of wood. It would take him nearly half a day to load the car with blackjack, and a half a day for the trip to Augusta. And then after he got there he might not be able to find anybody to buy it.

He still planned a crop for that year, though. He had by no means given up his plans to raise one. Ten or fifteen acres of cotton could be raised, if he could get the seed and guano. There was a mule over near Fuller he thought he could borrow, and he had a plow that would do; but it took money or an equal amount of credit to buy seed-cotton and guano. The merchants in Fuller had said they would not let him have anything on credit again, and it was useless to try to raise a loan in a bank in Augusta. He had tried to do that three or four times already, but the first thing they asked him was whom did he have to sign his notes, and what collateral had he to put up. Right there was where the deal fell through every time. Nobody would sign his notes, and he had nothing to put up for security. The men in the bank had told Jeeter to try a loan company.

The loan companies were the sharpest people he had ever had anything to do with. Once he had secured a two-hundred-dollar loan from one of them, but he swore it was the last time he would ever bind himself to such an agreement. To begin with, they came out to see him two or three times a week; some of them from the company's office would come out to the farm and try to tell him how to plant the cotton and how much guano to put in to the acre. Then on the first day of every month they came back to collect interest on the loan. He could never pay it, and they added the interest to the principal, and charged him interest on that, too.

By the time he sold his cotton in the fall, there was only seven dollars coming to him. The interest on the loan amounted to three per cent a month to start with, and at the end of ten months he had been charged thirty per cent, and on top of that another thirty per cent on the unpaid interest. Then to make sure that the loan was fully protected, Jeeter had to pay the sum of fifty dollars. He could never understand why he had to pay that, and the company did not undertake to explain it to him. When he had asked what the fifty dollars was meant to cover, he was told that it was merely the fee for making the loan. When the final settlement was made, Jeeter found that he had paid out more than three hundred dollars, and was receiving seven dollars for his share. Seven dollars for a year's labor did not seem to him a fair portion of the proceeds from the cotton, especially as he had done all the work, and had furnished the land and mule, too. He was even then still in debt, because he owed ten dollars for the hire of the mule he had used to raise the cotton. With Lov and Ada's help, he discovered that he had actually lost three dollars. The man who had rented him the mule insisted on being paid, and Jeeter had given him the seven dollars, and he was still trying to get the other three to pay the balance.

Jeeter swore that he would never again have anything to do with the rich people in Augusta. They had hounded him nearly every day, trying to tell him how he should cultivate the cotton, and in the end they came out and took it all away from him, leaving him three dollars in debt. He had done all the work, furnished the mule and the land, and yet the loan company had taken all the money the cotton brought, and made him lose three dollars. He told everybody he saw after that, that God was not working in a deal such as that one was. He told the men who represented the finance company the same thing, too.

"You rich folks in Augusta is just bleeding us poor people to death. You don't work none, but you get all the money us farmers make. Here I is working all the year myself, Dude plowing, and Ada and Ellie May helping to chop the cotton in summer and pick it in the fall, and what do I get out of it? Not a durn thing, except a debt of three dollars. It ain't right, I tell you. God ain't working on your side. He won't stand for such cheating much longer, neither. He ain't so liking of you rich people as you think He is. God, He likes the poor."

The men collecting for the loan company listened to Jeeter talk, and when he had finished, they laughed at him and got in their new automobile and drove back to Augusta.

That was one reason why Jeeter was not certain he could raise a crop that year. But he thought now that if he could get the seed and guano on credit from a man in Fuller, he would not be robbed. The people in Fuller were farmers, just as he was, or as he tried to be, and he did not believe they would cheat him. But every time he had said something about raising credit in Fuller, the merchants had waved him away and would not even listen to him.

"Ain't no use in talking no more, Jeeter," they had said. "There's farmers coming into Fuller every day from all over the country wanting the same thing. If there's one, there's a hundred been here. But we can't help you people none. Last year we let some of you farmers have seed-cotton and guano on credit, and when fall came there was durn little cotton made, and what there was didn't bring more than seven cents, middling grade. Ain't no sense in farming when things is like that. And we can't take no more chances. All of us has just got to wait until the rich give up the money they're holding back."

"But, praise God, me and my folks is starving out there on that tobacco road. We ain't got nothing to eat, and we ain't got nothing to sell that will bring money to get meal and meat. You store-keepers won't let us have no more credit since Captain John left, and what is we going to do? I don't know what's going to happen to me and my folks if the rich don't stop bleeding us. They've got all the money, holding it in the banks, and they won't lend it out unless a man will cut off his arms and leave them there for security."

"The best thing you can do, Jeeter," they had said, "is to move your family up to Augusta, or across the river in South Carolina to Horsecreek Valley, where all the mills is, and go to work in one of them. That's the only thing left for you to do now. Ain't no other way."

"No! By God and by Jesus, no!" Jeeter had said. "That's one thing I ain't going to do! The Lord made the land, and He put me here to raise crops on it. I been doing that, and my daddy before me, for the past fifty years, and that's what's intended. Them durn cotton mills is for the women folks to work in. They ain't no place for a man to be, fooling away with little wheels and strings all day long. I say, it's a hell of a job for a man to spend his time winding strings on spools. No! We was put here on the land where cotton will grow, and it's my place to make it grow. I wouldn't fool with the mills if I could make as much as fifteen dollars a week in them. I'm staying on the land till my time comes to die."

"Have it your own way, Jeeter, but you'd better think it over and go to work in the cotton mills. That's what nearly everybody else around Fuller has done. Some of them is in Augusta and some of them is in Horsecreek Valley, but they're all working in the cotton mills just the same. You and your wife together could make twenty or twenty-five dollars a week doing that. You ain't making nothing by staying here. You'll both have to go and live at the county poor-farm pretty soon if you stay here and try to raise cotton."

"Then it will be the rich who put us there," Jeeter had said. "If we has to go to the poor-farm and live, it will be because the rich has got all the money that ought to be spread out among us all and won't turn it loose and give me some credit to get seed-cotton and guano with."

"You ain't got a bit of sense, Jeeter. You ought to know by now that you can't farm. It takes a rich man to run a farm these days. The poor has got to work in the mills."

"Maybe I ain't got much sense, but I know it ain't intended for me to work in the mills. The land was where I was put at the start, and it's where I'm going to be at the end."

"Why, even your children has got more sense than you, Jeeter. They didn't stay here to starve. They went to work in the mills. Now, there's Lizzie Belle up there in——"

"Maybe some of them did, but that ain't saying it was right. Dude, he didn't go, noway. He's still here. He's going to farm the land some day, just like all of us ought to be doing."

"Dude hasn't got the sense to leave. If he had the sense your other children had, he wouldn't stay here. He would be able to see how foolish it is to try to farm like things is now. The rich ain't aiming to turn loose their money for credit. They're going to hold on to it all the time to run the mills with."

Jeeter remembered all that had been said, as he sat on his heels by the chimney, leaning against the warm bricks in the late February sun. He had heard men in Fuller say things like that dozens of times, and it always had ended in his walking out and leaving them. None of them understood how he felt about the land when the plowing season came each spring.

The feeling was in him again. This time he felt it more deeply than ever, because in all the past six or seven years when he had wanted to raise a crop he had kept his disappointment from crushing his spirit by looking forward to the year when he could farm again. But this year he felt that if he did not get the seed-cotton and guano in the ground he would never be able to try again. He knew he could not go on forever waiting each year for credit and never receiving it, because he was becoming weaker each day, and soon he would not be able to walk between the plow-handles even if credit were provided for him.

It was because of his discouragement that the odor of wood and sedge smoke and of newly turned earth now filling the air, was so strong and pungent. Farmers everywhere were burning over the woods and the broom-sedge fields, and plowing the earth in the old cotton lands and in the new grounds.

The urge he felt to stir the ground and to plant cotton in it, and after that to sit in the shade during the hot months watching the plants sprout and grow, was even greater than the pains of hunger in his stomach. He could sit calmly and bear the feeling of hunger, but to be compelled to live and look each day at the unplowed fields was an agony he believed he could not stand many more days.

His head dropped forward on his knees, and sleep soon overcame him and brought a peaceful rest to his tired heart and body.

Chapter XIV

Dude and Sister Bessie came back at sunset. Dude was blowing the horn a mile away, when Jeeter first heard it, and he and Ada ran out to the road to watch them come. The horn made a pretty sound, Jeeter thought, and he liked the way Dude blew it. He was pressing the horn button and taking his finger off every few seconds, like the firemen who blew the engine whistles when they were leaving the coal chute.

"That's Dude blowing the horn," Jeeter said. "Don't he blow it pretty, though? He always liked to blow the horn near about as much as he liked to drive an automobile. He used to cuss a lot because the horn on my car wouldn't make the least bit of a sound. The wires got pulled loose and I never had time to tie them up again."

Ada stood in the road watching the shiny new car come nearer and nearer. It looked like a big black chariot, she said, running away from a cyclone. The dust blown up behind did look like the approach of a cyclone.

"Ain't that the *prettiest* sight to see?" she said.

"That's Dude driving it, and blowing the horn, too," he said. "It makes a pretty sound when it blows, don't it, Ada?"

Jeeter was proud of his son.

"I wish all my children was here to see it," Ada said. "Lizzie Belle used to like to look at automobiles, and ride in them, too, more than anybody I ever saw. Maybe she's got herself one now. I wish I knowed."

Sister Bessie and Dude drove up slowly, and turned into the yard. Jeeter and Ada ran along beside the car until it stopped beside the chimney of the house. Ellie May saw everything from around the corner of the house.

"How far a piece did you go riding?" Jeeter asked Bessie as she opened the door and stepped out on the ground. "You been gone clear the whole afternoon. Did you go to Augusta?"

Bessie caught up the bottom of her skirt and began wiping off the dust. Ada and Ellie May were already at work on the other side of the car. The grandmother was thirty feet away, standing behind a chinaberry tree and looking around the trunk at the automobile. Dude sat under the steering-wheel blowing the horn.

"We went and we went till we went clear to McCoy," she said. "We just kept on going till we got there."

"That's about thirty miles, ain't it?" Jeeter asked excitedly. "Did you go clear that far and back?"

"That's what we did," Dude said. "I ain't never been that far away from here before. It's a pretty country down that way, too."

"Why didn't you go to Augusta?" Jeeter asked. "You went down to the crossroads and I thought sure you was going to Augusta."

"We didn't go that way," Dude said, "we went the other way—toward McCoy. And we went clear to McCoy, too."

Jeeter walked to the front of the car and looked at it. Dude climbed out and stopped blowing the horn for a while.

"Praise the Lord," Jeeter said, "what went and done that?"

He pointed to the right front fender and headlight. Everybody stopped dusting and gathered around the radiator. The fender was twisted and crumpled until it looked as if somebody had taken a sledge-hammer and tried to see how completely he could maul it. The right headlight had been knocked off. Only a piece of twisted iron and a small strand of insulated wire remained where it had been. The fender had been mashed back against the hood.

"It was a wagon what done that," Dude said. "We was coming back from McCoy, and I was looking out at a big turpentine still, and then the first thing I knowed we was smashed smack into the back end of a two-horse wagon."

Bessie looked at the mashed fender and missing headlight, but she said nothing. She could hardly blame it on the devil this time, as she had been riding in the car herself when the accident occurred, but it seemed to her that God ought to have taken better care of it, especially after she had stopped and prayed about it when she bought the automobile that morning in Fuller.

"It don't hurt the running of it none, though, does it?" Jeeter asked.

"It runs like it was brand new yet," Dude said. "And the horn wasn't hurt none at all. It blows just as pretty as it did this morning."

The fender had been crumpled beyond repair. It was lying against the hood of the car and, except for the jagged edges, it appeared as if it had been removed. Apparently nothing else, with the exception of the headlight, had been damaged; there were no dents in the body, and the wheels and axle seemed to stand straight and in line. The broken spring made the left rear end sag, however.

"That don't hurt it none," Jeeter said. "Don't pay no attention to it, Bessie. Just leave it be, and you'll never know it was any different than it was when you got it brand new."

"That's right," she said. "I ain't letting it worry me none, because it wasn't Dude's fault. He was looking at the big turpentine still alongside the road, and I was too, when the wagon got in our way. The nigger driving it ought to have had enough sense to get out of our way when he heard us coming."

"Wasn't you blowing the horn then, Dude?" Jeeter asked.

"Not right then I wasn't, because I was busy looking at the big still. I never saw one that big nowhere before. It was almost as big as a corn-liquor still, only it wasn't as shiny-looking."

"It's a shame to get the new car smashed up so soon already, though," Bessie said, going back and wiping off the dust. "It was brand new only a short time before noon, and now it's only sundown."

"It was that nigger," Dude said. "If he hadn't been asleep on the wagon it wouldn't have happened at all. He was plumb asleep till it woke him up and threw him out in the ditch."

"He didn't get hurt much, did he?" Jeeter asked.

"I don't know about that," Dude said. "When we drove off again, he was still lying in the ditch. The wagon turned over on him and mashed him. His eyes was wide open all the time, but I couldn't make him say nothing. He looked like he was dead."

"Niggers will get killed. Looks like there ain't no way to stop it."

The sun had been down nearly half an hour and the chill dampness of an early spring night settled over the ground. The grandmother had already gone into the house and got into bed. Ada went up on the porch, hugging her arms across her chest to keep warm, and Bessie started inside, too.

Dude and Jeeter stood around the car until it was so dark they could not see it any longer, and then they too went inside.

The glare of woods-fire soon began to light the sky on the horizons, and the smell of pine smoke filled the damp evening air. Fires were burning in all directions; some of them had been burning a week or longer, while others had been burning only since that afternoon.

In the spring, the farmers burned over all of their land. They said the fire would kill the boll-weevils. That was the reason they gave for burning the woods and fields, whenever anybody asked why they did not stop burning up young pine seedlings and standing timber. But the real reason was because everybody had always burned the woods and fields each spring, and they saw no cause for abandoning life-long habits. Burning fields and woods seemed to them to be as necessary as drilling guano in the cotton fields to make the plants yield a large crop. If the wood that was burned had been sawn into lumber or cut into firewood, instead of burning to ashes on the ground, there would have been something for them to sell. Boll-weevils were never killed in any great numbers by the fire; the cotton plants had to be sprayed with poison in the summer, anyway. But everybody had always burned over the land each spring, and they continued if only for the reason that their fathers had done it. Jeeter always burned over his land, even though there was no reason in the world why he should do it; he never raised crops any more. This was why the land was bare of everything except broom-sedge and blackjack; the sedge grew anew each year, and the hottest fire could not hurt those tough scrub oaks.

Inside the house the women gathered in the bedroom in the darkness and waited for Jeeter and Dude. The grandmother was already in bed, covered with her ragged quilts. Ellie May had gone out into the broom-sedge and had not yet returned. Bessie and Ada sat on the beds waiting.

The three beds had always held all the Lesters, even when there were sometimes as many as eight or nine of them there. Occasionally, some had slept on pallets on the floor in summer, but in winter it was much warmer for every one in the beds. Now that all of the children had left except Dude and Ellie May, there was just enough room for every one. Bessie had a house of her own, a three-room tenant house on the last sandhill at the river; but the roof was rotten, and the shingles had blown away, and when it rained everything in the three rooms was soaked with water.

Sometimes in the middle of the night when a storm came up suddenly, Bessie would wake up to find the bed filled with water, every piece of her clothes wet, and more water pouring down through the roof. She had told Ada that she did not want to stay there any more until she could have a new shingle roof put on the house. The building and the land around it belonged to Captain John Harmon; he never came out to the tobacco road any more, and he made no repairs to the buildings. He had told Jeeter and Bessie, and all the other people who lived out there, that they could stay in the houses until the buildings rotted to the ground and that he would never ask for a penny of rent. They understood the arrangement fully; he was not going to make any repairs to the roofs, porches, rotted under-sills, or anything about the buildings. If the houses fell down, he said, it would be too bad for them; but if they stood up, then Jeeter, Bessie, and all the others could remain in them as long as they wanted to stay.

Jeeter and Dude came into the house, stumbling through the darkness. There was a lamp in the house, but no kerosene had been bought that whole winter. The Lesters went to bed at dark, except in summer when it was warm enough to sit on the porch, and they got up at daylight. There was no need for kerosene, anyway.

Jeeter sat down on his bed beside Ada and pulled off his heavy shoes. The brogans fell on the floor like bricks dropped waist high.

"We stopped in every house we came to, and got out and visited a while," Bessie said. "Some of them wanted prayer, and some didn't. It didn't make much difference to me, because me and Dude was all excited about riding around. Some of the people wanted to know where I got all the money to buy a brand-new car, and why I married Dude, and I told them. I told them my former husband left me eight hundred dollars, and I said I married Dude because I was going to make a preacher out of him. Of course, that was only one reason why we got married, but I knew that would be enough to tell them."

"Nobody said things against you, did they, Sister Bessie?" Jeeter asked. "Some people has got a way of talking about people like us."

"Well, some of them did say a few things about me marrying Dude. They said he was too young to be married to a woman my age, but when they started talking like that, we just got in our new automobile and rode off. A lot of them said it was a sin and a shame for to take my husband's money and buy an automobile and get married to a young boy like Dude, but while they was doing the talking, me and Dude was doing the riding, wasn't we, Dude?"

Dude did not answer.

"I reckon Dude has gone to sleep," Jeeter said. "He worked pretty hard to-day, driving that automobile clear to McCoy and back again."

Ada sat up in bed.

"Take them overalls off, Jeeter," she said angrily. "I ain't never seen the like of it. You know I ain't going to let you sleep in the bed with them dirty pants on. I have to tell you about it nearly every time. They dirty-up the bed something bad. You ought to know I ain't going to stand for that."

"It's pretty cold again to-night," Jeeter said. "I get chilly when I don't sleep with my overalls on. It seems like I can't do nothing no more like I want to. Sleeping in overalls ain't going to hurt nothing, noway."

"You're the only man I ever knowed of who wanted to sleep in his overalls. Don't nobody else do like that."

Jeeter did not answer her. He got up out of bed and climbed out of his overalls and hung them on the foot of the bed. When he got back under the quilts, he was shivering all over.

Bessie could be heard over on the other side of the room stepping around in her stockinged feet getting ready for bed. She had kept her shoes on until she removed her clothes.

Jeeter lifted his head from under the cover and tried to look through the darkness of the room.

"You know, Bessie," he said, "it sort of makes me feel good like I was before I lost my health to have a woman preacher sleep in my house. It's a fine feeling I has about you staying here."

"I'm a woman preacher, all right," she said, "but I ain't no different in other ways from the rest of the women-folks. Jeeter, you know that, don't you?"

Jeeter raised himself on his elbow and strained his eyes to see through the darkness across the room.

"I hope you ain't leaving us no time soon," he said. "I'd be powerful pleased to have you sleep here all the time, Bessie."

Ada thrust her elbow into his ribs with all her strength, and he fell down groaning with pain on the bed beside her.

Bessie could be heard getting into her bed. The corn-shuck mattress crackled, and the slats rattled as she lay down and stretched out her feet. She lay still for several minutes, and then she began to stretch her hands out towards the other side, the impact of her arms making the shucks crackle more than ever.

Suddenly she sat up in bed, throwing the quilts aside.

"Where's Dude?" she demanded angrily, her voice gruff and unnatural. "Where is you, Dude?"

Not a sound was to be heard in the room. Ada had sat upright, and Jeeter had sprung to a sitting position on the side of the bed. Bessie's corn-shuck mattress crackled some more, and then the thump of her bare feet on the pine floor could be heard all over the house. Jeeter still did not attempt to speak or to move. He waited to catch every sound in the house.

"You Dude—you Dude!" Bessie cried from the centre of the room, trying to feel her way from bed to bed. "Where is you, Dude—why don't you answer me? You'd better not try to hide from me, Dude!"

"What's the matter, Bessie?" Jeeter said.

"Dude ain't in the bed—I can't find him nowhere at all."

Reaching for his overalls, Jeeter jumped to his feet. He began fumbling in his pockets for a match. At last he found one, and bending over, he struck it on the floor.

The flare of the match revealed every one in the room. Every one was there except Ellie May and Dude. Bessie was only a few feet away from Jeeter, and he tried to look at her. She was shielding her eyes from the light.

Ada crawled out of bed and stood behind Jeeter the moment she saw Bessie.

"Put them overalls on," she commanded Jeeter. "I don't know what you and her is up to, but I'm watching. You put them overalls on right now. I don't care if she is a woman preacher, she ain't got no right to stand in the floor in front of you like she is."

Jeeter hesitated, and the match burned down to his fingers. He stepped into his overalls, put one arm through a gallus, and reached into his pocket for another match.

Bessie was still standing beside Jeeter, but when he struck the match, she ran to Mother Lester's bed. She jerked back the covers, and saw Dude sound asleep. The grandmother was awake, and she lay trembling in her old torn black clothes.

Jeeter shook Dude awake and pulled him to the floor. Ada jerked him by the arm.

"What you mean by not getting in bed with Bessie?" Jeeter demanded, shaking him roughly by the collar.

Dude looked around him and blinked his eyes. He was unable to see anything in the flare of the match.

"What you want?" he asked, rubbing his eyes.

"Dude, he didn't know which bed to get in," Sister Bessie said tenderly. "He was so tired and sleepy he didn't look to see which one we was going to sleep in, did you, Dude?"

"Dude, you can't act that way," Jeeter said. "You got to keep your eyes open when you get married. Bessie, here, got powerful nervous when she didn't find you in bed."

Ada went back to bed, and Jeeter followed her. He did not take off his overalls, and Ada went to sleep without thinking about them.

Ellie May came in after a while and got into bed with her grandmother. No one spoke to her.

The grandmother had been wide awake all the time, but no one said anything to her, and she did not try to tell Bessie that Dude was in her bed. No one ever said anything to her, except to tell her to get out of the way, or to stop eating the bread and meat.

Dude and Bessie went to their bed and lay down. Sister Bessie tried to talk to Dude, but Dude was tired and sleepy. He did not answer her. The rustling sound of the corn-shuck mattress continued most of the night.

Chapter XV

Jeeter drank his third cup of chicory and cleared his throat. Dude had already left the kitchen and gone to the yard, and Sister Bessie was on the back porch combing her hair. Jeeter went down the back steps and leaned against the well.

"It would be a pretty smart deal if I was to take a load of wood to Augusta to-day," he said. "Me and Dude's got a big pile of it all cut and ready to haul. Now, if we was to pile it in the new automobile it wouldn't take no time to haul it to the city, would it, Bessie?"

She finished combing her hair, stuck half a dozen pins and the rhinestone comb into it, and walked with Jeeter over to the automobile.

"Maybe it would hold a load," she said. "There ain't so much room in the back seat, though."

"Mine holds a fair load, and it ain't no bigger than that one. They is the same kind of automobiles. The only difference being that yours is near about a brand-new one now."

Dude turned on the switch and raced the engine. The motor hummed perfectly. The tightness that had bothered Dude the day before had gone, and the engine was in good running order. He blew the horn several times, grinning at Jeeter.

"I'd sort of like to take a trip to Augusta, all right," Bessie said. "Me and Dude was going there yesterday, before we changed our mind and went down to McCoy instead."

"It won't take long to put a load of wood in the back seat," Jeeter said. "We can leave pretty soon. Dude—you drive the automobile out across the field yonder to that pile of wood we been cutting the past week. I'll get some pieces of baling wire to bind the load good and tight so it won't drop off."

Bessie got in beside Dude, and they started out across the old cotton field towards the grove of blackjack. The field had grown up into four-foot broom-sedge in the past few years. Once it had been the finest piece of tobacco land on the whole farm.

The rows of the last crop of cotton were still there, and as the car gathered speed, the bumps tossed Dude and Bessie up and down so suddenly and so often that they could not keep their seats. Dude grasped the steering-wheel tightly and held himself better than Bessie could; Bessie bobbed up and down as the car raced over the old cotton rows and her head hit the top every time there was a bump. They had gone about a quarter of a mile, and were almost at the edge of the grove where the pile of blackjack was, when suddenly there was a jarring crash that stopped the car dead in its tracks.

Dude was thrown against the steering-wheel, and Bessie shot forward off the seat and struck her head against the wind-shield. Where her forehead had hit the glass there were a hundred or more cracks, branching out like a wet spider-web in the sunshine. None of the glass shattered, though, and the wind-shield was still intact. She did not know what had happened.

"Praise the Lord," Bessie shouted, pulling herself out of her cramped position on the floorboards. "What's we done this time, Dude?"

"I reckon we rammed into a stump," he said. "I clear forgot about them old dead stumps out here in the sedge. I couldn't see nothing at all for the sedge. It covers everything on the ground."

Both of them got out and went to the front. A two-foot stump had stopped them.

The blackened pine stump, hidden from view by the four-foot wall of brown broom-sedge, stood squarely in front of the axle. It was partly decayed, and except for the heart of it, the car would have knocked it down and gone ahead without any trouble. As it was, the axle was not badly bent; actually, the car was going only about fifteen miles an hour, and there had not been enough force to twist the axle out of shape. The wheels had sprung forward a few inches, but aside from that, there was nothing to worry about. The car was still almost as good as new.

Jeeter came running up just then with his hands and arms full of rusty bailing wire, which he had found behind the corn-crib.

They did not have to tell him what had happened, because he could see just as well as they did that the front axle had hit the stump and sprung the wheels forward several inches.

"It don't appear to be hurt much," he said. "Maybe it ain't hurt none at all. We has got to haul a load of wood to Augusta to-day, because there ain't no more meal and chicory in the house to eat."

Bessie watched Dude start up the engine and back away from the stump. He swung around it, and drove carefully the remaining few yards to the pile of blackjack. Jeeter began picking up the pieces of scrub oak and hurling them like javelins into the back seat.

"I reckon I'd better put the top down," Dude said. "It won't hold much unless the top's down."

He began unfastening the set screws holding the top to the wind-shield, while Jeeter and Bessie continued to hurl blackjack into the back seat.

"There won't be no room for Ada to go along, too, will there?" Jeeter said. "She'll be powerful put out when she sees us drive off to

Augusta and not stopping to take her along. The last time me and Dude went up there in my car, she and Ellie May liked to had a fit, but it wasn't no use, because we needed all the room for wood."

"Well, I ain't going to stay at home," Bessie said. "I'm going just as big as the next one. You can't make me stay here."

"I'm going," Dude said. "Can't nobody make me stay here. I'm going to drive the car."

He had thrown the top back and was trying to tie it down. Most of it had been folded up, but some of it hung down as far as the rear axle. He could not find any means of making it stay folded, so he allowed it to hang down behind.

"I sure ain't going to miss going," Jeeter said. "It's my wood I'm taking to sell. I'm going to be the first one to go."

The scrub oak had been cut into varying lengths the past week when Jeeter and Dude had spent a day in the grove getting a load ready to sell. Some of it was a foot in length, but most of it was anywhere from three to six feet long. The length in which it had been cut was the length of the stunted trees after they had been hacked off with an axe at the stump. As soon as a tree was hacked down, Jeeter had taken the axe and broken the limbs off, and then the wood was ready to haul. The blackjack never grew much taller than a man's head; it was a stunted variety of oak that used its sap in toughening the fibres instead of growing new layers and expanding the old, as other trees did. The blackjack sticks were about two or three inches in diameter, and wiry and tough as heavy pieces of wire or small iron water-pipes.

It took them about half an hour to pile on as much wood as the back seat would hold. After that, Jeeter began binding it to the body with baling wire so none of it would drop off along the road while they were riding to Augusta. The ends of the blackjack protruded in all directions, sticking out several feet on each side and behind. Others had been jabbed straight into the upholstery, and they appeared to be the only ones that did not need fastening. The rusty baling wire broke nearly every time Jeeter attempted to fasten it to the door-handles, and he would have to stop and splice the ends, twisting them until they would hold. The task of loading the blackjack and tying it on to the car took nearly two hours, and even then several pieces of wood fell off when one of them touched the car or leaned against it.

With the wood in place, Dude drove back across the field towards the house, going no faster than a man's walk, but even then the wood persisted in falling off. Jeeter and Bessie came behind, picking up the sticks and carrying them to the house.

Ada and Ellie May were in the yard when they got there. The

grandmother waited behind a chinaberry tree to see what they were going to do. Ada stood squarely in front of the car, waiting to find out where she was going to sit. The grandmother went to the corner of the house and stood there, all except her face hidden from view.

"Where is I going to sit and ride?" Ada said. "I don't see no sitting place for nobody much, with all that wood you got loaded."

Jeeter waited several minutes, hoping that Bessie would undertake to answer Ada. When she did not, Jeeter got in and sat down beside Dude.

"There ain't no room for you," he said.

"Why ain't there no room for me, if there's room for you and Dude and that hussy, there?"

"Sister Bessie ain't no hussy," Jeeter said. "She ain't nothing like that. She's a woman preacher."

"Being a woman preacher don't keep her from being a hussy. That could help to make her a bigger one. Something acts that way, because she is a big old hussy."

"What makes you say that about Bessie?" he said.

"Last night she was walking all around the room with none of her clothes on. If I hadn't made you put on your overalls when I did, there ain't no telling what she might have done. She's a hussy."

"Now, Ada," he said, "you ought not to talk like that about Bessie. She's a woman preacher, and she's married to Dude, too."

"That don't make no difference. She's a hussy, all the same. She always fools around with the men-folks. She don't never stay in the house and help clean it up like I has to do. She's taking after the men-folks because she's a hussy. When she goes preaching, she always does the preaching to the men-folks and don't pay no attention to the women-folks at all."

"I ain't got nothing to say against Sister Bessie. She's a woman preacher, and what she does is the Lord's doings. He instructs her what to do."

"Ada is peeved because I married Dude and came here to stay," Bessie said to Jeeter. "She don't like it because I'm going to stay in the room."

"You shut your mouth now, Ada," Jeeter said, "and let us be going. I got to sell this load of wood in Augusta to-day."

Dude started the car, and Bessie got in and sat on the edge of the seat beside Jeeter. There was barely enough room for all three of them.

Ada ran towards them, trying to jump on the running-board, but Dude speeded up the car and she could not get on. When he suddenly cut the wheels and turned out of the yard into the tobacco road, the rear wheel barely missed running over Ada's feet. She shouted after them, but the car was going so fast by that time that it was useless to run after them and try to stop them. She went back into the yard and, with Ellie May, stood looking at the cloud of dust that hid the car from view. The grandmother came from behind the corner of the house and, picking up the old croker sack, started to the thicket for dead twigs. She was already hungry again, although she had had a cup of chicory only two or three hours before.

Dude slowed down when they approached the crossroad where they were to turn off the tobacco road and enter the State highway to Augusta. He did not slow down enough, however, because the momentum swung the load of blackjack to the offside, and the entire top of the pile fell in the road.

Jeeter and Dude worked half an hour getting the wood in place again, and with Bessie helping the little that she could, it was then ready to be tied down again. Jeeter went across the field to a Negro cabin and borrowed two plow-lines. He came back and threw them over the wood and tied the ends down tightly.

"Now, that will hold it, durn that blackjack," he said. "There ain't nothing else in the world like plow-lines and baling wire. The two together is the best in the world to do anything with. Give me a little of both and I can do any kind of job."

They were off again, speeding down the highway towards Augusta. The city was now only twelve miles away.

Dude was a good driver, all right; he swung out of the tracks just at the right moment everytime he met another automobile. Only two or three times did he almost run head-on into other cars. He was so busy blowing the horn that he forgot to drive on the right-hand side of the road until the last minute. Most of the cars they met gave them plenty of road when they heard the horn blowing.

Jeeter could not talk, because he was holding his breath most of the time. The swiftness of the car frightened him so badly he could not answer Bessie's questions. She looked grimly ahead most of the time, proud of her automobile and hoping that the Negroes and farmers they passed in the fields beside the road would know it belonged to her instead of thinking it was Jeeter's or Dude's.

It was between noon and one o'clock when they reached the halfway point. Augusta was then only a little over seven miles away, and when they got to the top of the last hill they would be able to see the city down in the valley beside the big muddy river.

The last hill they had to climb before reaching that point was a long one. It was a mile and a half from the creek at the bottom to the filling-station on top, and they were about half way up, when suddenly the car slowed down to a few miles an hour. The water was boiling in the engine and radiator, and steam shot higher than the top of the wind-shield. The engine was making a great noise, too. It sounded as if it were knocking in the same way that Jeeter's old car had, only a little harder and a little louder.

"What's the matter with us?" Bessie said, leaning over the door and looking around outside.

"It must have got hot climbing the hill," Dude said. "I don't know what else is wrong with it."

They went a hundred yards, and the car stopped. The engine choked down, and steam whistled out of the pipes like pistons on a freight train at the coal chute.

Jeeter jumped out and shoved a big rock under the rear wheel before Dude could put on the brakes. The car stopped rolling backward.

"What's the matter with it, Dude?" Bessie said again. "Is something gone wrong?"

"I reckon it just got hot," he said.

He made no effort to get out. He sat under the steering-wheel, grasping it tightly and jerking it from side to side as far as it would go. Presently he began blowing the horn again.

"That won't help it none, Dude," Jeeter said. "You'll wear out that durn horn before you know it, if you keep doing that all the time. Why don't you get out and try to do something?"

Several automobiles passed them at high speed, going up the hill and coming down, but none of them slowed up or stopped to offer help.

Another car was coming slowly up the hill behind them. It was coming very slowly in low gear, and it was steaming like Bessie's new car. As it chugged slowly past them, some of the Negroes leaned out and looked at the stalled automobile.

One of them called to Jeeter.

"What's the matter with your automobile, white-folks? It looks like it ain't going to run no more."

"By God and by Jesus!" Jeeter said, angrily. "What your name, nigger? Where you from?"

"We come from Burke County," he said. "What you want to know that for, white-folks?"

Before Jeeter could say anything more, the Negroes' car was a hundred yards up the hill, and gaining speed. Jeeter had been going to make them pull Bessie's car up the hill, if he could have stopped them.

Dude cranked up the engine and put the car into gear. Jeeter and Bessie hopped on the running-board just in time, because Dude soon had the car going fast. The engine had cooled, and they were going faster than the Negroes' car. They gained on the car ahead and were getting ready to pass it, when suddenly the engine began knocking louder than ever, and they came to a stop.

"This is the durndest automobile I ever saw," Jeeter said. "It don't do the same thing long enough to make me accustomed."

They had stopped this time on top of the hill. Dude was getting ready to let it roll down, when Jeeter saw the filling-station, and he told Dude to wait a minute.

"I'll bring some water and put it in," he said.

He crossed the road and went into the filling-station. He was back in a few minutes carrying a bucket of water. The man who ran the station came out with him.

While Jeeter was unscrewing the radiator cap, the other man was raising the hood to measure the oil.

"The trouble with you people, brother," he said, "is you ain't got a drop of oil in your car. Your bearings is burned out. How far did you come from?"

Jeeter told him they lived near Fuller on the old tobacco road.

"You've already ruined your new car," he said. "That's a shame. I hate to see people who don't know no better ruining automobiles."

"What's wrong with it now?" Bessie said.

"Your new car is ruined, sister. It'll take a gallon and a half of oil to put enough in it to run on. Do you want me to fill it up for you?"

"How much does it cost?" Bessie said.

"A dollar and a half."

"I didn't aim to pay out money on it."

"Well, it won't run no more unless you put oil in it. It looks to me like you didn't have enough in it to start with."

"I ain't got but two dollars," she said. "I was going to buy gasoline with most of that."

"Me and Dude ain't got none," Jeeter said. "But when I sell this load of wood, I'll have a dollar and a half, maybe."

"You pour the oil into it," Bessie said. "I don't want to ruin my new automobile. I bought it brand new in Fuller yesterday."

"It's already ruint, sister," the man said, "but you'll have to put oil in it if you're going in to Augusta and back to Fuller again."

They waited while he poured the oil in, and then Bessie gave him the money. She had the bills tied in a handkerchief, and it took her several minutes to untie the hard knots.

Dude started the engine, and they moved slowly off the hill-top and rolled down the long grade to Augusta. The car was running like new again by the time they reached the bottom of the hill, but the engine made more noise than the one in Jeeter's car. The bearings and connecting rods were so loose they made a jingling sound when the car was going more than fifteen miles an hour down hill.

Chapter XVI

THREE hours had already been spent in trying to sell the load of blackjack. Apparently there was not a man in Augusta who wanted to buy it. At some of the houses Jeeter went to, the people at first said they needed wood, but after they had asked him how much he wanted for it they were suspicious. Jeeter told them he was asking only a dollar, and then they asked him if he were selling split pine at that small price. He had to explain that it was blackjack, and not even sawn into stove length. The next thing he knew the door was slammed in his face, and he had to go to the next house and try again.

At a little after six o'clock the wood was still piled on the back seat of the car, and no buyer was in sight. Jeeter began stopping people on the streets in a final and desperate effort to dispose of the wood at fifty cents; but the men and women he approached took one look at the blackjack piled on the car and walked off, evidently thinking it was a joke of some kind. Nobody was foolish enough to buy blackjack when pine wood burned better and was less trouble to use.

"I don't know what we're going to do," Jeeter told Bessie. "It's getting almost too late to go back home, and nobody wants to buy wood no more. I used to sell it with no effort any time I brought a load up here."

Dude said he was hungry, and that he wanted to go somewhere and eat. Sister Bessie had half a dollar; Jeeter had nothing. Dude, of course, had nothing.

Jeeter had planned to sell the wood for a dollar, and then to buy some meat and meal to take home to eat; but he did not know what to do now. He turned to Bessie questioningly.

"Maybe we better start back toward Fuller," she said. "I can buy two gallons of gasoline, and that ought to be enough."

"Ain't we going to eat nothing?" Dude said. "My poor belly is as dry as the drought."

"Maybe we could sell something else," Jeeter said, looking at the automobile. "I don't know what we has got to sell, though."

"We ain't going to sell my new automobile," Bessie said quickly. "It was brand new only yesterday. That's one thing nobody ain't going to sell."

Jeeter looked the car over from front to back.

"No, I wouldn't think of doing nothing like that. But you know, Bessie, maybe we could sell a wee biddy piece of it, sort of."

He walked around the car and grasped the spare tire and wheel in his hands. He shook it violently.

"It's near about loose, anyhow," he said. "It wouldn't hurt the new car none, Bessie."

"Well, I reckon we got to," she said slowly. "That tire and wheel ain't doing us no good, noway. We can't ride on but four of them at a time, and five is a big waste."

They drove around the block until they found a garage. Jeeter went in and made inquiry. Presently a man came out, took the tire and wheel off, and rolled it through the garage door.

Jeeter came walking briskly across the street, holding out several green notes. He counted them one by one before Bessie and Dude.

"Ain't we lucky folks, though?" he said.

"How much money did it bring?" she asked.

"He said three dollars was more than enough, but that much sounded like a heap of money to me. And here it is! Ain't they pretty and new, though? Out there at Fuller all the money I ever saw was just about ready to fall apart, it was that worn out. Up here in Augusta the people has got good money."

The next stop was a small grocery store. Jeeter got out and bought a large sack of soda crackers and two pounds of yellow cheese. He came back to the car and offered the food to Dude and Bessie. They all broke off chunks of cheese and stuffed their mouths full of crackers.

"Just help yourself, Bessie," he said. "Take all you want. Run your hand in the poke and eat until you is full. Dude, there, might hog it all if you don't take care of your own wants."

Jeeter was feeling fine. It was the first time since he could remember that he had been to Augusta and could get something to eat when he wanted it. He smiled at Bessie and Dude, and waved to people passing along the street. When a woman passed, he took off his hat and bowed.

"Augusta is a fine place," he said. "All these people here is just like us. They is rich, but that don't make no difference to me. I like everybody now."

"Where is we going now?" Bessie said.

"There's a place to sleep right up above the store," Jeeter said. "Supposing we sleep in there to-night, and then to-morrow morning sell the wood—ain't that what we ought to do?"

Dude liked the suggestion, but Bessie hesitated. It looked to her as if it might cost a lot of money to spend the night in the hotel.

"Maybe it will cost too much," she said. "You go upstairs and see how much it costs."

Jeeter stuffed another handful of crackers and cheese in his mouth, and went up the flight of stairs where the hotel was. There was a small sign over the door, dimly lighted, which said it was a hotel.

He came back in less than five minutes.

"They'll let us stay for fifty cents apiece," he said. "They is pretty much crowded, and there ain't but one room vacant, but we can stay, if we wants to. I sure do, don't you, Bessie? I ain't never stayed all night in a hotel before."

Bessie by that time had set her heart on spending a night in a hotel in the city, and she was ready to go up the stairs when Jeeter said it would cost fifty cents for each of them.

"Now you hold on tight to that money, Jeeter," she said. "That's a heap of money to lose. You don't want to let it get away from you."

They walked up the narrow stairway and found themselves in a small, dusty room. It was the lobby. Half a dozen straight-back chairs and a table were in the dimly lighted room. The man who ran the hotel took them to the table and told them to sign their names on the register. Jeeter told him they would have to make their marks.

"What's your name?" he asked.

"Jeeter."

"Jeeter what?"

"Jeeter Lester, from out near Fuller."

"What's the boy's name?"

"Dude's name is Dude, the same as mine."

"Dude Lester?"

"That's right."

"And what's her name?" he asked, looking up at Bessie.

Bessie smiled at him, and he looked at her legs. She hunched her left shoulder forward and hung her head downward. He looked her over again.

"Her name is Mrs. Dude," Jeeter said.

The man looked at Dude and then at Bessie, and smiled. He was holding the pen for them to touch while he made the cross-marks opposite their names.

Jeeter gave him the money, and they were taken up another stairway to the third floor. The halls were dark, and the rooms shadowy and unventilated. He opened a door and told them to walk in.

"Is this where we sleep?" Jeeter asked him.

"This is the place. It's the only room I got left, too. We're pretty full tonight."

"This sure is a fine place," Jeeter said. "I didn't know hotels was such fine places before. I wish Lov was here to see me now."

There was only one bed in the room; it was large, flat, and high off the floor.

"I reckon we can crowd in the bed some way," Jeeter said. "I'll sleep in the middle."

"There's plenty of room for all of you," the man said, "but maybe I can find another bed for one of you."

He went out and shut the door.

Jeeter sat down on the bed and unlaced his brogans. The dusty shoes fell with heavy thuds on the bare floor. Dude sat in the chair and looked at the room, the walls, and the ceiling. The yellow plaster had dropped off in many places, and more hung loose, ready to fall the next time there was a vibration.

"We might as well go to bed," Jeeter said. "Ain't no sense in sitting up."

He hung his black felt hat on the bed-post and lay down. Bessie was standing before the wash-stand mirror taking down her hair.

"Ada ought to see me now," Jeeter said. "I ain't never slept the night in a hotel in all my days. I bet Ada won't believe I'm telling the truth when I tell her."

"You ain't got no business sleeping in bed with me and Bessie," Dude said. "You ought to get out on the floor."

"Now, Dude, you wouldn't begrudge me one night's sleeping, would you? Why, Bessie, there, is all willing, ain't you, Bessie?"

"You hush your mouth, Jeeter!" she said. "You make me feel so foolish when you say that!"

"It's only me and you, Dude," he said. "It's not like it was somebody else. I been wanting to sleep with you and Bessie for the longest time."

Some one knocked on the door and, before they could answer it, the man walked in.

"What did you say your name was?" he asked Bessie.

He walked over to the washstand where she stood, and waited close beside her.

"Mrs. Dude—" Jeeter said. "I told you that already once."

"I know—but what's her first name? You know what I mean—her girl's name."

Bessie put her dress over herself before she told him.

"Bessie," she said. "What do you want to know that for?"

"That's all right, Bessie," he said. "That's all I wanted to know."

He went out and shut the door.

"These city folks has got the queerest ways," Jeeter said. "You don't never know what they is going to ask you next."

Dude took off his shoes and coat and waited for Bessie to get into bed. She had sat down on the floor to take off her shoes and stockings.

Jeeter sat up in bed and waited for her to finish. A door nearby was slammed so hard that pieces of yellow plaster dropped off the ceiling to the bed and floor.

Suddenly some one knocked on the door again, and it was opened immediately. This time it was a man whom they had not seen before.

"Come on down the hall, Bessie," he said.

He waited outside until Bessie got up from the floor and went to the door.

"Me?" she said. "What you want with me?"

"Come on down to this other room, Bessie. It's too crowded up here."

"They must have found another bed for us," Jeeter said. "I reckon they found out that there was more beds empty than they thought there was."

He and Dude watched Bessie gather up her clothes and leave the room. She carried her dress, shoes, and stockings in one hand, and her hat in the other. After the door was closed, the building became quiet again.

"These city people has queer ways, don't they, Dude?" Jeeter said, turning over and closing his eyes. "They ain't like us folks out around Fuller."

"Why didn't you go to the other bed?" Dude said. "Why did the man tell Bessie to go?"

"You never can tell about the queer ways of city folks, Dude. They do the durndest things sometimes."

They both lay awake for the next half hour, but neither of them said anything. The light was still burning, but they did not try to turn it off.

A board in the hall floor squeaked, and Bessie came in carrying her clothes in her hands.

"Don't you like the place they provided you with in the other room?" Jeeter asked, sitting up. "What made you come back, Bessie?"

"I reckon I must have got in the wrong bed by mistake or something," she said. "Somebody else was in it."

Dude rubbed his eyes in the glare of the electric light, and looked at Bessie.

"Bessie is sure a pretty woman preacher, ain't she?" Jeeter said, looking at her.

"I didn't have time to dress again," she said. "I had to leave right away, and there wasn't no time to put my clothes on."

"That man ought to know what he was doing at the start. Ain't no sense in making people change beds all night long. He ought to let folks stay in one bed all the time and let us sleep some."

"Men sure is queer in a hotel," Bessie said. "They say the queerest things and do the queerest things I ever saw. I'm sure glad we stayed here, because I been having a good time to-night. It ain't like it is out on the tobacco road."

There was a tapping on the door again, and a man opened it. He looked at Bessie, and beckoned her to the door.

"Come here, Bessie," he said, "there's a room down at the other end of the hall for you."

He waited outside the partly opened door.

"I went to one room just a little while ago, and there was a man in the bed."

"Well, that's all right. Down at this other room is another bed for you. Come on, I'll go with you and show you how to get there."

"By God and by Jesus," Jeeter said. "I never heard of the likes of it in all my life. The men here is going to wear Bessie out, running her from one bed to another all night long. I don't reckon I'll ever come to this kind of a hotel again. I can't get no peace and sleep."

Bessie picked up her clothes and went out. The door was closed, and they heard her and the man walking down the hall.

"I reckon she's fixed up this time so she won't have to change beds again," Jeeter said. "I can't stay awake no longer to find out."

Dude went to sleep, too, in a few minutes.

At daybreak, Jeeter was up and dressed, and Dude got up a few minutes later. They sat in the room for the next half hour waiting for Bessie. At last Jeeter got up and went to the door and looked up the hall and down it.

"I reckon we'll have to go hunt Sister Bessie," he said. "Maybe she got lost and can't find this room. It was dark out there last night, and things look different in the day-time up here in the city."

They opened the door and walked to the end of the hall. All the doors were closed, and Jeeter did not know which one to open. The first two he opened were not occupied, but the next one was. He turned the knob and went inside. There were two people asleep in the bed, but the woman was not Bessie. Jeeter backed out of the room and closed the door. Dude tried the next room. The door of that one was unlocked, too, and Jeeter had to go across the room and look at the woman's face before he was satisfied she was not Bessie. In the other rooms they entered they failed to find Bessie, and Jeeter did not know what to do. The last room they entered had only a single bed and he was about to close the door, when the girl opened her eyes and sat up. Jeeter stood looking at her, not knowing what else to do. When the girl was fully awake, she smiled and called Jeeter to her.

"What you want?" he said.

"Why did you come in here?" she said.

"I'm looking for Bessie, and I reckon I'd better go hunt for her some more. I'm liable to disgrace myself if I stay here looking at you."

She called Jeeter again, but he turned his back and ran out of the room. Dude caught up with his father.

"By God and by Jesus, Dude," Jeeter said. "I never saw so many pretty girls and women in all my days. This hotel is just jammed with them. I'd sure lose my religion if I stayed here much longer. I've got to get out in the street right now."

At the foot of the stairway they saw the man who had rented them the room the night before. He was reading the morning paper.

"We're ready to leave now," Jeeter said, "but we can't find Sister Bessie."

"The woman who came in with you last night?"

"She's the one. Sister Bessie, her name is."

"I'll get her," he said, and started up the stairs. "What's wrong with her nose? I didn't notice it last night, but I saw it this morning. It gives me the creeps to look at it."

"She was born like that," Jeeter said. "Bessie ain't much to look at in the face, but she's a right smart piece to live with. Dude, here, he knows, because he's married to her."

"She's got the ungodliest-looking nose I ever saw," the man said, going up the stairs. "I hope I never get fooled like that again in the dark."

In about five minutes both he and Bessie came down the stairs. The man was in front and Bessie behind.

Out in the street, where they had left the car, Jeeter found the bag of crackers and cheese, and he began eating them hungrily. Dude took a handful of crackers and put them into his mouth. A few doors away was a store with a Coca-Cola sign on it, and all of them went in and got a drink.

"You don't look like you slept none too much last night," Jeeter said. "Couldn't you go to sleep, Bessie?"

She yawned and rubbed her face with the palms of her hands. She had dressed hurriedly, and had not combed her hair. It hung matted and stringy over her face.

"I reckon the hotel was pretty full last night," she said. "Every once in a while somebody came and called me to another room. Every room I went to there was somebody sleeping in the bed. Looked like nobody knowed where my bed was. They was always telling me to sleep in a new one. I didn't sleep none, except about an hour just a while ago. There sure is a lot of men staying there."

Jeeter led them outside the store and they got into the automobile and drove off towards the residential part of the city. Bessie yawned, and tried to take a nap on the front seat.

Selling the load of blackjack was no easier than it had been the afternoon before. Nobody wanted to buy wood, at least not the kind Jeeter had for sale.

By three o'clock that afternoon all of them were thoroughly tired of trying to find somebody to take the wood.

Sister Bessie wanted to go back home, and so did Jeeter. Bessie was sleepy and tired. Jeeter began swearing every time he saw a man walking along the street. His opinion of the citizens of Augusta was even less than it had been before he started the trip. He cursed every dollar in the city.

Dude was anxious to go back home, because he would have the opportunity of blowing the horn when they went around the long curves on the highway.

Bessie bought the gasoline and Jeeter paid for it out of the money they had left. No trouble with the engine developed, and they sailed along at a fast rate of speed for nearly ten miles.

"Let's stop a minute," Jeeter said.

Dude stopped the car without question and they all got out. Jeeter began untying the plow-lines and untwisting the baling wire around the load of blackjack.

"What you going to do now?" Bessie asked him, watching him begin throwing off the sticks.

"I'm going to throw off the whole durn load and set fire to it," he said. "It's bad luck to carry something to town to sell and then tote it back home. It ain't a safe thing to do, to take it back home. I'm going to pitch it all off."

Dude and Bessie helped him, and in a few minutes the blackjack was piled in the ditch beside the road.

"And I ain't going to let nobody else have the use of it, neither," he said. "If the rich people in Augusta won't buy my wood, I ain't going to let it lay here so they can come out and take it off for nothing."

He gathered a handful of dead leaves, thrust them under the pile, and struck a match to them. The leaves blazed up, and a coil of smoke boiled into the air. Jeeter fanned the blaze with his hat and waited for the wood to catch on fire and burn.

"That was an unlucky trip to Augusta," he said. "I don't know when I've ever had such luck befall me before. All the other times I've been able to sell my wood for something, if it was only a quarter or so. But this time nobody wanted it for nothing, seems like."

"I want to go back some time and spend another night at that hotel," Bessie said, giggling. "I had the best time last night. It made me feel good, staying there. They sure know how to treat women real nice."

They waited for the blackjack to burn so they could leave for home. The leaves had burned to charred ashes, and the flame had gone out. The scrub oak would not catch on fire.

Jeeter scraped up a larger pile of leaves, set it on fire, and began tossing the sticks on it. The fire burned briskly for several minutes, and then went out under the weight of the green wood.

Jeeter stood looking at it, sadly. He did not know how to make it burn. Then Dude threw some gasoline from the tank and poured it on the pile. A great blaze sprang up ten or twelve feet into the air. Before long that too died down, leaving a pile of blackened sticks in the ditch.

"Well, I reckon that's all I can do to that damn-blasted blackjack," Jeeter said, getting into the car. "It looks like there ain't no way to get rid of the durn wood. It won't sell and it won't burn. I reckon the devil got into it."

They drove off in a swirl of yellow dust, and were soon nearing the tobacco road. Dude drove slowly through the deep white sand, blowing the horn all the way home.

Chapter XVII

THE next automobile trip Jeeter had planned after the return from Augusta was a journey over into Burke County to see Tom. From the things Jeeter had heard repeated by various men who had been in that section of the country, he knew Tom was a successful cross-tie contractor. Those men who had had business that took them close to the cross-tie camp came back to Fuller and told Jeeter that Tom was making more money than anybody else they knew. Jeeter was almost as proud of Tom as he was of Dude.

Very little else was known about Tom Lester. That was one of the reasons why Jeeter wanted to go over there. He wanted to find out how much money Tom was making, first of all, and then he wanted to ask Tom to give him a little money every week.

Bessie and Dude were not thinking of staying at home either while the new car was in running order. The trip to Augusta had not caused them to lose any of their enthusiasm for automobile travel any more than it had Jeeter. Springing the front axle, cracking the wind-shield, scarring the paint on the body, tearing holes in the upholstery, and parting with the spare tire and extra wheel were considered nothing more than the ordinary hazards of driving a car. The mashed front fender and broken rear spring had softened everybody's concern for the automobile. After their first accident, when Dude ran into the back end of the two-horse wagon near McCoy and killed the colored man, anything else that happened to the car would not matter so very much, anyway.

Jeeter the next morning casually mentioned the fact that he would like very much to ride over to Burke County to see Tom.

Dude was filling the radiator at the time, and he stopped to hear what Bessie was going to say. She said nothing, and Dude picked up the bucket again and filled the radiator to overflowing. Jeeter walked away, waiting for Bessie to make up her mind. He went towards the rear of the house as if he were going to get out of sight until she had time to make up her mind definitely whether she would go or not. Jeeter did not go so far away that he could not keep his eye on the car. Bessie was liable to do most anything when his back was turned, and he did not want them to slip off and leave him.

"Jump in and let's go in a hurry, Dude," Bessie whispered excitedly, pushing him to the car. "Hurry, before your Pa sees us."

Jeeter was standing by the well, looking out across the broom-sedge, and he did not know they were getting ready to leave him.

When he heard Dude start the motor, he dashed for the automobile. By that time, Dude had got the gears engaged, and the car shot over the yard to the tobacco road.

He had swung the front wheels sharply, making a circle around the chinaberry trees, and he bumped over the ditch without slackening speed. They were away in a few short seconds, long before Jeeter could run to the road. He stood looking after them.

"Well, I never saw the likes of that," he said. "I don't know why they want to run off and leave me. I always treated Bessie fair and square. When a man gets old, folks seem to think that he don't care about riding around, and they go off and make him stay at home."

He stood watching them until the car was out of sight. Ada and Ellie May stood on the porch looking at the disappearing car. They had come to the door the moment they heard the car start. Both of them wanted to go somewhere, too; they had not been allowed inside the new car since it was bought.

Jeeter took a seat on the porch and sat down to wait for them to return. He was glum and silent the rest of the morning. When Ada told him to come into the kitchen at dinner time and eat some cheese and crackers, Jeeter did not move from his chair. Ada went back into the house without urging him to eat. There was so little food, she was glad he was not coming. The cheese and crackers that had been brought back from Augusta provided barely enough of a meal for one or two persons; and as he would not leave the porch, there would be more for her and Ellie May. It did not matter about the grandmother, because she was going to be given the cheese rinds and cracker crumbs that were left when they had finished. Jeeter always ate so fast that there was never time for anybody else to get his full share at any meal. Jeeter ate as if it were the last time he would ever taste food again.

Ada and Ellie May sat down to eat their meal, leaving Jeeter alone.

Late that afternoon when Bessie and Dude returned home, Jeeter was still waiting for them on the porch. He got up as they approached, and followed the car to its place beside the chimney. He was as angry as ever, but he had forgotten about it momentarily. He was anxious to know if they had found Tom.

"Did you see Tom?" he asked Bessie. "What was he doing? Did he send me some money?"

Ada came out to listen. The grandmother took her accustomed position behind a chinaberry tree, looking and listening. Ellie May came closer.

"Tom ain't at all like he used to be when I knowed him better," Bessie said, shaking her head. "I don't know what's come over Tom."

"Why?" Jeeter asked. "What did he do—what did he say? Where's the money he sent me?"

"Tom didn't send no money. He don't appear to be aiming to help you none. He's a wicked man, Tom is."

"You ought to have taken me along, Bessie," Jeeter said. "I know Tom better than I do my own self. He was my special boy all along. Me and Tom got along all right together. The other children was always fighting with me, looks like now. But Tom never did. He was a fine boy when he was growing up."

Bessie listened to Jeeter talk, but she did not want to stop and argue about going off and leaving him at home. It was all over now. The trip was finished, and they were back.

"Why didn't you let me go along and see Tom?" he said.

"Tom works about a hundred ox," Dude said. He was very much impressed by the large number of oxen his brother worked at the cross-tie camp. "I didn't know there was that many ox in the whole country."

"When did Tom say he was coming over here to see me?" Jeeter asked.

"Tom said he wasn't never coming over here again," Dude said. "He told me to tell you he was going to stay where he was at."

"That sure don't sound like Tom talking," Jeeter said, shaking his head. "Maybe he has to work so hard all the time that he can't get off."

"Ain't that," Bessie said. "Tom said just what Dude told you. Tom said he ain't never coming over here again. He don't want to."

"That don't sound like Tom talking. Me and Tom used to get along first-rate concerning everything. Me and him never had no difficulties like I was always having with my other children. They used to throw rocks at me and hit me over the head with sticks, but Tom never did. Tom was always a first-rate boy when I knowed him. Ain't no reason why he ought to change now, and be just like all the rest of them."

"I told him how bad off you was, and his Ma, too," Bessie said. "I told him you didn't have no meal or meat in the house half the time, and that you can't farm and raise a crop no more, and Tom says for you and Ada to go to the county poor-farm and stay."

"You made a mistake by telling Tom I wasn't going to farm no more. I'm going to raise me a big crop of cotton this year, if I can get hold of some seed-cotton and guano. The rest of what you told him is true and accurate, however. We is hungry pretty much of the time. That ain't no lie."

"Well, that's what he said, anyway. He told me to tell you and Ada to go to the county poor-farm and stay."

"That sure don't sound like Tom talking. Tom ain't never said nothing like that to me before. I can't see why he wants me and his Ma to go and live at the poor-farm. Looks like he would send me some money instead. I'm his daddy."

"I don't reckon that makes no difference to Tom now," she said. "He's looking after his own self."

"I wish I had my young age back again. I wouldn't beg of no man, not even my own son. But Tom ain't like he used to be. Looks like he would send me and his old Ma a little bit of money."

"Tom said to tell you to go to hell, too," Dude told Jeeter.

Bessie jumped forward, clutching Dude by the neck, and shook him until it looked as if his head would twist off and fall on the ground. She continued to shake him until he succeeded in escaping from her grasp.

"You shouldn't have told Jeeter that," she shouted at Dude. "That's a wicked thing to say. I don't know nothing more sinful. The devil is trying to take you away from me so I can't make a preacher out of you."

"Christ Almighty!" he shouted at her. "You come near about killing me! I didn't say that—Tom said it. I was just telling him what Tom said. I didn't say it! You ought to keep off me. I didn't do nothing to you."

"Praise the Lord," Bessie said. "You ain't never going to make a preacher if you talk like that. I thought you said you was going to stop your cussing. Why don't you quit it?"

"I ain't going to say that no more," Dude pleaded. He remembered that the automobile belonged to her. "I wouldn't have said it that time if you hadn't hurt my neck shaking me so hard."

Jeeter walked around the automobile, trying to recover from the shock of hearing what they told him Tom had said. He could not believe that Tom had developed into a man who would tell his father to go to hell. He knew Tom must have changed a great deal since he knew him.

He stopped at the rear of the automobile and was looking at the rack where the spare tire and extra wheel had been, when he saw the great dent in the body. He stared at it until Dude and Bessie stopped talking.

"You won't be fit to preach a sermon next Sunday if you cuss like that," she was saying. "Good folks don't want to have God send them sermons by cussing preachers."

"I ain't going to say it no more. I ain't never going to cuss no more."

Jeeter motioned to them to come to the back of the car. He pointed to the dent in the body. The centre of it had been knocked in about ten or twelve inches, dividing the body into two almost equal halves.

"What done that?" he asked, still pointing.

"We was backing out from the cross-tie camp and ran smack into a big pine tree," Bessie said hesitantly. "I don't know what made it happen. Looks like everything has tried to ruin my new automobile. Ain't nothing like it was when I paid eight hundred dollars for it in Fuller the first of the week."

Dude ran his hands over the dent. The cracked paint dropped to the white sand. He tried to make the dent look smaller by rubbing it.

"It ain't hurt the running of it none, though, has it?" Jeeter said. "That's only the body smashed in. It runs good yet, don't it?"

"I reckon so," Bessie said, "but it does make a powerful lot of noise when it's running down hill—and up hill, too."

Ada came over and looked at the dent in the back of the car. She rubbed her hands over it until more of the cracked black paint dropped off and fell on the white sand at her feet.

"What does Tom look like now?" Ada asked Bessie. "I reckon he don't look like he used to, no more."

"He looks a lot like Jeeter," she said. "There ain't much resemblance in him and you."

"Humph!" Ada said. "There was a time when I'd declared it was the other way around."

Jeeter looked at Ada, and then at Bessie. He could not understand what Ada was talking about.

"What did Tom say when you told him you and Dude was married now?" Jeeter said.

"He didn't say nothing much. Looked to me like he didn't care one way or the other."

"Tom said she used to be a two-bit slut when he knowed her a long time back," Dude said. "He told it right to her, but she didn't say nothing. I reckon he knowed what he was talking about, because she didn't say it was a lie."

Sister Bessie grabbed Dude around the neck again and shook him vigorously. Jeeter and Ada stood beside them watching. Ellie May had heard everything, but she had not come any closer.

Dude jerked away from Bessie more quickly than he had the first time. He was learning how to get away from her more easily.

"God damn you!" he shouted, striking at her face with his fist. "Why in hell don't you keep off me!"

"Now, Dude," Bessie pleaded tenderly, "you promised me you was not going to cuss no more. Good folks don't want to go and hear a Sunday sermon by a cussing preacher."

Dude shrugged his shoulders and walked away. He was getting tired of the way Bessie jumped on him and twisted his neck every time he said something she did not want to hear.

"When's Dude going to start being a preacher?" Jeeter asked her.

"He's going to preach a little short sermon next Sunday at the schoolhouse. I'm already telling him what to say when he preaches."

"Looks like to me he ought to know that himself," Jeeter said. "You don't have to tell him everything to do, do you? Don't he know nothing?"

"Well, he ain't familiar with preaching like I is. I tell him what to say and he learns to say it himself. It won't take him long to catch on and then I won't have to tell him nothing. My former husband told me what to say one Saturday night and I went to the schoolhouse the next afternoon and preached for almost three hours without stopping. It ain't hard to do after you catch on. Dude's already told me what he was going to preach about Sunday. He knows now what he's going to say when the time comes."

"What's he going to preach about Sunday?"

"About men wearing black shirts."

"Black shirts? What for?"

"You ask him. He knows."

"Black shirts ain't nothing to preach about, to my way of thinking. I ain't never heard of that before."

"You come to preaching at the schoolhouse Sunday afternoon and find out."

"Is he going to preach *for* black shirts, or *against* black shirts?"

"Against them."

"What for, Sister Bessie?"

"It ain't my place to tell you about Dude's preaching. That's for you to go to the schoolhouse and hear. Preachers don't want their secrets spread all over the country beforehand. Wouldn't nobody take the trouble to go and listen, if they did that."

"Maybe I don't know much about preaching, but I ain't never heard of nobody preaching about men wearing black shirts—against black shirts, at that. I ain't never seen a man wearing a black shirt, noway."

"Preachers has got to preach *against* something. It wouldn't do them no good to preach *for* everything. They got to be *against* something every time."

"I never looked at it that way before," Jeeter said, "but there might be a lot in what you say. Though, take for instance, God and heaven— you wouldn't preach *against* them, would you, Sister Bessie?"

"Good preachers don't preach about God and heaven, and things like that. They always preach *against* something, like hell and the devil. Them is things to be against. It wouldn't do a preacher no good to preach for God. He's got to preach against the devil and all wicked and sinful things. That's what the people like to hear about. They want to hear about the bad things."

"You sure is a convincing woman, Sister Bessie," he said. "God must be pretty proud of having a woman preacher like you. I don't know what He's going to think about Dude, though. Specially when he starts preaching *against* men wearing black shirts. I ain't never seen a man wearing a black shirt, noway, and I don't believe there's such things in the country."

Jeeter bent over and rubbed his hands on the dent in the body of the car. He scraped the surface paint with his fingernails until most of it had peeled off and fallen on the ground.

"Stop doing that to my automobile," Bessie said. "Ain't you got no sense at all? You and Ada has near about got all the paint off of it already doing that."

"You wouldn't talk to me like that, would you, Bessie?" he asked. "I ain't hurting the automobile no more than it's already done."

"Well, you keep your hands off it, anyhow."

Jeeter slouched away and leaned against the corner of the house. He looked sharply at Bessie, saying nothing.

"I near about ruined my new automobile letting you fool with it," she said. "I ought to had better sense than to let you get near it. Hauling that load of blackjack to Augusta tore holes all in the back seat."

"You ain't going to take me riding in it none?" he asked, standing erectly by the house.

"No, sir! You ain't going to ride in my new automobile no more. That's why I wouldn't let you go with me to see Tom this morning. I don't want you around it no more, neither."

"By God and by Jesus, if that's what you're aiming to do, you can get off my land," he said, shifting his weight from one foot to the other and pulling at the rotten weatherboards behind him. "I ain't none too pleased to have you around, noway."

Bessie did not know what to say. She looked around for Dude, but he was not in sight.

"You're going to make me leave?"

"I done started doing it. I already told you to get off my land."

"It don't belong to you. It's Captain John's land. He owns it."

"It's the old Lester place. Captain John ain't got no more right to it than nobody else. Them rich people up there in Augusta come down here and take everything a man's got, but they can't take the land away from me. By God and by Jesus, my daddy owned it, and his daddy before him, and I ain't going to get off it while I'm alive. But durned if I can't run you off it—now git!"

"Me and Dude ain't got no place to go. The roof is all rotted away at my house."

"That don't make no difference to me. I don't care where you go, but you're going to get off this land. If you ain't going to let me ride in the new automobile when I wants to, you can't stay here. I'm tired looking at them two dirty holes in your durn nose, anyhow."

"You old son of a bitch, you!" she cried, running to him and scratching his face with her fingernails. "You're nothing but an old dirty son of a bitch, you is! I hope God sends you straight to hell and never lets you out again!"

Ada came running around the corner of the house when she heard the cries of Bessie. The sight of Jeeter's bleeding face threw her into a fit of uncontrollable anger. She hit at Bessie with her fists and kicked her with her feet.

Dude came running, too. He stood looking at the fight while all three of them were striking and scratching one another. Ellie May grinned from behind a chinaberry tree.

Bessie retreated. Both Ada and Jeeter were fighting her, and she was unable to strike back. She ran to the automobile and jumped in. Jeeter picked up a stick and hit her with it several times before Ada took it from him and began poking Bessie in the ribs with it. The sharp point hurt her much more than Jeeter's blows on her head and shoulders had, and she screamed with pain.

Both Ellie May and the grandmother came out from behind the chinaberry trees and watched all that was taking place.

Dude jumped in and backed the car towards the road as fast as he could. His choice lay with Sister Bessie. He liked to drive an automobile too much to let hers get away from him on account of a little scrap like that.

Mother Lester, who had watched the fight from the start, ran across the yard to get behind another chinaberry tree where she could see from a better location everything that was happening. She had no more than reached a point midway between two chinaberry trees when the rear end of the automobile struck her, knocking her down and backing over her.

Bessie leaned out of the car, shaking her fists and making faces at Ada and Jeeter. They followed the automobile to the tobacco road.

"You old sons of bitches, you!" she yelled at them at the top of her high-pitched voice. "All of you Lesters is dirty sons of bitches!"

Ada picked up a big rock and hurled it at the car as hard as she could. By that time, Bessie and Dude were several hundred feet away, and Ada's big stone fell short of the mark by three-fourths of the distance. She should have known she did not have the strength to throw rocks as large as that. It was almost as big as a stove-lid.

Chapter XVIII

AFTER the dust had settled on the road, Ada and Jeeter came back into the yard. Mother Lester still lay there, her face mashed on the hard white sand. From the corner of the house, Ellie May looked at what had happened.

"Is she dead yet?" Ada asked, looking at Jeeter. "She don't make no sound and she don't move. I don't reckon she could stay alive with her face all mashed like that."

Jeeter did not answer her. He was too busy thinking of his hatred for Bessie to bother with anything else. He took another look at the grandmother and walked across the yard and around to the back of the house. Ada went to the porch and stood there looking back at Mother Lester several minutes, then she walked inside and shut the door.

Mother Lester tried to turn over so she could get up and go into the house. She could not move either her arms or her legs without unbearable pain, and her head felt as if it had been cracked open. The automobile had struck her with such force that she did not know what had hit her. Both of the left wheels had rolled over her, one of them across her back and the other on her head. She had not known what had happened. More than anything else she wanted to get up and lie down on her bed. She struggled with a final effort to raise her head and shoulders from the hard sand, and she managed to turn over. After that she lay motionless.

When he had finished getting a fresh drink of water at the well, Jeeter walked out into the broom-sedge, kicking the ground with the toes of his shoes to find out how dry it was. He believed the soil held just the right amount of moisture needed for plowing, but he wanted to be sure of it, because he was confident that he could borrow a mule somewhere and begin plowing and planting early the following week.

While he walked around in the waist-high broom-sedge, Lov was racing down the tobacco road, hatless and out of breath. Lov began shouting to Jeeter as soon as he reached the front yard, and Jeeter ran out of the sedge to meet him and find out what the trouble was.

Lov was dressed in his dirty black overalls, the pair he wore at the chute when he shovelled coal into the scoops. His hat had blown off when he started running to Jeeter's, and he had not waited to go back and pick it up. Lov's fiery red hair stood almost straight up; ordinarily, it was falling down over his forehead and getting into his eyes.

He saw the old grandmother lying in the yard and he slowed down to look at her, but he did not linger there. He ran until he was face to face with Jeeter.

"What you doing down here at this time of day, Lov?" Jeeter said. "Why ain't you working at the chute?"

Lov did not speak for several minutes. He had to wait until he could regain his breath. He sat on the ground, and Jeeter squatted on his heels beside him.

They were not far from the well. Ellie May was standing beside the stand drinking from the bucket when Lov reached Jeeter, but she did not run away immediately. She waited until Lov sat down, so she could hear what he had to tell Jeeter.

"What's the matter, Lov?" Jeeter asked. "What happened down at the chute that made you run here so fast?"

"Pearl—Pearl—she run off!"

"Run where to?" Jeeter asked calmly, disappointed because it was not something of more interest to him. "Where'd Pearl run to, Lov?"

"She's gone to Augusta!"

"Gone to Augusta!" Jeeter said, straightening up. "I thought maybe she just went off in the woods somewhere for a spell, like she was always doing. Reckon what she run off to Augusta for?"

"I don't know," Lov said, "but I reckon she just up and went. I don't know what else she done it for. I didn't hurt her none this morning. I didn't do nothing to her, except throw her down on the bed. She got loose from me, and I ain't seen her since."

"What was you trying to do to her?"

"Nothing. I was only going to tie her up with some plow-lines to see if I could do it. I figured she'd have to stay in the bed if I tied her there. I was going to turn her loose pretty soon."

"How you know she's run off to Augusta? Maybe she just went off in the woods somewhere again. Did she tell you she was going to run off to Augusta?"

"She didn't say nothing to me."

"Then what makes you think she went up there, instead of going off in the woods somewhere?"

"I didn't even know she was running off up there till Jones Peabody came by the chute and told me he met her up near Augusta when he was coming back to Fuller with an empty lumber truck. He said he stopped and asked her where she was going to, and if I knowed she'd left home, but she wouldn't talk to him. He said she looked like she was near about scared to death. He came and told me about it the first thing. He said he knowed I wouldn't know about it."

"Pearl, she was just like Lizzie Belle. Lizzie Belle up and went to Augusta just like that!" He snapped his fingers, jerking his head to one side. "I didn't know nothing about it till I seen her up there on the street once. I asked her what made her run off without saying nothing to her Ma and me about it, but she wouldn't talk none. I thought all the time that she was staying out in the woods somewhere for a while, but I knowed it was Lizzie Belle the first time I looked at her. She had on some stylish clothes and a hat, but they didn't fool me. I knowed it was Lizzie Belle, even if she wouldn't talk to me. She was working in a cotton mill across the river from there, all that time. I knowed then why she up and went there, because Ada told me. Ada said Lizzie Belle wanted to have some stylish clothes and a hat to wear, and she run off up there to work in a cotton mill so she could get them kind of things herself."

"Pearl never said nothing to me about wanting a stylish dress and a hat," Lov said. "I make a dollar a day at the chute, and I could have bought her a dress and a hat if she had told me she wanted them. But Pearl never said nothing to me—she never said nothing to nobody. She slept on that durn pallet on the floor and wouldn't answer my requests when I told her to do something I wanted done."

"I reckon about the best thing you can do, Lov, is to let her be. She wasn't satisfied living down here on the tobacco road, and if you was to bring her back, she'd run off again twice as quick. She's just like Lizzie Belle and Clara and the other gals. I can't recall all of their names right now, but it was every durn one of them, anyhow. They all wanted some stylish clothes. They wasn't satisfied with the pretty calico and gingham their Ma sewed for them. Well, Ada ain't satisfied neither, but she can't do nothing about it. That's how the gals took after their Ma. I sort of broke Ada of wanting to go off and do that. She don't talk no more about buying of stylish clothes and a hat, excepting a dress to die in and be buried in. She talks about getting a stylish dress to die in, but she ain't going to get it, and she knows she ain't. She'll die and be buried in the ground wearing that yellow calico she's got on now. I broke Ada of wanting to run off, but them gals was more than I could take care of. There was too durn many of them for only one man to break. They just up and went."

"Maybe she'll come back," Lov said. "Reckon she'll come back, Jeeter?"

"Who—Pearl? Well, I wouldn't put no trust in it. Lizzie Belle went off and she ain't never come back. None of the other gals came back, neither."

"I sort of hate to lose her, for some reason or another. She was a pretty little girl—all them long yellow curls hanging down her back always made me hate the time when she'd grow up and be old. I used to sit on the porch and watch her through the window when she was combing and brushing her hair in the bedroom——"

"That sure ain't no lie," Jeeter said. "Pearl had the prettiest yellow hair of any gal I ever saw. It was a plumb shame that she was so bad about wanting to stay by herself all the time, because I used to want to have her around me. I wish Ada had been that pretty. Even when Ada was a young gal, she was that durn ugly it was a sin. I ain't never seen an uglier woman in the whole country, unless it's that durn woman preacher Bessie. Them two dirty holes in her face don't do a man no good to look at."

"Pearl always took a long time to fix herself up, woman-like. I used to want to tell her there wasn't no other girl in the whole country who was nowhere as pretty as she was, but she wouldn't listen to me. And I lived with her so long I sort of got used to seeing her every day, and I don't know what I'm going to do now when she's gone to Augusta to stay. I'll miss them long yellow curls hanging down her back, and that pretty face of hers, too. Aside from that, I don't know of a prettier sight to see than to look in her pale blue eyes early in the morning before the sun got up so high it threw too much light in them. Early in the morning they was the prettiest things a man could ever want to look at. But they was pretty any time of the day, and sometimes I used to sit and shake all over, for wanting to squeeze her so hard. I don't reckon I'll ever forget how pretty her eyes was early in the morning just when the sun was rising."

"Maybe you would like to take Ellie May down to your house, Lov?" Jeeter suggested. "She ain't got a man, and it looks like she ain't never going to get one, unless you take a fancy to her. You and Ellie May was hugging and rubbing of the other the first of the week, around at the front of the house. Maybe you would want to do that some more?"

"Reckon if I was to go up to Augusta and find her, she would let

me bring her back home to stay?" Lov said. "Reckon she would,
Jeeter?"

"Who—Pearl?" Jeeter said. "No, I wouldn't recommend that. You'll
lose your time down there at the chute while you was looking for her,
and it's like I said at the start. Pearl is just like Lizzie Belle and Clara
and all the rest of the gals. They was plumb crazy for getting stylish
clothes. None of them gals of mine liked to wear the calico and gingham Ada sewed."

"But Pearl—she might get hurt up there in Augusta——"

"Lizzie Belle and Clara took care of themselves all right, didn't they?
They didn't get hurt none. Now, as I was saying about Ellie May. You
can take her to your house, Lov. Ellie May would be crazy about going
down there to stay all the time. She wouldn't be never getting down
on no durn pallet on the floor, neither."

"Seeing them long yellow curls hanging down her back used to
make me cry sometimes. I'd look at her pretty hair and eyes so long
that I thought I'd go crazy if I didn't touch her and see deep down
into her eyes. But she wouldn't never let me come close to her, and
that's what made the tears fall out of my eyes, I reckon. I been the
lonesomest man in the whole country, for the longest time. Pearl was
so pretty it was a sin for her to do like she done."

"Ellie May's got to get a man somewhere. She can't stay here all
the time. When me and Ada's dead and gone, there won't be nobody to
watch after her. If she stayed here at the house by herself the niggers
would haul off and come here by the dozens. The niggers would get
her in no time, if she was here by herself."

"The last pretty I got for Pearl was some green beads on a long
string. I gave them to her and she put them around her neck, and I
swear to God if it didn't make her the prettiest little girl I ever saw or
heard about in the whole country."

"If you want to take Ellie May with you now, I'll tell her to wash
herself up and get ready to go," Jeeter said.

"I might take Ellie May for a while, and I might not. I don't know
what I'm going to do about Pearl, yet. I wish I could get her to come
back."

"Ellie May's got——"

"Ellie May's got that ugly-looking face," Lov said. "I don't know
as how I would want to look at it all the time,"

"You would sort of get used to it, slow-like," Jeeter said. "It don't
bother me none now. I got used to looking at the slit and I don't notice
it no more."

Lov stood up and leaned against the well. He was silent for a long
time, looking out over the tall brown broom-sedge. Jeeter watched him,
and whittled on a little stick with his pocketknife.

Ellie May was behind another chinaberry tree then. She had moved from one to another while Lov and Jeeter were busy talking. She had at last come closer so she could hear what was being said.

Presently Lov turned around and looked at Ellie May. She jerked her head behind the chinaberry tree before he could see her face.

"I've got to be going back to the chute," he said. "That afternoon freight will be coming along pretty soon now, and it always empties all the scoops. I got to get back and fill them up before the passenger comes. They raise hell about the scoops being empty, because that makes the train have to wait until I can load them up."

He and Jeeter went around the house to the front yard. Neither of them had thought of Mother Lester again until they saw her lying on the sand. She was procumbent, and her face was mashed on the ground, but she had moved several feet closer to the house.

"What's wrong with her?" Lov said.

"Dude and Bessie backed the new automobile over her when they left. They was trying to get away before I could hit Bessie again, and they ran over her. I got it in good and heavy for that woman preacher now. I ain't letting her set foot on my land another time. She treated me bad about riding in the new automobile. She wouldn't let me go riding with her at all."

Lov walked over to where the old grandmother lay on the hard white sand. She had stopped bleeding, and she made no sound.

"Looks like she's dead," he said. "Is she dead, Jeeter?"

Jeeter looked down and moved one of her arms with his foot.

"She ain't stiff yet, but I don't reckon she'll live. You help me tote her out in the field and I'll dig a ditch to put her in."

They carried the body by the hands and feet, and put it down in the broom-sedge. Jeeter went to get a shovel from behind the corn-crib.

"You think that over what I said about Ellie May," Jeeter said. "I'll send her down to your house in time to cook your supper to-night. Ellie May won't treat you bad like Pearl done. Ellie May won't sleep on no durn pallet on the floor."

Lov started back down the tobacco road towards the coal chute. He shuffled his feet along the road, filling his shoes with sand. He did not look back.

Jeeter went out into the field with the shovel and began digging a grave to put his mother in. He dug in the earth for ten or fifteen minutes, and then called Ellie May. She had been standing in the yard behind a chinaberry tree waiting for Jeeter to tell her to go to Lov's.

"You wash yourself and go down to Lov's house and fix up for him," he told her, leaning wearily on the shovel handle. "He'll be coming home for supper to-night, and you cook him what he tells you."

Ellie May dashed into the house before Jeeter could finish giving her his instructions. She could not wait any longer.

He dug some more earth out of the ground, making the ditch a little longer.

Ellie May came out of the house in less than five minutes, running towards the road. Jeeter threw down the shovel and ran after her, calling her.

"You come back here in the morning after Lov goes to work and bring some victuals with you, do you hear?" he shouted. "Lov makes a dollar a day at the chute, and he's got rations for a lot of victuals. Me and your Ma ain't got nothing up here. We get pretty hungry sometimes. You remember that."

Ellie May had run all the way across the yard and was racing down the middle of the tobacco road as fast as she could. Before Jeeter could say anything else to her, she was a hundred yards away. He had wanted to tell her to bring him a pair of Lov's overalls too, the next morning when she brought the cooked food. She looked as if she was in such a great hurry to reach Lov's house that he let her go. She could make another trip the next day with the overalls.

Chapter XIX

THE time for spring plowing was over. Throughout the last two weeks of February the weather had been dry and the ground crumbly; there had been no finer season for plowing and planting in six or seven years. Usually at that time rains came every few days and kept the earth continually wet and soggy; but this year the season had begun in the middle of February with clearing skies, and a gentle breeze had been drying the moisture in the ground ever since the winter rains had stopped.

Farmers around Fuller who were undertaking to raise a crop of cotton this year had finished their plowing by the end of the month. With such an early start, there seemed to be no reason why, with plenty of hot weather during the growing season, the land should not yield a bale of cotton to the acre that fall. All farmers would put in as much guano as they could buy, and there was no limit to the number of pounds of cotton an acre would yield if fertilizer could be bought and used with a free hand. A bale to the acre was the goal of every cotton farmer around Fuller; but the boll-weevil and hard summer rains generally cut the crop in half. And on the other hand, if it was a good year for the raising of cotton, the price would probably drop lower than it had before. Not many men felt like working all year for six- or seven-cent cotton in the fall.

Jeeter had lived through the season for burning broom-sedge and pine woods, and through the time for spring plowing, without having done either. It was still not too late to begin, but Jeeter did not have a mule, and he did not have the credit to purchase seed-cotton and guano at the stores. Up until this year, he had lived in the hope that something would happen at the last moment to provide a mule and credit, but now it seemed to him that there was no use hoping for anything any more. He could still look forward to the following year when he could perhaps raise a crop of cotton, but it was an anticipation not so keen as it once had been. He had felt himself sink lower and lower, his condition fall further and further, year after year, until now his trust in God and the land was at the stage where further disappointment might easily cause him to lose his mind and reason. He still could not understand why he had nothing, and would never have anything, and there was no one who knew and who could tell him. It was the unsolved mystery of his life.

But, even if he could not raise a crop that year, he could at least make all preparations for one. He could burn over the broom-sedge and the groves of blackjack and the fields of young pine seedlings. He could have the land ready for plowing in case something happened that would let him plant a crop of cotton. He would have the land ready, in case——

It was late afternoon on the first of March. He walked across the old cotton field through the waist-high broom-sedge towards the blackjack grove at the rear of the house; he kicked at the crumbly earth lying exposed between the tufts of sedge, thinking there was still time in which to arrange for credit at the stores in Fuller. He knew the time for burning and plowing had ended the day before, but there still lingered in the warm March air something of the new season. The smell of freshly turned earth and the odor of pine and sedge-smoke hovered over the land even after burning and plowing was done. He breathed deeply of it, filling his body with the invigorating aroma.

"Maybe God will send some way to allow the growing of a crop," he said. "He puts the land here, and the sun and rain—He ought to furnish the seed and the guano, somehow or other."

Jeeter firmly believed that something would happen so he would be able to keep his body and soul alive. He still had hope left.

The late afternoon sun was still warm, and the air was balmy. There had been no cold nights for almost a week. People could sit on their front porches in the evening now without feeling the chill night air of February.

The breeze was blowing from the east. The white smoke of the broom-sedge fire coiled upward and was carried away towards the west, away from Jeeter's view of the house and tobacco road. He stood watching it burn slowly away from him, and at the fire eating along the ground under the brown broom-sedge. There were several hundred acres of the land to burn; the fields that had not been cultivated, some of them for ten or fifteen years, were matted with the dry grass. Beyond the fields lay the woods of yellow pine and blackjack. The fire would probably blaze and smoulder three or four days before it would burn itself out and die along the shores of the creeks farther away.

"If Tom and some of the older boys was here, maybe they could help get some seed-cotton and guano somehow," he said. "I know where I might could borrow a mule, if I had the seed-cotton and guano to plant. But a mule ain't no good without the rest of the things. Wouldn't nothing grow in the new rows except broom-sedge and blackjack sprouts."

He walked back to the house, to sit on the back steps a while before bed-time and watch the long line of yellow fire in the sedge.

It was long after dark before he got up and went into the house. From the rear bedroom window where he stood taking off his heavy shoes, Jeeter watched with fascination the distant fire that had melted into a vivid red with the fall of darkness. Some of the fire had gone far over the hills, and all that could be seen of it was the dull orange glow in the sky above it. Other sections of it had circled around the fields like cornered snakes, and burned on both sides of the house. In the centre, where he had stood that afternoon when he struck the match, there was a deep dark hole in the earth. The ground would remain black until it rained again.

He lay awake a long time after Ada was asleep. It was quiet in the house, now that there was no one else there to keep them company.

Jeeter tossed and turned, smelling the aroma of pine and broom-sedge smoke in the night air. With it came the strong odor of freshly turned earth somewhere a long way off. He looked straight up at the black ceiling, solemnly swearing to get up the next morning and borrow a mule. He was going to plow a patch to raise some cotton on, if he never did anything else as long as he lived.

He went to sleep then, his mind filled with thoughts of the land and its sweet odors, and with a new determination to stir the earth and cultivate plants of cotton.

The fire burned lustily through the night. It went farther and farther towards the west where the young pines grew, and it burned through the groves of blackjack, leaving the scrub-oak trees standing blackened and charred. They would not die, but the young pines would.

The dawn was beginning to break in the east, and the wind shifted to the north, blowing a final night breeze before daylight. The fire in the broom-sedge on each side of the house burst into renewed vigor in the path of the wind, and it burned back towards the centre where it had started. When it reached the point where the sedge ended at the rim of blackened ground, it would die out. In the meantime there were the fields on each side of the house to burn. After that, there would remain to be burned only the land far back in the woods and on the hills where the blue smoke and red flames climbed above the tree-tops.

Beside the house, the broom-sedge fire leapt higher in the early morning breeze. It came closer and closer to the house, and only a thin strip of sandy yard separated it from the building. If a brisk wind caught the fire at the moment when it was burning hardest, it would whirl the embers of grass against the house, under it, and onto the roof.

The moment when the sun came up, the wind caught the fire and sent it swirling through the dry grass. Torn by the wind, stems of flaming grass were showered on the house, some dying as they burned out, others leaving a glowing spark imbedded in the dry tinder-like shingles that had covered the house for fifty years or more. There were cracks in the roof where the more rotten shingles had been ripped and blown away by the strong autumnal winds, and in these the embers spread quickly.

Jeeter and Ada usually got up with the sun, and it was that time now. Neither of them came to the windows now, however, nor did either of them open the door. They were both asleep.

The fiery, red flaming roof was a whirling mass of showering embers in a short time. The dry tinder-like shingles, rotted by the autumn and winter rains and scorched by the searing spring and summer sun for two generations, blazed like coals in a forge. The whole roof was in flames in a few seconds, and after that it was only a matter of minutes until the rafters, dry and dripping with pine pitch, fell down upon the floor of the house and upon the beds. Half an hour after the roof had first caught, the house was in black smoking ashes. Ada and Jeeter had not known what had happened.

Several near-by farmers had seen the smoke and flames as they were getting up at sun-rise. Most of them hurried along the tobacco road and across the fields to the Lester place with the intention of helping to save some of the furniture. They had not realized how fast the dry pitch-dripped house had burned to the ground, until they reached it.

There was a crowd of twenty or thirty men standing around the ashes when Lov and Ellie May reached the place, and when Bessie and

Dude got there. There was nothing anybody could do then. There was nothing that could be saved. Jeeter's old automobile was a pile of rust-colored junk.

Some of the men took long blackjack poles and poked around in the mass of ashes, hoping to find the bodies and to take them out before they were burned any more, but the heat of the ashes drove every one back for a while.

"The Lord had a curse on this house," Bessie said. "He didn't want it to stand no longer. Praise the Lord!"

Nobody paid any attention to Bessie.

"Jeeter is better off now than he was," one of the farmers said. "He was near about starved to death half the time and he couldn't raise no crops. It looks to me like his children ought to have stayed at home and helped him run a farm."

Lov's first thought on seeing the smoking ashes was to remember Jeeter's prayerful plea about the care he wanted taken of his body when he died. Now it did not matter, because there was very little of it left.

After the coals had cooled, the men went into the ashes and carried out the two bodies and laid them down under the chinaberry tree beside the road. The tree's green limbs had been scorched, but it was too far away from the house to burn. The other chinaberry trees in the yard had been closer to the house, and they had burned almost as quickly as the house.

Preparations were begun at once to dig the grave. The men found two or three charred and broken-handled shovels and a pick behind the scorched and blistered corn-crib, and asked Lov where he wanted the grave dug. They decided to dig it in the blackjack grove, because if some one did decide to farm the land that year or the following ones, there would be no danger of the grave being plowed up so soon.

The men dug the grave, and carried the remains, stretched out on blackjack poles, to the grove. They were lowered into the ground. Some of the men asked Bessie to say a short prayer before the bodies were covered, but she refused to say anything for Jeeter or Ada. There was nothing, then, left to do but to throw the earth in and smooth the mounds with the back of the shovels.

Most of the farmers hurried back to their homes for breakfast. There was nothing else to be done.

Lov sat down by the lone chinaberry tree and looked at the blackened mass of ashes. Bessie and Dude stayed a while, too; they had to wait on Lov. Ellie May hovered in the distance, looking on, but never coming close enough to be noticed by Lov or the others.

"I reckon old Jeeter had the best thing happen to him," Lov said. "He was killing himself worrying all the time about the raising of a crop. That was all he wanted in this life—growing cotton was better than anything else to him. There ain't many more like him left, I reckon. Most of the people now don't care about nothing except getting a job in a cotton mill somewhere. But can't all of them work in the mills, and they'll have to stay here like Jeeter until they get taken away too. There ain't no sense in them raising crops. They can't make no money at it, not even a living. If they do make some cotton, somebody comes along and cheats them out of it. It looks like the Lord don't care about crops being raised no more like He used to, or He would be more helpful to the poor. He could make the rich people lend out their money, and stop holding it up. I can't figure out how they got hold of all the money in the country, anyhow. Looks like it ought to be spread out among everybody."

Dude poked around in the ashes looking for whatever he could find. There had been nothing of value in the house; but he liked to dig in the ashes and toss out the twisted tin kitchen dishes and china door-knobs. The charred and crusted iron casters of the wooden beds were there, and nails and screws; almost everything else in the house had been made of wood or cloth.

"Old Jeeter had one wish fulfilled," Lov said. "It wasn't exactly fulfilled, but it was taken care of, anyhow. He used to tell me he didn't want me to lock him up in the corn-crib and go off and leave him when he died. That's what happened to his daddy. When his daddy died, Jeeter and the men who were sitting up with the body locked it in the corn-crib at night while they rode to Fuller for tobacco and drinks. They put it in the crib so nothing would happen to it while they was gone. When they went to bury it the next day, a big crib rat jumped out of the box. It had gnawed into the coffin while it was shut up in the crib, and it had eaten all one side of the older Lester's face and neck. That was what Jeeter was afraid would happen to him, and he used to make me promise two or three times a day that I wouldn't lock him up in the crib when he died. There wasn't no use of him worrying so, because there ain't been no rats in the crib in many a year, except when they come back sometimes to look around and see if any corn has been put in it."

"I don't think the Lord took to Jeeter none too much," Sister Bessie said. "Jeeter must have been a powerful sinful man in his prime, because the Lord wasn't good to him like He is to me. The Lord knows us all like that. He knows when we're good and when the devil is in us."

"Well, it don't make no special difference now," Lov said. "Jeeter's dead and gone, and he won't be bothered no more by wanting to grow things in the ground. That's what he liked to do more than anything else, but somehow he never got a chance to do it much. Jeeter, he would lots rather grow a big crop of cotton than go to heaven."

"If he'd gone to Augusta and worked in the cotton mills like the rest of them done, he would have been all right. There ain't no money for a man like him farming all the time when he can't get no credit."

"I reckon Jeeter done right," Lov contended. "He was a man who liked to grow things in the ground. The mills ain't no place for a human who's got that in his bones. The mills is sort of like automobiles —they're all right to fool around in and have a good time in, but they don't offer no love like the ground does. The ground sort of looks out after the people who keeps their feet on it. When people stand on planks in buildings all the time, and walk around on hard streets, the ground sort of loses interest in the human."

Dude came out of the ashes, shaking the black flakes off his shoes and overalls. He sat on the ground and looked on silently. Ellie May still hovered in the distance, as if she were afraid to come any closer to the ashes of the house.

"Ada didn't get no stylish dress to die in, though," Lov said. "I sort of hoped she would, too. It's a pity about that, but it don't make no difference now. Her old dress was burned off of her in the fire, and she was buried just like God made her. Maybe that was better than having a stylish dress, after all. If she had died of age, or anything like that, she wouldn't have had no stylish dress, noway. She would have had to be buried in the old one she had. It sort of worked out just right for her. She didn't know she didn't have a stylish dress to die in. It didn't make no difference if it was the right length or not."

No one mentioned the old grandmother, but Lov was glad she had been killed the day before. He did not feel that it would have been right to bury her body in the same grave with Jeeter and Ada, or even in the same field. They had hated her so much that it would have been taking advantage of her death to put Mother Lester's body next to theirs. She had lived so long in the house with Jeeter and Ada that she had been considered nothing more than a door-jamb or a length of weather-boarding. But it could be said about her, Lov thought to himself, that she never complained of the treatment she received. Even when she was hungry, or sick, no word had passed her lips. She had lived so long with Ada and Jeeter that she had believed it was useless to try to protest. If she had said anything, Jeeter or Ada would have knocked her down.

Dude was the first to get into the automobile, and Sister Bessie soon followed. They waited for Lov to get in so they could go back to their house and cook breakfast. After he was in, Ellie May came and sat down beside him on the back seat. Dude steered the car out of the yard, and turned down the tobacco road towards the blackened coal chute and the muddy red river.

Almost immediately, Dude began blowing the horn.

When they were going over the first sand hill, Lov looked back through the rear curtain and saw the Lester place. The tall brick chimney standing blackened and tomb-like in the early morning sunlight was the only thing that he could see.

Dude took his hand off the horn-button and looked back at Lov.

"I reckon I'll get me a mule somewhere and some seed-cotton and guano, and grow me a crop of cotton this year," Dude said. "It feels to me like it's going to be a good year for cotton. Maybe I could grow me a bale to the acre, like Pa was always talking about doing."

GOD'S LITTLE ACRE

For Helen

Chapter I

SEVERAL yards of undermined sand and clay broke loose up near the top, and the land slid down to the floor of the crater. Ty Ty Walden was so angry about the landslide that he just stood there with the pick in his hands, knee-deep in the reddish earth, and swore about everything he could think of. The boys were ready to stop work, anyway. It was mid-afternoon then, and they had been down in the ground digging in the big hole since daylight that morning.

"Why in the pluperfect hell did that dirt have to break loose up there just when we were getting deep?" Ty Ty said, glaring at Shaw and Buck. "Now ain't that something!"

Before either of them could answer their father, Ty Ty clutched the pick handle in both hands and hurled it with all his might against the side of the crater. He let it go with that. There were times, though, when he was so provoked that he would pick up a stick and flail the ground with it until he dropped exhausted.

Buck gripped his knees with his hands and pulled his legs out of the loose earth and sat down to shake the sand and gravel out of his shoes. He was thinking of that great mass of earth they would have to shovel and carry out of the hole before they could begin digging again.

"It's time we were starting a new hole," Shaw told his father. "We've been digging in this one for about two months already, and we ain't struck nothing yet but a lot of hard work. I'm tired of this hole. We can't get anything out of this one, no matter how much deeper we dig."

Ty Ty sat down and fanned his hot face with his hat. There was no fresh air down in the big hole, and the crater was hotter than a pail of barbecue hash.

"The trouble with you boys is that you ain't found the patience that I've got," he said, fanning and wiping his face. "I've been digging in this land close on to fifteen years now, and I'm aiming to dig here fifteen more, if need be. But I've got a feeling the need won't be. I figure we're going to strike pay pretty soon. I feel it in my bones these hot days. We can't stop and start all over again every time a little loose dirt breaks away from the rim up there and comes sliding down. Wouldn't be no sense in starting a new hole all over again every time that happened. We've just got to keep plugging away like nothing ever happened. That's the only way to do. You boys are too impatient about little things."

"Impatient, hell!" Buck said, spitting into the red clay. "We don't need patience—what we need is a diviner. Looks like you would know better than to dig without one."

"There you go again talking like the darkies, son," Ty Ty said resignedly. "I wish you had the sense not to listen to what the darkies say. That ain't a thing in the world but superstition. Now, take me, here. I'm scientific. To listen to the darkies talk, a man would believe they have got more sense than I have. All they know about it is that talk about diviners and conjurs."

Shaw picked up his shovel and started climbing to the top of the ground.

"Well, I'm quitting for the day, anyway," Shaw said. "I want to go to town tonight."

"Always quitting work in the middle of the day to get ready to go to town," Ty Ty said. "You'll never get rich doing that. All you do when you go to town is to hang around the pool room a while and then go chasing after some woman. If you'd stay at home, we'd get somewhere."

Shaw got down on his hands and knees when he got halfway to the top and crawled the rest of the way to keep from slipping backward. They watched him go up the side of the crater and stand on the ground above.

"Who does he go to see in town so often?" Ty Ty asked his other son. "He'll be getting into trouble if he don't watch out. Shaw ain't used to women yet. They can do him dirty and he won't know about it till it's too late to stop the clock."

Buck sat on the other side of the hole from his father and crumbled the dry clay in his fingers.

"I don't know," he said. "Nobody in particular. He's got a new girl every time I hear about it. He likes anything with skirts on."

"Why in the pluperfect hell can't he let the women alone? There ain't no sense in a man going rutting every day in the whole year. The women will wear Shaw to a frazzle. When I was a young fellow, I never carried on like he does about the women. What's got into him, anyway? He ought to be satisfied just to sit at home and look at the girls in the house."

"Don't ask me. I don't care what he does in town."

Shaw had been out of sight for several minutes, but suddenly he appeared up above and called down to Ty Ty. They saw Shaw with surprise.

"What's the matter, son?" Ty Ty asked.

"There's a man coming across the field, Pa," he said. "He's coming from the house."

Ty Ty stood up, looking around in all directions as though he could see over the top of the hole twenty feet above.

"Who is he, son? What does he want out here?"

"I can't make out who he is yet," Shaw said. "But it looks like somebody from town. He's all dressed up."

Buck and his father gathered up the picks and shovels and climbed out of the crater.

When they reached the top of the ground, they saw a large fat man walking laboriously over the rough field towards them. He was coming slowly in the heat, and his pale blue shirt was plastered to his chest and stomach wth perspiration. He stumbled helplessly over the rough ground, unable to look down and see his feet.

Ty Ty raised his hand and waved.

"Why, that's Pluto Swint," he said. "Reckon what Pluto wants out here?"

"I couldn't recognize Pluto all dressed up like that," Shaw said. "I wouldn't have known him at all."

"Looking for something for nothing," Buck replied to his father. "That's all he ever does, that I've heard about."

Pluto came closer, and they went over to the shade of the live-oak tree and sat down.

"Hot weather, Ty Ty," Pluto said, stumbling over the ground. "Hello there, boys. How are you folks making out, Ty Ty? You ought to build a road out here to the holes so I could drive my car on it. You ain't quitting for the day, are you?"

"You ought to stay in town and wait for the cool of the evening before coming out here, Pluto," Ty Ty said.

"I wanted to drive out and see you folks."

"Ain't it hot, though?"

"Reckon I can stand it, if anybody can. How are you folks making out?"

"Ain't complaining," Ty Ty said.

Pluto sat down against the trunk of the live-oak tree and panted like a dog running rabbits in mid-summer. The perspiration oozed from the fat flesh on his face and neck, and trickled down upon his pale blue shirt, turning it several shades darker. He sat there for a while, too tired and hot to move or to speak.

Buck and Shaw rolled cigarettes and lit them.

"So you ain't complaining," Pluto said. "Well, that's something to be thankful for. I reckon there's enough to complain about these days if a fellow wants to belly-ache some. Cotton ain't worth the raising no longer, and the darkies eat the watermelons as fast as they ripen on the vine. There's not much sense in trying to grow things for a living these days. I never was much of a farmer, anyway."

Pluto stretched out and put his arms under his head. He was becoming more comfortable in the shade.

"Strike anything lately?" he asked.

"Nothing much," Ty Ty said. "The boys are after me to start a new hole, but I ain't decided yet. We've gone about twenty feet in that one, and the sides are starting to cave in. I reckon we might just as well go and dig somewhere else for a spell. A new one won't be any worse than an old one."

"What you folks need is an albino to help you out," Pluto said. "They tell me that a man ain't got as much of a chance as a snowball in hell without an albino to help."

Ty Ty sat up and looked at Pluto.

"A what, Pluto?"

"An albino."

"What in the pluperfect hell is an albino, Pluto? I never heard of one before. Where'd you hear of it?"

"You know what I'm talking about. You know you've heard about them."

"It's slipped my mind completely, if I have, then."

"He's one of these all-white men who look like they are made out of chalk or something just as white. An albino is one of these all-white men, Ty Ty. They're all white; hair and eyes and all, they say."

"Oh, that," Ty Ty said, sitting back again. "I didn't recognize what you were talking about at first. Sure, I know what one of those is. I've heard the darkies talking about it, but I don't pay no attention to what the colored people say. I reckon I could use one though, if I knew where to find it. Never saw one of the creatures in my whole life."

"You folks need one here."

"I always said I'd never go in for none of this superstition and conjur stuff, Pluto, but I've been thinking all the time that one of those albinos is what we need. You understand, though, I'm scientific all the way through. I wouldn't have anything to do with conjur. That's one thing in this world I ain't going to fool with. I'd heap rather sleep in the bed with a rattler than monkey around with conjur."

"A fellow was telling me he saw one the other day," Pluto said. "And that's a fact."

"Where?" Ty Ty asked, jumping to his feet. "Where'd he see it, Pluto? Somewhere around here, Pluto?"

"Down in the lower end of the county somewhere. He wasn't far away. You could go and get him and be back here with him inside of ten or twelve hours at the most. I don't reckon you'd have any trouble catching him, but it wouldn't do any harm to tie him up a little before starting back. He lives in the swamp, and he might not like the feel of solid ground."

Shaw and Buck moved closer to the tree where Pluto was sitting.

"A real honest-to-God albino?" Shaw asked.

"As real as the day is long."

"Alive and walking around?"

"That's what the fellow told me," Pluto answered. "And that's a fact."

"Where is he now?" Buck asked. "Reckon we could catch him easy?"

"I don't know how easy you folks can catch him, because it might take a powerful lot of persuading to get him to come up here on solid ground. But then, I reckon you folks know how to go about getting him."

"We'll rope him," Buck said.

"I didn't aim to say as much, but I reckon you folks caught on to what I had in mind. I don't go around recommending the breaking of laws as a rule, and when I hint at it, I expect folks to leave me out of it."

"How big is he?" Shaw asked.

"The fellow didn't recall."

"Big enough to do some good, I hope," Ty Ty said.

"Oh, sure. It's not the size that counts, anyway. It's the all-whiteness, Ty Ty."

"What's his name?"

"The fellow didn't recall," Pluto said. "And that's a fact."

Ty Ty broke off a double-sized chew of tobacco and hitched up his suspenders. He began walking up and down in the shade, looking at nothing save the ground at his feet. He was too excited to sit still any longer.

"Boys," he said, still walking up and down in front of them, "the gold-fever has got me steaming again. Go to the house and fix up the automobile for a trip. Make sure that all the tires are pumped up hard and tight, and put plenty of water in the radiator. We're going to take a trip right off."

"After the albino, Pa?" Buck asked.

"You're durn tooting, son," he said, walking faster. "We're going to get that all-white man if I have to bust a gut getting there. But there's not going to be any of this conjur hocus-pocus mixed up in it. We're going about this business scientifically."

Buck started towards the house at once, but Shaw turned and came back.

"What about the rations for those darkies, Pa?" he asked. "Black

Sam said at dinner-time that he's all out of meat and corn meal at his house, and Uncle Felix said he didn't have anything at his house this morning to eat for breakfast. They told me to be sure and say something to you about it so they could have something to eat for supper tonight. They both looked a little hollow-eyed to me."

"Now, son, you know good and well I ain't got the time to be worrying about darkies eating," Ty Ty said. "What in the pluperfect hell do you mean by bothering me right when I'm the busiest, and getting ready to go after that all-white man? We've got to get down to the swamps and catch that albino before he gets away. You tell Black Sam and Uncle Felix that I'll try to fix them up with something to cook just as soon as we find that albino and bring him back."

Shaw still did not leave. He waited for several minutes, glancing at his father.

"Black Sam said he was going to butcher that mule he's plowing with and eat him, if you don't give him some rations soon. He showed me his belly this morning. It's flat under his ribs."

"You go tell Black Sam that if he kills that mule and eats him, I'll take out after him and run his ass ragged before I quit. I ain't going to have darkies worrying me about rations at a time like this. You tell Black Sam to shut his mouth and leave that old mule alone and plow that cotton out there."

"I'll tell him," Shaw said, "but he's liable to eat the mule, anyway. He said he was so hungry he didn't know what he might take a notion to do next."

"You go tell him what I said, and I'll attend to him after we finish roping this albino."

Shaw shrugged his shoulders and started for the house behind Buck.

Across the field the two Negro men were plowing in the newground. There was very little land remaining under cultivation on the farm then. Fifteen or twenty acres of the place had been potted with holes that were anywhere from ten to thirty feet deep, and twice as wide. The newground had been cleared that spring to raise cotton on, and there was about twenty-five acres of it. Otherwise, there would not have been sufficient land that year for the two share-croppers to work. Year by year the area of cultivated land had diminished as the big holes in the ground increased. By that fall, they would probably have to begin digging in the newground, or else close to the house.

Pluto cut off a fresh chew of tobacco from the long yellow plug he carried in his hip pocket.

"How do you folks know there's gold in the ground, Ty Ty?" he asked. "You folks have been digging around here for the past fifteen years now, and you ain't struck a lode yet, have you?"

"It won't be long now, Pluto. With that all-white man to divine it, it's going to turn up for sure. I feel it in my bones right now."

"But how do you know there's gold in the ground on this farm. You've been digging here since 'way back yonder, and you ain't struck it yet. Everybody between here and the Savannah River talks about finding gold, but I ain't seen none of it."

"You're just hard to convince, Pluto."

"I ain't seen it," Pluto said. "And that's a fact."

"Well, I ain't exactly struck a lode yet," Ty Ty said, "but we're getting pretty durn near to it. I feel it in my bones that we're getting warm. My daddy told me there was gold on this land, and nearly everybody else in Georgia has told me so, and only last Christmas the boys dug up a nugget that was as big as a guinea egg. That proves to my satisfaction that there's gold under the ground, and I aim to get it out before I die. I ain't aiming to give up looking for it yet. If we can find that albino and rope him, I know good and well we're going to strike the lode. The darkies dig for gold all the time, all over the whole country, even up there in Augusta, I hear, and that's a pretty good sign there's gold somewhere."

Pluto screwed up his mouth and spat a stream of golden-yellow tobacco juice at a lizard under a rotten limb ten feet away. His aim was perfect. The scarlet lizard darted out of sight with his eyes stinging from Pluto's tobacco juice.

Chapter II

I DON'T know," Pluto said, looking over the tops of his shoes for some other object at which to spit tobacco juice. "I don't know. Somehow it seems to me like a waste of time to go digging these great big holes in the ground looking for gold. Maybe I'm just lazy, though. If I had the gold-fever like you folks, I reckon I'd be tearing up the patch like the rest. Somehow the gold-fever don't seem to cling to me like it does to you folks. I can throw it off just by sitting down and thinking about it some."

"When you get the real honest-to-goodness gold-fever, Pluto, you can't shake it loose to save your soul. Maybe you ought to be glad you ain't got the fever. I don't regret it none myself, now that it's in my blood, but I reckon I ain't like you. A man can't be lazy and have the fever at the same time. It makes a man be up and doing."

"I haven't got the time to spend digging in the ground," Pluto said. "I just can't spare it."

"If you had the fever, you wouldn't have time for nothing else," Ty Ty said. "It gets a man just like liquor does, or chasing women. When you get a taste for it, you ain't going to sit still till you get it some more. It just keeps up like that, adding up all the time."

"I reckon I understand it a little better now," Pluto said. "But I still ain't got it."

"I don't reckon you'll be apt to get it, either, till you train down so you can work some."

"My size don't hinder me. It gets in my way sometimes, but I get around that."

Pluto spat haphazardly to the left. The lizard had not come back, and he could find nothing to aim at.

"My only sorrow is that all my children wouldn't stay here and help," Ty Ty said slowly. "Buck and Shaw are still here helping me, and Buck's wife, and Darling Jill, but the other girl went off up to Augusta and got a job in a cotton mill across the river in Horse Creek Valley and married, and I reckon you know about Jim Leslie just as well as I could tell you. He's a big man up there in the city now, and he's as rich as the next one to come along."

"Yes, yes," Pluto said.

"Something got into Jim Leslie at an early age. He wouldn't have much to do with the rest of us, and still won't. Right now, he takes on like he don't know who I am. Just before his mother died, I took her up to the city one day to see him. She said she wanted to see him just one more time before she died. So I took her up there and went to his big white house on The Hill, and when he saw who it was at the door, he locked it and wouldn't let us in. I reckon that sort of hastened his mother's death, his acting that way, because she took sick and died before the week was out. He acted like he was ashamed of us, or something. And he still does. But the other girl is different. She's just like the rest of us. She's always pleased to see us when we go over to Horse Creek Valley to pay a call. I've always said that Rosamond was a right fine girl. Jim Leslie, though—I can't say so much for him. He's always looking the other way when I happen to meet him on the street in the city. He acts like he's ashamed of me. I can't see how that ought to be, though, because I'm his father."

"Yes, yes," Pluto said.

"I don't know why my oldest boy should turn out like that. I've always been a religious man, all my life I have. I've always done the best I could, no matter how much I was provoked, and I've tried to get my boys and girls to do the same. You see that piece of ground over yonder, Pluto? Well, that's God's little acre. I set aside an acre of my farm for God twenty-seven years ago, when I bought this place, and every year I give the church all that comes off that acre of ground. If it's cotton, I give the church all the money the cotton brings at market. The same with hogs, when I raised them, and about corn, too, when I plant it. That's God's little acre, Pluto. I'm proud to divide what little I have with God."

"What's growing on it this year?"

"Growing on it? Nothing, Pluto. Nothing but maybe beggar-lice and cockleburs now. I just couldn't find the time to plant cotton on it this year. Me and the boys and the darkies have been so busy with other things I just had to let God's little acre lie fallow for the time being."

Pluto sat up and looked across the field towards the pine woods. There were such great piles of excavated sand and clay heaped over the ground that it was difficult to see much further than a hundred yards without climbing a tree.

"Where'd you say that acre of land was, Ty Ty?"

"Over there near the woods. You won't be able to see much of it from here."

"Why did you put it 'way over there? Ain't that a sort of out-of-the-way place for it to be, Ty Ty?"

"Well, I'll tell you, Pluto. It ain't always been where it is now. I've been compelled to shift it around a heap during the past twenty-seven years. When the boys get to discussing where we'll start digging anew, it seems like it always falls on God's little acre. I don't know why that is, either. I'm set against digging on His ground, so I've been compelled to shift it around over the farm to keep from digging it up."

"You ain't scared of digging on it and striking a lode, are you, Ty Ty?"

"No, I wouldn't say that, but I'd hate to have to see the lode struck on God's little acre the first thing, and be compelled to turn it all over to the church. That preacher's getting all he needs like it is. I'd hate something awful to have to give all the gold to him. I couldn't stand for that, Pluto."

Ty Ty raised his head and glanced across the field potted with holes. At one place he could see nearly a quarter of a mile away, in a straight line between the mounds of earth. Over there in the newground Black Sam and Uncle Felix were plowing the cotton. Ty Ty always managed to keep an eye on them, because he realized that if they did not raise any cotton and corn, there would be no money and little to eat that fall and winter. The Negroes had to be watched all the time, otherwise they would slip off at the first chance and dig in the holes behind their cabins.

"I've got something I'd like to ask you, Ty Ty."

"Is that what brought you out here in the hot sun?"

"I reckon so. I wanted to ask you."

"What's on your mind, Pluto? Go ahead and ask it."

"Your girl," Pluto said weakly, swallowing a little tobacco juice accidentally.

"Darling Jill?"

"Sure, that's why I came."

"What about her, Pluto?"

Pluto took the chew of tobacco out of his mouth and threw it aside. He coughed a little, trying to get the taste of the yellow tobacco out of his throat.

"I'd like to marry her."

"You would, Pluto? You mean it?"

"I sure to God would, Ty Ty. I'd go and cut off my right hand to marry her."

"You've taken a liking to her, Pluto?"

"I sure to God have," he said. "And that's a fact."

Ty Ty thought a while, pleased to think that his youngest daughter had attracted a man with serious intentions so early in life.

"No sense in cutting off your hand, Pluto. Just go ahead and marry her when she's ready for you. I reckon maybe you would consent to let her stay here some and help us dig after you are married, and maybe come yourself and help some. The more we have helping to dig, the quicker we're going to strike that lode, Pluto. I know you wouldn't object to digging some, being as how you would be one of the family."

"I never was one to dig much," Pluto said. "And that's a fact."

"Well, we won't discuss it any more just now. There'll be plenty of time to talk about it when you get married."

Pluto felt the blood running over his face just beneath his skin. He took out his handkerchief and wiped his face with it for a long time.

"But there's one thing about it——"

"What's that, Pluto?"

"Darling Jill said she didn't like me with such a fat belly. I can't help it, Ty Ty."

"What in the pluperfect hell has your belly got to do with it?" Ty Ty said. "Darling Jill is just crazy some, Pluto. Don't pay no attention to what she says. Just go ahead and marry her and don't pay it no mind. She'll be all right after you get her off somewhere for a while. Darling Jill is crazy sometimes, and about nothing."

"And there was something else," Pluto said, turning his face away from Ty Ty.

"What is that?"

"I don't like to bring it up."

"Just go ahead and say it, Pluto, and after you've said it, it'll be done and can't be coming back to bother you."

"I heard that she ain't so particular about what she does some-times."

"Just like what, for example?"

"Well, I heard that she's been teasing and fooling with a lot of men."

"Has things been said about my daughter, Pluto?"

"Well, about Darling Jill."

"What do people say, Pluto?"

"Nothing much, except that she's been teasing and fooling with a lot of men."

"I'm tickled to death to hear that. Darling Jill is the baby of the family, and she's coming along at last. I sure am glad to hear that."

"She ought to quit it, because I want to marry her."

"Never mind, Pluto," Ty Ty said. "Don't pay no heed to it. Don't give it no attention. She is careless, to be sure, but she don't mean no harm. She's just made that way. It don't hurt her none, not so that you will notice it, anyway. I reckon a lot of women are like that, a little or more, according to their natures. Darling Jill likes to tease a man some, but she don't mean no real harm. A pretty girl like Darling Jill has got everything coming her way, anyhow, and she knows it. It's up to you to satisfy her, Pluto, and make her so pleased she'll leave off with everybody but you. She's just been acting that way because she's come along now and there's been nobody man enough to hold her down. You're man enough to keep her satisfied. I can see that in your eyes, Pluto. Don't let that bother you no more."

"It's a pity God can't make a woman like Darling Jill and then leave off before He goes too far. That's what He did to her. He didn't know when He had made enough of a good thing. He just kept on and on—and now look at her! She's so full of teasing and the rest that I don't know that I'd ever have a peaceful night's rest when we get married."

"Well, it might be God's fault that He didn't know when to stop, Pluto, but just the same Darling Jill ain't the only girl He has made like that. In my time I've run across a heap like her. And I wouldn't have to go a thousand miles from home to cite you one. Now, you take Buck's wife, there. Pluto, I declare I don't know what to make of so pretty a girl as Griselda."

"That's what you think now, but I don't see how it can be so, Ty Ty. I've seen lots of women a little like her, but I've yet to see one that's as crazy as she is. When I get to be sheriff, I wouldn't want to have her running loose all the time like she does now. It wouldn't be good for my political career. I've got to keep that in mind."

"You ain't elected yet, Pluto."

"No, not yet, but everything is pointing my way. I've got a lot of friends working for me night and day all over the county. If somebody don't come along and shuffle the deck again, I'll get the office with no trouble at all."

"Tell them not to come here to my place, Pluto. I pledge you my vote, and all the votes on the place. Just be sure and don't let none of your workers come here trying to shake hands with everybody on the farm. I declare, there's been a hundred candidates here this summer, if there's been one. I won't shake with none of them, and I've told my boys and Darling Jill and Griselda not to stand for it. Ain't much use in telling you why I don't want candidates coming here, Pluto. Some of them are spreading the itch every which way, and it's going to stick for seven long years. I ain't saying you got the itch, but a heap of candidates do have. There's going to be so many cases of it in the county this fall and winter it won't be safe to go to town till the seven years have passed."

"There wouldn't be so many candidates for the few offices open, if it wasn't for the hard times. Hard times bring out the candidates just like lye does the fleas on a hound's back."

Over in the yard beside the house, Buck and Shaw had rolled the car out of the garage and were busy pumping up the tires. Buck's wife, Griselda, was standing in the shade of the porch talking to them. Darling Jill was not within sight.

"I've got to be getting along now," Pluto said. "I'm way behind this afternoon. I've got to make calls on all the voters between here and the crossroads between now and sundown. I've got to be going."

Pluto sat against the trunk of the live-oak tree, waiting until he felt like getting up. It was comfortable there, and shady; out in the field, where there was no shade, the sun beat down as steadily as ever. Even the weeds were beginning to curl a little in the steady heat.

"Where are we going to locate that albino you mentioned a while ago, Pluto?"

"You folks drive down below Clark's Mill and take the right-hand road at the creek. About a mile beyond that fork is where the fellow saw him. He was out in a thicket, on the edge of the swamp, cutting wood, the fellow said. Just get out and start looking. He's somewhere around there, because he couldn't get far away in this short time. If I didn't have so much to do, I'd go with you folks and help the little I could. The sheriff's race is getting hotter every day now, though, and I've got to count votes all the time I can. I don't know what I'd do if I didn't get elected."

"I reckon we'll find him all right," Ty Ty said. "I'll take the boys along, and they can do most of the walking while I sit and watch for signs. It'll be a pretty smart deal to take along some plow-lines to rope him with when we locate him. I reckon he'll try to put up a stiff scrap when I tell him to come along up here. But we'll get him though, if he's in the country. We've been needing just what he is for the longest time. The darkies said an all-white man can divine a lode, and I reckon they know what they're talking about. They dig more of the time than me and the boys, and we're at it from daybreak to sundown most days. If Shaw hadn't got that notion to quit and go to town just a while ago, we'd be at it now, down in that big hole yonder."

Pluto made as if to rise, but the effort discouraged him. He sat back again, breathing hard, to rest a little longer.

"I wouldn't be too rough with that albino, Ty Ty," he advised. "I don't know what you're aiming to catch him with, so I can't say how to go about it, but I sure don't advise shooting him with a gun. Hurting him would be against the law, and if I was you folks I'd play safe and not hurt him no more than I could help. You need him here to help you too bad to take any chances on running up against the law needlessly, just when you've gone and caught what you need most right now. Just catch him as easy as you can, so he won't get hurt and have scars to show for the handling."

"He won't get hurt none," Ty Ty promised. "I'll be as gentle with him as I would a newborn babe. I need that albino too bad to be rough with him."

"I've got to be getting along now," Pluto said, still not moving.

"Ain't it hot, though?" Ty Ty said, looking out at the heat on the baked earth.

It made Pluto hot to think about it. He closed his eyes, but that made him feel no cooler.

"It's too hot to be out counting votes today," Pluto said. "And that's a fact."

They sat a while longer, watching Buck and Shaw working over the big automobile in the yard beside the house. Griselda sat on the porch steps and watched them. Darling Jill was still not within sight.

"We'll be needing all the help we can find after we rope that albino and get him home," Ty Ty said. "I reckon I'll have to put Darling Jill and Griselda to digging, too. I wish Rosamond was here. She could help us out a lot. Do you reckon you could come by here in a day or two and dig a little with us, Pluto? It would be a big help, if you would dig some. I can't say how much I would be obliged to you, for whatever digging you want to do."

"I've got to be out and electioneering, Ty Ty," Pluto said, shaking his head. "Those other candidates for sheriff are tearing up the patch night and day. I've got to keep after the voters every minute I can spare. These voters are queer people, Ty Ty. One will promise to vote for you, and then the first thing you know, he's promising the next fellow to come along the very same thing. I can't afford to lose this election. I declare, I wouldn't have a thing to do for a living, if I lost it.

I can't afford to lose a good job like that when I haven't a thing to do for a living."

"How many men running against you, Pluto?"

"For sheriff?"

"That's what I meant to say."

"There was eleven in the race when I last heard about it this morning, and by night there's liable to be two or three more. But the actual candidates are few besides all the workers they've got counting votes for them, expecting to be made deputies. Looks like now every time you go up to a voter and ask a man to vote for you it sort of puts a bug in his ear and the first thing you know, he's out running for some office himself. If these hard times don't slacken before fall, there's going to be so many candidates running for county offices that there won't be a common ordinary voter left."

Pluto was beginning to wish he had not left the shaded streets in town to come out into the country and bake in the hot sun. He had hoped that he would see Darling Jill, but now that he could not find her, he was thinking of returning to town without calling on the voters along the road.

"If you can get a little time off, Pluto, I wish you would come out this way in a day or two and give us a hand with a shovel. It'll help us a lot. And while you're digging, you ought not to forget about the three or four votes here on the place. Votes are things you are in need of right now."

"I'll try to come by some time soon, and if I do I'll try to dig a little for you, if the hole ain't too deep. I don't want to get down in something I can't get out of again. After you get that albino you won't have to work so hard, anyway. When you catch him, all your troubles are over, Ty Ty, and all you'll have to do will be to dig down and strike the lode."

"I wish it was so," Ty Ty said. "I've been digging fifteen years now, and I need a little encouragement."

"An albino can locate it," Pluto said. "And that's a fact."

"The boys are ready to start," Ty Ty said, getting up. "We've got to be up and on our way before night sets in. I aim to rope that all-white man before daybreak."

Ty Ty started down the path towards the house where his sons were waiting. He did not look back to see if Pluto had got up, because he was in a big hurry. Pluto got up slowly and followed Ty Ty down the path between the deep holes and the high mounds of earth toward his car where he had left it in the road in front of the house two hours before. He hoped he would see Darling Jill before he left, but she was not within sight.

Chapter III

WHEN Ty Ty and Pluto reached the house, they found the boys resting after their work. All the tires were tight and hard, and the radiator was filled to overflowing. Everything seemed to be ready for the trip. While waiting for their father to get ready to start, Shaw sat on the runningboard rolling a cigarette, and Buck sat on the steps beside his wife with his arm around her waist. Griselda was playing with his hair, ruffling it with her hands.

"Here he comes now," Griselda said, "but that's no sign he's ready to leave."

"Boys," Ty Ty said, walking over to the sycamore stump and sitting down to rest, "we've got to be up and doing. I aim to rope that all-white man before daybreak tomorrow morning. If he's in the country, we'll have him roped by then, if we don't catch him a heap sooner."

"You'll have to keep guard over him when you bring him back, won't you, Pa?" Griselda asked. "The darkies might try to take him off, as soon as they hear that you've got a conjur-man on the place."

"Now you be quiet, Griselda," Ty Ty said angrily. "You know good and well I don't take any stock in superstition and conjur and such things. We're going about this thing scientifically, and no fooling around with conjur. It takes a man of science to strike a lode. You've never heard of darkies digging up many nuggets with all their smart talk about conjur. It just can't be done. I'm running this business scientifically clear from the start. Now you be quiet, Griselda."

"The darkies get nuggets somewhere," Buck said. "I've seen plenty of them, and they come out of the ground some way. The darkies would catch an albino if they knew there was one in the county, or anywhere near. They would try to catch him, if they weren't too scared to go after him."

Ty Ty turned away, tired of arguing with them. He knew what he was going to do, but he was too exhausted after a hard day's work out in the big hole to try to convince them of his way of looking at it. He turned around and looked in another direction.

It was late in the afternoon, but the sun looked as if it were a mile high, and it was every bit as hot as it had ever been.

"Sorry I've got to rush right off like this, folks," Pluto said, sitting down on the shaded steps. "There's a ballot box full of votes between here and the crossroads, and I've got to count them all before sundown tonight. It never does pay to put things off. That's why I've got to rush off like this in the heat of the day."

Shaw and Buck looked at Pluto a moment and at Griselda, and laughed out loud. Pluto would not have noticed them if they had not kept on laughing.

"What's so funny, Buck?" he asked, looking around him in the yard, and finally down at his overflowing belly.

Griselda began laughing again when she saw him looking down at himself.

Buck nudged her with his elbow, urging her to answer Pluto.

"Mr. Swint," she said, "it looks like you will have to wait till tomorrow to count some more votes. Darling Jill went off down the road about an hour ago and she hasn't come back yet. She was driving your car."

Pluto shook himself like a dog that has been standing in the rain. He made as though to get up, but he could not rise from the steps. He looked across the yard where he had left his car earlier in the afternoon and it was not there. He could not see it anywhere.

Ty Ty leaned forward to hear what they were talking about.

Pluto had had plenty of time to make some reply, but he had uttered no intelligible sound. He was in a position where he did not know what to say or to do. He merely sat where he was and said nothing.

"Mr. Swint," Griselda said, "Darling Jill went off in your automobile."

"It's gone," he said weakly. "And that's a fact."

"Don't pay any attention to Darling Jill," Ty Ty said consolingly. "Pluto, Darling Jill is as crazy as hell sometimes, and about nothing."

Pluto sank back on the steps, his body spreading on the boards when he relaxed. He took a fresh chew of yellow plug. There was nothing else he could do.

"We ought to be starting, Pa," Shaw said. "It's getting late."

"Why, son," he said, "I thought you quit work an hour or two ago to go to town. What about that game of pool you were going to shoot?"

"I wasn't going to town to shoot pool. I'd rather go to the swamp tonight."

"Well, then, if you didn't aim to shoot pool in town tonight, what about that woman you would be after?"

Shaw walked away without a reply. When Ty Ty tried to make fun of him, he could only walk away. He could not explain some things to his father, and he had long before decided that the best course was to let him go ahead and talk as much as he wished.

"It's time to get started," Buck said.

"That ain't no lie," Ty Ty said, going down toward the barn.

He came back in a few moments carrying several plow-lines over his arm. He tossed the ropes into the back seat of the car and sat down on the stump again.

"Boys," he said, "I've just had a notion. I'm going to send for Rosamond and Will to come over here. We need them to help us dig some, now that we're going to have that albino to show us where the lode is, and Rosamond and Will ain't doing much now. The mill over there at Scottsville is shut down again, and Will ain't doing a thing in the world. He might just as well be over here helping us dig. Rosamond and Griselda can help a lot, and maybe Darling Jill, too. Now mind you, I don't say I'm asking girls to do work like the rest of us. They can do a lot to help us, though. They can cook food for us and carry water, and some other things. Griselda, there, and Rosamond will help all they can, but I ain't so sure about Darling Jill. I'll try to persuade her to do something for us out there in the holes. I wouldn't let a girl on my place work like a man, but I'll do my durndest trying to make Darling Jill want to help some."

"I'd just like to see you make Will Thompson dig," Shaw said, jerking his head at his father. "That Will Thompson is the laziest white man this side of Atlanta. I've never seen him work, not here, anyway. I don't know what he does over there in that cotton mill, when it's running, but I'll bet it's nothing to speak of. Will Thompson won't be doing much digging, even if he does go down in a hole and go through the motions of it."

"You boys don't seem to catch on to Will like I do. Now, Will is just as hard a worker as the next one. The reason he never likes to dig in the holes here for us is because he don't feel at home here. Will is a cotton mill man, and he can't get along in the country on a farm. But maybe Will will dig some this time. Will can dig as good as the next one, if he wants to. He might get the gold-fever over here this time, and go down in the ground and dig like nobody's business. You never can tell what will happen when the fever strikes a man; maybe you'll wake up some morning and go out there to find him digging for a fare-you-well. I ain't seen a man or a woman yet who won't get down in the ground and dig when the gold-fever strikes him. You get to thinking about turning up a handful of those little yellow nuggets, maybe with the next stroke of the pick, and—man alive—you dig and dig and dig! That's why I'm going to send for Rosamond and Will right away. We'll be needing all the help we can get, son. That lode might be thirty feet in the ground, and at a place we haven't started digging into yet."

"It might be on God's little acre," Buck said. "What would you do about that? You wouldn't dig nuggets when they were all going to the preacher and the church, would you? I know I wouldn't. All the gold I get is going into my pockets, at least my share of it. I wouldn't be giving it to the preacher at the church."

"We ought to give up that piece of ground till we can dig on it and make sure," Shaw said. "God's not in need of it, and the first thing you know, we're going to strike   lode on it. I'll be dog-goned if I'm going to dig for nuggets and see that preacher get them. I'm in favor of shifting that piece of land till we can see what's in it."

"All right, boys," Ty Ty agreed, "I'll move it again, but I ain't aiming to do away with God's little acre altogether. It's His and I can't take it away from him after twenty-seven years. That wouldn't be right. But there ain't nothing wrong with shifting it a little, if need be. It would be a heathen shame to strike the lode on it, to be sure, the first thing, and I reckon I'd better shift it so we won't be bothered."

"Why don't you put it over here where the house and barn are, Pa?" Griselda suggested. "There's nothing under this house, and you can't be digging under it, anyway."

"I'd never thought of doing that, Griselda," Ty Ty said, "but it sure sounds fine to me. I reckon I'll shift it over here. Now, I'm pretty much glad to get that off my mind."

Pluto turned his head and looked at Ty Ty.

"You haven't shifted it already, have you, Ty Ty?" he asked.

"Shifted it already? Why, sure. This is God's little acre we're sitting on right now. I moved it from over yonder to right here."

"You're the quickest man of action I've ever heard about," Pluto said, shaking his head. "And that's a fact."

Buck and Griselda went around the corner of the house out of sight. Shaw started to follow them, but he changed his mind and rolled a cigarette instead. He was ready to go on the trip, and he did not wish to delay the start any longer. He knew, though, that Ty Ty would not leave until he became tired of sitting still.

Pluto sat on the steps thinking of Darling Jill and wondering where she was. He wished she would return so he could sit beside her and put his arms around her. Sometimes she would let him sit beside her, and at other times she would not. She was as inconsistent about that as she was about everything else she did. Pluto did not know what to do about it; she was that kind of girl, and he knew of no way to change her. But as long as she would sit still and let him hug her, he was completely satisfied; it was when she slapped him on the face and hit him in the belly with her fists that he was wholly displeased.

An automobile passed the house in a cloud of red dust, powdering the roadside until the weeds and trees looked more dead than ever. Pluto glanced at the car, but he quickly saw that Darling Jill was not driving it, and he had no further interest in it. The car went out of sight around the bend in the road, but the dust lingered in the air long after it had gone.

The last time he had seen Darling Jill she had made him leave five minutes after he got there. It hurt Pluto, and he went back home and got into bed. He had come to see her for the evening that time, confidently expecting to be with her for several hours at least, but five minutes after he reached the house he was on his way home again. Darling Jill had told him to go roll his hoop. On top of that she slapped him on the face and hit him in the belly with her fists. Now he hoped that if there was a law of averages, or even a law of compensation, his meeting of her this time would be wholly different. This time she should, if there was any justice, be glad to see him; she should even let him hug her and, to make up for the previous visit, allow him to kiss her several times. Darling Jill should do all of that, but whether she would or not was something he did not know. Darling Jill was as uncertain as were his chances of being elected sheriff that fall.

The thought of the coming election stirred Pluto. He made as though to stand up, but he did not move from his seat. He could not get out in the heat of the day and walk down the dusty road calling on voters.

Buck and Griselda came back with two large Senator Watson watermelons and a salt-shaker. Buck also had a butcherknife in his hand. Pluto forgot his troubles when he saw the two large melons, and sat up. Ty Ty pulled himself out of his crouched position. After Buck and Griselda had put the melons on the porch, Ty Ty went over and cut them into quarters.

Griselda carried Pluto his portion, and he thanked her many times over for her consideration. There would have been no need for his getting up to go for his slice of watermelon inasmuch as Griselda was already standing. And if she had not brought it to him, he did not know whether he could have gone after it or not. She had sat down beside him and was watching him lower his face into the cool meat. The melons had been cooling on the bottom of the well for two days and they were ice-cold.

"Mr. Swint," she said, looking up at Pluto, "your eyes look like watermelon seeds."

Everyone laughed. Pluto knew she was right. He could almost see himself at that moment.

"Now, Griselda," he said, "you're just making fun of me again."

"I couldn't help saying it, Mr. Swint. Your eyes are so small and your face is so red, that you do look exactly like a watermelon with two seeds showing."

Ty Ty laughed again, louder than before.

"There's a time for fun, and a time for work," he said spitting out a mouthful of seeds, "and now is the time for work. We've got to be up and doing, boys. We've sat around the house here long enough for one day, and now we've got to be on our way. I aim to rope that albino sometime between now and daybreak tomorrow morning. Let's be up and doing."

Pluto wiped his hands and face and laid the rind aside. He wished to wink at Griselda, and to lay his hand on her knees. In a minute or two he found the courage to wink at her with his watermelon seeds, but try as he might he could not bring himself to touch her. The thought of laying his hand on her knees and maybe trying to push his fingers between her legs brought a blush to his face and neck. He drummed on the steps with his fingers in seven-eighths time, whistling under his breath, and scared to death that somebody would read his thoughts.

"Buck's got a fine-looking wife, hasn't he, Pluto?" Ty Ty asked him, spitting out another mouthful of watermelon seeds. "Did you ever see a finer-looking girl anywhere in the country? Just look at that creamy skin and that gold in her hair, not to mention all that pale blueness in her eyes. And while I'm praising her, I can't overlook the rest of her. I reckon Griselda is the prettiest of them all. Griselda has the finest pair of rising beauties a man can ever hope to see. It's a wonder that God ever put such prettiness in the house with an ornery old cuss like me. Maybe I don't deserve to see it, but I'm here to tell you I'm going to take my fill of looking while I can."

Griselda hung her head and blushed.

"Aw, now, Pa," she begged.

"Ain't I right, Pluto?"

"She's a perfect little female," Pluto said. "And that's a fact."

Griselda glanced up at Buck and blushed again. Buck laughed at her.

"Son," Ty Ty said, turning to Buck, "wherever in the world did you happen to find her, you lucky dog?"

"Well, there's no more where she came from," he said. "She was the pick of the crop."

"And I'll bet they've given up trying to raise any more, there at that place, after seeing you come and take away the beauty of them all."

"Now stop that, Pa, you and Buck," Griselda said, putting her hands over her face and trying to keep them from seeing her.

"I hate to cross you, Griselda," Ty Ty said determinedly. "Once I get started about you, I can't stop. I've just got to praise you. And I reckon any man would who has seen you like I have. The first time I saw you, when Buck brought you here from wherever it was you came from, I felt like getting right down there and then and licking something. That's a rare feeling to come over a man, and when I have it, it does me proud to talk about it for you to hear."

"Please, Pa," she said.

Ty Ty continued talking, but it was impossible for anyone to hear what he was saying. He sat on the stump talking to himself and looking down at the hard white sand at his feet.

Pluto moved his hands a little. He wished to get closer to Griselda, but he was afraid. He turned around to see if anyone were looking. The others were all looking elsewhere, and he quickly put his hand on her legs and leaned against her. Griselda turned and slapped him so quickly he did not know what had struck him. He felt the flow of blood rushing to his stinging cheeks and he heard the tinkle of bells in his ears. When he could open his eyes and look up, Griselda was standing on the ground in front of him, and Buck and Shaw were doubled up with laughter.

"I'll teach you not to get fresh with me, you big haystack!" she cried angrily. "Don't get me confused with Darling Jill. She may not always slap you, but I certainly shall. You'll know better than to try something like that again."

Ty Ty got up and came across the yard, looking at Pluto to see how badly he was hurt.

"Pluto didn't mean no harm, Griselda," Ty Ty said, trying to calm her. "Pluto wouldn't harm you, not with Buck around, anyhow."

"You'd better be going on down the road to count your votes, Mr. Swint," she said.

"Now, Griselda, you know good and well Pluto can't leave till Darling Jill comes back with his car."

"He can walk, can't he?" she asked, laughing at Pluto. "I didn't know he had got so he can't even walk any more."

Pluto looked around him frantically, as if he were looking for something to hold on to. The thought of getting out into the hot sun and walking in the red dust terrified him. He clutched the overlapping boards of the steps with both hands.

Shaw noticed someone coming towards the house from the barn. He looked again a moment later and saw that it was Black Sam. When the colored man came closer, Shaw left the yard and went to meet him.

"Mr. Shaw," Black Sam said, taking off his hat, "I'd like pretty much to have a word with your Pa. I need to see him."

"What do you want to see him about? I told you what he said about the rations."

"I know you did, Mr. Shaw, but I'm still hungry, I'd like to see your Pa, please, sir, boss."

Shaw called Ty Ty to the corner of the house.

"Mr. Ty Ty, I'm all out of something to eat at my house, and we ain't had nothing to eat all today. My old woman is downright hungry for something to eat."

"What in the pluperfect hell do you mean by coming to the house and bothering me, Black Sam?" Ty Ty shouted. "I sent you word that I'd get you some food when I get around to it. You can't come here to the house and bother me like this. Now get on home and stop worrying me. I'm going off to rope an all-white man tonight, and I've got to give all my thought to that. This all-white man is going to help me locate the lode."

"You ain't speaking of a conjur-man, is you, Mr. Ty Ty?" Black Sam asked fearfully. "Mr. Ty Ty, please, sir, white-folks, don't bring no conjur-man here. Mr. Ty Ty, please, sir, boss, I can't stand to see a conjur-man."

"Shut up, durn it," Ty Ty said. "It's none of your business what I do. Now go on home and stop coming here to the house when I'm busy."

The colored man backed away. He forgot for the time being about his hunger. The thought of seeing an albino on the place made him breathless.

"Now, wait a minute," Ty Ty said. "If you butcher that mule and eat him while I'm gone, when I get back I'll make you pay for him, and it won't be in money either, because I know you ain't got a penny."

"No, sir, Mr. Ty Ty, I wouldn't do nothing like that. I wouldn't eat up your mule, boss. I never thought of anything like that. But, please, sir, white-captain, don't bring no conjur-man around here."

Black Sam backed away from Ty Ty. His eyes were abnormally large and extraordinarily white.

When Ty Ty had turned and gone back to the front yard, Shaw went up to the colored man.

"After we leave," he said, "come around to the back door and Miss Griselda will give you something out of the kitchen. Tell Uncle Felix to come and get something, too."

Black Sam thanked him, but he did not remember hearing a word Shaw had said. He turned and ran towards the barn, moaning to himself.

Chapter IV

Buck walked back and forth between the porch and the car impatiently.

"Let's get started, Pa," he said. "We'll be tramping around in the swamp all night if we don't get an early start. I don't like the swamps much after dark, anyway."

"I thought you were going to send for Rosamond and Will," Griselda broke in, looking at her father-in-law. "You'd better write the letter now and mail it when you go through town."

"I didn't aim to mail a letter," Ty Ty said. "A letter would take too long to get there. I figured on sending after them. I reckon Darling Jill could go over there to Scottsville and bring them back all right. I'll send her on the bus to Augusta, and she'll get there early tonight. They could all start back tomorrow morning on the bus and maybe get here in time to start digging in the afternoon just as soon as dinner was over."

"Darling Jill isn't here," Buck said. "There's no way of knowing when she'll be back, either. If we have to wait for her, we'll never get started to the swamp."

Pluto sat up erectly and looked down the road. He would never get around to make a personal call on the voters at the rate he was going.

"She'll be back any minute now," Ty Ty said assuredly. "We'll wait and take her to Marion with us. When we get to town, we'll leave her at the bus station and go on to the swamp after that albino. That's the thing to do. Darling Jill will be home any minute now. Wouldn't be any sense in going off and leaving when she'll be here before long."

Buck shrugged his shoulders and walked up and down in the yard disgustedly. Two hours had already been wasted, and nothing had been accomplished by the delay.

"I would—" Pluto said, and then he hesitated.

"You'd do what?" Ty Ty asked him.

"Well, I was going to say——"

"Say what? Go on, Pluto. Speak your mind. We're all of a family here."

"If she wouldn't object, I thought——"

"What in the pluperfect hell has got into you, Pluto?" Ty Ty asked angrily. "You start out to say something, and then you get all red in the face and neck, and you carry on like you're scared to say it and scared not to. Go on and tell me what it is."

Pluto's face got red again. He looked from person to person, at last taking out his handkerchief and holding it over his face while he pretended to wipe it. When his face became less inflamed, he put it back into his pocket.

"I was going to say that I'd be pleased to drive Darling Jill over to Horse Creek Valley this evening, if she would bring my car back. I mean, I'd be pleased to take her over there if she'd let me."

"Why, that's real neighborly of you, Pluto," Ty Ty said enthusiastically. "Now I know you can count on our votes. If you'll take her over there, it'll save me some money in the end. I'll tell her to go with you. She won't mind it at all. What do you mean by saying if she'll let you? I'll tell her to, Pluto. Much obliged for the offer. I'll save a lot of money in the end by that deal."

"Do you reckon she'll go with me—I mean, do you reckon she'll consent to letting me drive her over there in my car if she brings it back?"

"I reckon she will when I tell her to go, and she ought to be real pleased to have you taking her," Ty Ty said emphatically, spitting upon a wild onion stem at his feet. "Don't make the mistake of thinking I ain't got a hand over my own children, Pluto. She'll go, all right, when I tell her to go. She won't mind it a bit."

"If Pluto is going to take her, then let's get started for the swamps, Pa," Buck said. "It's getting late. I want to get back here by midnight, if I can."

"Boys," Ty Ty said, "I'm mighty proud to hear you say you want to be up and doing. We'll start right off. Pluto, you drive Darling Jill over to Scottsville and leave her with Rosamond and Will. It's mighty fine of you. I'm mighty much obliged to you, Pluto."

Ty Ty ran up the porch steps and back to the yard again. He had forgotten for a moment how excited he was over the prospect of finding the albino.

"Griselda, when Darling Jill gets back, tell her to go over to Horse Creek Valley and bring Rosamond and Will back tomorrow morning. She'll have to explain what we want with them, and you can tell her what to say to them. We need them to help us dig. Tell Darling Jill that me and the boys have gone to the swamp after that all-white man, and tell her we're going to strike the lode in no time. I won't say when, but I can say in no time. I'll buy you and her both the finest clothes the merchants in the city can show. I'll get the same for Rosamond, when we strike the lode. I want Rosamond and Will to know we need their help pretty bad, so they'll come tomorrow and help us. We'll all start in as soon as dinner is over tomorrow, and dig and dig and dig."

Ty Ty fumbled in his pocket a moment, at length taking out a quarter and handing it to Griselda.

"Take this and buy yourself a pretty the next time you go to town," he urged. "I wish I had more to give you, because you're so much prettiness and when I look at you, I can't help it, but we ain't struck the lode yet."

"Let's get going, Pa," Shaw said.

Buck cranked up the big seven passenger car and idled the engine while his father was giving Griselda final instructions for Darling Jill. Just when Buck thought Ty Ty was ready to get into the car, he wheeled around and ran down to the barn. A few moments later he came running back with three or four more plow-lines. He tossed them into the back seat with the others.

Ty Ty stood looking at Pluto on the steps for several minutes, his brow wrinkled, intent upon him as if he were trying to remember something he had meant to tell him before leaving. Unable to recall it, he turned and climbed into the car with Buck and Shaw. Buck raced the engine, and a cloud of black smoke blew out of the exhaust pipe. Ty Ty turned around in his seat and waved good-by to Griselda and Pluto.

"Be sure and remember to tell Darling Jill what I told you," he said. "And tell her to come home the first thing tomorrow morning without fail."

Shaw had to reach over his father and shut the door that Ty Ty had been too excited to close. With a roar and a rank odor from the exhaust pipe, the big car shot out of the yard and rumbled into the highway. They were out of sight a moment later.

"I hope they find that albino," Pluto said, not particularly to Griselda. "If they don't find him, Ty Ty will come back swearing I lied about him. I swear to God, the fellow said he saw him down there. I didn't lie about it. The fellow said he saw him in the thicket on the edge of the swamp cutting wood as big as life. If Ty Ty doesn't find him and bring him home, he'll take his vote away from me. That'll be real bad. And that's a fact."

Griselda had gone to the porch while Pluto was talking. She could not hear what he was mumbling to himself, for one thing; and she did not care to stand out in the yard with him, for another. She sat down in a rocker and watched the back of Pluto's neck. From the position she was in, she could get a better view of the road, and she watched for the first sign of Darling Jill's returning home.

Pluto sat alone on the steps mumbling something to himself. He no longer raised his voice high enough for her to hear what he was saying. He was thinking of what Ty Ty Walden would say and do if he could not find the albino. He was beginning to feel sorry that he had ever mentioned the albino in the first place. He knew then that he should have kept his mouth shut about something he was not certain of.

Griselda stood up and looked down the road.

"Is that your car, Pluto?" she asked, pointing over his head towards the cloud of red dust rising from the road. "It looks like Darling Jill driving it, anyway."

Pluto got to his feet with effort. He stood up and took several steps in that direction. He waited beside the sycamore stump while the automobile came closer. It was making a lot of noise, but it did look like his car. He wondered why it was making so much noise. He had never noticed it when he drove.

"Yes," Griselda said. "That's Darling Jill, Pluto. Can't you recognize your own automobile?"

Darling Jill turned into the yard without slackening speed. The heavy sedan skidded a distance of ten or twelve feet, coming to an abrupt stop turned halfway around in the yard. One of the rear tires was as flat as a board, and the innertube, which was hanging from the rim, had been chewed all to pieces. Pluto looked at the tire with a feeling of great fatigue coming over him.

Pluto heard Griselda coming down the steps behind him and he moved out of her way a little.

"You had a puncture, Pluto," Darling Jill said. "See it?"

Pluto tried to say something, and he found that it was difficult to pull his tongue loose from the roof of his mouth. When it finally came loose, it fell between his lips and hung on the outside.

"What's the matter with you?" she asked, jumping out to the ground. "Can't you see it? You're not blind, are you?"

"Who had a puncture?" Pluto managed to ask. He realized how weak his voice was only after he had spoken. "Who?"

"You did, you big horse's ass," Darling Jill said. "What's the matter with you? Can't you see anything?"

Griselda came running up.

"Hush, Darling Jill!" she said. "Don't talk like that."

As soon as Pluto could recover, he began jacking up the wheel to change the spare on to it. He went about replacing the punctured tire, puffing and blowing, but he did not have a word to say to Darling Jill for rim-cutting a brand new tire and chewing up a new two-dollar innertube. Darling Jill watched him at work a moment, laughed at him, and started to the porch with Griselda.

"Who's been eating melons, and didn't save me some?"

"There's plenty left," Griselda said. "I saved you two large pieces in the kitchen."

"What is Pluto Swint doing around here?"

"Pa wants you to go over to Rosamond and Will's and bring them back," Griselda said, quickly remembering Ty Ty's messages. "Pa and Buck and Shaw have gone to the swamp to catch an albino to divine the lode for them, and he said he needs Rosamond and Will to help dig. Pluto will take you over there right away, and Pa said you and Rosamond and Will can come back tomorrow morning on the first bus. I wish I could go, too."

"Come on and go. Why can't you?"

"Buck said he might be back by midnight, and I want to be here when he comes home. I'll go over there some other time. You'd better hurry and dress."

"I'll be ready in a minute," Darling Jill said. "I've got to take a bath first, though. Don't let Pluto go off and leave me. I'll be ready in no time. It won't take me long."

"Oh, he'll wait for you," Griselda said, following her into the house. "He'll be here, all right. You couldn't pry him loose until you're ready to go with him."

She and Darling Jill went into the house, leaving Pluto alone in the yard to change the tire. He had already got the punctured tire off the wheel, and he was getting ready to put the spare on and tighten the lugs. He worked away in the heat, not mindful of the fact that Griselda and Darling Jill had left him alone in the yard.

When he had finished and had replaced the jack and lug wrench under the seat, he stood up and tried to dust his clothes. His face and arms were covered with dirt and perspiration, and his hands were grimy. He tried for a while to wipe it off with his handkerchief, but he had to give that up when he saw how hopeless it was. He started around the house to the well in the back yard where he could bathe his face and hands.

Pluto reached the corner of the house without raising his eyes from the ground. When he got to the corner, he looked up and saw Darling Jill in the yard.

First, he stepped back for a moment; then, he stepped forward again and looked at her the second time. After that he did not know what to do.

Griselda was sitting on the top step of the porch talking to Darling Jill. She had not looked in Pluto's direction. Darling Jill was standing over a large white enameled tub that had been hurriedly carried to the yard from the house and placed halfway between the porch and the well. She was busy talking to Griselda and soaping her arms when Pluto saw her.

It was at that moment when Pluto realized fully where he was. He did not wish to turn around and leave, but he was afraid to go closer.

"Well, darn my socks!" Pluto said, his mouth agape.

Darling Jill heard him and she looked at him. She paused with the soapy washcloth on her shoulder, and looked even more intently than before. Griselda turned to see what she was staring at so long.

For a while, Pluto thought that perhaps Darling Jill was trying to stare him out of countenance, or perhaps drive him back around the house, but he had remained there several minutes already, and he did not know what she intended to do. He was determined, after having stood there that long, to make her take the first move. Darling Jill did not attempt to run from his sight, and she did not try to cover herself with the washcloth or with anything else. She just stood over the white enameled bowl, staring at him.

"Well, darn my socks!" Pluto said again. "And that's a fact."

Darling Jill reached down into the bowl with both hands and, picking up all the suds she could hold, threw the soapy froth at Pluto. Pluto, only a few feet away, saw the suds coming towards him, but he could not force his body to move in time to escape them. By the time he finally moved a few steps, the soap was already stinging his eyes and running down the collar of his shirt. He could not see a thing. Somewhere in front of him he could hear both Griselda and Darling Jill laughing, but he was unable to protest. When he opened his mouth to say something, he tasted soap all over his tongue, and the inside of his mouth tasted just as disagreeable. He bent as far forward as he could and tried to spit out the taste of the soap.

"That will darn your socks," he heard Darling Jill say to him. "Maybe you'll think twice the next time you try to slip up on me while I'm naked. What can you see now, Pluto? See anything, Pluto? Why don't you look at me now—you could see something if you did!"

Griselda laughed at him again on the steps.

"I wish I could take a picture of him now," she said to Darling Jill. "He would make a pretty picture to show to the voters on election day, wouldn't he, Darling Jill? I'd call it the 'Soapy Sheriff of Wayne County Counting Votes.'"

"If he ever tries to slip up on me again while I'm naked, I'll duck him in a tub of suds until he learns to cry 'Uncle' in three languages. I never saw such a man in all my life. He's always trying to put his hands on me and squeeze something, or else trying to sneak up and grab me while I'm naked. I never saw such a man."

"Maybe he didn't know you were taking a bath in the back yard, Darling Jill. He wouldn't know it until he came around here and saw you."

"Don't you think he didn't know it. If you think that, then tell me why it is he comes around the corner of the house every time I'm taking one. Pluto isn't so dumb as he looks. He'll fool you by his looks."

There was a silence after that, and Pluto knew they had left the yard and gone into the house. He wrung his handkerchief again and attempted to wipe the soap out of his eyes. Feeling his way around to the front of the house, he reached the steps and sat down to wait for Darling Jill to dress and come out. He was not angry with her for throwing soap in his face; nothing could have made him angry with her. She had done things much worse than that to him many times. And she called him the worst names she could think of.

When he succeeded in drying the soap and in wiping the last of it from his face and hair, he was surprised to look up and see that the sun was almost down. He realized that he would not be able to call on any more of the voters that day. But as long as he was taking Darling Jill to Scottsville, he did not regret it. He would rather be with her than win an election.

The screendoor behind him squeaked, and Darling Jill and Griselda came out.

They stood on the porch at his back looking down at the top of his head and giggling a little. He could not turn around to see them without getting up, and he decided to wait until they came down the steps before looking at them.

"Darning your socks, aren't you, Pluto?" Darling Jill asked him. "You should have done that before you went around to the back yard."

Chapter V

IT was after ten o'clock when they reached Scottsville that evening. Pluto was lost in the maze of mill streets, but Darling Jill had been there many times before and she recognized the house before they got to it. Rosamond and Will's house was apparently like all the others, but Rosamond usually had blue curtains over the windows and Darling Jill had looked for those.

Pluto stopped the car but did not shut off the motor. Darling Jill turned the switch and took out the key.

"Wait a minute," Pluto said excitedly. "Don't do that, Darling Jill."

She dropped the key into her pocketbook and laughed at Pluto's protests. Before he could stop her, she had opened the door and stepped to the street. Pluto got out and followed her up the walk to the front door.

"I don't hear Will anywhere," she said, stopping and trying to see through the window.

They opened the door and went into the hall. The light was burning and all the other doors were open. From one of the rooms came the sound of someone crying. Darling Jill went into one of the dark rooms and snapped on the light. Rosamond was lying across the bed with part of a sheet covering her face. She was sobbing loudly.

"Rosamond!" Darling Jill cried. "What in the world is the matter!" She ran and fell across the bed with her sister.

Rosamond raised herself on her elbows and looked around the room. She dried the tears on her face and tried to smile.

"I wasn't expecting you," she said, throwing her arms around Darling Jill and bursting into tears again. "I'm glad you came when you did. I thought I was going to die. I must have been out of my head a little."

"What did Will do to you? Where is he?"

Pluto had been standing in the doorway, not knowing what else to do. He tried not to look at Rosamond until she had noticed him.

"Hello, Pluto," she smiled. "I certainly am glad to see you again. Take the clothes off the chair and sit down and make yourself at home."

"Where's Will?" Darling Jill asked again. "Tell me what happened, Rosamond."

"I suppose he's down the street somewhere," Rosamond said. "I don't know exactly where he is."

"But what's the matter?"

"He's been drunk all this week," Rosamond said. "And he won't stay at home with me. He talks about turning the power on at the mill when he's drunk, and when he's sober, he won't say anything. The last time he came home he hit me."

Her face was badly swollen. One of her eyes was slightly discolored, and blood had been flowing from her nose.

"Isn't he working?"

"No, of course not. The mill is still shut down. I don't know when it will start running again. Some people say it never will. I don't know."

Pluto stood up, twisting his hat in his hands.

"I've got to be gettin' back home," he said. "And that's a fact."

"Sit down, Pluto," Darling Jill told him. "And be quiet."

He sat down again, placing his hat under the chair and folding his hands in his lap.

"I came over to take you and Will home with me," Darling Jill said. "Pa says he wants you and Will to help some. He needs Will to help dig, and you can do whatever you like. Pa's got something on his mind about finding gold for sure this time. I don't know what got into him."

"Oh, he always has some new notion," Rosamond said. "There's no gold on that place, is there? If there was gold there, they would have found it long before now. Why can't he stop digging the land full of holes and farm some?"

"I don't know," Darling Jill said. "He and the boys think they're going to strike it soon. That's what keeps them at it all the time. I wish they would."

"The Waldens are worse than the darkies, always expecting to find gold somewhere."

"Pa wants you and Will to come, anyway."

"Will won't dig. Pa ought to know that by this time. Will's always restless when he is away from here."

"Pa has his head set on you and Will coming over there, anyway. You know how he is."

"We can't go tonight. Will isn't here, and I don't know when he'll come back."

"Tomorrow is soon enough. We'll spend the night. Pluto can sleep with Will, and I'll sleep with you."

Pluto started to protest that he had to get back to Marion that night, but neither of them noticed him.

"You're welcome to stay," Rosamond said, "but the bed isn't big enough for Will and Pluto. One of them will have to sleep on the floor."

"Pluto can," Darling Jill said. "Just give Pluto a pillow and a quilt and let him make himself a pallet in the hall. He won't mind."

Rosamond got up and fixed her hair and powdered her face. She looked better after that.

"I don't know when Will is coming home. Maybe not at all tonight. Sometimes he doesn't."

"He'll get sober when he goes back with us and digs a day or two. Pa will keep him sober, too."

All of them turned and listened. There was a noise on the front porch, followed by the sound of someone banging on the door.

"That's him now," Rosamond said. "He's still drunk, too. I can tell."

They waited in the room while he came through the hall and appeared at the door.

"Well, for God's sake!" Will said. "You back again?"

He stared at Darling Jill for several moments and started toward her, his hands leading him. She side-stepped, and he went into the wall.

"Will!" Rosamond said.

"And there's old Pluto, too! How's everything out there around Marion these days?"

Pluto got up and tried to shake hands with Will, but Will started sideways toward the other side of the room.

Will sat down in the corner against the wall and placed his head on his arms. He was quiet for such a long time that all of them thought he had gone to sleep. They were getting ready to tiptoe out of the room, and they had got as far as the door when Will looked up and called them back.

"Trying to slip off from me again, weren't you? Come back here, all of you, and keep me company."

Rosamond made a gesture of helplessness and sank wearily upon the bed. Pluto and Darling Jill laughed at Will and sat down.

"How's Griselda?" Will asked. "Is that girl as good-looking as ever? What part of the country did she come from? I'd like to go there some day and take my pick."

"Please, Will," Rosamond said.

"I'm going to get that girl yet," Will said determinedly, shaking his head from side to side. "I've been wanting her for a long time now, and I can't wait much more for her, either. I'm going to get her."

"Please shut your mouth, Will," Rosamond said.

He appeared not to have heard her.

"Tell me how Griselda's looking these days, Darling Jill. Does she still look ripe for picking? I'm going to get her, so help me God! I've had my eye on her ever since she moved in the house over there. Griselda's got the sweetest pair——"

"Will!" Rosamond said.

"Aw, what the hell is the matter with you," Will said irritatedly. "It's all in the family, ain't it? Why in the hell should you bawl me out for talking about her? Buck wouldn't care much if I did get her. He can't use her all the time. Nobody ought to howl about just one tiny little bit when nobody is getting hurt. You act like I was getting ready to run down the King of England's daughter."

"Please don't talk about it now, then," Rosamond begged.

"Now, listen to me," Will said. "Griselda can't keep from being the prettiest girl in the country, no more than I can keep from wanting to get her. So what the hell does that make you? I promised myself a piece when I saw her the first time over there in Georgia, and I'll be damned if I'm going to break my own promise. You get all you bargained for. I can't help it if you raise a howl, either."

"I'll talk about it some other time, Will, if you promise to stop talking now. Try to remember who's here."

"It's all in the family, ain't it? So, what the hell!"

Darling Jill looked at Pluto and laughed. Pluto felt the blood coming over his face again, and he turned his head toward the wall where the light would shadow it. Darling Jill burst out laughing again.

There was no use in any of them trying to talk as long as Will was there.

Rosamond suddenly began to cry.

"There ain't a bit of sense in taking on like that," Will said doggedly. "It's all in the family, ain't it? Well, what the hell! Old Pluto, there, is having a good time with Darling Jill, or would if he could, and I reckon I take you plenty of times, except when you get uppity and start talking about the God damn sacredness of approaching a female, or some such talk. So, why in hell can't I talk about getting Griselda if I want to? You can't expect a girl like Griselda to put a plug in herself. Why, that would be a God damn shame! It would be a heathen sin. I swear it would. That'd be the damnedest shame I ever heard about!"

He began to cry at the thought of it. He stood up and the tears ran down his face and he sounded as if his heart were breaking. He tried to stop the flow of tears by twisting his fists into his eyesockets, but the tears fell as heavily as ever.

Rosamond got up off the bed.

"I'm glad that's over with," she said, sighing. "He'll be all right now. Just leave him alone for a little while, and he'll be himself again. Come on into the other room. I'll turn the light out so it won't hurt his eyes."

Pluto and Darling Jill followed her, leaving Will crying in the corner.

When they had all found chairs in the other room, Rosamond turned to Pluto.

"I'm awfully ashamed of what happened in the next room, Pluto," she said. "Please try to forget it and not think of it again. When Will gets drunk, he doesn't know what he's saying. He didn't mean a word of it. I'm sure of that. I wouldn't have let him embarrass you for anything, if I could have helped it. Please forget all about what he said."

"Oh, that's all right, Rosamond," he said, blushing a little. "I don't hold anything against you or Will."

"Well, I don't suppose you would," Darling Jill broke in. "It's none of your business, anyway. Just sit tight, Pluto, and keep your mouth shut."

She and Rosamond began talking about something else then, and Pluto was unable to follow the conversation. He was almost on the other side of the room from them, and their voices were lowered. He sat uncomfortably in the little chair, wishing he could sit on the floor where he would have a wider seat.

Presently Will came to the door. His face was drawn, but he showed little indication of his drinking. Apparently he had sobered.

"Glad to see you, Pluto," he said, going over and shaking hands. "It's been a long time since I've seen you. It's been nearly a year, hasn't it?"

"I reckon it has, Will."

Will drew up a chair and sat down, leaning back to look at Pluto.

"What are you doing now, the same thing as usual?"

"Well, I'm a candidate for sheriff this year," Pluto told him. "I'm running for office."

"You'll make a humdinger," Will said. "It takes a big man to hold the office of sheriff. Why that is, I don't know, but it seems to be a fact. I don't remember ever seeing a skinny sheriff."

Pluto laughed good-naturedly. He went to the window and spat tobacco juice on the ground.

"I ought to be back home now," he said, "but I'm glad to have the chance of coming over here to see you and Rosamond. I've got to get back the first thing in the morning though, and do some canvassing. I didn't get a thing done all day. I reckon I started early enough, but I only got as far as the Waldens, and now here I am over here in Carolina."

"Are the old man and the boys still digging holes in the ground over there?"

"Night and day, almost. But they're going to get an albino from the swamps to divine it for them. That's where they are tonight. They left a little before we did."

Will laughed, slapping his legs with his broad hands.

"Conjur stuff now, huh? Well, I'll be damned. I didn't know Ty Ty Walden would start using conjur, old as he is. He's always been trying to tell me how scientific he is about digging for gold. And now he's using conjur stuff! I'll be a suck-egg mule!"

Pluto wished to make a defense of some kind, but Will was laughing so much he was afraid to bring it up.

"That might help some, at that," Will continued. "And then again it mightn't. The old man ought to know, though; he's been fooling around that farm digging for gold nearly fifteen years now, and he ought to be an expert at it by this time. Reckon there's gold in that ground, sure enough, Pluto?"

"I'd hate to say," Pluto replied, "but I reckon there must be, because people have been picking up nuggets all over the country around there ever since I can remember. There's gold somewhere around there, because I've seen the nuggets."

"Every time I hear about Ty Ty digging those holes I sort of get the fever myself," Will said. "But just take me over there and put me out in that hot sun, and I lose all interest in it. I wouldn't mind striking gold there, and that's no lie. Looks like there isn't much use of waiting around here to make a living in the mill. That is, unless we do something about it."

Will had turned and was pointing out the window towards the darkened cotton mill. There was no light in the huge building, but arc lights under the trees threw a thin coating of yellow glow over the ivy-covered walls.

"When's the mill going to start up again?" Pluto asked.

"Never," Will said disgustedly. "Never. Unless we start it ourselves."

"What's the matter? Why won't it run?"

Will leaned forward in his chair.

"We're going in there some day ourselves and turn the power on," he said slowly. "If the company doesn't start up soon, that's what we're going to do. They cut the pay down to a dollar-ten eighteen months ago, and when we raised hell about it, they shut off the power and drove us out. But they still charge rent for these God damn privies we have to live in. You know why we're going to run it ourselves now, don't you?"

"But some of the other mills in the Valley are running," Pluto said. "We passed five or six lighted mills when we drove over from Augusta tonight. Maybe they'll start this one again soon."

"Like so much hell they will, at a dollar-ten. They are running the other mills because they starved the loomweavers into going back to work. That was before the Red Cross started passing out sacks of flour. They had to go back to work and take a dollar-ten, or starve. But, by God, we don't have to do it in Scottsville. As long as we can get a sack of flour once in a while we can hold out. And the State is giving out yeast now. Mix a cake of yeast in a glass of water and drink it, and you feel pretty good for a while. They started giving out yeast because everybody in the Valley has got pellagra these days from too much starving. The mill can't get us back until they shorten the hours, or cut out the stretchout, or go back to the old pay. I'll be damned if I work nine hours a day for a dollar-ten, when those rich sons-of-bitches who own the mill ride up and down the Valley in five thousand dollar automobiles."

Will had got warmed to the subject, and once started, he could not stop. He told Pluto something of their plans for taking over the mill from the owners and running it themselves. The mill workers in Scottsville had been out of work for a year and a half already, he said, and they were becoming desperate for food and clothing. During that length of time the workers had reached an understanding among themselves that bound every man, woman, and child in the company town to a stand not to give in to the mill. The mill had tried to evict them from their homes for nonpayment of rent, but the local had got an injunction from a judge in Aiken that restrained the mill from turning the workers out of the company houses. With that, Will said, they were prepared to stand for their demands just as long as the mill stood in Scottsville.

Rosamond came over to Will and placed her hand on his shoulder. She stood silently beside him until he finished. Pluto was glad she had come. He felt uneasy in Scottsville then; Will talked as though there might be violence at any minute.

"It's time to go to bed, Will," she said softly. "If we're going back with Darling Jill and Pluto in the morning, we ought to get some sleep. It's after midnight now."

Will put his arm around her and kissed her on the lips. She lay in his arms with her eyes closed, and her fingers were interlocked with his.

"All right," he said, raising her from his lap. "I reckon it is time."

She kissed him again and went to the door. She stood there a moment, partly turned, looking at Will.

"Come on to bed, Darling Jill," she said.

They went into the bedroom across the hall and closed the door. Pluto began taking off his tie and shirt. After he had removed them, he began to unlace his shoes. He was ready after that to lie down on the floor and go to sleep. Will brought him a pillow and a quilt and tossed them on the floor at his feet. After leaving Pluto, he went into the room across the hall and closed the door.

"Where am I going to sleep?" he asked, standing in the middle of the room and watching Darling Jill undress.

"In the other bed, Will," Rosamond said. "Now please go along, Will, and don't bother Darling Jill. She's going to sleep with me. Please don't try to start a row. It's awfully late. It's after midnight."

Without another word he opened the door and went into the adjoining room. He took off his clothes and got into bed. It was too hot to sleep in nightclothes, or even in underwear. He stetched out on the bed and closed his eyes. He still felt a little drunk, and his head was beginning to hurt behind his temples. If he had not felt so badly just then, he knew he would have got up and argued with Rosamond about sleeping in the other room.

When Darling Jill and Rosamond had undressed, Rosamond turned out the light and opened the doors of all the rooms so there would be better circulation of air. Will could hear her open the door of his room, but he was too tired and sleepy by that time to open his eyes and call her. It was nearly one o'clock before they all went to sleep, and the only sound in the house was Pluto's snoring on his pallet across the hall.

Towards morning Will woke up and went to the kitchen for a drink of water. It was cooler then, but still too hot to get under covers. He came back and looked at Pluto on the floor, watching him in the flickering street light that shone through the windows. In the other room he went to the bed and looked down at Rosamond and Darling Jill. He stood beside the bed for several minutes, wide awake, looking down at their white bodies in the dim glow of the street light on the corner. Will thought for a moment of waking Darling Jill, but he felt a little sick and his head was beginning to throb again, and he turned away and went back to his room and closed his eyes. He did not remember anything else until the sun woke him by shining in his face. It was nearly nine o'clock then, and there was not a sound in the house.

Chapter VI

WILL was lying on his side, looking out the window at the yellow company house next door, when he felt something warm against his back, something that felt like a purring kitten against his bare skin. He turned over, wide awake, partly raised on his elbow.

"Well, for God's sake!" he exclaimed.

Darling Jill sat up and began teasing him. She pulled his hair and ran her hand over his face rather hard, mashing his nose.

"You wouldn't get mad at me, would you, Will?"

"Mad?" he said. "I'm tickled to death."

"Tickle me some, Will," she said.

He reached for her, and she squirmed out of his reach. He thought he had such a grip around her that she could never get away. Will lunged after her, catching her arm and pulling her back beside him. Darling Jill cuddled up in his arms, kissing his chest, while he laughed at her.

"Where's Rosamond?" he asked, suddenly remembering her.

"She's gone downtown for a box of hairpins."

"How long has she been gone?"

"Only a minute or so."

Will raised his head and tried to see over the foot of the bed.

"Where's Pluto?"

"Sitting on the front porch."

"Hell," Will said, letting his head fall upon the pillow, "he's too lazy to get up."

She cuddled closer, putting her arms securely around him. Will pressed her breast tightly in his hand.

"Don't do that so hard, Will. You hurt me."

"I'm going to hurt you more than that before I get through with you."

"Kiss me a little first, Will. I like it."

He drew her closer and kissed her. Darling Jill threw her arms around Will and pulled herself to him. When she was closer, Will kissed her more desperately.

"Take me, Will," Darling Jill begged. "Please, Will, right now."

The woman in the yellow company house next door leaned out the window and shook a dust-mop, striking it several times against the side of the building to shake loose the sand and lint.

"Take me, Will—I can't wait," she cried.

"You and me both," said he.

Will got on his hands and knees and raised Darling Jill's head until he could draw her hair from under her. He lowered her pillow, and her long brown hair hung over the bed and almost touched the floor. He looked down and saw that she had raised herself until she was almost touching him.

He awoke to hear Darling Jill screaming in his ear. He did not know how long she had been screaming. He had been oblivious to everything in the complete joy of the moment.

He raised his head after a while and looked into her face. She opened her eyes wide and smiled at him.

"That was wonderful, Will," she whispered. "Do it to me again."

He tried to free himself and arise, but she would not let him move. He knew she was waiting for him to answer her.

"Will, do it to me again."

"Damn it, Darling Jill, I can't right now."

He struggled once more to free himself and arise. She held him determinedly.

"When we get back to Georgia?"

"If it's as good in Georgia as it is in Carolina, you're damn right, Darling Jill."

"It's better in Georgia," she smiled.

"Strike me down," he said.

"I said, it's better in Georgia, Will."

"It had better be. If it's not, I'm going to bring you back to Carolina right away."

"But I would still be a Georgia girl, even if you did bring me back over here."

"All right, you win," he said, "but if all the Georgia girls are as good as you are, I'm going to stay over there."

Darling Jill raised her arm and rubbed the teethmarks where he had bitten her. Will wished he could get up and lie on his back, but she still refused to release him. He lay quietly for a while, with his eyes closed, feeling good all over.

Suddenly, like a stroke of lightning out of a cloudless sky, something hit him an awful whack on the buttocks. Will let out a yell and turned completely over in the air, falling on his back with his eyes almost popping out. He knew a bolt of lightning could not have frightened him any more thoroughly.

Before he could say anything, his eyes fell upon Rosamond at the side of the bed. She had the hairbrush raised threateningly in one hand, and with the other she was trying with all her might to turn Darling Jill over on her stomach. She succeeded in getting her sister turned over, and she whacked five or six times in quick succession, striking before Darling Jill could squirm out of reach.

Will realized that there was no sense in his attempting to get up, so he lay still, watching the hairbrush in Rosamond's hands and praying that she would not turn him over on his stomach and blister him again.

Darling Jill first laughed, but she was so badly blistered, and the blisters hurt so much, she started to cry. Will put his hand under himself and felt the big welt that had been raised on his body. He rubbed it, trying to make the stinging feeling leave. Darling Jill's buttocks were as red as fire all over, and there were ridges of scarlet welts on her tender flesh. He looked again and saw that there were even welts on top of welts, rising like oblong blocks the size and shape of Rosamond's hairbrush.

Pluto stood behind Rosamond looking pityingly at Darling Jill's trembling bare body and at her quivering blistered buttocks.

"Jesus," Will said, touching the blister behind.

"Is that all you got to say for yourself?" Rosamond asked him. "I went down the street to the store and was gone for fifteen or twenty minutes. And this is what you were doing while I was away! What do you suppose Pluto would say if he could talk? Don't you know he hopes to marry her? It's almost breaking his heart to see this. Suppose you had gone downtown and had come back and found me in bed with Pluto—what would you do about it? Can't you say anything but 'Jesus'?"

Darling Jill suddenly burst out laughing. She looked at Rosamond a moment, and at Pluto. She laughed louder.

"Not with that belly, Rosamond," Darling Jill said. "How could he with that belly of his?"

Rosamond choked back a smile, but Pluto's face became crimson. He turned his head, backing against the wall and trying to press himself into it out of sight. Darling Jill put her hand on the blisters and began crying again.

"Now, wait a minute, Rosamond," Will said.

Rosamond looked down at Will, resting the hand that held the hairbrush on the foot of the bed.

"I have to beg you to sleep with me sometimes, but Darling Jill comes to the house just for one night and you take her. She's no better-looking than I am, Will."

He could think of nothing to say. He could not think of a single word to utter in reply. She continued looking down at him, however; he knew he had to say something before she would move.

"Just once was all right, wasn't it, Rosamond?"

"Once! That's all you ever say. Every time I ask you why you did it, you say you only did it once. You've had every girl in town, once. It might just as well be a hundred times. Don't you ever stop to think how it makes me feel—you out somewhere with a girl you have no business being with, and here I am sitting at home wondering where you are and what you're doing?"

Will turned his head just enough to see Darling Jill out of the corners of his eyes.

"Maybe it's because she's a Georgia girl, Rosamond. I reckon that's why."

"That's no excuse—you can't even make one up. I'm a Georgia girl myself—at least I used to be before I married you and came over here to Carolina."

Will looked at Pluto, but Pluto apparently had no suggestion worth the offer. He stared back blankly at Will.

"Rosamond, honey," he said meekly, "I felt of her and kissed her some and then the first thing I knew about it was that I just had to do it. I didn't mean any harm. That's just how it was."

"If I had a baseball bat, I'd do a thing or two to you," Rosamond replied.

Will began to have a little more confidence in his ability to argue with Rosamond. He was not afraid of Rosamond any longer, and he knew he could take the hairbrush away from her if she tried to blister him again.

"Now, listen here, Rosamond," he said. "A girl like Darling Jill can't come around without someone getting her. She was made that way from the start."

Rosamond made as if to take the hairbrush and blister them both all over again, but she turned instead and ran to the dresser near the corner where Pluto was. She jerked open the top drawer and pulled out the little pearl-handled thirty-two she kept there. She ran back to the bed, holding it out in front of her.

"For God's sake, Rosamond!" Will shouted. "Rosamond, honey, don't do that!"

Darling Jill looked up from the pillow just in time to see the hammer go back and to hear it cock. Will sat up in bed, hugging the pillow in front of him.

"If I blister you, you won't stay blistered, but if I shoot you, you'll stay shot, Will Thompson."

"Honey," he begged, "if you'll put that down, I'll never do it again. I swear to God I won't, honey. If a girl tries to make me, I'll throw her in Horse Creek. I swear to God I'll never do it again as long as I live, Rosamond, honey."

Rosamond pulled the trigger and the room was full of white smoke. She had shot at Will's feet, but she had missed. Will jumped at Rosamond, with one hand out after the little revolver. Rosamond shot it again. The bullet went between his legs, and he was scared to death. He looked down to see if he had been shot, but he was afraid to take the time to look closely. He ran to the window and jumped out, landing on his hands and chest. He was up and out of sight around the corner of the house a second after he had struck the ground.

The woman in the yellow company house next door ran to the window and stuck out her head. She saw Will running naked across the front yard and down the street as fast as his heels would fly. After he had passed from sight, she turned and looked at Rosamond at the window with the little pearl-handled revolver shaking in her hand.

"Is that Will Thompson?" the woman asked.

Rosamond leaned out the window, looking up the street and down it.

"Where did he go?" Rosamond asked her.

"Down the street yonder," the woman said, unable to keep from laughing any longer. "It's something new for Will Thompson to get shot out of his own house, ain't it? I'll have to tell Charlie about Will when he comes home. He'll die laughing when he hears about it. And Will Thompson was as naked as a jay-bird, too. Ain't that something, though?"

Rosamond went back and put the revolver into the dresser drawer and shut it. Then she sat down in a chair and cried.

Pluto did not know what to do. He did not know whether to go after Will and try to bring him back home, or whether to stay in the room and try to quiet Rosamond and Darling Jill. Darling Jill had quieted down some, and she was not crying so loudly then. But Rosamond was. Pluto leaned over and put his hand on her arm and patted it. Rosamond threw his hand off and cried even more hysterically. Pluto decided then that the best thing for him to do was to do nothing for a while. He sat down again and waited.

Presently Rosamond got up and ran to the bed where her sister was. She threw herself upon the bed, hugging Darling Jill in her arms and bursting into tears once more. They both lay there consoling one another. Pluto looked on uneasily. He had expected to see them fly at each other, pulling hair, scratching, and calling each other names. But they were doing nothing of the sort. They were actually hugging one another and weeping together. Pluto could not understand why Rosamond did not try to shoot Darling Jill, or at least why she was not angry with her. To look at them at that moment, Pluto could not imagine how Rosamond had acted as she had a few minutes before. They were behaving as though suffering a common bereavement.

When Rosamond's sobs had almost ceased, she sat up and looked down at her sister. The red welts on Darling Jill's buttocks still throbbed with intense pain, and she could not lie upon them. Rosamond touched one of the welts tenderly with the tips of her fingers as though she might be able to soothe the hurt a little thereby.

"Lie where you are until I come back," Rosamond told her. "I'll only be gone a moment."

She ran to the kitchen and came back with a cup of lard and a large bath towel. She sat down on the side of the bed and dipped her fingers into the grease.

"Come here, Pluto," she said, not turning around to look at him. "You can help me."

Pluto came over to the bed, blushing to the tips of his ears at the sight of Darling Jill lying naked before him.

"Lift her gently, Pluto, and hold her across your lap," Rosamond instructed. "Now be careful. Don't irritate those welts, whatever you do."

Pluto put his arms under Darling Jill, laying the palms of his hands flat against her breasts and thighs. He jerked his hands from under her, his face and neck burning.

"Now, what's the matter?"

"Maybe you had better lift her."

"Don't be silly, Pluto. How can I? I'm not strong."

He put his hands under her again, closing his eyes and compressing his lips.

"Hurry, Pluto, and let me put this lard on those swollen places before they turn blue."

Pluto lifted her and turned around. He sat down on the side of the bed next to Rosamond with Darling Jill lying across his knees. Rosamond began applying the lard at once. Pluto would have watched her, but he could not take his eyes from Darling Jill's long brown hair hanging to the floor. He raised her a little so her hair would not touch it. She winced once or twice when Rosamond touched her, but she did not protest or try to get up. When the lard had been carefully spread, Rosamond wiped her fingers on a piece of cloth and began folding the towel until it was a long thick bandage. Pluto looked down at Darling Jill's soft buttocks with a sudden desire to touch them and try to soothe the pain. Each time he looked down at her in his lap, though, he began to blush all over again.

"Help her to her feet, Pluto," Rosamond said. "Lift her up and let her stand on her feet, Pluto."

Darling Jill stood up in front of Pluto and her sister while the towel was being fastened securely around her. Pluto's gaze was fixed on a point of her body that happened to be the closest. He looked straight ahead, moving his eyes neither to the right nor to the left. He knew Darling Jill was looking down at him, but he could not bring himself to raise his head and look up into her face.

He was not at all certain, but he believed she had leaned forward towards him.

"Like me, Pluto?" Darling Jill asked, smiling.

Pluto's face trembled, his neck stung with a sudden rush of blood, and he tried to look up and meet her eyes. It was an exertion for him to move his head upward and backward, but he forced himself to move it.

"I'm going to be angry if you won't say you like me now," she pouted.

"I'm crazy about you, Darling Jill," he said, partly choked. "And that's a fact."

"Why do you turn red in the face and neck when you see me like this, Pluto?"

He felt fresh blood rush in to embarrass him. He pulled at a loose thread in the counterpane without knowing what he was doing.

"I like it, though," he replied.

"Marry me, Pluto?"

"Right now, or anytime you say," he told her. "And that's a fact."

"But your belly is too big, Pluto."

"Aw, now, Darling Jill, don't let that stand in the way."

"If it wasn't so big, Pluto, you could stand closer."

"Aw, now, Darling Jill."

"And that's a fact," she said, mocking him.

"Aw, now, Darling Jill," he said, reaching out to put his arms around her waist.

She allowed him to draw her close enough to be kissed. Pluto drew her between his legs and stretched his head as high as he could but her lips were so far above his reach he knew he could never kiss her unless he stood up beside her or unless she bent down to him. He reasoned that it would be much easier for her to bend over than it would be for him to get to his feet, and he knew she was aware of it. But she remained standing erectly in his arms, tantalizing him by refusing to bend over and place her lips on his. When he did not know what to do, unless it was to get to his feet beside her, Darling Jill leaned against him and twisted her body a little. Before he realized how it had come about, he felt her warm breast against his face and he was kissing her madly.

"Stop it this instant, Darling Jill!" Rosamond said, getting up and pulling them apart. "Stop teasing Pluto like that. It's a shame to treat the poor boy the way you do all the time. Some of these days he's going to turn on you, and anything may happen."

Darling Jill, jerking herself out of his embrace, ran to the door and into the next room holding the towel around her buttocks. Pluto sat in a daze, his hands lifeless beside him, and his mouth hanging agape. Rosamond, turning, saw him; she felt so sorry for him that she came back and patted his cheek tenderly.

Chapter VII

AT NOON the whistles of the cotton mills up and down the Valley blew for the midday shutdown. Everywhere else there was a sudden cessation of vibration, and the men and women came out of the buildings taking cotton from their ears. In the company town of Scottsville the people did not move from the chairs on their porches. It was noon, and it was dinner-time; but in Scottsville the people sat with contracted bellies and waited for the end of the strike.

The woman in the yellow company house next door made a fire in the cook-stove and put on a pan of water to boil. Such as there was to eat, she and her husband and the children would devour without breaking the tightly drawn lines at the corners of their mouths. Each successive day was a victory; for eighteen months they had stood out against the mill, and they would never give in while there was hope.

Rosamond suggested making a freezer of ice cream. "Will would like some when he comes back," she said.

Pluto was sent down the street for a cake of ice. He went to the store at the corner, hurrying down and back as fast as he could walk, while Rosamond was scalding the freezer and paring the peaches. He was frightened every second he was in the Valley. He was afraid somebody would jump at him from behind a tree and slash his throat from ear to ear, and even in the house he was afraid to sit with his back to a door or window.

Darling Jill came out on the back porch while Rosamond was preparing the cream and sat down on a pillow in the shade. She had combed her hair but had not pinned it up. It hung down her back, covering her shoulders, and reached almost to the floor. Rosamond had lent her a dressing gown, and she wore that over the towel and the black silk stockings supported by canary yellow garters.

When Pluto returned with the cake of ice, the cream was ready to be frozen. He saw that it was up to him to turn the freezer.

It was cool on the shaded back porch, now that the sun was passing over the house. There was a breeze that blew occasionally, and the ninety-degree temperature at midday was bearable. Broad, green, cool Horse Creek looked like an oblong lake down below, stretching for miles up and down the Valley.

"I've got to be getting home," Pluto said. "And that's a fact."

"The voters won't miss you," Darling Jill told him. "They'll be glad you're not there today to worry them. Anyway, we're not ready to go back yet."

"I missed yesterday, and the day before, and two or three days before that. And now I'm missing today, too."

"When we get back, I'll campaign some for you, Pluto," Darling Jill said. "I'll get more votes than you will know what to do with."

"I wish I was back now, anyway," he said. "And that's a fact."

He turned the freezer faster, hoping to finish it in time to start back within the hour.

"I wish Will would come back," Rosamond said. "Do you suppose he'll stay away this time—and never come home?"

Darling Jill sighed and looked into the kitchen window of the yellow company house next door. The people over there were eating sandwiches and drinking iced tea. It made Darling Jill a little hungry to watch them eat.

Rosamond thought the cream was getting stiff. Pluto was having difficulty in turning the freezer at the pace he had started, and the perspiration rolled from his face and his mouth hung open with exhaustion. He held the freezer with one hand and turned doggedly with the other.

No one happened to be looking in that direction when Will stuck his head around the corner of the house and watched them for several minutes. When he saw that Pluto was freezing ice cream, he stepped around the corner and walked slowly along the path to the steps.

"Why, there's Will now," Darling Jill said, seeing him first.

Will stopped in his tracks and looked at Rosamond.

"Will!" she cried.

She jumped up and ran down the steps to meet him, throwing her arms around his neck and kissing him frantically.

"Will, are you all right?"

He patted her shoulder and kissed her. He was wearing only a pair of khaki pants he had borrowed somewhere, and he was barefooted and shirtless.

Rosamond drew him up the steps and made him sit down in her chair. Pluto stopped turning the crank to look at him. He had not expected to see Will again for a long time.

"The cream is stiff by this time, Pluto," Rosamond said. "Take off the top while we're getting the dishes and spoons. And be careful of the salt. Take out some of the ice before you forget it."

She was gone only a moment. Darling Jill took the large spoon and filled the dishes and passed them around. Rosamond remained with Will, refusing to leave him again. He took a bite of the peach cream and smiled at her.

"Did you hear anything about the mill opening?" she asked him.

"No," he replied.

The women in the yellow company houses asked that every day, but the men always said they had heard nothing.

"The other mills are still running, aren't they?"

"I reckon so," he said.

"When will ours start up?"

"I don't know."

The thought of the other mills operating regularly stiffened Will. He sat up erectly and stared down at the broad green water. Horse Creek lay down there as calm as a smooth lake. The thought of the other mills in the Valley running night and day started a vivid picture that began to unroll across his eyes. He could see the ivy-walled cotton mill beside the green water. It was early morning, and the whistle blew, calling eager girls to work. They were never men, the people who entered the mill now; the mill wished to employ girls, because girls never rebelled against the harder work, the stretching-out, the longer hours, or the cutting of pay. Will could see the girls running to the mill in the early morning while the men stood in the streets looking, but helpless.

All day long there was a quiet stillness about the ivy-walled mill. The machinery did not hum so loudly when the girls operated it. The men made the mill hum with noise when they worked there. But when evening came, the doors were flung open and the girls ran out screaming in laughter. When they reached the street, they ran back to the ivy-covered walls and pressed their bodies against it and touched it with their lips. The men who had been standing idly before it all day long came and dragged them home and beat them unmercifully for their infidelity.

Will woke up with a start to see Pluto and Rosamond and Darling Jill. He had been away, and when he returned, he was surprised to see them there. He rubbed his eyes and wondered if he had been asleep. He knew he had not been, though, because his dish was empty. It lay in his hands heavy and hard.

"Christ," he murmured.

He remembered the time when the mill down below was running night and day. The men who worked in the mill looked tired and worn, but the girls were in love with the looms and the spindles and the flying lint. The wild-eyed girls on the inside of the ivy-walled mill looked like potted plants in bloom.

Up and down the Valley lay the company towns and the ivy-walled cotton mills and the firm-bodied girls with eyes like morning-glories and the men stood on the hot streets looking at each other while they spat their lungs into the deep yellow dust of Carolina. He knew he could never get away from the blue-lighted mills at night and the bloody-lipped men on the streets and the unrest of the company towns. Nothing could drag him away from there now. He might go away and stay a while, but he would be restless and unhappy until he could return. He had to stay there and help his friends find some means of living. The mill streets could not exist without him; he had to stay there and walk on them and watch the sun set on the mill at night and rise on it in the morning. In the mill streets of the Valley towns the breasts of girls were firm and erect. The cloth they wove under the blue lights clothed their bodies, but beneath the covering the motions of erect breasts were like the quick movements of hands in unrest. In the Valley towns beauty was begging, and the hunger of strong men was like the whimpering of beaten women.

"Jesus Christ," he murmured under his breath.

He looked up to find Darling Jill filling his empty dish with peach-flecked ice cream. Before she could turn and go away, Will grabbed her arm and pulled her to him. He kissed her cheek several times, squeezing her hand tightly.

"For God's sake don't ever come over here and work in a mill," he begged. "You wouldn't do that, would you, Darling Jill?"

She started to laugh, but when she saw his face, she became anxious.

"What's the matter, Will? Are you sick?"

"Oh, nothing is the matter," he said, "but for God's sake don't ever go to work in a cotton mill."

Rosamond laid her hand on his and urged him to eat the cream before it melted.

He closed his eyes and saw the yellow company houses stretched endlessly through Scottsville. In the rear of the houses he saw tight-lipped women sitting at kitchen windows with their backs to the cold cookstoves. In the streets in front of the houses he saw the bloody-lipped men spitting their lungs into the yellow dust. As far as he could see, there were rows of ivy-walled mills beside broad, cool Horse Creek, and in them the girls sang, drowning out the sound of moving machinery. The spinning mills and the fabric mills and the bleacheries were endless, and the eager girls with erect breasts and eyes like morning-glories ran in and out endlessly.

"Pluto is going to take us over to Georgia," Rosamond said softly. "You'll have a good rest over there at home, Will. You'll feel lots better when we come back."

He was glad then that they were going to Ty Ty's for a while, but he hated to go away and leave the others there to sit and wait and stand out against the mill. When he got back, he would feel much better, though; perhaps they could then break open the steel-barred doors of the mill and turn on the power. He would like to come back to the Valley and stand in the mill and hear the hum of machinery, even if there was to be no cloth woven any time soon.

"All right," he said. "When do we start, Pluto?"

"I'm ready now," Pluto said. "I'd like to get back in time to count some votes before supper."

Rosamond and Darling Jill went into the house to dress. Will and Pluto sat looking down at the green water below. It looked cool, and it did make the breeze feel cooler after passing over it. But the temperature was even under the cloudless sky. The grass and weeds wilted in the sun, and the dust that blew down from the cultivated uplands settled on the ground and on the buildings like powdered paint.

Will went inside to take off the khaki pants and put on his own clothes.

They were ready to start and had locked the house when Will saw someone coming up the street.

"Where you going, Will?" the man asked, stopping and looking at them and at Pluto's car.

"Just over to Georgia for a day or two, Harry."

Will felt like a traitor, running off like that. He waited for Rosamond to go down the walk first.

"Are you sure you're not leaving for good, Will?" the man asked suspiciously.

"I'll be back in town in a few days, Harry. And when I get back, you'll know it."

"All right, but don't forget to come back. If everybody leaves, pretty soon the company is going to rush a crew of operators in here and start up without us. We've all got to stay here and hold out. If the mill ever once got started without us, we wouldn't have a chance in the world. You know that, Will."

Will went down the walk and got in front of Rosamond. He walked down the street with the other man, talking to him in a low voice. They stopped several yards away and began arguing. Will would talk a little while, tapping the other man on the chest with his forefinger; the other man would nod his head and glance down at the ivy-walled mill below. They turned and walked a little further, both talking at the same time. When they stopped again, the other man began talking to Will, tapping him on the chest with his forefinger. Will nodded his head, shook it violently, nodded again.

"We can't let anybody go in there and wreck the machinery," Will said. "Nobody wants to see that done."

"That's just what I've been trying to tell you, Will. What we want to do is to go in there and turn the power on. When the company comes and sees what's happening, they'll either try to drive us out, or else get down to business."

"Now listen, Harry," Will said, "when that power is turned on, nobody on God's earth is going to shut it off. It's going to stay turned on. If they try to turn it off, then we'll—well, God damn it, Harry, the power is going to stay turned on."

"I've always been in favor of turning it on and never shutting it off. That's what I've tried to tell the local, but what can you tell that son-of-a-bitch A.F.L.? Nothing! They're drawing pay to keep us from working. When we start to work, the money will stop coming in here to pay them. Well, God damn it, Will, we're nothing but suckers to listen to them talk about arbitration. Let the mill run three shifts, maybe four shifts, when we turn the power on, but keep it running all the time. We can turn out as much print cloth as the company can, maybe a lot more. But all of us will be working then, anyway. We can speed up after everybody gets back on the job. What we're after now is turning on the power. And if they try to shut off the power, then we'll get in there and—well, God damn it, Will, the power ain't going to be shut off once we turn it on. Now, God damn it, Will, I've never been in favor of wrecking anything. You know that, and so does everybody else. That son-of-a-bitch A.F.L. started that talk when they heard we were thinking about turning the power on. All I'm after is running the mill."

"That's what I've been saying at every local meeting since the shut-down," Will said. "The local is all hopped-up with the A.F.L. They've been saying nothing is going to get us our jobs back except by arbitrating. I've never been in favor of that. You can't talk to the company and get nothing but a one-sided answer. They're not going to say a thing but 'a dollar-ten.' You know that as well as I do. And how in the hell can a man pay rent on these stinking privies we live in out of a dollar-ten? You tell me how it can be done, and I'll be the first to vote for arbitrating. No, sir. It just can't be done."

"Well, I'm in favor of going in there and turning on the power. That's what I've been saying all the time. I've never said anything else, and I never will."

Rosamond came part of the way and called Will. He turned away from the other man and asked what she wanted. He had forgotten all about the trip to Georgia.

"Come on, Will," she said. "Pluto is all up in the air about waiting so long to start. He's running for sheriff back home, and he's got to canvass for votes. You and Harry can finish that argument when we come back in a day or two."

He and Harry talked for several moments, and Will turned and followed Rosamond to the car. Darling Jill was in the driver's seat, with Pluto beside her. Will sat down on the back seat with Rosamond. The motor had been idling for five minutes or longer while they waited.

Will leaned out of the car to wave to Harry.

"Try to get that meeting called for Friday night," he shouted. "By God, we'll show the A.F.L. and the company what we mean by turning the power on."

Darling Jill raced down the unpaved street and turned the corner recklessly. They were off in a cloud of dust that blew up and sifted thickly through the hot air to settle on the trees and front porches of the yellow company houses.

They sped along the hot concrete toward Augusta, passing an almost endless cluster of company houses. They passed through the other company towns, slowing down in the restricted zones and looking out at the humming mills. They could see the men and girls through the open windows and they could almost hear the hum of the moving machinery behind the ivy-covered walls. Along the streets there were few people to be seen. There were not nearly so many as there were on the streets of Scottsville.

"Hurry up and let's get to Augusta," Will said. "I want to get out of the Valley as soon as this car can take me out. I'm damn tired of looking at spinning mills and company houses every minute of the day and night."

He knew he was not tired of looking at them, or of living with them; it was the sight of so many open mills that irritated him.

Graniteville, Warrenville, Langley, Bath, and Clearwater were left behind, and out of the Valley they raced over the hot concrete at seventy miles an hour. When they got to the top of Schultz Hill, they could look down over the dead city of Hamburg and see the muddy Savannah and, on the Georgia side, the wide flood plain on which Augusta was built. Up above it was the Hill, clustered with skyscraping resort hotels and three-story white residences.

While coasting down the long hill toward the Fifth Street Bridge, Rosamond said something about Jim Leslie.

"He lives in one of those fine houses on The Hill," Will said. "Why doesn't the son-of-a-bitch ever come to see us?"

"Jim Leslie would come, if it wasn't for his wife," Rosamond said. "Gussie thinks she's too good to speak to us. She makes Jim Leslie call us lint-heads."

"I'd rather be a God-forsaken lint-head and live in a yellow company house than be what she and Jim Leslie are. I've seen him on Broad Street and when I spoke to him, he'd turn around and run off so people wouldn't see him talking to me."

"Jim Leslie didn't use to be that way," Rosamond said. "When he was a boy at home, he was just like all the rest of us. He married a society girl on The Hill, though, when he made a lot of money, and now he won't have anything to do with us. He was a little different from the rest of us at the start, though. There was something about him—I don't know what it was."

"Jim Leslie is a cotton broker," Will said. "He got rich gambling on cotton futures. He didn't make the money he's got—he crooked it. You know what a cotton broker is, don't you? Do you know why they're called brokers?"

"Why?"

"Because they keep the farmers broke all the time. They lend a little money, and then they take the whole damn crop. Or else they suck the blood out of a man by running the price up and down forcing him to sell. That's why they call them cotton brokers. And that's what Jim Leslie Walden is. If he was my brother, I'd treat him just like I would treat a scab in Scottsville."

Chapter VIII

IT WAS not quite dark, but the stars were beginning to come out, and lights in the houses beside the road blinked in the late twilight. When they were half a mile from home, they could see moving lights that looked as if lanterns were being carried by moving men.

There was a stir and a hum about the place that showed that something was going on. Darling Jill speeded up the car to find out what it was. She slowed down at the turn, burning the brake bands until the odor of rubber enveloped them in the dust.

Ty Ty came running around the house holding out a smoking lantern in front of him. His face was red with the day's heat, and his clothes were caked with dried clay that clung to the cloth like beggar-lice. They all jumped out to meet him.

"What's the matter, Pa?" Rosamond asked him excitedly.

"Great guns," he said, "we're digging like all get-out. We've sunk a hole twenty feet since this morning, and I don't mean maybe, either. We've been doing the fastest digging in ten years."

He pulled at them, urging them to follow him. He broke into a run, leading them across the yard and around the corner of the house. Stopping abruptly, they found themselves balanced on the rim of a lantern-lit crater at the side of the house. Down on the floor of it, Shaw and Buck and Black Sam were digging into the clay. On the other side of the crater, opposite them, was Uncle Felix with another smoking lantern and a shotgun. There was another man beside him, looking like a ghost in the flickering light.

"Who's that over there?" Will asked.

Ty Ty shouted down at Buck and Shaw. Griselda came suddenly into view, emerging from somewhere in the darkness.

"Boys," Ty Ty shouted, "we've been working since early this morning, and I reckon we'd better stop and rest some. Will's here now, and we'll all start in again tomorrow morning bright and early. Come on up and see the folks."

Buck threw down his shovel, but Shaw kept on picking away at the hard clay. Buck began arguing with him, trying to get him to stop for the night and rest. Black Sam was already climbing out of the hole.

Griselda and Darling Jill went into the house and lit the lamps.

"I'm hungry as all get-out, girls," Ty Ty said.

Uncle Felix picked up the smoking lantern at his feet, poking the other man with the end of the shotgun. He urged the strange man around the house towards the barn.

"Who's that?" Pluto asked. "Is he a voter?"

"That? Why, that's the all-white man you put me on the track of, Pluto. Great guns, Pluto, that's that albino we roped in the swamps."

They walked around the house behind the man and Uncle Felix. The colored man was urging him forward, talking to him while he poked with the end of the gun.

"I didn't tell you no lie about him, did I?" Pluto asked. "I said he was down there in the swamp, didn't I, Ty Ty?"

"You didn't tell no lie about him being there, but you sure overestimated the trouble he might cause. Why, that all-white man was no more trouble to bring home than a dead rabbit. He came along just as peaceful, Pluto. But I ain't taking no chances with him. He might be playing possum. That's why I keep Uncle Felix guard over him day and night."

"Did he divine for you, Ty Ty?"

"Just like four and four make eight," Ty Ty said. "When we got him here and told him what he was to do, why the first thing he did was to point out that spot where the new hole is now. He said that was the place to dig for the lode. And that's where it is."

"How do you know it is? Did you find any nuggets?"

"Well, not exactly. But we're getting warmer every minute."

"Can he talk?" Will asked.

"Talk? Well, I reckon he can, and then some. Why, that all-white man will talk your arm off if you give him half a showing. He can argue like nobody's business. My jaws are so tired now that they're almost locked down from talking with him. I ain't scared of him no

longer, either. He's just like me and you and everybody else, Will,
only he's all-white, including his hair and eyes. True, his eyes are a
little pinkish, but even that passes for white when the light ain't so
good."

"Did you mention to him that I am running for sheriff?" Pluto
asked.

"Now, Pluto," Ty Ty said, "I ain't got no time letting him off to cast
a vote. He's going to stay right where he is, day and night. We're going
to dig gold out of that hole, even if we have to go clear down to China
to raise it. But we're getting warm now. It ain't going to be long before
we strike that lode and start shoveling out those yellow guinea eggs."

Ty Ty stopped at the barn gate.

"I'm awfully hungry now," he said. "Let's go back to the house and
hurry up the girls cooking something to eat, and after supper we can
bring him up to the house and let everybody take a good look and see
what an albino looks like at close range."

Ty Ty turned and started back to the house. Will and Pluto followed
behind. They had wished to see the man in the barn right away, but
neither of them was anxious to go there unless Ty Ty was with them.

"You ought not to have let him set you digging right beside the
house," Will said. "That was the wrong thing to do, it looks like to
me. The house might tumble right down into the hole."

"I've seen to that," Ty Ty said. "Me and the boys and Black Sam
brace it up as we go along. We've got it propped so it can't fall in the
hole. It don't matter so much if it does, though; when we strike the
lode, we'll be rich enough to build any number of fine houses, lots
finer than that one is."

"I don't know so much about that part," Pluto said, "but it looks
like you're digging on God's little acre."

"Well, that won't worry you long," Ty Ty said. "I shifted God's
little acre clear over to the back side of the farm this morning. There
ain't no danger in us striking the lode on it for a while to come. God's
little acre is as safe over there as it would be down in Florida."

Ty Ty and Will went into the house, but Pluto sat down on the
porch where it was cooler.

Griselda and Rosamond were cooking supper, and Darling Jill was
setting the table. Black Sam had brought in an armful of fat pine knots,
and the cookstove was red hot on top. Everybody was hungry, but
it would not take long to boil the grits and bake the sweet potatoes
with the heat Black Sam had provided. Griselda had sliced half a ham
and it was frying on two griddles.

Everyone forgot about Pluto. Just as Will and Ty Ty were getting
up from the table, Darling Jill remembered that he had not had supper,
and she ran to find him. She brought him into the dining-room pro-

testing that he did not have time to stay. He kept on saying that he had to get out on the road and canvass the voters before bed-time that night.

"Now, Pluto," Ty Ty said, "you just sit and eat. When you finish, we're going to bring that all-white man up here from the barn and let everybody get a good look at him in the light. He has to come to eat just like the rest of us, and he can eat here just as well as he can in the barn. That'll give Uncle Felix a breathing spell, because he's been guarding him ever since we brought him back last night."

Buck and Shaw got ready to drive to Marion for some new shovels. Since beginning anew, they had broken one shovel handle, and one blade had bent. Ty Ty wished to get a new shovel for Will, and he himself thought he could dig better with a new one. Buck and Shaw washed and changed their clothes and got ready to leave.

Ty Ty took Will and Pluto into the living-room while the girls were clearing the table and stacking the dishes in the kitchen for Black Sam to wash. He was eager to tell them how the albino had been captured.

"Buck saw him first," Ty Ty began. "He's right proud of it, and I don't blame him none, either. We were down in that swamp below Marion waiting for the first sight of him when Buck said he thought he'd go up to a house just off the road and inquire about an all-white man. We drove up there in the car and stopped in the yard, and Buck got out and rapped on the porch. I was looking the other way at the time, thinking maybe I might see some sign of the albino in the distance, and I don't know what Shaw was doing. But Shaw wasn't looking the same way Buck was, because before I knew it I heard Buck yell, 'Here he is!'"

"Was he in the house, there?" Pluto asked.

"Was he?" Ty Ty said. "Well, I reckon he was. When I turned around, there he was, big as life, standing in the door looking like a man who's just been ducked in a flour barrel. He was wearing overalls and a blue work shirt, but he was white everywhere else I could see."

"Did he run?"

"Run nothing! He came out on the porch and asked Buck what we was after. Buck grabbed him around the legs, and Shaw and me jumped out on the ground with the plow-lines. We had him tied up in no time, just like you rope a calf to take to market. He yelled some, and kicked a great deal, but that didn't cut no ice with the boys and me. Then pretty soon a woman came to the door to see what all the fuss was about. She was like all women, and I mean by that, she wasn't all-white like the albino was. She said to me, 'What on earth are you folks doing?' And she said to the albino, 'What's the matter, Dave?' He didn't say anything for a while, and that's how we came to know what his name was. It's Dave. Directly he said, 'These sons-of-bitches have got me all roped up.' Then she started yelling and ran through the house and out the back door into the swamp, and that's the last I saw or heard of her. She was his wife, I reckon, but I can't see what an albino has got business of marrying for. It's a good thing we brought him away. I hate to see a white woman taking up with a coal-black darky, and this was just about as bad, because he is an all-white man."

"Now that you've got him, what can he do?" Will said.

"Do? Why, locate the lode for us, Will."

"That's not scientific, like you've always talked about being," Will said. "Now, tell the honest-to-God truth. Is it?"

"I reckon it is, if I know what I'm doing. Some folks say a well-diviner ain't a scientific man, but I maintain he is. And I stick up the same way for a gold-diviner."

"There's nothing scientific about breaking off a willow branch and walking over the ground with it looking for a stream of water underground. It's hit or miss. I've heard them say, 'Dig here,' and when the shaft had been sunk a couple of hundred feet, there wasn't a drop of water on the drill. You might just as well roll high-dice for water as to walk over the ground with a willow branch. Sure, a willow branch will dip sometimes, and other times it will rise up, too. If I was going to sink a well, I wouldn't try to divine water with a piece of willow limb. I'd roll high-dice for it before I'd make a fool out of myself doing that."

"You just haven't got a scientific mind, Will," Ty Ty said sadly. "That's the whole trouble with your talk. Now, take me. I'm scientific clear through to the marrow, and I've always been, and I reckon I'll be to the end. I don't laugh and poke fun at scientific notions like you do."

After the hearty supper of grits and sweet potatoes, hot biscuits and fried ham, both Ty Ty and Will were feeling good. Pluto had eaten as much, if not more than anyone in the house, but he was restless. He knew he ought to leave and go home so he could get up at break of day the next morning and make an early start campaigning. He was beginning to worry about the outcome of the election. If he were not elected sheriff, he did not know what he was going to do. He did not have a job, and the colored share-cropper who worked his sixty-acre farm could not make enough cotton to provide him with a living. He might be able to peddle something, if he could find some novelty that people would buy. He had been selling first one thing and then another for eight or ten years, but he had never been able to make much more than expense money for his car out of it. For one thing, he was never able to get around much. When he remained in town, he liked to sit in the big chair in the pool room and call shots, and to talk about politics. He knew he should not spend so much of his time in the pool room, but he just could not get out in the hot sun day after day trying to sell laundry bluing or furniture polish that people did not wish to buy, or if they did, not have enough money to pay for. But if he were elected sheriff, that would be another matter. He would draw a good salary, with fees in addition, and the deputies could go out and serve all the papers and make all the arrests. He could sit in the pool room most of the time and call shots across the table.

"I reckon I'd better be going home, now," he said.

He made no effort to rise from the chair, and no one paid any attention to him.

Darling Jill came in with Griselda and Rosamond and patted Pluto's bald head. She would not come in front of him where he could put his hands on her, and he was forced to submit to her play while he hoped she would soon consent to sit on his lap.

"When are you going to bring that albino up here so we can see him?" Will asked.

"Stay calm and hold your horses a little longer," Ty Ty told him. "Black Sam has got to finish washing the dishes first, and then I'll send him down to the barn for him. Uncle Felix can eat his supper while everybody is looking at the all-white man in here."

"I'm just crazy to see him," Darling Jill said, playing with Pluto's head.

"I've got to be going home," Pluto said. "And that's a fact."

Pluto's statement was completely ignored.

"I'd like to see him, too," Rosamond said, looking at Griselda. "What does he look like?"

"He's big and strong. And good-looking, too."

"Aw, hell," Will said, making a face, "ain't that just like a woman?"

"I don't aim to have no fooling around with him," Ty Ty told them. "You girls can just walk off and call crows, if that's what you've got on your minds. He's got to keep on the job for me all the time."

Darling Jill sat down on Pluto's lap. He was surprised, and pleased. He beamed with pleasure when she put her arms around his neck and kissed him.

"Why don't you and Pluto get married?" Ty Ty asked.

"I'm willing, day or night," Pluto said eagerly.

"I declare, it sure would be a big load off my mind if you would."

"I'm willing, day or night," Pluto repeated. "And that's a fact."

"You're willing for what?" Darling Jill asked.

"To get married anytime you say so."

"To me? Marry me?"

"You bet your boots," he said, jerking his head at her. "I'm crazy about you, Darling Jill, and I can't keep on waiting for it to happen. I want to get married right away."

"When you swallow that belly, I might think about it." She began pounding it with her fists, hitting him without mercy. "But I wouldn't marry you now, you horse's ass."

Not even Pluto spoke after that. There was not a word spoken for nearly a minute. Then Griselda got up and tried to make Darling Jill leave Pluto alone.

"Hush, Darling Jill," Griselda said; "don't talk like that. It isn't nice."

"Well, he is an old horse's ass, isn't he? What would you call him? A doll-baby? He looks like a horse's ass to me."

Ty Ty got up and went out of the room. Everyone supposed he was going down to the barn and bring back the albino. The others in the room sat still and tried not to look at Pluto. Pluto sat glumly alone, hurt by Darling Jill's treatment of him, but all the more eager to marry her.

Chapter IX

There was a stamping of heavy-shod feet on the front porch. Ty Ty's voice could be heard above the sound, however; he was telling Uncle Felix to take Dave into the house and show him off.

"Just shove him in," Ty Ty said. "The folks in there are waiting to get a look at him."

The albino was the first to appear in the door; Uncle Felix was behind him, shotgun leveled against his back, and looking scared to death. He was glad to be relieved of his responsibility, if only temporarily, when Ty Ty told him to go to the kitchen and eat his supper.

"Well, folks, here he is," Ty Ty said proudly. He laid the shotgun across the chair seat and led Dave into the room. "Take a seat and make yourself at home."

"What's your name, fellow," Will asked him, partly dazzled by the whiteness of his skin and hair.

"Dave."

"Dave how-many?"

"Dave Dawson."

"Can you divine a lode of gold?"

"I don't know. I've never tried it before."

"Well, then," Will said, "you'd better begin praying about it, because if you can't, all these folks are going to be pretty mad at you and I don't know what might be liable to happen to you."

"Sure, he can do it," Ty Ty broke in. "He can do it and don't know it."

"I want to see the gold you divine, fellow," Will told him. "I want to feel it in my hand, and bite it."

"Now don't get him all shy and scared, Will. When he grows up, he's going to be some almighty gold-diviner. He's young yet. Just give him time."

Darling Jill and Rosamond had been looking at the strange man without taking their eyes from him. Rosamond was a little afraid of him, and she drew back in her chair involuntarily. Darling Jill, though, leaned forward and gazed steadily into his eyes. He felt her staring at him and he looked at her. Dave bit his lip, wondering who she was. He had never seen a girl he thought so beautiful before, and he was trembling a little.

With their eyes upon him, Dave felt like an animal on exhibition. All of them were looking at him, and he could only look at one person at a time. His eyes went around the room, returning to Darling Jill. The more he saw her, the more he liked her. He wondered if she were the wife of one of the men in the room.

"How do you like it up here on solid ground, fellow?" Will asked.

"It's all right."

"But you'd rather be back home in the swamp, wouldn't you?"

"I don't know," he replied.

He looked again at Darling Jill. She was smiling at him, then, and he dared to smile back at her.

"Well, I'll declare," Ty Ty said, leaning back in his chair. "Just look at him and Darling Jill carry-on, would you, folks!"

Up until then Ty Ty had not for a moment considered Dave a human being. Since the night before, Ty Ty had looked upon him as something different from a man. But it dawned upon him when he saw Darling Jill's smile that the boy was actually a person. He was still an albino, though, and he was said to possess unearthly powers to divine gold. In that respect, Ty Ty still held him above all other men.

"What would your wife say, fellow, if she saw you here making eyes at Darling Jill?" Will asked him.

"She's pretty," the boy said simply.

"Who? Your wife?"

"No," he answered quickly, looking at Darling Jill. "She is."

"I don't reckon you're the first one to say that, fellow, but she's hard to get unless she's the one who's doing the getting. They're too many after her now, to make her come easy. See that fat man over there in the corner? Well, he's after her, for one. He's been trying God-knows-how-long, but he hasn't got her yet himself. You'll have to go some to get her, fellow, I'm telling you."

Pluto looked uneasily at the tall slim boy sitting in the straight-backed chair in the center of the room. He did not like the way Darling Jill made eyes at Dave, either. That kind of a beginning brought a dangerous ending.

"It's only fair to set the boy straight at the start, seeing as how he's a male and women are females," Ty Ty said. "I've had the side of my barn kicked off just because I was careless enough to lead a stud horse into the wind when I should have led him with the wind."

"Talking don't help much," Will broke in. "If you've got a rooster, he's going to crow."

"Don't listen to him," Ty Ty continued. "I know what I'm about. Now, see that girl sitting in the middle? That's Buck's wife and her name is Griselda and, if I do say so myself, God never made a finer-looking woman in His day. But leave her alone. Then the other one, there with the dimples is Rosamond. She's Will's wife. Leave her alone, too. And the one you're looking at is Darling Jill. She's nobody's wife yet, but that don't make her free for the asking, and I'm trying my best to make her marry Pluto. Pluto is the fat man in the corner. He's running for sheriff this year. I may let you off to vote for him when the time comes."

"It's no use telling him to leave Darling Jill alone," Will said. "It's a waste of words to say that. Just look at them make eyes at each other."

"I wasn't going to mention it, but since you brought it up, I reckon he might just as well know that I can't stop Darling Jill from what she sets her head on. She's as crazy as hell sometimes, and about nothing."

While Dave and Darling Jill were looking at each other, Ty Ty fell to talking again. His voice was not raised, but everyone in the room heard what he said.

"I reckon God was pretty good to me. He favored me with the finest-looking daughters and daughter-in-law a man could hope for. I reckon I've been lucky not to have had any more trouble than I've had. I get to thinking sometimes that maybe it's all not for the best. I think a lot about maybe having trouble with such pretty girls in the house. But so far, I've been spared that misery. Darling Jill acts crazy as hell some-times, and about nothing. But we've been living on the lucky side of the road so far."

"Now, Pa," said Griselda, "please don't start that again."

"I ain't ashamed of nothing," Ty Ty said heatedly. "I reckon Griselda is just about the prettiest girl I ever did see. There ain't a man alive who's ever seen a finer-looking pair of rising beauties as she's got. Why, man alive! They're that pretty it makes me feel sometime like getting right down on my hands and knees like these old hound dogs you see chasing after a flowing bitch. You just ache to get down and lick something. That's the way, and it's God's own truth as He would tell it Himself if He could talk like the rest of us."

"You don't mean to sit there and say you've seen them, do you?" Will asked, winking at Griselda and Rosamond.

"Seen them? Why, man alive! I spend all my spare time trying to slip up on her when she ain't looking to see them some more. Seen them? Man alive! Just like a rabbit likes clover! And when you've seen them once, that's only the start. You can't sit calm and peaceful and think about nothing else till you see them again. And every time you see them it makes you feel just a little bit more like that old hound dog I was talking about. You're sitting out there in the yard somewhere all calm and pleased and all of a sudden you'll get a notion in your head. You sit there, telling it to go away and let you rest, and all the time there's something getting up inside of you. You can't stop it, because you can't put your hands on it; you can't talk to it, because you can't make it hear. And so it gets up and stands right there on the inside of you. Then it says something to you. It's that same old feeling again, and you know you can't stop it now to save your soul. You can sit there all day long, till it's squeezed almost to death, but it won't leave you. And that's when you go stepping around the house on your toes trying to see something. Man alive! And don't I know what I mean!"

"Aw, now, Pa," Griselda said, blushing. "You promised to stop talking like that about me."

"Girl," he said, "you just don't know how I'm praising you in my talk. I'm saying the finest things a man can say about a woman. When a man gets that ache to get right down on his hands and knees, and lick—well, girl, it just makes a man—aw, shucks, Griselda."

Ty Ty fumbled in his pockets until he found a twenty-five cent piece. He laid it in Griselda's hand.

"Take that and buy yourself a pretty the next time you're in the city, Griselda. I wish I had more to give you."

"Now, listen here," Will said, winking at Rosamond and Griselda. "You're giving yourself away. If you don't watch out, you won't get a chance to see Griselda again like that. She'll keep out of your way after this, if you don't be quiet."

"That's where you're wrong, son," Ty Ty said. "I've lived a heap longer than you have, and I know a little more about the ways of women. Griselda won't be after keeping me from seeing her the next time, or any time. She won't come right out now and say so, but just the same she'll be pleased like all get-out when I do see her the next time. She knows good and well I appreciate what I saw. Now, ain't that the truth, Griselda?"

"Aw, now, Pa!"

"See there? Didn't I tell you the whole truth? She'll be in that room over there with the door wide open some of these days before long, and I'll be standing there looking at her for all I'm worth. A girl like her has a right to show off, too, if she wants to. I wouldn't blame her a bit if she did. Why, man alive! That's a sight for sore eyes!"

"Now, Pa, please stop," Griselda said, hiding her face in her hands. "You promised to stop saying that."

Ty Ty had been so busy talking he had not noticed that Darling Jill had got up and was pulling Dave by the hands to the door. He jumped to his feet in an instant when he saw the albino between him and the door. He jerked the shotgun off the chair-seat and pointed it at Dave.

"No, you don't!" he shouted. "Get back in the room where you were, now."

"Wait a minute, Pa," Darling Jill said, running to him and putting her arms around his neck. "Pa, just leave us alone for a little while. He isn't going to run away. We're only going out on the back porch to get a drink and sit in the cool. He wouldn't run away. You wouldn't run away, would you, Dave?"

"No, you don't!" Ty Ty said, not so firmly.

"Now, Pa," Darling Jill said, hugging him tighter.

"Now, I don't know about that."

"You wouldn't run away, would you, Dave?"

The boy shook his head vigorously. He was afraid to speak to Ty Ty, but if he had dared, he would have begged to be allowed to go with Darling Jill. He continued to shake his head, hoping.

"I don't like the looks of it," Ty Ty said. "When he gets out there in the dark with nobody to guard him, all he has to do is plunge off the porch, and he's gone for good. We couldn't ever find him out there in the dark. I wouldn't like to take that risk. I don't like the looks of it."

"Let him go with her," Will said. "That's not what they're going for. He won't try to get away. He sort of likes it here now a little since Darling Jill has come home. Isn't that right, fellow?"

The boy nodded his head, trying to make them believe he was not interested in running away. He kept on nodding his head until Ty Ty laid the gun down on the chair-seat.

"I still don't like the looks of it," Ty Ty said, "but I'll have to let you go for a little while. But I'll tell you something to remember. If you do run off, it'll be hell to pay when I catch you again. I'll forge some chains around your legs and bar you in the barn so tight you'll never get another chance to leave. I aim to keep you till you locate that lode for me. You'd better not try fooling with me, because when I get mad, I stay mad."

Darling Jill drew him out of the room, pulling him by the hands. They went through the dark hall to the back porch. The water bucket was empty, and they went to the well. Dave drew the water and poured it into the bucket.

"Don't you like me better than you do your wife?" Darling Jill asked him, hanging to his arm.

"I wish I had married you," he said, his hands trembling beside her. "I didn't know there was a girl so beautiful anywhere in the country. You're the prettiest girl I've ever seen. You're so soft, and you talk like bird-song, and you smell so good——"

They sat down on the bottom step. Shivers went over Darling Jill while she listened to Dave. She had never heard a man talk like that.

"Why are you white all over?" she asked him.

"I was born that way," he said slowly. "I can't help looking like I do."

"I think you are wonderful-looking. You don't look like any man I've ever seen, and I'm glad you are so different."

"Would you marry me?" he asked huskily.

"You're already married."

"I don't want to stay that way now. I want to marry you. I like you so much, and I think you are so beautiful."

"We wouldn't have to get married, if you like me a lot."

"Why?"

"Just because."

"But I couldn't do everything I wanted to."

"Don't be silly."

"I'd be a little afraid. They might beat me, or something. I don't know what they'd do to me."

"It was a shame for Pa to tie you up with ropes and bring you up here," she said. "But I'm glad he did."

"I am too, now. I wouldn't run away now if I had a chance. I'm going to stay so I can see you all the time."

Darling Jill moved closer to him, putting her arm around his waist and placing her head on his shoulder. He grabbed her madly.

"Would you like to kiss me?"

"Would you let me?"

"Yes, I would like it."

He kissed her, squeezing her to him. She could feel the swell of his muscles when his body touched hers and pressed so tightly.

Presently he picked her up and started across the yard. He ran with her in the dark, not knowing where he was going.

"Where are we going?"

"Out here so they can't bother us," he said. "I don't want them to come and make me go back to the barn yet."

He walked with her to the end of the yard and sat down with her on his lap under one of the water-oak trees. She could not bear to have him release her, and she locked her arms around him.

"When we find the gold, we'll take some of it and go away together," Darling Jill said. "You would do that, wouldn't you, Dave?"

"You bet I would. I'd go now, if you'd go."

"I don't care," she whispered. "I don't care what happens. I'll do anything you ask me to."

"Why do they call you Darling Jill?" he asked after a long silence.

"When I was a little girl, everybody called me 'Darling,' and my name is Jill. When I grew up, they still called me that. Now everyone calls me Darling Jill."

"It's a perfect name for you," he said. "I couldn't think of a better name to call you. You are a darling."

"Kiss me again," she said.

Dave bent over and drew her up until his lips touched hers. They lay on the ground unmindful of anything else in the world. The pressure of his arms and the swelling of his muscles made her tremble again and again.

Ty Ty and Will came out on the back porch looking for them. Ty Ty called, and then he swore. Will went back for a lantern, running into the house telling Ty Ty not to scare the boy away by his shouts. When he came back with the smoking lantern, Ty Ty grabbed it and started out across the yard, running back and forth in all directions. He shouted to Will, swearing at Dave and Darling Jill, and looking everywhere as fast as his feet would carry him.

Rosamond and Griselda came out of the house and stood by the well looking out in the darkness.

"I knew it," Ty Ty kept saying over and over again. "I knew it all the time."

"We'll find him," Will said. "They didn't go far."

"I knew it, I just knew it. My white-haired boy is gone for fair."

"I don't believe he ran off," Will protested. "I'll bet a pretty he's only lying low till you stop scaring him to death. When they left the room, they weren't trying to run off. He was more for going out in the dark so he could have a good time with her than he was for running off. Just look for her, and you'll find him at the same time. She had her mind made up to have him, and she's the one who took him off wherever it is they've gone."

"I knew it, I just knew it was going to happen. My white-haired boy is gone for fair."

Rosamond and Griselda called from the well.

"Have you found him yet, Pa?"

Ty Ty was so busy searching for the albino he did not stop to answer.

"They're out here somewhere," Will said. "They're not far off."

Ty Ty dashed around the house, making a complete circle of it, barely missing the black mouth of the crater. He skirted the big hole by inches, almost falling into it in his blind haste.

Once around the house, he struck out across the yard, running at random. When he got out near the water-oak trees, the light from the smoking lantern suddenly revealed the snow-white hair of Dave. Ty Ty ran nearer and saw them both sprawled on the ground. Neither of them was aware of his presence, even though the yellow light flickered in Darling Jill's eyes and twinkled like two stars when her eye-lids blinked.

Will saw Ty Ty standing still with the smoking lantern and he knew they had been found. He ran to see why Ty Ty was not calling him, and Rosamond and Griselda came behind.

"Did you ever see such a sight?" Ty Ty asked, looking around at Will. "Now, ain't that something?" ,

Will waited until Griselda got there, pointing down at Dave and Darling Jill. They stood silently for a moment, trying to see in the yellow lantern light.

Ty Ty suddenly found himself turned around and being pushed towards the house.

He whirled around.

"What's the matter with you girls, Rosamond?" he said stumbling with the lantern. "What makes you push me like that?"

"You ought to be ashamed of yourself, Pa, you and Will, standing here looking at them. Go on away, both of you, now."

Ty Ty found himself standing beside Will several yards from them.

"Now, look here," he protested; "I don't like to be shoved around like a country-cousin. What's the matter with you girls, anyhow?"

"Shame on you, Pa, you and Will," Griselda said. "You were standing here looking all the time. Now, go on off and stop looking."

"Well, I'll be a suck-egg mule," Ty Ty said. "I wasn't doing a thing in the world but standing there. And here you girls come running up and say, 'Shame on me.' I ain't done a blessed thing to be ashamed of. What's wrong with you, Griselda and Rosamond?"

Will and Ty Ty moved away, walking slowly towards the house. Just before reaching the well, Ty Ty stopped and looked back.

"Now, what in God's name did I do wrong?"

"Women don't like men to stand around and see one of them getting it," Will said. "That's why they raised such a howl about you being there. They only wanted to get me and you away."

"Well, dog my cats," Ty Ty said. "Is that what was going on back there! I never would have known it, Will, I declare I wouldn't. I only thought they was lying there hugging one another. That's the truth if I know it. I couldn't see a thing in that pale light."

Chapter X

THEY had been at work since sunrise in the new crater, and at eleven o'clock the heat was blistering. Buck and Shaw had little to say to Will. They had never been able to get along together, and even the prospect of turning up a shovelful of yellow nuggets any moment did not serve to bind them any closer. If Buck had had his way, Will would never have been sent for in the first place. All the gold that was turned up was going into their own pockets, anyway; if Will should try to take some, they would die fighting before they would allow him to share in it.

Will leaned on his shovel and watched Shaw pick the clay. He laughed a little, but neither Buck nor Shaw paid the least attention to him. They went on as though he were nowhere near.

"It looks to me like you boys would have better sense than to let Ty Ty egg you on to digging all these big holes in the ground. He gets all this hard work out of you, and it doesn't cost him a penny. Why don't you boys go off somewhere and get a real job that pays something when Saturday comes? You don't want to stay countrymen all your lives, do you? Tell Ty Ty to shovel his own dirt, and walk off."

"Go to hell, you lint-head," Shaw said.

Will rolled a cigarette while he watched them dig and sweat. He did not mind being called a lint-head by people of his own world, but he could never stand being called that by Buck and Shaw. They knew it was the quickest and most effective way either to silence him outright or to make him fighting mad.

Buck looked up at the rim of the crater to see if Ty Ty were near. If there was going to be trouble, he wished to have Ty Ty there to help them. Their father had always sided with them when they had an argument with Will, and he would this time as well.

But Ty Ty was not within sight. He was over in the newground with the two colored men trying to get the cotton banked. The crop had been planted late that year, as they had been so busy digging that there had been no opportunity to plant it until June, and Ty Ty wished to

hurry it along as much as possible, if it was within his power to make
it grow and mature, in order to get some money by the first of September. He had already bought to the limit of his credit in the stores at
Marion, and he had been unable to get a loan at the bank. If the cotton
did not thrive, or if the boll weevils ruined it, he did not know what he
was going to do the coming fall and winter. There were two mules
to feed, in addition to the two colored families, and his own household.

"There ain't no more gold in this ground than there is in the toes of
my socks," Will said derisively. "Why don't you boys go up to Augusta
or Atlanta or somewhere and have a good time? I'll be damned if I'd
stay a clodhopper all my life just because Ty Ty Walden wants you
to dig in the ground for him."

"Aw, go to hell, you Valley town lint-head."

Will looked at Buck, debating momentarily whether to hit him.

"Got any message to send your folks?" he asked finally.

"If you want to play the dozens, you're at the right homestead,"
Shaw said.

Will threw down his shovel with both hands and picked up a dried
clod of clay. He ran several steps toward them, rolling the dead cigarette to the corner of his mouth with his tongue.

"I didn't come over here to have trouble with you boys, but if
you're looking for it, you're barking up the right tree now."

"That's all you've ever done," Shaw said, gripping the shovel handle
in both hands. "Barking is all you've ever done."

Will wished to fight Buck, if there was going to be a fight. He had
nothing against Shaw, but Shaw would side with his brother always.
Will disliked Buck. He had disliked him from the first. He did not
hate him personally, but Griselda was Buck's wife, and Buck was
always standing between them. They had already had several tussles,
not over Griselda any more than for any other reason, and they were
likely to have others. As long as Griselda was married to Buck, and
lived with him, Will would fight him whenever he had the opportunity.

"Drop that clod," Buck ordered.

"Come and make me," Will retorted.

Buck stepped back and whispered something to Shaw. Will stepped
forward and threw the clod with all his might just as Buck ran towards
him with the raised shovel. The shovel handle struck Will a glancing
blow on the shoulder, flying off to the ground. The clod had missed
Buck, but it hit Shaw squarely in the pit of the stomach. He bent over
with pain, falling to the ground and groaning weakly.

When Buck turned and saw Shaw doubled into a knot behind him,
he thought surely Will had injured him seriously. He ran forward,

raising the shovel over his head, and hit Will on the forehead with all his might.

The blow stunned Will, but it did not knock him out. He was up on his feet, angrier than ever, and running after Buck before the shovel could be raised for another blow.

"All you damn Waldens think you're tough, but we're tougher where I come from," Will said. "It would take you and six more like you to beat me up. I'm used to it—I have a couple of fights every morning before breakfast where I come from."

"You damn lint-head," Buck said contemptuously.

Shaw got to his hands and knees, blinking his eyes. He looked around for a weapon of any nature, but there was nothing within his reach. His shovel was on the other side of Will.

"You damn lint-head," Buck repeated, sneering.

"Come on, both of you sons-of-bitches," Will shouted. "I'll take you both down at the same time. I wasn't raised to be scared of country-men."

Buck raised his shovel, but Will reached up and jerked it out of his hands, tossing it out of reach behind him. With a well-aimed blow he struck Buck on the jaw, knocking him flat on his back. Shaw ran towards him, crouched low over his knees. Will swung at him with both fists, one after the other. Shaw's knees gave way, and he fell at Will's feet.

Buck was up again. He jumped on Will, hurling him to the ground and pinning his arms under him. Before Will could twist free, Buck had begun pounding him on the head and back. All of them were in an ugly temper by that time.

From the top of the crater Ty Ty shouted at them. He came running down the side at once, jumping into the midst of the fists and kicks. He pried Buck and Will apart, and flung them sprawling to the ground on each side of him. Ty Ty was as large as any one of the others, and he had always been able to handle a fight between them. He stood panting and blowing, looking down at them.

"That's enough of that," he said, still breathing hard. "What in the pluperfect hell have you boys got to fight about so much, anyhow? That ain't digging for the lode. Fighting among yourselves won't find it."

Buck sat up and held his swollen jaw. He glared at Will, still unde-feated.

"Send him back where he belongs, then," Buck said. "The son-of-a-bitch hasn't any business over here. This ain't no place for lint-heads to hang out."

"I'll go when I get damn good and ready and not a minute before. Just try and make me go before then. Just try it!"

"What in the pluperfect hell did you boys go and do that for, any-how," Ty Ty asked Shaw, turning to see if he was all right. "There ain't nothing for you boys to fight about like this. When we strike the lode, it's all going to be divided up fair and square, and nobody is going to get a larger share than the next one. I aim to see to that. Now, what made you boys start scrapping one another like that?"

"Nothing started it, Pa," Shaw said. "And it wasn't about sharing the gold. It wasn't about anything like that. It just happened, that's all. Every time that son-of-a-bitch comes over here he invites a beating. It's just the way he talks and acts. He acts like he's better than we are, or something. He acts like he's better because he works in a cotton mill. He's always calling Buck and me countrymen."

"Now that ain't nothing to get all heated up about," Ty Ty said. "Boys, it's a shame we can't keep a peaceful family all the time. That's what I've aimed all my life to have."

"Make him leave Griselda alone then," Buck said.

"Is Griselda in this?" Ty Ty asked in wonder. "Why, I didn't know she was all mixed up in this fight."

"You're a damn liar," Will shouted. "I never said a word about her."

"Now, boys," Ty Ty said, "don't start scrapping all over again. What's Griselda got to do with all this?"

"Well, he didn't say anything about her," Buck replied, "but it's just the way he looks and acts. He acts like he's getting ready to do something to her."

"That's a lie," Will shouted.

"Now, Buck, you maybe just imagine all that. I know it ain't so, because Will is married to Rosamond and they get along first-rate together. He ain't after Griselda. Just forget that part."

Will looked at Buck but said nothing. He was angry because Ty Ty had separated them before he could strike the last blow.

"If he would stay where he belongs, and not come over here raising hell, I'd be satisfied," Buck stated. "The son-of-a-bitch is a lint-head, anyway. He ought to stay with his own kind. We don't want to mix with him."

Will got to his feet again, looking around for the shovel.

Ty Ty ran and pushed him to the other side of the crater. He held Will with both hands, pushing him back against the side of the hole.

"Will," he said calmly, "don't pay any attention to Buck. That heat's got his dander up, and about nothing. Now stay here and leave him alone."

He ran back to the other side of the hole and pushed Buck down. Shaw was out of it then. He made no further signs of going in again.

"You boys all get up on top of the ground and cool off," Ty Ty ordered. "You got all heated up down here in the hole, and fresh air is the only way to get it out of you. Now go on up there and cool off a while."

He waited while Buck and Shaw climbed out and disappeared from sight. After giving them plenty of time to get away, he urged Will to get up and climb to the top for air. Ty Ty followed close behind in case Shaw and Buck were waiting just out of sight to jump on Will and resume the fight. When they got to the surface above, Shaw and Buck had gone from sight.

"Don't give them no more thought, Will," he said. "Just sit down in the shade and cool off."

They went to the side of the house and sat down in the shade. Will was still angry, but he was willing to drop the fight where it was, even if Buck had had the last blow. The sooner he got back to Scottsville the better would he be pleased. He would never have come in the first place if Rosamond and Darling Jill had not begged him so much. Now he wished to get back to the Valley and talk to his friends before the meeting of the local Friday night. The sight of bare land, cultivated and fallow, with never a factory or mill to be seen, made him a little sick in his stomach.

"You ain't made up your mind to leave so soon, have you, Will?" Ty Ty asked. "I hope you ain't aiming to do that."

"Sure, I'm leaving," Will said. "I can't be wasting my time digging holes in the ground. I'm no damn doodle-bug."

"I aimed to have you help us till we struck the lode, Will. I need all the help I can get right now. The lode is there, sure as God made little green apples, and I ache to get my hands on it. I've been waiting fifteen years, night and day, for just that."

"You ought to be out making cotton," Will said shortly. "You can raise more cotton on this land in a year than you can find gold in a lifetime. It's a waste of everything to dig these holes all over the place."

"I wish now I had spent a little more time on the cotton. It looks like now that I'm going to be short of money before the lode is struck. If I had twenty or thirty bales of cotton to tide me over the fall and winter, I could devote all the rest of the time to digging. I sure do need a lot of cotton to sell the first of September."

"Well, it's too late to plant any more cotton this year. You're out of luck, if you don't do something else."

"There ain't but one thing I can do, and that's dig."

"This house is going to topple over into the hole if you dig much more in it. The house is leaning a little now. It won't take much to tip it over."

Ty Ty looked at the pine logs that had been dragged from the woods and propped against the building. The logs were large enough and strong enough to hold the house where it was, but if it were undermined too much, it would surely fall in, and then turn over. When it did that, it would either be lying on one side in the big hole, or else it would be upside down on the bottom of it.

"Will, when the gold-fever strikes a man, he can't think about nothing else to save his soul. I reckon that's what's wrong with me, if anything is. I've got the fever so bad I can't be bothered about planting cotton. I'm bent on getting those little yellow nuggets out of the ground. Come heaven, hell, or high water, I reckon I'll just have to keep on digging till I strike the lode. I can't stop to do nothing else now. The gold-fever has water-logged me through and through."

Will had cooled off. He was no longer restless to get up, and he did not care whether he ever saw Buck and Shaw again to renew the fight. He was willing to let them alone until the next time.

"If you're hard up for money, why don't you go up to Augusta and borrow some from Jim Leslie?"

"Do what, Will?" Ty Ty asked.

"Get Jim Leslie to lend you enough to see you through the fall and winter. You can plant a big crop of cotton next spring."

"Aw, shucks, Will," Ty Ty said, laughing a little, "there wouldn't be no sense in that."

"Why not? He's got plenty of money, and his wife is as rich as a manure pile."

"He wouldn't help me none, Will."

"How do you know he wouldn't? You've never tried to borrow off of him, have you? Well, how do you know he wouldn't lend you a little?"

"Jim Leslie won't speak to me on the street, Will," he replied sadly, "and if he won't speak to me on the street, I know durn well he wouldn't lend me money. Wouldn't be no sense in trying to ask him. It would be just a big waste of time trying."

"Hell, he's your boy, ain't he? Well, if he's your boy, he ought to listen to you when you tell him how much hard luck you're having trying to strike the lode."

"That wouldn't make much difference to Jim Leslie now. He left home just on that account. He said he wasn't going to stay here and be made a fool of digging for nuggets all his life. I don't reckon he's changed much since then, either."

"How long ago was that?"

"Nearly fifteen years ago, I reckon."

"All that's worn off of him by this time. He'll be tickled to death to see you. You're his daddy, ain't you?"

"Yes, I reckon. But that won't make much difference to him. I've tried to speak to him on the street, but he won't look my way at all."

"I'll bet he'll listen to you when you tell him about the hard luck, anyway."

"Well, this here now lode might turn up, if I could afford to keep digging," Ty Ty said, rising to his feet.

"Sure, it might," Will told him. "That's just what I've been trying to make you see."

"If I had a little money, maybe two or three hundred dollars, this here now lode might could be located. It takes time, and a durn heap of patience to locate gold, Will."

"Why don't you go up to Augusta and talk to him about it then? That's the thing to do."

Ty Ty started around the house. He stopped at the corner and waited for Will to catch up with him. They went across the yard and down to the barn where Dave and Uncle Felix were. Shaw and Buck were sitting on the stall partition talking to the albino and Uncle Felix.

"Boys," Ty Ty said, "we've got to be up and doing. I've made up my mind to go up to Augusta right away. Come and wash up some so we can get started."

"What for?" Buck asked sourly.

"What for? Why, to see Jim Leslie, son."

"I reckon I'll stay here then," Buck stated.

"Now, boys," Ty Ty pleaded, "I need you to drive me up there in the car. You know good and well I can't drive an automobile in the big city. Why, I'd wreck the whole shooting-match up there the first thing off the bat."

First Buck and then Shaw climbed down off the stall partition and left the barn. Ty Ty walked behind them, telling them over and over his reason for wishing to see Jim Leslie.

Will stuck his head through the feed-rack and looked at Dave.

"How you feeling, fellow?"

"All right," the boy said.

"Would you like to get out and go home now?"

"I'd rather stay here."

Will pulled his head out, laughing at the albino. He turned away, walking out the barn towards the house.

"You might just as well cool your heels a while," he called back. "Darling Jill won't be here tonight. She's going up to Augusta with the rest of us."

He left Dave and Uncle Felix with no other word. On the way to the house he began to feel sorry for Dave. He hoped Ty Ty would turn him free in a few days and let him go back home if he wished to.

Buck was on the back porch washing his face and hands in the basin, but Will did not look in that direction. He went around to the front of the house and sat down on the steps to wait for Ty Ty to get ready to leave. Pluto had gone home that morning to change his shirt and socks, and Will missed him. He had said something about getting an early start to canvass for votes, and Will hoped he would come by the house before they left. Pluto might be elected sheriff, if his friends who expected to be appointed deputies worked hard enough for him. But Pluto alone could never gather enough support.

Griselda was the first to come out of the house ready to leave. She smiled at Will, and he winked at her. She was wearing a new floral print afternoon frock with a large hat that had a brim covering her shoulders. Will wondered if he had ever seen a girl so good-looking as Griselda. He hated to think of having to go back to Scottsville without having an opportunity of seeing her alone. He might even have to come back with them that night from Augusta, instead of going to the Valley, just so he could have the chance of being with her.

Chapter XI

WHEN they reached Augusta in the early evening, Buck stopped the car at the curb on Broad Street near Sixth. Nothing had been said about stopping downtown, and Ty Ty leaned forward to ask Buck and Shaw why they had stopped. Jim Leslie's house was on The Hill, several miles away.

"What did you do this for, Buck?"

"I'm getting out here to go to the movies," Buck answered, not looking around. "I'm not going up there to Jim Leslie's."

Shaw got out with him and they stood on the street. They waited to see if anyone else was going with them. After a moment's hesitation, Darling Jill and Rosamond got out.

"Now, you folks wait a minute," Ty Ty said excitedly. "You folks are just going to shove it all off on me. Why can't somebody go with me up there and help convince Jim Leslie how much in need of money I am?"

"I'll go with you, Pa," Griselda said.

"You won't need me," Will stated, getting out. "I couldn't talk to him without getting mad and batting him down."

"Go on with Pa, Will," Darling Jill urged. "Pa needs you along."

"Why don't you go? You're telling everybody else to go, but you don't go yourself."

"Don't be scared of Jim Leslie, Will," Griselda said. "He can't hurt you."

"Who said I was scared of anybody? Me—scared of him?"

"It's time to go," Ty Ty said. "We'll be sitting here arguing all night if we don't make up our minds right away."

Buck and Shaw started up the street towards the brightly lighted theaters. Rosamond ran and caught up with them.

"Oh, I'll go," Darling Jill said. "I don't mind."

"We three are enough, unless Will wants to go."

"That's all right with me," Will said. "I'll hang around here till you get back."

Darling Jill got out of the back seat and sat under the steeringwheel. Griselda got in with her, leaving Ty Ty alone in the rear.

"I'll stick around here somewhere," Will said, looking up and down the street.

He walked slowly away, keeping close to the curb and glancing up at the windows on the second storeys. The buildings all had iron-grilled balconies, three or four feet wide, and people were sitting in the windows and leaning over the iron railings looking down on the sidewalk.

Somebody further down the street called Will's name. He walked down there, looking up at the faces overhead.

"There goes Will," Griselda said hopelessly.

One of the girls overhead was leaning over the railing talking to him. Will walked away looking up at other balconies. The girl who had tried to talk to him cursed and called him all the obscene names she could think of.

Darling Jill giggled and whispered something to Griselda. They spoke in undertones for a while, and Ty Ty was unable to overhear a word they said.

"Let's be going, girls," he said. "It's a sin and a shame to stay here."

Darling Jill made no effort to start the car. One of the girls above them on the balcony was pointing at Ty Ty. He had already seen them up there, and he refused to look in any direction except down at his feet.

He was biting his tongue with fear that one of the girls up there would speak to him before Darling Jill would start the car.

"Hello, grandpa," the girl who had pointed said. "Come on up a while and have a good time."

Ty Ty looked at Darling Jill and Griselda when they turned to see what he was going to do. He was wishing they would only hurry and drive away before the girls on the second-storey balconies could say anything else to him. He would not have minded being spoken to under any other circumstances, but he did not feel free to answer anybody up there while he was with Darling Jill and Griselda. He leaned forward, poking Darling Jill with his finger, urging her to drive away.

"Why don't you go up there and see what's going on, Pa?" she asked, giggling again.

"Man alive!" Ty Ty said, blushing through his tanned skin.

"Go on up, Pa," Griselda urged. "We'll wait for you. Go on up and have a good time."

"Man alive!" Ty Ty said again. "I'm way past that age. Wouldn't be no sense in that."

The girl who had been watching Ty Ty beckoned to him with her finger, jerking her head and pointing to the stairs that opened on the street. She was a small girl, not much older than sixteen or seventeen, and when she leaned over the iron railing and looked down into the car, Ty Ty could not keep from glancing up and wishing he could go up the stairs to see her. His hands clutched the thin roll of soiled one-dollar bills in his pocket, and perspiration dampened his brow. He knew Darling Jill and Griselda were waiting for him to get out and walk up the stairs, but he did not have the courage to go in their presence.

"Don't be a tightwad, grandpa," the girl said out of the corner of her lips. "You'll never be young but once."

Ty Ty glanced at the backs of Griselda's and Darling Jill's heads. They were watching the girl on the balcony above, and talking about her in undertones.

"Go on up, Pa," Griselda said. "You'll have a good time up there. You ought to have a little fun sometimes after working so hard at home in the holes."

"Now, Griselda," Ty Ty protested weakly, "I'm way past that now. Don't tease me so much. It makes me feel like I don't know what I'm liable to do with myself."

The girl had left the little iron-grilled balcony. Ty Ty looked up and felt a relief. He leaned forward, prodding Darling Jill with his finger, urging her to drive away.

"Wait just another minute," she said.

He could see that they were watching the stairs that opened on the street. Out of the gray darkness of the building the girl suddenly appeared in the glow of the whiteway lights.

Ty Ty saw her and sank down in the seat hoping to get out of sight. She walked straight for the automobile, stepping off the curb and into the street beside Ty Ty on the back seat.

"I know what's wrong with you—you're bashful."

Ty Ty blushed and sank lower. He could see Darling Jill and Griselda watching him in the little mirror on top of the windshield.

"Come on upstairs and jazz a little."

Darling Jill giggled outright.

Ty Ty said something, but no one could hear what it was. The girl put her foot on the runningboard and reached for Ty Ty's arm to pull him out. He moved to the middle of the seat, evading her fingers.

Darling Jill turned around and glanced at the girl's powdered breasts in the low-cut dress. She turned back and whispered something to Griselda. Both laughed.

"What's the matter with you, grandpa? Have you got a boil on you, or don't you have any money?"

Ty Ty vaguely wondered if she would go away and let him alone if he told her he had no money.

He shook his head at her, moving further away.

"You're a cheap son-of-a-bitch," she said. "Why can't you spend a little money at the end of the week? If I had known you were such a tight-fisted son-of-a-bitch I wouldn't have bothered to come down here."

Ty Ty did not answer her, and he thought she would go on back into the building. She did not even remove her foot from the running-board, but stood waiting beside the car and looking sullenly at him.

"Let's go, girls," he urged. "We've got to be on our way."

Darling Jill started the motor and engaged the gears. She turned around to see if the girl had removed her foot from the car. She backed several feet. The girl's foot was dragged off the runningboard, and she stood at the curb cursing Ty Ty. When they were clear of the curbing, Darling Jill started down the street and turned the corner. In a few minutes they were in a boulevard bound for The Hill.

"I'm sure thankful you girls got me away from there," Ty Ty said. "It looked like we was never going to get away. I'd have gone up there with her just to make her be quiet if we hadn't left when we did. I hate to be out in the main street and have a woman swear at me like that for all the people to hear. I never could stand being cussed by a woman right in the middle of the city."

"Oh, we weren't going to let you go up there, Pa," Griselda said. "We were only fooling. We wouldn't have let you go up there and get diseased. It was only a joke on you."

"Well, I ain't saying I wanted to go, and I ain't saying I didn't. But I sure hate to have a woman swear at me like that on the main street. It doesn't sound nice, for one thing. I never could put up with it."

They crossed the canal and entered another boulevard. The Hill was still two miles distant, but the car was in a fast-moving stream of traffic, and they sped up the gradually rising elevation. Ty Ty was still a little nervous after his encounter with the girl who lived in the room behind the iron balcony, and he was glad it was over. He had known several girls who lived in that part of town, but that was ten to fifteen years earlier, and the ones he knew had gone away and others much younger had taken their places. Ty Ty felt uneasy in the presence of the new generation of girls down there, because they were no longer willing to stay in their rooms, or even on the balconies. Now they came down to the street and dragged men out of their cars. He shook his head, glad he was in another section of the city.

"Man alive!" Ty Ty said. "She was a she-devil, all right. I don't know when I've seen such a regular little hell-cat."

"Are you still thinking about that girl, Pa?" Griselda asked. "If you say so, we'll turn around and go back."

"Great guns," he shouted, "don't do that! Keep on the way we're going. I've got to see Jim Leslie. I can't be fooling away my time down there again."

"Do you know which way to go now?" Darling Jill asked him, slowing down at an intersection of three streets.

"Take the right-hand one," he said, pointing with his hand.

They drove for several blocks along a tree-lined street. There were large houses in that part of the city. Some of the large houses occupied an entire block. Up above them they could see the high towers on the Bon Air-Vanderbilt. They were in the midst of the resort hotels.

"It's a big white house with three storeys and a big front porch," Ty Ty said. "Now go slow while I look out for it."

They drove two more blocks in silence.

"They all look alike at night," Ty Ty said. "But when I see Jim Leslie's, I'll know it without fail."

Darling Jill slowed down to cross a street. Just beyond was a large white house with three storeys and a large porch with white columns rising to the roof.

"That's it," Ty Ty said, prodding them with his finger. "That's Jim Leslie's as sure as God makes little green apples. Stop right where we are."

They got out and looked up at the big white house behind the trees. There were lights in all the windows downstairs, and in some of the windows on the middle floor. The front door was open, but the screen door was closed. Ty Ty became worried about the screen door. He was afraid it was locked.

"Don't stop to knock or ring a bell, girls. If we did that, Jim Leslie might see who we are and lock the door before we can get inside."

Ty Ty went ahead and tiptoed up the steps and across the wide porch. Darling Jill and Griselda stayed close behind so they would not be locked outside. Ty Ty opened the screen door noiselessly, and they went into the wide hall.

"We're on the inside," Ty Ty whispered, much relieved. "He'll have a hard time putting us out now before I can tell him what I'm after."

They walked slowly to the wide door on the right. Ty Ty stopped there, looking into the room.

Jim Leslie heard them and glanced up from the book he was reading with a frown on his face. He was alone in the room at the time. His wife was somewhere else in the house, probably on the floor above, Ty Ty supposed.

He walked into the room with his son.

"What are you doing here?" Jim Leslie said. "You know I don't let you come here. Get out!"

He glanced over Ty Ty's shoulder and saw his sister and Griselda. He frowned again, looking at them harder still.

"Now, Jim Leslie," Ty Ty began, "you know you're pleased to see us. We ain't seen you in a long long time, now have we, son?"

"Who let you in?"

"We let ourselves in. The door was open, and I knew you were here, because I saw you through the window, so we just walked in. That's the way we do out at home. Nobody ever has to knock on my door, or ring bells either, to come into the house. Out there everybody is welcome."

Jim Leslie looked again at Griselda. He had seen her once or twice before, at a distance, but he had not realized that she was so pretty. He wondered why a girl so beautiful had married Buck and had gone to live in the country. She would have looked much more at home in a house like this. He sat down, and the others found seats for themselves.

"What did you come here for?" he asked his father.

"It's important, son," Ty Ty said. "You know good and well I wouldn't come to your house uninvited unless I was in great trouble."

"Money, I suppose," Jim Leslie said. "Why don't you dig it out of the ground?"

"It's in there, all right, but I just can't seem to get it out right away."

"That's what you thought ten or twelve years ago. It looks like you ought to learn some sense in fifteen years. There's no gold out there. I told you that before I left."

"Gold or no gold, I've got the fever, son, and I can't stop digging. But you're wrong about that, because the gold is there, if I could only locate it. I've got an albino now, though, and I'm aiming to strike the lode any day now. All the folks say an albino can divine it if it's in the country."

Jim Leslie grunted disgustedly. He looked helplessly at his father, not knowing what to say to a man who talked so foolishly.

"Don't be a damn fool all your life," he said finally. "That talk about diviners is Negroes' talk. They're the only people I ever heard of who took such things seriously. A white man ought to have better sense than to fall for such superstition. You grow worse every year."

"You might call it that, but I'm going about the digging of the nuggets scientifically. I've done that clear from the start. The way I'm doing is scientific, and I know it is."

Jim Leslie had nothing further to say about it. He turned and looked at the bookcase.

Ty Ty looked around at the richly furnished room. He had never been in the house before, and its rugs and furnishings were a revelation to him. The rugs were as soft and yielding as freshly plowed ground, and he walked over them feeling at home. He turned once to look at Griselda and Darling Jill, but they were watching Jim Leslie and did not meet his eyes.

Presently Jim Leslie slumped down in the large overstuffed chair. He locked his hands under his chin and studied Griselda. Ty Ty saw that he was looking at her steadily.

Chapter XII

THAT's Buck's wife, Griselda," Ty Ty said.

"I know," Jim Leslie replied without turning.

"She's a mighty pretty girl."

"I know."

"The first time I saw her I said to myself: 'Man alive! Griselda is a mighty pleasing dish to set before a man.'"

"I know," he said again.

"It's a shame your wife ain't so pretty as Griselda," Ty Ty said sympathetically. "It's a dog-gone shame, Jim Leslie, if I do say it myself."

Jim Leslie shrugged his shoulders a little, still looking at Griselda. He could not keep his eyes away from her.

"They tell me that your wife has got diseased," Ty Ty said, moving his chair closer to his son's. "I've heard the boys say a lot of these rich people up here on The Hill have got one thing and another wrong with them. It's a dog-gone shame you had to marry her, Jim Leslie.

I feel downright sorry for you, son. Did she get you cornered so you couldn't worm out of marrying her?"

"I don't know," Jim Leslie said wearily.

"I sure hate to see you married to a diseased wife, son. Now just look at those two girls, there. Neither of them is diseased. Darling Jill is all right, and so is Griselda. And Rosamond ain't diseased either. They're all nice clean girls, son, the three of them. I'd hate to have a girl in my house diseased. I'd feel so ashamed of it that I'd hide my face when people came to see me at the house. It must be pretty hard for you to have to live with a diseased woman like your wife. Why is it, anyhow, that so many of these rich girls here in Augusta have got the diseases, son?"

"I don't know," he replied weakly.

"What is it she's got, anyhow?"

Jim Leslie tried to laugh at Ty Ty, but he could not even force a smile to his lips.

"Don't you know the name of it, son?"

Jim Leslie shook his head, indicating that he had no answer to give.

"The boys said she has gonorrhea. Is that right, son? That's what I heard, if I remember right."

Jim Leslie nodded his head almost imperceptibly. As long as he could sit there and look at Griselda he was willing to let Ty Ty's questions pass over his head. He had no interest in them as long as Griselda was there.

"Well, I'm sorry for you, son. It's a dog-gone shame you had to marry a girl with a disease. I reckon, though, you wouldn't have done it if she hadn't cornered you so you couldn't worm out of it. If you couldn't get out of it, then that's something God Himself couldn't have helped. You deserve a little better, though. It's a dog-gone shame you had to do it."

Ty Ty moved his chair closer to Jim Leslie's. He leaned forward, nodding his head towards Griselda.

"It's a dog-gone shame about your wife, son, if I do say it myself. Now, just take Griselda, there. She ain't diseased, and she's the prettiest girl you can ever hope to see. Just look at her! Now, you know good and well you've never seen a prettier girl, all over, have you, son?"

Jim Leslie smiled, but said nothing.

"Aw, now, Pa," Griselda begged anxiously, "please don't say those things again now. Don't say things like that in front of him, Pa. It's not nice, Pa."

"Now you just wait, Griselda. I'm mighty proud of you, and I aim to praise you. We ain't strangers here, anyhow. Ain't Jim Leslie one of the family, just like Darling Jill, there, and the rest of them? I aim to praise you mightily, Griselda. I'm as proud of you as a hen is of a lone chick."

"But don't say any more then, please, Pa."

"Son," Ty Ty said, turning towards Jim Leslie, "Griselda is the prettiest girl in the whole State of Georgia, and I reckon that's something to be proud of. Why, man alive! She's got the finest pair of rising beauties a man ever laid eyes on. If you could see them there under the cloth, you'd know I'm telling the truth as only God Himself could tell it if He could only talk. And you wouldn't be the first one to go plumb wild just looking at them, either."

"Oh, Pa!" Griselda begged, covering her face and trying to hide from sight. "Please don't say any more, Pa. Please don't!"

"Now you just sit and be quiet while I praise you mightily, Griselda. I know what I'm doing. I'm proud to discuss you, too. Jim Leslie has never seen the likes of what I'm talking about. His wife don't appear to be in the running at all. She looks like she's all mashed down on the chest and can't rise up. It's a shame and a pity, I'll be dog-gone if it ain't, that he had to marry a girl with her awful looks. It's a wonder he can stand it, on top of the disease. Now, don't try to stop me while I'm praising you, Griselda. I'm mighty proud of you, and I aim to praise you skyhigh."

Griselda was already beginning to cry a little. Her shoulders shook in jerks and she had to hold the handkerchief tight against her eyes so the tears would not fall on her lap.

"Son," Ty Ty said, "ain't she the prettiest little girl you ever did see? When I was a young man, I used to think that all girls were alike, more or less, after allowing for a little natural difference, and I reckon maybe you've thought the same up till now; but when you've got an eyeful of Griselda, there, you know durn well you've been missing a heap thinking such foolishness all your life. Son, I reckon you know what I mean. You sit there and look at her and you get to feeling something trying to stand up on the inside of you. That's it. I ain't been around much outside of Georgia, and so I can't speak for the other parts of the world, but I've sure-God seen a heap in my time in Georgia, and I'm here to tell you that it ain't no use to go no further away when it comes to looking for such prettiness. Man alive! Griselda totes around with her so much prettiness that it's a shame to look sometimes."

Griselda cried brokenly.

Ty Ty felt in his pocket for a quarter, finally picking it out of a handful of nails, harness brads, and loose change. He gave it to Griselda.

"Now, ain't I right, Jim Leslie?"

Jim Leslie glanced at his father and back again at Griselda. He appeared to be far less angry with his father than he had been earlier in the evening. He wished he could say something to Griselda, or to Ty Ty about her.

"Maybe that wasn't a fair question," Ty Ty said. "I reckon I'd best take that back, son. You ain't had a chance to see Griselda like I have, and you can't be expected to take my word for what you ain't seen. When the time comes to see her, though, you'll remember that I didn't lie about it, not one word. She's got all the prettiness I said she has, and then some. If you'll just sit there and look at her, you'll get to feeling it in no time. Her prettiness comes right through everything if you're there to see it."

Jim Leslie suddenly sat up and listened. There was the distinct sound of a person walking somewhere in the house. He jumped to his feet, nodding almost imperceptibly at Darling Jill and Griselda, and ran from the room.

Darling Jill got up and walked across the room and stood by the mantelpiece looking at the bric-a-brac. She turned and called Griselda.

"Did you ever see such beautiful things in all your life, Griselda?"

"But we shouldn't touch anything, Darling Jill. None of it is ours. It belongs to them."

"Jim Leslie is my brother, so why shouldn't we do what we like in his house?"

"It's her house, too."

Darling Jill turned up her nose and made a face that both Griselda and Ty Ty could plainly see.

"Jim Leslie lives in fine style all right," Ty Ty said. "Just look at all the fine furniture in this room. To look at him now, a man wouldn't think that he came from out near Marion when he was a boy. I don't reckon he's got all the way used to such things, though. I'll bet a pretty he wishes sometimes he was out at home with Buck and Shaw and the rest of us helping dig in the holes. Jim Leslie ain't no different from the whole of us, Griselda. Don't let a fine suit of clothes try to tell you different. I wouldn't be scared in his house if I was you."

Darling Jill put her hand on the mahogany endtable and felt the smooth beauty of it. She called Griselda to admire it with her.

"There is a picture as big as a window sash," Ty Ty remarked, getting up and going to the wall to inspect it more closely. "Now, it took a lot of time and patience to do a job like that. I'll bet there was two months' work put into that. Just look at all the trees with red leaves."

They looked for a moment at the landscape Ty Ty admired so much, and went to the windows to look at the curtains. Ty Ty was left to himself, puzzled over the oil painting. He stood back and looked at it with his head to one side, and then he walked closer to study the texture of it. He liked the picture best of anything he had noticed in the house.

"The man who painted that knew what he was doing, all right," Ty Ty said. "He didn't put in all the limbs on the trees, but I'll be dog-goned if he didn't make the picture more like a real woods than woods really are. I've never seen a grove of trees like that in all my life, but dog-gone if it ain't better than the real thing. I sure would like to have a picture like that out at Marion. Those old Black-Draught calendars ain't nothing once you have seen a picture like this. Even those Coca-Cola signs they put up around Marion look pretty sick up beside something fine like this. I sure wish I could persuade Jim Leslie to part with it and let me take it home with me tonight."

"Pa, please don't ask for anything," Griselda begged in haste. "All this belongs to her, too."

"If Jim Leslie wants to give me something out of the bounty of his heart, I'll take it. And if she tries to stop me, then I'll just be compelled to ride right over her. What do I care for her!"

Ty Ty turned about, and in turning he knocked a china vase from a little table he had not known was in existence. He looked quickly at Darling Jill and Griselda.

"Now I've gone and done it," he said meekly. "What will Jim Leslie say to that!"

"Quick," Griselda said, "we must pick up every piece before she comes into the room."

She and Ty Ty got down on the floor and swept the chips of thin china into a pile. Darling Jill would not help. She acted as though she did not care whether the pieces were picked up or left lying on the floor for everyone to see. Ty Ty trembled all over when he thought of what Jim Leslie's wife would say if she saw what he had so carelessly done.

"Where in the world can we put the pieces?" Griselda asked excitedly.

Ty Ty looked wildly around the room. He did not know what he was looking for, but the windows were closed and he saw the fireplace held no ashes to bury them in.

"Here," he said, holding out both hands. "Put everything in here."

"But what are we going to do with them?"

Ty Ty slipped the broken china into his pocket, smiling up at both of them. He walked away holding the pocket with his hand.

"That's the finest place in the world. When we get on the outside of town, I'll just cast them away and won't nobody ever know the difference."

Darling Jill looked into the next room through the wide glass doors. She could see nothing in the darkness, but she imagined it was the dining-room. Both she and Griselda wished to see everything they could during the short time they would be there.

Ty Ty sat down in a chair to wait for Jim Leslie's return. He had been gone for ten or fifteen minutes, and Ty Ty was anxious for him to come back. He felt lost in the big house.

Jim Leslie came to the door. Ty Ty got up and walked toward his son.

"What did you wish to see me about?"

"Well, I'm hard up, son. Black Sam and Uncle Felix didn't get much cotton planted this year, what with taking time off every day or so to dig some for the lode on their own account, and when September comes, I won't hardly have a red penny to my name. I'm aiming to strike that lode out there any day now, but I can't say when it will be. And I need a little money to tide me over."

"I can't be lending you money, Pa. All I've got is tied up in real estate, and it takes all I can make from day to day to run this house. You've got the impression that people here in Augusta go around carrying big rolls of money with them, and that's wrong; people with money have to invest it, and when it's invested, you just can't pick it up one moment and lay it down the next."

"Your wife has got some."

"Well, I suppose she has, but it's not mine."

Jim Leslie turned and looked down the hall as though he expected to see Gussie. She was still in another part of the house.

"How much do you think you've got to have?"

"Two or three hundred dollars would see me through the fall and winter. Next spring we'll be able to get a big crop of cotton planted. All I need now is enough to see us through the fall and winter."

"I don't know if I can let you have that much. I tell you, I'm hard up myself right now. I've got some tenements downtown, but I can't collect much rent these days. I've had to put out seven or eight families already, and vacant rooms don't bring in a cent."

"Ask your wife for it then, son."

"When do you have to have it?"

"Right now. I need it to buy feed for the mules and rations for the household and two share-croppers. It takes a lot of money to run a farm these days when it's all going out and durn little coming in."

"I wish you could see me later. I'd be better fixed in another month. I've attached some furniture that ought to bring me in some money when it's sold. You don't know how hard up I am when I can't collect rent."

"I'm sorry to hear that you're selling poor people's household goods, son. That would make me ashamed of myself if I was you. I don't reckon I could bring myself to be so hard on my fellow-creatures."

"I thought you came here to borrow money. I can't stand here all night listening to your talk."

"Well, I've got to have some money, son," Ty Ty said. "Mules and share-croppers and my own household can't wait. We've got to eat, and eat quick."

Jim Leslie took out his pocketbook and counted an amount in ten- and twenty-dollar bills. He folded the money once and handed it to his father.

"That's a great help, son," Ty Ty said gratefully. "I sure do thank you from the bottom of my heart for helping me out at a time like this. When the nuggets come in, there won't be any need for borrowing more."

"That's all I can let you have. And don't come up to me on the street and ask for more. I can't let you have any more. You ought to stop trying to find gold out there and raise cotton and something to eat. There's no sense in a man with a hundred acres and two mules having to run to town every time he needs a bunch of beets. Raise it on the land out there. That's good land. It's been lying fallow, most of it, for twelve or fifteen years. Make those two share-croppers raise enough vegetables to feed themselves."

Ty Ty nodded his head at everything Jim Leslie said. He felt good now. The flat roll of money in his pocket raised him to a level with any man. Three hundred dollars was all he had wished for, and he had not expected to get any.

"I reckon we'll be going on home now," Ty Ty said.

Ty Ty went to the library and called Darling Jill and Griselda. They came into the hall and moved toward the door.

Jim Leslie was the last to leave the house. He followed them across the wide porch and down the steps to the walk. After they had seated themselves in Ty Ty's automobile, Jim Leslie came to the side where Griselda was and laid his hand on the door. He leaned against the car, looking at Griselda.

"Sometime when you're in town, come to see me," he said slowly, writing something on a card with his fountain pen and handing it to her. "I'm going to expect you, Griselda."

Griselda lowered her head to escape his eyes.

"I couldn't do that," she said.

"Why not?"

"Buck wouldn't like it."

"To hell with Buck," Jim Leslie said. "Come anyway. I'd like to talk to you."

"You'd better leave her alone and attend to your wife," Darling Jill said.

"I don't give a damn about her," he replied heatedly. "I'm going to look for you, Griselda."

"I can't do that," Griselda said again, shaking her head. "It wouldn't be fair to Buck. I'm his wife."

"I said to hell with Buck. I'm going to get you, Griselda. If you don't come to see me in my office the next time you're in town, I'm coming out there after you. Do you hear? I'm coming out there and bring you back here."

"Buck would shoot you, too," Darling Jill said. "He's had enough trouble with Will already."

"Will who? Who in hell is Will? What's he got to do with her?"

"You know Will Thompson."

"That lint-head? Good God, Griselda, you wouldn't let Will Thompson have anything to do with you, would you? That damn Horse Creek Valley lint-head?"

"What if he does live in a company town?" Darling Jill asked quickly. "He's a lot better than some of the people who live in these fine houses."

Jim Leslie put his arm over the back of the seat and dropped it closely around Griselda. She tried to move away from him, but he pulled her back. When she was still again, he leaned forward and tried to kiss her.

"You leave her alone, son, and let us be going home before trouble starts," Ty Ty said, standing up. "This here now pulling at her has got to stop."

"I'll drag her out of this damn automobile," he answered. "I know what I want."

Darling Jill started the car and it moved rapidly away. After it had gone several yards, Jim Leslie found that he could not remain there much longer. He knew Darling Jill might intentionally drive close to one of the trees along the curb and he would be knocked to the ground. He made one more effort to reach Griselda before he was forced from the runningboard. He reached for her, catching the open collar of her floral print frock in his fingers. He could feel the cloth suddenly give way, and he looked down at her and tried to see in the semidarkness. Before he could lean closer, Darling Jill swerved the car to the other side of the street, hurling him to the pavement.

He landed heavily on his hands and knees, but he was not so badly hurt as he thought he would be. The force of his fall made his hands and knees sting with pain, but he got to his feet immediately, brushing his clothes and watching the fast disappearing car in the distance.

At the next corner they all looked back and saw Jim Leslie standing under the street light dusting the dirt from his suit. There was a tear in the knee of one of his trouser legs, but he had not yet discovered it.

"I reckon you did the right thing," Ty Ty said, speaking to Darling Jill. "Jim Leslie didn't mean no harm to Griselda, but anything in God's world might have happened if he had kept on. He said something about dragging her out of the car, and he's man enough to do it, too. I'd hate, though, to have to leave here without her and have to face Buck downtown when he asked where she was."

"Oh, Jim Leslie is all right, Pa," Griselda said. "He didn't hurt me a bit. He didn't even scare me. He's too nice to be ugly."

"Well, it's mighty white of you to say that about him, but I don't know. Jim Leslie is a Walden, and the Walden men ain't so well known for their timidness as they are for their getting what they're after. Maybe I'm wrong about that, though. Maybe I'm the only one with the name who's that way."

Coasting down the long steep grade to the brightly lighted city on the flood plain below, Ty Ty leaned forward to see what made Griselda's shoulders jerk so much. He could hear her trying to hold back sobs, but there were no tears in her eyes that he could see.

"Maybe Jim Leslie would have dragged her out, after all," he said to himself. "I don't know what else could be wrong with her, unless it is that. It takes a Walden to make the girls all wrought up."

He leaned further forward, crouching on his knees so he would not be hurled from the open car if Darling Jill should suddenly turn a corner while he was not expecting it. He looked forward and saw that Griselda was trying to fasten the tear in her new dress. It had been ripped down the front almost to her waist, exposing the creamy whiteness of her body. Ty Ty looked again before she pinned the dress securely together. He wondered if it had been anything he said that evening that was the cause of her dress being torn like that.

After a while he sat back on the seat, stretching his legs against the footrest, and clutched more tightly in his moist palm the roll of three hundred dollars Jim Leslie had let him have.

Chapter XIII

Rosamond, Buck, and Shaw were waiting on the downtown corner when they arrived. Will, though, was not in sight. They rode up to the curb and stopped, shutting off the motor. The second story windows behind the iron-grilled balconies were still open and lights were burning in most of them. Ty Ty tried not to look higher than the plate glass windows on the street level.

"Did you get it, Pa?" Rosamond asked, the first to reach the car.

"I reckon I did," he said proudly. "Just look at this big wad of greenbacks!"

Buck and Shaw were drawn to the side of the car to see it. Everyone looked pleased.

"I need a new raincoat," Shaw said.

"Son," Ty Ty said, shaking his head and pushing the roll of money back into his pocket out of sight, "son, when it rains, just peel off your clothes and let your skin take care of the rest. God never made a finer raincoat than a man's skin, anyhow."

"What are you going to do with all that money, Pa?" Buck said next. "You can spare a little of it, can't you? I haven't had any spending-money since a month ago Sunday."

"And you won't get none of this in a month of Sundays. You boys talk like this was nuggets I've got, expecting it to be shared. Jim Leslie let me have all this money to see us through the fall and winter. We've got to eat on this, and share with the mules besides."

Ty Ty craned his neck to find Will. He was anxious to leave for home, because it was nearly midnight then and he wished to get an early start in the morning. He was planning to resume digging at sunrise.

"Where's Will?"

"He was here a minute ago," Rosamond said, getting into the car and sitting down beside Ty Ty on the back seat. "He'll be back any second now."

"Will ain't gone and done it again, has he?" Ty Ty asked. "Ain't no sense in a man going to the dogs ever so often."

"Will didn't go to the dogs this time," Shaw said, winking at Griselda. "He went with a good-looking blonde. I reckon he's through with her by now, though, because the last time I saw him pass by he was getting ready to ditch her."

Rosamond choked back a sob.

"Will never means no harm," Ty Ty said. "Tomorrow morning bright and early we're all going to go out and get a good start digging in the holes. That'll straighten Will out."

"It looks like rain now," Shaw said. "Won't be no early start in the morning if it rains hard tonight."

"It can't rain now," Ty Ty said assuredly. "I'm against it raining for yet a while. We've got to dig in the holes without fail."

Each time there was a hard rain, the holes filled up with water, sometimes two or three feet deep. The only thing they could do in cases like that was to siphon it out with the long hose. They would put one end of the long hose in the hole they were digging, the other end in a hole situated lower on a hillside, and siphon the water from one to the other. Before Ty Ty had bought the second-hand fire hose from the Augusta Fire Department, they had had many trying days of labor. They had to carry out the water in buckets in those days, and if the water was deep, a day or two was lost after every rain before they could resume excavating the earth. With the fire hose now they could siphon out several feet of water in an hour or less.

Ty Ty continued to crane his neck, looking up the street and down it.

"Here comes Will now."

Rosamond turned around to see in which direction Ty Ty was looking. She began to sob again.

Will sauntered up to the car, his hat tilted precariously on the side of his head, and leaned against the front mudguard on Ty Ty's side. He took off his hat and fanned his face.

"Have any luck?" he shouted at Ty Ty. "Get the money, fellow?"

He could be heard for several blocks. People as far away as the next corner stopped and turned around and looked back to see what the disturbance was.

"Hush, Will," Griselda said.

She was the closest to him and she believed it was her duty to try to quiet him until they could get out of town.

"Why, hello there, good-looking!" Will shouted at her. "Where'd you come from? I didn't see you when I drove up."

Buck and Shaw stood nearby and laughed at Will's behavior. The others were anxious to get him into the car and drive away before a patrolman came by.

"I'm sure-God thankful I ain't a man of drinking habits," Ty Ty said. "Once I got started I wouldn't know when to stop. I'd go the whole hog, as sure as God makes little green apples."

Buck and Shaw helped Will into the back seat, in spite of his violent protest. Rosamond pulled up the auxiliary seats and gave Will her place beside Ty Ty. Buck sat with her while Shaw and Ty Ty held Will down between them.

"You folks ain't doing me fair and square," Will protested, kicking his feet against Ty Ty's shins. "I'm not getting justice. Don't you know I can't leave the city till the last shot is fired? Just look at everybody still up and walking the streets. Let me out of here."

Darling Jill pulled away from the curb and started out the street that led to the Marion highway.

"Now wait a minute," Will said. "Where we going? I'm going home tonight. Turn around and take me to the Valley."

"We're going home, Will," Ty Ty said. "Now just sit back and cool off in the night air."

"That's a lie," he said, "because we're going toward Marion. I've got to get back to the Valley tonight. I've got to see about turning on the power in the mill."

"He's out of his head a little," Ty Ty said. "He drank too much raw corn."

"He talks about turning on the power even when he's sober, though," Rosamond said. "He even talks about it in his sleep at night now."

"Well, I don't know what he's talking about. I can't make head nor tail out of it. What power? What's he going to turn it on for?"

"Will says they're going to take the mill away from the company and turn on the power and run it themselves."

"That's just some more of those crazy cotton-mill workers' doings," Ty Ty said. "Farmers ain't never talking like that. Farmers are peace-loving creatures, taking it all in all. It looks like those fools in the Valley ain't got a bit of sense. Neither Will nor any of the rest of them. He ought to stay and farm some and dig a little in the holes on the side. I'm in favor of making him stay away from Horse Creek Valley before he gets his head shot off."

"He wouldn't be content to do that," Rosamond said. "I know Will. He's a loomweaver through and through. I don't suppose there ever was a man who loves a cotton mill as much as he does. Will talks about a loom just like it was a baby, sometimes. He wouldn't be content on a farm."

Will had stretched out on the seat, his feet propped against the footrest, and his head thrown back on top of the seat. He had not closed his eyes, however, and he looked as if he were aware of every word spoken.

They had left the city far behind. Each time they went over the crest of a sand hill they could look back and see the yellow glow of the lighted city behind them on the flood plain. Far up above it, looking as if it were built in the sky, the lighted streets of The Hill appeared like a castle in the clouds.

The big seven passenger car was rushing through the night, its two long beams of light looking like the feelers of a fast flying insect as it broke through the wall of darkness ahead. Darling Jill had driven over the highway hundreds of times, and she knew when each curve was coming. The hot tires sang on the smooth concrete.

The fifteen miles to Marion was driven in twenty minutes. Just before they reached the town, the car slowed down and they turned off the paved highway on the sand-clay road home. The house was only a mile and a half away, and they were there in a few minutes.

Ty Ty got up reluctantly. He always enjoyed riding in an automobile at night.

"This has been my lucky day, folks," he said, climbing out and stretching. "Man alive! I feel like nobody's business!"

He walked over the yard, feeling the familiar hard white sand under his shoes. It was a wonderful sensation to come back home and walk around the yard. He liked to take trips to Marion and to Augusta merely for the opportunity it gave him to come back and walk over the hard white sand and to stand and look at the big piles of earth scattered over the farm like magnified ant hills.

Will sat up and stared at the shadowy outline of the house and barn. He rubbed his eyes and looked again, leaning forward in order to see better.

"Who brought me out here?" he asked. "I had to go home tonight."

"That's all right, Will," Rosamond said soothingly. "It was late, and Pa wanted to come home and go to bed. We'll get back tomorrow some way. If Darling Jill can't take us, we can go on the bus."

She put her arm around his waist and led him toward the house. He followed her resignedly.

"I'm going to turn the power on," he said.

"Of course you are, Will."

"If it's the last thing I ever do, I'm going to turn the power on."

"Of course, Will."

"They can't stop me. I'm going in there and throw those switches on, so help me God!"

"Let's go to bed now," Rosamond said tenderly. "When we get into bed, I'll rub your head and sing you to sleep."

They stumbled up the steps in the darkness and entered the house. Darling Jill and Griselda went behind them and lighted the lamps.

"I've been wondering how that Dave is," Ty Ty said. "Come on, boys, and we'll step down to the barn to see."

"I'm tired," Shaw said. "I want to go to bed."

"It won't take a minute, son. Just a minute."

They walked down to the barn silently. There was no moon, but the sky was clear and the stars were bright. The threatening clouds had disappeared, and there was little possibility of rain before morning. They went through the barn gate and on into the barn where the stalls were.

There was no sound, except that of somebody snoring. Even the mules were quiet.

Ty Ty struck a match and lighted the lantern that always hung by the barn door. He carried it to the stall where Dave slept at night.

"Well, I'll be a suck-egg mule," Ty Ty exclaimed in a low husky undertone.

"What's the matter, Pa?" Buck asked, coming up and looking through the hay rack.

"Now ain't that something, son?"

Shaw and Buck looked at Dave and at Uncle Felix. Both of them were sound asleep. Uncle Felix's shotgun was standing in the corner of the stall, and he was propped uncomfortably against the stall partition, with his head on his shoulder, snoring loud enough to be heard all the way to the other end of the barn. Dave had stretched out on his back and rested his head on a bundle of fodder. He looked as peaceful as a newborn babe, Ty Ty thought, and he turned away so Dave would not be disturbed.

"Don't bother them, boys," he said, backing off. "Uncle Felix couldn't help going to sleep. He looks dog-tired, sitting up there snoring to beat-the-band. And I don't reckon Dave is after getting loose. If he was, he'd be gone long before now. He's content to stay, it appears to me. Just leave them alone. He won't run off before morning, anyhow."

On the way back to the house, Buck walked beside his father.

"That Dave is after Darling Jill, Pa. You ought to stop him from taking up with her. The first thing you know, she'll be running off with him."

Ty Ty walked along thinking for several moments.

"He's already had her once," he said. "They went out under that oak tree yonder the other night, and that's where Will and me found them. What I'm thinking now is that I don't reckon I need to worry about them running off. A man and a girl only run off when they can't do what they're after at home. So I reckon there won't be nothing for them to run off together about. I've got a notion that Darling Jill is done with him, anyhow. She is set up all she wants."

Buck walked ahead a little distance. He spoke to his father over his shoulder. "You ought to make her behave herself, Pa. She's going to get ruined the way she's headed."

"Not if she keeps an eye on the curvature of the moon, she won't," he replied. "And I reckon Darling Jill can take care of herself all right. She knows what she's doing, most of the time. She's crazy as hell sometimes, and about nothing. But that don't keep her from knowing which is straight up and which is straight down."

Buck went into the house without further comment. Shaw went to the back porch for a drink of water before going to bed. Ty Ty was left in the hall alone.

The bedroom doors were open, and the rest of the house was getting ready for bed. Rosamond was undressing Will, pulling off his trousers by the cuffs while he sat on a chair falling asleep again. Ty Ty stood and watched them for several moments.

"See if you can't talk Will into staying here and working on the farm, Rosamond," he said, coming to the door. "I need somebody to oversee the crops. Me and the boys can't spare the time, because we've got to dig all the time, and those two darkies invite watching. They like to dig in their own holes better than they do plowing the crops."

"I couldn't make him do that, Pa," she said, shaking her head and looking up at Will. "It would break his heart if he had to leave the Valley and come over here to live. He's not made for farming and such things. He was raised in a mill town, and he's grown up in one. I couldn't think of trying to make him leave now."

Ty Ty walked away disappointed. He saw that it would be useless for the present to try to argue her into it.

At the door of Buck and Griselda's room he stopped and looked inside. They also were getting ready for bed. Buck was sitting on a chair taking off his shoes, and Griselda was sitting on the rug taking off her stockings.

They looked up when Ty Ty stopped at the door.

"What do you want, Pa?" Buck asked irritatedly.

"Son," he said, "I just can't help admiring Griselda, there. Ain't she the prettiest little girl you ever did see?"

Buck tossed his shoes and socks under the bed and lay down. He turned over, his back to Ty Ty, and pulled the sheet around his head.

Griselda shook her head at Ty Ty disapprovingly.

"Now, Pa," she said, looking up at him, "please don't start that now. You promised not to say that anymore, too."

Ty Ty put one foot inside the room and leaned against the door frame. He watched her roll and unroll her stockings and hang them over the back of the chair. She got up quickly and stood at the foot of the bed.

"You wouldn't begrudge me a little thing like that, now would you, Griselda?"

"Aw, now, Pa," she said.

Griselda waited for him to leave so she could finish undressing and put on her nightgown. Ty Ty waited in the doorway, one foot inside the room, admiring her. She finally began to unfasten her dress, glancing at him each moment. When she had unpinned it, she slipped her arms from the sleeves, holding it against her. With her other hand she put the nightgown over her head. Dexterously, she allowed the dress to drop to the floor while the nightgown slipped down over her shoulders and hips, but in the fraction of a second Ty Ty opened his eyes wider to see that there had been at least several inches between the top of the dress and the hem of the gown when they both slipped downward. He rubbed his eyes to see what had happened.

"Dog-gone my hide," he said, walking away into the dark hall. "Dog-gone it!"

Griselda blew out the light and jumped into bed.

Chapter XIV

IT LOOKED to Ty Ty as if there would be trouble before evening. Since early that morning when they had started to work in the big hole beside the house, Buck had been uttering threats at Will, and Will had sat sullen and alone on the porch cursing Buck under his breath. All of them were digging, including Buck, Sam and Uncle Felix; everyone was working except Will, and he still refused to go down into the hole and shovel sand and clay in the hot sun.

Buck was in an ugly temper, and the increasing heat of midday in the hole, where there was not a breath of fresh air, made his anger more and more dangerous. All morning Ty Ty had done his best to keep Buck down there.

"I'll kill the son-of-a-bitch," Buck said for the fourth time.

"Will ain't going to bother Griselda, Buck," Ty Ty told him. "Now go on and dig and leave him out of your mind."

Buck was not impressed by Ty Ty's assurances, even if he did remain quiet for a while. Ty Ty climbed out of the hole to cool off a little. He got on top of the ground and looked around for Will, just to make sure that he was not bothering Griselda. When he found him, Will was sitting peacefully on the front porch, cursing Buck under his breath.

Down in the crater, Dave was working with the rest. Ty Ty had come to the conclusion that the albino boy could be of greater service for the present if he would help dig. He had already divined the lode for Ty Ty, and Ty Ty thought it would be a good idea to let him help them strike it. The shotgun had been replaced on the rack in the dining-room, and he was no longer under guard. Uncle Felix had been singing that morning for the first time since Dave had been brought from the swamp. The colored man was glad to have the responsibility off his mind and to be allowed to dig with the rest of them.

When Ty Ty told Dave that he was not to be kept under guard any longer, the boy had acted as though he were afraid that Ty Ty would tell him to leave. When he was told to get down into the hole with Buck and Shaw, however, he was delighted. He had hoped that

Darling Jill would come and talk to him, but she had not appeared. Dave was beginning to fear by that time that she was not going to have anything more to do with him. If she still cared for him, he believed she would have come to the crater and at least smiled at him.

"Will," Ty Ty said, sitting down and fanning himself with his straw hat, "what in the pluperfect hell do you boys want to scrap about, anyhow? That ain't no way for a family like us to be doing. I'm ashamed of the way you and Buck act."

"Listen," he answered quickly. "You tell him to keep his mouth shut, and you won't hear another word out of me. The only reason why I've ever said anything to him was because he's always calling me a lint-head, and saying he's going to kill me. Tell him to keep his mouth shut, and you won't be able to kick about what I say."

Ty Ty sat and thought a while. The mystery of human life was not nearly so obscure to him as it was to most men, and he wondered why everyone could not see as he did. Will Thompson probably came as close to understanding the secrets of the mind and body as he himself understood them, but Will was not the kind of man to tell what he knew. He went about his life keeping his thoughts to himself, and acting, when the time came, without revealing, save through his actions, the secrets of his knowledge. Ty Ty knew that the whole trouble between Will and Buck was over Griselda, and Buck was undoubtedly justified in being suspicious of Will's intentions. Griselda was certainly not to blame for anything; she had never made an advance toward Will during the whole time she had been in the house. She always appeared to be trying so hard to keep Will away from her, and to make Buck believe that she cared only for him. Ty Ty knew she had had ample opportunity to deceive Buck if she had wished to; the truth was that she did not wish to deceive him. But she could not keep men from admiring her and being drawn to her and from trying to take her away from her husband. Ty Ty wondered what could be done about it.

"If there's one thing I've tried all my life to do, it's to keep peace in the family," he told Will. "I reckon I'd just fold up and die away if I saw blood spilled on my land. I'd never be able to get over the sight of it. I'd die to keep that from happening. I couldn't stand to see blood on my land."

"There's not going to be blood spilt, if Buck keeps his mouth shut and minds his own business. I've never tried to pick a fight with him. He always starts it, just like he started it this morning. I never even went close enough to him to say anything. He just came up and looked mean and started calling me a son-of-a-bitch and a lint-head, and the rest. That's all right with me. I don't intend to fight your boys for a little thing like that. But he keeps it up, rubbing it in all the time, and there's where the trouble is going to really start. If he'd say what it is he's got to say, and let it go with that, then it would be all right with me. But he hangs around saying it all day long. Tell him to shut up, if you don't want to see blood spilt on your land."

Ty Ty cocked his ears and listened. An automobile was slowing down to turn into the yard. Pluto Swint drove in and stopped under the shade of one of the live-oak trees. He got out laboriously, compressing his big round belly with the palms of his hands so he could squeeze himself between the door and the steeringwheel.

"I'm glad to see you, Pluto," Ty Ty said. He remained beside Will on the steps and waited for Pluto to come over and sit down. "I sure am glad to see you, Pluto. You got here just when I like to see you most. Somehow, it seems like you sort of bring a calming influence when you come. I can sit here now and feel satisfied that there won't be nothing to cause harm to me or mine."

Pluto blew and puffed and wiped his face free of perspiration, taking a seat on the steps. He looked at Will, nodding his head. Will spoke to him.

"Counted many votes today, so far?" Ty Ty asked.

"Not yet," Pluto answered, still blowing and puffing. "I couldn't get an early start today, and this is all the distance I've gone."

"Ain't it hot?"

"It's sizzling today," Pluto said. "And that's a fact."

Will took out his pocketknife and broke off a splinter on the steps and began whittling it. He could hear Buck saying something about him down in the hole around the house, but he was not interested in what he was saying.

"Me and Rosamond have got to go home today."

Ty Ty looked at him quickly, on the verge of protesting, but he held his tongue after a moment's thought. He wished to have Will there to help them dig, but Will would not dig, and he was of no help. That being the case, Ty Ty reasoned that it would be better for Will and Rosamond to go back to Scottsville. As long as Will remained there, Buck was going to make threats, and Will might not be so reasonable after another day. The safest and wisest course, Ty Ty said to himself, would be to let Will and Rosamond go home.

"I reckon we could have taken you last night when we were in Augusta," he said, "but it was pretty late, for one thing, and everybody wanted to come back and go to bed."

"I'll get Darling Jill to take us to Marion and we'll catch a bus. I've got to get back before night."

Ty Ty was relieved to think that perhaps there would be no trouble between Buck and Will after all. If they left soon, Buck would not have a chance to challenge Will.

"I'll go tell Darling Jill to get ready and drive you and Rosamond into town," he said, rising.

"Sit down," Will told him, "and let's wait a while. There's no hurry. It's only about eleven o'clock now. We'll wait till after dinner."

Ty Ty sat down uneasily. The best he could hope for was that Will and Buck would not meet before then.

"How's politics now, Pluto?" he asked, trying to take his mind off such an unpleasant subject.

"Getting hot," Pluto said. "The candidates ain't content to count a vote once any longer; they're going out now and counting them over again to make sure they ain't lost them to somebody else. This running around all over the country has got me worn to a frazzle already. I don't see how I can keep up the chase like this for another six weeks."

"Now Pluto," Ty Ty said confidently, "you know you'll win in a walk. Every man I've talked with since New Year's Day has told me he was going to vote for you."

"Saying he's going to vote for me and doing it when the time comes is as far apart as the land and the sky. I don't put any trust in politics. I've been mixed up in them since I was twenty-two years old, and I know."

Ty Ty studied the smooth white sand in the yard, his eyes following the line of small round pebbles under the eaves of the porch where the water drained to the ground.

"I was just thinking, Pluto, that maybe you'd like to drive a little trip today."

"Where to?"

"Taking Will and Rosamond over to Horse Creek Valley in your car. I know the girls would be tickled to death to ride over there and back with you."

"I've got to be getting on down the road to count votes," Pluto protested. "And that's a fact."

"Now, you know you'd be pleased to ride over there and back, Pluto, carrying such fine-looking girls in your car. You ain't going to count votes sitting here in the yard, anyhow."

"I've got to get out and count votes all day long."

Ty Ty got up and went into the house, leaving Will and Pluto on the steps. Will rolled a cigarette and borrowed a match from Pluto. The sound of the picks striking the hard clay in the bottom of the crater around the house rose and fell in their ears to the rhythm of Uncle Felix's work-song. Pluto would have liked to have gone to the hole and looked down into it to see how deep it had been dug, but it was too much of an exertion for him to get up. He sat listening to the sound of the picks, trying to determine from the sound how deep the hole was. After he had thought about it a while, he was glad he had not gone around the house to look into it. He did not particularly care how deep it was, anyway; and, on top of that, if he had gone, the sight of seeing Buck and Shaw, the two darkies, and Dave sweating in the air-tight hole would have made him much hotter than he was already.

He looked up to see Darling Jill standing behind him. She was freshly dressed, swinging a wide-brimmed hat in her hands. She looked as if she were getting ready to go somewhere without consulting him. Will moved over a little and she sat down between them, putting her arm through Pluto's and placing her cheek against his shoulder.

"Pa said you were going to take Griselda and me for a ride to Scottsville," she smiled. "I didn't know anything about it until he came just now and told me."

Will laughed, leaning forward to see Pluto's face.

"I can't do that," Pluto protested.

"Now, Pluto, if you loved me a little you would."

"Well, I do that, anyway."

"Then you'll take us over with you when you take Will and Rosamond home."

"I've got to get out and count some votes," he said.

She reached up and kissed him on the cheek. Pluto beamed. He leaned closer so she would do it again.

"You can't be wasting your time canvassing for votes today, Pluto."

"I don't reckon I can," he said. "Can't you do that another time?"

"Once before we leave, and once before we start back," she promised.

"I sure can't get elected like this," Pluto said. "And that's a fact."

"There'll be plenty of time after today, Pluto."

She allowed his hand to rest on her knees, and watched him closely while he lifted her skirt and slipped his fingers under her garter.

"You're nothing but a big overgrown baby, Pluto. You're always wanting something you can't have."

"What do you say to getting married, Darling Jill?" he asked, his face flushing.

"It's not time yet."

"Why isn't it time yet?"

"Because I'd have to be a few months gone before I'd do that."

"It won't be long then," Will said, winking at Pluto.

Pluto was slow to understand what Darling Jill meant. He started to ask her, but he was silenced by Darling Jill's and Will's laughter.

"It won't be long if that fellow from the swamp stays here another week or so," Will said.

"Dave?" Darling Jill asked, making a face. "He's nothing. I wouldn't hurt Pa's little white-haired boy."

Pluto smiled contentedly when he heard her dismiss the albino so completely.

"Well, if you're going to forget him," Will said, "was I something, or wasn't I?"

"To tell the truth," she confessed, "you've got me worried."

"You ought to be. When I drive a nail into a plank, it stays driven."

"What's that you're talking about got to do with getting married, Darling Jill?" Pluto asked.

"Oh, nothing," she replied, winking at Will. "Will was just counting the daisies he picked."

"Well, I'm ready to get married," Pluto said.

"Well, I'm not," she said. "And that's a fact, too."

Will got up, laughing at Pluto, and went into the house to get ready to leave. Pluto put his arm around Darling Jill and hugged her. He knew he was going to drive them to Scottsville, because he would have done anything in the world Darling Jill asked. She sat close to him, submissive, while he squeezed her in his arms. She liked him, she knew she did. She thought she loved him, too, and in spite of his protruding stomach and his laziness. When the time came, she would marry him. She had already settled that much. What she did not know, was when the time would be.

Sitting so close to him then, she wished to tell him that she was sorry she had treated him so meanly at times, and had called him such vulgar names. When she turned to speak to him, however, she was afraid to say anything. She began to wonder of the wisdom of telling Pluto she was sorry she had been free with Will and Dave and with all the others while refusing him. She decided in that moment not to say anything about it, because it would not matter to him that she did not say it. She loved Pluto too much to see him hurt needlessly.

"Maybe next week we can get married, Darling Jill?"

"I don't know, Pluto. I'll tell you when I'm ready."

"I can't keep on waiting all the time," he said. "And that's a fact."

"But if you know you are going to marry me, you can wait a little while longer."

"That would be all right, maybe," he agreed, "if it wasn't that I'm scared somebody is going to come along and take you off some day."

"If I do go away with somebody, Pluto, I'll come back in time to marry you."

Pluto hugged her with both arms, trying to hold her so tightly that the impression of her body against his would be in his memory forever. She at last freed herself and stood up.

"It's time to leave, Pluto. I'll go get Will and Rosamond. Griselda ought to be ready by now."

Pluto walked out toward his car in the shade. He turned just in time to see Buck crawl out of the big hole and walk around the corner of the house. He met Griselda as she ran out the front door.

"Where are you going?" he demanded.

"Darling Jill and I are going to ride over to Scottsville with Pluto," she said, trembling. "We'll be back soon."

"I'll kill the son-of-a-bitch," he said, running up the steps.

Buck was angry and hot. His clay-soiled clothes and his perspiration-matted hair gave him the appearance of a man suddenly become desperate.

"Please, Buck," she begged.

"Where is he now?"

She tried to talk to Buck, but he would not listen to her. Just then Ty Ty came out of the house and took Buck by the arm.

"You'd better leave me alone, now," he told Ty Ty.

"Let the girls go for the ride, Buck. There ain't no harm in that."

"You'd better turn me loose, now."

"It's all right, Buck," Ty Ty argued. "Darling Jill and Rosamond will be along, and Pluto in the car, too. Let the girls go along for the ride. Can't no harm come of that."

"I'll kill the son-of-a-bitch, now," Buck said unchanged. He was not impressed by his father's assurance of Griselda's safety.

"Buck," Griselda begged, "please don't be angry. There's nothing to talk like that about."

Ty Ty led him down the steps into the yard and tried to talk with him.

"You'd better leave me alone, now," he said again.

They began walking up and down in the yard, Ty Ty leading him by the arm. After a while, Buck pulled away and went back to the crater beside the house. He was not so angry as he had been, and not nearly so hot, and he was willing to go back to work and let Griselda go in the car to Scottsville. He went back where Shaw and Dave and the two colored men were without saying another word.

When they were certain Buck had gone to the crater to stay, Darling Jill and Rosamond stopped holding Will in the house and allowed him to come out and get into the car.

Chapter XV

THEY reached Scottsville in the upper end of the Valley two hours later.

Will had jumped out of the car when they stopped in front of the house and had run down the street, shouting back over his shoulder for them to stay until he came home. That had been in the middle of the afternoon, and at six he had not returned.

Pluto was anxious to get back to Georgia, and Griselda was frantic. She did not know what Buck might do to her for not returning home immediately, and it frightened her to think about it. She was glad to stay as long as she could, though, because it was the first time she had ever been in Horse Creek Valley, and the feeling of the company town gave her a pleasure she had never before experienced. The rows of yellow company houses, all looking alike to the eye were individual homes to her now. She could look into the yellow company house next door and almost hear the exact words the people were saying. There was nothing like that in Marion. The houses in Marion were buildings with closed doors and uninviting windows. Here in Scottsville there was a murmuring mass of humanity, always on the verge of filling the air with a concerted shout.

Pluto and Darling Jill had made a freezer of ice cream while they were waiting for Will to come home. At dark when he still had not returned, they ate the cream with graham crackers for the evening meal. Pluto was still restless, wishing to get back to Georgia. He felt uncomfortable in Horse Creek Valley and he did not like to think too much of the probability of being there long after dark. For some reason he was suspicious of cotton mill towns, and firmly believed that after dark people came out of hiding and preyed upon strangers, robbing them and beating them if not actually murdering them.

"I really believe Pluto is scared to go out of the house after dark," Darling Jill said.

Pluto trembled at the suggestion, clutching his chair. He was afraid, and if one of them asked him to go to the store down the street on an errand he would refuse to leave the house. At home in Marion he was afraid of nothing; the darkness of night had never cowed him before in all his life. But here in the Valley he trembled with acute fear; he did not know at what minute somebody would run through the unlocked door and strike him dead in his tracks.

"Will can't possibly stay out much longer," Rosamond said. "He always comes home for supper at night."

"I wish we could go, anyway," Griselda said. "Buck will be wild."

"Both of you are scared to death," Darling Jill laughed. "There's nothing to be scared of here, is there, Rosamond?"

Rosamond laughed. "Of course not."

Through the open windows the soft summer night floated into the room. It was a soft night, and it was warm; but with the evening air there was something else that excited Griselda. She could hear sounds, voices, murmurs that were like none she had ever heard before. A woman's laughter, a child's excited cry, and the faint gurgle of a waterfall somewhere below all came into the room together; there was a feeling in the air of living people just like herself, and this she had never felt before. The new knowledge that all those people out there, all those sounds, were as real as she herself was, made her heart beat faster. Never had the noises of Augusta sounded like these; in the city there were other sounds of another race of people. Here in Scottsville the people were as real as she herself was at that moment.

Will came in then, surprising her, and walked as noiselessly as a soft-toed animal. Griselda felt like running to him and throwing her arms around his neck when she first saw him. He was one of the persons she had felt in the night air.

He stood in the door of the room looking at them.

There was a look on Will's face that forced Griselda to suppress a cry that rose to her throat. She had never seen an expression on anyone's face such as he had. There was a painful plea in his eyes, a look that she had seen wounded animals have. And the lines of his face, the position of his head on his shoulders, something, whatever it was, was horrifying to look upon.

He seemed to be trying to say something. He looked as if he were bursting with words that he could not turn loose. All the things she had ever heard Rosamond say about the cotton mill down there below were written on his face more plainly than human words could express.

Will was speaking to Rosamond. His lips moved in the form of words long before she heard them. It was like looking through a pair of binoculars at a man speaking afar off, and seeing his lips move before the sound reached her ears. She looked at him wild-eyed.

"We had the meeting," he told Rosamond. "But they wouldn't listen to Harry and me. They voted to arbitrate. You know what that means."

"Yes," Rosamond said simply.

Will turned and looked at Griselda and the others.

"So we're going ahead and do it anyway. To hell with the damn local. They draw pay for arguing with us. To hell with them. We're going to turn the power on."

"Yes," Rosamond said.

"I'll be damned if I sit still and see them starve us with a dollar-ten, and charging rent on what we live in. There are enough of us to get in there and turn the power on. We can run the damn mill. We can run it better than anybody else. We're going down there in the morning and turn it on."

"Yes, Will," his wife said.

A light was switched on in one of the rooms of the yellow company house next door.

"We're going to turn the power on, and I'm man enough to do it. You'll see. I'm as strong as God Almighty Himself is now. You'll hear about the power being turned on tomorrow. Everybody will hear about it."

He sat down in silence and buried his head in his hands. No one spoke. He was the one to speak, if anyone did.

A darkness enveloped everything. For a while the whole memory of his life passed across his eyes. He squeezed the lids over the eyeballs, straining to forget the memory. But he could not forget. He could see, dimly at first, the mills in the Valley. And while he looked, everything was as bright as day. He could see, since the time he could first remember, the faces of the wild-eyed girls like morning-glories in the mill windows. They stood there looking out at him, their bodies firm and their breasts erect, year after year since he could first remember being alive. And out in the streets in front of the mills stood bloody-lipped men, his friends and brothers, spitting their lungs into the yellow dust of Carolina. Up and down the Valley he could see them, count them, call them by their names. He knew them; he had always known them. The men stood in the streets watching the ivy-covered mills. Some of them were running night and day, under blinding blue lights; some of them were closed, barred against the people who starved in the yellow company houses. And then the whole Valley was filled with the people who suddenly sprang up. There again were the girls with eyes like morning-glories and breasts so erect, running into the ivy-covered mills; and out in the street, day and night, stood his friends and brothers, looking, and spitting their lungs into the yellow dust at their feet. Somebody turned to speak to him, and through his parted lips issued blood instead of words.

Will shook his head, hitting the sides of it with the heels of his hands, and looked around him in the room. Pluto and Darling Jill, Griselda and Rosamond, were looking at him. He drew the back of his hand over his mouth, wiping away the dried blood and the warm blood he thought he felt on his lips.

"I told you to stay till I got back, didn't I?" he said, looking steadily at Griselda.

"Yes, Will."

"And you stayed. Thank God for that."

She nodded.

"We're going to turn the power on the first thing in the morning. That's settled. We're going to do that, no matter what happens."

Rosamond looked at him anxiously. She believed for a moment that he was out of his mind. It was something in the way he spoke, something that sounded strange in his voice; she had never heard him talk like that before.

"Are you all right, Will?" she asked.

"Oh, God, yes," he said.

"Try not to think so much about the mill tonight. It will make you so restless you won't be able to go to sleep."

Murmurs passed through the company streets of the company town, coming in rhythmic tread through the windows of the company house. It was alive, stirring, moving, and speaking like a real person. Griselda felt her heart ache with sharp pain.

"You've never worked in a spinning mill, have you, Pluto?" he asked suddenly, turning upon Pluto.

"No," he answered weakly. "I've got to be getting back home right away."

"You don't know what a company town is like, then. But I'll tell you. Have you ever shot a rabbit, and gone and picked him up, and when you lifted him in your hand, felt his heart pounding like—like, God, I don't know what! Have you?"

Pluto stirred uneasily in his chair. He turned to look at Griselda beside him and saw a convulsive shiver envelop her.

"I don't know," Pluto said.

"God!" Will murmured hoarsely.

They looked at him, trembling, all of them. Somehow, they had felt exactly what he had meant when he said that. They were frightened by the revelation.

A new murmur passed through the company house, floating softly through row after row of other yellow company houses.

"You think I'm drunk, don't you?" he asked.

Rosamond shook her head. She knew he was not.

"No, I'm not drunk. I've never been as sober as I am now. You think I'm drunk because I talk like that. But I'm sober, as sober as a stick of wood."

Rosamond said something to him, something tenderly soft and understanding.

"Back there in Georgia, out there in the middle of all those damn holes and piles of dirt, you think I'm nothing but a dead sapling sticking up in the ground. Well, maybe I am, over there. But over here in the Valley, I'm Will Thompson. You come over here and look at me in this yellow company house and think that I'm nothing but a piece of company property. And you're wrong about that, too. I'm Will Thompson. I'm as strong as God Almighty Himself now, and I can show you how strong I am. Just wait till tomorrow morning and walk down the street there and stand in front of the mill. I'm going up to that door and rip it to pieces just like it was a window shade. You'll see how strong I am. Maybe you'll go back to those God damn pot holes in Marion and think a little different after tomorrow."

"You'd better go to bed now, Will, and get some sleep. You'll have to get up early in the morning."

"Sleep! To hell with sleep! I'm not going to sleep now, or any time tonight. I'll be as wide awake when the sun rises as I am now."

Pluto wished to be able to get up and leave, but he was afraid to say anything while Will was talking. He did not know what to do. He looked at Darling Jill and at Griselda, but neither of them seemed anxious to go home now. They sat enthralled before Will.

Griselda sat before Will looking up at him as if he were a precious idol come to life. She felt like getting down on the floor in front of him and throwing her arms around his knees and begging for the laying of his hand on her head.

He was looking at her when she found the courage to look up. He was looking at her as if he had never seen her before.

"Stand up, Griselda," he said calmly.

She stood up immediately, rising eagerly at his command. She waited for anything he might tell her to do next.

"I've waited a long time for you, Griselda, and now is the time."

Rosamond made no move to speak or to get up. She sat calmly in her chair, her hands folded in her lap, waiting to hear what he would say the next moment.

"Ty Ty was right," Will said.

All of them wondered what Will meant. Ty Ty had said many things, so many things that it was impossible for them to know what Will had in mind.

But Griselda knew. She knew precisely the words he had used and to which Will now referred.

"Before you go any further, Will," Darling Jill said, "you'd better not forget Buck. You know what he said."

"He said he would kill me, didn't he? Well, why doesn't he come and do it? He had the chance to try it this morning. I was over there among those God damn pot holes. Why didn't he do it then?"

"He can still do it. There'll be time enough for it."

"I'm not scared of him. If he ever makes a move at me, I'll twist his neck off and throw it into one of those God damn pot holes, and him into another."

"Will," Rosamond said, "please be careful. Buck can't be stopped once he sets his head on doing something. If you put your hands on Griselda, and Buck ever hears about it, he'll kill you as sure as the world we stand on."

He was no longer interested in hearing them express their fear of what Buck would do.

Griselda stood before him. Her eyes were closed, and her lips were partly open, and her breath came rapidly. When he told her to sit down, she would sit down. Until then she would remain standing for the rest of her life.

"Ty Ty was right," Will said, looking at her. "He knew what he was talking about. He told me about you, lots of times, but I didn't have sense enough to take you then. But I'm going to now. Nothing in God's world can stop me now. I'm going to have it, Griselda. I'm as strong as God Almighty Himself now, and I'm going to do it."

Darling Jill and Pluto moved nervously in their seats, but Rosamond sat calmly quiet with folded hands in her lap.

"I'm going to look at you like God intended for you to be seen. I'm going to rip every piece of those things off of you in a minute. I'm going to rip them off and tear them into pieces so small you'll never be able to put them together again. I'm going to rip the last damn thread. I'm a loomweaver. I've woven cloth all my life, making every kind of fabric in God's world. Now I'm going to tear all that to pieces so small nobody will ever know what they were. They'll look like lint when I get through. Down there in the mill I've woven ginghams and shirting, denim and sheeting, and all the rest; up here in this yellow company house I'm going to tear hell out of the cloth on you. We're going to start spinning and weaving again tomorrow, but tonight I'm going to tear that cloth on you till it looks like lint out of a gin."

He went toward her. The veins on the backs of his hands and around his arms swelled and throbbed, looking as if they would burst. He came closer, stopping at arm's length to look at her.

Griselda stepped backward out of his reach. She was not afraid of Will, because she knew he would not hurt her. But she stepped backward out of his reach, afraid of the look in his eyes. Will's eyes were not cruel, and they were not murderous—he would not hurt her for anything in the world—they were too tender for that now—and his eyes were coming closer and closer.

Will caught the collar of her dress, a hand on each side, and flung his arms wide apart. The thin printed voile disintegrated in his hands like steam. He had ripped it from her, tearing it insanely in his hands, quickly, eagerly, minutely. She watched him with throbbing excitement, following the arcs of his flying fingers and the motions of his arms. Piece by piece he tore like a madman, hurling the fluffy lint in all directions around the room while he bent forward over the cloth. She watched him unresistingly when he flung the last of the dress aside and ripped open the white slip as though it were a paper bag. He was working faster all the time, tearing, ripping, jerking, throwing the shredded cloth around him and blowing the flying lint from his face. The final garment was silk. He tore at it frantically, even more savagely than he had at the beginning. When that was done, she was standing before him, waiting, trembling, just as he had said she would stand. Perspiration covered his face and chest. His breathing was difficult. He had worked as he had never done before, and the shredded cloth lay on the floor at his feet, covering them.

"Now!" he shouted at her. "Now! God damn it, now! I told you to stand there like God intended for you to be seen! Ty Ty was right! He said you were the most beautiful woman God ever made, didn't he? And he said you were so pretty, he said you were so God damn pretty, a man would have to get down on his hands and knees and lick something when he saw you like you are now. Didn't he? Yes, so help me God, he did! And after all this time I've got you at last, too. And I'm going to do what I've been wanting to do ever since the first time I saw you. You know what it is, don't you, Griselda? You know what I want. And you're going to give it to me. But I'm not like the rest of them that wear pants. I'm as strong as God Almighty Himself is now. And I'm going to lick you, Griselda. Ty Ty knew what he was talking about. He said that was what a man would do to you. He's got more sense than all the rest of us put together, even if he does dig in the ground like a God damn fool."

He paused for breath, going toward her. Griselda backed toward the door. She was not trying to escape from him now, but she had to go away from him until he caught her and dragged her to another part of the house. He ran, throwing his hands on her.

Chapter XVI

For a long time after they had gone Darling Jill sat squeezing her fingers with savage excitement. She was afraid to look across the room at her sister then. The beating within her breast frightened her, and she was almost choked with nervousness. Never before had she felt so completely aroused.

But when she did not look at her sister, she was afraid of being alone. She turned boldly and looked at Rosamond, and she was surprised to see such composure as Rosamond possessed. She was rocking a little in the chair, folding her hands and unfolding them without haste. There was an expression of sereneness on Rosamond's face that was beautiful to behold.

Beside her, Pluto was bewildered. He had not felt the things she had. She knew no man would. Pluto was speechless with wonder at Will and Griselda, but he was unmoved. Darling Jill had felt the surge of their lives pass through the room while Will stood before them tearing Griselda's clothes to shreds, and Rosamond had. But Pluto was a man, and he would never understand how they felt. Even Will, who brought it, had acted only with the guidance of his want of Griselda.

Through the open doors they could see the restless flicker of the street light breaking through the leaves of the trees and falling on the bed and floor of the room. Over there, in that room, were Will and Griselda. They were not in hiding, because the doors were open; they were not in secret, because their voices were strong and distinct.

"I'll pick up some of the lint now," Rosamond said calmly. She got down on her knees and began gleaning the minute particles of cotton fiber from the floor, piling them carefully beside her. "I don't need any help."

Darling Jill watched her while she gathered the threads and torn cloth slowly and with care. She bent over, her face obscured, and picked piece by piece the clothes torn from Griselda. When she had finished, she went to the kitchen and brought back a large paper bag. Into it she placed the torn voile and underclothing.

It seemed to Darling Jill that Will and Griselda had been in the room across the hall for hours. They no longer were talking, and she began to wonder if they had gone to sleep. Then she remembered that Will had said he would not sleep that night, and she knew he would be awake even if Griselda were not. She waited for Rosamond to return from the kitchen.

Rosamond came back and sat down across from her.

"Buck is going to kill Will when he hears about this," Darling Jill said.

"Yes," Rosamond replied. "I know."

"He'll never find out from me, but he'll learn of it in some way. Maybe he'll just feel it or something. But he will certainly know what happened."

"Yes," Rosamond said.

"He may be on his way over here now. He expected Griselda to come straight back."

"I don't believe he will come tonight. But he may come tomorrow."

"Will ought to go away somewhere, so Buck won't be able to find him."

"No. Will wouldn't go anywhere. He'll stay here. We couldn't make him leave."

"But Buck will kill him, Rosamond. If he stays here, and Buck hears about it, he'll be killed as sure as the world. I'm certain of that."

"Yes," Rosamond said. "I know."

Rosamond went to the kitchen to see what time it was by the clock. It was between three and four in the morning then. She came back and sat down, folding her hands and unfolding them without haste.

"Aren't we ever going home?" Pluto asked.

"No," Darling Jill said. "Shut up."

"But I've got to——"

"No, you haven't. Shut up."

Will appeared noiselessly at the door, barefooted. He was wearing only a pair of khaki pants, and he looked like a loomweaver, barebacked and sleep-refreshed, ready to go to work.

He sat down in the room with them, holding his hands around his head. He had the appearance of someone trying to protect his head from an enemy's fists.

Darling Jill felt the returning surge of savage excitement grip her. She could never again look at Will without that feeling coming over her. The memory of seeing Will stand in front of Griselda tearing her clothes to threads like a madman, hearing him talk like Ty Ty, watching him clutch Griselda with swollen muscles, that memory was branded upon her as if it had been seared upon her body with white-hot irons. She stood it as long as she could, and then she ran and fell at his feet, hugging his knees and kissing him all over. Will laid his hand on her head and stroked her hair.

She stirred jerkily, rising to her knees and thrusting her body between his legs, and locked her arms around his waist. Her head was buried against him, and she hugged him with her arms and shoulders. It was only when she could find his hands that she lay still against him. One after the other she kissed his fingers, pushing them between her lips and into her mouth. But after that, she still was not satisfied.

He continued to stroke her hair, slowly and heavily. His head was thrown back and his other arm was thrown around his face and forehead.

"What time is it?" he asked after a while.

Rosamond got up and went again to the kitchen and looked at the clock.

"It's twenty past four, Will," she said.

He covered his face again, trying to blot out the light from his eyes.

His mind was so clear he could follow a thought through the endless tube of his brain. Each thought reached to endless depths, but each time it returned after the whirling journey of his brain. Each thought raced around and around in his head, flowing smoothly from cell to cell, and he closed his eyes and knew at each moment the exact point on his skull where he could place the tip of his finger and locate it.

Up and down the Valley his mind raced, biting eagerly at the doors of the yellow company houses and at the windows of the ivy-walled mills. At Langley, at Clearwater, at Warrenville, at Bath, at Graniteville, he stopped for a moment to look at the people going into the spinning mills, the bleacheries, the weaving mills.

He came back to the room in the yellow company house in Scottsville and listened to the early morning hum of motor trucks and trailers and the whirr of passenger cars and busses on the Augusta-Aiken highway speeding over the wide concrete up and down the Valley. When the sun rose, he would be able to see the endless regiments of wild-eyed girls with erect breasts, firm-bodied girls who looked like morning-glories through the windows of the ivy-walled mills. But out in the streets, in the early morning shadow of the sun, he would see the endless rows of bloody-lipped men, his friends and brothers, standing with eyes upon the mills, spitting their lungs into the yellow dust of Carolina.

At sunrise, in the cool black-and-white of morning, Griselda came to the door. She had not been asleep. She had lain upon the bed in the other room prolonging with bated breath the night that so inevitably merged into day. It was day now, and the red glow of the sun rising over the house-tops covered her with a glow of warmth that flushed her face again and again while she stood in the doorway.

Rosamond got up.

"I'll cook breakfast now, Will," she said.

They went out, the three of them, going first to one of the other rooms to clothe Griselda.

Later in the kitchen Will heard them at the table and at the stove. First there was the smell of chewed grain, the boiling grits; then the smell of frying meat, the hunger for food; and finally there was the smell of coffee, the start of a new day.

Through the window he could see someone in the kitchen of the yellow company house next door making a fire in the cook-stove. Soon there came the curl of blue wood smoke from the chimney top. People were getting up early today; for the first time in eighteen months the mill was going to run. Down at the mill beside cool, broad, dammed-up Horse Creek they were going to turn on the power. The machinery would turn, and men would be standing in their places, stripped to the waist, working again.

He went to the kitchen impatiently. He wished to fill his stomach with warm food and to run down the street calling to his friends in the yellow company houses on both sides of the street. They would come to the door, shouting to him. On the way down to the mill the mass of men would grow, piling into the green in front of the mill, chasing away the sheep that had grazed so fat for eighteen months while men and women and children had grown hollow-eyed on grits and coffee. The barb-wire steel fence would be up-rooted, the iron posts and the concrete-filled holes would be raised into the air, and the first bar would be lowered.

"Sit down, Will," Rosamond said.

He sat down at the table, watching them prepare a place for him hurriedly, easily, lovingly. Darling Jill brought a plate, a cup, and a saucer. Griselda brought a knife, a spoon, and a fork. Rosamond filled a glass of water. They ran over the kitchen, jumping from each other's way, weaving in and out in the small room hurriedly, easily, lovingly.

"It's six o'clock." Rosamond said.

He turned and looked at the face of the clock on the shelf over the table. They were going to turn the power on that morning. They were going in there and turn it on and if the company tried to shut it off, they were going to—well, God damn it, Harry, the power is going to stay turned on.

"Here's the sugar," Griselda said.

She put two spoonfuls into the coffee cup. She knew. It wasn't every woman who would know how much sugar to put into his cup. She's got the finest pair of rising beauties a man ever laid eyes on, and when you once see them, you're going to get right down on your hands and knees and lick something. Ty Ty has got more sense than all of us put together, even if he does stay out there among those God damn pot holes digging for what he'll never find.

"I'll bring a dish for the ham," Darling Jill said.

Rosamond stood behind his chair, watching him cut the meat and place hungry bites into his mouth. It was the thirty-pound ham Ty Ty had given them.

"What time will you be home for lunch?" she asked.

"Twelve-thirty."

Already men were walking down the street towards the ivy-walled mill by the side of broad Horse Creek. Men who had been up all night, sitting at windows, looking at the stars, left as soon as they had finished breakfast, walking down the street towards the mill in khaki pants. No one looked at the ground on which he walked. Down at the ivy-walled mill the windows reflected the early morning sun, throwing it upon the yellow company houses and into the eyeballs of men walking down the streets. We're going in there and turn the power on and if the company tries to shut it off—well, God damn it, Harry, it's going to stay turned on.

"Could you get us jobs in the mill, Will?" Darling Jill asked him. "For Buck and Shaw and me?"

He shook his head.

"No," he said.

"I wish you would, Will, so we could move over here."

"This is no place for you, or the others."

"But you and Rosamond live here."

"That's different. You stay in Georgia."

He shook his head again and again.

"I wish I could come," Griselda said.

"No," he said.

Rosamond brought him his shoes and socks. She knelt on the floor at his feet, putting them on his feet. He worked his shoes on and she tied them. Then she got up and stood behind his chair.

"It's nearly seven o'clock," she said.

He looked up at the clock above. The minute hand was between ten and eleven.

People passed the yellow company house faster, all going swiftly in one direction. Women and children were among them. The local draws pay for sitting on their tails on the platform and shaking their heads when somebody says something about turning the power on. The sons-of-bitches. The union sends money in here to pay those sons-of-bitches who run the local, and the rest of us grow hollow-eyed on grits and coffee. The people were walking faster down the street, their eyes on a level with the sun-red mill windows. Nobody looked down at the ground on which he walked. Their eyes were on the sun-bright windows of the ivy-walled mill. The children ran ahead, looking up at the windows.

Somebody came through the house and into the kitchen. He found and jerked a chair. He sat down beside Will, his head a little on one side, his other hand on the back of Will's chair. He watched Will Thompson eat grits and ham. Where'd you get the ham, Will? Jesus Christ, it looks good!

"They've brought down some plain-clothes guards from the Piedmont, Will."

"When did you find that out, Mac?"

He swallowed the ham unchewed.

"I saw them when they got here. I was just getting up, and I looked out the window and saw three cars of them drive around to the rear of the mill. You can tell those bastards from the Piedmont a mile off."

Will got up and went to the front of the house. Mac followed him, his eyes sweeping the girls as he left. They could be heard talking in the front room where Pluto was asleep in the chair.

Griselda began washing the dishes. None of them had eaten anything. But they drank coffee while they washed the dishes and tried to hurry. There was no time to waste. They had to hurry.

"We ought to start back home, but I would rather stay," Griselda said.

"We are going to stay," Darling Jill said.

"Buck might come."

"He will come," Rosamond said. "We can't stop him."

"I'm sorry," Griselda said.

They knew without asking further what she meant.

"I would rather you wouldn't be. I wish you wouldn't say that. I'd rather that you weren't sorry."

"It's all right, Griselda," Darling Jill spoke. "I know Rosamond better than you do. It's all right."

"If Buck ever finds out about it, he'll kill Will," Rosamond said. "That's all I'm sorry about. I don't know what I would do without Will. But I know Buck's going to kill him. I'm certain of it. Nothing can stop him when he finds it out."

"But there is something we can do, isn't there?" Griselda said. "I couldn't let that happen. It would be awful."

"I don't know anything to do. I'm afraid Pluto might say something when he gets back, too."

"I'll attend to him," Darling Jill promised.

"But you never can tell what may happen. If Buck asks him a question, he can read his face. Pluto couldn't hide anything."

"I'll talk to Pluto before we get back. He'll be careful after I get through talking to him."

They went into the front of the house. Pluto was still asleep, and Will and Mac had left. They began getting ready quickly.

"Oh, let Pluto sleep," Darling Jill said.

Griselda put on some of Rosamond's clothes. She had her own slippers. Rosamond's dress looked well on her. They each stopped and admired it.

"Where's Will gone to?" Darling Jill asked.

"To the mill."

"We've got to hurry. They're going to turn the power on."

"It's nearly eight o'clock. They may not wait much longer. We can't wait any longer."

They ran out of the house, one behind the other. Down the street they ran towards the ivy-walled mill trying to keep together in the crowd. Everyone's eyes were on a level with the windows that the sun shone so redly upon.

"Buck will kill him," Griselda said, breathless.

"I know it," said Rosamond. "We can't stop him."

"He'll have to shoot me too, then," Darling Jill cried. "When he points a gun at Will, I'll be the first to be shot. I would rather die with Will than live after he was killed by Buck. Buck will have to shoot me."

"Look!" Rosamond cried, pointing.

They stopped, raised their heads above the crowd. Men were gathering around the company fence. The three sheep so fat that had grazed on the green for eighteen months were being chased away. The fence was raised into the air—iron posts, concrete holes, and the barb-wire and steel mesh.

"Where's Will?" Griselda cried. "Show me Will!"

Chapter XVII

THERE they go!" Rosamond said, clutching the arms of her sister and Griselda. "Will is at the door now!"

Women all around them were crying hysterically. After eighteen months of waiting it looked as if there would again be work in the mill. Women and children pushed forward, stronger than the force of the walled-up water in Horse Creek below, pushing close behind the men at the mill door. Some of the older children had climbed up the trees and they were above the crowd now, hanging to the limbs and shouting at their fathers and brothers.

"I can't believe it's true," a woman beside them said. She had stopped crying long enough to speak.

All around them women and girls were crying with joy. When the men had first said they were going to take over the mill and turn on the power, the women had been afraid; but now, now when they were crushed against the mill, it looked as if everything would come true. Here in the mill yard now were the wild-eyed Valley girls with erect breasts; behind the mill windows they would look like morning-glories.

"It's open!" somebody shouted.

There was a sudden surge of closely pressed bodies, and Rosamond and Darling Jill and Griselda were pushed forward with the mass.

"We'll have something beside fat-back and Red Cross flour now," a little woman with clenched fists said in a low voice beside them. "We've been starving on that, but we won't any longer. The men are going to work again."

Already the mass of men were pouring through the opened doors. They fought their way in silently, hammering at the narrow doors with their fists and pushing them with their muscles, angry because the doors were not wide enough to admit them quicker. Windows on the first floor were being tilted open. The crowd of women and children could follow the advance of the men by watching the opening of the mill windows one after the other. Before the first floor windows were all opened, several on the second floor were suddenly tilted wide.

"There they are," Rosamond said. "I wonder where Will is now."

Somebody had said that the company had hired fifteen additional guards and placed them in the mill. The new guards had arrived that morning from the Piedmont.

The entire mill was occupied. The third and fourth floor windows were being opened. Already men were running to the windows on all floors, jerking off their shirts and flinging them to the ground. When men in the Valley went back to work after a long lay-off, they took off their shirts and threw them out the windows. Down on the green, where the three company sheep so fat had grazed for eighteen months, the ground was covered with shirts. The men on the last two floors were throwing out their shirts, and down on the ground the piled shirts were knee deep on the green.

"Hush!" the whisper went over the crowd of women and girls and yelling children in the trees.

It was time for the power to be turned on. Everyone wished to hear the first concerted hum of the machinery behind the ivy-walled building.

"I wonder where Will is," Rosamond said.

"I haven't seen him at the window yet," Griselda said. "I've been looking for him."

Darling Jill stood on her toes, straining to see over the heads of the people. She clutched Rosamond, pointing to a window above.

"Look! There's Will! See him at the window?"

"What's he doing?"

"He's tearing his shirt to pieces!" Rosamond cried.

They stood on their toes trying their best to see Will before he left the window.

"It is Will!" Griselda said.

"Will!" Darling Jill cried, urging all the strength of her body into her lungs so he might hear her above the noise. "Will! Will!"

For a moment they thought he had heard her. He stopped and bent far out the window trying to see down into the densely packed mass below. With a final tear he balled the ripped cloth in his hands and threw it out into the crowd. The women nearest the mill reached up and fought for the torn strips of cloth. The ones who caught parts of it quickly took it from the reach of the others who wished to have a part of it.

Rosamond and Darling Jill and Griselda could not get close enough to fight for Will's torn shirt. They had to stand where they were and see the other women and girls struggle over it until there was none left.

"Let's hear the machinery, Will Thompson!" an excited woman cried.

"Turn the power on, Will Thompson!" another girl cried at him.

He turned and ran out of sight. The crowd below was as still as the empty mill yard had been before they came. They waited to hear the first hum of the machinery.

Rosamond's heart beat madly. It was Will whom the crowd begged to turn the power on. It was he whom they had acknowledged by acclamation as their leader. She wished to climb up high above the mass of crying women and shout that Will Thompson was her husband. She wished to have all the people there know that Will Thompson was her Will.

Through the tilted glass windows they could see the men at their places, waiting for the wheels to turn. Their voices were raised in shouts that burst through the windows, and their bare backs gleamed in the rising sun like row after row of company houses in the early morning.

"It's on!" somebody cried. "The power is on!"

"Will has turned on the power," Griselda said, dancing with joy. She was on the verge of bursting into tears again. "Will did it! It was Will! Will turned the power on!"

All of them were too excited to speak coherently. They jumped up and down on their toes, each trying to see over the head of the other. Men ran to the windows shaking their fists into the air. Some of them were laughing, some were cursing, some were standing as though they were in a daze. When the machinery turned, they ran back and stood in their accustomed positions beside the looms.

There was a sound of sudden small explosions in the eastern end of the mill. It sounded like small firecrackers bursting. In the roar of the machinery it had almost been drowned out, but it was loud enough to be heard.

Everyone turned his head to look down at the eastern end of the mill. Down there the power room was located.

"What was that?" Griselda asked, clutching Rosamond.

Rosamond was like a ghost. Her face was drawn and white, and her pale lips were dry like cotton.

The other women began talking excitedly among themselves. They spoke in whispers, in hushed undertones that made no sound!

"Rosamond, what was that!" Griselda cried frantically. "Rosamond, answer me!"

"I don't know," she murmured.

Darling Jill trembled beside her sister. She could feel a convulsive throb surge through her heart and head. She leaned heavily upon Griselda for support.

A man on one of the middle floors ran to a window and shook his fist into the air, cursing and shouting. They could see warm blood trickle from the corners of his lips, dropping to his bare chest. He raised his fists into the air, screaming to the heavens.

Soon others ran to the windows excitedly, staring down into the crowd of wives and sisters below, cursing and shouting while their fists shook into the air.

"What's the matter!" a woman in the crowd cried. "What happened! Dear God, help us!'

The windows were filled with cursing, bare-chested men who looked down into the faces of the women and girls.

Suddenly there was a cessation of noise in the mill. The machinery whirled to a stop, dying. There was not a sound anywhere, not even in the crowd below. Women turned to each other, helplessly.

First one man, his bare chest gleaming in the sun, appeared at the big double-doors below. He came out slowly, his hands holding fists that were too weak to remain doubled any longer. Another man came behind him, then two, then others. The door was filled with men walking slowly, turning at the steps until the glow of the sun covered their pale backs with thin blood.

"What happened?" a woman cried. "Tell us what happened! What's wrong?"

Rosamond and Darling Jill and Griselda were not close enough to hear what the men answered in weak voices. They stood on tiptoes, clutching each other, waiting to see Will and to hear from him what the trouble was.

A woman nearby screamed, sending shudders through Griselda. She cried with the pain of the woman's scream.

They pushed and fought their way towards the men coming from the mill. Griselda clung to Rosamond, Darling Jill clung to Griselda. They went forward slowly, pushing frantically through the crowd to the men coming so slowly from the mill.

"Where's Will?" Griselda cried.

A man turned and looked at them. He came toward them to speak to the three of them.

"You're Will Thompson's wife, aren't you?"

"Where is Will?" Rosamond cried, throwing herself upon the man's bare chest.

"They shot him."

"Who shot him?"

"Will! Will! Will!"

"Those Piedmont guards shot him."

"Dear God!"

"Is he badly hurt?"

"He's dead."

That was all. There was no more to hear.

The women and girls behind them were silent like people in slumber. They pressed forward, supporting Will Thompson's widow and sisters-in-law.

More men filed out, walking slowly up the hill towards the long rows of yellow company houses, while the muscles on their bare backs hung like cut tendons under the skin. There was a man with blood on his lips. He spat into the yellow dust at his feet. Another man coughed, and blood oozed through the corners of his tightly compressed mouth. He spat into the yellow dust of Carolina.

Women were beginning to leave, running to the sides of the men and walking beside them up the hill towards the long rows of yellow company houses. There were tears in the eyes of the girls so beautiful who walked homeward with their lovers. These were the girls of the Valley whose breasts were erect and whose faces were like morning-glories when they stood in the windows of the ivy-walled mill.

Rosamond was not beside Griselda and Darling Jill when they turned to put their arms around her. She had run towards the mill door. She fell against the side of the building, clutching in her hands the ivy that grew so beautifully.

They ran to be with her.

"Will!" Rosamond cried frantically. "Will! Will!"

They put their arms around her and held her.

Several men stepped out the door and waited. Then several others came out slowly, carrying the body of Will Thompson. They tried to keep his wife and sisters-in-law back, but they ran closer until they could look at him.

"Oh, he's dead!" Rosamond said.

She had not realized that Will was dead until she saw his limp body. She still could not believe that he would not come to life. She could not believe that he would never be alive again.

The men in front took Rosamond and Darling Jill and Griselda up the hill towards the long rows of yellow company houses, holding them and supporting them. The bare backs of the men were strong with their arms around Will Thompson's wife and sisters-in-law.

When they reached the front of the house, the body was kept in the street until a place could be provided for it. The three women were carried to the house. Women from the yellow company houses up the street and down it came running to help.

"I don't know what we're going to do now," a man said. "Will Thompson isn't here any more."

Another man looked down at the ivy-walled mill.

"They were afraid of Will," he said. "They knew he had the guts to fight back. I don't reckon there'll be any use of trying to fight them without Will. They'll try to run now and make us take a dollar-ten. If Will Thompson was here, we wouldn't do it. Will Thompson would fight them."

The body was carried to the porch and placed in the shade of the roof. His back was bare, but the three drying blood-clogged holes were hidden from sight.

"Let's turn him over," somebody said. "Everybody ought to know how Will Thompson was shot in the back by those sons-of-bitches down there."

"We'll bury him tomorrow. And I reckon everybody in Scottsville will be at the funeral. Everybody but those sons-of-bitches down there."

"What's his wife going to do now? She's all alone."

"We'll take care of her, if she'll let us. She's Will Thompson's widow."

An ambulance came up the street and the strong bare-backed men lifted the body from the porch and carried it out to the street. The three women in the house came to the door and stood close together while the bare-backed men carried Will from the porch and put him into the ambulance. He was Will Thompson now. He belonged to those bare-backed men with bloody lips. He belonged to Horse Creek Valley now. He was not theirs any longer. He was Will Thompson.

The three women stood in the door watching the rear end of the ambulance while it went slowly down the street to the undertaker. The body would be prepared for burial, and the next day there would be a funeral in the cemetery on the hill that looked down upon Horse Creek Valley. The men with blood-stained lips who carried him down to his grave would some day go back to the mill to card and spin and weave and dye. Will Thompson would breathe no more lint into his lungs.

Inside the house one of the men was trying to explain to Pluto how Will had been killed. Pluto was more frightened than ever. Until that time he had been scared of only the darkness in Scottsville, but now he was afraid of the day also. Men were killed in broad daylight in the Valley. He wished he could make Darling Jill and Griselda go home right away. If he had to remain in the yellow company house another night, he knew he probably would not sleep. The man with the bare chest and back sat in the room with Pluto, talking to him about the mill, but Pluto was not listening any longer. He had become afraid of the man beside him; he was afraid the man would suddenly turn with a knife in his hand and cut his throat from ear to ear. He knew then that he was out of place in a cotton mill town. The country, back at home in Marion, was the place for him to go as quickly as possible. He promised himself he would never again leave it if only he could get back safely this time.

Late that evening some of the women from the yellow company houses on the street came and prepared the first meal any of them had had that day. Will had eaten breakfast early that morning, but none of the others had. Pluto felt starved after missing two meals. He had never been so hungry in all his life. Back home in Marion he had never been forced to go hungry for the lack of food. He could smell the cooking food and the boiling coffee through the open doors, and he was unable to sit still. He got up and went to the door just as one of the women came to call him to the kitchen. Out in the hall he became frightened again and would have gone back, but the woman took his arm and went with him to the kitchen.

While he was there, Darling Jill came in and sat down beside him. He felt much safer then. Somehow, he felt that she was a protection in a foreign country. She ate a little, and when she had finished, she remained seated beside him.

Later, Pluto ventured to ask Darling Jill when they could go back to Georgia.

"Tomorrow as soon as the funeral is over," she said.

"Can't we go now?"

"Of course not."

"They can bury Will all right without us," he suggested. "They'll do it all right. I wish I could go home right away, Darling Jill. I don't feel safe in Scottsville."

"Hush, Pluto. Don't be such a child."

He remained silent after that. Darling Jill took his hand and led him to one of the dark rooms across the hall. He felt exactly as he once had many years before when he was a small boy holding the hand of his mother in a dark night.

Outside the windows was the sound of the Valley town with all its strange noises and unfamiliar voices. He was glad the street light shone through the leaves of the tree and partly lighted the room. It was safer with a little light, and he was not so afraid as he had been earlier that evening. If somebody should come to the window and crawl inside to slit his throat from ear to ear he would be able to see them before he felt the blade under his chin.

Darling Jill had brought him to the bed and had made him lie down upon it. He was reluctant then to release her hand, and when he saw that she was going to lie down beside him, he was no longer afraid. The Valley was still there, and the strange company town, but he had Darling Jill to lie beside him, her hand in his, and he could close his eyes without fear.

Just before both of them dropped off to sleep, he felt her arms around his neck. He turned to her, holding her tightly. There was nothing to be afraid of then.

Chapter XVIII

Ty ty was waiting for them on the front porch when they reached home late that afternoon. He got up when he recognized Pluto's car, and walked across the yard to meet them before the automobile was brought to a stop.

"Where in the pluperfect hell have you folks been the past two days, anyhow?" he demanded severely. "Me and the boys are near about starved for woman's cooking. We've been eating, yes, but a man can't get the proper nourishment out of just eating. We crave woman's cooking to satisfy us. You folks have been aggravating me like all get-out."

Pluto was ready to explain why they had not come back sooner, but Darling Jill made him be quiet.

"Where's Will Thompson?" Ty Ty asked. "Did you bring that good-for-nothing Will Thompson back again? I don't see him in the car, though."

"Hush, Pa," Griselda said, starting to cry.

"Of all the fool women, I never heard the like. Why can't I ask about Will? I only asked one question, and all of you girls started to cry. I'll be dog-gone if I ever seen the like of it."

"Will isn't here any more," Griselda said.

"What the pluperfect hell do you take me to be, anyhow? Don't you reckon I can see he ain't here?"

"Will was shot yesterday morning."

"Shot? What with—corn?"

"Killed with a pistol, Pa," Darling Jill said. "We buried Will this afternoon in the Valley. He's dead now, and covered with earth."

Ty Ty was speechless for a moment. He leaned against the car, searching each face before him. When he saw Rosamond's face, he knew it was true.

"Now, you don't mean Will Thompson," Ty Ty said. "Not our Will! Say it ain't so!"

"It is so, Pa. Will is dead now, and covered with earth over there in Horse Creek Valley."

"Trouble at the mill then, I'll bet a pretty. Or else over a female."

Rosamond got out and ran to the house. The others got out slowly and looked strangely at the buildings in the twilight. Pluto did not know whether to remain where he was or whether to go home immediately.

Ty Ty sent Darling Jill into the house to cook supper without loss of time.

"You stay here and tell me what happened to Will Thompson," he told Griselda. "I can't let our Will pass on without knowing all about it. Will was one of the family."

They left Pluto sitting on the runningboard of his car, and walked across the yard to the front steps. Ty Ty sat down and waited to hear what Griselda had to tell him about Will. She was still crying a little.

"Did they shoot him for breaking into company property, Griselda?"

"Yes, Pa. All the men in Scottsville went into the mill and tried to start it. Will was the one who turned the power on."

"Oh, so that's what he was always talking about when he said he was going to turn the power on? Well, I never did fully understand what he had in mind when he said that. And our Will turned the power on!"

"Some company police from the Piedmont shot him when he turned it on."

Ty Ty was silent for several minutes. He gazed out through the gray dusk, seeing through it to the boundaries of his land. He could see each mound of earth that had been excavated, each deep round hole they had dug. And far beyond them all he could see the cleared field beyond the woods where God's little acre lay. For some reason he wished then to bring it closer to the house where he might be near it all the time. He felt guilty of something—maybe it was sacrilege or desecration—whatever it was, he knew he had not played fair with God. Now he wished to bring God's little acre back to its rightful place beside the house where he could see it all the time. He had very little in the world to live for anyway, and when men died, he could find consolation only in his love of God. He brought God's little acre back from the far side of the farm and placed it under him. He promised himself to keep it there until he died.

Ty Ty had no eulogy for Will Thompson. Will would never help them dig for gold. He laughed at them when Ty Ty asked him to help. He said it was foolish to try to find gold where there was no gold. Ty Ty knew there was gold in the ground, and he had always been a little angry with Will for laughing at his efforts to find it. Will had always seemed to be more interested in getting back to Horse Creek Valley than he was in staying there and helping Ty Ty.

"Sometimes I wished Will would stay here and help us, and sometimes I was glad he didn't. He was a fool about cotton mills, I reckon, and couldn't pretend to be a farmer. Maybe God made two kinds of us, after all. It looks like now, though I used to never think so, that God made a man to work the ground and a man to work the machinery. I reckon I was a fool to try to make Will Thompson take an interest in the land. He was always saying something about spinning and weaving, and about how pretty the girls and how hungry the men were in the Valley. I couldn't always make out what he was talking about, but sometimes I could just about feel something inside that told me all the things he said were true. He used to sit here and tell me how strong men were in the Valley when they were young and how weak they were when they grew up breathing cotton lint into their lungs and dying with blood on their lips. And Will used to say how pretty the girls were when they were young and how ugly they were when they were old and starving with pellagra. But he didn't like the land, anyway. He was one of the people of Horse Creek Valley."

Griselda pushed her hand into his. He held her hand awkwardly, not knowing why she wished him to touch her.

"You and Will were not different in every way," she said softly.

"Which way is that? It looks to me like I just finished telling you how different we were. Will was a mill man, and I'm a man of the land."

"You and Will were the only two men I've ever known who treated me as I liked to be treated."

"Now, now, Griselda. You're just all wrought up over seeing Will get shot over there in the Valley. Don't take on so about him. Everybody dies in this world sooner or later, and Will died sooner. That's all the difference."

"You and Will were real men, Pa."

"Now what in the pluperfect hell do you mean by that? I can't make heads or tails of it?"

Griselda stopped crying until she could tell Ty Ty. She pushed her hands tighter into his, laying her head on his shoulder.

"You remember what you said about me sometimes—you used to say that and I'd try to make you stop—and you never would stop—that's what I mean."

"Now, I don't know. Maybe I do."

"Of course you know—those things about what a man would want to do when he saw me."

"I reckon I do. Maybe I do know what you mean."

"You and Will were the only two men who ever said that to me, Pa. All the other men I've known were too—I don't know what to say—they didn't seem to be men enough to have that feeling—they were just like all the rest. But you and Will weren't like that."

"I reckon I know what you mean."

"A woman can never really love a man unless he's like that. There's something about it that makes everything so different—it's not just liking to be kissed and things like that—most men think that's all. And Will—he said he wanted to do that—just like you did. And he wasn't afraid, either. Other men seem to be afraid to say things like that, or else they aren't men enough to want to do them. Will—Will took my clothes off and tore them to pieces and said he was going to do that. And he did, Pa. I didn't know I wanted him to do it before, but after that I was certain. After a woman has that done to her once, Pa, she's never the same again. It opens her up, or something. I could never really love another man unless he did that to me. I suppose if Will had not been killed, I would have stayed over there. I couldn't have left him after that. I would have been like a dog that loves you and follows you around no matter how mean you are to him. I would have stayed with Will the rest of my life. Because when a man does that to a woman, Pa, it makes love so strong nothing in the world can stop it. It must be God in people to do that. It's something, anyway. I have it now."

Ty Ty patted her hand. He could think of nothing to say, because there beside him sat a woman who knew as he did a secret of living. After a while he breathed deeply and lifted her head from his shoulder.

"Just try to get along with Buck somehow, Griselda. Maybe Buck will be like that when he grows older. He's not as old as Will was, and he hasn't had time to learn the things he should. Help him along as much as you can. He's my boy, and I want him to keep you. There's not another girl in ten thousand like you. If you left him, he'd never find another wife as fine as you are."

"He'll never learn, Pa. Buck just isn't like you and Will. A man has to be born that way at the start."

Ty Ty got up. "It's a pity all folks ain't got the sense dogs are born with."

Griselda put her hand on his arm and got to her feet. She stood beside him unsteadily for several moments, trying to balance herself.

"The trouble with people is that they try to fool themselves into believing that they're different from the way God made them. You go to church and a preacher tells you things that deep down in your heart you know ain't so. But most people are so dead inside that they believe it and try to make everybody else live that way. People ought to live like God made us to live. When you sit down by yourself and feel what's in you, that's the real way to live. It's feeling. Some people talk about your head being the thing to go by, but it ain't so. Your head gives you sense to show you how to deal with people when it comes to striking a bargain and things like that, but it can't feel for you. People have got to feel for themselves as God made them to feel. It's folks who let their head run them who make all the mess of living. Your head can't make you love a man, if you don't feel like loving him. It's got to be a feeling down inside of you like you and Will had."

He walked to the edge of the porch and looked up at the stars. She waited beside him until he was ready to leave.

"We'd better go in and see how supper is cooking," he told her.

They walked through the dark hall, smelling the aroma of freshly ground coffee. Nearer the kitchen they could smell frying ham on the stove.

Buck looked up at Griselda from his chair behind the partly opened door when they walked into the brightly lighted kitchen where the others were. She had to turn her head and shoulders halfway around in order to see him. He glared at her surlily.

"I reckon if he hadn't been shot, you'd still be over there, wouldn't you?"

The words were on the tip of her tongue to shout at him that she would, but she bit her lips and tried to keep from speaking just then.

"You and him got pretty thick, didn't you?"

"Please, Buck," she begged.

"Please, what? Don't want me to talk about it, huh?"

"There's nothing to talk about. And anyway, you ought to have some regard for Rosamond."

He looked at Rosamond. She stood with her back to him turning the ham in the griddles.

"What's wrong with me? Why did you have to chase off after him? Don't you think I'm good enough for you, huh?"

"Please, Buck, not now."

"If you were going to run around with your legs spread open, why in hell didn't you take better aim? That son-of-a-bitch was a lint-head. A lint-head from Horse Creek Valley!"

"There's no particular spot in the world where real men live," Darling Jill said. "You can find just as many in Horse Creek Valley as you can on The Hill in Augusta, or on farms around Marion."

Buck turned and looked her up and down.

"You talk like you've been pricked, too. What in hell went on over there, anyhow?"

Ty Ty thought it was time to step in before things went too far. He laid his hand on Buck's shoulder and tried to quiet him. Buck threw his father's hand off, moving his chair to another part of the kitchen.

"Now, son," he said, "don't go and get all heated up over nothing."

"To hell with that talk," he shouted. "You stay out of this and stop trying to take up for her."

The girls began carrying the supper dishes into the next room and placing them on the wide table. They all went into the dining-room and sat down. Buck had not said all he wished to say, by any means. He merely transferred the scene from one room to the other.

"Go get Pluto, Darling Jill," Ty Ty said. "He'll sit out there in the yard all night and not get a bite to eat if somebody doesn't look out for him."

Griselda sat with lowered head, her eyes averted. She hoped Buck would not say anything else while Rosamond was in the room. It hurt her to have Buck talk about Will in Rosamond's presence, and so soon after the funeral, too.

Pluto came back with Darling Jill and took his accustomed seat at the table. He could feel the tension in the room, and he took care to keep his mouth shut unless he was spoken to. He was afraid that Buck was going to ask him what had happened in Scottsville.

After several minutes of silence, Ty Ty tried to take advantage of it to change the subject.

"A man was out here watching us dig yesterday, and he tried to tell me I called the lode by the wrong name. He said he used to mine gold up in North Georgia, and up there a lode was a streak of gold in the rock. He said what we were aiming at was placering. I told him as long as we struck gold, I didn't give a dog-gone what name he called it by."

"He was right," Shaw said. "In high school the teachers said placer mining was getting gold out of dirt or gravel. Lode mining is by blasting it out of rock and crushing it and cooking it out with heat."

"Well, he still may be right, and you too, son," Ty Ty said, shaking his head, "but a load of gold is what I've got my heart set on. That will be my ship coming in, and I don't give a dog-gone for the name you call it. You can call it lode mining or placer mining, whichever you want, but when I get a load of it, I'll know dog-gone well my ship has come in."

"The man said the only way nuggets could get into the ground around here would be by a flood washing them down a long time ago, and then being covered up with silt."

"The man you mention don't know no more about digging for gold on my land than one of those mules out there. I've been doing it for nearly fifteen years, and I reckon if anybody knows what I'm doing, I do. Let the man have his say, but don't pay him no heed, son. Too many men talking will get you all balled up, and you won't know which way is straight up and which is straight down."

Buck leaned over the table.

"I reckon if I was to put my hands on you now, you'd say, 'Ouch! Don't do that, Buck. I'm sore there.' " He looked at Griselda steadily. "Can't you talk? What's the matter with you?"

"Of course, I can talk, Buck," she pleaded. "Please don't say such things now."

Pluto looked at Darling Jill uneasily. He dreaded for the time to come when Buck would ask him what had happened in Scottsville.

"Well, he's dead now," Buck said, "and I can't do much about it, to him. But if he wasn't, I'd sure do something you wouldn't forget. I'd take that gun hanging up there and do plenty. It's a God damn shame you can't kill a man but once. I'd like to kill him just as long as I could buy shells to fire at him."

Rosamond cried. She laid down her knife and fork and ran from the room.

"Now, see what you've done!" Darling Jill said. "You ought to be ashamed of yourself for doing a thing like that."

"You and her," he said, pointing his fork at Griselda, "you and her don't look ashamed for anything. If I was married to you, I'd choke hell out of you. You're as loose as a busted belly-band on a gray mule."

"Now, son," Ty Ty said. "She's your sister."

"What of it? She's loose, ain't she, sister or no sister? I'd choke hell out of her if she was my wife."

"If you're not man enough to hold your wife, you ought to be too ashamed to say anything," Darling Jill told him. "You ought to go somewhere and hide your face."

"We're going on like this all the time," Ty Ty said wearily, "and we're getting further and further away from the happy life. All of us ought to sit down and think a little about living, and how to do it. God didn't put us here to scrap and fight each other all the time. If we don't have a little more love for each other, one of these days there's going to be deep sorrow in my heart. I've tried all my life to keep a peaceful family under my roof. I've got my head set on having just that all my days, and I don't aim to give up trying now. You folks see if you can't stop your scrapping and laugh just a little, and I'll feel much better. That's the finest cure in the world for scrapping and fighting."

"You talk like a damn fool," Buck said disgustedly.

"Maybe it does sound that way to you, Buck. But when you get God in your heart, you have a feeling that living is worth striving for night and day. I ain't talking about the God you hear about in the churches, I'm talking about the God inside of a body. I've got the greatest feeling for Him, because He helps me to live. That's why I set aside God's little acre out there on the farm when I was just a young man starting

in. I like to have something around me that I can go to and stand on
and feel God in."

"He ain't got a penny out of it yet," Shaw said laughing a little.

"You boys don't seem to catch on, son. It ain't so important that I get
money out of God's little acre to give to the church and the preacher,
it's just the fact that I set that up in His name. All you boys seem to
think about is the things you can see and touch—that ain't living. It's
the things you can feel inside of you—that's what living is made for.
True, as you say, God ain't got a penny of money out of that piece of
ground, but it's the fact that I set God's little acre aside out there that
matters. That's the sign that God's in my heart. He knows I ain't
striking it rich down here, but He ain't interested in how much money
a man makes. What tickles Him is the fact that I set aside a part of my
land for Him just to show that I have got some of Him inside of me."

"Why don't you go to church more than you do then?" Shaw asked.
"If you believe so much in God, why don't you go there oftener?"

"That ain't a fair question, son. You know good and well how tired
I am when Sunday comes, after digging all week long in the holes.
God doesn't miss me there, anyhow. He knows why I can't come. I've
spoken to Him about such things all my life, and He knows pretty well
all about it."

"What's all that got to do with her?" Buck asked, pointing his fork
at Griselda. "I was talking about her before you butted in about something else."

"Nothing, son. It ain't got a thing in the world to do with her. She
already knows about it. I was talking for your benefit so you could
learn more about living. If I was you, son, when I went to bed tonight,
I'd get down on my knees in the dark and talk to God about it. He
can tell you things nobody else can, and maybe He'll tell you how
you ought to act with Griselda. He'll tell you, if you'll only take the
time and trouble to listen, because if there's anything in the world He's
crazy about, it's seeing a man and a woman fools about each other. He
knows then that the world is running along as slick as grease."

Chapter XIX

Ty ty stayed up late that night trying to talk to Buck. He knew it
was a duty he owed his children to convince them that living was
deeper than the surface they saw. The girls seemed to realize that, but

the boys did not. Ty Ty knew there would be plenty of time later to talk to Shaw, and he gave all his attention to Buck for Griselda's sake. Buck was irritated by the things he tried to explain and he acted as though he did not wish to understand.

"You boys just don't seem to catch on," Ty Ty said, dropping his hands at his sides. "You boys seem to think that if you have a little money to spend and a new raincoat or some such knickknack and a belly full of barbecue, there ain't another thing to be concerned about. I wish I could tell you all about it. It's a ticklish thing to try to explain, because I don't know none too much about using words, and if I did know, it wouldn't help matters much because it's something you've got to feel. It's just like the fellow said: 'It's there, or it ain't there, and there are only two ways about it.' You boys appear like it ain't there. Just take a walk off by yourself some time and think about it, and maybe it will come to you. I don't know what else to tell you to do."

"I don't know what in hell you're trying to say," Buck broke in, "but if it's what Griselda's got, I don't want it. She went over there to Horse Creek Valley and got shot full of something. And if you ask me, I'll say it was some of Will Thompson. That lint-head!"

"Will Thompson was a real man," Darling Jill said.

"A real man, huh? And you got a shot, too, didn't you? It's a damn good sign when you come back here with your mind made up to marry Pluto Swint all of a sudden. You'd be in a mess now if he wouldn't marry you."

"Will was a real man, anyway."

"What in hell is a real man? Will Thompson wasn't any bigger than I am. He wasn't any stronger, either. I could throw him any morning before breakfast."

"It wasn't the way he looked that made him different. It was how he was made inside. He could feel things, and you can't."

Buck got up and looked at them for a moment from the door.

"What do you take me for, anyway—a sucker? Don't you reckon I know damn well you and Griselda are making up that for an excuse? I'm not all that dumb. You can't suck me in with that kind of talk."

He left the house and no one knew where he had gone. Ty Ty waited a while, thinking Buck might come back in a few minutes and listen with more reason after he had cooled off in the night, but at twelve he had not returned. Ty Ty got up then to go to bed.

"Buck will come around all right when he gets a little older, Griselda. Just try to be patient with him till he lives a little more. It takes some people a lifetime, almost, to learn some things."

"I'm afraid he'll never learn," she said. "Not before it's too late, anyway."

Ty Ty patted her shoulder.

"You girls are all wrought up over Will getting killed. Just go to bed now and get a good night's sleep. Tomorrow morning things will look a lot different."

"But he's dead," Darling Jill said. "I can't forget that he's dead."

"Maybe it's best that he is, now. The three of you couldn't have stayed over there in Scottsville. Rosamond was married to him, and you and Griselda would have made a mess that the law doesn't allow."

Long after everybody else in the house was asleep, Ty Ty lay awake thinking. Buck had not returned, and Griselda was alone in the room across the hall, crying. For nearly an hour he had lain on his side listening to the restless toss of her body as she lay sleepless upon the bed. But she finally became quiet, and he knew she had fallen to sleep at last. Ty Ty wondered where Buck had gone. There was no need for him to get up and go out in the night looking for him, so he tried to dismiss Buck from his thoughts.

Some time in the night he heard Darling Jill go to the back porch for a drink of water. He could hear her walking in her soft-soled slippers through the hall past his door. She remained on the porch only a minute and came back into the house. Ty Ty turned over and looked through the door into the dark hall when he heard her returning. He could see dimly the moving light of her nightgown, and he could have reached out and touched her with the tips of his fingers when she passed the door. He was about to ask her if she were ill, but he thought better of it. He knew she was not sick, anyway; there was nothing the matter with her except that which also made Rosamond and Griselda restless. He allowed her to go back to her bed without speaking. All three of them would feel much better after several hours of sleep. When breakfast was over, he would try to say something to them.

At daybreak Buck still had not returned to the house. Ty Ty lay a little while staring at the beginning of light on the ceiling, turning later to watch the gray dawn break into day. When he heard Black Sam and Uncle Felix talking in an undertone in the yard, he jumped out of bed and dressed quickly. He looked out the window and saw the two colored men sitting on the rim of the crater, their feet hanging over the side, waiting for him to start them to work.

He left the room and walked out into the yard.

"Did you see Buck anywhere?" he asked Uncle Felix.

Uncle Felix shook his head.

"Mr. Buck didn't get up this early already, did he?" Black Sam asked.

"He stayed out somewhere all night. I reckon he'll show up before long."

"Trouble in your house, boss?" Uncle Felix asked cautiously.

"Trouble?" Ty Ty repeated. "Who said there was trouble in the house?"

"When white folks don't stay in the house to sleep, there's pretty nearly always trouble."

Ty Ty sat down several feet away, looking down into the big hole at his right. He knew it was useless to try to lie to Negroes. They always knew.

"Maybe there was trouble," he said. "It's about over with now, though. One of them got killed, and I don't look for much after today. It's all over with now, I hope."

"Who got killed?" Black Sam asked. "I didn't hear about anybody getting killed, Mr. Ty Ty. That's news to me."

"It was Will Thompson, over there in Horse Creek Valley. Somebody shot him over there day before yesterday. The girls got all excited about it, and I've had a hard time trying to calm them down."

"I sure reckon you do have a hard time trying to do that, boss. It's pretty hard to calm the women folks down after the male man's gone."

Ty Ty turned around quickly, looking at Black Sam.

"What in the pluperfect hell are you talking about, anyhow?"

"Nothing, Mr. Ty Ty. Nothing at all."

"Go on to work," he said shortly. "The sun's been up half an hour already. We can't get nothing done if we're going to wait till after the sun rises before we start digging. The only way to strike that lode, I've been thinking, is to dig and dig and dig."

The two colored men went down into the ground. Black Sam was singing a little, but Uncle Felix was waiting for Ty Ty to leave so he could talk to Black Sam about the trouble in the house. Presently he looked up to the top where Ty Ty had been standing. Ty Ty had gone from sight.

"That Buck would have killed him pretty soon himself," Uncle Felix said. "He would have done it first if he hadn't been so slow to catch on. I saw that look in his wife's eyes a long long time ago when Will Thompson first started coming over here to Georgia. She was getting ready to make way for him then. It didn't look to me like she knew it herself, but I could see it a mile off. That other girl was getting ready for the same thing, too. They just had to make way for Mr. Will. Wasn't no stopping them."

"Who you mean?"

"Darling Jill's the other one I mean."

"Man, man! black fellow, that wasn't nothing new for her. That white girl's always been like that. I've stopped paying any attention to her. But I reckon she was getting ready for it a heap sooner than she generally does, because Mr. Will just naturally made them all that way. But that Griselda is the one to watch. She makes a man itch all over till he don't know where to scratch first."

"Lord, Lord!"

"I was born unlucky. I wish I was a white man myself. She's got what I'm talking about."

"Lord, Lord!"

"One day I was passing the window around yonder and I looked in."

"What did you see, nigger? The moon rising?"

"What I saw made me just want to get right straightaway down on my hands and knees and lick something."

"Lord, Lord!"

"I was born unlucky."

"Ain't it the truth!"

"Trouble in the house."

"Lord, Lord!"

"One man's dead."

"And trouble in the house."

"The male man's gone."

"He can't prick them no more."

"Lord, Lord!"

"Trouble in the house."

"My mammy was a darky——"

"My daddy was too——"

"That white gal's frisky——"

"Good Lord, what to do——"

"Lord, Lord!"

"The time ain't long."

"Somebody shot the male man."

"He can't prick them no more."

"And trouble in the house."

"Lord, Lord!"

Ty Ty shouted down into the hole from the ground above. They picked the clay without looking up. Ty Ty slid down into the crater, bringing a yard of loose sand and clay with him.

"Buck's come back, and I don't want you to say anything to him about staying out all night. I've got enough trouble on my hands, Uncle Felix, without making more. Just leave him alone and don't ask him where he's been. I've got all the trouble now I can stand."

They nodded while he looked at them.

"Somebody shot the male man," Black Sam said aloud.

Ty Ty wheeled around.

"What did you say?"

"Yes, sir, boss. Yes, sir. We won't say nothing to him."

He started up the side of the hole.

"He can't prick them no more."

Ty Ty stopped. Suddenly he jumped from the side of the crater, turning around in the air.

"What in the pluperfect hell are you darkies saying?"

"Yes, sir, boss. Yes, sir. We won't say nothing to Mr. Buck. We won't say nothing at all."

Once more he started climbing to the top.

"Trouble in the house," Black Sam said aloud.

Ty Ty stopped for the third time, but he did not turn around. He waited there, listening.

"Yes, sir, boss. Yes, sir. We won't say nothing to Mr. Buck. We won't say nothing at all."

"He'll be down here in a little while, and I want him left alone. If I hear you talking to him about staying out all night, I'll come down in here with a singletree and knock your blocks clear off your shoulders."

"Yes, sir, boss," Black Sam said. "Yes, sir, white-boss. We ain't saying nothing to Mr. Buck."

Ty Ty climbed up the side of the hole, leaving the colored men silent. He was confident that they would obey his orders. They were smart Negroes.

Up on the ground Ty Ty met Buck coming to work. He put his arm around his son's shoulder when they met. Neither of them said anything, and after a moment Buck turned from Ty Ty and slid down into the crater with the two colored men. Ty Ty stood above for several minutes watching them shovel the clay. Later he left and walked around to the front yard.

Coming down the road from the Marion-Augusta highway was a big car blowing up a cloud of dust. At first Ty Ty thought it was Pluto, but the car was traveling twice as fast as Pluto ever dared drive, and, besides that, it was a larger car and it was shiny black with nickeled trimming that glistened in the sun like new half-dollars.

"Now, who can that be?" Ty Ty asked himself, stopping at the water-oak to watch its approach.

The automobile was at the yard before he realized it. The driver slowed down in a quickly enveloping cloud of yellow dust, coming to a stop so suddenly that the dust passed on in front of it.

Ty Ty ran several steps towards the large black car. It came into the yard then, swaying on the deep springs and roaring in its long motor.

With mouth agape he saw Jim Leslie step out and come towards him. He could not imagine seeing Jim Leslie there. It was the first time in nearly fifteen years that he had set foot on the place.

"Well, I'll declare!" Ty Ty said, running forward to grasp his son's hand.

"Glad to see you, Pa," Jim Leslie said. "Where's Griselda?"

"Who?"

"Griselda."

"You didn't come out here to ask that, did you, son?"

"Where is she?"

"You must be all balled up, Jim Leslie. Didn't you come to see the whole family?"

Jim Leslie started towards the house. Ty Ty ran and caught up with him, pulling his arm and stopping him quickly.

"Now, wait a minute, son. Just hold your horses. What do you want to see Buck's wife about?"

"I haven't got time to talk to you now. I'm in a big hurry. Turn my arm loose."

"Now, listen, son," Ty Ty begged, "there's sorrow here in the house now."

"What about it? What's the matter?"

"Will Thompson was killed the other day over in Scottsville. The girls in the house are nervous and sad. I don't want you to come here and make a mess. You come on out to the hole and sit and talk to the boys and me. When you get tired of staying, then just turn around and go on back to Augusta. We'll all take a trip up there next week to see you when the girls have calmed down some."

"There's nothing the matter with Griselda. What's she got to do with Will Thompson getting killed? He wasn't anything to her. She wouldn't get mixed up with a lint-head from Horse Creek Valley."

"Now, son, I know a heap more right now than you do, and I ask you not to go in there. Women are queer creatures, and man don't always understand them. I can't tell you about it now, but I ask you to stay out of that house. Just get back into your car and turn around and go on back to Augusta where you came from. Now go on, son, before trouble starts."

"What's that got to do with me?" Jim Leslie asked crossly. "Will Thompson is out of this. Griselda wouldn't have anything to do with a lint-head."

"Will Thompson being a lint-head, as you call him, hasn't anything to do with it, either."

"Turn me loose, then. I'm in a big hurry. I haven't got time to stand here arguing with you. I know what I want, and I came after it."

Ty Ty saw that he was powerless to keep Jim Leslie from the house, but he was determined to do all he could to keep trouble from starting. He decided that the best thing to do was to call Buck and Shaw, and the three of them would be able to force Jim Leslie back into his car.

He called Buck, and waited, still holding Jim Leslie's arm. Jim Leslie looked all around, expecting to see Buck suddenly appear at any moment.

"It won't do any good to call him, because I'm not scared of him. Where is he, anyway?"

"He's down in the hole digging."

Ty Ty called again, listening for Buck's answer.

"Still digging for gold," Jim Leslie laughed. "And even Buck and Shaw. It looks like you and the rest of them would have learned your lesson by now. You ought to go to work raising something on this land. Raising piles of dirt is the nearest you've come to it yet."

"I aim to strike the lode soon."

"That's the same thing you said fourteen or fifteen years ago. Age didn't bring you any sense."

"I've got sense you don't know about, son."

Buck came around the corner of the house. He was surprised to see Jim Leslie there, but he came forward to find out why he had been called. Several feet away he stopped and looked at his older brother suspiciously.

"What do you want?" he asked.

"I didn't call you," Jim Leslie said. "Ask him. He was the one who called."

Ty Ty turned to Jim Leslie.

"Now, son, I ask you once more to get in your car and go back to Augusta before trouble starts. You know I can't stop Buck once he gets started, and I don't want no trouble here on the place."

Ty Ty waited a moment, hoping that Jim Leslie would do as he had been asked. He made no reply to his father. Even the appearance of Buck did not deter him from his announced intentions.

"Now, son," Ty Ty said, "Jim Leslie is here. We don't want to have no trouble. He's as welcome as the day is long. But if he starts in the house, well—he just ain't going in there, that's all."

Jim Leslie turned his back on them and started up the porch steps. He was halfway up when he felt his arm being twisted in its socket.

"No, you don't," Buck said, releasing him. "You stay in the yard, or you leave."

Ty Ty yelled for Shaw to come running.

Chapter XX

Now, son," Ty Ty said to Buck, "Jim Leslie has come out here and I want him to leave in a peaceful manner. I've aimed all my life to have a peaceful family, and I can't stand here and see you boys scrap. You just tell Jim Leslie, son, that we don't want no trouble out here. If he'll get in his car and turn around and go on back to Augusta, everything will be all right and like it was before he came. I wouldn't know what to think of myself if it turned out that you boys would scrap all over the place."

Ty Ty saw the two colored men at the corner of the house looking at the scene in the yard. Only their heads were showing, and their eyes were the shade of whitewash on a sunny day. When they had first heard Ty Ty calling for Buck, they knew something was about to happen up on top of the ground, and they had come up to see what the trouble was. Hearing Ty Ty order Jim Leslie into his car, they turned and walked softly out of sight around the other side of the house. After passing the rear of the building, they tiptoed towards the barn, holding their hats in their hands, and trying their best not to look back over their shoulders.

"What do you want out here?" Buck asked his brother, blocking his way on the porch.

" I didn't come out here to talk to you," Jim Leslie replied curtly.

"If you can't talk, then get to hell away from here, and be quick about it."

"Now, son," Ty Ty said.

Jim Leslie turned his back again and started up the steps to the porch. Buck still blocked the way, but Jim Leslie pushed past him.

"Now, wait a minute, you son-of-a-bitch."

"This here now scrapping has got to quit," Ty Ty shouted. "I don't aim to have it on my land."

"Wait?" Jim Leslie replied to his brother. "What for? I'm in a hurry. I can't wait."

Buck struck him on the jaw, knocking him against the side of the house. Jim Leslie crouched low over his knees and sprang at Buck.

When he saw what had happened, Ty Ty ran between them, trying his best to pry them apart. He had to duck his head every moment or two in order to keep from being hit by one of the four fists that flew all around him. He succeeded in pushing Jim Leslie against the wall, and then he tried to hold Buck.

"Now, wait a minute, boys," he said. "You boys are brothers, the three of you. You know good and well you don't want to fight each other. Every one of you wants to be peaceful, and I aim to keep you that way. Let's all just walk down to the barn and talk things over calmly and without scrapping like a pack of bobcats. I've got some things to tell you down there. There's a heap I can explain if you will only be calm while I try to talk. It's a sin and a shame for you to scrap like this. Now, come on and let's all walk down to the barn."

"I'll kill the son-of-a-bitch, now," Buck said, impatient with his father for talking so much.

"Let's not use swear-words at each other," Ty Ty begged. "I'm against so much swearing among brothers. It's all right at some times and places, but not among brothers."

Ty Ty thought that Buck appeared at that moment to be willing to listen if Jim Leslie would.

"He can't come out here—I'll kill him. I know what you're after. I'm no damn fool."

Shaw had not said anything, but he was standing beside Buck ready to help him the moment his help was needed. He would take up for Buck any time the choice was required. Ty Ty knew that he and Jim Leslie never got along very well together, anyway.

"This here now squabbling over women has got to stop on my land," Ty Ty said with sudden determination. He had at last realized how hopeless his efforts to make peace had been. "I've tried to settle this argument peacefully, but I ain't going to stand for you boys scrapping each other over women no longer. It's going to stop right now. You get in your car, son, Jim Leslie, and go on back to Augusta. Buck, you and Shaw go on back to the hole and dig. I've let this scrapping go as far as I'm going to stand for. Go on now, all of you. This here now squabbling over women has got to stop on my land."

"I'll kill the son-of-a-bitch, now," Buck said. "I'll kill him if he goes in that house, now. He can't come out here and take Griselda off, now."

"Boys, this here now squabbling over women on my land has got to stop. You-all boys go on and do like I told you to do just now."

Jim Leslie saw his opportunity, and he sprang for the door and was in the house before they could stop him. Buck was only three steps behind him, however, and Ty Ty and Shaw ran after them. Jim Leslie ran through the first door he reached, and on into another room. He did not know where Griselda was, and he continued through the house in search of her.

"Stop him, Buck!" Shaw shouted. "Make him come back through the hall—don't let him get away through the back door!"

In the dining-room when Ty Ty reached it a moment later, Jim Leslie was in the middle of the room, with the table between Buck and himself, and they were cursing each other. Over in the corner the three girls were huddled behind a chair they had pulled in front of them. Griselda was crying, and so was Rosamond. Darling Jill looked as if she did not know whether to cry or to laugh. Ty Ty could not stop to look at them any longer, and he did not try to protect them so long as they were in no immediate danger, but began shouting at the boys again. He soon saw it was useless. They did not hear a word he said; they appeared to be unaware of his presence in the room.

"Come out of that corner, Griselda," Jim Leslie told her. "You're going with me. Come out of that corner and get into the car before I have to come and pull you out."

"You stay where you are and don't move," Buck told her out of the corner of his mouth, his eyes still on his brother.

Ty Ty turned to Shaw in desperation.

"You'd better go get Black Sam and Uncle Felix to help us. It looks like we can't handle him alone."

"You stay here, Shaw," Buck said. "I don't need any help. I can handle him by myself."

"Come out of that corner before I drag you out, Griselda," Jim Leslie said again.

"You came to get her, huh? Why didn't you say that in the yard? I knew damn well what it was, but I've just been waiting to hear you say it. You came to get her, huh?"

"This here now squabbling over women on my land has got to quit," Ty Ty said determinedly. "I just ain't going to stand for it no longer."

"Come out of that corner, Griselda," Jim Leslie said for the third time.

"I'll kill the son-of-a-bitch, now," Buck said.

He stepped back, relaxing his muscles.

"This here now squabbling over women on my land has got to stop," Ty Ty said, banging his fists on the table between his two sons.

Buck stepped back to the wall behind him and reached for the shotgun on the rack. He unbreeched it, looking down a moment to see if both barrels were loaded.

When Jim Leslie saw Buck with the gun, he ran out the door into the hall and on through the house to the front yard. Buck was behind him, holding out the gun in front of him as though it were a snake on a stick.

Out in the yard, Ty Ty realized it was useless for him to try to stop Buck. He could not wrestle the gun away from him; Buck was too strong. He would throw him aside without much effort. So, instead of running out into the yard, Ty Ty sank to his knees on the porch and began praying.

Behind him in the hall stood Griselda and Rosamond and Darling Jill, afraid to come any further, but scared to stay alone in the house. They huddled behind the front door, peeping through the crack to see what was happening in the yard.

Ty Ty looked up from his prayer, one eye open in fright, one eye closed in supplication, when he heard Buck shout to Jim Leslie to stop running. Jim Leslie was in front of his automobile, and he could easily have jumped behind it for protection, but instead he stopped where he was and shook his fist at Buck.

"I reckon you'll leave her alone now," Buck said.

The gun was already leveled at Jim Leslie. Ty Ty could almost see through the sights from where he was on the porch, and he was certain he could feel Buck's finger tighten on the trigger. He closed his eyes prayerfully a second before the explosion in the barrel. He opened his eyes to see Jim Leslie reach forward for something to grip for support, and heard almost immediately the explosion of the second shell. Jim Leslie stood upright for a few short seconds, and then his body twisted to one side and he fell heavily on the hard white sand under the water-oak tree.

Griselda and Rosamond and Darling Jill screamed behind the door at the same moment. Ty Ty closed his eyes again, trying to erase from his mind each horrible detail of the scene. He hoped, opening them, to find that it had all vanished. It was no different than before, however, except that Buck was standing over Jim Leslie pushing new shells into the gun. Jim Leslie twisted and doubled up into a round ball.

Ty Ty got up and ran down into the yard. He pushed Buck away and bent over Jim Leslie trying to speak to him. Without help he lifted his son in his arms and carried him to the porch. Shaw came and looked down at his brother, and the girls stood in the doorway with their hands over their faces. Every moment or so one of them would scream. Buck sat down on the steps, dropping the shotgun at his feet.

"Say you ain't going to die, son," Ty Ty begged, getting down beside him on the floor.

Jim Leslie looked up at him, closing his eyes in the glare of the sun. His lips moved for a number of seconds, but Ty Ty could not hear a sound.

"Can't we do something for him, Pa?" Rosamond asked him. She was the first to come from the hall. "What can we do, Pa?"

She knelt down with him, holding her throat with her hands. Griselda and Darling Jill came a little closer, looking down at Jim Leslie.

Ty Ty nodded to Rosamond.

"Hold his hand, Rosamond," he said. "That's what his mother would do if she was here now."

Jim Leslie opened his eyes and looked up at her when he became conscious of her hands over his.

"Can't you say something, son?" Ty Ty asked. "Just a little something, son."

"I haven't anything to say," he answered weakly, closing his eyes again.

The handkerchief in Ty Ty's hand slipped from the wound in Jim Leslie's chest and fell to the porch. Jim Leslie's eyes had opened for the last time, and they glistened in the sun, glazed and motionless.

Ty Ty got up stiffly and walked down into the yard. He walked up and down in front of the steps trying to say something to himself. He walked slowly, from one corner of the house to the other, not looking higher than the white sand he tramped upon. Griselda and Darling Jill had fallen to their knees beside Rosamond, and the three of them knelt there, breathless before the sobs came to their throats. Ty Ty did not look to see them. He knew they were there without looking.

"Blood on my land," he said. "Blood on my land."

The sound of Rosamond's running into the house behind Griselda and Darling Jill awakened him. He looked up and saw Black Sam and Uncle Felix racing across the fields towards the woods on the other side of the farm. The sight of the two colored men running away made him wonder for the first time that day where Dave was. He remembered then that he had not seen Dave since early that morning. He did not know where Dave had gone, and he did not care. He could get along somehow without him.

On the bottom step of the porch, Buck sat with his head dropped over his chest. The shotgun was still lying on the ground where it had fallen from his hands. Ty Ty turned completely around to escape the sight of it.

"Blood on my land," he muttered.

The farm before him looked desolate. The piles of red clay and yellow sand, the wide red craters between, the red soil without vegetation —the land looked desolate. In the shade of the water-oak tree where he stood, Ty Ty felt completely exhausted. He no longer felt strength in his muscles when he thought of the gold in the earth under his farm. He did not know where the gold was, and he did not know how he was going to be able to dig any longer without his strength. There was gold there though, because several nuggets had been found on the farm; he knew there was gold there, but he did not know whether he would be able to continue his search for it. At that moment he felt that there was no use in ever doing anything again. All his life he had lived with the determination of keeping peace in his family. Now it did not matter; nothing mattered now. Nothing mattered any longer, because blood had been spilled on his land—the blood of one of his children.

He thought himself talking to Buck in the dining-room the evening before.

"The trouble with you boys is that you don't seem to catch on."

The glare of the sun in his eyes reminded him of something else.

"Blood on my land," he repeated. "Blood on my land."

The three girls in the house were crying through the open doors and windows. While he walked up and down, they came to the porch again, standing there and looking.

"Go get an undertaker or a doctor or something, son," he told Shaw, nodding his head wearily.

Shaw got into Ty Ty's car and started to Marion. They stood on the porch watching the cloud of yellow dust left behind to settle over the roadside.

Ty Ty tried to force his eyes upon the floor so he would not lift them to look at his desolate land. He knew if he looked at it again he would feel a sinking sensation in his body. Something out there repelled him. It was no longer as it had been before. The big piles of earth had always made him feel excitement; now they made him feel like turning his head away and never looking out there again. The mounds even had a different color now, and the soil of his land was nothing like earth he had ever seen before. There had never been any vegetation out there, but he had never realized the lack of it before. Over on the other side of the farm, where the newground was, there was vegetation, because the top soil in the newground had not been covered with piles of sand and clay in one place, and big yawning holes in others. He wished then that he had the strength to spread out his arms and smooth the land as far as he could see, leveling the ground by filling the holes with the mounds of earth. He realized how impotent he was by his knowledge that he would never be able to do that. He felt heavy at heart.

"Son," he said to Buck, looking off into the distance, "son, the sheriff——"

Buck raised his head for the first time and looked up into the day. He heard his father speaking to him, and he knew what had been said.

"Oh, Pa!" Rosamond screamed, standing in the door.

Ty Ty waited to hear if she would say anything else. He knew there was nothing else to say. There was no more for him to hear.

He got up and walked from one corner of the house to the other, passing in front of Buck, his lips compressed grimly, his eyes feeble.

"Son," he said, stopping at the steps, "son, the sheriff will be hearing about it when Shaw gets to town."

The girls came running down the steps to his side. Rosamond threw her arms around Buck, hugging him with all her might. Griselda was beside him crying.

"The good Lord blessed me with three of the prettiest girls a man ever had in his house. He was good to me that way, because I know I don't deserve it all."

Darling Jill had begun to cry audibly. They were all close to Ty Ty, hugging Buck in their arms.

"The good Lord blessed me that way, but he puts sorrow in my heart to pay for it. It looks like a good thing and a bad thing always have to go hand-in-hand. You don't get the one without the other, ever."

Griselda held Buck's head against her breast, stroking his hair and kissing his face. She tried to make Buck speak to her, but he closed his eyes and said nothing.

"There was a mean trick played on us somewhere. God put us in the bodies of animals and tried to make us act like people. That was the beginning of trouble. If He had made us like we are, and not called us people, the last one of us would know how to live. A man can't live, feeling himself from the inside, and listening to what the preachers say. He can't do both, but he can do one or the other. He can live like we were made to live, and feel himself on the inside, or he can live like the preachers say, and be dead on the inside. A man has got God in him from the start, and when he is made to live like a preacher says to live, there's going to be trouble. If the boys had done like I tried to get them to do, there never would have been all this trouble. The girls understand, and they are willing to live like God made them to live; but the boys go off and hear fools talk and they come back here and try to run things counter to God. God made pretty girls and He made men, and there was enough to go around. When you try to take a woman or a man and hold him off all for yourself, there ain't going to be nothing but trouble and sorrow the rest of your days."

Buck stood up, straightening his shoulders. He had one arm around Griselda, holding her while she clung to him and kissed him.

"I feel like the end of the world has struck me," Ty Ty said. "It feels like the bottom has dropped completely out from under me. I feel like I'm sinking and can't help myself."

"Don't talk like that, Pa," Darling Jill said, hugging him. "It makes me feel so bad when you say that."

Buck broke Griselda's grip around him and pushed her hands from him. She ran and threw herself upon him frantically. He could not move with her holding him.

"Son," Ty Ty said, looking out across the field piled high with earth, "son, the sheriff——"

Buck bent over and kissed Griselda full on the lips, pressing her closely for a long time. Then he pushed her away.

"Buck, where are you going?" she cried.

"I'm going for a walk," he said.

She fell upon the steps and covered her face. Darling Jill sat beside her, holding her head in her lap.

Buck went out of sight around the corner of the house, and Ty Ty followed him a moment later, walking slowly behind him. Buck climbed the fence on the other side of the well and walked in a straight line across the fields towards the newground on the other side of the farm. Ty Ty stopped at the fence and went no further. He stood there, leaning against it for support, while Buck walked slowly over the field to the newground.

He remembered then that God's little acre had been brought back to the house, and all the more acutely he realized that Jim Leslie had been killed upon it. But it was Buck that Ty Ty was thinking of at that moment, and he willed that God's little acre follow Buck, stopping when he did so that he would always be upon it. He watched Buck go towards the newground, and he was glad he had thought of God's little acre in time to have it follow Buck, stopping where Buck stopped so that his son would be upon it no matter where he went.

"Blood on my land," Ty Ty said aloud. "Blood on my land."

After a while he could no longer see Buck, and he turned towards the house and walked to the side of the big hole. The moment he looked down into the crater, he felt a consuming desire to go down to the bottom of it and dig. He went down into the hole slowly. His back was a little stiff, and his knees were weak. He was getting to be old, digging in the holes. Soon he would be too old to dig any more.

He picked up Shaw's shovel and began throwing loose earth over his shoulders. Some of it rolled back, but most of it remained up above. When the platform was full, he would have to climb up there and shovel the earth to the next platform. They were so deep now that the earth had to be handled four or five times before it was finally thrown out at the top. The hole was widening, too. The house would be undermined if some additional supports were not cut in the woods and drawn by the mules. He would have to send Black Sam and Uncle Felix with the mules to draw six or seven large logs the next morning.

Ty Ty did not know how long he had been digging when he heard Griselda calling him from the top of the ground.

"What's the matter, Griselda?" he asked, leaning wearily against the shovel.

"Where's that shotgun, Pa?" she asked. "Have you seen it?"

He waited a little while before answering her. He was too tired to speak until he had rested for a few moments.

"No, Griselda," he said finally. "I haven't seen it. I haven't got time to help you look for it now."

"Where in the world is it then, Pa? It was lying in the yard, and it's not there now."

"Griselda," he said, dropping his head so he would not have to look up at her, "Griselda, when Buck went for a walk, he carried it with him."

There was no sound above him on the rim of the crater, and presently he looked up to see if Griselda was still looking down at him. She was not within sight, but he distinctly heard the voices of Darling Jill and Rosamond raised in excitement somewhere up there on the top of the ground. He bent over his shovel, kicking the blade into the clay with his foot, and wondering how soon Shaw would come back to help him dig.

APPENDIX TO THE FIFTH PRINTING

OF *God's Little Acre*

On May 2, 1933, The New York Society for the Suppression of Vice, through its agent, John S. Sumner, brought The Viking Press into court on an obscenity charge for publishing *God's Little Acre*. Counsel for The Viking Press, Wolfgang S. Schwabacher, fought the charge on the ground that the book was an honest work of literature, which could not be considered obscene if read as a whole, and introduced in support of his case letters of protest from leading citizens, including many writers and reviewers, as well as excerpts from newspaper and magazine reviews praising the book for its literary qualities. On May 23, Magistrate Benjamin Greenspan dismissed the case in a memorable opinion, which declared that the book was "very clearly not a work of pornography." The publishers deem his opinion of sufficient importance to the cause of literature to be worth reprinting in full in the following pages.

The author and the publishers take this occasion to thank the sixty or more individuals who sent written protests against the attempt to suppress the book, as well as the newspapers and the general public, which rallied to their support in defending it.

MAGISTRATE'S COURT, CITY OF NEW YORK
FOURTH DISTRICT, BOROUGH OF MANHATTAN

THE PEOPLE OF THE STATE OF NEW YORK,
                              Plaintiff,

—*against*—

THE VIKING PRESS, INC., and HELEN SCHILLER,
                              Defendants.

HAROLD FRANKEL, Deputy Assistant District Attorney
for the Plaintiff.

HAYS, HERSHFIELD, KAUFMAN AND SCHWABACHER,
(Wolfgang S. Schwabacher and James M. Grossman
of counsel) for the Defendant.

BENJAMIN E. GREENSPAN, City Magistrate.

This prosecution is instituted by The New York Society for the Suppression of Vice, through Mr. John S. Sumner, its Secretary and Attorney, against The Viking Press, Inc., the publishers of a certain book by one ERSKINE CALDWELL entitled *God's Little Acre*, and against HELEN SCHILLER, a clerk in the employ of the publishers, who sold the book to an agent of the Society.

It is claimed that the sale of the book is a violation of Section 1141 of the Penal Law and that the book is, within the meaning of that statute, "obscene, lewd, lascivious, filthy, indecent, and disgusting." In order to sustain the prosecution, the Court must find that the tendency of the book as a whole, and indeed its main purpose, is to excite lustful desire and what has been rather fancifully called "impure imaginations." PEOPLE *v.* MULLER, 96 N. Y. 408. The statute is aimed at pornography, and a pornographic book must be taken to be one where all other incidents and qualities are mere accessories to the primary purpose of stimulating immoral thoughts.

The courts have strictly limited the applicability of the statute to works of pornography and they have consistently declined to apply it to books of genuine literary value. If the statute were construed more broadly than in the manner just indicated, its effect would be to prevent altogether the realistic portrayal in literature of a large and important field of life. The Court of Appeals has consistently frowned upon such an interpretation of the statute. PEOPLE *v.* WENDLING, 258 N. Y. 451; HALSEY *v.* N. Y. SOCIETY FOR THE SUPPRESSION OF VICE, 234 N. Y. 1. See also the opinion of the Appellate Division, 1st Dep't, in PEOPLE *v.* BRAINARD, 192 App. Div. 816, regarding the book called *Madeleine,* an anonymous autobiography of a prostitute.

It is claimed, on behalf of the defendants, that the book in the instant case, Caldwell's *God's Little Acre,* has high literary merit. In support of this claim, counsel for the defendants have collected and presented to this Court a large number of testimonials from people eminent in the literary life of this city and country, as well as from others distinguished in social work, education, and other fields. Some of these testimonials were written especially for presentation to this Court. Others are culled from literary reviews and newspapers. Among the latter, which are necessarily to be given more weight than those written especially for the purpose of defeating this prosecution, the Court finds praise of the merits of the book by the following: Franklin P. Adams in the *New York Herald Tribune* of January 28th, 1933; William Soskin in the *New York Evening Post* of April 29th, 1933; Horace Gregory in the *New York Herald Tribune Book Review* of February 5th, 1933; an unnamed reviewer in the *London Times Literary Supplement* of March 23rd, 1933; James T. Farrell in the *New York Sun* of February 7th, 1933; Louis Kronenberger in the *New York Times* of February 5th, 1933; a reviewer in the *New York Evening Post* of February 7th, 1933, who refers to the book as "a passionately honest book"; Gilbert Seldes in the *New York Journal* of February 11th, 1933, who describes the book as "engaging and impressive at once"; Jonathan Daniels in the *Saturday Review of Literature,* as quoted in the Raleigh, North Carolina, *News Observer* of March 5th, 1933; and Joseph Henry Jackson in the *San Francisco Chronicle* of February 17th, 1933. The Court regards this as a fair cross-section of American literary opinion, by a group of men competent to judge with reasonable accuracy the value of contemporary American books.

The brief presented to this Court by Mr. Sumner makes the following references to these reviews: "We have seen this attempted before and the question arises as to whether a criminal prosecution is to be determined by interested parties having access to the newspapers and no interest in public welfare or by the Courts existing for that purpose and representing the whole people and not only the literati." Mr. Sumner also refers to the following quotation from PEOPLE *v.* PESKY, 230 App. Div. 203: "These matters must be judged by normal people and not by the abnormal. Conditions would be deplorable if abnormal people were permitted to regulate such matters." Mr. Sumner then says: "Substitute the word 'literati' for 'abnormal people' and we have an exact explanation of the letters, reviews, and other favorable comments presented in behalf of this book and its author."

Letters have been presented to this Court praising the value of the book in question, from Mark Eisner, President of the Board of Higher Education of the City of New York; Lewis Gannett of the *New York Herald Tribune;* John Mason Brown, Dramatic Critic of the *New York Evening Post;* Sidonie M. Gruenberg of the Child Study Association of America; Solomon

Lowenstein, Executive and Director of the Federation for the Support of Jewish Philanthropic Societies; Marc Connelly; Horace M. Kallen, Honorary Vice-President of the American Jewish Congress; Carl Van Doren, a distinguished literary critic; Herbert Bayard Swope, former Editor of the *New York World*; J. Donald Adams, Editor of the *New York Times Book Review*; Prof. Raymond Weaver, of the English Department of Columbia University; Malcolm Cowley, one of the Editors of the *New Republic*; Henry S. Canby, the veteran Editor of the *Saturday Review of Literature*; Nathan Ottinger; Elmer Rice, Playwright; John Cowper Powys; and finally Sinclair Lewis.

This Court cannot subscribe to Mr. Sumner's opinion of the capacity for fair judgment of these leaders of American literary and educational thought. The Court declines to believe that so large and representative a group of people would rally to the support of a book which they did not genuinely believe to be of importance and literary merit. The Court is of the opinion, moreover, that this group of people, collectively, has a better capacity to judge of the value of a literary production than one who is more apt to search for obscene passages in a book than to regard the book as a whole.

This Court has carefully read the book in question. It is an attempt at the portrayal, in a realistic fashion, of life as lived by an illiterate Southern white farm family. A daughter of this family is married to a worker in a Southern mill town. There is inter-action between the run-down farm life and the mill town life. Both on the farm and in the mill town the people are primitive and impoverished. They are deprived of the opportunity for development, and their activities are largely sexual. They are of a simple nature, and savage passion is found close to the surface.

This Court is not sufficiently familiar with conditions in the portion of the country described to say, at first hand, that the description is accurate. Nothing in this opinion is to be construed as an expression by the Court as to whether or not the book is an accurate piece of reporting. As fiction, however, it contains internal evidence that it was written with a sincere attempt to present with truth and honesty a segment of life in the Southern United States. The author has set out to paint a realistic picture. Such pictures necessarily contain certain details. Because these deails relate to what is popularly called the sex side of life, portrayed with brutal frankness, the Court may not say that the picture should not have been created at all. The language, too, is undoubtedly coarse and vulgar. The Court may not require the author to put refined language into the mouths of primitive people.

The book as a whole is very clearly not a work of pornography. It is not necessary for the Court to decide whether it is an important work of literature. Its subject matter constitutes a legitimate field for literary effort and the treatment is also legitimate. The Court must consider the book as a whole even though some paragraphs standing by themselves might be objectionable. "No work may be judged from a selection of such paragraphs alone. Printed by themselves, they might, as a matter of law, come within the prohibition of the statute. So might a similar selection from Aristophanes or Chaucer or Boccaccio or even from the Bible. The book, however, must be considered broadly as a whole." HALSEY v. N. Y. SOCIETY FOR THE SUPPRESSION OF VICE, 234 N. Y. 1, at page 4. The test is whether "not in certain passages, but in its main purpose and construction," HALSEY v. N. Y. SOCIETY FOR THE SUPPRESSION OF VICE, 234 N. Y. 1, at page 10, the book is obscene and lewd, and, therefore, violative of the statute.

The Court holds that it is not. This is not a book where vice and lewdness are treated as virtues or which would tend to incite lustful desires in the normal mind. There is no way of anticipating its effect upon a disordered or diseased mind, and if the courts were to exclude books from sale merely because they might incite lust in disordered minds, our entire literature would very likely be reduced to a relatively small number of uninteresting and barren books. The greater part of the classics would certainly be excluded. In conclusion, *God's Little Acre* has no tendency to inspire its readers to behave like its characters, therefore, it has no tendency to excite "lustful desire." Those who see the ugliness and not the beauty in a piece of work are unable to see the forest for the trees. I personally feel that the very suppression of books arouses curiosity and leads readers to endeavor to find licentiousness where none was intended. In this book, I believe the author has chosen to write what he believes to be the truth about a certain group in American life. To my way of thinking, *Truth* should always be accepted as a justification for literature.

No complaint will be entertained against the defendants and the summons herein will be dismissed.

SHORT STORIES

Almost every short story writer and novelist who creates the characters that people his fiction is beset by readers demanding affidavits that such characters "actually exist." No writer worth his salt is ever guilty of such gross adynamia as the demand implies. All fictional characters are created from the materials of human experience, but rarely are they replicas of living persons. It is to the credit of fiction as a form of art that readers are moved to ask for proof, but it also shows a lack of discrimination on the part of readers when they are unable to distinguish between fantasy and reality.

August Afternoon

Vic Glover awoke with the noon-day heat ringing in his ears. He had been asleep for only half an hour, and he was getting ready to turn over and go back to sleep when he opened his eyes for a moment and saw Hubert's wooly black head over the top of his bare toes. He stretched his eyelids and held them open in the glaring light as long as he could.

Hubert was standing in the yard, at the edge of the porch, with a pine cone in his hand.

Vic cursed him.

The colored man once more raked the cone over Vic's bare toes, tickling them on the under-side, and stepped back out of reach.

"What do you mean by standing there tickling me with that dad-burned cone?" Vic shouted at Hubert. "Is that all you can find to do? Why don't you get out in that field and do something to them boll-weevils? They're going to eat up every boll of cotton on the place if you don't stop them."

"I surely hated to wake you up, Mr. Vic," Hubert said, "but there's a white man out here looking for something. He won't say what he's looking for, but he's hanging around waiting for it."

Vic sat up wide awake. He sat up on the quilt and pulled on his shoes without looking into the yard. The white sand in the yard beat the glare of the sun directly into his eyes and he could see nothing beyond the edge of the porch. Hubert threw the pine cone under the porch and stepped aside.

"He must be looking for trouble," Vic said. "When they come around and don't say anything, and just sit and look, it's trouble they're looking for."

"There he is, Mr. Vic," Hubert said, nodding his head across the yard. "There he sits up against that wateroak tree yonder."

Vic looked around for Willie. Willie was sitting on the top step at the other end of the porch, directly in front of the strange white man. She did not look at Vic.

"You ought to have better sense than to wake me up while I'm taking a nap. This is no time of the day to be up in the summertime. I've got to get a little sleep every now and then."

"Boss," Hubert said, "I wouldn't never wake you up at all, not at any time, but Miss Willie just sits there high up on the steps showing her pretty and that white man has been out there whittling on a little stick a long time without saying nothing. I'm scared about something happening when he whittles that little stick clear through, and it's just about whittled down to nothing now. That's why I waked you up, Mr. Vic. Ain't much left of that little whittling-stick."

Vic glanced again at Willie, and from her he turned to stare at the stranger sitting under the wateroak tree in his front yard.

The piece of wood had been shaved down to paper thinness.

"Boss," Hubert said, shifting the weight of his body uneasily, "we ain't aiming to have no trouble today, is we?"

"Which way did he come from?" Vic asked, ignoring the question.

"I never did see him come from nowhere, Mr. Vic. I just looked up, and there he was, sitting against that wateroak out yonder and whittling on that little stick. I reckon I must have been drowsy when he came, because when I opened my eyes, there he was."

Vic slid down over the quilt until his legs were hanging over the edge of the porch. Perspiration began to trickle down his neck as soon as he sat up.

"Ask him what he's after, Hubert."

"We ain't aiming to have no trouble today, is we, Mr. Vic?"

"Ask him what he wants around here, I said."

Hubert went almost halfway to the wateroak tree and stopped.

"Mr. Vic says what can he do for you, white-folks?"

The man said nothing. He did not even glance up from the little stick he was whittling.

Hubert came back to the porch, the whites of his eyes becoming larger with each step.

"What did he say?" Vic asked him.

"He ain't said nothing yet, Mr. Vic. He acts like he don't hear me at all. You'd better go talk to him, Mr. Vic. He won't give me no attention. Appears to me like he's just sitting there and looking at Miss Willie on the high step. Maybe if you was to tell her to go in the house and shut the door, he might be persuaded to give some notice to what we say to him."

"Ain't no sense in sending her in the house," Vic said. "I can make him talk. Hand me that stillyerd."

"Mr. Vic, I'm trying to tell you about Miss Willie. Miss Willie's been sitting there on that high step showing her pretty and he's been looking at her a right long time, Mr. Vic. If you won't object to me saying so, Mr. Vic, I reckon I'd tell Miss Willie to go sit somewhere else, if I was you. Miss Willie ain't got much on today, Mr. Vic. Just only that skimpy outside dress, Mr. Vic. That's what I've been trying to tell you. I walked out there in the yard this while ago to see what he was looking at so much, and when I say Miss Willie ain't got much on today, I mean she's got on just only that skimpy outside dress, Mr. Vic. You can go look yourself and see if I'm lying to you, Mr. Vic."

"Hand me that stillyerd, I said."

Hubert went to the end of the porch and brought the heavy iron cotton-weighing steelyard to Vic. He stepped back out of the way.

"Boss," Hubert said, "we ain't aiming to have no trouble today, is we?"

Vic was getting ready to jump down into the yard when the man under the wateroak reached into his pocket and pulled out another knife. It was about ten or eleven inches long, and both sides of the handle were covered with hairy cowhide. There was a spring-button in one end. The man pushed the button with his thumb, and the blade sprang from the case. He began playing with both knives, throwing them up into the air and catching them on the backs of his hands.

Hubert moved to the other side of Vic.

"Mr. Vic," he said, "I ain't intending to mess in your business none, but it looks to me like you got yourself in for a peck of trouble when you went off and brought Miss Willie back here. It looks to me like she's got up for a city girl, more so than a country girl."

Vic cursed him.

"I'm telling you, Mr. Vic, you ought to marry yourself a wife who hadn't ought to sit on a high step in front of a stranger, not even when she's wearing something more than just only a skimpy outside dress. I walked out there and looked at Miss Willie, and, Mr. Vic, Miss Willie is as bare as a plucked chicken, except for one little place I saw."

"Shut up," Vic said, laying the steelyard down on the quilt beside him.

The man under the wateroak closed the blade of the small pen-knife and put it into his pocket. The big hairy cowhide knife he flipped into the air and caught it easily on the back of his hand.

"Mr. Vic," Hubert said, "you've been asleep all the time and you don't know like I do. Miss Willie has been sitting there on that high step showing off her pretty a long time now, and he's got his pecker up. I know, Mr. Vic, because I went out there myself and looked."

Vic cursed him.

The man in the yard flipped the knife into the air and caught it behind his back.

"What's your name?" he asked Willie.

"Willie."

He flipped the knife again.

"What's yours?" she asked him, giggling.

"Floyd."

"Where are you from?"

"Carolina."

He flipped it higher than ever, catching it underhanded.

"What are you doing in Georgia?"

"Don't know," he said. "Just looking around."

Willie giggled, smiling at him.

Floyd got up and walked across the yard to the steps and sat down on the bottom one. He put his arms around his knees and looked up at Willie.

"You're not so bad-looking," he said. "I've seen lots worse-looking."

"You're not so bad yourself," Willie giggled, resting her arms on her knees and looking down at him.

"How about a kiss?"

"What would it be to you?"

"Not bad. I reckon I've had lots worse."

"Well, you can't get it sitting down there."

Floyd climbed the steps on his hands and feet and sat down on the next to the top step. He leaned against Willie, putting one arm around her waist and the other under her knees. Willie slid down the step beside him. Floyd pulled her to him, making a sucking-sound with his lips.

"Boss," Hubert said, his lips twitching, "we ain't aiming to have no trouble today, is we?"

Vic cursed him.

Willie and Floyd moved down a step without loosening their embrace.

"Who is that yellow-headed sapsucker, anyhow?" Vic said. "I'll be dad-burned if he ain't got a lot of nerve—coming here and fooling with Willie."

"You wouldn't do nothing to cause trouble, would you, Mr. Vic? I surely don't want to have no trouble today, Mr. Vic."

Vic glanced at the eleven-inch knife Floyd had stuck into the step at his feet. It stood on its tip, twenty-two inches high, while the sun was reflected against the bright blade and made a streak of light on Floyd's pants-leg.

"Go over there and take that knife away from him and bring it to me," Vic said. "Don't be scared of him."

"Mr. Vic, I surely hate to disappoint you, but if you want that white-folk's knife, you'll just have to get it your own self. I don't aim to have myself all carved up with that thing. Mr. Vic, I surely can't accommodate you this time. If you want that white-folk's knife, you'll just be bound to get it your own self, Mr. Vic."

Vic cursed him.

Hubert backed away until he was at the end of the porch. He kept looking behind him all the time, looking to be certain of the exact location of the sycamore stump that was between him and the pine grove on the other side of the cotton field.

Vic called to Hubert and told him to come back. Hubert came slowly around the corner of the porch and stood a few feet from the quilt where Vic was sitting. His lips quivered and the whites of his eyes grew larger. Vic mentioned for him to come closer, but he would not come an inch farther.

"How old are you?" Floyd asked Willie.

"Fifteen."

Floyd jerked the knife out of the wood and thrust it deeper into the same place.

"How old are you?" she asked him.

"About twenty-seven."

"Are you married?"

"Not now," he said. "How long have you been?"

"About three months," Willie said.

"How do you like it?"

"Pretty good so far."

"How about another kiss?"

"You just had one."

"I'd like another one now."

"I ought not to let you kiss me again."

"Why not?"

"Men don't like girls who kiss too much."

"I'm not that kind."

"What kind are you?"

"I'd like to kiss you a lot."

"But after I let you do that, you'd go away."

"No, I won't. I'll stay for something else."

"What?"

"To get the rest of you."

"You might hurt me."

"It won't hurt."

"It might."

"Let's go inside for a drink and I'll show you."

"We'll have to go to the spring for fresh water."

"Where's the spring?"

"Just across the field in the grove."

"All right," Floyd said, standing up. "Let's go."

He bent down and pulled the knife out of the wood. Willie ran down the steps and across the yard. When Floyd saw that she was not going to wait for him, he ran after her, holding the knives in his pocket with one hand. She led him across the cotton field to the spring in the pine grove. Just before they got there, Floyd caught her by the arm and ran beside her the rest of the way.

"Boss," Hubert said, his voice trembling, "we ain't aiming to have no trouble today, is we?"

Vic cursed him.

"I don't want to get messed up with a heap of trouble and maybe get my belly slit open with that big hairy knife. If you ain't got objections, I reckon I'll mosey on home now and cut me a little firewood for the cookstove."

"Come back here!" Vic said. "You stay where you are and stop making moves to go off."

"What is we aiming to do, Mr. Vic?"

Vic eased himself off the porch and walked across the yard to the wateroak. He looked down at the ground where Floyd had been sitting, and then he looked at the porch steps where Willie had been. The noon-day heat beat down through the thin leaves overhead and he could feel his mouth and throat burn with the hot air he breathed.

"Have you got a gun, Hubert?"

"No, sir, boss," Hubert said.

"Why haven't you?" he said. "Right when I need a gun, you haven't got it. Why don't you keep a gun?"

"Mr. Vic, I ain't got no use for a gun. I used to keep one to shoot rabbits and squirrels with, but I got to thinking hard one day, and I traded it off the first chance I got. I reckon it was a good thing I traded, too. If I had kept it, you'd be asking for it like you did just now."

Vic went back to the porch and picked up the steelyard and hammered the porch with it. After he had hit the porch four or five times, he dropped it and started out in the direction of the spring. He walked as far as the edge of the shade and stopped. He stood listening for a while.

Willie and Floyd could be heard down near the spring. Floyd said something to Willie, and Willie laughed loudly. There was silence again for several minutes, and then Willie laughed again. Vic could not tell whether she was crying or laughing. He was getting ready to turn and go back to the porch when he heard her cry out. It sounded like a scream, but it was not exactly that; it sounded like a shriek, but it wasn't that, either; it sounded more like someone laughing and crying simultaneously in a high-pitched, excited voice.

"Where did Miss Willie come from, Mr. Vic?" Hubert asked. "Where did you bring her from?"

"Down below here a little way," he said.

Hubert listened to the sounds that were coming from the pine grove.

"Boss," he said after a little while, "it appears to me like you didn't go far enough away."

"I went far enough," Vic said. "If I had gone any farther, I'd have been in Florida."

The colored man hunched his shoulders forward several times while he smoothed the white sand with his broad-soled shoes.

"Mr. Vic, if I was you, the next time I'd surely go that far, maybe farther."

"What do you mean, the next time?"

"I was figuring that maybe you wouldn't be keeping her much longer than now, Mr. Vic."

Vic cursed him.

Hubert raised his head several times and attempted to see down into the pine grove over the top of the growing cotton.

"Shut up and mind your own business," Vic said. "I'm going to keep her till the cows come home. Where else do you reckon I'd find a better-looking girl than Willie?"

"Boss, I wasn't thinking of how she looks—I was thinking of how she acts. That white man came here and sat down and it wasn't no time before she had his pecker up."

"She acts that way because she ain't old enough yet to know who to fool with. She'll catch on in time."

Hubert followed Vic across the yard. While Vic went towards the porch, Hubert stopped and leaned against the wateroak where he could almost see over the cotton field into the pine grove. Vic went up on the porch and stretched out on the quilt. He took off his shoes and flung them aside.

"I surely God knowed something was going to happen when he whittled that stick down to nothing," Hubert was saying to himself. "White-folks take a long time to whittle a little piece of wood, but when they whittle it down to nothing, they're going to be up and doing before the time ain't long."

Presently Vic sat upright on the quilt.

"Listen here, Hubert——"

"Yes, sir, boss!"

"You keep your eye on that stillyerd so it will stay right where it is now, and when they come back up the path, you wake me up in a hurry."

"Yes, sir, boss," Hubert said. "Are you aiming to take a little nap now?"

"Yes, I am. And if you don't wake me up when they come back, I'll break your neck for you when I do wake up."

Vic lay down again on the quilt and turned over on his side to shut out the blinding glare of the early afternoon sun that was reflected upon the porch from the hard white sand in the yard.

Hubert scratched his head and sat down against the wateroak, facing the path from the spring. He could hear Vic snoring on the porch above the sounds that came at intervals from the pine grove across the field. He sat staring down the path, drowsy, singing under his breath. It was a long time until sun-down.

Undoubtedly some day a Professor Horatio Perkins will be found leafing through this book in search of a peg to hang his hat on. He will feel discouraged at the start because he will find his cardinal rule, "never end a sentence with a preposition," has been broken; but, nonetheless, he will feel it is his duty to keep on. It is his hope, of course, to discover for himself, so that he may impart to his students, the secret of story telling. When he has finished his research, the chances are that he will write a book and call it "The Eleven Ways to Write a Short Story." I dislike depriving him of his royalties, but I think my grandfather anticipated him by a number of years by saying that the only satisfactory way of doing what you set out to do is to do it the best way.

Horse Thief

I DIDN'T steal Lud Moseley's calico horse.

People all over have been trying to make me out a thief, but anybody who knows me at all will tell you that I've never been in trouble like this before in all my life. Mr. John Turner will tell you all about me. I've worked for him, off and on, for I don't know exactly how many years. I reckon I've worked for him just about all my life, since I was a boy. Mr. John knows I wouldn't steal a horse. That's why I say I didn't steal Lud Moseley's, like he swore I did. I didn't grow up just to turn out to be a horse thief.

Night before last, Mr. John told me to ride his mare, Betsy. I said I wanted to go off a little way after something, and he told me to go ahead and ride Betsy, like I have been doing every Sunday night for going on two years now. Mr. John told me to take the Texas saddle, but I told him I didn't care about riding saddle. I like to ride with a bridle and reins, and nothing else. That's the best way to ride, anyway. And where I was going I didn't want to have a squeaking saddle under me. I wasn't up to no mischief. It was just a little private business of my own that nobody has got a right to call me down about. I nearly always rode saddle Sunday nights, but night before last was Thursday night, and that's why I didn't have a saddle when I went.

Mr. John Turner will tell you I'm not the kind to go off and get into trouble. Ask Mr. John about me. He has known me all my life, and I've never given him or anybody else trouble.

When I took Betsy out of the stable that night after supper, Mr. John came out to the barnyard and asked me over again if I didn't want to take the Texas saddle. That mare, Betsy, is a little rawboned, but I didn't mind that. I told Mr. John I'd just as lief ride bareback. He said it was all right with him if I wanted to get sawn in two, and for me to go ahead and do like I pleased about it. He was standing right there all the time, rubbing Betsy's mane, and trying to find out where I was going, without coming right out and asking me. But he knew all the time where I was going, because he knows all about me. I reckon he just wanted to have a laugh at me, but he couldn't do that if I didn't let on where I was headed. So he told me it was all right to ride his mare without a saddle if I didn't want to be bothered with one, and I opened the gate and rode off down the road towards Bishop's crossroads.

That was night before last—Thursday night. It was a little after dark then, but I could see Mr. John standing at the barnyard gate, leaning on it a little, and watching me ride off. I'd been plowing that day, over in the new ground, and I was dog-tired. That's one reason why I didn't gallop off like I always did on Sunday nights. I rode away slow, letting Betsy take her own good time, because I wasn't in such a big hurry, after all. I had about two hours' time to kill, and only a little over three miles to go. That's why I went off like that.

II

Everybody knows I've been going to see Lud Moseley's youngest daughter, Naomi. I was going to see her again that night. But I couldn't show up there till about nine-thirty. Lud Moseley wouldn't let me come to see her but once a week, on Sunday nights, and night before last was Thursday. I'd been there to see her three or four times before on Thursday nights that Lud Moseley didn't know about. Naomi told me to come to see her on Thursday nights. That's why I had been going there when Lud Moseley said I couldn't come to his house but once a week. Naomi told me to come anyway, and she had been coming out to the swing under the trees in the front yard to meet me.

I haven't got a thing in the world against Lud Moseley. Mr. John Turner will tell you I haven't. I don't especially like him, but that's to be expected, and he knows why. Once a week isn't enough to go to see a girl you like a lot, like I do Naomi. And I reckon she likes me a little, or she wouldn't tell me to come to see her on Thursday nights, when Lud Moseley told me not to come. Lud Moseley thinks if I go to see her more than once a week that maybe we'll take it into our heads to go get married without giving him a chance to catch on.

That's why he said I couldn't come to his house but once a week, on Sunday nights.

He's fixing to have me sent to the penitentiary for twenty years for stealing his calico horse, Lightfoot. I reckon he knows good and well I didn't steal the horse, but he figures he's got a good chance to put me out of the way till he can get Naomi married to somebody else. That's the way I figure it all out, because everybody in this part of the country who ever heard tell of me knows I'm not a horse thief. Mr. John Turner will tell you that about me. Mr. John knows me better than that. I've worked for him so long he even tried once to make me out as one of the family, but I wouldn't let him do that.

So, night before last, Thursday night, I rode off from home bareback, on Betsy. I killed a little time down at the creek, about a mile down the road from where we live, and when I looked at my watch again, it was nine o'clock sharp. I got on Betsy and rode off towards Lud Moseley's place. Everything was still and quiet around the house and barn. It was just about Lud's bedtime then. I rode right up to the barnyard gate, like I always did on Thursday nights. I could see a light up in Naomi's room, where she slept with her older sister, Mary Lee. We had always figured on Mary Lee's being out with somebody else, or maybe being ready to go to sleep by nine-thirty. When I looked up at their window, I could see Naomi lying across her bed, and Mary Lee was standing beside the bed talking to her about something. That looked bad, because when Mary Lee tried to make Naomi undress and go to bed before she did, it always meant that it would take Naomi another hour or more to get out of the room, because she had to wait for Mary Lee to go to sleep before she could leave. She had to wait for Mary Lee to go to sleep, and then she had to get up and dress in the dark before she could come down to the front yard and meet me in the swing under the trees.

III

I sat there on Betsy for ten or fifteen minutes, waiting to see how Naomi was going to come out with her sister. I reckon if we had let Mary Lee in on the secret she would have behaved all right about it, but on some account or other Naomi couldn't make up her mind to run the risk of it. There was a mighty chance that she would have misbehaved about it and gone straight and told Lud Moseley, and we didn't want to run that risk.

After a while I saw Naomi get up and start to undress. I knew right away that that meant waiting another hour or longer for her to be able to come and meet me. The moon was starting to rise, and it was getting to be as bright as day out there in the barnyard. I'd been in the habit of opening the gate and turning Betsy loose in the yard, but I was scared to do it night before last. If Lud Moseley should get up for a drink of water or something, and happen to look out toward the barn and see a horse standing there, he would either think it was one of his and come out and lock it in the stalls, or else he would catch on it was me out there. Anyway, as soon as he saw Betsy, he would have known it wasn't his mare, and there would have been the mischief to pay right there and then. So I opened the barn door and led Betsy inside and put her in the first empty stall I could find in the dark. I was scared to strike a light, because I didn't know but what Lud Moseley would be looking out the window just at that time and see the flare of the match. I put Betsy in the stall, closed the door, and came back outside to wait for Naomi to find a chance to come out and meet me in the swing in the yard.

It was about twelve-thirty or one o'clock when I got ready to leave for home. The moon had been clouded, and it was darker than everything in the barn. I couldn't see my hand in front of me, it was that dark. I was scared to strike a light that time, too, and I felt my way in and opened the stall door and stepped inside to lead Betsy out. I couldn't see a thing, and when I found her neck, I thought she must have slipped her bridle like she was always doing when she had to stand too long to suit her. I was afraid to try to ride her home without a lead of some kind, because I was scared she might shy in the barnyard and start tearing around out there and wake up Lud Moseley. I felt around on the ground for the bridle, but I couldn't find it anywhere. Then I went back to the stall door and felt on it, thinking I might have taken it off myself when I was all excited at the start, and there was a halter hanging up. I slipped it over her head and led her out. It was still so dark I couldn't see a thing, and I had to feel my way outside and through the barnyard gate. When I got to the road, I threw a leg over her, and started for home without wasting any more time around Lud Moseley's place. I thought she trotted a little funny, because she had a swaying swing that made me slide from side to side, and I didn't have a saddle pommel to hold on to. I was all wrought up about getting away from there without getting caught up with, and I didn't think a thing about it. But I got home all right and slipped the halter off and put her in her stall. It was around one or two o'clock in the morning then.

The next morning after breakfast, when I was getting ready to catch the mules and gear them up to start plowing in the new ground again, Lud Moseley and three or four other men, including the sheriff, came riding lickety-split up the road from town and hitched at the rack. Mr. John came out and slapped the sheriff on the back and told him a funny story. They carried on like that for nearly half an hour, and then the sheriff asked Mr. John where I was. Mr. John told him I was getting ready to go off to the new ground, where we had planted a crop of corn that spring, and then the sheriff said he had a warrant for me. Mr. John asked him what for, a joke or something? And the sheriff told him it was for stealing Lud Moseley's calico horse, Lightfoot. Mr. John laughed at him, because he still thought it just a joke, but the sheriff pulled out the paper and showed it to him. Mr. John still wouldn't believe it, and he told them there was a mix-up somewhere, because, he told them, I wouldn't steal a horse. Mr. John knows I'm not a horse thief. I've never been in any kind of trouble before in all my life.

They brought me to town right away and put me in the cellroom at the sheriff's jail. I knew I hadn't stole Lud Moseley's horse, and I wasn't scared a bit about it. But right after they brought me to town, they all rode back and the sheriff looked in the barn and found Lud Moseley's calico horse, Lightfoot, in Betsy's stall. Mr. John said things were all mixed up, because he knew I didn't steal the horse, and he knew I wouldn't do it. But the horse was there, the calico one, Lightfoot, and his halter was hanging on the stall door. After that they went back to Lud Moseley's and measured my foot tracks in the barnyard, and then they found Betsy's bridle. Lud Moseley said I had rode Mr. John's mare over there, turned her loose, and put the bridle on his Lightfoot and rode him off. They never did say how come the halter came to get to Mr. John's stable, then. Lud Moseley's stall door was not locked, and it wasn't broken down. It looks now like I forgot to shut it tight when I put Betsy in, because she got out someway and came home of her own accord sometime that night.

Lud Moseley says he's going to send me away for twenty years where I won't have a chance to worry him over his youngest daughter, Naomi. He wants her to marry a widowed farmer over beyond Bishop's crossroads who runs twenty plows and who's got a big white house with fifteen rooms in it. Mr. John Turner says he'll hire the best lawyer in town to take up my case, but it don't look like it will do much good, because my footprints are all over Lud Moseley's barnyard, and his Lightfoot was in Mr. John's stable.

I reckon I could worm out of it someway, if I made up my mind to do it. But I don't like to do things like that. It would put Naomi in a bad way, because if I said I was there seeing her, and had put Betsy in the stall to keep her quiet, and took Lightfoot out by mistake in the dark when I got ready to leave—well, it would just look bad, that's all. She would have to say she was in the habit of slipping out of the house to see me after everybody had gone to sleep, on Thursday nights, and it would just look bad all around. She might take it into her head some day that she'd rather marry somebody else than me, and by that time she'd have a bad name for having been mixed up with me—and slipping out of the house to meet me after bedtime.

Naomi knows I'm no horse thief. She knows how it all happened—that I rode Lud Moseley's calico horse, Lightfoot, off by mistake in the dark, and left the stall door unfastened, and Betsy got out and came home of her own accord.

Lud Moseley has been telling people all around the courthouse as how he is going to send me away for twenty years so he can get Naomi married to that widowed farmer who runs twenty plows. Lud Moseley is right proud of it, it looks like to me, because he's got me cornered in a trap, and maybe he will get me sent away sure enough before Naomi gets a chance to tell what she knows is true.

But, somehow, I don't know if she'll say it if she does get the chance. Everybody knows I'm nothing but a hired man at Mr. John Turner's, and I've been thinking that maybe Naomi might not come right out and tell what she knows, after all.

I'd come right out and explain to the sheriff how the mix-up happened, but I sort of hate to mention Naomi's name in the mess. If it had been a Sunday night, instead of night before last, a Thursday, I could—well, it would just sound too bad, that's all.

If Naomi comes to town and tells what she knows, I won't say a word to stop her, because that'll mean she's willing to say it and marry me.

But if she stays at home, and let's Lud Moseley and that widowed farmer send me away for twenty years, I'll just have to go, that's all.

I always told Naomi I'd do anything in the world for her, and I reckon this will be the time when I've got to prove whether I'm a man of my word, or not.

This story was first published in The Atlantic Monthly.
This is its fifth appearance in print.

The Negro In the Well

Jule robinson was lying in bed snoring when his foxhounds struck a live trail a mile away and their baying woke him up with a start. He jumped to the floor, jerked on his shoes, and ran out into the front yard. It was about an hour before dawn.

Holding his hat to the side of his head like a swollen hand, he listened to the trailing on the ridge above the house. With his hat to deflect the sound into his ear, he could hear the dogs treading in the dry underbrush as plainly as his own breathing. It had taken him only a few seconds to determine that the hounds were not cold-trailing, and he put his hat back on his head and stooped over to lace his shoes.

"Papa," a frightened voice said, "please don't go off again now—wait till daybreak, anyway."

Jule turned around and saw the dim outline of his two girls. They were huddled together in the window of their bedroom. Jessie and Clara were old enough to take care of themselves, he thought, but that did not stop them from getting in his way when he wanted to go fox-hunting.

"Go on back to bed and sleep, Jessie—you and Clara," he said gruffly. "Those hounds are just up on the ridge. They can't take me much out of hollering distance before sunup."

"We're scared, Papa," Clara said.

"Scared of what?" Jule asked impatiently. "There ain't a thing for two big girls like you and Jessie to be scared of. What's there to be scared of in this big country, anyway?"

The hounds stopped trailing for a moment, and Jule straightened up to listen in the silence. All at once they began again, and he bent down to finish tying his shoes.

Off in the distance he could hear several other packs of trailing hounds, and by looking closely at the horizon he could see the twinkle of campfires where bands of fox-hunters had stopped to warm their hands and feet.

"Are you going, anyway, Papa?" Clara asked.

"I'm going, anyway," he answered.

The two girls ran back to bed and pulled the covers over their heads. There was no way to argue with Jule Robinson when he had set his head on following his foxhounds.

The craze must have started anew sometime during the holidays, because by the end of the first week in January it looked and sounded as if everybody in Georgia were trading foxhounds by day and bellowing "Whoo-way-oh!" by night. From the time the sun went down until the next morning when it came up, the woods, fields, pastures, and swamps were crawling with beggar-liced men and yelping hounddogs. Nobody would have thought of riding horseback after the hounds in a country where there was a barbwire fence every few hundred yards.

Automobiles roared and rattled over the rough country roads all night long. The fox-hunters had to travel fast in order to keep up with the pack.

It was not safe for any living thing with four legs to be out after sundown, because the hounds had the hunting fever too, and packs of those rangy half-starved dogs were running down and devouring calves, hogs, and even yellow-furred bobcats. It had got so during the past two weeks that the chickens knew enough to take to their roosts an hour ahead of time, because those packs of gaunt hunt-hungry hounds could not wait for sunset any more.

Jule finished lacing his shoes and went around the house. The path to the ridge began in the back yard and weaved up the hillside like a cowpath through a thicket. Jule passed the well and stopped to feel in his pockets to see if he had enough smoking tobacco to last him until he got back.

While he was standing there he heard behind him a sound like water gurgling through the neck of a demijohn. Jule listened again. The sound came even more plainly while he listened. There was no creek anywhere within hearing distance, and the nearest water was in the well. He went to the edge and listened again. The well did not have a stand or a windlass; it was merely a twenty-foot hole in the ground with boards laid over the top to keep pigs and chickens from falling into it.

"O Lord, help me now!" a voice said.

Jule got down on his hands and knees and looked at the well-cover in the darkness. He felt of the boards with his hands. Three of them had been moved, and there was a black oblong hole that was large enough to drop a calf through.

"Who's that?" Jule said, stretching out his neck and cocking his ear.

"O Lord, help me now," the voice said again, weaker than before.

The gurgling sound began again, and Jule knew then that it was the water in the well.

"Who's down there muddying up my well?" Jule said.

There was no sound then. Even the gurgling stopped.

Jule felt on the ground for a pebble and dropped it into the well. He counted until he could hear the *kerplunk* when it struck the water.

"Doggone your hide, whoever you are down there!" Jule said. "Who's down there?"

Nobody answered.

Jule felt in the dark for the water bucket, but he could not find it. Instead, his fingers found a larger pebble, a stone almost as big around as his fist, and he dropped it into the well.

The big rock struck something else before it finally went into the water.

"O Lord, I'm going down and can't help myself," the voice down there said. "O Lord, a big hand is trying to shove me under."

The hounds trailing on the ridge swung around to the east and started back again. The fox they were after was trying to back-trail them, but Jule's hounds were hard to fool. They had got to be almost as smart as a fox.

Jule straightened up and listened to the running.

"Whoo-way-oh!" he called after the dogs.

That sent them on yelping even louder than before.

"Is that you up there, Mr. Jule?" the voice asked.

Jule bent over the well again, keeping one ear on the dogs on the ridge. He did not want to lose track of them when they were on a live trail like that.

"This is me," Jule said. "Who's that?"

"This is only Bokus Bradley, Mr. Jule," the voice said.

"What you doing down in my well, muddying it up like that, Bokus?"

"It was something like this, Mr. Jule," Bokus said. "I was coming down the ridge a while ago, trying to keep up with my hounds, and I stumbled over your well-cover. I reckon I must have missed the path, somehow or other. Your well-cover wouldn't hold me up, or something, and the first thing I knew, here I was. I've been here ever since I fell in. I reckon I've been down here most of the night. I hope you ain't mad at me, Mr. Jule. I just naturally couldn't help it at all."

"You've muddied up my well-water," Jule said. "I ain't so doggone pleased about that."

"I reckon I have, some," Bokus said, "but I just naturally couldn't help it none at all."

"Where'd your dogs go to, Bokus?" Jule asked.

"I don't know, Mr. Jule. I haven't heard a sound out of them since I fell in here. They was headed for the creek when I was coming down the ridge behind them. Can you hear them anywhere now, Mr. Jule?"

Several packs of hounds could be heard. Jule's on the ridge was trailing east, and a pack was trailing down the creek toward town. Over toward the hills several more packs were running, but they were so far away it was not easy to tell to whom they belonged.

"Sounds to me like I hear your dogs down the creek, headed for the swamp," Jule said.

"Whoo-way-oh!" Bokus called.

The sound from the well struck Jule like a blast out of a megaphone.

"Your dogs can't hear you from 'way down there, Bokus," he said.

"I know they can't, Mr. Jule, and that's why I sure enough want to get out of here. My poor dogs don't know which way I want them to trail when they can't hear me talk to them. Whoo-way-oh!" Bokus shouted. "O Lord, help me now!"

Jule's dogs sounded as if they were closing in on a fox, and Jule jumped to his feet.

"Whoo-way-oh!" he shouted, cupping his hands around his mouth. "Whoo-way-oh!"

"Is you still up there, Mr. Jule?" Bokus asked. "Please, Mr. Jule, don't go away and leave me down here in this cold well. I'll do anything for you if you'll just only get me out of here. I've been standing neck-deep in this cold water near about all night long."

Jule threw some of the boards over the well.

"What you doing up there, Mr. Jule?"

Jule took off his hat and held the brim like a fan to the side of his head. He could hear the panting of the dogs while they ran.

"How many foxhounds have you got, Bokus?" Jule asked.

"I got me eight," Bokus said. "They're mighty fine fox-trailers, too, Mr. Jule. But I'd like to get me out of this here well before doing much more talking with you."

"You could get along somehow with less than that, couldn't you, Bokus?"

"If I had to, I'd have to," Bokus said, "but I sure enough would hate to have fewer than my eight dogs, though. Eight is just naturally the right-sized pack for me, Mr. Jule."

"How are you figuring on getting out of there?" Jule said.

"I just naturally figured on you helping me out, Mr. Jule," he said. "Leastaways, that's about the only way I know of getting out of this here well. I tried climbing, but the dirt just naturally crumbles away every time I dig my toes into the sides."

"You've got that well so muddied up it won't be fit to drink out of for a week or more," Jule said.

"I'll do what I can to clean it out for you, Mr. Jule, if I ever get up on top of the solid ground again. Can you hear those hounds of mine trailing now, Mr. Jule?"

"They're still down the creek. I reckon I could lower the water bucket, and I could pull a little, and you could climb a little, and maybe you'd get out that way."

"That just naturally would suit me fine, Mr. Jule," Bokus said eagerly. "Here I is. When is you going to lower that water bucket?"

Jule stood up and listened to his dogs trailing on the ridge. From the way they sounded, it would not be long before they treed the fox they were after.

"It's only about an hour till daybreak," Jule said. "I'd better go on up the ridge and see how my hounds are making out. I can't do much here at the well till the sun comes up."

"Don't go away and leave me now, Mr. Jule," Bokus begged. "Mr. Jule, please, sir, just lower that water bucket down here and help me get out. I just naturally got to get out of here, Mr. Jule. My dogs will get all balled up without me following them. Whoo-way-oh! Whoo-way-oh!"

The pack of fox-trailing hounds was coming up from the creek, headed toward the house. Jule took off his hat and held it beside his ear. He listened to them panting and yelping.

"If I had two more hounds, I'd be mighty pleased," Jule said, shouting loud enough for Bokus to hear. "Just two is all I need right now."

"You wouldn't be wanting two of mine, would you, Mr. Jule?" Bokus asked.

"It's a good time to make a trade," Jule said. "It's a mighty good time, being as how you are down in the well and want to get out."

"Two, did you say?"

"Two is what I said."

There was silence in the well for a long time. For nearly five minutes Jule listened to the packs of dogs all around him, some on the ridge, some down the creek, and some in the far-off hills. The barking of the hounds was a sweeter sound to him than anything else in the world. He would lose a night's sleep any time just to stay up and hear a pack of foxhounds live-trailing.

"Whoo-way-oh!" he called.

"Mr. Jule!" Bokus shouted up from the bottom of the well.

Jule went to the edge and leaned over to hear what the Negro had to say.

"How about that there trade now, Bokus?"

"Mr. Jule, I just naturally couldn't swap off two of my hounds, I just sure enough couldn't."

"Why not?" Jule said.

"Because I'd have only just six dogs left, Mr. Jule, and I couldn't do much fox-hunting with just that many."

Jule straightened up and kicked the boards over the top of the well.

"You won't be following even so few as one hound for a while," he said, "because I'm going to leave you down in the bottom where you stand now. It's another hour, almost, till daybreak, and I can't be wasting that time staying here talking to you. Maybe when I get back you'll be in a mind to do some trading, Bokus."

Jule kicked the boards on top of the well.

"O Lord, help me now!" Bokus said. "But, O Lord, don't make me swap off no two hounds for the help I'm asking for."

Jule stumbled over the water bucket when he turned and started across the yard toward the path up the ridge. Up there he could hear his dogs running again, and when he took off his hat and held it to the side of his head he could hear Polly pant, and Senator snort, and Mary Jane whine, and Sunshine yelp, and the rest of them barking at the head of the trail. He put on his hat, pulled it down hard all around, and hurried up the path to follow them on the ridge. The fox would not be able to hold out much longer.

"Whoo-way-oh!" he called to his hounds. "Whoo-way-oh!"

The echo was a masterful sound to hear.

A writer's reputation would not be worth comment if word got around that every piece he turned out was up to a certain standard, because some slick coiner of phrases would be certain to immortalize the thought by saying that so-and-so's latest story was as well-made and highly polished as his previous one. When that kind of talk began going around, naturally the prospective reader would say to himself that so-and-so's stuff must be coming out of a machine these days. And so, with no compunction whatever, he would bestow his patronage upon some other writer—a writer who had not been blighted by all this talk of standardization and the machine-made.

Honeymoon

Never mind what put Claude Barker up to getting married. Nearly everybody does something like that sometime or other. They'll be going along minding their own business for months at a time, and then all at once they come across a girl that sort of—well, never mind about that, either.

If it had been anybody else than Claude, nobody would have thought much about it. He was one of the bunch that had been hanging around town, mostly at the poolroom, doing nothing most of the time, for five or six years, maybe ten or twelve. Claude said he was waiting for a job at the filling station, but everybody else who wasn't working said that, too.

Jack and Crip were sitting in the sun in front of the filling station when Claude went by the first time. That was about ten o'clock that morning, and Claude was on his way to the courthouse to get a license.

"What's Claude up to?" Crip said.

The car Claude had borrowed early that morning from Jack sounded as if it would never make the trip to the courthouse and back.

"Search me," Jack said. "Maybe he thinks he knows where he can find a job."

"Yeah," Crip said, spitting. "But whoever would have thought of borrowing a car to run away from it? If a job ever hears of Claude, it'll wish it hadn't by the time it catches up with him. He'd turn around and fan its tail all the way from here to Atlanta and back again. His old man . . ."

Claude's old man, sitting on the bench in front of the post office, said he thought he knew why Claude had suddenly taken it into his head to get married. Everybody was waiting for the cotton-gin whistle to blow so he could go home to dinner. Claude had been to the court-house and back, and somebody had seen him drive out to the preacher's house on the edge of town half an hour before.

Claude's old man said he reckoned he knew why Claude was getting married. "By God, it wouldn't pain a man much to make a guess like that," somebody said. "No, but it would be a hell of a come-off if there were no more girls like Willeen Howard left in the country." "That ain't no lie," somebody else said. "When that time comes, I'll be ready to turn the country over to niggers and boll weevils and screw-worms and sell out from here."

The ginnery whistle down the railroad tracks blew for the twelve-thirty lay-off. Claude's old man stood up to go home to see what his wife had cooked up for dinner.

"I'll tell you people what put the marrying bug on Claude. The boy is young yet, and he wasn't used to fooling around with white girls. He's been of the habit . . ."

The crowd broke up like a rotten egg hitting the side of a barn.

"Claude's been in the habit . . ."

Old man Barker didn't have time to finish. He had to hurry home and eat his meal before his wife let the victuals get cold.

Downtown at the noon hour was quiet except for a handful of Negroes from the country who were sitting on the shaded railroad-station platform eating rat-trap cheese and soda crackers. Occasionally an automobile would plow through town on its way to Atlanta or Savannah, leaving the air tasting like ant poison for half an hour afterward.

Claude and Willeen came rattling down the street, across the square, Jack's old car hitting the railroad irons with a sound like a brick running through a cotton gin. Claude drove up to the filling station and stopped. Crip woke up and ran out to see who it was. Claude had lifted the seat and was unscrewing the gas-tank cap.

"Boy, you need lots of gas today," Crip said, putting the nozzle into the tank and looking at Willeen at the same time.

"Give me two gallons," Claude said.

"What you two going to do now?" Crip asked, turning the pump crank.

"That ain't no lie," Claude said, winking at Willeen.

Crip hung up the hose while Claude was counting out the change for the gasoline. He took a quick look into the back seat to see if Claude and Willeen had any baggage for a trip. There was not a thing. He looked again to be sure.

Crip did not have time to do any more looking around, because he had to have one more look at Willeen before Claude drove off with her. It was too late then to ask her why she had not told him something about it. If he had known about it in time, he could have asked her himself. It would not have been any trouble for him to get married. He could have done it just as easily as Claude did. But, God Almighty, what a funny feeling Willeen gave you when you looked at her real hard. It made you feel as if you were eating a clingstone peach and had got down almost to the last of it, and the more you sucked it, and bit the stone, the better the peach tasted, and you began to feel sort of hoggish but didn't give a damn how you acted when you couldn't get enough of it.

Willeen got back into the front seat and sat down. Claude grabbed up the water bucket and began filling the radiator.

It would have been easy enough to have married her, if you had only thought about it before Claude did. You'd make a monkey of yourself, all over the place, any day of the week, for some of that. By that time your eyes felt dry and stuck in your head when you had blinked them for so long, and when you shut them for a moment to get them moistened, you were ready to start all over again. After that you couldn't help seeing all the pretty things she had and you forgot all about tending the filling station and got to thinking that maybe I could fix it up someway or other. It wasn't so long ago that Willeen told you you could throw her down if you wanted to. You were a damn fool not to do it when she gave you the chance. But that wasn't now by a long shot.

They drove off down the street leaving Crip standing there looking like a cow mired in quicksand.

Claude drove around the square seven or eight times, warming up the engine, and finally stopped in front of the poolroom. It made him itch all over when he thought of having a cue-stick in his hands. There was no reason why he should not take time to shoot a couple of games. He might be able to win half a dollar, and then he could buy another couple gallons of gas. They could ride twice as far if they had two more.

It was time for the one-thirty ginnery whistle to blow, and people were already on their way back from dinner. A game was just starting when Claude went inside, and he grabbed a cue-stick from the rack and got in. They played five rounds of three-handed straight, and Claude came out even, after all.

Somebody in the street was blowing an automobile horn. Upton

Daniels came in, and Claude started a two-handed game of rotation with him. Claude broke, and made the seven- and fifteen-ball.

"Boy, what a shot!" he said. "I wouldn't take dollars for this stick of mine. There's never been one like it before."

Upton made a face by pushing out his mouth.

"You ought to have seen me ring them in last night," said Claude. "Seven and eleven were pay-balls, and I rang them in nine games in a row. It takes a good man to do that."

"Pig's butt," Upton said.

Upton shot and missed an easy one. He banged his cue-stick on the floor and made another face with his mouth.

Claude ran in three balls, missed the fourth, but Upton was left sewn up behind the fourteen. Upton jerked up his cue and scattered the balls with the heavy end.

"That gives a man away every time," Claude said, chalking his cue-tip. "The first thing I learned about shooting pool was to keep my head. That's why I'm the best shot in town. If you was as good as I am, you could make yourself a little money now and then off the drummers who come to town. I know you've made runs of thirty-seven and thirty-eight every once in a while, but that was just luck."

"Pig's butt," Upton said.

The horn out in the street started blowing again. When they finished the game, Claude went out to the front of the poolroom and looked into the street to see who was making so much racket. He had missed a couple of easy shots on that account.

When he saw Willeen sitting in the car, he shoved his cue-stick at Upton and ran outside. Willeen looked angry.

"God Almighty," Claude said under his breath, getting into the car and driving off.

It was about five o'clock in the afternoon then, and there were only two gallons of gasoline in the tank. Ten miles out of town, Claude turned around and came back. When they reached his house, it was time for supper.

"I'll go inside and fix things up first," he told Willeen. "It won't take long."

He got out and started up the steps. Willeen called him back, and he went to the car.

"I'd like to go home first and get a few things, Claude," she said. "You wouldn't mind, would you?"

"Sure, that's all right," he said, starting the car. "By the time you're ready, I'll have got things fixed up here. I'll be by for you about ten o'clock."

"You don't have to wait that long, Claude," Willeen said. "I'll be ready in just a few minutes."

"I've got to see a fellow downtown," Claude said. "It might take me a couple of hours to find him. We'd better make it ten o'clock, like I said. I've got to take this car back where I got it from, for another thing."

On his way back after leaving Willeen at her father's house, Claude stopped at the poolroom a minute. Somebody gave him a drink of corn, and after that he decided to shoot a few games of pool with Upton before going home to fix things up for Willeen.

Claude's old man was downtown early the next morning. When he passed the filling station, Jack and Crip asked him where Claude was.

"He and Willeen are still asleep," Claude's old man said. "But I reckon you'll be seeing Claude most anytime now. Is there anything in particular you boys want to see him about? Is that job ready for him?"

"He's still got my car," Jack said. "He ought to bring it back. I only let him have it for a couple hours yesterday, and he kept it all day and all night."

"Don't worry about your car, son," old man Barker said. "It's standing up there in the front yard of the house right this minute. Claude'll be coming downtown with it before very long."

He went across the square and sat down in the shade in front of the post office. There were three or four men over there who had been talking about the news in the morning paper.

After he had sat down, somebody asked him how Claude was getting along now that he was married to Willeen Howard. Old man Barker nodded his head. Somebody else spat into the dust. "This would sure-God be a puny country if it got cleaned out of girls like that. If the time ever comes when they don't invite a throw-down, then it's time to let the niggers and boll weevils and screw-worms run wild." Claude's old man sort of chuckled to himself. The boy wasn't up when he left home. "What did Claude have to say when he woke up this morning? I'll bet it was the same thing I said when I was in his place once," the fellow said, winking.

About an hour later Claude drove Jack's car down to the filling station. They were waiting for him.

"How's everything, Claude?" Jack said.

"Couldn't be better," Claude told him.

"It's a funny feeling, though, I bet," Jack said.

Claude turned and looked at Crip a moment. Crip looked straight at him, but he had nothing to say to Claude.

"Funny?" Claude said, laughing a little and going to the gas pump and leaning against it. "Funny ain't no name for it, Crip."

Crip looked at him between the eyes.

"I still can't seem to get over it somehow," Claude said. "This morning I woke up and opened my eyes and I saw a bare arm lying over me. When I saw it, I was scared to death. I jumped out of bed in a hurry, thinking to myself, 'What in hell am I doing sleeping in bed with a white girl?' "

Crip kicked at the tires on Jack's old car to see how well they were holding up. He walked all the way around it a couple times. Nobody had said anything after Claude finished talking.

After a while Claude walked off down the street towards the poolroom. Jack pushed the car behind the filling station where it would be out of the way. While he was back there, he took the cap off the gas tank to see if Claude had left any gas in it. There was almost a whole gallon inside. Jack thought that was funny, because Claude had started off into the country as if he had figured on taking a trip somewhere.

It is possible that I was impelled to write this story because I have never been able to recall a time when I did not want a new straw hat. For some reason, though, I was never able to get one. Either an old one had to do, or else I went without.

A Day's Wooing

W<small>HEN</small> Tuffy Webb woke up that morning, the first thing he saw was his new straw hat hanging on the back of the cane-bottomed chair beside the bed. The red, orange, and blue silk band around the hat looked as bright in the sunshine as the decorations in the store windows in town on circus day. He reached out and felt the rough crown and brim, running his fingers over the stiff brown straw. He would never have to step aside for anybody, in a hat like that. That was all he needed, to get the world by the tail.

"Maybe that won't knock a few eyes out!" Tuffy said, throwing off the covers and leaping to the floor. "They'll all be cross-eyed from looking at it."

He placed the hat carefully on his head and walked over to the mirror on the wall. The new straw hat looked even finer Sunday morning than it had Saturday night, when he tried it on in the store.

"When Nancy sees this lid, she'll come tumbling," Tuffy said, stepping back and tilting the hat a little on one side of his head and winking at himself under the brim.

He walked past the mirror several times, free and easy in his loose knee-length nightshirt, turning his eyes to see himself in passing. It was easy to get up courage in a hat like that.

"I could have all the girls after me now if I wanted them," he said to himself.

Tuffy got dressed in a hurry and made a fire in the cookstove. He pulled the hat down carefully over his head so it would not fall off and hit the floor while he was cooking breakfast.

During all the time he was in the kitchen he kept thinking to himself that he would not have to keep bach much longer after that, not after Nancy saw him in his new hat. She would be tickled to death to marry him now, the first time she saw him walking up to her house with the straw sailor tilted over one ear, sort of like a cock's comb that always looked like it was going to fall off but never did.

After breakfast Tuffy had to drive the cows to the pasture on the other side of the creek because it had become time for them to have a change of feed, and the johnson grass over there was ready for grazing.

He started off with his hat on his head, but he got to thinking about it and finally decided he ought to leave it at the house. Sometimes a yearling took to heels and bolted off into a thicket, and he did not like to think of taking any chances of having the hat fall off into the briers and mud, and maybe being trampled by the cows. Now that he was thinking about it, he remembered seeing a cow chew up a straw hat once and swallow it.

He hurried back to the house and hung the hat on the cane-bottomed chair beside the bed.

Tuffy got back from the pasture at about eleven o'clock, and he changed his clothes right away, putting on his coat and the hat. After that he still had almost an hour to wait before he could leave home, because he did not wish to get to the Millers' while they were eating dinner. If he did that, one of the Millers would be certain to say that he had got there then to get something to eat.

He walked out on the porch and leaned against the railing for a while. The sun was almost directly overhead, and there was not a cloud in sight. He knew he could not have chosen a finer day to go calling on Nancy in a new straw hat. There was not a single drop of rain in the whole sky above.

"This would be a dandy time to speak to Nancy about us getting married," he said, going out into the yard and walking first around the chinaberry tree and then around the willow. "All I'd have to do would be to ask her, and I know already what Nancy'll say. She's just as willing as I am, and she knows it. It wouldn't do her any good to try to show otherwise."

Tuffy leaned against the willow, picking at the bark with his thumb-nail.

"If I go right up to her and say, 'Nancy, how about me and you hitching up together?' she'll say, 'When, Tuffy?' and I'll say, 'The sooner the better suits me.' Then she'll say, 'Nothing would please me more.' That's all there will be to it, and it'll be all planned and settled. All I'll have to do is get a preacher to marry us, and then me and Nancy'll be married for a fare-you-well. Getting married wouldn't take long, maybe no longer than tomorrow noon. We'll probably start right in tomorrow some time. That's none too soon for me, and I know it won't be none too soon for Nancy."

Tuffy went over and sat on the woodpile.

"I'll go over there to old Berry Miller's and walk right up to where they're all sitting on the porch and lose no time about it. Berry'll probably want to know what I came for, all dressed up like this in a coat and a new straw hat, and I'll soon tell him, too. 'Well,' I'll say, 'I came to marry Nancy, Berry. How do you like that? Me and her are getting married right off.' He won't scare me a bit, no matter what he says. He might have some little fault to find to begin with, but there's no objection I know about that's good enough to stop me from going ahead and getting married to Nancy. I'll walk right up to where she's sitting on the porch and put my arm around her and show those Millers I mean business and don't mean maybe."

Tuffy picked up a piece of stovewood and began tearing splinters out of it with his fingernails. He piled the splinters in a little stack between his feet.

"If old Berry Miller makes any show of getting his bristles up, I'll reach right down and kiss her in front of all the Millers, and then pick her up and walk off with her without so much as looking back at them even once. That'll show Berry that when I set out to get married, I don't let nothing in the whole wide world stop me. Those Millers can't put the scare into me."

He hurled the stick of stovewood across the yard. It narrowly missed hitting one of his hens asleep in a dust hole under the chinaberry tree. The hen woke up and ran squawking for her life. The other chickens got scared and followed her under the house.

Tuffy took out his handkerchief and wiped the sweatband of his new straw hat. It was a scorching hot day, especially out in the sun at midday, and the heavy wool coat had never felt so tight before.

"If I had thought to get the license yesterday, me and Nancy could have got married today," he said disgustedly, kicking at the ground. "Now, why didn't I think about that yesterday? I'll have to wait till tomorrow before I can go to the courthouse now."

He got up and walked to his car. He had not intended getting inside, because it was still about half an hour too soon for him to leave, but he could not wait any longer. He would have to drive around ten or fifteen miles an hour, and maybe stop at the creek and wait a while, but he was too anxious to be on his way to Nancy's house to wait around home any longer. He started the car and drove off, pushing the new straw hat tightly on his head so the wind could not blow it off.

It was half past twelve o'clock when Tuffy Webb drove up to the Berry Miller place and stopped his car in the shade. He had not got there a minute too soon, because the Millers were at that minute coming out on the porch from the dinner table. It was getting hotter all the time, and Tuffy sat in his car for several minutes trying to cool off before getting out and going up to the house.

Before looking at the Millers on the porch, he took out his handkerchief and tried to wipe off some of the perspiration that trickled down his cheeks and down the back of his neck. When he finished, he took off his hat and wiped the sweatband good and dry.

Old man Berry Miller waved at him from the porch. One of the Miller boys rose up on his elbow from the porch floor to see what Tuffy was doing.

Tuffy got out and walked stiff and erect across the yard to the house. He was uncomfortable all over, and it made his face flush red when he realized what he was doing there. The Millers had a way of staring at him that made him forget what he was doing sometimes.

"Come on in on the porch out of that hot sun and have a slice of watermelon fresh out of the bottom of the well," Berry Miller said. "There's not much left, but what there is, you're welcome to it. It's only the leavings."

Berry brushed away the flies with his hat. They swarmed around the porch for a few moments and then settled back again on the rinds and watermelon seed scattered about on the floor.

"Well, howdy, folks," Tuffy said.

One of the boys waved his arm at Tuffy, and both the girls giggled. Berry's wife rocked back and forth in her chair without saying a thing. A watermelon seed had stuck to her chin and was drying there. Tuffy wondered why nobody told her to brush it off.

"Mighty hot day today," he said, flushing red again when his eyes swept the porch and saw the two girls.

Their white dresses were starched so stiffly that they looked as if corset stays had been sewn into the cloth.

"Sort of," Berry said. "Can't complain, though. Heat's due us."

The boys on the other end of the porch sat up.

"What are you all dressed up for, Tuffy?" Henry asked him. "Going somewhere?"

Tuffy's eyes dropped and he dug the toe of his shoe into the sandy yard.

Nancy, the oldest girl, giggled again.

Tuffy looked up quickly, hoping to see her plain.

"You're dressed up fit to kill, ain't you, Tuffy?" Henry said.

Berry kicked a piece of watermelon rind off the porch.

"That's a mighty fine-looking straw hat you've got on there, Tuffy," Berry said. "You must have bought that at a big store somewhere, and paid a lot of money for it, in the bargain. A pretty all-colored band like that don't come on everyday hats."

Tuffy nodded his head.

The other Miller boy on the porch, Clyde, scraped up a handful of watermelon seed and began shooting them between his fingers.

Presently one of the seed hit Tuffy in the face, making him jump as if somebody had taken a slingshot and hit him in the eye with a hickory nut. Tuffy would not look at Clyde, because he and Clyde never had got along any too well. They had had several fist fights already that summer.

Berry's wife moved to and fro in her rocker, looking disinterestedly at Tuffy. The watermelon seed had dried on her chin and was stuck there for good. He glanced at her, and their eyes met. Whenever she looked at him, it always made Tuffy feel as if she were looking at some object directly behind him. She had never spoken a word to him in all her life.

Nancy smoothed out the skirt of her starched white dress, bending the stiff hem down over her knees. He could still see where her stockings ended on her legs. Nancy's sister looked at Tuffy and giggled.

"I just thought I'd drop by," Tuffy said at last. "I didn't have much else to do today."

"Had any watermelon today so far?" Berry asked him.

"No," Tuffy said.

"If you don't mind eating the leavings," Berry said, waving his hand at the rind-strewn porch, "you're welcome to have some."

Tuffy looked to see what Nancy was doing, but he could not see the expression on her face when his eyes were watching the black and white garter-line on her legs. She bent the starched hem over again, but when she leaned back, it straightened out again and her legs above the stocking tops were as bold as ever.

"Ain't you staying?" Berry asked.

"I don't care if I do," Tuffy said. "I was just riding around, and I thought I'd stop by."

Clyde picked up a piece of rind and threw it at the tree in the yard.

"It's been quite a while since I last saw you all dressed up like that," Berry said. "If I remember correctly, the last time was at the baptizing over at the church about a month ago. Wasn't you all dressed up that day, Tuffy?"

Nancy giggled and hid her face against her sister's shoulder. Tuffy blushed again.

"I didn't have this new hat then, though," he said.

"So you didn't!" Berry said. "That is right, ain't it? That hat looks so natural on your head that I forgot all about it. But you did have on a coat that day, didn't you?"

Tuffy nodded, digging the toe of his shoe into the yard.

"I wish you had come by a little sooner," Berry said. "It's pretty late now to get any of the good part of the melons. The leavings ain't much to offer a body. But of course, now, if you ain't particular, just go ahead and help yourself."

One of the boys kicked a piece of rind across the porch and it fell into the yard near Tuffy's feet. He looked at it, all covered with sand.

"Where you going, Tuffy?" Henry asked him.

"Nowhere much," Tuffy said.

"How about me and you going off a piece?" Henry said, winking. "There's some easy pickings on Sunday afternoons over beyond Hardpan."

Tuffy glanced at Nancy. There was a peculiar look on her face that made him uneasy. The garter-line on her legs wavered in his sight when she rocked in her chair. He dropped his eyes to the ground once more.

"I don't reckon I can right now," he told Henry, blushing red all over.

The two girls began whispering at each other. Every once in a while Nancy glanced up at Tuffy, and then she quickly looked the other way. Tuffy took off his hat and fanned his face with it.

"It's about time to do some thinking about a little foxhunting, ain't it, Tuffy?" Berry said. "These nights now are beginning to have a little nip in them, along about midnight, and the foxes will be running before you know it. Anyway, it don't hurt none to sort of warm up the hounds. They've been laying around here all summer and have got as lazy as can be. I been thinking lately of going out some night pretty soon and giving them a short run."

Tuffy nodded his head, but he did not say anything.

"I been thinking about making a trade of some kind for a couple more hunters," Berry said. "That Blackie is still a little lame from last year, and that Elsie is weighted down with pups. That Rastus looks like he takes to cold-trailing more and more every year, and I'm a little upset. I don't reckon it would do any harm to make a trade of some kind, if I could find exactly what I'm looking for. I've got a mule that's stove-up pretty bad, and I figure I need hunting dogs a lot more now than I do a blamed stiff-legged mule."

Tuffy glanced up at Nancy, looking as if he were bursting with something to say. He looked at her so desperately that she reached over and bent the starched hem and held it down. He could do no more than swallow hard and flush red all over. It made his skin feel prickly under the heavy coat when she looked at him.

Clyde sat up and slid down to the edge of the porch. He sat swinging his legs over the edge and looking at Tuffy. Tuffy was becoming more and more uncomfortable. He had been standing for half an hour in the hot sun, and he caught himself swaying on his feet.

"I sure admire that new straw hat of yours, Tuffy," Berry said. "Especially that all-colored pretty band around it."

Tuffy looked desperately at Nancy, and then glanced at the rest of the family. Everyone, except Nancy, stared right back at him. Nancy hung her head when their eyes met.

Henry crossed the yard between him and the house, taking something out of his pocket. He began pulling on it, making it snap like elastic. When he stopped in front of Tuffy, Tuffy looked to see what Henry was playing with. It was a girl's garter, bound in pink silk, and tied in a bow with a red rosebud sewn into it. Tuffy jumped as if he had been pricked with a pin.

Tuffy backed off, taking short steps towards his car.

"Not going so soon?" Berry said. "Why, it hardly seems like more than a minute ago when you got here."

Tuffy stopped. Henry had kept up with him, snapping the garter. He put one end against Tuffy's arm, pulled the other end back a foot or two, and turned it loose. Tuffy jumped when the elastic stung him.

"Where you going, Tuffy?" Henry asked him.

Tuffy looked at the porch where Nancy was. She had sat upright in the chair, leaning slightly forward, and stopped rocking. The starched flare of her skirt had straightened out once more, and he was glad she wore yellow garters.

He started backing away again. Henry followed him, springing the elastic rosebud-trimmed garter at him.

"Let's me and you ride over beyond Hardpan, Tuffy," Henry urged. "It won't be no trouble at all to find us a couple of girls, and we can make a lot of headway on a Sunday afternoon. How about it, Tuffy, huh?"

Tuffy backed away faster, shaking his head. When he got to the tree where his car was, he turned around and jumped into the front seat.

Nancy ran into the house. She could be heard crying all the way to the back porch.

When Tuffy got his car started, Berry got up and walked out into the yard. He watched the automobile disappear over the hill, trying to turn his ear away from Henry's cursing.

"I hate to see a man rush off like that," Berry said. "I'd have swore he came here for some purpose to begin with."

He stood with his back to the house while Clyde left the porch and crossed the field to get some more watermelons to cool in the bottom of the well.

Of course, it is a despicable trait in human nature, but we might as well admit that all of us derive a feeling of self-satisfaction from the act of cheating when no one is looking. There is probably not a solitaire player alive today who could hold a straight face and say he has never slipped a red jack from the discard when he needed it badly enough. In recognition of this trait, I suggest that this story be skipped while nobody is looking.

Where the Girls Were Different

NOBODY could ever explain exactly why it was, but the girls who lived in all the other parts of Oconee County were different from the ones in our section. All the girls in Woodlawn, which was the name of the town where we lived, were the sassy kind. They were always slapping and biting, too. I suppose all of them were tomboys. That's about the worst thing you can call a girl when she is growing up. But the girls who lived at Macy's Mill, and at Bradford, and especially in Rosemark, were a different kind. We used to talk about it a lot, but nobody knew why it was.

"How are the Rosemark girls different?" I asked Ben, when we were talking about it one day.

"Jiggers," he said, "I don't know exactly."

I never went around like Ben and the other boys did, because I had a girl who lived in town and I went to see her two or three times a week, and that was as many nights as my folks would let me go out. They did not believe in letting me go all over the county to see girls. So I stayed at home and went to see Milly pretty often.

But those girls in other parts of the county were not like the ones at home. The other boys used to go off nearly every night to see girls at Bradford and Macy's Mill and Rosemark, Rosemark especially. I don't know why that was, either. There was just something about those girls down in Rosemark that made a man act kind of funny.

Ben went down to Rosemark three or four nights every week to see girls. The strange part of it was he rarely went to see the same girl more than once. He had a new girl almost every time he went down there. The other boys did the same way, too. They had a new girl every time. Shucks, I had to stay at home and go to see Milly and nobody else.

I asked Ben in a confidential way what it was about the girls down in Rosemark that made them so different from the ones around home.

Ben was my first cousin and I didn't mind asking him personal questions.

"Jumping jiggers!" he said. "You've never been down there to see a Rosemark girl, have you, Fred?"

I told him how it was about Milly. I did not want to go to see her all the time, but I never had a chance to go down to Rosemark like the other boys.

"Well," he said, "you are a fool to go to see her all the time. She's just like all the other girls around here. You've got to go down to Rosemark and see some real girls. They're not like these around Woodlawn."

"What are they like, Ben?" I asked him again. Everybody said they were different, but nobody ever said in what way they were different. "What do they do that's different?"

"Well, that's hard to say. They act just like all the girls do—but they are different."

"Tell me about them, Ben."

"I'll tell you this," he said. "You got to be careful down there. Every girl in Rosemark that's got an old man or a brother is watched pretty close. I guess that's because they are pretty wild."

"How are they wild?" I asked him. "What do they do?"

"That's hard to say, too. You can't put your finger on it exactly—they are just different. You've got to go down there."

"But how can I get a date with one of them?"

"Oh, that's easy," he said. "You just go down there some Sunday night and wait outside a church until they come out. Then pick one out and ask her to let you take her home. That's the way to do it."

"Can I do that? Would she let me take her home?"

"Sure. That's one way they are different. You can get any girl you want if you ask her before somebody else does. You go down Sunday night and try it. Jiggers, Fred, you got to see those Rosemark girls! The ones around here aren't fit to fool with."

I hated to tell my folks the next Sunday night that I was going to see Milly when I wasn't, but—gee—I had to go down to see those girls in Rosemark. I drove the old car down and got there just before the churches let out.

I picked out the biggest church I could find and waited outside the door. I figured that the bigger the church the better chance I would have because there would be more girls in it.

Shucks, it wasn't any trouble at all. I asked the first girl that came out by herself if I could take her home and she said, "Sure," just as nice. Gee, this was the way to see girls. Up at home the girls acted sassy about letting you take them home. These Rosemark girls were different that way.

"Where do you live?" I asked her.

"About five miles out in the country," she said. She talked nice and soft like all girls would if they knew what was good for themselves. "Do you want to take me?"

"You bet I do," I told her. "I don't care how far it is."

Five miles wasn't anything. It was fine, because I'd have a longer time to find out about her. I could tell right away she was different.

She showed me the way to go and we started out. The old car was running good, but there was no hurry to get there.

"What's your name?" I asked her.

"Betty," she said.

No girl up in Woodlawn had a name like that. I was beginning to see why all the boys at home liked to come down to Rosemark.

Gee, she was different! She sat real close to me and sort of hunched her shoulders forward like she was awfully pleased. I had never seen a girl act so nice in all my life. She put her arm through mine and sort of leaned against me a lot and I had a devil of a time trying to keep our old car in the road.

As soon as we got outside of town a little distance another automobile came up behind us real close. I drew over to the side of the road so it could pass, but whoever was running it wouldn't try to pass. I thought that was funny, because I was driving only about ten miles an hour and making a lot of dust behind, too. The man who was running the other car was crazy not to pass us and go on ahead.

Betty sat closer and closer all the time and was so nice I didn't know what to make of it.

"The devil," I said to myself, "I'm going to take a chance and kiss her."

That was a reckless thing to do, because all the girls I knew up home were pretty particular about things like that and they didn't mind slapping you good and hard, either.

Gee whiz! I reached down and kissed her and she wouldn't let me stop. The old car rocked from one side of the road to the other as dizzy as a bat. I couldn't see to steer it because Betty wouldn't let me stop kissing her, and I had to wait until we ran into a ditch almost before I knew which way to turn the wheel. Gee whiz! The girls in Rosemark were certainly different, all right.

Finally I got away from her and got back my breath and saw which way to guide the old car.

"Don't you like to kiss me?" she asked, hunching her shoulders forward again like a girl does when she wants to make you feel funny.

Shucks, I couldn't let her get away with that! I reached my right arm around her and kissed her as hard as I could. She didn't mind how rough I was, either. I guess she liked it, because she put both of her arms around my neck and both of her legs across my lap and hugged the life out of me. *Gee whiz!* I didn't know girls did like that! Ben said the girls down in Rosemark were different, but I didn't expect anything like this to happen to me. Holy cats! The girl was sitting on my lap under the steering-wheel and I was having a devil of a time trying to kiss her for all I was worth and steer the old car at the same time.

Right then I knew I was coming down to Rosemark again as soon as I could get away. Ben sure knew what he was talking about when he said the girls down here were nothing like the ones at home. Shucks, those old girls up at home were not anything.

By this time we had got to the place where she lived and she looked up just at the right moment to tell me where to turn in. Before I could steer the old car into the driveway the automobile that had been behind us all the time beat me to it and I had to jerk on the brakes to keep from running smack into it.

"Who is that fool?" I asked Betty.

"That's Poppa," she said.

I started to say something pretty mean about him for doing a thing like that, but I thought I had better not if I wished to come back to see her. I was going to ask her for a lot of dates as soon as we got in the yard.

She took her arms down and moved over to her side of the seat just as if nothing in the world had happened.

I shut off the engine and reached over and opened the door for her. She jumped out just as nice and I was right behind her. I got as far as the running-board when the man who had beaten us to the gate pushed me back into the seat. He shoved me so hard I hurt my spine on the steering-wheel.

"Where do you think you're going?" he growled at me. "Start up that car and get away from here and don't ever let me see you again."

He came closer and shoved me again. I then saw for the first time that he had a great big rusty pistol with a barrel about a foot and a half long in his other hand.

"If I ever catch you around Betty again I'll use this gun on you," he said.

I didn't lose any time getting away from there. I hated to go away and not see Betty again, so I could ask her for a lot of dates next week, but it wouldn't do any good to have dates if I couldn't come back.

I drove the old car back home and went to bed. I knew now why Ben never went to see the same girl twice. He knew what he was doing, all right. And I knew why he said the girls down there were different. They sure were different. It was hard to say what the difference was, but if you ever went down there it was easy to feel it all over yourself.

The next morning I saw Ben and told him about going down to Rosemark the night before. After a while I told him about the way Betty kissed me and how she wanted to sit on my lap under the steering-wheel.

"What!" he said, his eyes wide open.

I told him about it again, and how she wouldn't let me stop kissing her and how she put her legs across my lap.

"Jumping jiggers, that's funny. None of them ever let me kiss her, and none of them ever sat on my lap."

"Gosh, Ben," I said, "then why did you think they were different?"

"Jumping jiggers!" he said again, frowning all over. "I don't know."

As a rule I do not read the stories I write. This case is an exception. I read the first part of this story and immediately wrote the second. Afterwards I went back and read the first part for the second time, and straightway wrote the third part. By now the reader may wonder why I did not write a fourth part. The reason is, simply, That I did not read it again.

My Old Man

(*in Three Parts*)

I. THE NIGHT MY OLD MAN CAME HOME

THE dogs barked at a little before midnight, and Ma got up to look out the window. It was a snowy night about two weeks before Christmas. The wind had died down a little since supper, but not enough to keep it from whistling around the eaves every once in a while. It was just the kind of white winter night when it felt good to be in bed with plenty of covers to keep warm.

The light was burning in the hall, because we always kept one light on all night. Ma did not turn on the light in the room right away. She could see better what was going on outside when the room was dark.

She did not say a word for quite a while. The dogs growled some, and then started in barking again. They were kept chained at the side of the house all night; if they had been allowed to run loose, they would have chewed up a lot of people who came out that way after dark. It was a good thing for my old man, too; they would have chewed him up as quick as they would have somebody they had never smelt before. My old man was away from home so much he was just like a stranger, anyway. The last time he was there was in the summer, and he only stayed about five minutes then. He came back for a pair of pants he had left hanging on a nail in the woodshed the winter before.

"That's him, all right," Ma said, tapping the window-sill with the door key. She was no more mad than usual, but that was enough. When she tapped the woodwork with things like the door key, it was the only sign anybody needed to know how she was feeling.

Presently there was a rumble that sounded like a two-horse wagon crossing a plank bridge. Then a jar shook the house like somebody had taken a sledge hammer and knocked most of the foundation from under it.

That was my old man trying out the front steps and porch in the dark to see if they would hold his weight. He was always afraid somebody was going to set a trap for him when he came home, something like loosening the boards on the porch in such a way that he would fall through and have to lie there until Ma could reach him with the broom or something.

"He's going to come home like this just once too many some of these times," Ma said. "I'm getting sick and tired of it."

"I want to get up and see him," I said. "Please, Ma, let me."

"You stay right where you are, William, and pull those covers up over your head," Ma said, tapping some more on the sill with the door key. "When he gets in here, he's not going to be any fit sight for you to look at."

I got up on my knees and elbows and pulled the covers over my head. When I thought Ma had stopped looking that way, I pulled the covers back just enough so I could see out.

The front door banged open, almost breaking the glass in the top part. My old man never did act like he cared anything about the glass in the door, or about the furniture, or about anything else in the house. He came home once and picked Ma's sewing machine to pieces, and Ma had a dickens of a time saving up enough to get it fixed.

I never knew my old man could make so much racket. It sounded like he was out in the hall jumping up and down to see if he could stomp the floor clear through the ground. All the pictures on the wall shook, and some of them turned cockeyed. Even the big one of Grandpa turned sidewise.

Ma turned the light on and went to the fireplace to kindle the fire. There were lots of embers in the ashes that glowed red when she fanned them with a newspaper and laid some kindling over them. As soon as the kindling began to blaze, she put on two or three chunks of wood and sat down on the hearth with her back to the fire to wait for my old man to come into the room.

He was banging around out in the hall all that time, sounding like he was trying to kick all the chairs down to the far end next to the kitchen. In the middle of it he stopped and said something to somebody he had with him.

Ma got up in a hurry and put her bathrobe on. She looked in the mirror a time or two and straightened her hair. It was a big surprise for him to bring somebody home with him like that.

"You cover up your head and go to sleep like I told you, William," Ma said.

"I want to see him," I begged her.

"Don't argue with me, William," she said, patting her bare foot on the floor. "Go and do like I told you once already."

I pulled the covers up, but slipped them back enough to see out.

The door to the hall opened a couple of inches. I got up on my knees and elbows again so I could see better. Just then my old man kicked the door open with his foot. It flew back against the wall, knocking loose dust that nobody knew was there before.

"What do you want, Morris Stroup?" Ma said, folding her arms and glaring at him. "What do you want this time?"

"Come on in and make yourself comfortably at home," my old man said, turning around and jerking somebody into the room by the arm. "Don't be backward in my own house."

He pulled a girl about half the size of Ma into the room and pushed her around until they were over against Ma's sewing machine. Ma turned on her feet, watching them just like she had been a weather-vane following the wind.

It was pretty serious to watch my old man drunk and reeling, and to see Ma so mad she could not get a word out of her mouth.

"Say 'Howdy,'" he told the girl.

She never said a thing.

My old man put his arm around her neck and bent her over. He kept it up, making her bow like that at Ma, and then he got to doing it too, and pretty soon they were keeping time bowing. They did it so much that Ma's head started bobbing up and down, just like she could not help herself.

I guess I must have snickered out loud, because Ma looked kind of silly for a minute, and then she went and sat down by the fire.

"Who's she?" Ma asked, acting like she was pretty anxious to find out. She even stopped looking cross for a little while. "Who is she, Morris?"

My old man sat down heavy enough to break the bottom out of the chair.

"She?" he said. "She's Lucy. She's my helper nowadays."

He turned around in the chair and looked over at me on my knees and elbows under the cover.

"Howdy, son," he said. "How've you been?"

"Pretty well," I said, squeezing down on my knees and trying to think of something to say so I could show him how glad I was to see him.

"Still growing, ain't you, son?" he said.

"A little, I reckon," I told him.

"That's right. That's the thing to do. Just keep it up, son. Some day you'll be a man before you know it."

"Pa, I——"

Ma picked up a piece of kindling and slung it at him. It missed him and hit the wall behind him. My old man jumped up on his feet and danced around like it had hit him instead of the wall. He reeled around like that until he lost his footing, and then he slid down the wall and sat on the floor.

He reached over and got his hands on a straight-back chair. He looked it over carefully, and then he started pulling the rungs out. Every time he got one loose, he pitched it into the fireplace.

When all the rungs and legs were out, he started picking the slats out of the back and throwing them into the fire. Ma never said a word. She just sat and looked at him all the time.

"Let's go, Morris," the girl Lucy said. It was the first thing she had said since she got there. Both Ma and me looked at her sort of surprised, and my old man cut his eyes around too, like he had forgotten she was there. "Morris, let's go," she said.

Lucy looked all but scared to death, it was easy to see. Everybody had stared at her so much, and Ma was acting so mad, that it was no wonder.

"Sit down and make yourself comfortable," my old man told her. "Just sit, Lucy."

She reached for one of the chairs and sat down just like he told her to.

The way she was sitting there, and Ma's mad streak on, and my old man picking the chair to pieces was a funny sight to see. I guess I must have snickered again out loud, because Ma turned around at me and shook her finger and motioned for me to pull the covers up over my head, and to go to sleep too, I guess. But I could never go to sleep while all that was going on, when I had not seen my old man for so long a time, and Ma must have known it. I just squeezed down on my elbows and knees as much as I could, and kept on looking.

"When you get that chair picked to pieces, Morris Stroup, you can just hand me over seven dollars to pay for a new one," Ma said, rocking back and forth.

"Shucks, Martha," my old man said. "Shucks, I don't believe there's a chair in the whole world that I'd give more than a dollar, maybe two, for."

Ma jerked out of her spell like a snapped finger. She jumped up and grabbed the broom from the side of the mantelpiece and started for him. She beat him over the head with it until she saw how much damage she was doing to the broomstraw, and then she stopped. She had beat out so much straw that it was scattered all over the floor.

After that she turned the broom around and began poking him with the handle.

My old man got up in a hurry and staggered across the room to the closet, throwing what was left of the chair into the fire as he passed it. He opened the closet door and went inside. He did something to the lock, because no matter how hard Ma tried, she could not make the door open after he had closed it.

By that time Ma was so mad she did not know what she was doing. She sat down on the edge of the bed and pinned her hair up a little.

"This is nice goings-on at this time of night, Morris Stroup!" she yelled at him through the door. "What kind of a child can I raise with things like this going on in the house?"

She did not even wait for my old man to answer her. She just spun around toward Lucy, the girl my old man had brought along with him.

"You can have him," Ma said, "but you've got to keep him away from here."

"He told me he wasn't married," Lucy told Ma. "He said he was a single man all the time."

"Single man!" Ma yelled.

She got red in the face again and ran to the fireplace for the poker. Our poker was about three feet long and made of thick iron. She jabbed it into the crack of the closet and pried with it.

My old man began to yell and kick in the closet. I never heard such a racket as when the dogs started their barking again. People who heard them must have thought robbers were murdering all of us that night.

About then Lucy jumped up, crying.

"Stop that!" she yelled at Ma. "You're hurting him in that closet!"

Ma just turned around, swinging her elbow as she went.

"You leave me be!" Ma told her. "I'll attend to what I'm doing, sister!"

I had to squirm all around to the other side of the bed to keep up with what they were doing at the closet door. I never saw two people carry on so funny before. Both of them were mad, and scared to do much about it. They acted like two young roosters that wanted to fight but did not know how to go about it. They were just flapping around, trying to scare each other.

But Ma was as strong as the next one for her size. All she had to do when she made up her mind was drop the poker, grab Lucy, and give her a shove. Lucy sailed across the room and landed up against the sewing machine. She looked scared out of her wits when she found herself there so quick.

Ma picked up the poker again and she pried with all her might and, *Bang!* the door sprang open. There was my old man backed up against the closet wall all tangled up in Ma's clothes, and he looked like he had been taken by surprise and caught red-handed with his fist in the grocer's cash drawer. I never saw my old man look so sheepish before in all my life.

As soon as Ma got him out of the closet and into the room, she went for Lucy.

"I'm going to put you out of my house," Ma told her, "and put a stop to this running around with my husband. That's one thing I won't stand for!"

She grabbed at Lucy, but Lucy ducked out of reach. Then they came back at each other just exactly like two young roosters that had finally got up enough nerve to start pecking. They jumped around on the floor with their arms flapping like wings and Ma's bathrobe and Lucy's skirt flying around like loose feathers. They hopped around in a circle for so long that it looked like they were riding on a merry-go-round. About that time they got their hands in each other's hair and started pulling. I never heard so much screaming before. My old man's eyes had just about got used to the light again, and he could see them, too, every once in a while. His head kept going around and around, and he missed a lot of it.

Ma and Lucy worked across the room and out the door into the hall. Out there they scuffled some more. While it was going on, my old man stumbled across the room, feeling for another chair. He picked up the first one he could put his hands on. It was Ma's high-back rocker, the one she sat in all the time when she was sewing and just resting.

By that time Ma and Lucy were scuffling out on the front porch. My old man shut the door to the hall and locked it. That door was a thick, heavy one with a spring thumb lock as well as a keyhole lock.

"No use talking, son," he said, sitting down on the bed and pulling off his shoes, "there's nothing else in the world like a couple of females at odds. Sometimes——"

He slung his shoes under the bed and turned out the light. He felt his way around the bed, dragging Ma's high-back rocker with him. I could hear the wood creak in the chair when he strained on the rungs. He pulled the covers up, then began picking the chair to pieces and throwing them toward the fire. Once in a while one of the pieces hit the mantelpiece; as often as not one of them struck the wall.

By then Ma and Lucy had got the dogs started again. They must have been out in the front yard scuffling by that time, because I could not hear them on the porch.

"Sometimes, son," my old man said, "sometimes it appears to me like the good Lord ought never put more than one woman in the world at a time."

I snuggled down under the covers, hugging my knees as tight as I could, and hoping he would stay at home all the time, instead of going off again.

My old man broke the back off the rocker and slung it in the dark toward the fireplace. It hit the ceiling first, and then the mantelpiece. He began picking the seat to pieces next.

It sure felt good being there in the dark with him.

II. HANDSOME BROWN AND THE AGGRAVATING GOATS

"If it's not one thing your Pa's done," Ma said, looking all helpless and worn, "it's something else. I declare, sometimes I think I'll never have a minute's peace as long as I live."

She walked up and down in the backyard wringing her hands, trying to think of something to do.

The goats that Pa and our Negro houseboy, Handsome Brown, had brought home from our farm in the country were standing on top of the house chewing and looking down at us. The big billy goat had long white chin whiskers that made him look exactly like Mr. Carter who lived across the street.

"What in the world am I going to do?" Ma said, still walking up and down. "I've invited the Ladies' Social Circle to meet here this afternoon, and if those goats are still up on top of the house when they get here, I'll simply die of mortification."

The two nanny goats were chewing, too, but their whiskers were not nearly as long as the big goat's. In addition to the three grown goats up on the rooftop, there were two little kids up there. The kids were only two months old and they were only a quarter the size of the billy, but all five of them up there together on top of the house looked like a lot of goats.

"William, tell Handsome to go downtown and find your Pa and tell him to come home and get those goats down right away," she said to me.

Handsome was cleaning up in the kitchen, and all I had to do was go to the edge of the porch and call him. He came out and asked me what we wanted.

"The first thing I want you to do, Handsome Brown," Ma said angrily, "is to tell me what on earth you meant by bringing those goats here."

"I only done what Mr. Morris told me to do, like I always does when you or Mr. Morris tells me to do something, Miss Martha," he said, shifting from one foot to the other. "Mr. Morris said he wanted them goats brung home and he told me to drive them, and I done just that. You oughtn't blame me too much for what Mr. Morris told me to do, Miss Martha."

"Why didn't you tell Mr. Morris he ought to ask me first, then?" she said. "You thought of that, didn't you?"

"Yes, mam, I thought of it, but when I got ready to mention it to Mr. Morris, Mr. Morris said, 'the devil you say,' just like that, and that's why I ended up driving them here like I done."

Ma got madder than ever. She picked up a piece of stove wood and slung it at the goats on top of the house, but the stick fell half-way short of reaching them. It slammed against the side of the house, making a big noise and leaving a mark on the weatherboarding.

"Go downtown this instant and find Mr. Morris," she told Handsome, "and tell him I want to see him right away. Look in the barbershop and the hardware store and every place he loafs until you find him. And don't you dare come back without him, Handsome Brown. I don't want to hear any excuses from you this time."

"Yes, mam, Miss Martha," Handsome said, trotting off to look for Pa.

The goats walked along the ridgeplate on the roof, looking down into the backyard at Ma and me part of the time, and the rest of the time looking down the other side into the street. They had got up there by hopping from the woodpile to the woodshed, from there to the porch roof, then leaping up on top of the kitchen roof, and from there to the main part of the house. They were about two stories and a half high above us on the ground, and it was a funny sight to see the three large goats and the two little kids walking Indian-file across the top of the roof.

The next time they stopped and looked down at us, the billy chewed some more, making his whiskers sway, and it looked exactly as though he were making faces at us.

Ma tried to find another stick of wood to throw at him, but she was too mad then to look for one. She shook her fist at all five of them and then went running into the house.

I sat down on the steps for a minute, but Ma came back and pulled me up by the arm.

"William, go out in the front and watch for your Pa," she said, shoving me down the steps, "and the minute you see him coming up the street, you run and tell me. The women will be getting here any time now."

I went around the corner of the house and stood by the front gate watching down the street. I did not have to wait long, because the first thing I knew I heard Pa and Handsome talking. They came walking fast.

"What's the matter, son?" Pa asked, looking up at the five goats on the rooftop. "What's gone wrong?"

"Ma says to get the goats down off the house before the women start coming to the meeting," I told him.

"That's easy enough," he said, hurrying around the corner of the house to the backyard. "Come on, Handsome, and get a hustle on."

"Me, Mr. Morris, you're talking to?" Handsome said. Handsome was big and heavy and he could not walk fast. He always said his arches hurt him when he tried to walk fast. When he did have to hurry, he trotted.

"Hurry up, Handsome," Pa told him. "Stop complaining."

We got to the backyard and Pa studied the goats on the ridgeplate for a while before saying anything. He liked the goats just about as much as I did, and that was why he wanted them in town where he could see them every day. When they stayed out in the country on the farm, we did not see them sometimes for as long as a week at a time, because we did not go out there every day.

The goats had stopped walking back and forth on the roof and were looking down at us to see what we were up to.

"Handsome," Pa said, "go get the ladder and put it up against the porch roof."

Handsome got the ladder and stood it up the way Pa told him to.

"Now, what to do, Mr. Morris?" Handsome asked.

"Go up there and chase them down," Pa said.

Handsome looked up at the big billy goat. He backed away from the ladder.

"I'm a little scared to go up there where that big billy goat is, Mr. Morris," he said. "He's got the meanest-looking set of horns I ever looked at in all my life. If it's all the same to you, Mr. Morris, I just don't feel like going up there. My arches has been hurting all day. I don't feel good at all."

"Stop that talking back to me, Handsome," Pa said, "and go on up there like I told you. There's nothing wrong with your arches today, or any day."

Just then Ma came out, pinning the white starched collar on her dress that she wore when she dressed up for company. She came as far as the steps and stood looking down at Pa and me.

"Now, Martha," Pa said, talking fast, "don't you worry yourself one bit. Handsome and me will have those goats down from there in a jiffy."

"You'd better get them down from there in a jiffy," Ma said. "I've never been so mortified in all my life. All these women will be coming here to the circle meeting any minute now. What will people say if they see a lot of goats walking around on the roof of my house?"

"Now, calm yourself, Martha," Pa said. "Handsome is on his way up there now."

Handsome was still backing away from the ladder. Pa walked over to where he was and gave him a shove.

"Hurry up and do like I told you," Pa said, shoving him towards the ladder again.

Handsome fidgeted a lot, killing all the time he could by hitching up his pants and buttoning his shirt, but he finally made a start to-wards the ladder. He climbed to the top and stepped to the porch roof. Then he started backing down again.

"Handsome Brown," Ma said, running out into the yard where we were, "if you come down that ladder before getting those goats off the roof, I'll never give you another bite to eat as long as I live. You can just make up your mind to go off somewhere else and starve to death, if you don't do what Mr. Morris told you."

"But, Miss Martha, my arches has started paining me again some-thing awful."

"I've warned you, Handsome Brown," Ma said, tapping her shoe on the ground, "and I mean exactly what I said."

"But, Miss Martha, I——"

"I've warned you once and for all," Ma said.

Handsome looked up at the goats, then down at Ma again, and after that he climbed up on top of the kitchen roof. When he had got that far, he cut his eyes down at us to see if we were watching him.

Just then Ma heard some of the women coming up the street. We could hear them talking almost a whole block away. Ma shook her finger at Handsome and ran inside to lock the front door so the women could not get into the house. She figured they would sit on the porch if she did that, because otherwise they might just walk on through the house and come out on the back porch and see what was going on.

Pa and me sat down on the woodpile and watched Handsome. Handsome had gone as far as the top of the kitchen roof, and he was sprawled on the ridgeplate hugging the shingles. He looked awfully small up there.

"Don't you dare let one of those goats get hurt, or fall off," Pa shouted at him. "And take care that those little kids don't get caught in a stampede and get shoved off to the ground. I'll skin you alive if anything happens to those goats."

"I hear every word you say, Mr. Morris," Handsome shouted down. "I swear, I never saw such a slippery place before. But I'm doing the best I can. Every time I move I'm scared I'm about to fall off on that hard ground, I'm scared to breathe, Mr. Morris."

He waited, killing time, to hear if Pa was going to say anything more. After a while, he found out that Pa was not going to answer him, and he inched himself along the ridgeplate towards the main roof. When he got to the top of the pitch, he gave one more look down at the ground. He shut his eyes when he saw it and did not look down at us again.

"Take care those goats don't get hurt," Pa shouted.

"Yes, sir, Mr. Morris," Handsome said, sounding far off. "I'm taking the best care I can."

He got to the edge of the main roof and climbed on it. From there to the top where the ridgeplate was looked as far again as Handsome had already climbed. He inched his way up the sloping side until his fingers got a grip on the ridgeplate. It was easy enough for him to climb the rest of the way to the top. When he got up there, he threw one leg across and sat astride the ridgeplate, hugging it for all he was worth.

The goats had gone down to the far end of the roof, getting out of Handsome's way. In order to chase the goats down, he would have to slide himself along the ridgeplate to where they were and make them turn around and come back to the kitchen roof, where they could jump to the porch and woodshed, and finally to the woodpile.

Handsome had got half-way across when it looked as if the billy had taken it into his head to come back of his own accord. When the billy started, all the goats came, the big one in front, the medium-sized ones in the middle, and the little kids behind. Handsome saw them coming, especially the billy, because the billy lowered his head until his horns stuck up in the air like lightning-rods.

"Wait a minute!" Handsome yelled at the big goat. "Wait there a minute, I said!"

The goat kept on towards him. When he got four or five feet from Handsome, he stopped, chewed half a dozen strokes, and looked Handsome in the eye.

While Handsome and the billy goat were up there staring each other in the eye, Ma came running out into the yard to see if the goats had been chased off the roof.

Just then the billy gave a lunge, and went flying at Handsome with his head tucked down and hooves flying out behind. Handsome saw the goat coming at him in time to duck, but the trouble was that there was not any place he could go except flatter on his stomach. Handsome dug into the shingles with his fingers and held on for all he was worth.

"Look out, Handsome!" Pa yelled when he saw what was happening.

Pa jumped to his feet and started waving his arms at the goat. None of that did any good, though, because the goat flew into Handsome headlong with all his might. For an instant it was hard to tell what was going to happen, because after the billy had butted Handsome, both of them sort of stopped short, like two boards coming together in mid-air.

"Hold on, Handsome!" Pa yelled up there at him.

The next thing we knew, Handsome was coming down the slope of the roof, backward, on the seat of his pants. He slid about half-way down, and then he started spinning around like a top. We had no more than seen that when he left the roof and was coming down into the yard. The first thing we thought of was where Handsome was going to land. The yard was hard and sandy, and there was not a thing there, such as the woodpile at the other end of the yard, to break his fall. But before we knew what had happened, he missed the yard completely and was out of sight. He had gone through the well-cover like a bullet.

"My heavenly day!" Ma screamed. "Handsome's gone!"

She tottered and fell in the yard in a dead faint. Pa stooped to pick her up, but he dropped her after he had raised her part way off the ground, and ran to the well to see what had become of Handsome. Everything had taken place so suddenly that there was no time to think about it then. The boards covering the well had been bashed in as if a big two-hundred-pound rock had landed on them.

Me and Pa tore across the yard to the well. When we got there and looked down inside, we could not see a thing at first. It was pitch-black down there. Pa yelled at Handsome, and the echo bounced back like a rubber ball and blasted our ears.

"Answer me, Handsome!" Pa shouted some more. "Answer me!"

Ma got up and staggered across the yard to where we were. She had a hard time steadying herself, and she came reeling towards us like Mr. Andy Howard on Saturday night. She was still dizzy from her faint when she reached us.

"Poor Handsome Brown," Ma said, clutching at the well-stand to support herself. "Poor Handsome Brown. He was the best darkey we ever had. Poor old Handsome Brown."

Pa was busy unwinding the windlass, because he wanted to get the rope and bucket down into the well as quick as he could.

"Shut up, Martha!" he said out of the corner of his mouth; "don't you see how busy I am trying to get this rope and bucket down in here?"

"Poor old Handsome Brown," Ma said, brushing some tears from her eyes and not paying any attention to Pa at all. "I wish I hadn't scolded him so much while he was alive. He was the best darkey we ever had. Poor old Handsome Brown."

"Shut your mouth, Martha!" Pa shouted at her. "Can't you see how busy I am at what I'm doing?"

By that time Ma had got over her fainting spell, and she was able to stand up without holding onto anything. She leaned over the well-stand and looked down inside.

"Are you down there, Handsome?" Pa shouted into the well.

There was no answer for a while. We leaned over as far as we could and looked down. At first there was not a thing to be seen, but slowly two big, round, white balls started shining down in the bottom. They looked as if they were a mile away. Pretty soon they got brighter and then they looked like two cat eyes on a black night when you turn a flashlight on them.

"Can you breathe all right, Handsome?" Pa shouted down at him.

"I can breathe all right, Mr. Morris," Handsome said, "but my arches pain me something terrible."

"Fiddlesticks," Pa said. "There's nothing wrong with your arches. Can you see all right?"

"I can't see a thing," Handsome said. "I've done gone and got as blind as a bat. I can't see nothing at all."

"That's because you're in the bottom of the well," Pa told him. "Nobody could see down there."

"Is that where I am?" Handsome asked. "Lordy me, Mr. Morris, is that why there's all this water around me? I thought when I come to that I was in the bad place. I sure thought I had been knocked all the way down to there. When is you going to get me out of here, Mr. Morris?"

"Grab hold the bucket on the rope, and I'll have you out of there in no time," Pa told him.

Handsome caught the bucket and shook the rope until Pa leaned over again.

"Mr. Morris, please, sir?" Handsome asked.

"What do you want now?"

"When you get me out of here, you ain't going to make me go back up on that roof again where them goats is, is you?"

"No," Pa told him, turning the windlass. "Them aggravating goats can stay on top of the house until they get hungry enough to come down of their own accord."

We had forgotten all about the goats, we had been so busy worrying about Handsome. Ma turned and looked up on the roof. She shook her fist at them, hard. All of them had crossed to the other end of the roof, the end near the kitchen, and they were standing up there looking down at us.

The billy goat looked Ma straight in the eye, and he stopped chewing as he did it. Ma and the billy acted as if they were trying to see which could stare the other down first.

Just then fifteen or twenty of the women who had come to the circle meeting stuck their heads around the corner of the house and looked at us in the backyard. They had got together when they found the front door locked and decided to come around there and see what was going on. They had been able to see the goats on the roof when they came up the street, and they were curious to see what we were making so much racket about back there.

"My sakes alive, Martha Stroup," one of them said, "what's going on here? Those goats up on top of your house is the funniest sight I ever saw!"

Ma wheeled around and saw the women. She did not say a word, but her hands flew to her face, as though she were trying to hide it, and then she ran into the house through the back door. She slammed it shut and locked it behind her. Pretty soon the women went to the front door, but after they had knocked on it a long time, they gave up trying to get in, and all of them started down the street. They kept looking back over their shoulders at the goats on the roof and laughing loud enough to be heard all over our part of town.

III. MY OLD MAN HASN'T BEEN THE SAME SINCE

When I got up to eat breakfast, my old man was sitting at the kitchen stove, leaning back on two legs of the chair and eating hot biscuits and sorghum molasses for all he was worth. He had put his plate on the apron in front of the firebox as he always did, because he could sit there with the oven door open and reach inside for a hot biscuit without having to get up. My old man was a fool about hot biscuits and sorghum molasses.

He had his mouth full when I went in, and he didn't say anything at first. He looked up at me, though, and winked.

"Howdy, Pa," I said, awfully glad to see him. He had been away for almost a whole week that time.

He didn't say anything until he reached into the oven and got another biscuit. He broke it open, spread butter on it, and laid it on the plate, open. Then he picked up the molasses jug from the floor and poured a good cupful of it on the bread.

"How's your copperosticks, son?" he said, squeezing his fingers around my arm.

"All right," I said.

He felt my muscles.

I sure was glad to see him.

Ma came in then and set my plate at the kitchen table and helped

me to bread and molasses and a little bacon. She did not say a word
to anybody during the whole time she was fixing my breakfast for
me. She stirred around after that, making a lot of noise and racket
with the pots and pans. She was as mad as a wet hen.

Pa sat looking across the kitchen, cocking an eye at her every once
in a while, waiting for her to say something. Me and him both knew
the best thing to do when she was like that was to just wait her out.
It only made things worse if we tried to talk to her until she was ready
to be talked to. Pa sat in his chair as meek as a tramp asking for a
bite to eat.

When I had almost finished eating, she came and stood at the stove,
hands on hips, staring Pa down.

"Where have you been this time, Morris Stroup?" she said, suddenly raising her hand and brushing the hair back from her face.

"Now, Martha," Pa said, ducking his head to one side when he saw
her raise her hand, "I haven't been anywhere much."

"Going away from home and staying the-Lord-knows-where four or
five days at a time may be your idea of not going anywhere much,
but it's not mine. Where have you been?"

"Now, Martha," he said, "I just went down the country a little
way."

"Where's that good-for-nothing rooster of yours?" she asked.

"College Boy's out in the chicken pen," he said.

"If I ever get my hands on him," Ma said, stamping her foot, "I'm
going to wring his neck off."

Pa's fighting cock, College Boy, was the champion of Merryweather
County, Georgia. We had had him for about six months, and when
Pa brought him home the first time he said the cock was as smart as
people with a college education. That's why Pa named him College
Boy. He might have been the champion of the whole nation if Pa
could have taken him to all the mains. But Pa didn't have any money
to ride on the trains with, and we didn't have an automobile to drive,
and the only places Pa could go were the ones he could walk to. That
was the reason he had to be away from home so much. It sometimes
took him several days to walk where there was going to be a cock
fight, because they had to keep changing the places from one part of
Merryweather County to another so the sheriff couldn't catch up with
Pa and the other men who owned game cocks and pitted them.

Pa hadn't answered Ma, because we know better than to say anything that would sound as if we were taking up for College Boy. Ma
hated the cock worse than sin.

"If you don't think I'm asking too big a favor of you," Ma said, "go
down to Mrs. Taylor's and get her washing—if you're not ashamed
for people to see you bringing home washing for me to do."

"Now, Martha," he said, "you know that's not a proper thing to say. You know I always like to help out."

She went to the kitchen door and looked out into the backyard to see how the fire was burning under the washpot.

"William," she said, turning around to me, "go out in the backyard and throw some more pineknots under that washpot."

I got up and started outside to do what she told me to do. When I got as far as the door, she turned on Pa again.

"And when you see Mrs. Taylor, Morris Stroup, you can tell her, and everybody else in Fairfield, how I break my back taking in washing while you go tramping around the country with a good-for-nothing rooster under your arm." She stared Pa down some more. "I'd like to get my fingers around that rooster's neck—and yours, too—just once!"

"Now, Martha——"

"The Lord only knows what would become of us if I didn't take in washing," she said. "You haven't done an honest day's work in ten years."

Pa got up and came out in the yard where I was feeding the fire under the pot. He stood and watched me.

"Son," he said, lowering his voice so Ma couldn't hear, "do you know where you can find a handful of corn somewhere for College Boy?"

He didn't wait for me to answer him, because he knew that I knew what to do. He went out the back gate and down the street towards Mrs. Taylor's house three blocks away. After Ma had gone back into the kitchen, I went to the hen house and got an egg out of a nest and put it into my pocket. I knew exactly what Pa wanted me to do, because he always sent me to Mr. Brown's grocery at the corner when he needed corn for College Boy.

I took the egg to the store and traded it for a poke of corn just like Pa did when I went along with him. Mr. Brown said he had heard that Pa won three dollars at a cocking down near Nortonsville the day before, and he wanted to know why we were trading an egg for the corn instead of paying some of the money Pa had made. I told him I didn't know anything about that, because Pa hadn't said a word about how College Boy did at Nortonsville since he got back. Mr. Brown told me to tell Pa that he wanted a chance to see College Boy in a pit the next time they had one near Fairfield. I went back up the street with the poke of corn in my shirt so Ma wouldn't see it and take it away from me.

Pa was already back from Mrs. Taylor's with the washing, and he had come out behind the chicken house to see if I had brought the corn. The chicken house was about a hundred and fifty feet from the backyard where Ma was washing, and we could stay out there and be out of sight. But we had to keep from talking loud, though, or she could hear us.

He was squatting on the ground holding College Boy and wiping him off with a damp rag. College Boy had lost quite a lot of feathers, and he was pretty well tired out. His right leg was sore where the skin had rubbed off when a spur worked loose. Pa said for a while he was afraid College Boy wasn't going to be able to come through, on account of the loose spur, but when he found out he couldn't do any damage with the right one, he went to work with the left one. Pa said it was the closest call College Boy had had since his first pit fight. He said he was going to let College Boy rest until his leg healed up, because he didn't want to run any risks.

Pa wiped him down good, and he let me help him. When he finished with the damp rag, he let me hold College Boy in my arms. It was the first time he had ever let me touch the cock, and I asked Pa if I could go along with him the next time he went to a pit fight. Pa said he wanted me to wait until I was older, but he said it wouldn't be long.

"Your Ma would skin me alive if I took you now," he said. "There's no telling what she wouldn't do to you and me both."

I held College Boy in my arms and he sat there just as if he never wanted to leave. He was a fine-looking cock with bright red feathers on his neck and wings and dull yellow feathers underneath. His comb folded over on the right side of his head like a cow-lick. I had never known how little he was until then. He wasn't a bit bigger than a medium-sized pullet, but you could tell how strong and quick he was by holding him in your arms. Pa said there wasn't a finer cockaldrum in the whole nation.

I handed him back to Pa, and Pa told me to crack the corn. I got a flat piece of iron and a rock and cracked the corn and Pa scooped it up and held it in his hand for College Boy. He ate it as though it were the best thing in the world, and he acted as if he couldn't get enough. He ate up the corn as fast as I could crack it.

All the time we were out behind the chicken house, Ma was in the backyard boiling the washing. She was doing Mrs. Taylor's washing then, but there were six or seven others that she did every week, too. It looked as if she washed every day and ironed all night.

We stayed out there a long time watching College Boy. He had a dust-bed in one corner of the run, and he liked to lie there in the shade and flap dust under his feathers with his wings.

I told Pa I hoped he wasn't going away again soon, because I wanted him to stay at home and let me help him crack corn and feed College Boy every day. He said he wasn't going anywhere for a while, anyway, because he thought College Boy needed at least a week's rest.

We sat there on the ground in the shade a long time until noon. Then Ma called to us to come and eat.

When we had finished, she told Pa she wanted him to carry Mrs. Dolan's washing to her. Mrs. Dolan lived on the other side of town, and it was a long walk over there and back. I asked Ma if I could go along and help carry the washing, and she said I could.

We took the washing right after we finished eating, and I thought we would get back in time to go out and see College Boy again before it was too dark. But it was late when we came through town on our way back, and Pa said he wanted to stop at the post office and talk to some men for a while. We must have stayed there two or three hours, because when we did get home, it was pitch-dark. Ma heard us on the front porch and she came out and asked Pa for the money he had collected for Mrs. Dolan's washing. Pa gave her the seventy-five cents and asked her how long before supper would be ready. She said it would be soon, and so we sat down on the porch.

It felt good to be sitting on the front porch with my old man, because he was away from home so much I never had a chance to be with him very often. My old man lighted a cigar stub he had been saving, and we sat there and he puffed on it in the dark, and the smoke drifted across the porch, smelling good in the night breeze.

"Son," he said after a while, "as soon as you've had your breakfast in the morning, I want you to go down to Brown's grocery. Get another egg out of the chicken house and take it down and swap it for some more corn. As soon as breakfast is over, I'll want to feed College Boy. He's pretty well tuckered out, and I want to feed him well so he'll get his strength back."

"All right, Pa," I told him. "I sure will."

We sat there in the dark thinking about the cock.

Ma called us in a little while and we went inside and sat down at the supper table. There wasn't much on the table to eat that night, except a big chicken pie. It was in a big deep pan with a thick brown crust over it, and Pa helped me first, and then Ma. After that he took a big helping for himself.

Ma didn't have much to say, and Pa was scared to talk. He never started in talking much, anyway, until he was sure of his ground. We sat at the table eating the chicken pie and not saying anything much until the pie was all gone. Pa leaned back and looked at me, and it was easy to see that he thought a lot of Ma's cooking.

It was as quiet as the inside of a church after the congregation had left.

"Morris," Ma said, laying her knife and fork in a neat row on her plate, "I hope this will be a lesson to you."

"Hope what will, Martha?" he said.

She looked down at the way she had laid her knife and fork on the plate, moved them just a little, and then looked him straight in the face.

"I hope you'll never bring another game rooster to this house as long as you live," she said. "I had to do something desperate——"

"What?" he said, leaning over the table towards her.

"I made this chicken pie out of the one——"

"College Boy!" Pa said, pushing his chair back a little.

Ma nodded her head.

My old man's face turned white and his hands dropped down beside him. He opened his mouth to say something, but he made no sound. I don't know how long it was, but it seemed as though it were half the night before anybody moved after that.

Ma was the first one to say anything.

"It was a harsh thing to do, Morris," she said, "but something drastic had to be done."

"That was College Boy, Ma," I said, "you shouldn't——"

"Be quiet, William," she said, turning to me.

"You shouldn't have done that, Martha," Pa said, pushing his chair back and getting to his feet. "Not to College Boy, anyway. He was——"

He did not say anything more after that. The next thing he did was to turn around and go through the house to the front porch.

I got up and went through the house behind him. It was darker than ever on the porch and I couldn't see anything at all after being where the light was. I felt on all the chairs for him, but he was not there. The cigar stub he had left on the porch railing when we went inside to supper was still burning, and it smelled just like my old man. I hurried down the steps and ran down the street trying to catch up with him before it was too late to find him in the dark.

The End of Christy Tucker

CHRISTY TUCKER rode into the plantation town on muleback late in the afternoon, whistling all the way. He had been hewing new pickets for the fence around his house all morning, and he was feeling good for having got so much done. He did not have a chance to go to the plantation town very often and, when he could go, he did not lose any time in getting there.

He tied up the mule at the racks behind the row of stores, and the first thing he noticed was the way the other Negroes out there did not seem anxious to speak to him. Christy had been on friendly terms with all the colored people on the plantation ever since he and his wife had moved there three months before, and he could not under-stand why they pretended not to see him.

He walked slowly down the road towards the plantation office wondering why nobody spoke to him.

After he had gone a little farther, he met Froggy Miller. He caught Froggy by the arm before Froggy could dodge him.

"What's the matter with you folks today?" he said. Froggy Miller lived only a mile from his house in a straight line across the cotton field, and he knew Froggy better than anyone else on the plantation. "What's the matter, anyway, Froggy?"

Froggy, a big six-foot Negro with close-cropped hair, moved away.

He grabbed Froggy by the arm and shook him.

"Now, look here!" Christy said, getting worried. "Why do you and everybody else act so strange?"

"Mr. Lee Crossman sent for you, didn't he?" Froggy said.

"Sure, he sent for me," Christy said. "I reckon he wants to talk to me about the farming. But what's that got to do with——"

Before he could finish, Froggy had pulled away from him and walked hurriedly up the road.

Without wasting any more time, Christy ran towards the plantation office to find out what the trouble was.

The plantation bookkeeper, Hendricks, and Lee Crossman's younger brother, Morgan, were sitting in the front office with their feet on the

344

window sill when he ran inside. Hendricks got up when he saw
Christy and went through the door into the back room. While the
bookkeeper was in the other room, Morgan Crossman stared sullenly
at the Negro.

"Come here, you," Hendricks said, coming through the door.

Christy turned around and saw Lee Crossman, the owner and boss
of the plantation, standing in the doorway.

"Yes, sir," Christy said.

Lee Crossman was dressed in heavy gray riding breeches and tan
shirt, and he wore black boots that laced to his knees. He stood aside
while Christy walked into the back room, and closed the door on the
outside. Christy walked to the middle of the room and stood there
waiting for Lee Crossman.

Christy had moved to the Crossman plantation the first of the year,
about three months before. It was the first time he had ever been in
Georgia, and he had grown to like it better than Alabama, where he
had always lived. He and his wife had decided to come to Georgia
because they had heard that the land there was better for sharecrop-
ping cotton. Christy said he could not be satisfied merely making a
living; he wanted to get ahead in life.

Lee Crossman still had not come, and Christy sat down in one of
the chairs. He had no more than seated himself when the door opened.
He jumped to his feet.

"Howdy, Mr. Lee," he said, smiling. "I've had a good chance to
look at the land, and I'd like to be furnished with another mule and
a gang plow. I figure I can raise twice as much cotton on that kind
of land with a gang plow, because it's about the best I ever saw.
There's not a rock or stump on it, and it's as clear of bushes as the
palm of my hand. I haven't even found a gully anywhere on it. If
you'll furnish me with another mule and a gang plow, I'll raise more
cotton for you than any two sharecroppers on your plantation."

Lee Crossman listened until he had finished, and then he slammed
the door shut and strode across the room.

"I sent for you, nigger," he said. "You didn't send for me, did you?"

"That's right, Mr. Lee," he said. "You sent for me."

"Then keep your black face shut until I tell you to open it."

"Yes, sir, Mr. Lee," Christy said, backing across the room until he
found himself against the wall. Lee Crossman sat down in a chair and
glared at him. "Yes, sir, Mr. Lee," Christy said again.

"You're one of these biggity niggers, ain't you?" Lee said. "Where'd
you come from, anyway? You ain't a Georgia nigger, are you?"

"No, sir, Mr. Lee," Christy said, shaking his head. "I was born and
raised in Alabama."

"Didn't they teach you any better than this in Alabama?"

"Yes, sir, Mr. Lee."

"Then why did you come over here to Georgia and start acting so biggity?"

"I don't know, Mr. Lee."

Christy wiped his face with the palm of his hand and wondered what Lee Crossman was angry with him about. He began to understand why the other Negroes had gone out of their way to keep from talking to him. They knew he had been sent for, and that meant he had done something to displease Lee Crossman. They did not wish to be seen talking to anyone who was in disfavor with the plantation owner and boss.

"Have you got a radio?" Lee asked.

"Yes, sir."

"Where'd you get it?"

"I bought it on time."

"Where'd you get the money to pay on it?"

"I had a little, and my wife raises a few chickens."

"Why didn't you buy it at the plantation store?"

"I made a better bargain at the other place. I got it a little cheaper."

"Niggers who live on my plantation buy what they need at my plantation store," Lee said.

"I didn't want to go into debt to you, Mr. Lee," Christy said. "I wanted to come out ahead when the accounts are settled at the end of the year."

Lee Crossman leaned back in the chair, crossed his legs, and took out his pocketknife. He began cleaning his fingernails.

There was silence in the room for several minutes. Christy leaned against the wall.

"Stand up straight, nigger!" Lee shouted at him.

"Yes, sir," Christy said, jumping erect.

"Did you split up some of my wood to hew pickets for the fence around the house where you live?"

"Yes, sir, Mr. Lee."

"Why didn't you ask me if I wanted you to do it?"

"I figured the fence needed some new pickets to take the place of some that had rotted, and because I'm living in the house I went ahead and did it."

"You act mighty big, don't you?" Lee said. "You act like you own my house and land, don't you? You act like you think you're as good as a white man, don't you?"

"No, sir, Mr. Lee," Christy protested. "I don't try to act any of those ways. I just naturally like to hustle and get things done, that's all. I just can't be satisfied unless I'm fixing a fence or cutting wood or picking cotton, or something. I just naturally like to get things done."

"Do you know what we do with biggity niggers like you in Georgia?"

"No, sir."

"We teach them to mind their own business and stay in their place."

Lee Crossman got up and crossed the room to the closet. He jerked the door open and reached inside. When he turned around, he was holding a long leather strap studded with heavy brass brads. He came back across the room, slapping the strap around his boot-tops.

"Who told your wife she could raise chickens on my plantation?" he said to Christy.

"Nobody told her, Mr. Lee," Christy said. "We didn't think you'd mind. There's plenty of yard around the house for them, and I built a little hen house."

"Stop arguing with me, nigger!"

"Yes, sir."

"I don't want chickens scratching up crops on this plantation."

"Yes, sir," Christy said.

"Where did you get money to pay on a radio?"

"I snared a few rabbits and skinned them, and then I sold their hides for a little money."

"I don't want no rabbits touched on my plantation," Lee said.

He shook out the heavy strap and cracked it against his boots.

"Why haven't you got anything down on the books in the plantation store?" Lee asked.

"I just don't like to go into debt," Christy said. "I want to come out ahead when the accounts are settled at the end of the year."

"That's my business whether you come out owing or owed at the end of the year," Lee said.

He pointed to a crack in the floor.

"Take off that shirt and drop your pants and get down on your knees straddle that crack," the white man said.

"What are you going to do to me, Mr. Lee?"

"I'll show you what I'm going to do," he replied. "Take off that shirt and pants and get down there like I told you."

"Mr. Lee, I can't let you beat me like that. No, sir, Mr. Lee. I can't let you do that to me. I just can't!"

"You black-skinned, back-talking coon, you!" Lee shouted, his face turning crimson with anger.

He struck Christy with the heavy, brass-studded strap. Christy backed out of reach, and when Lee struck him the second time, the Negro caught the strap and held on to it. Lee glared at him at first, and then he tried to jerk it out of his grip.

"Mr. Lee, I haven't done anything except catch a few rabbits and raise a few chickens and things like that," Christy protested. "I didn't mean any harm at all. I thought you'd be pleased if I put some new pickets in your fence."

"Shut your mouth and get that shirt and pants off like I told you," he said, angrier than ever. "And turn that strap loose before I blast it loose from you."

Christy stayed where he was and held on to the strap with all his might. Lee was so angry he could not speak after that. He ran to the closet and got his pistol. He swung around and fired it at Christy three times. Christy released his grip on the strap and sank to the floor.

Lee's brother, Morgan, and the bookkeeper, Hendricks, came running into the back room.

"What happened, Lee?" his brother asked, seeing Christy Tucker lying on the floor.

"That nigger threatened me," Lee said, blowing hard. He walked to the closet and tossed the pistol on the shelf. "You and Hendricks heard him threaten to kill me. I had to shoot him down to protect my own life."

They left the back room and went into the front office. Several clerks from the plantation store ran in and wanted to know what all the shooting was about.

"Just a biggity nigger," Lee said, washing his hands at the sink. "He was that Alabama nigger that came over here two or three months ago. I sent for him this morning to ask him what he meant by putting new pickets in the fence around his house without asking me first. When I got him in here, he threatened me. He was a bad nigger."

The clerks went back to the plantation store, and Hendricks opened up his books and went to work on the accounts.

"Open up the back door," Lee told his brother, "and let those niggers out in the back see what happens when one of them gets as biggity as that coon from Alabama got."

His brother opened the back door. When he looked outside into the road, there was not a Negro in sight. The only living thing out there was the mule on which Christy Tucker had ridden to town.

As a fellow member of the writing craft, I have always felt proud of the accomplishments of those who chose to become reviewers. For their purposes, they have boiled down the English language from some six hundred thousand to a hundred words. As each new book appears, they juggle their hundred words with such dexterity that they never seem at first glance to be the same words that were used the day before. It would be a mistake, however, to assume that all reviewers employ the same hundred words, because each reviewer has carefully selected his own handful for individual use. Over the years the reading public has come to associate certain words with certain reviewers. Most readers are well aware of the fact, for example, that "masterpiece" and "magnificent" are to be found exclusively in Joe Doakes' daily book column; that "epoch-making" and "earth-shaking" are heard only in Sylvester Judd's weekly book chat.

Balm of Gilead

Back in January, about the middle of the first week, Ned Jones received a letter from the fire insurance agent's office in Bangor. The letter said that the company, effective January 1st, last, had discontinued allowing a discount on premiums covering farm houses and barns which were equipped with lightning rods. Therefore, the letter said, the cost for protection on his buildings would be raised to twenty-two-fifty from twenty-fifty.

However, the letter went on, if the rods were already installed on the buildings, a lightning rod expert would call and inspect the terminals, ground wires, brads, and so forth, and if the expert found them in first-class condition, the discount would be reinstated. The charge for all of this, the letter concluded, would be three dollars for the inspector's time.

"Thunderation," Ned said when he had finished reading the letter the third time. "Hell and thunderation!"

It did not take him long to figure out that he would save a dollar by not having the lightning rods inspected, but even so he could see that it was going to cost him two dollars a year more to keep his buildings covered by insurance.

"That's thunderation," he said.

His wife, Betty, was silent about the whole matter. She always froze up inside whenever something came up like that and threatened to cost an extra penny.

The insurance premium was not due and payable until February 1st, but a week before that time, Ned got ready to make a trip to Bangor and pay a call at the insurance agent's office.

He and his wife started out to Bangor after breakfast, driving the old car slowly along the black-top road, taking care to stay as far on the right-hand side of the road as possible. The law was that a car owner would not have to carry liability and property damage insurance as long as he did not have a mishap. Ned was set on not having that first accident on the highways that would force him to pay insurance premiums for the right to drive his car. It was an old car anyway, about twelve years old, and he did not intend buying another one when it was worn out.

They got to Bangor just before ten o'clock in the forenoon, and, after finding a safe place to park and leave the automobile, Ned and his wife went straight to the agent's office.

They sat down on a bench in the hall and waited for several minutes, and then a girl took them to see Mr. Harmsworth.

"Now, about that insurance on my stand of buildings out at Gaylord," Ned said, shaking his head and his finger at the agent.

"I take it you're upset about the new lightning rod clause, effective January 1st, last," Mr. Harmsworth said, smiling at Ned and his wife. "You see, Mr. Jones, and Mrs. Jones, the company at the home office in New Hampshire rewrites the contracts, and we agents have nothing whatever to do with the terms the company dictates."

"What do people in New Hampshire know about lightning rods anyway?" Ned said. "Now let me tell you. I once knew a man in New Hampshire who——"

"Let's not get off the subject, Mr. Jones, and Mrs. Jones," Mr. Harmsworth said. "After all, both my parents were born and raised in New Hampshire, and I'm sure there is a New Hampshire connection somewhere in your family, too."

He smiled at Mrs. Jones, beaming upon her all the force of what he knew was a sunny smile. Betty refused to be disarmed. She was frozen up inside, and she intended to remain unthawed as long as the insurance company refused to make an adjustment that would not cost them an extra penny.

"Now, I've lived down here in the State of Maine for all my life," Ned said, "and I'm sixty and more right now, and lightning rods are the only things in the world that'll keep lightning from striking and setting fire to a house or barn. All my life I've seen lightning strike a spire and run down the cable into the ground without even so much as smoking up the roof and clapboards. If it wasn't for lightning rods——"

"Are you sure lightning runs down lightning rods, Mr. Jones, and Mrs. Jones?" Mr. Harmsworth said. "I was under the impression it ran up the rods, or rather made contact on the point of the spire. However——"

"Lightning is lightning, whether it runs up or down, or slantwise, if it has a mind to," Ned said, rising up.

"I see you know a lot more about such things than I do," Mr. Harmsworth laughed, beaming upon Mrs. Jones, "I was raised here in the city, and I never had a chance to observe how lightning behaves when it comes in contact with a rod-equipped building. But, just the same, there's nothing either you or I can do about this here clause, because the home office rewrote the contract and sent us the printed forms, and I'm merely their representative. I carry out their orders, but I have no authority to alter a clause in a contract."

Ned looked at his wife, and she shook her head. That was all he wanted to know. No insurance company, with a home office in New Hampshire, run by New Hampshire people, was going to tell him whether they thought lightning rods were protection or not. He looked at his wife again, and shook his head. Betty tightened her mouth, freezing tighter inside, and nodded at Ned.

Mr. Harmsworth shuffled some papers on his desk, and, bringing one out with much crinkling and creasing, laid it before Ned.

"This is your bill for fire protection coverage, due February 1st," he said, glancing quickly at Ned, but not looking at Mrs. Jones.

Ned pushed it back at him.

"Now, about this Balm of Gilead," Ned said, edging forward in his chair.

"What Balm of Gilead?" Mr. Harmsworth asked, startled. "What's that?"

Ned looked at his wife, and Betty nodded. That was what he wanted to know from her. He pulled his chair closer to the desk.

"My Balm of Gilead," he said. "I've got one in my dooryard, fourteen feet from the west wall of my dwelling house, and twenty-two feet from the east wall of my barn."

"What's a Balm of Gilead?" Mr. Harmsworth asked, still startled. "Wasn't that something in the Bible? How'd you get something that was in the Bible?"

Ned and Betty looked at each other, but neither of them made any motion of the head.

"Balm of Gilead is a tree," Ned said. "My Balm of Gilead was set out by my father, seventy-seven years ago, and it stands in my dooryard."

"What about it?" Mr. Harmsworth asked, wild-eyed.

"It's a lightning rod," Ned said. "It's the finest lightning rod on earth. After a Balm of Gilead——"

"You want us to give you a discount because you have a tree——" Mr. Harmsworth began, sitting forward in his chair.

"—passes its fiftieth year, it turns into a lightning rod," Ned continued doggedly. "Lightning won't strike any other thing within fifty yards of it. Lightning strikes the Balm of Gilead every time."

"I don't know what you're driving at exactly," Mr. Harmsworth said, "but I wouldn't suppose you expect to get any discount on your fire insurance for having a tree like that."

Betty stiffened her backbone.

"I don't know why not," Ned said. "Why shouldn't I get a discount when I've got a Balm of Gilead located almost half-way between my two buildings, and the farthest is twenty-two feet from it. A tree like that is two or three times more protection than rods on the buildings. Why, it even makes the buildings proof against lightning! I figure I'm due five or six dollars discount for having that tree where it is."

Mr. Harmsworth scratched his head and took a swift look at Mrs. Jones. He had time to see that her mouth was drawn in a tight line across her face. He did not look at her again.

"If you insist upon it," he said, "I'll take it up with the home office in New Hampshire. I won't be able to do a thing until I hear from them. But I shouldn't think they would allow anybody a discount on fire insurance for having a Balm of Gilead tree."

"If they wasn't those New Hampshire people," Ned said, "they'd know how much protection a tree like that is."

"I'll write you a letter and let you know what the home office has to say just as soon as I get their answer," he said, standing up.

Ned and Betty got up and went out into the hall. Mr. Harmsworth followed them trying to shake hands with at least one of them. Betty kept her hands clasped tightly across her waist. Ned outwalked the agent to the street.

"Ignorant young cuss," Ned said. "Associates with New Hampshire people."

Betty nodded her head.

They bought a few things in a store, and then got into their car and drove home. Neither of them mentioned the insurance during the rest of the day.

During the remainder of the week, and through the first three days of the following one, both Ned and his wife watched the mail for the letter from the agent in Bangor. On the third day the letter came.

They went into the kitchen and sat down in the chairs by the window before opening it. Ned first took out his glasses and carefully polished the lenses. Betty put her handkerchief to her nose, and then put it away. Ned read the letter aloud.

"Dear Mr. Jones: I have taken up the matter of the Balm of Gilead tree in your dooryard with the home office in New Hampshire, and I am herewith advising you of their decision. It seems that the company thought it was all a joke or something because, in their own words, they wished to know if your Balm of Gilead tree would 'catch mice, scare crows away, and cure painter's colic.' Further along in their letter they state most emphatically that under no circumstances would a discount on fire insurance premiums be allowed for possession of a Balm of Gilead tree."

The letter did not end there, but Ned read no farther. He handed the letter to his wife, and she laid it aside on the table, drawing her mouth into a thin straight line across her face.

"I never did waste any feelings for the people of New Hampshire," Ned said, putting away his glasses, getting his hat, and standing up.

His wife did not say a word when he left the kitchen and went out into the dooryard.

When she saw him come out of the woodshed with the ax and the crosscut saw, she put on her jacket and went out to help him.

First he cut a notch in the Balm of Gilead on the side in order to fell it in the direction where he wanted it to fall. When that was done, he picked up one end of the crosscut, and Betty picked up the other end. They began sawing silently, their faces bright but drawn in tight lines, and both hoping that an electrical storm would come early in the spring, and each of them praying silently that lightning would strike the house and burn it to a heap of ashes on the ground.

One morning in the early spring of 1930 I arrived in New York with a suitcase full of stories. I had been writing and submitting stories to editors for five years with no success whatever, and I had decided to try door-to-door salesmanship. At the end of the first day I had left one or more in the office of every magazine in town. After two days I began collecting my manuscripts. I got back all but four. One had been taken to New Jersey, hurriedly printed, and was being hawked by whispering men standing in dark doorways. One was in the locked drawer of an editorial desk used by a young woman who said the magazine could not buy it but that she had always wanted to marry a writer. The third manuscript burned up when somebody laid a lighted cigarette on it. The fourth manuscript was accepted by a magazine editor who called me on the phone and asked me how much I wanted for it. "About—" I began. "I'm afraid we can't pay you that much," he said. "But—" I protested. "You'll have to come down in your price—the best we can pay is two fifty," he said. "I think I ought to have at least two seventy-five for it," I insisted. "All right, two hundred and seventy-five, then!" he said. "Dollars?" I asked. "Of course! What did you think I meant!" he said.

The Mating of Marjorie

He was coming—he was coming—God bless him! He was coming to marry her—coming all the way from Minnesota!

Trembling, breathless, Marjorie read the letter again and again, holding it desperately in the ten fingers of her hands. Then at last, her eyes so blurred she could no longer see the handwriting, she placed the letter against the bareness of her breasts where she could breathe into it all the happiness of her heart. All the way from Minnesota he was coming—coming all that great distance to marry her!

The letter's every word, every mark of careless punctuation, was burned inerasably on her memory. The thought of the letter was like a poem running through her—like the chill of sudden warmth—fragments of lines repeating themselves like the roar in a furnace-pipe.

His letter was not a proposal of marriage, but he did say he liked the way she looked in the picture she sent him. And why would he be coming all the way from Minnesota if he did not intend asking her to be his wife? Surely he wanted her.

Marjorie had his picture, too. She could actually feel the untiring strength of the lean muscles stretching over his face to the chin. Her fingers stole over his face excitedly, filling her with passion for the man with whom she would mate. He was a strong man. He would do with her as he pleased.

Surely he would like her. He was a mature man, and men who are mature seek beauty of soul and body when they marry. Marjorie was beautiful. Her beauty was her youth and charm. He wrote Marjorie that her eyes and her face and her hair were the loveliest he had ever seen. And her body was beautiful, too. He would see that when he came. Her slender limbs were cool and firm like the young pine trees in winter. Her heart was warm and eager. He would like her—surely he would.

Should she please him, and should he want her, and naturally he would when he saw her, Marjorie would give him her soul. Her soul would be her greatest gift to him. First she would give him her love, then her body, and at last her soul. No one had ever possessed her soul. But neither had her body or her love been possessed.

He had written frankly in all his letters. He said he wanted a wife. It was lonely, he said, living alone in Minnesota. Marjorie was lonesome, too. She had lived the long five years since her mother's death, alone. She understood. She had always been lonesome.

Marjorie prepared a room for him and waited his coming. She laundered the linen sheets and pillow-cases three times. She dried the linen each time on the limbs of the fir trees and ironed it in the early morning while it was still damp with the pine-scented air.

The day of his coming Marjorie was awake long before the sun rose. The sun rose cool and swift.

Before laying out the new clothes she would wear for him, she ran to the room and patted the pillows and smoothed the coverlet for the last time. Then hurriedly she dressed and drove to the depot nineteen miles away.

He arrived on the noon train from Boston. He was much larger than she had expected him to be, and he was much more handsome than she had hoped.

"Are you Marjorie?" he asked huskily.

"Yes," Marjorie answered eagerly. "I am Marjorie. You are Nels?"

"Yes," he smiled, his eyes meeting hers. "I am Nels."

Marjorie led Nels to the automobile. They got in and drove away. Nels was a silent man, speaking crisply and infrequently. He looked at Marjorie all the time. He looked at her hands and face intently. She was nervous and self-conscious under his non-committal scrutiny. After they had gone several miles he placed his arm across the back of the seat. Only once or twice did Marjorie feel his arm. The bumpy roads tossed them both as the car sped across-country. Nels' arms were as strong and muscular as a woodsman's.

Late that afternoon Marjorie and Nels walked down through the wood to the lake. There was a cold icy wind out of the northeast and the lake rose and tossed as if a storm were upon it. While they stood on a boulder at the lakeside watching the waves, a sudden gust of wind threw her against his shoulder. Nels braced her with his steel-like arms and jumped to the ground. Later she showed Nels the ice-house and pointed out to him the shed where the boats were stored in winter. Then they walked home through the pines and firs.

While Marjorie prepared supper Nels sat in the parlor smoking his pipe. Several times Marjorie ran to the open door for a hurried glimpse of the man she was to marry. The only motion about him was the steady flow of tobacco-smoke boiling from the bowl of his pipe. When the meal was ready, Marjorie quickly changed her dress and called Nels. Nels enjoyed the meal before him. He liked the way she had prepared the fish. Her skin was so hot she could not bear to press her knees together. Nels ate with full appetite.

After Marjorie had hastily carried the dishes to the kitchen she again changed her dress and went into the room where Nels sat by the fireplace. They sat in silence until she brought him the album and showed him the pictures. He looked at them silently.

All through the evening she sat hoping he would soon take her in his arms and kiss her. He would later, of course, but she wanted now to be in his arms. He did not look at her.

At ten-thirty Nels said he should like to go to bed. Marjorie jumped up and ran to his room. She turned back the pine-scented covers and smoothed the pillows. Bending over the bed, she laid her flushed cheek against the cool soft linen. Tearing herself away, she went back into the room where Nels sat silently by the fire.

After Nels had gone to his room and closed the door behind him, Marjorie went to her own bedroom. She sat down in a rocking-chair and looked out upon the lake. It was after midnight when she got up and undressed. Just before retiring she tiptoed to the door of Nels' room. She stood there several minutes listening intensely. Her fingers touched the door softly. He did not hear her. He was asleep.

Marjorie was awake at five. Nels came into the kitchen at seven while she prepared breakfast. He was freshly clean, and under his loose tweed suit she all but felt the great strength of his body.

"Good-morning," he said.

"Good-morning, Nels," she greeted him eagerly.

After breakfast they sat in the parlor while Nels smoked his pipe. When he finished smoking, he stood up before the fireplace. He took out his watch and glanced at the time. Marjorie sat hushed behind him.

"What time does the train leave for Boston?" he asked.

With stilled breath she told him.

"Will you take me to the train?" he asked her.

She said she would.

Marjorie immediately went into the kitchen and leaned heavily against the table. Nels remained in the parlor re-filling his pipe. Marjorie ran toward the parlor several times, but each time she turned back when she reached the door. She wanted to ask Nels if he were coming back. She picked up a plate and it crashed to the floor. It was the first piece of china she had broken since the morning of her mother's death. Trembling, she put on her hat and coat. Of course he was coming back! How foolish it was to think he would not! He was probably going to Boston to get some presents for her. He would come back—of course he would!

When they reached the depot, Nels held out his hand. She placed her hand in his. It was the first time his skin had touched her skin.

"Good-by," he said.

"Good-by, Nels," she smiled at him. "I hope you enjoyed your visit."

Nels picked up his traveling-bag and started towards the waiting-room.

Marjorie's arms and legs had the numbness of death in them. She started the motor uncertainly. He had not said he would return!

"Nels!" she cried desperately, gripping the door of the automobile with bloodless fingers.

Nels stopped and turned around, facing her.

"Nels, you are welcome to come back any time you want to," she begged unashamedly.

"Thank you," he replied briefly, "but I'm going home to Minnesota and I'll not be back again."

"What!" she cried, her lips quivering so violently she could barely make them speak. "Where are you going——?"

"To Minnesota," he replied.

Marjorie drove home as fast as her car would take her. As soon as she reached the house she ran to Nels' room.

In Nels' room Marjorie stood by the side of the bed and looked at the crumpled sheets and pillows with tear-blinded eyes. With a sob she threw herself between the sheets where Nels had lain. In her arms she hugged the pillows and dampened them with her tears. She could feel his body against hers. She kissed his face and held her lips for him to kiss.

It was night when she arose from the bed. The sun had gone down and the day was over. Only the cool clear twilight was left to shadow the room.

Throwing a blanket around her shoulders, Marjorie jerked the sheets and pillow-cases from the bed and ran blindly to her own room. She opened the cedar chest and tenderly folded the crumpled sheets and pillow-cases. She laid the linen in the chest and dragged the chest to the side of her bed.

Marjorie turned out the light and lay down between the sheets of her own bed.

"Good-night, Nels," she whispered softly, her fingers touching the smooth lid of the cedar chest at her side.

I believe this story would have been far superior if it could have been told orally.

An Autumn Courtship

AMOS WILLIAMS had been carrying a jug of his last year's cider over to Esther Tibbetts' every Sunday night for two months or more and he thought it was about time for something to happen. Amos had been trying all summer to marry Esther, but Esther owned a good farm and a fine set of buildings and she thought she was very well off just as she was. Every Sunday night Esther seemed to be ready to say she would marry Amos, but by that time the cider was all gone and he had to go away and wait for another week to pass before he could try again.

When he went back to work at the skewer-mill Monday morning, the other men wanted to know if anything had happened the night before. Everybody in the mill knew that Amos was trying his hardest to marry Esther before winter and cold weather came. Amos had begun taking Esther a jug of cider because one of the men there had said that if a woman drank enough hard cider she would marry anybody.

"What did Esther say last night, Amos?" one of the men asked him, winking at the others. "Did she say she would get married to you?"

Amos said nothing for a few minutes. The mill was turning out candy-sticks for all-day suckers this week because there was a big stock of meat-skewers on hand and a large order for candy-sticks had been received over the week-end. Amos picked up a wrench and adjusted the turning-machine on his bench while everybody stood around waiting to hear about Esther.

"The cider gave out too quick, I guess," he said. "I thought for a while she was going to say she would get married, but I guess there wasn't enough cider."

"What you should do, Amos," another of the men said seriously, "is to take two jugs of cider with you next Sunday night. When I was courting my wife, I couldn't do a thing with her until I began taking two jugs with me when I went to see her. You should take two jugs of cider, Amos. That will make things happen, all right."

"I'll have to do something about it," Amos said. "My cider-barrel is getting low. I've only got five or six gallons left in it now. And winter is coming on, too. If Esther don't marry me pretty soon, I'll have to buy some new blankets."

"You take Esther two jugs next Sunday night, Amos, and if all that cider won't make something happen for you I'll give you five gallons out of my own barrel."

Amos pulled the belt on his machine and went to work turning candy-sticks. He was getting uneasy now that winter was coming. He had planned to marry Esther before it began to be cold at night so he would not have to buy any new blankets. His sister had taken all his quilts when she was married that past spring and now he could not get them away from her. Esther had a lot of quilts and if he could marry her they would use hers that winter. Everything would work out just fine if Esther would only say she would marry him. He would live in Esther's house because it was a mile closer to the skewer-mill than his own, and he would not have to walk so far when he went to work.

By the end of the week Amos was desperate. Since Tuesday there had been a heavy frost every night and the only bed-covering he had was the old yellow quilt his sister said she would not have. It would have been a foolish waste of money to go to the store and buy two or three sets of blankets, considering the fact that Esther had dozens and dozens of quilts which they would use if she would only marry him before winter and cold weather came.

Early Sunday evening Amos filled two jugs with his last-year's cider and took them with him to see Esther. When he got there, he wanted Esther to begin drinking with him right away. Esther liked cider, especially when it was a year old, and they drank one jug empty before nine o'clock. Amos had not said a word the whole evening about marrying. He figured that it would be better to wait and talk about that when they started on the second jug.

Esther took a good stiff drink from the new jug and danced a few steps before she sat down again.

"This is good cider, Esther," he said preliminarily.

Esther put her hand over her mouth and swallowed two or three times in quick succession.

"You always have good apple-juice, Amos," she smiled at him.

Amos rubbed the palms of his hands nervously over his knees, trying to erase the indigo stain of white birch from the skin. He liked to hear Esther praise his cider.

"The boys at the skewer-mill promised to give me a whole barrel of cider when I get married," he lied shamelessly.

He glanced at Esther, hoping to find on her face some sign of the effect the carefully planned story should have had on her. Esther looked blankly at the ceiling, as though she did not know why Amos came to see her every Sunday night with his last-year's cider. Amos poured her another glass from the jug.

While she drank the cider, Amos studied the pile of thick quilts and comforters on the foot of her bed in the next room. Seeing Esther's quilts made him more than ever determined to marry her right away. He could see no sense in his coming to her house every week and bringing her his good cider when, if she would marry him, he could be there every night and have all his cider for himself.

And this time, when he brought two jugs, he knew he had the best opportunity of his life. If Esther drank both jugs of cider and still continued to say that she would not marry him, then there would be no use in wasting any more of his cider on her.

Esther finished the glass and gave it to Amos. He put it on the table and turned around just in time to see Esther lifting her skirt near the hem with a thumb and forefinger and carelessly throwing one leg across the other. He knew at once that the second jug was doing all it should do, because Esther had never crossed her legs so gaily during all the other times he had been bringing one jug. He poured her another glass, and rubbed his birch-stained hands together enthusiastically while she was placing the glass to her lips.

"Esther, I've got more than seven thousand dollars in the savings-bank," he began. That was the first thing he said each time he asked her to marry him. "My farm and buildings are worth three thousand dollars, and I haven't any debts."

Esther lifted her eyelids and looked at Amos. Her eyes were sleepy-looking but she was wide awake.

"I don't want to be married," she said, beginning to giggle a little for the first time. "I want to stay like I am, Amos."

This was the only time he had ever been with Esther when she had a cider-giggle. He watched her anxiously, startled by her prompt refusal.

"But blankets—" he cried out nervously.

"What blankets?" she asked, raising herself on her elbow and guiding herself across the room. The cider-giggle was getting beyond her control.

"Winter is coming—cold weather!" he shouted desperately.

"What about cold weather, Amos?" she giggled again.

"I was just thinking about blankets," he said hopelessly.

Esther went to the door and looked into her bedroom. Amos came and stood beside her.

"I haven't any blankets, Amos," she giggled, "but I've got a lot of quilts and comforters."

Amos looked hopefully over her shoulder at the pile of quilts and comforters on her bed.

"I want us to get married, Esther," he said thickly. "How would you like to marry me?"

Esther pushed Amos roughly aside and went back into the room. She was giggling so foolishly she could not speak.

Amos went to the table and poured her another glass of cider. While she drank it he glanced at the almost empty jug, realizing that he would have to hurry Esther if he was to get her consent before all the cider was gone.

When she handed him the empty glass, Amos put it on the table and caught her hands before she could jerk away from him. Then, holding her arms so she could not push him away, he kissed her. Knowing that she would try to push him away when he did that, he put his arms around her and held her while he talked to her about marrying him.

"I want that you should marry me, Esther," he struggled with her strength, "because if you don't I'll have to buy some blankets for the winter."

Esther pushed and scratched but Amos held her all the tighter. He could see that she was mad, but at the same time she could not keep from giggling just as sillily as ever. Amos poured out the last glass of cider for her while he held her with one hand.

Still holding her with one hand he tried to force the cider into her mouth. Suddenly she shoved Amos with all her might, and both of them fell on the floor. Amos was not hurt, but Esther struck her knee on a chair and cut a deep gash in her leg. The blood ran through her stocking and dripped on the floor beside them.

"Esther, I want that you should marry me right away before—" he began a second time.

Before he could say another word Esther had grabbed the nearest cider-jug and hit him over the head with it. The blow was glancing, and the jug only stunned him for a moment. She had swung the jug so hard, though, that it was jerked from her fingers and crashed against the cast-iron stove. She immediately reached for the second jug, but Amos was too quick for her. He ran to the door and out into the yard before she could throw it at him. When he got to the road, she had reached the door, and with all her strength she hurled the stone jug at Amos. Amos dodged out of the way and ran down the road toward his house.

When he got home, there was nothing to do but drink some cider and go to bed. He was so mad about the way things turned out that he drank almost three times as much cider as he usually did when he went down into his cellar.

By the time Amos started to the skewer-mill the next morning he was resigned to his inability to marry Esther. His only regrets now were that he had wasted all his last-year's hard cider on her and would have to buy two or three sets of blankets, after all.

When he got to the mill, a stranger was standing in the doorway. The man made no effort to move when Amos tried to enter.

"Your name is Amos Williams, isn't it?" he asked.

"Amos Williams it's been ever since I can remember," Amos said sourly, trying to get into the mill.

"Well, you will have to come along with me to the county jail," he said, holding out a folded paper.

"What for?" Amos demanded.

"The paper says 'Assault on the Person of Esther Tibbetts.'"

The man who had promised Amos five gallons of cider the week before, when he suggested that Amos take Esther two jugs, came up the road to the mill door. He asked Amos what the trouble was and Amos told him.

"You got me into all this trouble," Amos swore at him. "You said two jugs would make her marry me, and now she's had me arrested for assault."

"Well, it's too bad you've got to go to jail and lose all that time here at the mill, Amos, but it was all your own fault."

"How was it my fault?"

"It's like this, Amos. There are three kinds of women. There are one-jug, two-jug, and three-jug women. You should have told me at the start that Esther was a three-jug woman. If you had done that, I could have told you to take her three jugs of cider instead of only two."

If Professor Perkins is still following me, I will gladly explain for his benefit the method I employ in writing these comments. When I have no comment to make, I merely say as much.

Priming the Well

WHEN I was a little fellow my mother, who was half damyankee, used to tell me the story about wooden nutmegs. Even now I can clearly remember her picturing the early peddlers with pouches of painted nutmegs going from farm to farm along the Potomac, selling the spice with all the solemnity of a Methodist circuit-rider. That the nutmegs were easily sold and eagerly bought is beside the story; the wonder is that we Southerners were so dumb we did not know the difference.

For some reason I never fully understood, my mother and father, when I was still quite young, went Down East and bought a farm in the Kennebec River Valley. Then, when I was eleven years old and my sister nine, they decided that they would sell the farm and move back to Virginia. This was the easiest phase of the decision, because finding somebody who wanted to invest six thousand dollars in a Maine farm was a problem difficult to solve. Even when we did find a purchaser it was by mere accident that the sale was so easily made.

It was a three-months' drought that finally brought a buyer to us. And that was chance, too; because droughts for more than three or four weeks were uncommon where we were.

In the late spring, about four months before the drought came to an end,—the last rain fell on the first day of June—there were two men who were very anxious to buy our farm. The price either of them was willing to pay at that time, however, was not much more than one half the figure my father had placed on it. Mr. Geroux, a Frenchman, was one of the prospective purchasers, and Elisha Goodwin the other. Mr. Geroux was a native of New Brunswick, but he had lived in Maine thirty years or longer. He had become unusually prosperous in recent years because of the rising market for seed potatoes, and during all that time he had been acquiring that same cautious mind Elisha Goodwin had inherited from six generations of forefathers. Both of these men, however, realized the value of our farm and both knew it was worth every dollar of six thousand. Neither of them was willing, though, to pay the price asked until he was sure it could not be bought for less. And, as we were told afterwards, Mr. Geroux would have paid almost anything up to ten thousand for the farm, because its improvements, fertility, and location were making it increasingly valuable.

In the month of August, the beginning of the last month of the terrible drought, both Mr. Geroux and Elisha Goodwin came to see my father in regard to purchasing our farm. They did not come together, of course, because each of them wanted to buy it before the other did. At the same time, each of them wanted to close the deal before he was forced to bid against the other. The month of August was the dryest ever to be recorded in the State of Maine. Everyone was certain of that. No rain had fallen since the first of June. The Kennebec River was so low that it was out of the question for the paper-mills to float pulpwood, and all of those which were not importing Scandinavian baled pulp had to close down. Even the lakes in the back-country were so low that at least fifty per cent of the fish had already died. There was nothing that could be done about the weather, though, and everybody just had to wait for fall to come, bringing rain or snow. Towards the end of the month the water famine was becoming dangerous. The farmers, whose wells had gone dry and who had been drawing water from the river and lakes, were faced with additional danger when the river went completely dry along with most of the lakes. The stock on every farm was dropping dead day and night. There had been no milk in the valley for nearly a month, and the horses, steers, and sheep were hungry and thirsty. The month of August was without exception the most damaging month in the history of the entire Kennebec River Valley.

There was a deep lake on our farm about a mile and a half from the buildings and we were fortunate in having some water for our stock and ourselves. We drew water to the house every day from the lake. Our well had gone dry just as quickly as all the other wells in the valley.

We had been drawing water in three barrels every day from the lake. After six weeks of this my father became tired of having to go to the lake every day. He decided that we would draw twenty-five or thirty barrels one day a week and store it on the farm. This would save us the trouble of having to go every day and give us time to do some other work that was needed. The real problem, however, was where and how to store a week's supply of water. It would have been foolish to buy twenty-five or thirty barrels, or even half that many, when we could use them at the most only two or three weeks longer. Then they would have to be stored away and they would dry and warp until they were valueless. I believe it was my mother who made the suggestion of storing the water in the well. At least, it was she who said it was the only place she knew about. At first my father was of the opinion that the water would run or seep out of the well faster than we could haul it, but he was willing to try it, anyway. The plan worked, much to my mother's joy. All of us—my father, my sister, and myself—congratulated her on making such a wise suggestion.

We went to work at once and all that day we drew water from the lake and poured it into the well. By late afternoon we had transferred about thirty or thirty-five barrels of lake water to the well. That evening all we had to do was to lower the bucket and bring up as much water as we needed for the stock. The next day it was the same. The water was still there and apparently none had seeped away. It was a great improvement over the way we had been doing before.

It was by accident that Elisha Goodwin stopped at our house that afternoon. His horse had thrown a shoe and he came up to the barn to draw out the nails so the hoof would not be injured. He came up to the barn where we were at the time.

"Well, Mr. Langley," he said to my father, "what are we going to do about this here drought? The whole State of Maine will be ruined if this keeps up another two weeks. There ain't a drop of water on my whole farm."

"The drought is terrible," my father said. "I won't have even a peck of potatoes out of the whole farm to sell this year. But, strange to say, I've got plenty of water in my well."

"What?" Mr. Goodwin shouted unbelievingly. "You say you got water in your well?"

"Plenty of it."

"Well, I don't believe it. Nobody else has got any water in their wells. How comes it you got water in your'n?"

"I water my stock from it twice a day and we have plenty of water for the kitchen besides. It's just as full as it's ever been."

Elisha Goodwin thought we were joking with him about having plenty of water in the well, but he went over to see for himself just the same.

My father sent my sister into the house.

Elisha Goodwin picked up three or four pebbles and leaned far over the well looking down into it and trying to see the water. He dropped one of the pebbles into the well and cocked his head sideways, listening for the *ker-plunk* the stone made when it struck the water. He repeated this as long as his pebbles lasted. Then he stood up and looked at us. By watching his face we could tell that he was getting ready to say something important.

He stood up looking at us and scratching the top of his head with three of his fingers while his hatbrim was held tightly by the other two. His chin-whiskers moved up and down faster than I could count.

"How much is it you're asking for this place of your'n?"

My father told him how much we were holding it for.

"You haven't closed a deal with anybody yet, have you?"

"Well, not exactly," my father stated. "Though Mr. Geroux has asked me to give him a two-months' option on the place."

"Did you let him have it?" Elisha Goodwin asked hurriedly.

"I'm to let him know tomorrow about it," my father said.

"You come with me to the village," Elisha Goodwin said. "We'll fix up a sale before sundown. I'm going to buy your place. It's the only farm in the whole gol-darned State that's got any well-water on it."

"Are you sure you want to buy it, Mr. Goodwin?" my father asked him. "You know the price and terms. It's six thousand dollars cash."

"I don't give a gol-darn what your terms are. I'm going to pay you six thousand dollars in cash for it as soon as you go to the village with me and draw up a bill of sale and turn over the deed. I ain't going to let that good-for-nothing Canuck get his hands on the best farm in the whole gol-darned country. Come on to the village and get it settled right away."

Instead of driving to the village in the buggy, he and my father went in our automobile. He left his horse and buggy hitched at our barn. They were gone about two hours.

When they came back, they shook hands with each other and Elisha Goodwin drove home at a fast clip. He must have forgotten about his horse throwing a shoe.

My mother came out with my sister and asked us what agreement had been made. My father told her all about it. She smiled a little but did not say anything just then. While I carried water to the stock and while my sister went down into the cellar to get some potatoes for supper, they walked across the pasture talking to themselves about something they did not want us to overhear. When they came back, we all went into the kitchen while supper was cooking.

"Well, we are moving back to Virginia next week," my father told us, smiling at my mother. "As soon as we can pack everything we want to take with us we're leaving."

He called my sister to him and lifted her on his knee. He stroked her curls absent-mindedly several times.

"Louise," he smiled at her, "tell me: are you a little Virginia girl, or are you a little New Englander?"

My sister answered without a moment's hesitation.

"I'd rather be a little Virginia lady."

"But your mother is a damyankee—don't you want to be like her?"

He always smiled to himself when he called my mother a dam-yankee.

Before my sister could reply, my mother came over where we were and lifted her to the floor from my father's lap.

"Louise, you and Tommy run out into the yard and play until supper is ready. Run along, now."

We left the kitchen and went out on the porch. Hardly before we were down the front steps, we heard two people laughing as though they had just seen the funniest thing in the world. We tiptoed to the kitchen window and looked in to see what was so funny. Both my mother and father were standing in the middle of the kitchen floor holding on to each other and laughing so hard I thought they would burst open if they kept it up much longer.

My sister pulled me by the arm and pointed down the river. The sky down there was the blackest I have ever seen. The black clouds were coming closer and closer all the time, like somebody covering you with a big black blanket at night. Away down the valley we could see the tops of trees bending over so far that many of them broke off and fell to the ground.

"Look!" my sister said, clutching my arm. She was trembling all over. "Look!"

Holding each other tightly by the hand, we ran into the house as fast as we could.

The writing of the stories in this volume was made possible through the courtesy of the following individuals and corporations, to whom thanks are hereby extended: The Axton-Fisher Tobacco Company (for carton Spuds); The Coca-Cola Company (for case of Coca-Cola); The Matson Navigation Company (for passage to Hawaii); Rogers Peet Company (for red feather for my hat); The Roosevelt Hotel of New Orleans (for basket of assorted fruit); Bennett Cerf (for copy of novel "The Day of the Locust," by Nathanael West); The Sal-Sagev Hotel of Las Vegas (for lending me ten dollars); Clare Boothe Luce (for instruction in dove shooting); Metro-Goldwyn-Mayer (for permission to use typewriter).

Ten Thousand Blueberry Crates

No one in the village had ever heard of a wood-turning mill called the Yankee Dowel Company when the stranger asked to be directed to it. He said he was positive the plant was in the town of Liverpool, because he had a letter in his pocket with the postmark on it and the name and address of the company printed on the letter-head. There were six or seven mills of that kind in the town, the largest being over in East Liverpool and owned by Walt Brown.

"Who signed the letter you got there?" Nate Emmonds asked him.

"A man by the name of Brown," he said, looking at the letter again. "Walter J. Brown."

"Walt Brown, eh?" Nate said, glancing around at the men in the store. "Walt Brown signed the letter, and he calls himself the Yankee Dowel Company. I wonder what he could be up to now?"

A knowing wink passed from man to man around the stove.

"He used to be the Eastern Barrel Hoop Corporation," someone said, slapping his hands on his knees and having a good laugh with the other men, "but I ain't heard much about that corporation since wooden flour barrels went out of use. Walt's been doing his durndest trying to sell me a load of barrel-hoops to stake tomato-plants with. He thinks up the queerest notions to get rid of his hoops of any man I ever saw. Who ever heard of staking tomato-plants with barrel-hoops, anyhow?"

It was several minutes before the crowd stopped laughing at Walt. He had been up to some crazy schemes in his lifetime. Only a month or two before that, he was all excited over a plan of his to make a new kind of wooden clothes-pin at his mill. Now there was something else up his sleeve. The trouble with Walt was he was always letting somebody get the better of him when it came to business deals. He got along all right as long as he stuck to his lumber business, but whenever he tried to branch out into fancy woodwork he was always licked from the start. Everybody thought he had learned his lesson after losing a lot of money in the barrel-hoop deal, and believed that he would stick to his planing and stop trying to get rich by taking up fancy doweling. Apparently, though, he was going in for it again.

"Sure," Nate said, "I know Walt Brown. But what's your name, and what do you want to see him for?"

The man looked at Nate and then at the crowd around the stove before he said anything. He knew the men would not tell him how to find the mill until he told them his name and business.

"I'm Bullock," he said, "from over at The Falls. I buy and sell wooden products."

Androscoggin Falls was a town forty-five miles northeast of Liverpool. There were several shoe-factories there, with a dozen or more mills turning out wooden products of various kinds.

Nate slapped his hands on his knees and winked at the men around him.

"So you're a Bullock from over at The Falls, eh? I don't guess you give milk then, do you?"

Everybody in the store broke out laughing again. The man from The Falls could not keep from laughing either.

"No," he said, suddenly getting red in the face and looking angry. "No, I don't give milk, but I'm a damn hard butter when I get wild and loose."

The crowd took it all in without a sign. The men knew Nate had run up against a man every bit as sharp-witted as he was. Nate looked at Bullock very hard for a moment, but he had nothing to say to that answer.

"Come on outside," Nate told him, "and I'll show you how to find Walt Brown's mill."

When they were out in the street, Nate offered him some smoking tobacco and admired his automobile. It was not long before both of them were laughing and telling each other jokes.

Bullock said finally that he was in a hurry to find the mill and get back to The Falls. Nate told him to take the upper lake road three miles to East Liverpool. Walt's mill was at the end of the lake where the State road crossed the stream.

It did not take him long to go the three miles in his car. When he reached East Liverpool, he walked into the mill and found Walt operating one of the wood-turning machines. There were five or six other men working in the plant with him.

"You're Walter Brown, aren't you?" Bullock asked him.

"I'm the one," Walt said. "What do you want?"

"I'm Bullock, from over at The Falls. You sent me some prices on cider-jug handles last week. I came over to talk business with you."

Walt brightened up immediately. He shut off the machine he was running and took Bullock to his office in the house across the street.

"That's a fairly good price you gave me on fifty gross," Bullock said. "I've got a chain store begging for some right away, so if I were to double that number could you shade the price a little?"

"Well, I guess maybe I can," Walt said. "And I guess maybe we can do business together."

Walt was very much excited over the prospect of getting a big order for wooden handles. When he had sent Bullock the quotation the week before, he had not expected it to amount to anything. Some people said his prices were too high, and that his plant was too far away from the railroad for him to get much business without offering f. o. b. shipments like the rest of the mill men. It cost a lot of money to truck twenty-seven miles to the depot.

Bullock signed the order for a hundred gross of the jug handles and gave Walt shipping directions. He knew he would have to pay trucking costs in addition to the freight, but he had figured all that into the cost before he left The Falls. Even then he was getting the handles cheaper than ever before, and he was pleased with Walt's price. The wooden jug handles had been costing him from fifty to seventy-five cents more a gross from the mills at The Falls.

When he was about to leave, he happened to see a stack of barrel-hoops in the mill. He asked Walt if he turned out hoops too. Walt explained that it was some left-over stock he had been unable to sell because people had stopped buying flour in barrels as they used to and bought it now in sacks instead.

Bullock went in and looked the lot over. Walt watched him break one of the hoops over his knee to inspect the grain in the wood. Bullock's business was dealing in wooden products on commission, but he had not had a hoop to pass through his hands in more than three years.

"I can't do anything with barrel-hoops either, these days, but I'll tell you one thing I've never been able to get enough of."

"What's that?" Walt asked quickly.

"Blueberry crates," he said. "I can't get enough of them. I could have sold five hundred only last week to a man over in New Hampshire if I could have got my hands on some. The blueberry-crate business is better this year than it ever has been. Everybody wants crates this year to ship berries to market."

Walt thought a while about blueberry crates and walked around in circles. He had made almost everything in wooden products during his lifetime, but a blueberry crate was one thing he had never thought of. He knew he could do it, though, because his machines would turn out practically anything.

"I can make blueberry crates," he said.

"If you can make delivery of them by the end of this month I can use them," Bullock said. "I'll pay the ruling price on them at the time you make delivery, too. That's a better deal for you than setting a price beforehand, because the market will be up when the season opens. I'll take as many as you can get out in that time, too. But they'll have to be ready before the end of the month, because after that the season will be too far advanced."

Walt went to his office to get an order-blank for Bullock to sign, but when he came back to the mill Bullock had gone. Walt did not like that, because he never wanted to make up an order when it hadn't been signed in advance. In that case he could not bring suit to collect if the man refused to take the lot. But Bullock looked all right, and he talked as if he meant to take them. In the matter of blueberry crates a signed order did not mean much anyway, because if a man decided to cancel an order all he had to do was to claim the crates were not up to standard specifications.

Walt went ahead with his plans for making the crates anyway. But first he started getting out the wooden jug-handles and had his men begin work on them right away. They would finish that job in a few days, and in the meantime they could begin getting the machines ready for the crates.

He went to the village the next morning to buy some nails with which to put the crates together. He had made a sample crate the night before, and with the weight of the nails he used he had figured out an estimate for the entire lot.

When he reached the village he went to Pat Hobb's store and told Pat he wanted some crate nails. Pat talked a while about the road money, and how it was being wasted by putting in a gravel fill by the North Schoolhouse. Walt was on the town road commission but he did not have much to say. He was in a hurry for the nails so he could get back to the mill.

Pat went over to the keg and picked it up. There were not more than ten pounds of nails in it.

"How many do you want?" he asked Walt.

"How many have you got?"

"About eight to ten pounds, maybe twelve."

"I want all of those, and I'll need a lot more besides."

"But I can't sell you all I've got, Walt. Suppose somebody else came in and said they wanted some?"

"Good God, I can't help that," Walt said. "You've got them to sell, ain't you? Well, sell them to me. I'm the one that wants to buy them."

"I couldn't do that, Walt," Pat said, putting the keg on the floor again. "I wouldn't have none left if I sold them all to you."

"Good God," said Walt, "ain't you in the selling business? What do you keep store for if it ain't to sell?"

"I know, but somebody——"

"Good God, Pat, don't make me mad. You can get some more nails, can't you? I'll want a lot more myself before I'm done buying. Why, do you know how many blueberry crates I'm going to make?"

"No," Pat said. "How many?"

"Ten thousand."

"Ten thousand blueberry crates?"

"That's what I said."

"Good God, Walt, that's a heap of blueberry crates. I never heard of a man making ten thousand of them before. What are you going to do with them?"

Walt did not know just then, himself. When he had said *ten thousand* it was done to impress Pat, so he could get all the nails he wanted, but when he began to think it over he was not sure that Bullock could take that many. It would take a lot of quart baskets of blueberries to fill that many crates, and there were other mills making crates too. But Walt knew he could never back down now. Pat would tell Nate Emmonds about it, and that would make Nate take back a lot of the things he had been saying about Walt and his wooden-products business.

"I've got an order from Bullock over at The Falls for that many. Maybe more, too."

Pat remembered Bullock's coming into the store and asking for Walt a few days before that. He would tell Nate about the big number of crates Walt was making as soon as he came into the store again.

"I'll take what nails you got there, Pat," Walt said. "And I'll be back in a few days for a lot more. I'll need a pile of nails to put all those crates together."

"All right," Pat agreed, "you can take them. But I know I ain't doing best. Somebody will be sure to come in and ask for crate nails and I won't have none at all."

"You order some right away. I'll be in again soon for two or three kegs full."

Walt went back to the mill and got to work on the crates. The wooden handles for the cider and vinegar jugs would be ready by the end of the next day. After he got them off to Bullock he could put all his men to work on the crates.

Everybody in town had heard about the large number of blueberry crates Walt was going to make, and by the middle of the following day men began coming in to ask Walt for a job helping make them. Walt took on fifteen new men and went to work. By the end of the week they were turning crates out at the rate of a thousand a day. The stack in the millyard got higher and higher, and it was not long before crates were piled twenty feet high in every available place.

The piles of crates attracted the attention of a man passing through East Liverpool in his car late Tuesday afternoon of the following week. He stopped, turned around, and drove back to the mill where Walt was. Walt was too busy to stop work.

"What kind of crates are those?" he asked Walt.

"Blueberry," Walt said without turning around.

"If you had said raspberry, I couldn't have told the difference. Raspberry crates are exactly like those. And I ought to know, because raspberry crates is my business."

"What do you want?" Walt asked him. "I can't waste time talking when I've got work to do."

"I want to buy those crates," the man said. "I had just started on a buying trip to get raspberry crates for my customers. I buy and sell wooden products on commission, and if you'll meet my offer halfway we can do business. I'll take all the crates you've got and haul them away in my own trucks starting tomorrow. You'll sell them to me, won't you?"

"Nope," Walt said, "I won't sell them to you. And those ain't raspberry crates, either—them are blueberry crates. And anyway, they are already bargained for. I'm making them on order."

Walt could not understand why the man called them raspberry crates. If he had learned the business of making crates before he jumped into it, he would have known the blueberry crates had to be made up in bundles because most of them were shipped several hundred miles down East on the coast, while raspberry crates were usually nailed together at the time they were made because they were used in this section of the State and it was cheaper and a saving of time to truck them to the fields directly from the mills. A distance of fifty miles was all that was necessary at times to change the name and use of a crate.

"This is the first time I ever saw blueberry crates put together at the mill. All the blueberry people I know want the parts shipped to them in bundles, and then they knock the crates together right in the fields where——"

"When you've been in the wooden-products business for as long a time as——"

"Then you're not going to sell me those raspberry crates even if I——"

"These blueberry crates are already bargained for. And if they was raspberry crates I wouldn't sell——"

"I've got to be going," the man said. "I can't waste my time standing here talking all day to a blundering fool."

"If you don't get going I'll have to waste some of my time looking for a piece of four-by-four to start you off with."

The man knew he could never persuade Walt to sell the crates, no matter what name he called them by, so he went back to his car and drove away. He had been dealing with mill men in that section of the State for thirty years, and he knew that whenever one of them talked as Walt did there was never anything but time and temper lost in trying to buy something from him.

Two days before the crates would be finished, Walt wrote Bullock a letter telling him when they would be ready and asking for shipping instructions.

Bullock drove over from The Falls the same day he received Walt's letter. He did not know what to do with the crates just then, because the season would be over in another week or two. But he figured that Walt would have only two or three, or at the most, five hundred crates, and he could take them to The Falls and carry them over to the next season and still make a good profit.

When he reached East Liverpool and saw the millyard, he almost had a heart-attack. He had never seen so many blueberry crates in all his life, and he had been dealing in them for twenty years.

When he had first talked to Walt about making crates, he had no idea Walt intended making them, at least not in such quantities, and he was certain he had not signed an order for them. But he wanted to continue getting wooden jug-handles at the good price Walt had made him. There was no other mill in the whole State that would sell handles to him at that figure. Bullock knew if he told Walt he had not ordered the crates, Walt would be angry about it and perhaps refuse to sell him any more cider-jug handles.

Before Walt came out of the mill, Bullock had a few minutes to think about what he was going to say. He knew it would ruin him to take that many blueberry crates merely to please Walt.

Walt came out of the mill and met Bullock at his car. Bullock was sitting on the running-board looking at the crates in the millyard stacked higher than the buildings themselves.

"Well, Bullock," Walt said, shaking his hand, "they're ready.

The last durn one of them. There's ten thousand waiting for you."

"Ten thousand!" Bullock gasped. "Ten thousand what?"

"Crates, man—blueberry crates."

"Ten thousand blueberry crates?"

"Sure," Walt said. "When I undertake a job I finish it. I made ten thousand of them for you, and I could get out half that many more by the end of the week if you want them. I've got fifteen extra men helping in the mill."

"Ten thousand," Bullock said again, still unable to realize that there were that many blueberry crates in the world.

"What's your shipping instructions? Where do you want them sent —over to The Falls?"

Bullock rose to his feet and supported himself against the side of his automobile.

"Good God," he said, wiping his face with the back of his hand.

"What's the matter?" Walt asked him.

"I'm afraid there's been a mistake," he said. "A pretty bad mistake, too. I guess probably I should have told you about it in the first place, because I've found that nearly every mill man in the State makes the same mistake when he undertakes to make blueberry crates. And naturally it's pretty hard on the mill man."

"What do you mean? There ain't no mistake. You said you wanted as many crates as I could make, didn't you? You said you'd take all I made. There ain't no mistake on my part."

"Yes, it's a bad mistake," Bullock said, gravely shaking his head from side to side. "You see, your business is in dowels principally, isn't it? And going back to the bottom of things, you are in the lumber business. That's your main business. All this kind of work making crates and hoops and jug handles is a sort of side-line with you. Well, that shows you're not a blueberry-crate man at all. That's why you didn't know you were making a mistake. A blueberry-crate man would never have done that."

"Done what?" Walt begged. "What's the matter with the crates I made?"

"Your crates are put together. They would have to be knocked down and bundled before they would be of any use to me. Why, man, it would cost a fortune to truck those empty crates to the depot and ship them by freight to my customers all over the State. That many empty crates would take up more space than the railroad has got boxcars to put them in. That's the mistake. You'll have to knock them down before I can use them."

"But this other man said he would haul raspberry crates away just like they stand now, if——"

"Good God, man," Bullock said, "we're talking about blueberry crates. I didn't say anything about raspberry——"

"That's right," Walt said. "I just got mixed up in what I was saying."

Walt wished Bullock would go away and leave him alone. He felt very cheap there with Bullock, having all those crates on his hands, whatever kind they were now. But no matter how hard he tried to think his way out of the trouble he was in, he still knew the crates had been thrown back on him. If he hired the men to knock the crates down and bundle them he would lose at least two or three hundred dollars on the deal. He could not afford that. And he knew he could not force Bullock to take them, because there was no signed contract. He remembered about the pile of barrel-hoops stacked up in the mill, too. They had been left on his hands because he nailed them together. Instead of nailing the ends together they should have been bundled and shipped flat. And now there was no market for hoops of any kind. Then his mind raced back to the crates. He wished he had asked the man who wanted to buy them for raspberry crates to leave his name and address. He could ask Bullock to put him in touch with the raspberry-crate man, because Bullock would probably know every wooden-products buyer in the State, but Walt didn't want to do that. The other man had been angry when he left, and he would probably refuse to have anything to do with Walt after being ordered away from the mill.

"Well, I guess I'll keep them," Walt said. "I don't want to knock them down. There wouldn't be any sense in doing that."

"Suit yourself," Bullock said. "But I can't use them as they are now. They would have to be knocked down and bundled. Now, if I was in the *raspberry*-crate business I could take every one you've got. Raspberry crates——"

"These ain't raspberry crates," Walt said stiffly. "Them are blueberry crates."

Walt went back into the mill. Bullock followed him, saying something about signing an order for fifty gross of cider-jug handles that he wanted added to the first order. Walt brought him an order-blank and watched him fill it in and sign it. The moment Bullock finished writing his signature he got into his automobile and started towards The Falls as fast as he could.

When Bullock was out of sight, Walt went to the millyard and looked at the stacks of blueberry crates a while. Then he went back into the mill and looked at the barrel-hoops. He was wondering what Nate Emmonds would say about him this time.

This story, over a period of years, was rejected by practically every magazine in the United States. Aside from that, I found it to be an interesting experience, because editors, not content with merely turning it down, felt called upon to accompany their refusals with advice that the story was (a) not true to life, (b) a denial of man's nobility, (c) injurious to my reputation, (d) an incitation to violence, (e) not understandable to readers (Hello, Bill!), and (f) evidence of a disordered mind. The story was finally accepted and published by The Yale Review. Subsequently, it was given the Yale Review Award for Fiction. This is its seventh appearance in print.

Country Full of Swedes

THERE I was, standing in the middle of the chamber, trembling like I was coming down with the flu, and still not knowing what god-awful something had happened. In all my days in the Back Kingdom, I never heard such noises so early in the forenoon.

It was about half an hour after sun-rise, and a gun went off like a coffer-dam breaking up under ice at twenty below, and I'd swear it sounded like it wasn't any farther away than my feet are from my head. That gun shot off, pitching me six-seven inches off the bed, and, before I could come down out of the air, there was another roar like somebody coughing through a megaphone, with a two weeks' cold, right in my ear. God-helping, I hope I never get waked up like that again until I can get myself home to the Back Kingdom where I rightfully belong to stay.

I must have stood there ten-fifteen minutes shivering in my nightshirt, my heart pounding inside of me like a ram-rod working on a plugged-up bore, and listening for that gun again, if it was going to shoot some more. A man never knows what's going to happen next in the State of Maine; that's why I wish sometimes I'd never left the Back Kingdom to begin with. I was making sixty a month, with the best of bed and board, back there in the intervale; but like a God damn fool I had to jerk loose and came down here near the Bay. I'm going back where I came from, God-helping; I've never had a purely calm and peaceful day since I got here three-four years ago. This is the damnedest country for the unexpected raising of all kinds of

378

unlooked-for hell a man is apt to run across in a lifetime of traveling. If a man's born and raised in the Back Kingdom, he ought to stay there where he belongs; that's what I'd done if I'd had the sense to stay out of this down-country near the Bay, where you don't ever know, God-helping, what's going to happen next, where, or when.

But there I was, standing in the middle of the upstairs chamber, shaking like a rag weed in an August wind-storm, and not knowing what minute, maybe right at me, that gun was going to shoot off again, for all I knew. Just then, though, I heard Jim and Mrs. Frost trip-trapping around downstairs in their bare feet. Even if I didn't know what god-awful something had happened, I knew things around the place weren't calm and peaceful, like they generally were of a Sunday morning in May, because it took a stiff mixture of heaven and hell to get Jim and Mrs. Frost up and out of a warm bed before six of a forenoon, any of the days of the week.

I ran to the window and stuck my head out as far as I could get it, to hear what the trouble was. Everything out there was as quiet and peaceful as midnight on a backroad in middlemost winter. But I knew something was up, because Jim and Mrs. Frost didn't make a practice of getting up and out of a warm bed that time of forenoon in the chillish May-time.

There wasn't any sense in me standing there in the cold air shivering in my night-shirt, so I put on my clothes, whistling all the time through my teeth to drive away the chill, and trying to figure out what God damn fool was around so early shooting off a gun of a Sunday morning. Just then I heard the downstairs door open, and up the steps, two at a time, came Jim in his breeches and his shirt-tail flying out behind him.

He wasn't long in coming up the stairs, for a man sixty-seven, but before he reached the door to my room, that gun went off again: BOOM! Just like that; and the echo came rolling back through the open window from the hills: *Boom! Boom!* Like fireworks going off with your eyes shut. Jim had busted through the door already, but when he heard that *Boom!* sound he sort of spun around, like a cock-eyed weathervane, five-six times, and ran out the door again like he had been shot in the hind parts with a moose gun. That *Boom!* so early in the forenoon was enough to scare the daylights out of any man, and Jim wasn't any different from me or anybody else in the town of East Joloppi. He just turned around and jumped through the door to the first tread on the stairway like his mind was made up to go somewhere else in a hurry, and no fooling around at the start.

I'd been hired to Jim and Mrs. Frost for all of three-four years, and I was near about as much of a Frost, excepting name, as Jim himself was. Jim and me got along first-rate together, doing chores and haying and farm work in general, because neither one of us was ever trying to make the other do more of the work. We were hitched to make a fine team, and I never had a kick coming, and Jim said he didn't either. Jim had the name of Frost, to be sure, but I wouldn't ever hold that against a man.

The echo of that gun-shot was still rolling around in the hills and coming in through the window, when all at once that god-awful cough-like whoop through a megaphone sounded again right there in the room and everywhere else, like it might have been, in the whole town of East Joloppi. The man or beast or whatever animal he was who hollered like that ought to be locked up to keep him from scaring all the women and children to death, and it wasn't any stomach-comforting sound for a grown man who's used to the peaceful calm of the Back Kingdom all his life to hear so early of a Sunday forenoon, either.

I jumped to the door where Jim, just a minute before, leaped through. He didn't stop till he got clear to the bottom of the stairs. He stood there, looking up at me like a wild-eyed cow moose surprised in the sheriff's corn field.

"Who fired that god-awful shot, Jim?" I yelled at him, leaping down the stairs quicker than a man of my years ought to let himself do.

"Good God!" Jim said, his voice hoarse, and falling all to pieces like a stump of punk-wood. "The Swedes! The Swedes are shooting, Stan!"

"What Swedes, Jim—those Swedes who own the farm and buildings across the road over there?" I said, trying to find the buttonholes in my shirt. "Have they come back here to live on that farm?"

"Good God, yes!" he said, his voice croaking deep down in his throat like he had swallowed too much water. "The Swedes are all over the place. They're everywhere you can see, there's that many of them."

"What's their name, Jim?" I asked him. "You and Mrs. Frost never told me what their name is."

"Good God, I don't know. I never heard them called anything but Swedes, and that's what it is, I guess. It ought to be that, if it ain't."

I ran across the hall to look out a window, but it was on the wrong side of the house, and I couldn't see a thing. Mrs. Frost was stepping around in the downstairs chamber, locking things up in the drawers and closet and forgetting where she was hiding the keys. I could see her through the open door, and she was more scared-looking than Jim was. She was so scared of the Swedes she didn't know what she was doing, none of the time.

"What made those Swedes come back for, Jim?" I said to him. "I thought you said they were gone for good, this time."

"Good God, Stan," he said, "I don't know what they came back for. I guess hard times are bringing everybody back to the land, and the Swedes are always in the front rush of everything. I don't know what brought them back, but they're all over the place, shooting and yelling and raising hell. There are thirty-forty of them, looks like to me, counting everything with heads."

"What are they doing now, Jim, except yelling and shooting?"

"Good God," Jim said, looking behind him to see what Mrs. Frost was doing with his things in the downstairs chamber. "I don't know what they're not doing. But I can hear them, Stan! You hurry out right now and lock up all the tools in the barn and bring in the cows and tie them up in the stalls. I've got to hurry out now and bring in all of those new cedar fence posts across the front of the yard before they start pulling them up and carrying them off. Good God, Stan, the Swedes are everywhere you look out-doors! We've got to make haste, Stan!"

Jim ran to the side door and out the back of the house, but I took my time about going. I wasn't scared of the Swedes, like Jim and Mrs. Frost were, and I didn't aim to have Jim putting me to doing tasks and chores, or anything else, before breakfast and the proper time. I wasn't any more scared of the Swedes than I was of the Finns and Portuguese, anyway. It's a god-awful shame for Americans to let Swedes and Finns and the Portuguese scare the day-lights out of them. God-helping, they are no different than us, and you never see a Finn or a Swede scared of an American. But people like Jim and Mrs. Frost arc scared to death of Swedes and other people from the old countries; Jim and Mrs. Frost and people like that never stop to think that all of us Americans came over from the old countries, one time or another, to begin with.

But there wasn't any sense in trying to argue with Jim and Mrs. Frost right then, when the Swedes, like a fired nest of yellow-headed bumble bees, were swarming all over the place as far as the eye could see, and when Mrs. Frost was scared to death that they were coming into the house and carry out all of her and Jim's furniture and household goods. So while Mrs. Frost was tying her and Jim's shoes in pillow cases and putting them out of sight in closets and behind beds, I went to the kitchen window and looked out to see what was going on around that tall yellow house across the road.

Jim and Mrs. Frost both were right about there being Swedes all over the place. God-helping, there were Swedes all over the country, near about all over the whole town of East Joloppi, for what I could see out the window. They were as thick around the barn and pump and the woodpile as if they had been a nest of yellow-headed bumble bees strewn over the countryside. There were Swedes everywhere a man could see, and the ones that couldn't be seen, could be heard yelling their heads off inside the yellow clapboarded house across the road. There wasn't any mistake about there being Swedes there, either; because I've never yet seen a man who mistakes a Swede or a Finn for an American. Once you see a Finn or a Swede you know, God-helping, that he is a Swede or a Finn, and not a Portugee or an American.

There was a Swede everywhere a man could look. Some of them were little Swedes, and women Swedes, to be sure; but little Swedes, in the end, and women Swedes too, near about, grow up as big as any of them. When you come right down to it, there's no sense in counting out the little Swedes and the women Swedes.

Out in the road in front of their house were seven-eight autos and trucks loaded down with furniture and household goods. All around, everything was Swedes. The Swedes were yelling and shouting at one another, the little Swedes and the women Swedes just as loud as the big Swedes, and it looked like none of them knew what all the shouting and yelling was for, and when they found out, they didn't give a damn about it. That was because all of them were Swedes. It didn't make any difference what a Swede was yelling about; just as long as he had leave to open his mouth, he was tickled to death about it.

I have never seen the like of so much yelling and shouting anywhere else before; but down here in the State of Maine, in the down-country on the Bay, there's no sense in being taken-back at the sights to be seen, because anything on God's green earth is likely and liable to happen between day and night, and the other way around, too.

Now, you take the Finns; there's any God's number of them around in the woods, where you least expect to see them, logging and such. When a Finn crew breaks a woods camp, it looks like there's a Finn for every tree in the whole State, but you don't see them going around making the noise that Swedes do, with all their yelling and shouting and shooting off guns. Finns are quiet about their hell-raising. The Portuguese are quiet, too; you see them tramping around, minding their own business, and working hard on a river dam or something, but you never hear them shouting and yelling and shooting off guns at five-six of a Sunday morning. There's no known likeness to the noise that a houseful of Swedes can make when they get to yelling and shouting at one another early in the forenoon.

I was standing there all that time, looking out the window at the Swedes across the road, when Jim came into the kitchen with an armful of wood and threw it into the woodbox behind the range.

"Good God, Stan," Jim said, "the Swedes are everywhere you can look out-doors. They're not going to get that armful of wood, anyway, though."

Mrs. Frost came to the door and stood looking like she didn't know it was her business to cook breakfast for Jim and me. I made a fire in the range and put on a pan of water to boil for the coffee. Jim kept running to the window to look out, and there wasn't much use in expecting Mrs. Frost to start cooking unless somebody set her to it, in the shape she was in, with all the Swedes around the place. She was so up-set, it was a downright pity to look at her. But Jim and me had to eat, and I went and took her by the arm and brought her to the range and left her standing there so close she would get burned if she didn't stir around and make breakfast.

"Good God, Stan," Jim said, "those Swedes are into everything. They're in the barn, and in the pasture running the cows, and I don't know what else they've been into since I looked last. They'll take the tools and the horses and cows, and the cedar posts, too, if we don't get out there and put everything under lock and key."

"Now, hold on, Jim," I said, looking out the window. "Them you see are little Swedes out there, and they're not going to make off with anything of yours and Mrs. Frost's. The big Swedes are busy carrying in furniture and household goods. Those Swedes aren't going to tamper with anything of yours and Mrs. Frost's. They're people just like us. They don't go around stealing everything in sight. Now, let's just sit here by the window and watch them while Mrs. Frost is getting breakfast ready."

"Good God, Stan, they're Swedes," Jim said, "and they're moving into the house across the road. I've got to put everything under lock and key before——"

"Hold on, Jim," I told him. "It's their house they're moving into. God-helping, they're not moving into your and Jim's house, are they, Mrs. Frost?"

"Jim," Mrs. Frost said, shaking her finger at him and looking at me wild-eyed and sort of flustered-like, "Jim, don't you sit there and let Stanley stop you from saving the stock and tools. Stanley doesn't know the Swedes like we do. Stanley came down here from the Back Kingdom, and he doesn't know anything about Swedes."

Mrs. Frost was partly right, because I've never seen the things in my whole life that I've seen down here near the Bay; but there wasn't any sense in Americans like Jim and Mrs. Frost being scared of Swedes. I've seen enough Finns and Portuguese in my time in the Back Kingdom, up in the intervale, to know that Americans are no different from the others.

"Now, you hold on a while, Jim," I said. "Swedes are no different than Finns. Finns don't go around stealing another man's stock and tools. Up in the Back Kingdom the Finns are the finest kind of neighbors."

"That may be so up in the Back Kingdom, Stan," Jim said, "but Swedes down here near the Bay are nothing like anything that's ever been before or since. Those Swedes over there across the road work in a pulp mill over to Waterville three-four years, and when they've got enough money saved up, or when they lose it all as the case may be, they all move back here to East Joloppi on this farm of theirs for two-three years at a time. That's what they do. And they've been doing it for the past thirty-forty years, ever since I can remember, and they haven't changed none in all that time. I can recall the first time they came to East Joloppi; they built that house across the road then, and if you've ever seen a sight like Swedes building a house in a hurry, you haven't got much else to live for. Why! Stan, those Swedes built that house in four-five days—just like that! I've never seen the equal to it. Of course now, Stan, it's the damnedest-looking house a man ever saw, because it's not a farm house, and it's not a city house, and it's no kind of a house an American would erect. Why! those Swedes threw that house together in four-five days—just like that! But whoever saw a house like that before, with three stories to it, and only six rooms in the whole building! And painted yellow, too; Good God, Stan, white is the only color to paint a house, and those Swedes went and painted it yellow. Then on top of that, they went and painted the barn red. And of all the shouting and yelling, at all times of the day and night, a man never saw or heard before. Those Swedes acted like they were purely crazy for the whole of four-five days, and they were, and they still are. But what gets me is the painting of it yellow, and the making of it three stories high, with only six rooms in the whole building. Nobody but Swedes would go and do a thing like that; an American would have built a farm house, here in the country, resting square on the ground, with one story, maybe a story and a half, and then painted it lead-white. But Good God, Stan, those fool Swedes had to put up three stories, to hold six rooms, and then went and painted the building yellow."

"Swedes are a little queer, sometimes," I said. "But Finns and Portuguese are too, Jim. And Americans sometimes——"

"A little queer!" Jim said. "Why! Good God, Stan, the Swedes are the queerest people on the earth, if that's the right word for them. You don't know Swedes, Stan. This is the first time you've ever seen those Swedes across the road, and that's why you don't know what they're like after being shut up in a pulpwood mill over to Waterville for four-five years. They're purely wild, I tell you, Stan. They don't stop for anything they set their heads on. If you was to walk out there now and tell them to move their autos and trucks off of the town road so the travelers could get past without having to drive around through the brush, they'd tear you apart, they're that wild, after being shut up in the pulp mill over to Waterville these three-four, maybe four-five, years."

"Finns get that way, too," I tried to tell Jim. "After Finns have been shut up in a woods camp all winter, they make a lot of noise when they get out. Everybody who has to stay close to the job for three-four years likes to act free when he gets out from under the job. Now, Jim, you take the Portuguese——"

"Don't you sit there, Jim, and let Stanley keep you from putting the tools away," Mrs. Frost said. "Stanley doesn't know the Swedes like we do. He's lived up in the Back Kingdom most of his life, tucked away in the intervale, and he's never seen Swedes——"

"Good God, Stan," Jim said, standing up, he was that nervous and up-set, "the Swedes are over-running the whole country. I'll bet there are more Swedes in the town of East Joloppi than there are in the rest of the country. Everybody knows there's more Swedes in the State of Maine than there are in the old country. Why! Jim, they take to this State like potato bugs take to——"

"Don't you sit there and let Stanley keep you back, Jim," Mrs. Frost put in again. "Stanley doesn't know the Swedes like we do. Stanley's lived up there in the Back Kingdom most of his life."

Just then one of the big Swedes started yelling at some of the little Swedes and women Swedes. I'll swear, those big Swedes sounded like a pastureful of hoarse bulls, near the end of May, mad about the black-flies. God-helping, they yelled like they were fixing to kill all the little Swedes and women Swedes they could get their hands on. It didn't amount to anything, though; because the little Swedes and the women Swedes yelled right back at them just like they had been big Swedes too. The little Swedes and women Swedes couldn't yell hoarse bull bass, but it was close enough to it to make a man who's lived most of his life up in the Back Kingdom, in the intervale, think that the whole town of East Joloppi was full of big Swedes.

Jim was all for getting out after the tools and stock right away, but I pulled him back to the table. I wasn't going to let Jim and Mrs. Frost set me to doing tasks and chores before breakfast and the regular time. Forty dollars a month isn't much to pay a man for ten-eleven hours' work a day, including Sundays, when the stock has to be attended to like any other day, and I set myself that I wasn't going to work twelve-thirteen hours a day for them, even if I was practically one of the Frosts myself, except in name, by that time.

"Now, hold on a while, Jim," I said. "Let's just sit here by the window and watch them carry their furniture and household goods inside while Mrs. Frost's getting the cooking ready to eat. If they start taking off any of you and Mrs. Frost's things, we can see them just as good from here by the window as we could out there in the yard and road."

"Now, Jim, I'm telling you," Mrs. Frost said, shaking all over, and not even trying to cook us a meal, "don't you sit there and let Stanley keep you from saving the stock and tools. Stanley doesn't know the Swedes like we do. He thinks they're like everybody else."

Jim wasn't for staying in the house when all of his tools were lying around in the yard, and while his cows were in the pasture unprotected, but he saw how it would be better to wait where we could hurry up Mrs. Frost with the cooking, if we were ever going to eat breakfast that forenoon. She was so excited and nervous about the Swedes moving back to East Joloppi from the pulp mill in Waterville that she hadn't got the beans and brown bread fully heated from the night before, and we had to sit and eat them cold.

We were sitting there by the window eating the cold beans and brown bread, and watching the Swedes, when two of the little Swedes started running across Jim and Mrs. Frost's lawn. They were chasing one of their big yellow tom cats they had brought with them from Waterville. The yellow tom was as large as an eight-months collie puppy, and he ran like he was on fire and didn't know how to put it out. His great big bushy tail stuck straight up in the air behind him, like a flag, and he was leaping over the lawn like a devilish calf, newborn.

Jim and Mrs. Frost saw the little Swedes and the big yellow tom cat at the same time I did.

"Good God," Jim shouted, raising himself part out of the chair. "Here they come now!"

"Hold on now, Jim," I said, pulling him back to the table. "They're only chasing one of their tom cats. They're not after taking anything that belongs to you and Mrs. Frost. Let's just sit here and finish eating the beans, and watch them out the window."

"My crown in heaven!" Mrs. Frost cried out, running to the window and looking through. "Those Swedes are going to kill every plant on the place. They'll dig up all the bulbs and pull up all the vines in the flower bed."

"Now you just sit and calm yourself, Mrs. Frost," I told her. "Those little Swedes are just chasing a tom cat. They're not after doing hurt to your flowers."

The big Swedes were unloading the autos and trucks and carrying the furniture and household goods into their three story, yellow clapboarded house. None of them was paying any attention to the little Swedes chasing the yellow tom over Jim and Mrs. Frost's lawn.

Just then the kitchen door burst open, and the two little Swedes stood there looking at us, panting and blowing their heads off.

Mrs. Frost took one look at them, and then she let out a yell, but the kids didn't notice her at all.

"Hey," one of them shouted, "come out here and help us get the cat. He climbed up in one of your trees."

By that time, Mrs. Frost was all for slamming the door in their faces, but I pushed in front of her and went out into the yard with them. Jim came right behind me, after he had finished calming Mrs. Frost, and telling her we wouldn't let the Swedes come and carry out her furniture and household goods.

The yellow tom was all the way up in one of Jim's young maple shade trees. The maple wasn't strong enough to support even the smallest of the little Swedes, if he should take it into his head to climb to the top after the cat, and neither Jim nor me was hurting ourselves trying to think of a way to get the feline down. We were all for letting the cat stay where he was, till he got ready to come down of his own free will, but the little Swedes couldn't wait for anything. They wanted the tom right away, then and there, and no wasting of time in getting him.

"You boys go home and wait for the cat to come down," Jim told them. "There's no way to make him come down now, till he gets ready to come down of his own mind."

But no, those two boys were little Swedes. They weren't thinking of going back home till they got the yellow tom down from the maple. One of them ran to the tree, before Jim or me could head him off, and started shinnying up it like a pop-eyed squirrel. In no time, it seemed to me like, he was up amongst the limbs, jumping around up there from one limb to another like he had been brought up in just such a tree.

"Good God, Stan," Jim said, "can't you keep them out of the trees?"

There was no answer for that, and Jim knew there wasn't. There's no way of stopping a Swede from doing what he has set his head on doing.

The boy got almost to the top branch, where the yellow tom was clinging and spitting, when the tree began to bend towards the house. I knew what was coming, if something wasn't done about it pretty quick, and so did Jim. Jim saw his young maple shade tree begin to bend, and he almost had a fit looking at it. He ran to the lumber stack and came back dragging two lengths of two-by-fours. He got them set up against the tree before it had time to do any splitting, and then we stood there, like two damn fools, shoring up the tree and yelling at the little Swede to come down out of there before we broke his neck for being up in it.

The big Swedes across the road heard the fuss we were making, and they came running out of that three story, six room house like it had been on fire inside.

"Good God, Stan," Jim shouted at me, "here comes the Swedes!"

"Don't turn and run off, Jim," I cautioned him, yanking him back by his coat-tail. "They're not wild beasts; we're not scared of them. Hold on where you are, Jim."

I could see Mrs. Frost's head almost breaking through the window-glass in the kitchen. She was all for coming out and driving the Swedes off her lawn and out of her flowers, but she was too scared to unlock the kitchen door and open it.

Jim was getting ready to run again, when he saw the Swedes coming toward us like a nest of yellow-headed bumble bees, but I wasn't scared of them, and I held on to Jim's coat-tail and told him I wasn't. Jim and me were shoring up the young maple, and I knew if one of us let go, the tree would bend to the ground right away and split wide open right up the middle. There was no sense in ruining a young maple shade tree like that, and I told Jim there wasn't.

"Hey," one of the big Swedes shouted at the little Swede up in the top of the maple, "come down out of that tree and go home to your mother."

"Aw, to hell with the old lady," the little Swede shouted down. "I'm getting the cat by the tail."

The big Swede looked at Jim and me. Jim was almost ready to run again by that time, but I wasn't, and I held him and told him I wasn't. There was no sense in letting the Swedes scare the day-lights out of us.

"What in hell can you do with kids when they get that age?" he asked Jim and me.

Jim was all for telling him to make the boy come down out of the maple before it bent over and split wide open, but I knew there was no sense in trying to make him come down out of there until he got good and ready to come, or else got the yellow tom by the tail.

Just then another big Swede came running out of that three story, six room house across the road, holding a double-bladed ax out in front of him, like it was red-hot poker, and yelling for all he was worth at the other Swedes.

"Good God, Stan," Jim said, "don't let those Swedes cut down my young maple!"

I had lots better sense than to try to make the Swedes stop doing what they had set their heads on doing. A man would be purely a fool to try to stop it from raining from above when it got ready to, even if he was trying to get his corn crop planted.

I looked around again, and there was Mrs. Frost all but popping through the window-glass. I could see what she was thinking, but I couldn't hear a word she was saying. It was good and plenty though, whatever it was.

"Come down out of that tree!" the Swede yelled at the boy up in Jim's maple.

Instead of starting to climb down, the little Swede reached up for the big yellow tom cat's tail. The tom reached out a big fat paw and harried the boy five-six times, just like that, quicker than the eye could follow. The kid let out a yell and a shout that must have been heard all the way to the other side of town, sounding like a whole houseful of Swedes up in the maple.

The big Swede covered the distance to the tree in one stride, pushing everything behind him.

"Good God, Stan," Jim shouted at me, "we've got to do something!"

There wasn't anything a man could do, unless he was either a Swede himself, or a man of prayer. Americans like Jim and me had no business getting in a Swede's way, especially when he was swinging a big double-bladed ax, and he just out of a pulp mill after being shut up making paper four-five years.

The big Swede grabbed the ax and let go at the trunk of the maple with it. There was no stopping him then, because he had the ax going, and it was whipping around his shoulders like a cow's tail in a swarm of black-flies. The little maple shook all over every time the ax-blade struck it, like wind blowing a corn stalk, and then it began to bend on the other side from Jim and me where we were shoring it up with the two-by-fours. Chips as big as dinner plates were flying across the lawn and pelting the house like a gang of boys stoning telephone insulators. One of those big dinner-plate chips crashed through the window where Mrs. Frost was, about that time. Both Jim and me thought at first she had fallen through the window, but when we looked again, we could see that she was still on the inside, and madder than ever at the Swedes.

The two-by-fours weren't any good any longer, because it was too late to get to the other side of the maple in time to keep it from bending in that direction. The Swede with the double-bladed ax took one more swing, and the tree began to bend towards the ground.

The tree came down, the little Swede came down, and the big yellow tom came down on top of everything, holding for all he was worth to the top of the little Swede's head. Long before the tree and the boy struck the ground, the big yellow tom had sprung what looked like thirty feet, and landed in the middle of Mrs. Frost's flowers and bulbs. The little Swede let out a yell and a whoop when he hit the ground that brought out six-seven more Swedes from that three story, six room house, piling out into the road like it was the first time they had ever heard a kid bawl. The women Swedes and the little Swedes and the big Swedes piled out on Jim and Mrs. Frost's front lawn like they had been dropped out of a dump-truck and didn't know which was straight up from straight down.

I thought Mrs. Frost was going to have a fit right then and there in the kitchen window. When she saw that swarm of Swedes coming across her lawn, and the big yellow tom cat in her flower bed among the tender plants and bulbs, digging up the things she had planted, and the Swedes with their No. 12 heels squashing the green shoots she had been nursing along—well, I guess she just sort of caved in, and fell out of sight for the time being. I didn't have time to run to see what was wrong with her, because Jim and me had to tear out behind the tom and the Swedes to try to save as much as we could.

"Good God, Stan," Jim shouted at me, "go run in the house and ring up all the neighbors on the line, and tell them to hurry over here and help us before the Swedes wreck my farm and buildings. There's no telling what they'll do next. They'll be setting fire to the house and barn the next thing, maybe. Hurry, Stan!"

I didn't have time to waste talking to the neighbors on the telephone line. I was right behind Jim and the Swedes to see what they were going to do next.

"I pay you good pay, Stan," Jim said, "and I want my money's worth. Now, you go ring up the neighbors and tell them to hurry."

The big yellow tom made one more spring when he hit the flower bed, and that leap landed him over the stonewall. He struck out for the deep woods with every Swede on the place behind him. When Jim and me got to the stonewall, I pulled up short and held Jim back.

"Well, Jim," I said, "if you want me to, I'll go down in the woods and raise hell with every Swede on the place for cutting down your young maple and tearing up Mrs. Frost's flower-bed."

We turned around and there was Mrs. Frost, right behind us. There was no knowing how she got there so quick after the Swedes had left for the woods.

"My crown in heaven," Mrs. Frost said, running up to Jim and holding on to him. "Jim, don't let Stanley make the Swedes mad. This is the only place we have got to live in, and they'll be here a year now this time, maybe two-three, if the hard times don't get better soon."

"That's right, Stan," he said. "You don't know the Swedes like we do. You would have to be a Swede yourself to know what to tell them. Don't go over there doing anything like that."

"God-helping, Jim," I said, "you and Mrs. Frost ain't scared of the Swedes, are you?"

"Good God, no," he said, his eyes popping out; "but don't go making them mad."

The technique of fiction writing is comparable to the dynamics of teetering. The principle involved is that of deftly drawing the reader to his toes and then gently setting him back on his heels. The master of the craft is able to accomplish this movement in page after page until, finally, the reader is so dizzy that merely the sudden cessation of motion is sufficient to send him on his way physically reeling and emotionally groggy.

A Swell-Looking Girl

NOTHING much ever happened in the upper part of Pine County until Lem Johnson went over into the next county and married a swell-looking girl named Ozzie Hall. About eight or ten years before there had been a shotgun wedding in the lower part of the county, it's true; but Pine County was so large nobody in the upper part ever took much interest in what those countrymen down there were doing.

Lem Johnson was a farmer. He worked a two-horse crop with a Negro called Dan. Lem lived by himself in a four-room house. The Negro, Dan, lived across the road in a cabin with his wife and half a dozen pickaninnies. Dan, the Negro, worked for Lem on shares.

When Lem went over into the next county and married Ozzie Hall, it was the biggest event that had taken place in the Lucyville section of Pine County since anybody could remember. A man could live a lifetime and never see a thing like that happen again. She was a swell-looking girl, all right.

Before Lem went over and married Ozzie Hall he was the biggest sport in the whole county. He liked to go out with the girls and have a good time. He had always gone somewhere every Saturday night, again all day Sunday, and Sunday night. Sometimes he would drive up in front of a girl's house and call for her. She would come out and stand by the buggy while Lem sat back with his feet on the dashboard and had a good time with her. Other times he would drive up and ask a girl to go riding with him. All the girls liked that, too.

And all this time Lem was anxious to get married.

When he went to town on Saturday afternoon, he always said something about getting married. The boys teased Lem a lot about wanting to marry a girl.

"I'm a-rearing to get married," Lem told them.

"Want a woman all-time, eh Lem?" they teased him.

"That's right," he said earnestly, "I don't want to have to wait all week for Sunday."

The boys sat in front of the store and wondered what girl Lem was going to marry.

"Say, Lem," one of them yelled after him down the road as he was leaving, "you ain't going buggy-riding every night when you get married, are you?"

Everybody whooped and shouted and Lem prodded the mule and drove away blushing.

All the girls in the Lucyville section knew Lem was thinking of getting married, too. But Lem did not ask any of them to marry him. They were not classy enough to suit him. He wanted a swell-looking girl. He had seen pictures of the kind of girl he wanted in the mail-order catalogues.

Lem heard that there was a girl just like he wanted over in the next county. One Saturday morning he hitched up the mule and drove away. It was late in the afternoon when he got there, but sure enough there she was, as classy as any girl he had ever seen in the mail-order catalogues.

Lem got her to marry him right away, and brought her home to Pine County Sunday night.

Ozzie had a lot of fine clothes and silk stockings and she certainly was good-looking. And she had a lot of things just like Lem had seen in the mail-order catalogues, besides some things he had never seen before.

Lem went right out the first thing and told everybody about Ozzie. He told everybody how good-looking she was and how much silk underwear she had.

Right there was where he made the biggest mistake of his life. All the boys began coming around at once to take a look at Ozzie, hoping to get a chance to see some of the things Lem talked about so much. They rode up three in a buggy, two on horseback, and a lot of them walked.

Lem took Ozzie out on the front porch to show her off. The boys had come a long way to see her.

"Well, Lem," Tom said, "you sure got yourself a swell-looking girl, ain't you?"

"Listen, Tom," Lem whispered confidentially, "Ozzie here is the swellest-looking girl in the whole country. You ought to see all the pink little things she's got."

Ozzie sat down in a chair and looked at the boys. There were twenty or more sitting on the edge of the porch looking up at her. Some of them said a lot of awfully fresh things when Lem was not listening.

"What kind of pink little things?" Tom asked him.

"All sorts of things, Tom. There's a lot I ain't learned the names of yet."

"I don't believe it," Tom stated.

"You don't believe it?" Lem asked in surprise. "You don't believe she's got some of those things on now?"

"Naw, I don't. The girls in this part of the county don't wear things like that: City girls do. Country girls like the ones around here don't. The girls in this part of the county wear underwear made out of ten-cents-a-yard cotton mill-ends."

"Ozzie don't!"

"I'll bet she does, too. All country girls wear mill-end underclothes. They buy the cloth at ten cents a yard."

"Ozzie don't!"

"Sure she does. Ain't she a country girl, too?"

"I'll prove she don't!"

"How?" Tom wanted to know. "Where?"

"Hell, right here!" Lem was good and mad at Tom for not believing what he told him.

Ozzie sat looking at the boys, with her legs crossed high. The boys were having the time of their lives looking at Ozzie from where they sat. She was a swell-looking girl, all right.

Lem walked over to Ozzie and told her to stand up. The boys crowded around to see what Tom and Lem were up to now.

Lem reached down and lifted the hem of Ozzie's skirt above her knees. Her stockings ended there, but there was no pink thing to be seen. All the boys could see where Ozzie's stockings ended. Tom could see, too; but he still did not believe she wore the things Lem said she did. Ozzie covered her face with her hands and peeped at the boys through her fingers.

Tom poked Lem with his thumb, nodding his head. Lem lifted her dress a little higher, looking for something pink. There was not anything yet, except more of her legs showing. Lem was determined to prove to Tom that Ozzie did not wear ten-cents-a-yard cotton mill-end underclothes. He lifted her dress a little higher and a little higher. Nothing appeared that would prove to Tom the things Lem had said on the other end of the porch were true. The boys crowded closer and closer to Ozzie.

Lem was sweating all over. The perspiration popped out on his hands and face and he felt a tickling sensation running up and down his back. He was beginning to wish he had never started to prove to Tom what he said about Ozzie. But there was no way out of it now. He had to keep it up until he proved that he knew what he was talking about.

Tom poked him again with his thumb.

"By God, Tom, I know what I'm talking about!" he shouted, jerking Ozzie's dress over the top of her head. "Now look!"

Lem stood there, staring pop-eyed at Ozzie while she was fighting to get her dress down and cover up her nakedness. The boys were making little whistling sounds and rubbing their eyes to make sure they were seeing right. Ozzie had on nothing at all under her dress. She ran into the house as fast as she could.

Tom took Lem by the arm and they went to the other end of the porch. The boys were out in the yard now, standing around talking and whispering in groups of twos and threes. They had a lot to talk about. She was a swell-looking girl, all right.

"Well, Lem," Tom said, swallowing hard two or three times, "you sure got mixed up that time, didn't you?"

"Tom, I swear before God she had a lot of those pink little things on last night."

"Maybe she wears them some days, and some days she don't wear nothing at all," Tom said.

Lem was trying hard to think about it, trying hard to figure out some sort of answer. To save his soul he could not understand why she did not wear the things all the time. He sat down on the edge of the porch, thinking as hard as he could about it.

"Well, she's a swell-looking girl, Lem. How did you ever find one like that?"

Lem did not bother to answer Tom. He sat on the edge of the porch trying to figure out why Ozzie wore those things one day and took them off the next.

Tom jumped to the ground and stood close to Lem.

"Lem, if I was you I'd keep her just like she is," he whispered. "Ten-cent mill-ends ain't good enough for a girl like you got in there."

Tom went out in the yard where the rest of the boys were. They stood around in front of the house talking for two or three hours until the sun went down. Then they began to leave.

Authors awaiting the impending publication of their first book, and subsequent reviews, would do well to occupy their time in the interim by familiarizing themselves with the recognized, or rote, methods of newspaper and magazine criticism. Once an author has made a thorough study of reviewing, he will be able to sort his notices as follows: (a) reviews beginning, "This book is by no means as good as Shakespeare, the Bible, or 'The Origin of Species'"; (b) the review by the newspaper owner's wife (or daughter); (c) the review written by the author of last year's bestseller; (d) the review written by one of the office boys who copied the blurb from the jacket; and (e) the review written by the professional critic, who wants his name mentioned in the publisher's advertisements, beginning "Far and away the greatest . . ."

Savannah River Payday

A QUARTER of a mile down the river the partly devoured carcasses of five or six mules that had been killed during the past two weeks by the heat and overwork at the sawmill, lay rotting in the mid-afternoon sun. Of the hundred or more buzzards hovering around the flesh, some were perched drowsily on the cypress stumps, and some were strutting aimlessly over the cleared ground. Every few minutes one of the buzzards, with a sound like wagon-rumble on a wooden bridge, beat the sultry air with its wings and pecked and clawed at the decaying flesh. Dozens of the vultures glided overhead hour after hour in monotonous circles.

The breeze that had been coming up the river since early that morning shifted to the east and the full stench of sun-rotted mule-flesh settled over the swamp. The July sun blazed over the earth and shriveled the grass and weeds until they were as dry as crisp autumn leaves. A cloud of dense black smoke blew over from the other side of the river when somebody threw an armful of fat pine on the fire under the moonshine still.

Jake blew his nose on the ground and asked Red for a smoke. Red gave him a cigarette.

"What time's it now, Red?"

Red took his watch from his overalls pocket and showed it to Jake.

"Looks to me like it's about three o'clock," he told Red.

Red jerked the pump out of the dust and kicked at the punctured tire. The air escaped just as fast as he could pump it in. There was nothing in the old car to patch the tube with.

Jake spat at the Negro's head on the running-board and grabbed Red's arm.

"That nigger's stinkin' worse than them mules, Red. Let's run that tire flat so we can git to town and git shed of him. I don't like to waste time around that smell."

Red was open to any suggestion. The sweat had been running down his face and over his chest and wetting his breeches. He had been pumping for half an hour trying to get some air into the tire. It had been flat when they left the sawmill.

Jake cranked up the engine and they got in and started up the road towards town. It was three miles to town from the sawmill.

The old automobile rattled up the road through the deep yellow dust. The sun was so hot it made the air feel like steam when it was breathed into the lungs. Most of the water had leaked from the radiator, and the engine knocked like ten-pound hammers on an anvil. Red did not care about the noise as long as he could get where he was going.

Half a mile up the road was Hog Creek. When they got to the top of the hill Red shut off the engine. The car rolled down to the creek and stopped on the bridge.

"Git some water for the radiator, Jake," Red said. He reached in the back seat and pulled out a tin can for Jake to carry the water in.

Jake crawled out of the car and stretched his arms and legs. He wiped the sweat off his face with his shirt-tail.

"Don't hurry me," Jake said, leaning against the car. "Ain't no hurry for nothin'."

Red got tired holding the can. He threw it at Jake. Jake dodged it and the can rolled off the bridge down into the creek. Red propped his feet on the windshield and got ready to take a nap while Jake was going for the water.

Jake walked around to the other side of the car and looked at the Negro. The hot sun had swollen the lips until they curled over and touched the nose and chin. The Negro had tripped-up that morning when he tried to get out of the way of a falling cypress tree.

"What's this nigger's name?" he asked Red.

"Jim somethin'," Red grunted, trying to sleep.

Jake turned the head over with his foot so he could see the face. He happened to think that he might have known him.

"God Almighty!" he said, shaking Red by the arm. "Hand me that monkey-wrench quick, Red."

Red lifted up the back seat and found the monkey-wrench. He got out and handed it to Jake.

"What's the matter, Jake? What's the matter with the nigger?"

Jake picked up a stick and pushed back the Negro's lips.

"Look at them gold teeth, Red," he pointed.

Red squatted beside the running-board and tried to count the gold teeth.

"Here, Red, you take this stick and hold his mouth open while I knock off that gold."

Red took the stick and pushed the lips away from the teeth. Jake choked the monkey-wrench half-way and tapped on the first tooth. He had to hit it about six or seven times before it broke off and fell on the bridge. Red picked it up and rubbed the dirt off on his overalls.

"How much is it worth, Jake?" he asked, bouncing the tooth in the palm of his hand trying to feel the weight.

"About two dollars," Jake said. "Maybe more."

Jake took the tooth and weighed it in his hand.

"Hold his mouth open and let me knock out the rest of them," Jake said. He picked up the monkey-wrench and choked it half-way. "There's about three or four more, looks like to me."

Red pushed the Negro's lips away from the teeth while Jake hammered away at the gold. The sun had made the teeth so hot they burned his fingers when he picked them off the bridge.

"You keep two and give me three," Red said. "It's my car we're totin' him to town in."

"Like hell I will," Jake said. "I found them, didn't I? Well, I got the right to keep three myself if I want to."

Red jerked the monkey-wrench off the running-board and socked Jake on the head with it. The blow was only hard enough to stun him. Jake reeled around on the bridge like he was dead drunk and fell against the radiator. Red followed him up and socked him again. A ball of skin and hair fell in the dust. He took all the gold teeth and put them into his overalls pocket.

Jake was knocked out cold. Red shook him and kicked him, but Jake didn't move. Red dragged him around to the back seat and threw him inside and shut the door. Then he cranked up the car and started to town. The tire that was punctured had dropped off the wheel somewhere down the road and there was nothing left except the rim to ride on.

Red had gone a little over a mile from the bridge when Jake came to himself and sat up on the back seat. He was still a little dizzy, but he knew what he was doing.

"Hold on a minute, Red," he shouted. "Stop this automobile."

Red shut off the engine and the car rolled to a stop. He got out in the road.

"What you want now, Jake?" he asked him.

"Look, Red," he pointed across the cottonfield beside the road. "Look what's yonder, Red."

A mulatto girl was chopping cotton about twenty rows from the road. Red started across the field after her before Jake could get out. They stumbled over the cotton rows kicking up the plants with every step.

Jake caught up with Red before they reached the girl. When they were only two rows away, she dropped her hoe and started running towards the woods.

"Hey, there!" Jake shouted. "Don't you run off!"

He picked up a heavy sun-baked clod and heaved it at her as hard as he could. She turned around and tried to dodge it; but she could not get out of the way in time, and it struck her full on the forehead.

Red got to her first. The girl rubbed her head and tried to get up. He pushed her down again.

Jake came running up. He tried to kick her dress above her waist with his foot.

"Wait a minute," Red said. He shoved Jake off his feet. "I got here first."

"That don't cut no ice with me," Jake said. He started for Red and butted him down. Then he stood over him and tried to stomp Red's head with his heels.

Red got away and picked up the girl's hoe and swung it with all his might at Jake's head. The sharp blade caught Jake on the right side of his head and sliced his ear off close to his face. Jake fell back and felt his face and looked at the ear on the ground.

Red turned around to grab the girl, but she was gone. She was nowhere in sight.

"Come on, Jake," he said. "She run off. Let's git to town and dump that nigger. I want 'bout a dozen good stiff drinks. I don't work all week and let payday git by without tankin' up good and plenty."

Jake tore one of the sleeves out of his shirt and made a bandage to tie around his head. It did not bleed so much after that.

Red went back to the car and waited for Jake. The dead Negro on the running-board was a hell of a lot of trouble. If it had not been for him, the girl would not have got scared and run away.

They got into the car again and started to town. They had to get to the undertaker's before six o'clock, because he closed up at that time; and they did not want to have to carry the dead Negro around with them all day Sunday.

"What time's it now, Red?" Jake asked him.

Red pulled out his watch and showed it to Jake.

"Looks like it's about five o'clock," Jake told him.

Red put the watch back into his overalls pocket.

It was about a mile and a half to town yet, and there was a black cloud coming up like there might be a big thunder-storm. The old car had got hot again because they did not get the water at Hog Creek, and the engine was knocking so hard it could be heard half a mile away.

Suddenly the storm broke overhead and the water came down in bucketfuls. There was no place to stop where they could get out of the rain and there was no top on the car. Red opened the throttle as wide as it would go and tried to get to town in a hurry. The rain cooled the engine and made the car run faster.

When they got to the edge of town, the old car was running faster than it ever had. The rain came down harder and harder all the time. It was a cloudburst, all right.

Then suddenly one of the cylinders went dead, and the machine slowed down a little. In a minute two more of the cylinders went dead at the same time, and the car could barely move on the one that was left. The rain would drown that one out, too, in a little while.

The car went as far as the poolroom and stopped dead. All the cylinders were full of water.

"Git out, Red," Jake shouted. "I'll bet you a quart of corn I can beat you five games of pool."

Red was right behind Jake. The rain had soaked every thread of their clothes.

The men in the poolroom asked Jake and Red where they got the Negro and what they were going to do with him.

"We're takin' him to the undertaker's when the shower's over," Red said. "He got tripped-up down at the sawmill this mornin'. Right on payday, too."

Some of the hounds that were not too lazy went out in the rain and smelled the Negro on the running-board.

One of the men told Jake he had better go to the drugstore and have his head fixed. Jake said he couldn't be bothered.

Jake beat Red the first four games, and then Red wanted to bet two quarts that he could win the last game. He laid a ragged five-dollar bill on the table, for a side bet. Jake covered that with a bill that was even more ragged.

Red had the break on the fifth game. He slammed away with his stick and lucked the eleven-ball, the fifteen, the nine, and the four-ball.

"Hell," Jake said, "I'll spot you that thirty-nine and beat you." He chalked his stick and got ready to make a run, after Red missed his next shot. "All I want is one good shot and I'll make game before I stop runnin' them. We shoot pool where I come from."

Jake made the one, two, three, and lucked the twelve-ball. He chalked his cue again and got ready to run the five-ball in.

Just as he was tapping the cue-ball somebody on the other side of the table started talking out loud.

"He ain't no pool shot," the man laughed. "I bet he don't make that five-ball."

Jake missed.

Before anybody knew what was happening, Jake had swung the leaded butt-end of his cue-stick at the man's head with all his might. The man fell against another table and struck his head on a sharp-edged spittoon. A four-inch gash had been opened on his head by the stick, and blood was running through a crack in the floor.

"I'll teach these smart guys how to talk when I'm shootin' pool," Jake said. "I bet he don't open his trap like that no more."

The man was carried down to the doctor's office to get his head sewed up.

Red took two shots and made game. Jake was ready to pay off.

They went out the back door and got the corn in a half-gallon jug. Jake took half a dozen swallows and handed the jug over to Red. Red drank till the jug was half full. Then they went back into the poolroom to shoot some more pool.

A man came running in from the street and told Jake and Red the marshal was outside waiting to see them.

"What does he want now?" Red asked him.

"He says he wants you-all to tote that nigger down to the undertaker's before he stinks the whole town up."

Jake took another half-dozen swallows out of the jug and handed it over to Red.

"Say," Jake said, falling against one of the tables, "you go tell that marshal that I said for him to take a long runnin' start and jump to hell.—Me and Red's shootin' pool!"

When an author completes a new book, it is customary for it to be read by various persons before it can be sent to the printer. Most authors allot twelve or fourteen months for this reading period, but that is because most authors are by nature optimistic. Taking into consideration not only the number of pre-publication readers involved, but the types of readers as well, it is nowadays considered remarkable when these readings can be accomplished within a year and a half. It is extremely unlikely that any book was ever published without first being read by (a) the author's wife, who studies the manuscript minutely in an endeavor to find out if the proceeds from its sale will enable her to buy a new frock; (b) the author's literary agent, who reads it in order to be able to estimate how much commission he can safely count on receiving; (c) the publisher's editorial adviser, who weighs it carefully for literary merit and circulating library appeal; (d) the publisher's sales manager, who must consider its potential commercial value after the jobber in Boston, who hates yellow, sees the binding; (e) the publisher's attorney, who scans the manuscript for passages that may be construed to be libelous in Los Angeles; (f) the publisher's wife, who passes judgment on the author's wife's taste in clothes; and (g) the publisher's secretary, so she will be able to tell her boss what the book is about in case it becomes a bestseller.

Nine Dollars' Worth of Mumble

You couldn't see no stars, you couldn't see no moon, you couldn't see nothing much but a measly handful of sparks on the chimney spout. It was a mighty poor beginning for a courting on a ten o'clock night. Hollering didn't do a bit of good, and stomping up and down did less.

Youster swung the meal sack from his right shoulder to his left. Carrying around a couple of hobbled rabbits wasn't much fun. They kicked and they squealed, and they kept his mind from working on a way to get into that house where Sis was.

He stooped 'way down and felt around on the road for a handful of rocks. When he found enough, he pitched them at the house where they would make the most noise.

"Go away from here and stop pestering us, Youster Brown," that old pinch-faced woman said through the door. "I've got Sis right where my eyes can see her, and that's where she's going to stay. You go on and get yourself away from here, Youster Brown."

"Woman," Youster shouted, "you shut your big mouth and open up that door! I reckon you must be so pinched-faced, you scared of the night-time."

"The night-time is one time when I ain't scared, even when you're in it, Youster Brown. Now, go yourself on off somewhere and stop worrying Sis and me."

"Old pinched-faced woman, why you scared to open the door and let me see Sis?" he asked, creeping up closer to the house.

"Because Sis is saving up for a man her worth. She can't be wasting herself on no half-Jim nigger like you. Now, go on off, Youster Brown, and leave us be."

Youster crept a little closer to the door, feeling his way up the path from the road. All he wanted was to see that door unlatch just one little inch, and he would get his way in.

"I've got a little eating-present here for Sis," he said when he got to the doorstep. He waited to hear if that old pinched-faced Matty would come close to the door. "It'll make some mighty good eating, I'm telling you."

"Don't you go bringing no white-folks' stole chickens around here, Youster Brown," she said. "I don't have nothing to do with white-folks' stole chickens, and you know I don't."

"Woman, these here ain't chickens. They ain't nothing like chickens. They ain't even got feathers on them. These here is plump rabbits I gummed in my own cotton patch."

"Lay them on the doorsill, and then back off to the big road," she said. "I wouldn't leave you get a chance to come in that door for a big white mansion on easy street, Youster Brown."

"What you got so heavy against me, Matty?" he asked her. "What's eating on you, anyhow?"

There was no sight or sound for longer than he could hold his breath. When Matty wasn't at the hearth to poke the fire, the sparks stopped coming out the chimney.

"If you so set on knowing what's the matter, you go ask Sally Lucky. She'll tell you in no time."

"Sally Lucky done give me a charm on Sis," Youster said. "I handed over and paid her three dollars and six bits only last week. I'm already sunk seven dollars in Sally Lucky, and all the good she ever done me was to say to come see Sis on every black night there was. That's why I'm standing out here now like I am, because it's a black night, and Sally Lucky says come when it's like it is now."

"You go give Sally Lucky two dollars more right now, and see what happens, Youster Brown. For all that money you'll have a lot coming to you. But you won't never find out nothing standing around here. Sally Lucky'll tell you, so you'll be told for all time."

Youster laid the sack with the two hobbled rabbits in it on the doorstep. Then he backed out to the road. It wasn't long before the door opened a crack, then a foot. Matty's long thin arm reached out, felt around, grabbed the meal sack, and jerked it inside. When she closed the door and latched it, the night was again as black as ever.

He waited around for a while, feeling the wind, and smelling the chimney smoke. He couldn't see why Sis had to grow up and live with an old pinched-faced woman like Matty.

When he got to thinking about Matty, he remembered what she said. He cut across the field toward Sally Lucky's. It didn't take him long when he had no time to lose. When he got to the creek, he crossed it on the log and jogged up the hollow to Sally Lucky's shack.

"Who's that?" Sally Lucky said, when he pounded on the door.

"Youster Brown," he said as loud as he could.

"What you want, Youster?"

"I want a working charm on Sis, or something bad on that old pinched-faced Matty. I done paid you seven, all told, dollars, and it ain't worked for me none yet. It's time it worked, too. If I give you two more dollars, will you make the charm work, and put something bad on Matty, too?"

The shriveled-up old Sally Lucky opened the door and stuck her head out on her thin neck. She squinted at him in the dark, and felt to see if he had a gun or knife in his pockets. She had been putting up her hair for the night, and half was up on one side of her head, and half down on the other. She looked all wore out.

"You sure look like you is the right somebody to put things on folks," Youster said, gulping and shaking. "If you is, now's the time to prove it to me. Man alive, I'm needing things on folks, if ever I did."

"Let me see your money, Youster," she said, taking him inside and sitting down in her chair on the hearth. "What kind of money you got on you?"

He took out all the money he had in the world—four half-dollar pieces—and put it on the fingers of her hand.

"I'm getting dog-tired of handing you over all my money, and not getting no action for it," Youster said. "Look here, now, woman, is you able to do things or ain't you?"

"You know Ham Beaver, don't you?"

"I reckon I know Ham. I saw him day before yesterday. What about him?"

"I gave him a charm on a yellow girl six miles down the creek, and he went and got her all for himself before the week was over."

"Maybe so," Youster said. "But I paid you seven dollars, all told, before now, for a charm on Sis, and I ain't got no sign of action for it. That old pinched-faced woman Matty just locks up the door and won't let me in when I want in."

"What you need is a curse on Matty," Sally Lucky said. "A curse is what you want, and for nine dollars, all told, you appear to be due one, Youster."

"It won't get me in no trouble with the law, will it?" he asked, shaking. "The law is one thing I don't want no trouble with no more at all."

"All my charms and curses are private dealings," she said, shaking her finger at him until he trembled more than ever. "As long as you do like I tell you, and keep your mouth shut, you won't have no trouble with the law. I see to that."

"I has bought charms before, and they didn't make no trouble for me. But I ain't never before in my life bought a curse on nobody. I just want to make sure I ain't going to get in no trouble with the law. I'm positive about that."

He studied the hickory-log fire for a while, and spat on an ember. He couldn't be afraid of the law as long as he had Sally Lucky on his side. And he figured nine dollars' worth was plenty to keep her on his side.

Sally Lucky picked up her poker and began sticking it into the fire. Sparks swirled in the fireplace and disappeared out of sight up the chimney. Youster watched her, sitting on the edge of his chair. He was in a big hurry, and he hoped it wouldn't take her long this time to see what she was looking for in the fire.

All at once she began to mutter to herself, saying things so fast that Youster could not understand what the words were. He got down on his hands and knees and peered into the blazing fire, trying to see with his own eyes what Sally Lucky saw. While he was looking so hard, Sally Lucky started saying things faster and faster. He knew then that she was talking to Matty, and putting the curse on her.

He was as trembly as Sally Lucky was by then. He crept so close to the fire that he could barely keep his eyes open in that heat. Then as suddenly as she had begun, Sally Lucky picked up a rusty tomato-can partly filled with water, and dashed it into the fire. The water sizzled, and the logs smoked and hissed, and a sharp black face could be seen in the fire.

Youster got back on his chair and waited. Sally Lucky kept on mumbling to herself, but the double-talk was dying down, and before long no sound came through her jerking lips.

"You sure must be real sure enough conjur, Sally Lucky," Youster said weakly.

She put a small tin snuff-can into his hand, closing her fingers over it. He could feel that it was heavy, heavier than a can of snuff. It rattled, too, like it had been partly filled with BB shot.

Sally Lucky didn't say another thing until she took him to the door. There she pushed him outside, and said:

"Whenever you think the curse ain't working like it ought to, just take out that snuff-can, Youster, and shake it a little."

"Like it was dice?"

"Just exactly like it was dice."

She shut the door and barred it.

Youster put the can into his pocket, and kept his hand in there with it so he wouldn't have a chance in the world to lose it. He ran down the creek as fast as he could, crossed it on the log, and cut across the field toward the big road where Sis and Matty lived.

There still was no light anywhere in the night. When he got closer to the house, he could see a handful of sparks come out the chimney spout every once in a while when Matty poked the hickory-log fire.

He strode up to the front door as big as a bill-collector. There wasn't nothing to make him scared of that old pinched-faced Matty no more.

"Open up," he said, pounding on the door.

"That you, Youster Brown, again?" Matty said on the inside.

"I reckon it is," Youster said. "It ain't nobody else. Open this here door up, woman, before I take it off its hinges. I ain't got no time to lose."

"You sure do talk big for a half-Jim nigger, Youster Brown. Ain't you got no sense? Don't you know that big talk don't scare me none at all?"

"The talk maybe don't, but the conjur do," Youster said. "Woman, I got a curse on you."

"You is?"

"Don't you feel it none?"

"I don't feel nothing but a draft on my back."

Youster took the snuff-can out of his pocket and shook it in his hand. He shook it like it was a pair of dice.

"Come on, can, do your work," he said to the snuff-box in his hand. "Get down on your knees and do your nine dollars' worth!"

While he waited for the can to put the curse into action, he listened through the door. There was no sound in there, except the occasional squeak of Matty's rocking-chair on the hearth.

"I don't hear Sis in there," Youster said. "Where you at, Sis?"

"Sis is minding her own business," Matty told him. "You go on off somewhere and mind yours. Sis ain't studying about you, anyhow."

"Why ain't she?" Youster shouted. "Sis is my woman, and my woman ought to be studying about me all the time."

"You sure do talk like all the big-headed half-Jim niggers I ever knew," Matty said. "Just because you paid seven dollars to Sally Lucky for a charm on Sis, you get the notion in the head that Sis's your woman. Nigger, if I had only your sense, I wouldn't know which end to stand on."

"That talk don't fool me none," Youster told her. "The way that gal cut her eyes at me last Sunday showed me the way to go home. I reckon I know when the best is yet to come."

Youster rubbed the snuff-box in his hands, feeling its slick surface and good warmth. He held his breath while he listened through the door.

"I can afford to put off getting her for a while," he said through the cracks, "being as how this curse is going to be working on you."

"What curse?" Matty said.

"The curse I just a while ago got Sally Lucky to put on you for me, that's what. I paid her two dollars for it. That makes nine, all told, dollars I've paid out. All I don't feel right about is that I waited all this time before I got a curse put on you. I ought to have had it working on you all this past summer and fall."

"If you paid nine dollars to Sally Lucky for putting something on me, Youster Brown, all you got was just nine dollars' worth of mumble."

"How come?" Youster said.

"Because I paid Sally Lucky three dollars for a curse on you the first time I ever saw you, that's how come," Matty said. "And that's how come all your big talk about getting a charm on Sis and a curse on me won't never come to nothing. Charms and curses won't cross, Youster Brown, because it's the one that's taken out first that does the work, and that's how come the curse I took out on you took, and the ones you took out on Sis and me won't take. I saw you coming, Youster Brown, and I didn't lose no time taking out the curse on you."

Youster sat down on the step. He looked down the path toward the road and across the field toward Sally Lucky's. He fingered the snuff-can for a while.

There came a squeak from the chair through the door, but there was no other sound. The black night was pulling down all around him. He couldn't see nothing, nowhere. There wasn't no sense in night being black like the bottom of a hole. After a while he got up and went off down the road. He was trying his best to think of some way to get his nine dollars back. Nine dollars was a lot of money to pay for mumble.

Candy-Man Beechum

It was ten miles out of the Ogeechee swamps, from the saw mill to the top of the ridge, but it was just one big step to Candy-Man. The way he stepped over those Middle Georgia gullies was a sight to see.

"Where you goin', Candy-Man?"

"Make way for these flapping feet, boy, because I'm going for to see my gal. She's standing on the tips of her toes waiting for me now."

The rabbits lit out for the hollow logs where those stomping big feet couldn't get nowhere near them.

"Don't tread on no white-folks' toes, Candy-Man," Little Bo said. "Because the white-folks is first come."

Candy-Man Beechum flung a leg over the rail fence just as if it had been a hoe-handle to straddle. He stood for a minute astride the fence, looking at the black boy. It was getting dark in the swamps, and he had ten miles to go.

"Me and white-folks don't mix," Candy-Man told him, "just as long as they leave me be. I skin their mules for them, and I snake their cypress logs, but when the day is done, I'm long gone where the white-folks ain't are."

Owls in the trees began to take on life. Those whooing birds were glad to see that setting sun.

The black boy in the mule yard scratched his head and watched the sun go down. If he didn't have all those mules to feed, and if he had had a two-bit piece in his pocket, he'd have liked to tag along with Candy-Man. It was Saturday night, and there'd be a barrelful of cat-fish frying in town that evening. He wished he had some of that good-smelling cat.

"Before the time ain't long," Little Bo said, "I'm going to get me myself a gal."

"Just be sure she ain't Candy-Man's, boy, and I'll give you a helping hand."

He flung the other leg over the split-rail fence and struck out for the high land. Ten miles from the swamps to the top of the ridge, and his trip would be done. The bushes whipped around his legs, where his legs had been. He couldn't be waiting for the back-strike of no swamp-country bushes. Up the log road, and across the bottom land, taking three corn rows at a stride, Candy-Man Beechum was on his way.

There were some colored boys taking their time in the big road. He was up on them before they had time to turn their heads around.

"Make way for these flapping feet, boys," he shouted. "Here I come!"

"Where you going, Candy-Man?"

They had to do a lot of running to keep up with him. They had to hustle to match those legs four feet long. He made their breath come short.

"Somebody asked me where I'm going," Candy-Man said. "I got me a yellow gal, and I'm on my way to pay her some attention."

"You'd better toot your horn, Candy-Man, before you open her door. Yellow gals don't like to be taken by surprise."

"Boy, you're tooting the truth, except that you don't know the why-for of what you're saying. Candy-Man's gal always waits for him right at the door."

"Saturday-night bucks sure have to hustle along. They have to strike pay before the Monday-morning whistle starts whipping their ears."

The boys fell behind, stopping to blow and wheeze. There was no keeping up, on a Saturday night, with the seven-foot mule skinner on his way.

The big road was too crooked and curvy for Candy-Man. He struck out across the fields, headed like a plumb-line for a dishful of frying catfish. The lights of the town came up to meet him in the face like a swarm of lightning-bugs. Eight miles to town, and two more to go, and he'd be rapping on that yellow gal's door.

Back in the big road, when the big road straightened out, Candy-Man swung into town. The old folks riding, and the young ones walking, they all made way for those flapping feet. The mules to the buggies and the sports in the middle of the road all got aside to let him through.

"What's your big hurry, Candy-Man?"

"Take care my dust don't choke you blind, niggers. I'm on my way."

"Where to, Candy-Man?"

"I got a gal what's waiting right at her door. She don't like for to be kept waiting."

"Better slow down and cool those heels, Candy-Man, because you're coming to the white-folks' town. They don't like niggers stepping on their toes."

"When the sun goes down, I'm on my own. I can't be stopping to see what color people be."

The old folks clucked, and the mules began to trot. They didn't like the way that big coon talked.

"How about taking me along, Candy-Man?" the young bucks begged. "I'd like to grab me a chicken off a henhouse roost."

"Where I'm going I'm the cock of the walk. I gouge my spurs in all strange feathers. Stay away, black boy, stay away."

Down the street he went, sticking to the middle of the road. The sidewalks couldn't hold him when he was in a hurry like that. A plateful of frying catfish, and he would be on his way. That yellow gal was waiting, and there was no time to lose. Eight miles covered, and two short ones to go. That saw-mill fireman would have to pull on that Monday-morning whistle like it was the rope to the promised land.

The smell of the fish took him straight to the fish-house door. Maybe they were mullets, but they smelled just as good. There wasn't enough time to order up a special dish of fins.

He had his hand on the restaurant door. When he had his supper, he would be on his way. He could see that yellow gal waiting for him only a couple of miles away.

All those boys were sitting at their meal. The room was full of hungry people just like him. The stove was full of frying fish, and the barrel was only half-way used. There was enough good eating for a hundred hungry men.

He still had his hand on the fish-house door, and his nose was soaking it in. If he could have his way about it, some of these days he was going to buy himself a whole big barrel of catfish and eat them every one.

"What's your hurry, Candy-Man?"

"No time to waste, white-boss. Just let me be."

The night policeman snapped open the handcuffs, and reached for his arms. Candy-Man stepped away.

"I reckon I'd better lock you up. It'll save a lot of trouble. I'm getting good and tired of chasing fighting niggers all over town every Saturday night."

"I never hurt a body in all my life, white-boss. And I sure don't pick fights. You must have the wrong nigger, white-boss. You sure has got me wrong. I'm just passing through for to see my gal."

"I reckon I'll play safe and lock you up till Monday morning just the same. Reach out your hands for these cuffs, nigger."

Candy-Man stepped away. His yellow gal was on his mind. He didn't feel like passing her up for no iron-bar jail. He stepped away.

"I'll shoot you down, nigger. One more step, and I'll blast away."

"White-boss, please just let me be. I won't even stop to get my supper, and I'll shake my legs right out of town. Because I just got to see my gal before the Monday-morning sun comes up."

Candy-Man stepped away. The night policeman threw down the handcuffs and jerked out his gun. He pulled the trigger at Candy-Man, and Candy-Man fell down.

"There wasn't no cause for that, white-boss. I'm just a big black nigger with itching feet. I'd a heap rather be traveling than standing still."

The people came running, but some of them turned around and went the other way. Some stood and looked at Candy-Man while he felt his legs to see if they could hold him up. He still had two miles to go before he could reach the top of the ridge.

The people crowded around, and the night policeman put away his gun. Candy-Man tried to get up so he could be getting on down the road. That yellow gal of his was waiting for him at her door, straining on the tips of her toes.

"White-boss, I sure am sorry you had to go and shoot me down. I never bothered white-folks, and they sure oughtn't bother me. But there ain't much use in living if that's the way it's going to be. I reckon I'll just have to blow out the light and fade away. Just reach me a blanket so I can cover my skin and bones."

"Shut up, nigger," the white-boss said. "If you keep on talking with that mouth of yours, I'll just have to pull out my gun again and hurry you on."

The people drew back to where they wouldn't be standing too close. The night policeman put his hand on the butt of his gun, where it would be handy, in case.

"If that's the way it's to be, then make way for Candy-Man Beechum, because here I come."

When you moved into this Hollywood picture factory, you soon found out that the important thing was to learn how to keep your couch. You lost face overnight if somebody stuck his head through your office door and saw that your couch was missing. Getting into the swing of the thing was tough at first. One day you would get down to business and turn in a thick pile of script, and of course the word would travel along the grapevine and before you know it you would look up and see two hefty guys lugging in your couch. The next day, let us say, you would feel like letting things go for a while, and not turn in any script at all, and before long these same two guys would come in and lug out your couch. After a couple of weeks of that sort of thing you would catch on to what those masterminds in the front office were doing to you. You could then beat them at their own game by writing up a big batch of script one day and turning it in in driblets, a little every day, and you never lost your couch again after that.

We Are Looking at You, Agnes

THERE must be a way to get it over with. If somebody would only say something about it, instead of looking at me all the time as they do, when I am in the room, there wouldn't be any more days like this one. But no one ever says a word about it. They sit and look at me all the time—like that—but not even Papa says anything.

Why don't they go ahead and say it—why don't they do something— They know it; everyone knows it now. Everybody looks at me like that, but nobody ever says a word about it.

Papa knows perfectly well that I never went to business college with the money he sent me. Why doesn't he say so— He put me on the train and said, Be a good little girl, Agnes. Just before the train left he gave me fifty dollars, and promised to send me the same amount monthly through October. When I reached Birmingham, I went to a beauty-culture school and learned how to be a manicurist with the money he sent me. Everybody at home thought I was studying shorthand at the business college. They thought I was a stenographer in Birmingham, but I was a manicurist in a three-chair barbership. It was not long until in some way everybody at home found out what I was doing. Why didn't they tell me then that they knew what I was doing— Why didn't they say something about it——

Ask me, Papa, why I became a manicurist instead of learning to be a stenographer. After you ask me that, I'll tell you why I'm not even a manicurist in a three-chair barbershop any longer. But say something about it. Say you know it; say you know what I do; say anything. Please, for God's sake, don't sit there all day long and look at me like that without saying something about it. Tell me that you have always known it; tell me anything, Papa.

How can you know what I am by sitting there and looking at me— How do you know I'm not a stenographer— How am I different from everybody else in town——

How did you know I went to Nashville—ask me why I went there, then. Say it; please, Papa, say it. Say anything, but don't sit there and look at me like that. I can't stand it another minute. Ask me, and I'll tell you the truth about everything.

I found a job in a barbershop in Nashville. It was even a cheaper place than the one in Birmingham, where the men came in and put their hands down the neck of my dress and squeezed me; it was the cheapest place I had ever heard about. After that I went to Memphis, and worked in a barbershop there a while. I was never a stenographer. I can't read a single line of shorthand. But I know all about manicuring, if I haven't forgotten it by this time.

After that I went to New Orleans. I wished to work in a fine place like the St. Charles. But they looked at me just like you are doing, and said they didn't need anyone else in the barbershop. They looked at me, just like Mamma is looking at me now, but they didn't say anything about it. Nobody ever says anything about it, but everybody looks at me like that.

I had to take a job in a cheap barbershop in New Orleans. It was a cheaper place than the one in Memphis, or the one in Nashville. It was near Canal Street, and the men who came in did the same things the men in Birmingham and Nashville and Memphis had done. The men came in and put their hands down the neck of my dress and squeezed me, and then they sat down and talked to me about things I had never heard of until I went to Birmingham to be a stenographer. The barbers talked to me, too, but nobody ever said anything about it. They knew it; but no one ever said it. I was soon making more money on the outside after hours than I was at the table. That's why I left and went to live in a cheap hotel. The room clerk looked at me like that, too, but he didn't say anything about it. Nobody ever does. Everyone looks at me like that, but there is never a word said about it.

The whole family knows everything I have done since I left home nearly five years ago to attend business college in Birmingham. They sit and look at me, talking about everything else they can think of, but they never ask me what I'm doing for a living. They never ask me what company I work for in Birmingham, and they never ask me how I like stenography. They never mention it. Why don't you ask me about my boss— But you know I don't work for a company. You know everything about me, so why don't you say something to me about it——

If somebody would only say it, I could leave now and never have to come back again once a year at Christmas. I've been back once a year for four years now. You've known all about it for four years, so why don't you say something— Say it, and it then will be all over with.

Please ask me how I like my job in Birmingham, Mamma. Mamma, say, Are your hours too long, Agnes—have you a comfortable apartment—is your salary enough for you— Mamma, say something to me. Ask me something; I'll not tell you a lie. I wish you would ask me something so I could tell you the truth. I've got to tell somebody, anybody. Don't sit there and look at me once a year at Christmas like that. Everyone knows I live in a cheap hotel in New Orleans, and that I'm not a stenographer. I'm not even a manicurist any longer. Ask me what I do for a living, Mamma. Don't sit there and look at me once a year at Christmas like that and not say it.

Why is everyone afraid to say it—I'll not be angry; I'll not even cry. I'll be so glad to get it over with that I'll laugh. Please don't be afraid to say it; please stop looking at me like that once a year at Christmas and go ahead and say it.

Elsie sits all day looking at me without ever asking me if she may come to visit me in Birmingham. Why don't you ask me, Elsie— I'll tell you why you can't. Go ahead and ask if you may visit me in Birmingham. I'll tell you why. Because if you went back with me you'd go to New Orleans and the men would come in and put their hands down the collar of your frock. That's why you can't go back to Birmingham with me. But you do believe I live in Birmingham, don't you, Elsie— Ask me about the city, then. Ask me what street I live on. Ask me if my window in Birmingham faces the east or west, north or south. Say something, Elsie; isn't anyone ever going to ask me anything, or say something——

I'm not afraid; I'm a grown woman now. Talk to me as you would to anyone else my age. Just say one little something, and I'll have the chance to tell you. After that I'll leave and never come back again once a year at Christmas.

An hour ago Lewis came home and sat down in the parlor, but he didn't ask me a single question about myself. He didn't say anything. How does he know— Lewis, can you tell just by looking at me, too— Is that how everyone knows— Please tell me what it is about me that everyone knows. And if everyone knows, why doesn't someone say something about it— If you would only say it, Lewis, it would be all over with. I'd never have to come home again once a year at Christmas and be made to sit here and have everyone look at me like that but never saying anything about it.

Lewis sits there on the piano stool looking at me but not saying anything to me. How did you find it out, Lewis— Did someone tell you, or do you just know— I wish you would say something, Lewis. If you will only do that, it will be all over with. I'd never have to come back home once a year at Christmas and sit here like this.

Mamma won't even ask me what my address is. She acts as though I went upstairs and slept a year, coming down once a year at Christmas. Mamma, I've been away from home a whole year. Don't you care to ask me what I've been doing all that time— Go ahead and ask me, Mamma. I'll tell you the truth. I'll tell you the perfect truth about myself.

Doesn't she care about writing to me—doesn't she care about my writing to her— Mamma, don't you want my address so you can write to me and tell me how everyone is— Every time I leave they all stand around and look at me and never ask when I'm coming back again. Why don't they say it— If Mamma would only say it, instead of looking at me like that, it would be better for all of us. I'd never have to come back home again, and they'd never have to sit all day and look at me like that. Why don't you say something to me, Mamma— For God's sake, Mamma, don't sit there all day long and not say a word to me.

Mamma hasn't even asked me if I am thinking of marrying. I heard her ask Elsie that this morning while I was in the bathroom. Elsie is six years younger than me, and Mamma asks Elsie that but she has never asked me since I went to Birmingham five years ago to study shorthand. They don't even tell me about the people I used to know in town. They don't even say good-by when I leave.

If Papa will only say something about it, instead of looking at me like that all the time, I'll get out and stay out forever. I'll never come home again as long as I live, if he will only say it. Why doesn't he ask me if I can find a job for Lewis in Birmingham— Ask me to take him back to Birmingham and look after him to see that he gets along all right from the start, Papa. Ask me that, Papa. Please, Papa, ask me that; ask me something else then, and give me a chance to tell you. Please ask me that and stop sitting there looking at me like that. Don't you care if Lewis has a job— You don't want him to stay here and do nothing, do you— You don't want him to go downtown every night after supper and shoot craps until midnight, do you, Papa— Ask me if I can help Lewis find a job in Birmingham; ask me that, Papa.

I've got to tell somebody about myself. You know already, but I've got to tell you just the same. I've got to tell you so I can leave home and never have to come back once a year at Christmas. I went to Birmingham and took the money to study manicuring. Then I found a job in a barbershop and sat all day long at a little table behind a screen in the rear. A man came in and put his hand down the neck of my dress and squeezed me until I screamed. I went to Nashville, to Memphis, to New Orleans. Every time I sat down at the manicurist's table in the rear of a barbershop, men came in and put their hands down my dress.

If they would only say something it would be all over with. But they sit and look, and talk about something else all day long. That's the way it's been once a year at Christmas for four or five years. It's been that way ever since I took the money Papa gave me and went to Birmingham to study stenography at the business college. Papa knows I was a manicurist in a barbershop all the time I was there. Papa knows, but Papa won't say it. Say something, Papa. Please say something, so I can tell you what I do for a living. You know it already, and all the others, too; but I can't tell you until you say something about it. Mamma, say something; Lewis, say something. Somebody, anybody, say something.

For God's sake, say something about it this time so I won't have to come back again next year at Christmas and sit here all day in the parlor while you look at me. Everybody looks at me like that, but nobody ever says it. Mamma makes Elsie stay out of my room while I'm dressing, and Papa sends Lewis downtown every hour or two. If they would only say something, it would be all over with. But they sit all day long in the parlor, and look at me without saying it.

After every meal Mamma takes the dishes I have used and scalds them at the sink. Why don't they say it, so I'll never have to come back——

Papa takes a cloth soaked in alcohol and wipes the chair I've been sitting in every time I get up and leave the room. Why don't you go ahead and say it——

Everyone sits in the parlor and looks at me all day long. Elsie and Lewis, Mamma and Papa, they sit on the other side of the room and look at me all day long. Don't they know I'll tell them the truth if they would only ask me— Ask me, Papa; I'll tell you the truth, and never come back again. You can throw away your cloth soaked in alcohol after I've gone. So ask me. For God's sake, say something to me about it.

Once a year at Christmas they sit and look at me, but none of them ever says anything about it. They all sit in the parlor saying to themselves, We are looking at you, Agnes.

This story was begun in New York, thrown away in Pittsburgh, begun again in Chicago, and completed in New York.

Kneel to the Rising Sun

A SHIVER went through Lonnie. He drew his hand away from his sharp chin, remembering what Clem had said. It made him feel now as if he were committing a crime by standing in Arch Gunnard's presence and allowing his face to be seen.

He and Clem had been walking up the road together that afternoon on their way to the filling station when he told Clem how much he needed rations. Clem stopped a moment to kick a rock out of the road, and said that if you worked for Arch Gunnard long enough, your face would be sharp enough to split the boards for your own coffin.

As Lonnie turned away to sit down on an empty box beside the gasoline pump, he could not help wishing that he could be as unafraid of Arch Gunnard as Clem was. Even if Clem was a Negro, he never hesitated to ask for rations when he needed something to eat; and when he and his family did not get enough, Clem came right out and told Arch so. Arch stood for that, but he swore that he was going to run Clem out of the country the first chance he got.

Lonnie knew without turning around that Clem was standing at the corner of the filling station with two or three other Negroes and looking at him, but for some reason he was unable to meet Clem's eyes.

Arch Gunnard was sitting in the sun, honing his jack-knife blade on his boot top. He glanced once or twice at Lonnie's hound, Nancy, who was lying in the middle of the road waiting for Lonnie to go home.

"That your dog, Lonnie?"

Jumping with fear, Lonnie's hand went to his chin to hide the lean face that would accuse Arch of short-rationing.

Arch snapped his fingers and the hound stood up, wagging her tail. She waited to be called.

"Mr. Arch, I——"

Arch called the dog. She began crawling towards them on her belly, wagging her tail a little faster each time Arch's fingers snapped. When she was several feet away, she turned over on her back and lay on the ground with her four paws in the air.

Dudley Smith and Jim Weaver, who were lounging around the filling station, laughed. They had been leaning against the side of the building, but they straightened up to see what Arch was up to.

Arch spat some more tobacco juice on his boot top and whetted the jack-knife blade some more.

"What kind of a hound dog is that, anyway, Lonnie?" Arch said. "Looks like to me it might be a ketch hound."

Lonnie could feel Clem Henry's eyes boring into the back of his head. He wondered what Clem would do if it had been his dog Arch Gunnard was snapping his fingers at and calling like that.

"His tail's way too long for a coon hound or a bird dog, ain't it, Arch?" somebody behind Lonnie said, laughing out loud.

Everybody laughed then, including Arch. They looked at Lonnie, waiting to hear what he was going to say to Arch.

"Is he a ketch hound, Lonnie?" Arch said, snapping his finger again.

"Mr. Arch, I——"

"Don't be ashamed of him. Lonnie, if he don't show signs of turning out to be a bird dog or a fox hound. Everybody needs a hound around the house that can go out and catch pigs and rabbits when you are in a hurry for them. A ketch hound is a mighty respectable animal. I've known the time when I was mighty proud to own one."

Everybody laughed.

Arch Gunnard was getting ready to grab Nancy by the tail. Lonnie sat up, twisting his neck until he caught a glimpse of Clem Henry at the other corner of the filling station. Clem was staring at him with unmistakable meaning, with the same look in his eyes he had had that afternoon when he said that nobody who worked for Arch Gunnard ought to stand for short-rationing. Lonnie lowered his eyes. He could not figure out how a Negro could be braver than he was. There were a lot of times like that when he would have given anything he had to be able to jump into Clem's shoes and change places with him.

"The trouble with this hound of yours, Lonnie, is that he's too heavy on his feet. Don't you reckon it would be a pretty slick little trick to lighten the load some, being as how he's a ketch hound to begin with?"

Lonnie remembered then what Clem Henry had said he would do if Arch Gunnard ever tried to cut off his dog's tail. Lonnie knew, and Clem knew, and everybody else knew, that that would give Arch the chance he was waiting for. All Arch asked, he had said, was for Clem Henry to overstep his place just one little half-inch, or to talk back to him with just one little short word, and he would do the rest. Everybody knew what Arch meant by that, especially if Clem did not turn and run. And Clem had not been known to run from anybody, after fifteen years in the country.

Arch reached down and grabbed Nancy's tail while Lonnie was wondering about Clem. Nancy acted as if she thought Arch were playing some kind of a game with her. She turned her head around until she could reach Arch's hand to lick it. He cracked her on the bridge of the nose with the end of the jack-knife.

"He's a mighty playful dog, Lonnie," Arch said, catching up a shorter grip on the tail, "but his wagpole is way too long for a dog his size, especially when he wants to be a ketch hound."

Lonnie swallowed hard.

"Mr. Arch, she's a mighty fine rabbit tracker. I——"

"Shucks, Lonnie," Arch said, whetting the knife blade on the dog's tail, "I ain't never seen a hound in all my life that needed a tail that long to hunt rabbits with. It's way too long for just a common, ordinary, everyday ketch hound."

Lonnie looked up hopefully at Dudley Smith and the others. None of them offered any help. It was useless for him to try to stop Arch, because Arch Gunnard would let nothing stand in his way when once he had set his head on what he wished to do. Lonnie knew that if he should let himself show any anger or resentment, Arch would drive him off the farm before sundown that night. Clem Henry was the only person there who would help him, but Clem . . .

The white men and the Negroes at both corners of the filling station waited to see what Lonnie was going to do about it. All of them hoped he would put up a fight for his hound. If anyone ever had the nerve to stop Arch Gunnard from cutting off a dog's tail, it might put an end to it. It was plain, though, that Lonnie, who was one of Arch's share-croppers, was afraid to speak up. Clem Henry might; Clem was the only one who might try to stop Arch, even if it meant trouble. And all of them knew that Arch would insist on running Clem out of the country, or filling him full of lead.

"I reckon it's all right with you, ain't it, Lonnie?" Arch said. "I don't seem to hear no objections."

Clem Henry stepped forward several paces, and stopped.

Arch laughed, watching Lonnie's face, and jerked Nancy to her feet. The hound cried out in pain and surprise, but Arch made her be quiet by kicking her in the belly.

Lonnie winced. He could hardly bear to see anybody kick his dog like that.

"Mr. Arch, I . . ."

A contraction in his throat almost choked him for several moments, and he had to open his mouth wide and fight for breath. The other white men around him were silent. Nobody liked to see a dog kicked in the belly like that.

Lonnie could see the other end of the filling station from the corner of his eye. He saw a couple of Negroes go up behind Clem and grasp his overalls. Clem spat on the ground, between outspread feet, but he did not try to break away from them.

"Being as how I don't hear no objections, I reckon it's all right to go ahead and cut it off," Arch said, spitting.

Lonnie's head went forward and all he could see of Nancy was her hind feet. He had come to ask for a slab of sowbelly and some molasses, or something. Now he did not know if he could ever bring himself to ask for rations, no matter how much hungrier they became at home.

"I always make it a habit of asking a man first," Arch said. "I wouldn't want to go ahead and cut off a tail if a man had any objections. That wouldn't be right. No, sir, it just wouldn't be fair and square."

Arch caught a shorter grip on the hound's tail and placed the knife blade on it two or three inches from the rump. It looked to those who were watching as if his mouth were watering, because tobacco juice began to trickle down the corners of his lips. He brought up the back of his hand and wiped his mouth.

A noisy automobile came plowing down the road through the deep red dust. Everyone looked up as it passed in order to see who was in it.

Lonnie glanced at it, but he could not keep his eyes raised. His head fell downward once more until he could feel his sharp chin cutting into his chest. He wondered then if Arch had noticed how lean his face was.

"I keep two or three ketch hounds around my place," Arch said, honing the blade on the tail of the dog as if it were a razor strop until his actions brought smiles to the faces of the men grouped around him, "but I never could see the sense of a ketch hound having a long tail. It only gets in their way when I send them out to catch a pig or a rabbit for my supper."

Pulling with his left hand and pushing with his right, Arch Gunnard docked the hound's tail as quickly and as easily as if he were cutting a willow switch in the pasture to drive the cows home with. The dog sprang forward with the release of her tail until she was far beyond Arch's reach, and began howling so loud she could be heard half a mile away. Nancy stopped once and looked back at Arch, and then she sprang to the middle of the road and began leaping and twisting in circles. All that time she was yelping and biting at the bleeding stub of her tail.

Arch leaned backward and twirled the severed tail in one hand while he wiped the jack-knife blade on his boot sole. He watched Lonnie's dog chasing herself around in circles in the red dust.

Nobody had anything to say then. Lonnie tried not to watch his dog's agony, and he forced himself to keep from looking at Clem Henry. Then, with his eyes shut, he wondered why he had remained on Arch Gunnard's plantation all those past years, share-cropping for a mere living on short-rations, and becoming leaner and leaner all the time. He knew then how true it was what Clem had said about Arch's share-croppers' faces becoming sharp enough to hew their own coffins. His hands went to his chin before he knew what he was doing. His hand dropped when he had felt the bones of jaw and the exposed tendons of his cheeks.

As hungry as he was, he knew that even if Arch did give him some rations then, there would not be nearly enough for them to eat for the following week. Hatty, his wife, was already broken down from hunger and work in the fields, and his father, Mark Newsome, stone-deaf for the past twenty years, was always asking him why there was never enough food in the house for them to have a solid meal. Lonnie's head fell forward a little more, and he could feel his eyes becoming damp.

The pressure of his sharp chin against his chest made him so uncomfortable that he had to raise his head at last in order to ease the pain of it.

The first thing he saw when he looked up was Arch Gunnard twirling Nancy's tail in his left hand. Arch Gunnard had a trunk full of dogs' tails at home. He had been cutting off tails ever since anyone could remember, and during all those years he had accumulated a collection of which he was so proud that he kept the trunk locked and the key tied around his neck on a string. On Sunday afternoons when the preacher came to visit, or when a crowd was there to loll on the front porch and swap stories, Arch showed them off, naming each tail from memory just as well as if he had had a tag on it.

Clem Henry had left the filling station and was walking alone down the road towards the plantation. Clem Henry's house was in a cluster of Negro cabins below Arch's big house, and he had to pass Lonnie's house to get there. Lonnie was on the verge of getting up and leaving when he saw Arch looking at him. He did not know whether Arch was looking at his lean face, or whether he was watching to see if he were going to get up and go down the road with Clem.

The thought of leaving reminded him of his reason for being there.

He had to have some rations before suppertime that night, no matter how short they were.

"Mr. Arch, I . . ."

Arch stared at him for a moment, appearing as if he had turned to listen to some strange sound unheard of before that moment.

Lonnie bit his lips, wondering if Arch was going to say anything about how lean and hungry he looked. But Arch was thinking about something else. He slapped his hand on his leg and laughed out loud.

"I sometimes wish niggers had tails," Arch said, coiling Nancy's tail into a ball and putting it into his pocket. "I'd a heap rather cut off nigger tails than dog tails. There'd be more to cut, for one thing."

Dudley Smith and somebody else behind them laughed for a brief moment. The laughter died out almost as suddenly as it had risen.

The Negroes who had heard Arch shuffled their feet in the dust and moved backwards. It was only a few minutes until not one was left at the filling station. They went up the road behind the red wooden building until they were out of sight.

Arch got up and stretched. The sun was getting low, and it was no longer comfortable in the October air. "Well, I reckon I'll be getting on home to get me some supper," he said.

He walked slowly to the middle of the road and stopped to look at Nancy retreating along the ditch.

"Nobody going my way?" he asked. "What's wrong with you, Lonnie? Going home to supper, ain't you?"

"Mr. Arch, I . . ."

Lonnie found himself jumping to his feet. His first thought was to ask for the sowbelly and molasses, and maybe some corn meal; but when he opened his mouth, the words refused to come out. He took several steps forward and shook his head. He did not know what Arch might say or do if he said "no."

"Hatty'll be looking for you," Arch said, turning his back and walking off.

He reached into his hip pocket and took out Nancy's tail. He began twirling it as he walked down the road towards the big house in the distance.

Dudley Smith went inside the filling station, and the others walked away.

After Arch had gone several hundred yards, Lonnie sat down heavily on the box beside the gas pump from which he had got up when Arch spoke to him. He sat down heavily, his shoulders drooping, his arms falling between his outspread legs.

Lonnie did not know how long his eyes had been closed, but when he opened them, he saw Nancy lying between his feet, licking the docked tail. While he watched her, he felt the sharp point of his chin cutting into his chest again. Presently the door behind him was slammed shut, and a minute later he could hear Dudley Smith walking away from the filling station on his way home.

II

Lonnie had been sleeping fitfully for several hours when he suddenly found himself wide awake. Hatty shook him again. He raised himself on his elbow and tried to see into the darkness of the room. Without knowing what time it was, he was able to determine that it was still nearly two hours until sunrise.

"Lonnie," Hatty said again, trembling in the cold night air, "Lonnie, your pa ain't in the house."

Lonnie sat upright in bed.

"How do you know he ain't?" he said.

"I've been lying here wide awake ever since I got in bed, and I heard him when he went out. He's been gone all that time."

"Maybe he just stepped out for a while," Lonnie said, turning and trying to see through the bedroom window.

"I know what I'm saying, Lonnie," Hatty insisted. "Your pa's been gone a heap too long."

Both of them sat without a sound for several minutes while they listened for Mark Newsome.

Lonnie got up and lit a lamp. He shivered while he was putting on his shirt, overalls, and shoes. He tied his shoelaces in hard knots because he couldn't see in the faint light. Outside the window it was almost pitch-dark, and Lonnie could feel the damp October air blowing against his face.

"I'll go help look," Hatty said, throwing the covers off and starting to get up.

Lonnie went to the bed and drew the covers back over her and pushed her back into place.

"You try to get some sleep, Hatty," he said; "you can't stay awake the whole night. I'll go bring Pa back."

He left Hatty, blowing out the lamp, and stumbled through the dark hall, feeling his way to the front porch by touching the wall with his hands. When he got to the porch, he could still barely see any distance ahead, but his eyes were becoming more accustomed to the darkness. He waited a minute, listening.

Feeling his way down the steps into the yard, he walked around the corner of the house and stopped to listen again before calling his father.

"Oh, Pa!" he said loudly. "Oh, Pa!"

He stopped under the bedroom window when he realized what he had been doing.

"Now that's a fool thing for me to be out here doing," he said, scolding himself. "Pa couldn't hear it thunder."

He heard a rustling of the bed.

"He's been gone long enough to get clear to the crossroads, or more," Hatty said, calling through the window.

"Now you lay down and try to get a little sleep, Hatty," Lonnie told her. "I'll bring him back in no time."

He could hear Nancy scratching fleas under the house, but he knew she was in no condition to help look for Mark. It would be several days before she recovered from the shock of losing her tail.

"He's been gone a long time," Hatty said, unable to keep still.

"That don't make no difference," Lonnie said. "I'll find him sooner or later. Now you go on to sleep like I told you, Hatty."

Lonnie walked towards the barn, listening for some sound. Over at the big house he could hear the hogs grunting and squealing, and he wished they would be quiet so he could hear other sounds. Arch Gunnard's dogs were howling occasionally, but they were not making any more noise than they usually did at night, and he was accustomed to their howling.

Lonnie went to the barn, looking inside and out. After walking around the barn, he went into the field as far as the cotton shed. He knew it was useless, but he could not keep from calling his father time after time.

"Oh, Pa!" he said, trying to penetrate the darkness.

He went further into the field.

"Now, what in the world could have become of Pa?" he said, stopping and wondering where to look next.

After he had gone back to the front yard, he began to feel uneasy for the first time. Mark had not acted any more strangely during the past week than he ordinarily did, but Lonnie knew he was upset over the way Arch Gunnard was giving out short-rations. Mark had even said that, at the rate they were being fed, all of them would starve to death inside another three months.

Lonnie left the yard and went down the road towards the Negro cabins. When he got to Clem's house, he turned in and walked up the path to the door. He knocked several times and waited. There was no answer, and he rapped louder.

"Who's that?" he heard Clem say from bed.

"It's me," Lonnie said. "I've got to see you a minute, Clem. I'm out in the front yard."

He sat down and waited for Clem to dress and come outside. While he waited, he strained his ears to catch any sound that might be in the air. Over the fields towards the big house he could hear the fattening hogs grunt and squeal.

Clem came out and shut the door. He stood on the doorsill a moment speaking to his wife in bed, telling her he would be back and not to worry.

"Who's that?" Clem said, coming down into the yard.

Lonnie got up and met Clem half-way.

"What's the trouble?" Clem asked then, buttoning up his overall jumper.

"Pa's not in his bed," Lonnie said, "and Hatty says he's been gone from the house most all night. I went out in the field, and all around the barn, but I couldn't find a trace of him anywhere."

Clem then finished buttoning his jumper and began rolling a cigarette. He walked slowly down the path to the road. It was still dark, and it would be at least an hour before dawn made it any lighter.

"Maybe he was too hungry to stay in the bed any longer," Clem said. "When I saw him yesterday, he said he was so shrunk up and weak he didn't know if he could last much longer. He looked like his skin and bones couldn't shrivel much more."

"I asked Arch last night after suppertime for some rations—just a little piece of sowbelly and some molasses. He said he'd get around to letting me have some the first thing this morning."

"Why don't you tell him to give you full rations or none?" Clem said. "If you knew you wasn't going to get none at all, you could move away and find a better man to share-crop for, couldn't you?"

"I've been loyal to Arch Gunnard for a long time now," Lonnie said. "I'd hate to haul off and leave him like that."

Clem looked at Lonnie, but he did not say anything more just then. They turned up the road towards the driveway that led up to the big house. The fattening hogs were still grunting and squealing in the pen, and one of Arch's hounds came down a cotton row beside the driveway to smell their shoes.

"Them fattening hogs always get enough to eat," Clem said. "There's not a one of them that don't weigh seven hundred pounds right now, and they're getting bigger every day. Besides taking all that's thrown to them, they make a lot of meals off the chickens that get in there to peck around."

Lonnie listened to the grunting of the hogs as they walked up the driveway towards the big house.

"Reckon we'd better get Arch up to help look for Pa?" Lonnie said. "I'd hate to wake him up, but I'm scared Pa might stray off into the swamp and get lost for good. He couldn't hear it thunder, even. I never could find him back there in all that tangle if he got into it."

Clem said something under his breath and went on towards the barn and hog pen. He reached the pen before Lonnie got there.

"You'd better come here quick," Clem said, turning around to see where Lonnie was.

Lonnie ran to the hog pen. He stopped and climbed half-way up the wooden-and-wire sides of the fence. At first he could see nothing, but gradually he was able to see the moving mass of black fattening hogs on the other side of the pen. They were biting and snarling at each other like a pack of hungry hounds turned loose on a dead rabbit.

Lonnie scrambled to the top of the fence, but Clem caught him and pulled him back.

"Don't go in that hog pen that way," he said. "Them hogs will tear you to pieces, they're that wild. They're fighting over something."

Both of them ran around the corner of the pen and got to the side where the hogs were. Down under their feet on the ground Lonnie caught a glimpse of a dark mass splotched with white. He was able to see it for a moment only, because one of the hogs trampled over it.

Clem opened and closed his mouth several times before he was able to say anything at all. He clutched at Lonnie's arm, shaking him.

"That looks like it might be your pa," he said. "I swear before goodness, Lonnie, it does look like it."

Lonnie still could not believe it. He climbed to the top of the fence and began kicking his feet at the hogs, trying to drive them away. They paid no attention to him.

While Lonnie was perched there, Clem had gone to the wagon shed, and he ran back with two singletrees he had somehow managed to find there in the dark. He handed one to Lonnie, poking it at him until Lonnie's attention was drawn from the hogs long enough to take it.

Clem leaped over the fence and began swinging the singletree at the hogs. Lonnie slid down beside him, yelling at them. One hog turned on Lonnie and snapped at him, and Clem struck it over the back of the neck with enough force to drive it off momentarily.

By then Lonnie was able to realize what had happened. He ran to the mass of hogs, kicking them with his heavy stiff shoes and striking them on their heads with the iron-tipped singletree. Once he felt a stinging sensation, and looked down to see one of the hogs biting the calf of his leg. He had just enough time to hit the hog and drive it away before his leg was torn. He knew most of his overall leg had been ripped away, because he could feel the night air on his bare wet calf.

Clem had gone ahead and had driven the hogs back. There was no other way to do anything. They were in a snarling circle around them, and both of them had to keep the singletrees swinging back and forth all the time to keep the hogs off. Finally Lonnie reached down and got a grip on Mark's leg. With Clem helping, Lonnie carried his father to the fence and lifted him over to the other side.

They were too much out of breath for a while to say anything, or to do anything else. The snarling, fattening hogs were at the fence, biting the wood and wire, and making more noise than ever.

While Lonnie was searching in his pockets for a match, Clem struck one. He held the flame close to Mark Newsome's head.

They both stared unbelievingly, and then Clem blew out the match. There was nothing said as they stared at each other in the darkness.

Clem walked several steps away, and turned and came back beside Lonnie.

"It's him, though," Clem said, sitting down on the ground. "It's him, all right."

"I reckon so," Lonnie said. He could think of nothing else to say then.

They sat on the ground, one on each side of Mark, looking at the body. There had been no sign of life in the body beside them since they had first touched it. The face, throat, and stomach had been completely devoured.

"You'd better go wake up Arch Gunnard," Clem said after a while.

"What for?" Lonnie said. "He can't help none now. It's too late for help."

"Makes no difference," Clem insisted. "You'd better go wake him up and let him see what there is to see. If you wait till morning, he might take it into his head to say the hogs didn't do it. Right now is the time to get him up so he can see what his hogs did."

Clem turned around and looked at the big house. The dark outline against the dark sky made him hesitate.

"A man who short-rations tenants ought to have to sit and look at that till it's buried."

Lonnie looked at Clem fearfully. He knew Clem was right, but he was scared to hear a Negro say anything like that about a white man.

"You oughtn't talk like that about Arch," Lonnie said. "He's in bed asleep. He didn't have a thing to do with it. He didn't have no more to do with it than I did."

Clem laughed a little, and threw the singletree on the ground between his feet. After letting it lie there a little while, he picked it up and began beating the ground with it.

Lonnie got to his feet slowly. He had never seen Clem act like that before, and he did not know what to think about it. He left without saying anything and walked stiffly to the house in the darkness to wake up Arch Gunnard.

III

Arch was hard to wake up. And even after he was awake, he was in no hurry to get up. Lonnie was standing outside the bedroom window, and Arch was lying in bed six or eight feet away. Lonnie could hear him toss and grumble.

"Who told you to come and wake me up in the middle of the night?" Arch said.

"Well, Clem Henry's out here, and he said maybe you'd like to know about it."

Arch tossed around on the bed, flailing the pillow with his fists.

"You tell Clem Henry I said that one of these days he's going to find himself turned inside out, like a coat-sleeve."

Lonnie waited doggedly. He knew Clem was right in insisting that Arch ought to wake up and come out there to see what had happened. Lonnie was afraid to go back to the barnyard and tell Clem that Arch was not coming. He did not know, but he had a feeling that Clem might go into the bedroom and drag Arch out of bed. He did not like to think of anything like that taking place.

"Are you still out there, Lonnie?" Arch shouted.

"I'm right here, Mr. Arch. I——"

"If I wasn't so sleepy, I'd come out there and take a stick and—I don't know what I wouldn't do!"

Lonnie met Arch at the back step. On the way out to the hog pen Arch did not speak to him. Arch walked heavily ahead, not even waiting to see if Lonnie was coming. The lantern that Arch was carrying cast long flat beams of yellow light over the ground; and when they got to where Clem was waiting beside Mark's body, the Negro's face shone in the night like a highly polished plowshare.

"What was Mark doing in my hog pen at night, anyway?" Arch said, shouting at them both.

Neither Clem nor Lonnie replied. Arch glared at them for not answering. But no matter how many times he looked at them, his eyes returned each time to stare at the torn body of Mark Newsome on the ground at his feet.

"There's nothing to be done now," Arch said finally. "We'll just have to wait till daylight and send for the undertaker." He walked a few steps away. "Looks like you could have waited till morning in the first place. There wasn't no sense in getting me up."

He turned his back and looked sideways at Clem. Clem stood up and looked him straight in the eyes.

"What do you want, Clem Henry?" he said. "Who told you to be coming around my house in the middle of the night? I don't want niggers coming here except when I send for them."

"I couldn't stand to see anybody eaten up by the hogs, and not do anything about it," Clem said.

"You mind your own business," Arch told him. "And when you

talk to me, take off your hat, or you'll be sorry for it. It wouldn't take much to make me do you up the way you belong."

Lonnie backed away. There was a feeling of uneasiness around them. That was how trouble between Clem and Arch always began. He had seen it start that way dozens of times before. As long as Clem turned and went away, nothing happened, but sometimes he stayed right where he was and talked up to Arch just as if he had been a white man, too.

Lonnie hoped it would not happen this time. Arch was already mad enough about being waked up in the middle of the night, and Lonnie knew there was no limit to what Arch would do when he got good and mad at a Negro. Nobody had ever seen him kill a Negro, but he had said he had, and he told people that he was not scared to do it again.

"I reckon you know how he came to get eaten up by the hogs like that," Clem said, looking straight at Arch.

Arch whirled around.

"Are you talking to me . . . ?"

"I asked you that," Clem stated.

"God damn you, yellow-blooded . . ." Arch yelled.

He swung the lantern at Clem's head. Clem dodged, but the bottom of it hit his shoulder, and it was smashed to pieces. The oil splattered on the ground, igniting in the air from the flaming wick. Clem was lucky not to have it splash on his face and overalls.

"Now, look here . . ." Clem said.

"You yellow-blooded nigger," Arch said, rushing at him. "I'll teach you to talk back to me. You've got too big for your place for the last time. I've been taking too much from you, but I ain't doing it no more."

"Mr. Arch, I . . ." Lonnie said, stepping forward partly between them. No one heard him.

Arch stood back and watched the kerosene flicker out on the ground.

"You know good and well why he got eaten up by the fattening hogs," Clem said, standing his ground. "He was so hungry he had to get up out of bed in the middle of the night and come up here in the dark trying to find something to eat. Maybe he was trying to find the smokehouse. It makes no difference, either way. He's been on short-rations like everybody else working on your place, and he was so old he didn't know where else to look for food except in your smokehouse. You know good and well that's how he got lost up here in the dark and fell in the hog pen."

The kerosene had died out completely. In the last faint flare, Arch had reached down and grabbed up the singletree that had been lying on the ground where Lonnie had dropped it.

Arch raised the singletree over his head and struck with all his might at Clem. Clem dodged, but Arch drew back again quickly and landed a blow on his arm just above the elbow before Clem could dodge it. Clem's arm dropped to his side, dangling lifelessly.

"You Goddamn yellow-blooded nigger!" Arch shouted. "Now's your time, you black bastard! I've been waiting for the chance to teach you your lesson. And this's going to be one you won't never forget."

Clem felt the ground with his feet until he had located the other singletree. He stooped down and got it. Raising it, he did not try to hit Arch, but held it in front of him so he could ward off Arch's blows at his head. He continued to stand his ground, not giving Arch an inch.

"Drop that singletree," Arch said.

"I won't stand here and let you beat me like that," Clem protested.

"By God, that's all I want to hear," Arch said, his mouth curling. "Nigger, your time has come, by God!"

He swung once more at Clem, but Clem turned and ran towards the barn. Arch went after him a few steps and stopped. He threw aside the singletree and turned and ran back to the house.

Lonnie went to the fence and tried to think what was best for him to do. He knew he could not take sides with a Negro, in the open, even if Clem had helped him, and especially after Clem had talked to Arch in the way he wished he could himself. He was a white man, and to save his life he could not stand to think of turning against Arch, no matter what happened.

Presently a light burst through one of the windows of the house, and he heard Arch shouting at his wife to wake her up.

When he saw Arch's wife go to the telephone, Lonnie realized what was going to happen. She was calling up the neighbors and Arch's friends. They would not mind getting up in the night when they found out what was going to take place.

Out behind the barn he could hear Clem calling him. Leaving the yard, Lonnie felt his way out there in the dark.

"What's the trouble, Clem?" he said.

"I reckon my time has come," Clem said. "Arch Gunnard talks that way when he's good and mad. He talked just like he did that time he carried Jim Moffin off to the swamp—and Jim never came back."

"Arch wouldn't do anything like that to you, Clem," Lonnie said excitedly, but he knew better.

Clem said nothing.

"Maybe you'd better strike out for the swamps till he changes his mind and cools off some," Lonnie said. "You might be right, Clem."

Lonnie could feel Clem's eyes burning into him.

"Wouldn't be no sense in that, if you'd help me," Clem said. "Wouldn't you stand by me?"

Lonnie trembled as the meaning of Clem's suggestion became clear to him. His back was to the side of the barn, and he leaned against it while sheets of black and white passed before his eyes.

"Wouldn't you stand by me?" Clem asked again.

"I don't know what Arch would say to that," Lonnie told him haltingly.

Clem walked away several paces. He stood with his back to Lonnie while he looked across the field towards the quarter where his home was.

"I could go in that little patch of woods out there and stay till they get tired of looking for me," Clem said, turning around to see Lonnie.

"You'd better go somewhere," Lonnie said uneasily. "I know Arch Gunnard. He's hard to handle when he makes up his mind to do something he wants to do. I couldn't stop him an inch. Maybe you'd better get clear out of the country, Clem."

"I couldn't do that, and leave my family down there across the field," Clem said.

"He's going to get you if you don't."

"If you'd only sort of help me out a little, he wouldn't. I would only have to go and hide out in that little patch of woods over there a while. Looks like you could do that for me, being as how I helped you find your pa when he was in the hog pen."

Lonnie nodded, listening for sounds from the big house. He continued to nod at Clem while Clem was waiting to be assured.

"If you're going to stand up for me," Clem said, "I can just go over there in the woods and wait till they get it off their minds. You won't be telling them where I'm at, and you could say I struck out for the swamp. They wouldn't ever find me without bloodhounds."

"That's right," Lonnie said, listening for sounds of Arch's coming out of the house. He did not wish to be found back there behind the barn where Arch could accuse him of talking to Clem.

The moment Lonnie replied, Clem turned and ran off into the night. Lonnie went after him a few steps, as if he had suddenly changed his mind about helping him, but Clem was lost in the darkness by then.

Lonnie waited for a few minutes, listening to Clem crashing through the underbrush in the patch of woods a quarter of a mile away. When he could hear Clem no longer, he went around the barn to meet Arch.

Arch came out of the house carrying his double-barreled shotgun and the lantern he had picked up in the house. His pockets were bulging with shells.

"Where is that damn nigger, Lonnie?" Arch asked him. "Where'd he go to?"

Lonnie opened his mouth, but no words came out.

"You know which way he went, don't you?"

Lonnie again tried to say something, but there were no sounds. He jumped when he found himself nodding his head to Arch.

"Mr. Arch, I—"

"That's all right, then," Arch said. "That's all I need to know now. Dudley Smith and Tom Hawkins and Frank and Dave Howard and the rest will be here in a minute, and you can stay right here so you can show us where he's hiding out."

Frantically Lonnie tried to say something. Then he reached for Arch's sleeve to stop him, but Arch had gone.

Arch ran around the house to the front yard. Soon a car came racing down the road, its headlights lighting up the whole place, hog pen and all. Lonnie knew it was probably Dudley Smith, because his was the first house in that direction, only half a mile away. While he was turning into the driveway, several other automobiles came into sight, both up the road and down it.

Lonnie trembled. He was afraid Arch was going to tell him to point out where Clem had gone to hide. Then he knew Arch would tell him. He had promised Clem he would not do that. But try as he might, he could not make himself believe that Arch Gunnard would do anything more than whip Clem.

Clem had not done anything that called for lynching. He had not raped a white woman, he had not shot at a white man; he had only talked back to Arch, with his hat on. But Arch was mad enough to do anything; he was mad enough at Clem not to stop at anything short of lynching.

The whole crowd of men was swarming around him before he realized it. And there was Arch clutching his arm and shouting into his face.

"Mr. Arch, I . . ."

Lonnie recognized every man in the feeble dawn. They were excited, and they looked like men on the last lap of an all-night foxhunting party. Their shotguns and pistols were held at their waist, ready for the kill.

"What's the matter with you, Lonnie?" Arch said, shouting into his ear. "Wake up and say where Clem Henry went to hide out. We're ready to go get him."

Lonnie remembered looking up and seeing Frank Howard dropping yellow twelve-gauge shells into the breech of his gun. Frank bent forward so he could hear Lonnie tell Arch where Clem was hiding.

"You ain't going to kill Clem this time, are you, Mr. Arch?" Lonnie asked.

"Kill him?" Dudley Smith repeated. "What do you reckon I've been waiting all this time for if it wasn't for a chance to get Clem. That nigger has had it coming to him ever since he came to this county. He's a bad nigger, and it's coming to him."

"It wasn't exactly Clem's fault," Lonnie said. "If Pa hadn't come up here and fell in the hog pen, Clem wouldn't have had a thing to do with it. He was helping me, that's all."

"Shut up, Lonnie," somebody shouted at him. "You're so excited you don't know what you're saying. You're taking up for a nigger when you talk like that."

People were crowding around him so tightly he felt as if he were being squeezed to death. He had to get some air, get his breath, get out of the crowd.

"That's right," Lonnie said.

He heard himself speak, but he did not know what he was saying.

"But Clem helped me find Pa when he got lost looking around for something to eat."

"Shut up, Lonnie," somebody said again. "You damn fool, shut up!"

Arch grabbed his shoulder and shook him until his teeth rattled. Then Lonnie realized what he had been saying.

"Now, look here, Lonnie," Arch shouted. "You must be out of your head, because you know good and well you wouldn't talk like a nigger-lover in your right mind."

"That's right," Lonnie said, trembling all over. "I sure wouldn't want to talk like that."

He could still feel the grip on his shoulder where Arch's strong fingers had hurt him.

"Did Clem go to the swamp, Lonnie?" Dudley Smith said. "Is that right, Lonnie?"

Lonnie tried to shake his head; he tried to nod his head. Then Arch's fingers squeezed his thin neck. Lonnie look at the men wild-eyed.

"Where's Clem hiding, Lonnie?" Arch demanded, squeezing.

Lonnie went three or four steps towards the barn. When he stopped, the men behind him pushed forward again. He found himself being rushed behind the barn and beyond it.

"All right, Lonnie," Arch said. "Now which way?"

Lonnie pointed towards the patch of woods where the creek was. The swamp was in the other direction.

"He said he was going to hide out in that little patch of woods along the creek over there, Mr. Arch," Lonnie said. "I reckon he's over there now."

Lonnie felt himself being swept forward, and he stumbled over the rough ground trying to keep from being knocked down and trampled upon. Nobody was talking, and everyone seemed to be walking on tiptoes. The gray light of early dawn was increasing enough both to hide them and to show the way ahead.

Just before they reached the fringe of the woods, the men separated, and Lonnie found himself a part of the circle that was closing in on Clem.

Lonnie was alone, and there was nobody to stop him, but he was unable to move forward or backward. It began to be clear to him what he had done.

Clem was probably up a tree somewhere in the woods ahead, but by that time he had been surrounded on all sides. If he should attempt to break and run, he would be shot down like a rabbit.

Lonnie sat down on a log and tried to think what to do. The sun would be up in a few more minutes, and as soon as it came up, the men would close in on the creek and Clem. He would have no chance at all among all those shotguns and pistols.

Once or twice he saw the flare of a match through the underbrush where some of the men were lying in wait. A whiff of cigarette smoke struck his nostrils, and he found himself wondering if Clem could smell it wherever he was in the woods.

There was still no sound anywhere around him, and he knew that Arch Gunnard and the rest of the men were waiting for the sun, which would in a few minutes come up behind him in the east.

It was light enough by that time to see plainly the rough ground and the tangled underbrush and the curling bark on the pine trees.

The men had already begun to creep forward, guns raised as if stalking a deer. The woods were not large, and the circle of men would be able to cover it in a few minutes at the rate they were going forward. There was still a chance that Clem had slipped through the circle before dawn broke, but Lonnie felt that he was still there. He began to feel then that Clem was there because he himself had placed him there for the men to find more easily.

Lonnie found himself moving forward, drawn into the narrowing circle. Presently he could see the men all around him in dim outline. Their eyes were searching the heavy green pine tops as they went forward from tree to tree.

"Oh, Pa!" he said in a hoarse whisper. "Oh, Pa!"

He went forward a few steps, looking into the bushes and up into the tree tops. When he saw the other men again, he realized that it was not Mark Newsome being sought. He did not know what had made him forget like that.

The creeping forward began to work into the movement of Lonnie's body. He found himself springing forward on his toes, and his body was leaning in that direction. It was like creeping up on a rabbit when you did not have a gun to hunt with.

He forgot again what he was doing there. The springing motion in his legs seemed to be growing stronger with each step. He bent forward so far he could almost touch the ground with his fingertips. He could not stop now. He was keeping up with the circle of men.

The fifteen men were drawing closer and closer together. The dawn had broken enough to show the time on the face of a watch. The sun was beginning to color the sky above.

Lonnie was far in advance of anyone else by then. He could not hold himself back. The strength in his legs was more than he could hold in check.

He had for so long been unable to buy shells for his gun that he had forgotten how much he liked to hunt.

The sound of the men's steady creeping had become a rhythm in his ears.

"Here's the bastard!" somebody shouted, and there was a concerted crashing through the dry underbrush. Lonnie dashed forward, reaching the tree almost as quickly as anyone else.

He could see everybody with guns raised, and far into the sky above the sharply outlined face of Clem Henry gleamed in the rising sun. His body was hugging the slender top of the pine.

Lonnie did not know who was the first to fire, but the rest of the men did not hesitate. There was a deafening roar as the shotguns and revolvers flared and smoked around the trunk of the tree.

He closed his eyes; he was afraid to look again at the face above. The firing continued without break. Clem hugged the tree with all his might, and then, with the far-away sound of splintering wood, the top of the tree and Clem came crashing through the lower limbs to the ground. The body, sprawling and torn, landed on the ground with a thud that stopped Lonnie's heart for a moment.

He turned, clutching for the support of a tree, as the firing began once more. The crumpled body was tossed time after time, like a sackful of kittens being killed with an automatic shotgun, as charges of lead were fired into it from all sides. A cloud of dust rose from the ground and drifted overhead with the choking odor of burned powder.

Lonnie did not remember how long the shooting lasted. He found himself running from tree to tree, clutching at the rough pine bark, stumbling wildly towards the cleared ground. The sky had turned from gray to red when he emerged in the open, and as he ran, falling over the hard clods in the plowed field, he tried to keep his eyes on the house ahead.

Once he fell and found it almost impossible to rise again to his feet. He struggled to his knees, facing the round red sun. The warmth gave him the strength to rise to his feet, and he muttered unintelligibly to himself. He tried to say things he had never thought to say before.

When he got home, Hatty was waiting for him in the yard. She had heard the shots in the woods, and she had seen him stumbling over the hard clods in the field, and she had seen him kneeling there looking straight into the face of the sun. Hatty was trembling as she ran to Lonnie to find out what the matter was.

Once in his own yard, Lonnie turned and looked for a second over his shoulder. He saw the men climbing over the fence at Arch Gunnard's. Arch's wife was standing on the back porch, and she was speaking to them.

"Where's your pa, Lonnie?" Hatty said. "And what in the world was all that shooting in the woods for?" Lonnie stumbled forward until he had reached the front porch. He fell upon the steps.

"Lonnie, Lonnie!" Hatty was saying. "Wake up and tell me what in the world is the matter. I've never seen the like of all that's going on."

"Nothing," Lonnie said. "Nothing."

"Well, if there's nothing the matter, can't you go up to the big house and ask for a little piece of streak-of-lean? We ain't got a thing to cook for breakfast. Your pa's going to be hungrier than ever after being up walking around all night."

"What?" Lonnie said, his voice rising to a shout as he jumped to his feet.

"Why, I only said go up to the big house and get a little piece of streak-of-lean, Lonnie. That's all I said."

He grabbed his wife about the shoulders.

"Meat?" he yelled, shaking her roughly.

"Yes," she said, pulling away from him in surprise. "Couldn't you go ask Arch Gunnard for a little bit of streak-of-lean?"

Lonnie slumped down again on the steps, his hands falling between his outspread legs and his chin falling on his chest.

"No," he said almost inaudibly. "No. I ain't hungry."